PRAISE FOR

The Gentleman Jewel Thief

"The fabled Hope Diamond is the centerpiece of Peterson's charming trilogy, where she mixes one very bad-boy gentleman with a headstrong heroine, a stolen gem, a duel, a band of acrobats, and an exiled French king . . . She peppers [*The Gentleman Jewel Thief*] with steamy love scenes, wild escapades, and a laugh or two . . . [and] keeps the pace flying and readers hanging on to their utter joy."

—*RT Book Reviews* (4 Stars)

"Deliciously fun! What a lovely, witty book—I can't wait to see what Jessica Peterson does next!"

—Kate Noble, author of *If I Fall*

"Sexy and sparkling with wit, *The Gentleman Jewel Thief* overflows with adventure, suspense, and fast-paced action. Jessica Peterson is a fresh new voice in historical romance."

—Shana Galen, author of *The Spy Wore Blue*

Berkley Sensation titles by Jessica Peterson

THE GENTLEMAN JEWEL THIEF
THE MILLIONAIRE ROGUE

The Millionaire Rogue

JESSICA PETERSON

BERKLEY SENSATION, NEW YORK

THE BERKLEY PUBLISHING GROUP
Published by the Penguin Group
Penguin Group (USA) LLC
375 Hudson Street, New York, New York 10014

USA • Canada • UK • Ireland • Australia • New Zealand • India • South Africa • China

penguin.com

A Penguin Random House Company

THE MILLIONAIRE ROGUE

A Berkley Sensation Book / published by arrangement with Peterson Paperbacks, LLC

For information, address: The Berkley Publishing Group,
a division of Penguin Group (USA) LLC,
375 Hudson Street, New York, New York 10014.

ISBN: 978-0-425-27208-4

PUBLISHING HISTORY
Berkley Sensation mass-market edition / January 2015

PRINTED IN THE UNITED STATES OF AMERICA

10 9 8 7 6 5 4 3 2 1

Cover art by Aleta Rafton.
Cover design by George Long.
Interior text design by Kelly Lipovich.

For my parents, who had an awkward,
often difficult, weirdly imaginative daughter,
and loved her anyway.
This one is for you, Mom and Dad,
even though it makes me squirm
when I think about you reading it.
Love you.

Acknowledgments

Wow. So many exciting things have happened since book one of the Hope Diamond Trilogy, *The Gentleman Jewel Thief*, was published—things that wouldn't have happened without the help and thoughtfulness of the following people.

My husband, Ben. You know how to throw one hell of a party. I hope to one day repay you by putting you on the cover of my books. In a kilt. I love you.

As always, my talented and inspiring agent, Alexandra Machinist; my fabulous editor, Leis Pederson, who always knows the right thing to say to put my author crazies to bed; and Jessica Brock, my publicist, who has helped a clueless author figure out the ins and outs of book promotion. I look forward to working with all of you in the years ahead!

To Shana Galen and Kate Noble, for their generous offer of time and talent. I so appreciate the wonderful blurbs you provided for *The Gentleman Jewel Thief.* I can only hope to one day be the masters you both are.

To all the bloggers, authors, and readers who have reached out over the past year—especially Alyssa Alexander. Having author friends is really the coolest thing on the planet.

And finally, to my family and friends. Y'all are the best, and none of this would be possible without your love, support, and nights spent drinking too much wine. Thanks to all our friends who have made *The Gentleman Jewel Thief* their book club selection; thanks to all our friends who have purchased and read the book. Your kindness means the world to me! Happy reading.

Prologue

The French Blue: A History of the World's Greatest Diamond

Vol. I.

By Thomas Hope

Across lands dry and rivers wide, through centuries of bloodshed and the downfall of great kingdoms, the French Blue's siren call has, like forbidden fruit, proven irresistible to royal and common man alike.

It all began in that mythic land across the great sea: India. Nearly three hundred years ago, a blue-gray diamond the size of a snuffbox was mined from the bowels of the earth. The great Shah Jehan, an emperor the likes of which the world had never seen, made an offering of the jewel to the goddess Sita; he commissioned a great statue of his goddess, the diamond glittering from the center of her forehead as an all-seeing third eye.

It was during this time that a Frenchman by the name of Jean Baptiste Tavernier traveled to the court of Shah Jehan. Being French, Tavernier was by nature dirty, wily, a born thief, and, of course, a libertine. Goading the Shah with false gifts and flattery, Tavernier gained his trust, and the love of his court.

It is impossible to know what, exactly, happened next; but it is widely assumed that, just as the Shah pressed Tavernier to his breast as brother and friend, Tavernier betrayed him. Some accounts even posit the Frenchman slit his host's throat; others, that Tavernier poisoned him and half his glorious court.

The goddess Sita was witness to the violence; and when Tavernier pried the jewel from her forehead with a dagger thieved from Shah Jehan's still-warm body, Sita cursed the Frenchman and all those who would come to own the diamond after him.

Sewn into the forearm of a slave girl, the diamond was brought to Europe, where Tavernier sold it to Louis XIV for the princely sum of two hundred thousand *livres*. The Sun King recut the jewel to improve its luster and wore it slung about his royal breast on a blue ribbon. As part of the crown jewels of France, the diamond would be henceforth known as the French Blue.

Alas, the jewel that bewitched the Frenchman and the king would also bring doom upon their heads; Sita would see her curse satisfied. Tavernier, living out his last days exiled in the wilds of Russia, was torn limb from lip by a pack of wild dogs, and buried in an unmarked grave.

Neither were the kings of France immune to Sita's curse; it was on a bitterly cold day in January when the last king, Louis XVI, lost his crown, his fortune, and his head before a crowd of angry Parisians.

And yet Sita's thirst for vengeance is not yet satisfied. The French Blue, along with most of the crown jewels, was thieved in late 1791 from the Garde Mueble, a royal warehouse on the outskirts of Paris. No one knows who stole it, or where it might be hidden away; in a Bavarian duke's treasure chest, perhaps, or the dirty pocket of a serving wench in Calais. The diamond could be anywhere.

While the trail grows cold, Sita's thirst burns hot. The French Blue is far too glorious a gem to remain hidden forever. Only when it is again brought into the light; only when it is claimed by whomever is brave, or perhaps daft, enough to claim it; only *then* will Sita's lust for blood be satisfied, and her curse at last fulfilled.

One

City of London
Duchess Street, near Cavendish Square
Spring 1812

Resisting the impulse to leap from his chair, fists raised, with a great *Huzzah!*, Mr. Thomas Hope thrust the quill into its holder beside the inkwell. He gathered the pages scattered across his desk and settled in to read the *History*.

The gray afternoon light was fading, and he drew the oil lamp closer so that he might read his masterwork without having to squint. For a masterwork it was, surely; how could it not be, after the years Hope dreamed of the diamond, researched its origins and the fantastic claims behind its curse?

But as his eyes traveled the length of each sentence, it became abundantly clear that Hope's *History* was no masterwork. Indeed, it was something else altogether.

Dear God, it was *awful*. Dramatic to the extreme, like an opera, but without the painted prima donna to compensate for its lack of narrative savvy. *The size of a snuffbox*. Whence had come *that* rubbish?

Tossing the pages onto the desk, Hope tugged a hand through his tangle of wayward curls. He was reading too much of that brooding, wicked man Lord Byron, and it was starting to take its toll on his pen.

He didn't have time for such frivolity besides. Hope had a goodly bit of work waiting for him back at the bank, and an even larger bit—a barrel, actually—of cognac to drink this evening.

Literary aspirations all but shot to hell, Hope was about to crumple the pages into his fists, when a strange noise, sounding suspiciously like muffled laughter, broke out over his shoulder.

His blood rushed cold. Not one of his men, the butler or a steward or a cashier from the bank. He was not expecting any visitors, and the hour for social calls had long passed.

Hope glanced across the gleaming expanse of his desk. His eyes landed on a silver letter opener, winking from its place beside the inkwell. Then there was the pistol in the top right drawer, of course, and the bejeweled Italian dagger in its box on the shelf; and his fists, he couldn't very well discount *those* weapons—

He swallowed, hard. Those days were behind him. The time for violence and subterfuge had passed; Hope was a respectable man of business now, like his father, and his father before him.

Respectable men of business did *not* greet visitors with a sock to the eye or a bejeweled dagger thrust at their throats.

At least not in England.

Removing his spectacles one ear at a time, he carefully placed them beside the pages on his desk. For a moment he closed his eyes, pulse racing.

Hope spun about in his chair. The breath left his body when his gaze fell on the hulking figure that loomed half a step behind him.

"Oh, God." Hope gaped. "Not you. Not now."

Smirking in that familiar way of his—one side of his mouth kicked up saucily, provokingly—Mr. Henry Beaton Lake reached past Hope and lifted the *History* from the desk.

"'Forbidden fruit'?" Lake wheezed. "Oh God indeed! That's bad, old man, very bad. I advise you to leave alliteration to the feebleminded, poets and the like. And the curse!"

Here Mr. Lake whooped with laughter, going so far as to bend over and slap his knee with great jollity. "Brilliant, I say, brilliant! Reading your little history, I'd almost venture you believed it. Heavens, what a good laugh you've given me, and how in the gloom of these past months I've needed it!"

Hope snatched the pages from Mr. Lake's pawlike hand and stuffed them into a drawer. "It's a work in progress," he growled. "I wasn't expecting to share it, not yet. What in hell are you doing here, and in daylight? Someone could have seen you."

Lake turned and leaned the backs of his enormous thighs against the desk. He crossed his ankles, then his arms, and looked down at Hope. "Anxious as always, old friend. You haven't changed a bit—well, except for those clothes. You look like a peacock."

Hope watched as Lake's penetrating gaze lingered a moment on Hope's crisply knotted cravat, his simple but exquisitely cut kerseymere waistcoat, and the onyx-studded watch peeking from his pocket.

"And you, Lake, look like a pirate out of *Robinson Crusoe*. What of it?" Hope took in Lake's broad shoulders, the corded muscles in his neck. He wore the black patch over his eye as some men wore a well-cut dinner jacket: with pride and a sort of impudent, knowing smile, confident any female in the vicinity would find him a little dangerous, wholly debonair, and far too tempting to resist.

"Thank you for the compliment." Lake's smile broadened. "And you needn't worry about being seen associating with the likes of me. I used the alley, and came in through the drawing room window."

"Of course you did. Still up to your old tricks, then?"

"King and country, Hope," Mr. Lake sighed, the laughter fading from his face. "Boney didn't stop when you and I parted ways. Someone needed to stay and fight."

Hope looked away, blinking back the sting of Lake's words. A beat of uncomfortable silence settled between them.

At last Lake pushed to his feet and made his way to the sideboard.

Hope watched the man limp across the room, his right leg remaining stiff at the knee. For a moment sadness and regret pressed heavy into his chest. Too many memories; memories that Hope did not care to revisit.

Mr. Lake held up an etched decanter. "Mind if I pour us a finger, or three?"

"I do indeed mind, very much," Hope replied.

But as he expected, Lake paid him no heed. His guest busied

himself at the sideboard, and a moment later returned with a generous pour of brandy in each of two bulbous snifters.

"I've too many engagements this evening to begin with brandy, and at so early an hour," Hope said, but even as the words left his mouth he found himself reaching for the snifter Lake had set before him. Something about the man's stone-set gaze made Hope feel as if he'd need a drink, and then some, after Mr. Lake revealed what he'd come for.

Hope watched Lake lower himself with a wince into the high-backed chair on the other side of the desk. He took a long pull of brandy and, after he felt the familiar fire relax his limbs, asked, "How's the leg?"

Lake finished his own pull before replying. "Good, bad, it's all the same. Scares off the right people, attracts all the wrong ones. I rather prefer it that way."

Hope scoffed, grinning wistfully at his brandy. "And you. You haven't changed, either. Not a bit."

Again charged silence stretched across the desk. Hope gulped his liquor. Lake did the same.

"The outcome of the war in Spain shall be decided in the coming weeks." Lake's voice was low. He did not meet Hope's gaze. "Wellington marches for Madrid; when the battle comes, it shall turn the tide of our fortunes there. For better or worse, I cannot say. That wastrel Frenchman Marmont, damn him, has the luck of the devil. The lives of thousands, tens of thousands, of British soldiers hang in the balance. My men—good men, smart men—they will die. Men like you."

"I was never one of your men, Lake. I was a refugee in need of aid and asylum. You gave me what I needed, and in return I gave you the same." Hope looked down at his glass. "I was never one of your men."

Lake's one pale eye snapped upward. "Yes, you were. You still are."

Hope tried not to flinch as he waited for what he knew came next.

"We need you," Lake said. "Your country needs you. To turn the tide in our favor."

Ah, so there it was. Hope knew he should run and hide, for those very words spelled the death of hundreds of England's finest men.

But with his earnest eye—the one eye the surgeon managed to save, after the accident—Lake pinned Mr. Hope to his chair.

"I would help if I could." Hope splayed his palms on the desk. "But it's the same as it was ten years ago. I was born to count, Lake, not to spy. My father was banker to the great houses of Europe, and his father before that. After I fled the Continent, I dreamed of restoring Hope and Company to its former glory. And now I've done that. I'm a respectable man of business—"

"Man of business, yes, but the respectable bit is questionable."

Hope chewed the inside of his lip to keep from rolling his eyes. "Regardless, I've a lot at stake. People depend on me, lots of people. Clients, employees. I can't risk the livelihood of thousands of families—never mind my own, my brothers, bless their black souls—by engaging in your sort of intrigue. It's bad business. I've worked long and hard to build my reputation. I won't see that work undone, and millions lost along the way."

Hope sipped his brandy, then swirled it in its glass. "But you knew I would say all that. So, Lake. Tell me why you are here."

Lake drained his glass and smacked his lips. "I'm here because of that diamond you write so very *ardently* about."

"The French Blue?" Hope eyed his visitor. "Quite the coincidence, that you should appear out of the ether just as I am finishing my history."

"I thought together we might begin a new chapter of your lovely little history," Lake said. "And you know as well as I do it's no coincidence. You've heard the rumors, same as me. You're going to buy the diamond from her, aren't you?"

Hope looked down at his hands. Damn him, how did Lake know everything? He assumed the existence of the French Blue in England was a well-kept secret. The Princess of Wales made sure of that, seeing as she likely came into possession of the diamond through illegal, perhaps even treasonous, means.

But Hope assumed wrong. He should have known better, especially when it came to Henry Beaton Lake, privateer-cum-spy extraordinaire. The man sniffed out secrets as a bloodhound would a fox: instinctively, confidently, his every sense alive with the hunt.

"Perhaps." Hope swept back a pair of curls with his fingers. "I admit I am looking to expand my collection. And diamonds—jewels—they are good investments. In the last decade alone—"

"Psh!" Lake threw back his head. "You're buying it for a woman, aren't you?"

This time Hope did not hold back rolling his eyes. "I avoid attachments to women for the very same reasons I avoid the likes of you. Much as I admire the female sex."

"You did a great deal more than admire said sex when we were in France."

"That was almost ten years ago, and hardly signifies."

Lake leveled his gaze with Hope's. "The distractions of women aside. You are attempting to buy the French Blue from Princess Caroline. I'm asking you to buy it for me. For England."

Hope choked on his brandy. Before he could protest, Lake pushed onward.

"We've tried to buy the stone from the princess, but she is holding it hostage from her husband the prince and, by extension, our operation. Relations between them are worse than ever. I'm shocked, frankly, that they haven't yet tried to poison one another."

"Would that we were so lucky as to be delivered from that nincompoop they have the nerve to call regent."

Lake waved away his words. "I'll pretend I didn't hear that. If we manage to obtain the French Blue, we could very well change the course of the war. For years now old Boney's been on the hunt for the missing crown jewels of France. We have reason to believe he'd trade valuable concessions for the largest and most notorious of those jewels. In exchange for the French Blue, that blackhearted little toad might hand over prisoners, a Spanish city or two. We could very well save hundreds, if not thousands, of lives, and in a single stroke."

Hope let out a long, hot breath. "You're shameless, Lake. Absolutely shameless. I refuse to be cowed into thinking I'm a selfish bastard for wanting to protect the interests of those who depend on me for their livelihoods, and their fortunes. I care for the thousands of lives you'll save, I do, but—"

"But." Lake held up his finger. "You *are* a selfish bastard, then."

Hope gritted his teeth, balling his palms into fists. "I've too much at stake," he repeated. "Princess Caroline has been a client of Hope and Company for years. She is more dangerous than she appears, and wily besides. I'm sunk if she uncovers the plot. I won't do it."

For a long moment Lake looked at Hope, his one pale eye unblinking. He shifted in his chair and winced, sucking in a breath as he slowly rested his weight on the bad leg.

The leg that had saved Hope from becoming a cripple, or a corpse, himself.

"Not even for me, old friend?" Lake's face was tensed with pain, and glowing red.

Hope shook his head. "Shameless." He laughed, a mirthless sound. "How do you know I'm worthy of the task? I am not the nimble shadow I once was. These days, a daring evening is a few too many fingers of liquor and a long, deep sleep—alone, sadly—in my bed."

All traces of pain disappeared from Lake's face as he grinned. "You are not as handsome as you once were, I'll give you that. But I wouldn't have asked you if I didn't believe you were a capable partner in crime. We shall work together, of course."

"Of course." Hope sighed in defeat. "So. What's the play?"

Lake leaned forward, resting his forearms on his knees, and rubbed his palms together with a look of fiendish glee. "Those engagements you have—cancel them. We make our move tonight."

Two

London
King Street, St. James's Square

A debutante of small name and little fortune would, surely, commit any number of unspeakable acts in exchange for a voucher to Almack's Assembly Rooms. For there lurked unmarried gentlemen of the rich, titled variety, the kind with palaces in the country and interests in exotic things like shiny boots and perfectly coiffed sideburns.

So why did Miss Sophia Blaise's pulse thump with something akin to relief, exhilaration, even, when one of said gentlemen excused himself from her company and disappeared into the crush?

The Marquess of Withington was not the handsomest peer, but he was the richest, and quite the Corinthian besides. His sideburns were surely the most perfect and the most coiffed, and his boots very shiny indeed. Every heiress and duke's daughter would willingly claw out the other's eyes for a chance to be courted by the marquess; such crimes were tolerated, welcomed, even, while on the hunt for this season's most eligible quarry.

Even now, as Sophia teetered awkwardly on the edge of the ballroom, she felt the sting of stares from venomous female passersby. Her two-minute conversation with the marquess was apparently grounds for preemptive attack by her fellow fortune hunters.

But Sophia was nothing if not ambitious. She took a

certain pride in being the object of such naked envy. Perhaps she did have a chance at making the brilliant match to which she'd always aspired, after all. Perhaps the marquess—the filthy-rich, swoon-worthy *marquess!*—was not so far out of reach.

The conversation itself had been a moderate success—his eyes had remained glued to her bosom, yes, but he *had* laughed at her jests—and even in the wake of her relief at his departure, Sophia felt the satisfaction of a job well done.

Now she had only to dread their next interaction.

"It will get easier," her mother counseled earlier that evening, swaying in time with the carriage.

"You mustn't take it too seriously," Cousin Violet said. She took a swig from her flask and let out a small hiss of satisfaction. "Men like Withington are in possession of little wit, and even less intelligence. You've nothing to fear from them."

It certainly *hadn't* gotten easier, or any less serious, as the beginning weeks of the season passed with alarming speed.

For as long as Sophia could remember, she desired two things above all else: to make a brilliant match with the season's most eligible bachelor, and a suitably large castle to go with him. Having grown up in a family teetering on the edge of penury, Sophia desired stability, security, too, and a man like the marquess could provide her all that and more: the titles, the crests, the fortune and fame.

She was not prepared, however, for just how difficult it would be to fulfill her ambitions. Nor did she anticipate how intimidating, how repellent, she would find a goodly majority of the gentlemen who belonged to said titles and crests.

Her first season, in short, was turning out to be quite a disaster. Yes, *quite*.

Sophia's shoulders slumped.

But even as the weight of that sobering truth bore down upon her heart, a flicker of anticipation pulsed there. Faint at first, it flamed hotter as the minutes passed. The hour of her departure from Almack's drew near; which meant, of course, Sophia was that much closer to her *second* engagement of the evening.

And this one, praise God, had nothing at all to do with sideburns or castles.

Sophia shivered with anticipation when at last the family's musty, creaking carriage jostled its occupants away from Almack's door on King Street later that evening, making for the family's ramshackle manse in Grosvenor Square.

"You're smiling." Violet eyed Sophia from across the carriage. "What's wrong?"

Sophia bit the inside of her lip, hoping to hide her grin of excitement. "Nothing out of the usual, Cousin. I very likely offended a marquess. Being the graceful swan that I am, I stepped on Lord Pealey's feet—yes, both of them—during the minuet."

Violet shrugged. "That makes for a better turn at Almack's than last week."

Lady Blaise said nothing as she swatted back Cousin Violet's attempt at another swig from her flask.

Violet tilted her head back and swigged anyway, draining every last drop.

Sophia sighed and looked out the window. *One more hour. One more hour until my escape.*

Grosvenor Square

Pulling her hood over her nose, Sophia leaned against the crumbling brick of her uncle's house and stepped into her boots, one stockinged foot at a time. She straightened and peered into the shadows, long and sinister in the flickering light of the gas lamps. Satisfied no one was about, she stole into the square, pressing to her breast the pages hidden in her cloak.

The night was cool and clammy; there would be rain. Above, the stars hid behind a thin layer of gray cloud, while the light of the full moon shone through like a lone, opaque eye, following her as she moved through the dark.

With each step her pulse quickened. The daring of it all, the risk—reputation, ruination, retribution—was immense. And exhilarating, all at once.

Whatever this feeling was, it far outshone the anxiety, and the disappointment, she'd experienced while in the Marquess of Withington's presence at Almack's.

It was not far to The Glossy. While Sophia had no occasion on which to dwell on such things, it had surprised her nonetheless that establishments such as La Reinette's populated Mayfair as thickly as potbellied peers.

Those potbellied peers, Sophia had quickly discovered, were possessed of wicked appetites in more ways than one.

The Glossy occupied a stately spot between Viscount Pickering's massive pile and the Earl of Sussex's broad, tired-looking townhouse. Now Sophia understood why Sussex was such a jolly fellow, despite a succession of sour-faced wives.

Its namesake shutters were lacquered deep blue, the slick paint glittering in the low light of lanterns on either side of the front door. Sophia slipped past The Glossy's facade onto a narrow lane that descended along one side of the house. She stopped at a hedgerow—wait, yes, this was the one—and ducked into the boxwood's firm grasp.

For several heartbeats she scraped through the darkness, complete and sweet smelling. She emerged onto a small but immaculately groomed courtyard, illuminated by exotic-looking torches standing guard around the perimeter. With light footsteps she crossed to a door, half-hidden by a budding vine of wisteria. She knocked once. Twice.

Waited a beat.

Then knocked twice more.

The door opened. A tall mulatto emerged, his enormous bulk occupying the whole of the threshold. His black eyes sparked with recognition as they fell upon Sophia's half-hidden face.

"Good evening, miss." He bowed. "Please, come in. The madam is waiting for you. Lily will show you up."

Sophia stepped into the hall but did not remove her hood.

The scent of fresh-cut flowers, mingled with a vivid musk Sophia had yet to name, filled her nostrils. She followed Lily, a yellow-haired woman so beautiful it was difficult not to stare, down a wide gallery and up a curving stair.

The Glossy was as lovely as Sophia remembered. Lovelier even than the first-rate homes of the *ton*, for La Reinette eschewed overstuffed severity in favor of feminine flair. Enormously tall ceilings were frescoed in the Italian style, blues and pinks and naked bodies aflutter. Light sparkled from heavy crystal chandeliers. The gilt furniture was upholstered in various shades of ivory and pink. Paintings lined the walls, depicting lovers past in various states of repose—Tristan and Isolde, Diana and Actaeon, Romeo and Juliet.

When at last Lily drew up before a pair of painted doors, Sophia was dizzy, intoxicated by her surroundings. Lily opened the doors and Sophia stepped mutely over the threshold, blinking to bring her blood back to life.

Before she could thank her guide, the doors swung shut behind her. A voice, thick and seductive, called out from inside the room.

"Ah, *mademoiselle*! *S'il vous plaît, entrez, entrez*!"

La Reinette approached, knotting the tasseled belt of her Japanese silk robe. She dropped into an elegant curtsy, and in her excitement Sophia did the same. La Reinette was more legend than lady; really, how did one greet the mistress to prime ministers and Continental royalty? She was called the little queen—*la reinette*—for good reason.

Madame clucked her tongue and lifted Sophia by her elbows. She drew back Sophia's hood and smiled in that languid way only Frenchwomen could, placing her palms on Sophia's neck.

Her spine tingled at La Reinette's touch. "Good evening, Madame. I am happy to see you again."

"And I am very happy, yes." Madame nodded at a table and chairs set before the fire. On the table, several quills were placed beside a mother-of-pearl inkwell and a quire of fine paper. "Come, let us sit. I am most eager to see the work you have done with my tales."

Sophia settled into her chair and placed the pages, bound in thin red ribbon, on the table. She watched as La Reinette hovered at a sideboard, pouring red wine into elegant goblets. Without asking, Madame placed a goblet on the table before Sophia and swept into the chair opposite.

"Drink it," Madame said. "It is very good, from my country. Not the vinegar that is made in Italy. It helps me to remember. I think it will help you to write."

Sophia brought the glass to her lips, gaze flicking to meet Madame's. In the glow of the fire her eyes appeared wholly black, like a stag's; a striking foil to her pale skin and hair.

Sophia pushed the bound pages across the table. "The edits from our first meeting are complete, and I compiled everything you gave me from the second. I—" Sophia blushed. "I enjoyed this week's tales. Thoroughly. That spy you knew, back in France—the one with the curls, who could fell a girl with his gaze alone? He is my favorite gentleman yet."

Again Madame smiled. "Yes," she said. "He is my favorite, too."

She placed a reticule, woven with pink thread, before Sophia on the table.

"Five pounds, as we agreed, and a bonus." Madame held up a thin, elegant hand at Sophia's protest. "It is no small risk you take, visiting me like this."

"I have come to enjoy our meetings, very much." Sophia squirreled away the reticule in the folds of her cloak. "The adventure you have seen, and the gentlemen you have known—they certainly don't make them like that in England."

Madame raised an eyebrow. "Your prince, you have not found him yet? But this is your season!"

"No prince. Not yet. Perhaps it is not my season, after all." Sophia set down her wine and picked up a quill, examining its sharpened nib. "But I'd rather discuss *your* princes. Where did we leave off last week? Oh yes, the spy, the one with the gaze. Together you were boarding a ship bound for Southampton—"

Sophia started at an enormous sound, the walls set trembling as if by thunder. The *thump thump thump* of heavy footsteps followed—running, whomever the footsteps belonged to was running—and drew closer with each passing heartbeat. So many footsteps it sounded as if The Glossy were being invaded by the whole of the French army.

She ducked at the violent, throaty crack of—dear God, was that a *pistol*? It couldn't be, not here, not in Mayfair, not in the madam's inner sanctum . . .

Sophia's thoughts ran riot. Madame had promised her discretion, protection too, and assured her she would not be seen by any guest, man or woman. But what if, by some accident, she *were* to be seen? And by, God forbid, someone she knew—someone who mattered?

"Are you expecting visitors?"

"No." La Reinette's mouth was a tight white line. She set

down her goblet and twisted in her chair at the sudden racket by the doors.

They catapulted open, banging against the walls.

To Sophia's very great horror, Mr. Thomas Hope sprang breathlessly into La Reinette's chamber, dark tendrils of hair curling from his forehead in a disheveled—and rather dashing—manner. A small but deep cut on his cheek oozed blood in thick, languorous drops.

His wide blue eyes swept over Sophia before landing on the madam.

With an authority that startled Sophia from her staring, he said, "Hide me. Now."

Three

It began as a familiar tingle at the back of Hope's neck, a spider of suspicion waking long-dormant senses as Lake, playing coachman, jostled the carriage into evening traffic.

They were being followed.

Darkness had fallen early, but even so Hope could see two blurs of blackness, blacker even than shadow, following them down the lane. Riders, their cloaks billowing about them in a close breeze.

With practiced nonchalance, Hope sat straight-backed beside the window. He yanked his beaver hat over his unruly curls and watched his new friends from the corner of his eye.

They were sufficiently sinister-looking, and held back just far enough, to confirm Hope's suspicion that these men were out for blood.

His blood. Lake's, too.

Why, he couldn't say. Except that half the world was out for Lake's blood, and for good reason.

Hope cursed under his breath. Not two hours with Mr. Henry Beaton Lake and already they courted just the kind of attention Hope wished to avoid.

He banged his fist to the roof. "We've got company."

"Haha!" came Lake's muffled reply. "And so the plot thickens!"

Hope was thrown back in his seat as Lake jolted the team into a canter. He cursed again. Moving this fast through the streets of Mayfair made them as conspicuous as highwaymen on the run.

Bad for business, his arse. If Hope made it out of this little assignment alive, he would be ruined, and quite thoroughly at that.

Amid the shouts of outraged groomsmen and foulmouthed pedestrians, Hope continued to watch the riders. They kept pace with the carriage, the hooves of their horses pounding the cobblestones in perfect synchronicity. With each stride they drew nearer, making Hope's pulse leap.

He tucked a curl behind one ear. "They're gaining."

"I see that!" Lake replied, voice edged with annoyance.

The carriage lurched forward, the horses now in an all-out gallop. Hope swallowed, hard, and watched as the street lamps whisked by with alarming speed. He dug his fingers into the velvet upholstery of his seat. Images of an overturned carriage, his mangled body slung across one of its wheels as Lake skipped away, whistling, filled his head.

"We've got to do something!" he called. "They're going to catch us!"

"Distract them!" Lake growled in reply.

Hope pitched forward onto the floor as Lake narrowly avoided mauling a woman and her husband in full ballroom attire. Lake was many things—spy, mentor, pirate, scoundrel—but a coachman he was not.

"Distract them? How?"

"I can't do everything!" Lake shouted. "*Think*, you idiot!"

Think. Hope gritted his teeth and pushed off the floor into his seat. If the front wall of the carriage didn't separate them, he would *think* about smashing his fist into Lake's face.

By now the riders were so close, Hope could hear their horses snorting with effort as they kept pace. His heart pummeled his ribs, and for a moment panic threatened to drown what little sanity he had left.

Think. Think what? He was trapped in a runaway carriage, chased down by men he didn't know for reasons he couldn't begin to guess. He had a pistol tucked into the pocket of his jacket, yes, but he couldn't very well start a firefight in the middle of a busy lane.

No, there would be no confrontation. At least not here, for all of Mayfair to see. That would be *very* bad business indeed.

What the hell did Lake expect him to do?

Hope dared another peek out into the night. A familiar

stuccoed facade, windows framed by shiny blue shutters, passed by the window. Hope's blood leapt in sudden recognition.

Of course!

The Glossy.

Why hadn't Hope thought of it before? La Reinette was one of his oldest clients, and a friend besides. Her house, being what it was, was filled with secret stairways, trapdoors, and hidden rooms; a more perfect place for avoiding certain capture and death did not exist in all England.

Hope peered down at the lane below. He'd have to jump; if Lake stopped the coach, the riders would be on them in half a heartbeat.

He blinked, fear clawing its way through him.

He blinked again. He had to act fast, or he would not act at all.

He raised his foot and pounded it against the carriage door with all the strength he could muster.

He nearly laughed when the door did not budge. And then on second thought, he nearly cried.

Again and again he pounded against the door until it suddenly swung open, banging violently against the outside of the carriage.

Lake was shouting something; the horses were screaming and the cobblestones of the lane below dashed together with dizzying speed. A rider drew close, his face hidden by the collar of his jacket.

Hope crouched, holding either side of the door opening. Without further ado, he closed his eyes and leapt forward, out into the night.

He landed, hard, on his feet, pain radiating up his shins to land screaming in his knees. He sucked in his breath, wincing, but didn't resist the forward momentum of his body. He ran for The Glossy and leapt over the low wall that bordered the property, clearing it with nary an inch to spare.

Behind him he heard shouts, and the whinnying of horses as the cloaked riders rode after him. Hope pumped his arms and legs harder, harder, so hard it felt as if his heart would break free from his chest. He struggled to breathe, lungs burning with the need for air.

Unfamiliar voices rang out over his shoulder, followed by the crunch of footsteps on the gravel drive. The riders were on his heels and gaining ground.

Hope ducked into the familiar hedge. Too late did he think to draw up his fists to protect his face, as an errant branch poked boldly into his cheek. He gritted his teeth against the sting—perhaps like Lake he would at last have a dashing souvenir of his daring—and pushed through onto the courtyard.

He didn't wait for Umberto to open the door, and instead rammed against it with his shoulder. To his very great surprise—so great, in fact, that Hope lost his footing entirely—the door splintered beneath his weight.

Catapulting arse over head into the foyer, Hope pushed clumsily to his feet. He waved away Umberto's pistol and pointed out to the night.

"Them," he wheezed. "Get them!" He turned and took off running through the house.

Hope climbed the stairs three at a time, but tripped to his knees on the top step at the sound of a pistol shot. His heart turned over in his chest. In the close quarters of the house it might as well have been heavy cannon it was so loud; the chandelier was still shivering above Hope's head as he grappled to his feet.

He tore down the second-story gallery, pulse roaring when he heard the footsteps, heavy, hurried, behind him.

At least one of the riders had made it past Umberto.

Hope swallowed the panic that rose in his chest. He pushed through the tall doors at the end of the gallery, his every sense alive with pain.

And then he nearly swallowed his tongue at the scene before him.

A pretty—*very* pretty—dark-haired girl sat, mouth agape, beside La Reinette.

Why the devil was Miss Sophia Blaise, exhaustingly virginal debutante, meeting with La Reinette in the middle of the night—and on a *Wednesday*?

As the cousin of one of Hope's largest investors—Lady Violet Rutledge and her father were some of Hope's oldest and best clients—her very presence threatened Hope's attempt to keep his clandestine activities exactly that.

So much for discretion. Mr. Lake and his follies were very bad for business indeed.

In a single glance, Hope took in Sophia's expression, equal parts curiosity and horror; the small reticule, heavy with coin, tucked into her long cloak; and her long, ink-stained fingers, clutching at the worn collar of her simple gown.

A puzzle, and an intriguing one at that.

But Hope didn't have time for puzzles. Especially not tonight, with the pounding footsteps of his pursuers drawing closer with each passing moment.

With some effort he turned his gaze to the madam, which she returned steadily, expressionless.

"Hide me," he panted. "Now."

Miss Blaise sprang to her feet, eyes so wide he had to resist the impulse to hold out his hand to catch them should they pop free of her head.

"Hide you?" Her voice rose with panic. "Hide *me*!"

God above.

He did *not* have time for this. But he didn't have time to protest, either; the riders were hot on his heels.

And so he reached for Miss Blaise, wrapping his fingers around her elbow as he tugged her alongside him. He ignored her gasp as he followed La Reinette across the room, the madam's footsteps silent amid those, drawing closer, of his pursuers.

La Reinette drew up before the far wall, embellished in elaborate gilt plasterwork. She placed both hands on one side of a framed painting and pushed.

A panel the width of Hope's forearm swung open to reveal a closet set into the wall. A high shelf held a red lacquer box and a haphazard stack of books.

Everything was covered in a furry layer of dust.

Beside Hope, Sophia gaped at the closet in horror.

La Reinette met his eyes over Sophia's head.

"It is this, or the certain death," Madame said. She reached out and with her thumb swiped at the cut on his cheek. He felt the warm smear of blood on his skin. She pulled back with a frown, rubbing his blood between the pads of her thumb and forefinger.

The footsteps in the gallery grew louder. Hope heard the

labored breathing of his assailants as they cursed their way toward La Reinette's chamber.

Hope pulled Sophia against him, her breast to his belly. With a look that implored her to silence, he wrapped an arm about her shoulders and ducked both their bodies into the closet.

His shoulders—*gah!*—got stuck halfway in. Hope was forced to pull Sophia tightly against him—so tightly she let out a little gasp of pain as at last they slid into the tiny space.

La Reinette shoved the panel back into place, pressing it against the side of Hope's body with such force his shoulder cracked to fit inside.

Darkness settled over Hope and Miss Blaise, along with a hysterical silence.

Well. This was awkward.

"Are you all right?" he whispered.

"No. No, most certainly not all right," came her muffled reply.

"Excellent." He tried to stand very still, not daring even to breathe. "Me neither."

Her chest heaved rather invitingly against his as she attempted to catch her breath. He was suddenly aware of her warmth, her every limb pressed against his own. Knees, forearms, hips, and even her nose, which grazed the sensitive skin at the base of his throat.

He took a deep, steadying breath, inhaling her scent as he did so. She smelled of fresh air and wine; not a hint of perfume. It was lovely, made lovelier by the novelty of it. Debutantes of her shape and stripe usually inhabited clouds of sickly-sweet tuberose and ambergris; he could always smell a fortune hunter long before he saw one.

Needless to say, Hope's deep breath had the opposite of its intended effect.

Hope felt Miss Blaise tremble as the sound of male voices filled La Reinette's chamber. He sensed her rising panic and quickly covered her mouth with his free hand, his own heart racing as La Reinette exchanged words with his pursuers.

There were two men, and they were responding to the madam's queries in rapid-fire French. To Hope's surprise, the intruders spoke the sort of airy, refined French of the ancien régime.

They were well-bred, aristocrats.

Or, at the very least, pretending to be.

In a voice like gravel, one of the men told Madame they were looking for a dangerous man, dark-haired with blue eyes, very tall.

Recognition pulsed in Hope's chest. *That voice!* It was vaguely familiar—he knew it in another time and place, another life—though he struggled to place it.

La Reinette responded to the intruder's queries with convincing bafflement, warning that while she had seen no such man, she would not allow them to bother her clients in the other rooms.

The men ignored La Reinette, and began to ransack the room. Drawers opened, pages scattered, a heavy piece of furniture skidded with a crash across the wood floor.

One of the men was pacing the room, his footsteps growing louder until Hope sensed his presence nary a hairsbreadth from the wall behind which Hope now cowered.

Suddenly the closet was filled with a strange, hoarse scraping noise. The intruder, running his hands along the gilded expanse of the wall.

Hope's heart sank even as it raced faster and faster with each passing second. The man's hands were now passing directly over the wall panel that hid Hope and Miss Blaise; Hope heard the man's labored breathing, the crinkling of his cloak as he bent to inspect the baseboard.

As noiselessly as he could manage, Hope tried to reach for the pistol in his jacket. But Miss Blaise was wound too tightly in his arms for him to access it; he had no room in which to move besides.

The scraping sound of the intruder's hand halted just as suddenly as it began. Hope nearly choked with relief; Miss Blaise remained stiff and shivering against him.

Hope removed his hand from her mouth. As if on cue, Miss Blaise whimpered, a small but succinct sound.

She froze. He froze. The voices in the room went silent.

La Reinette tried to pass the sound off as her own, and began offering her unwanted guests the company of her girls.

But they were not listening.

Their footsteps were impatient and heavy as they hurried

toward the closet, cursing with glee in their native tongue. With their gloved hands they pressed against the panel where it met with Hope's shoulder. He gritted his teeth against the tight burn that laced through his arm. He pulled Sophia against him, and braced himself for—

Well. For whatever came next.

Four

Yes, Sophia was in a state of most acute distress; yes, she was, in the next five minutes, likely to face death and dismemberment; and yes, she was in the arms of an apparently dangerous, definitely handsome man, the crisp lapels of his dinner jacket sliding up and down her breasts with each breath he took, his scent of sandalwood and lemon faint but delicious.

Even in the midst of such ghastly circumstances, she marveled at her stupidity. Though the whimper had escaped her lips instinctively, without invitation, she cursed herself for ruining their chances of escaping these goons unscathed.

Never mind the fact that the whimper had nothing at all to do with said goons. She'd whimpered not out of fear or distress or panic. No.

Sophia had whimpered at the loss of Mr. Thomas Hope's touch. Oh, that *touch*.

It was confident and urgent and very warm. A lovely little shiver had raced through her at the sensation of his skin pressed against her own. Combined with the heat of their tangled limbs, it was enough to fill Sophia's head with all sorts of salacious imaginings. How it would feel, for example, if it were his lips pressed against her mouth, instead of his palm. How that palm might make its way down the slope of her neck to cup her shoulder, then her breast—

Good God. La Reinette's tales of romance and adventure had certainly taken root in Sophia's fertile imagination.

But now that Sophia was in the midst of her own adventure—the romance bit had yet to materialize, but she apparently longed for it, madly—she was making a muck of it. Indeed, if she kept whimpering—really, who *whimpered*?—this was going to be her first, and last, adventure. Ever.

Sophia's bare hands were caught between their bodies, her palms pressed against Mr. Hope's broad, solid chest. She felt his heart pounding beneath the layers of his clothes, and pound yet harder when the men chasing him began clawing at the panel behind which she and Hope were hiding.

This was bad. Very, *very* bad.

Panic sliced through her. Instinctively her fingers clenched on Hope's chest, pulling at the fine fabric of his jacket. The first two fingers stilled when they gathered between them something jarringly hard and shapely tucked into his waist-coat.

Her fingers went to work, tracing the outline of what felt to be—oh dear, it was indeed—a pistol.

Her blood jumped. *A pistol!* Hysteria sparked at the back of her throat, stoked to flames by the intruders' incessant pounding against the closet panel. She tried to draw her hand away but Mr. Hope held her too tightly, pressing her hand firmly against his weapon.

La Reinette would have used just such a euphemism in her tales, Sophia thought wildly, and together they would have laughed about it over their pages and their wine.

The thought calmed Sophia, and she wondered what, exactly, would La Reinette, that great admirer of dangerous men, do in this situation?

As soon as she asked the question, Sophia knew the answer.

La Reinette would take matters into her own hands. Literally.

Mr. Hope's pistol pressed invitingly against Sophia's palm. She knew he could not reach the pistol himself, his arms stuck akimbo in the tiny closet. In the darkness she tapped twice on the gun, and while she could not see his face, she felt his eyes upon her. A beat of understanding passed between them; Hope loosened his grip on her so that she might grasp the pistol.

She curled her fingers around the metal, warm after having been tucked against the heat of his body. The weight of it nearly snapped her wrist as she pulled it from Hope's waistcoat. It was bigger than she'd imagined, and felt sinister in her hand.

Another euphemism that would have made La Reinette proud.

"Be careful," Mr. Hope hissed. "Have you ever shot before?"

"No-o?"

"Well," he answered tightly. "There's a first time for everything, isn't there, Miss Blaise?"

The intruders' pounding became unbearable. The wall that hid Sophia and Hope clattered against its frame, and finally splintered with a heartrending *crack*.

"Careful!" Hope breathed into her ear as the light from Madame's chamber flooded the closet.

The intruders, their masked, unshaven faces feral, peered over the debris like two red-eyed raccoons. They pulled what was left of the panel away from the closet. One of them—Sophia knew he was the cigar-voiced man, just by looking at him—sneered and lunged forward.

Mr. Hope propelled their bodies out of the closet, tucking Sophia behind his broad shoulders. She glanced down at the pistol, able to see it at last in the light.

It was enormous.

Not only that. It was enormously complicated-looking.

Oh dear.

The sneering intruder was on them now, swinging at Hope. He ducked just in time, allowing Sophia the perfect shot: the intruder's wide chest was exposed as he fell headfirst toward her.

She stepped forward and raised the gun, using both arms to support its weight. Slipping her finger into the inviting arc of the trigger, she gritted her teeth and pulled.

And pulled.

And pulled.

Nothing happened.

"Deuced thing!" she cried.

Before she could try again, Mr. Hope was behind her, wrapping his arms around her own as he took the pistol in his hand. In the space of a single blink—really, that's all it took—he pulled back what appeared to be another trigger on top of the gun and fired it.

Sophia started at the awesome force of it, the sound so loud that for several seconds afterward she couldn't hear much of anything. A cloud of singed smoke enveloped them, and in the fog Sophia felt the floor beneath her feet vibrate with a single, distinct thud.

The intruder had fallen.

Behind her Mr. Hope was shouting, and La Reinette was shouting back from somewhere in the chamber. Their voices were curiously faint.

And then she and Hope were running, her legs moving as if through water; they were at once heavy and weightless, taking her out of Madame's chamber, through the gallery, and down a narrow, winding stair hidden behind an iron balustrade.

Sophia looked down to see her hand clasped firmly in Mr. Hope's. She looked up to see the gleaming line of his jaw twitch with murderous intent, his dark curls wild around the inviting curve of his ear.

Behind them came the sound of heavy footsteps. One or both of those dreadful Frenchmen were still in pursuit.

Hope increased his pace without looking back, tugging Sophia along behind him. Her heart knocked painfully against her lungs, her every muscle begging her to stop the assault.

Just when she thought she might collapse, they stumbled through an unfamiliar door and out onto a dark lane that stank of refuse and horse manure. The night was close and complete here; Sophia found it difficult to breathe.

"This way!" Hope skidded on the gravel around a corner and broke into an all-out sprint. He glanced back at Sophia, his blue eyes translucent in the darkness.

"Not," he panted, "much. Farther."

She began to fall back, and felt herself become a weight on Mr. Hope's arm. Dear God, she was going to collapse. The air was too thick, her legs too heavy.

But then the sound of hurried footsteps again broke out behind them. Her panic propelled her forward, her gait pulling her in line with Hope.

Together they skidded around another corner and drew up before the dark shadow of an unmarked coach. Tendrils of smoke rose from its recently extinguished lamps.

"Get in!" a man called from the coachman's bench. He snapped the reins, and the horses began to move, leading the carriage out into the lane.

Hope reached for the carriage door and pried it open, trotting beside the vehicle as it quickened pace.

"You. First," he said to Sophia. He pulled her against him and looped his palms through her underarms. "Pull. And I. Will push!"

Sophia reached for the carriage and managed to grasp either side of the door opening. Gritting her teeth against the pain of her exertion, she pulled with what was left of her strength. The force of Hope's push knocked her breathless as she somersaulted into the coach.

Somewhere in the back of her mind she knew her ungainly leap had exposed a goodly bit of thigh, and probably more than that. But such virginal considerations seemed to hardly signify in the face of pistols and feral Frenchmen.

She didn't know why any of this was happening, or where the carriage would take her. But this was just the sort of adventure that she so admired in La Reinette's tales, and if such adventure involved nudity, then so be it.

By now the horses were in an all-out gallop, the carriage heaving violently behind them. Sophia scrambled to her feet and reached out for Hope. He took her hands and with an ungainly leap fell into the coach, his legs dangling out the open door.

When at last she managed to wiggle the rest of his great bulk into the carriage, Sophia collapsed on the floor, gasping for air. Mr. Hope rose to his knees as he reached for the door, which was swinging wildly in time to the coach's erratic movement.

"Who the devil. Was that?" Mr. Hope called out the open door.

"Who the devil is *she*?" came the coachman's shout.

Mr. Hope slammed the door shut in reply, and with a tremendous sigh fell heavily on the ground beside Sophia.

Shoulder to shoulder, they sat together gasping for several beats.

"Oh. Miss Blaise." Hope turned his head to look at her. "You visited La. Reinette on the wrong. Night I'm. Afraid."

Sophia glanced up to meet his eyes. *Those eyes*. He was looking at her closely, carefully. With great interest.

Looking at her like no one—man or woman, save perhaps her dearest mama—had ever looked at her before.

She quickly looked away, focusing her gaze on her lap. A moment ago she believed her heart beat as quickly and as vigorously as it could as she ran side by side with Hope from The Glossy.

Now she knew differently. It seemed with his gaze alone, Mr. Hope could very well coax her heart to explode from the prison of her ribs.

She swallowed. Hard.

"Is this what you do every Wednesday night?" She smiled into her lap. "If I had known bankers lived such exciting lives I would've angled to become one myself."

Mr. Hope paused, taken aback by her words; and then he laughed, laughed and put his hand on her knee. "Oh. Miss Blaise," he said again. "If I experienced such excitement every Wednesday, I daresay I'd be dead."

Sophia stared at his hand in the darkness, feeling the warmth of his fingers through the thin muslin of her gown. They were handsome fingers, broad but well kept and elegant, capable-looking, just like the rest of him.

She felt the heat rising to her cheeks. So much *touching*. It made her want to reach out and touch him back, to feel the heat of someone else's thrill beneath her palm.

Mr. Hope must have noticed, for he cleared his throat and pulled his hand away.

Sophia shifted uncomfortably as a beat of awkward silence stretched between them. She let her head fall back against the side of the coach, and tried not to wince as they clattered over a particularly jarring bump.

"You mustn't tell anyone," she said, closing her eyes. "Everything. Anything. I know Violet trusts you, but—"

"You have my word, Miss Blaise. I daresay I must ask the same courtesy of you. You see, I don't usually—"

The carriage lurched; suddenly the pounding of hooves, not far behind, filled the night.

The Frenchman was back, and in hot pursuit on horseback. Sophia's blood ran cold at the memory of his greedy eyes peeking over the debris of the plasterwork.

"Bloody hell." Hope rose into a seat and carefully pulled Sophia up beside him as the carriage bumped and jostled them against one another. He pounded the ceiling with his fist. "He's back!"

"I *see* that!" the coachman replied.

As if on cue, the rider appeared by the window at Sophia's side. She could see the gleam of his teeth as he grinned at her, holding the reins in one hand while in the other he brandished a pistol—Hope's pistol.

Sophia screamed. She heard the discharge of the gun just as the carriage jerked forward, Mr. Hope pressing her head into his lap. The window shattered and there was a great, billowing sound, like close thunder.

She managed to glance up at Mr. Hope. He was grinning. "He missed!" he shouted.

The carriage bolted left, throwing them against the far wall; then it bolted right, and Sophia nearly careened out the broken window before Mr. Hope grabbed her by her wrists and hauled her back against him.

For what seemed an eternity the chase continued in such a fashion, the coach leaping and groaning as it hurtled toward God knew where. Sophia was possessed of a strong stomach, but even so she felt the threat at the back of her throat of losing dinner more than once. Together she and Hope held on for dear life as they raced through the streets of Mayfair.

At last the sound of their pursuer's horse grew distant, and then disappeared altogether. She dared sit straight, her person once again in the line of fire, only when the carriage drew to a halt.

Hope let out a long, hot sigh. Sophia, however, was too shaken to feel any sense of relief. Or, perhaps, too enthralled.

She looked out the broken window and started, a now-familiar panic tingling to life in her chest.

"Where are we?" Her voice was tight. "We haven't left London, have we?"

Mr. Hope stuck his head out the broken window and considered their surroundings. The night was ravenous here, swallowing everything in its path. New grass and open space filled the air. It was damp; the rain would come any minute now.

"Well. I cannot be sure. But I've never known London to smell like *this*." Mr. Hope ducked back into the carriage, his smile fading as his eyes fell on her face. "You needn't worry, Miss Blaise, I'll have you back—"

The carriage door swung open, revealing a tall, sinister shadow with pale hair that gleamed blue in the faint light of the clouds above. Sophia jumped, nearly landing in Mr. Hope's lap.

"Terrifying, I know," Hope said.

"Terrifyingly handsome, you mean," the shadow said. He raised a lantern, illuminating his face, one side of his mouth kicked up in a devilish smirk. Sophia practically clawed Mr. Hope at the sight of the black patch covering one of the man's eyes, the sinister intent glittering in the other.

Dear God, pirates really *did* exist, despite her mother's assurances to the contrary!

"I thought you said you didn't like women," the shadow said, his eyes—his one eye—never leaving Sophia.

She leaned further into the solid warmth of Hope's chest. It was obvious this man was no coachman.

Mr. Hope tucked back the curls from his forehead and sighed. "I said that I *avoided* women, not that I didn't *like* them. Besides, it isn't what you think."

"Who is she? One of La Reinette's girls?"

"No," Hope replied. He rose to his feet and pushed the shadow from the threshold. Leaping to the ground, Mr. Hope turned and held up his hands.

"Who is she?" the shadow asked again.

Hope put his hands to Sophia's ribs, grazing the underside of her breasts with his thumbs.

She couldn't help it. She had to sigh as he lifted her to the ground. In the dark his hands lingered on her body a beat longer than was necessary.

Her heart hiccupped in her chest.

Too soon, he pulled away.

"I'm not above leaving her here if you don't tell me who she is."

Mr. Hope looked from Sophia to Lake and back again. He ran a hand through the tangle of his curls and sighed.

"If I vouch for each of you," he said, "might I make the introduction? You've my word as a banker and a friend, anything that happens this night shall remain between the three of us."

The shadow harrumphed. "Your word as a banker? Best run for the hills, then."

Sophia swallowed. He was even more enormous up close. His neck appeared to be as big around as her leg.

She glanced at her surroundings. They were stopped on the edge of a poorly tended road, a copse of trees to their left, a fallow field to their right. She hadn't a clue where they were, or why, or if the Frenchman would return to slit their throats.

Sophia looked back to the shadow. She risked everything by revealing herself to him. But she risked even more doing nothing.

There was something dangerous about this man. A character straight out of La Reinette's tales, he stank of intrigue and adventure. She had no doubt she would experience both in spades if she followed him, and Mr. Hope, into the night.

Dropping into a curtsy, she bowed her head and spoke before Hope could stop her. "Sophia Blaise. I am your servant."

To her surprise the shadow sketched an elegant bow. Just low enough, no groveling for him; he was, she realized, a gentleman.

"Well now, that wasn't so difficult! I am Henry Beaton Lake. Tell me, Miss Blaise, since we are on the subject of service; how do you feel about aiding in the fight against those nasty libertines the French? King and country, my dear. Tonight they require your aid."

Severed from rational thought, the word escaped her lips in a rush. "Yes."

"No," Hope said. "You'll not involve her in this."

Mr. Lake shrugged. "She's here. Nothing we can do about that now—begging your pardon, Miss Blaise. Indeed, I do believe this is a most happy surprise, for as I have looked upon your most lovely face, I've been struck by a novel idea. But first you must swear upon your very life that you shall tell no one what we share with you this night. I do so hate killing those who betray our cause." He held aloft the lantern, its yellow light illuminating his wolfish grin.

Five

Montague House was a pile of soot-blackened stones and tiny, squinting windows that lent it the appearance of an elderly fellow suffering a bout of digestive distress.

Appropriate, thought Hope, for the residence of Her Majesty the Princess of Wales.

Together with Miss Blaise he ascended the shallow front steps, her arm tucked snugly into the crook of his own. She held her shoulders square, but by the way she rolled her bottom lip between her teeth, he could tell she was nervous.

Oh, that *lip*. A just-bitten shade of pink, swollen from her ministrations. For a heartbeat he imagined himself finishing the job, taking the top lip and working it between his own.

Miss Blaise looked at him from the corner of her eye and caught him staring. He snapped his eyes to Montague House's front door, painted a garish shade of red, and felt himself flush the same color.

"Keep calm." He spoke as much to himself as he did to her. "And as I told you before, Miss Blaise, it is best not to stare."

She arched a brow. "'Miss Blaise'? If I am to play your betrothed, shouldn't you call me Sophia?"

The heat in his cheeks burned hotter. He cleared his throat and gave his cravat a ruthless tug. "Of course. Sophia."

"Of course. Thomas." Her grin was impish, her gold eyes dancing. He blinked. Hope had never seen her like this; during his visits to her family, Sophia always played the proper, if somewhat bland, young lady. But now he saw that mischief suited her. Hell, the girl had attempted to shoot a man not an hour ago. Though the attempt was unsuccessful, Sophia appeared all the more alive and eager for having done it.

Sophia. Thomas. The sound of his given name on her lips. He hadn't been called Thomas in years, not since he left his family and fortune behind in Amsterdam.

And now here he was, risking all he'd earned back with a lie on his tongue and a damnably alluring debutante at his side.

There were no two ways about it. He was mad.

Together with Sophia, Hope mounted the top step and raised his hand, knocking soundly on the door. He stepped back and waited in breathless silence, the muffled sounds of the house loud in his ears. Music, laughter, the strangled barking of small dogs.

Hope swallowed his surprise when a handsomely middle-aged man opened the door and bowed them inside. The butler was exceedingly normal, charming even, for a member of Princess Caroline's entourage.

"You are just in time." The butler took Sophia's cloak, and held out a hand for Hope's hat and coat. "Her Majesty is expecting you."

He led them up a short, squat stair to a wide gallery decorated in the Prussian style. Heavy dark moldings enclosed the space, and enormous paintings and banners hung from the walls in an excessive and self-conscious proclamation of Princess Caroline's exalted lineage.

The music and laughter grew louder and reached a crescendo when the butler paused outside a low, wide doorway, and motioned them inside.

Sophia glanced up at Hope. He nodded and let go of her arm, trailing his hand down her side to rest on the small of her back. He felt her spine harden as she took a deep breath, the butler's voice clear and proud as he announced their presence.

Hope followed her into the small chamber, a tower room with curving walls and a tall beamed ceiling that rose to a fine point high above their heads. Sophia fell into a deep curtsy as he sketched his finest bow. They rose, and he heard Sophia's sharp intake of breath as her eyes fell upon the scene before them.

A pair of nubile young men, eyes narrowed to slits with

drink, were laid out upon a sofa. Hope could tell they were Bavarians by their frilly dress and long, unkempt hair. They said nothing, but peered at Hope with a hostile glitter in their eyes, mouths agape as if waiting for an open pour of wine.

Sophia stood very still beside him. She was trying—and failing—not to stare at the figure seated across the room.

Her Majesty the Princess of Wales rose behind a gilded harpsichord, a passel of spaniels at her feet. Hope didn't know where to look first—the painted eyebrows, arching tragically over her tiny black eyes? The grotesquely huge bosom, bursting from a satin gown that Caroline's meaty girth seemed to be swallowing from the inside out? Or the enormous pearl earbobs dangling from her ears, an unfashionable foil to the fist-sized emerald slung from a diamond chain about her neck?

Definitely the eyebrows, Hope decided. They were painted black and far too thick for the princess's round, ruddy face.

"Your Majesty." Hope cocked his lips into a smile. "You look ravishing, as always."

A grin broke out on Caroline's face, the wrinkles about her eyes deepening with genuine pleasure. She smoothed the bodice of her gown with a wide, fat hand. "I am glad you have come to visit, Mr. Hope. So few friends I have now in London, and the gossip." She sighed, looking away. "It is worse than ever. Please, do sit."

Mr. Hope and Sophia sat on a settee across from the reclining Bavarians. One of them had fallen asleep, his head thrown back over the sofa's edge, and was snoring softly. The princess lifted a dog into the crook of her arm, cooing to it, and took a seat in a chair beside Mr. Hope with a frown.

"There, on your face." She peered at the cut, dry now, that made his whole cheek sting. "Whatever happened?"

Hope resisted the urge to bring his fingers to his face. "An unfortunate run-in with. Ah. A fork?"

Caroline wrinkled her nose. "A fork?"

"Yes." Hope swallowed. "A fork."

"Indeed." Caroline leaned forward, the chair gasping beneath its burden, to get a closer look at Sophia. "And who is this? A pretty one."

Hope cleared his throat and glanced at Sophia. "I've some news, Majesty. Though I haven't a clue what I did to deserve her, this lovely woman has agreed to be my wife. Miss Sophia Blaise and I shall be married come June."

Princess Caroline gasped. The dog dropped from her arm with a dissatisfied *yap*, and the princess clapped together her hands in a show of childlike joy. "Oh, lovers, let them love! How marvelous! Miss Blaise, you have my sincerest congratulations. Mr. Hope shall prove a wonderful husband." She sighed. "There must be no greater happiness in life than making a love match."

Sophia smiled, warmth radiating from her features. "He is very kind, and decently handsome."

"Decently?" Hope turned his head to look at Sophia. "Not terribly? Wholly? Drop-dead?"

The little minx shrugged her shoulders. "Decently should do, don't you think, Majesty?"

Caroline tittered in a fit of giggles. "Look at the two of you, squabbling like children in the nursery. It tickles my poor old heart." She glanced down at Sophia's hands, clasped neatly in her lap. "But you have no ring! Of all men, Mr. Hope, *you* should know better than to wed without a diamond! My jewels may be the only companions I have left in this world—aside from Gunter and Frederick there, of course—but they have never disappointed me. Nor has their beauty faded to fat, like a certain gentleman of our mutual acquaintance."

Sophia coughed, covering her mouth with a fist to hide the smile that rose unbidden to her lips. Watching her smother her laughter made Hope want to burst with his own.

He cleared his throat. Hope moved to cover Sophia's hands with one of his in her lap. He felt her start beneath his touch but just as quickly warm to him as her laughter faded.

"That is why we have called upon you," Hope said. "You see, Majesty, I was struck very low by Cupid's arrow the moment I laid eyes upon Miss Blaise."

"Love at first sight." Princess Caroline closed her eyes and, clutching a hand to her ample chest, sucked a loud breath through her nose. "Oh, it slays me, this love! I didn't think you capable of such romance, Mr. Hope, what with the bad numbers and worse news you usually bring me."

"I wasn't. Not until I met Miss Blaise. I loved her from the moment we met, and set out to find the most perfect, most flawless gem, for only such a stone would be worthy of her beauty."

Understanding unfurled across Princess Caroline's features. She grinned. "You have not yet found such a stone. And so you come to me." She fingered the emerald at her neck, and batted her eyes. "Tell me what you are looking for."

Hope settled back into the settee. For a moment he contemplated stretching out his arms and legs in a yawning show of nonchalance, but decided against it. Not only did it smack of melodrama, even in the midst of one of Lake's schemes, it would make an even bigger fool of the princess. She was strange, certainly, but kind, and her happiness for Hope and Sophia's pretend engagement was touching. He hated the idea of pulling the wool over her eyes, especially on behalf of that fat gentleman of their mutual acquaintance—the prince regent.

And so he decided on the second best option: candor.

"The French Blue," Hope said, meeting the princess's dark eyes. "I dare not presume you are in possession of that infamous jewel, but if you are, I've twenty thousand pounds in my pocket I'd give you in exchange for that diamond."

He reached into his jacket for said pocket and produced a fresh, if slightly wrinkled, note. He placed it on the marble-topped side table between himself and Princess Caroline.

Silence clouded the chamber as the Princess of Wales surveyed the note. Her expression was inscrutable. Hope's heart began to pound, and the room suddenly felt scorching, airless. He glanced at Sophia. She was playing with her lip again, damn her, and now the room felt *unbearably* hot, sweat breaking out under his collar and along his temples.

He squeezed her hand in his own and the lip popped free of her teeth. She glanced at him, eyes widening as they fell upon his stricken face, then turned her attention to Princess Caroline.

"I told Thomas that he needn't gift me a diamond, for his affection and attentions—" Sophia stopped as her voice tightened. He watched in fascination as she closed her eyes and cleared her throat. "Well. They have been gift enough, your Majesty."

Sophia then proceeded to burst into sobs.

Hope froze.

What in hell? Either he'd done something to offend Sophia, or she was a *much* better actress than she was a shot.

"Oh, my dear, dear girl." Princess Caroline hurried to Sophia's side and nestled her head into her rather epic bosom. "There there, there there. Ah, *el amor*, it is bittersweet, no? But the lovers. We must let them love!"

She released Sophia with a kindly pat on the cheek. "Stay right here, my dear, and I shall return straightaway. No more tears, only happiness!"

The princess swept out of the room in a flash of pearlescent satin and sour perfume, the dogs' nails tinkling as they followed her out. Hope stared at Sophia, unsure what, exactly, he should do next.

Across from them on the sofa, either Gunter or Frederick snorted in his sleep, while the other drooled on a fine tasseled pillow. Whoever these men were—Caroline's lovers, her cousins, the dukes of Bavaria—they were not very good company.

Hope turned to Sophia, who was sniffling beside him. He offered her his handkerchief. "Are you all right?"

She took the handkerchief but did not use it, and instead picked at it with the fingers of one hand while she held it in the other. "Yes. Quite all right. It was your story of Cupid's arrow that got me. Laid *very* low, indeed."

And then they were laughing, their heads bent together as they tried to suppress the sounds of their mirth. If he'd realized how ridiculous he'd sounded, Hope would never have said the words; but then again he and Miss Blaise wouldn't be laughing just now, hard, over the shared joke.

Just as *real* lovers would do.

Lovers, let them love. It did have a nice ring to it.

As Hope and Sophia were gasping for air, Princess Caroline returned, the posse of tinkling dogs at her ankles.

Her face was grave. In her portly hands she grasped a large, exquisitely carved lacquered box, black with looping curls set in silver.

Hope's heart turned over in his chest as a pulse of excitement shot through him.

The French Blue. After all this time, his misadventures, and the implausible, sometimes tragic, history of which Hope had been a part—after all that, was he at last to lay eyes upon the jewel that had fascinated first his father, then him, for years? And in the Princess of Wales's close, puce-colored drawing room, no less!

Caroline settled into her chair and unclasped the box's tiny gilt lock. With bated breath, Hope watched as she opened the lid and held out the box for Sophia and Hope to see.

"My God," he heard Sophia murmur as they straightened in unison to get a better look.

The box was lined in finest white velvet, so fine and silken as to appear pearlescent in the molten light of the room. Against this background the diamond glittered very clear and blue, a transparent color that reminded Hope of the open-air pools in the sultan's palace in Constantinople, gleaming beneath a wide, hot sun.

The jewel was somehow smaller than he'd imagined, but much more beautiful. Seductive even, like a woman with a wicked smile and sphinxlike eyes. He sensed trouble. He knew he couldn't, shouldn't, could never have her; but this desire, it was unlike anything he'd ever known, and the impulse to indulge it was overwhelming.

Cut into an irregular oval, the French Blue was about the size of a small rose bloom. Hope wondered how large it had been when Jean Baptiste Tavernier had brought it, rough and uncut, to France from India some two centuries before. The Sun King's jeweler had done the diamond justice, however; it was brilliant and near flawless. Hope understood where the curse had come from, understood why emperors had toppled kingdoms to possess the jewel; understood why the French Blue meant so much to Lake, and how much it would mean to Napoleon. This power the French Blue possessed over men, it was nothing short of hypnotic.

At last Princess Caroline spoke, breaking the diamond's spell.

"Will this suit my young lovers?" She glanced down at the note on the table beside her. "I do believe it is a fair bargain."

Hope pried his eyes from the diamond and looked at the princess. "The French Blue went missing some twenty years ago in Paris. Some believed it lost forever to the wars that followed. How did you find it?"

The princess blinked and looked away, her smile small and knowing. "Your twenty thousand only goes so far, Mr. Hope. Suffice it to say I came into possession of the French Blue through channels that shall forever remain unknown to history."

Hope swallowed his curiosity. They were so close—so very close to getting what they'd come for. He knew that if he pushed Princess Caroline any further she might renege on the deal.

Still. Something told him that the story of how Caroline came to own the diamond was an intriguing one, a missing piece of the puzzle he'd been trying to solve for years.

Beside him, Sophia squeezed his hand. He met her eyes. *Let's go*, she pleaded, *before she changes her mind.*

Hope looked back at the princess. It bothered him, this glaring gap in the jewel's history—what if she'd stolen the diamond? Bought if off a French spy? Was *working* as a French spy?—but he knew there would be time to unravel it later.

He smiled so wide it hurt. "It's perfect. Wouldn't you say, darling?"

Sophia demurred, her cheeks a convincing shade of pink. "You are too generous, Thomas. I shall have my wedding gown made to match it, though it's too large for a ring. Shall I wear it as a necklace or a brooch?"

"Oh, a necklace, definitely a necklace. You shall look ravishing, my dear." The princess closed the box and handed it to Hope. She picked up the note, and without looking at it folded it twice lengthwise and tucked it into the puckered crease between her breasts.

Mr. Hope's pulse skittered as he held the box in his hands. *The French Blue*. Here, right now, in his very hands. Hands that began to shake. He squeezed the box, willing them to be still.

"Thank you, Majesty, you have made a dream come true

this night. You may contact me at the bank tomorrow to arrange the transfer of funds."

"I am sorry to see it go, but as you can see, my husband keeps me in penury." The princess flapped a hand at her surroundings. "Your note brings me comfort of mind and of purse, and for that I must thank you. Perhaps you shall name your firstborn after me? Oh, lovers."

The princess beamed at them. Hope shifted uncomfortably in his seat, his jaw beginning to ache from smiling.

"Well, your Highness," he began, "it's been a pleas—"

"Aren't you going to kiss?" Caroline asked, looking from Hope to Sophia. "It is no small gift, the French Blue, wouldn't you say, Miss Blaise?"

Hope laughed nervously and glanced at Sophia. Her cheeks had gone from pink to persimmon, but her hazel eyes slanted invitingly, sparking with something akin to curiosity.

This was trouble.

"Kiss?" Hope said. "Well. That would hardly be proper, given the circumstances—"

"Not proper? Why, there were never more proper circumstances for a kiss in the history of mankind! Now go on. *Kiss!*"

Hope swallowed for what felt like the hundredth time that night. He turned his head to Sophia and met those warm, inviting eyes of hers. His heart raced, his blood wild.

It's only a kiss, he reminded himself. King and country, saving lives, for England, Harry, and St. George—he could kiss Sophia for all those reasons.

But kissing her for *his* reasons—reasons that now danced in that wild blood of his—that was another matter entirely. He'd already broken a promise he'd made to himself by joining Lake in this wild goose chase. Hope wouldn't—couldn't—break another by seducing Miss Sophia Blaise.

And yet here she was, those eyes and those lips. Oh, those lips, they just begged to be kissed. His groin tightened as he remembered her working that bottom lip earlier that evening. How he'd longed to work it himself, the top lip, too, and—

Again the twist of desire between his legs.

The urge rolled over him as swift and sure as the tide. He

couldn't say no, not when she looked at him like that, confident and terrified and curious all at once.

Thomas set the box in his lap and reached out and cradled her face in his palm, his thumb gently holding her chin in place. His eyes never leaving hers, he leaned forward, wondering vaguely if he even remembered how to do it, and do it well.

Six

Thomas knew how to kiss very well indeed.

Not that Sophia had any experience with things like kisses.

But God *above* it was a special sort of heaven, the firm but sensual press of his lips to hers, the obvious care he took in applying just enough pressure but never too much.

It had all happened so quickly. She watched with bated breath as he'd leaned forward, his blue eyes suddenly serious and clouded. Something about the lean slant of his neck as he tilted his head, just so, made her entire being pulse with longing. Mr. Hope—Thomas—was deucedly handsome. Devilishly, deucedly handsome.

When he drew too close, and she could no longer bear the anticipation, her eyes fluttered shut. And then his breath was soft and sweet upon her face, and she felt herself leaning into him.

And then.

And *then*.

Their lips met. The kiss was tender; the warmth of it surprised her, the intimacy of it terrifying. She had to resist the impulse to pull away, and yet her body yearned for more.

Hope's thumb grazed the line of her jaw, and suddenly the kiss deepened, so much so that Sophia could feel it all the way in her knees. Pleasure coursed through her when his lips moved against hers, slowly, skillfully, and she felt herself falling into the kiss, moving her mouth in time to his.

The assault was endless, and Sophia reveled in the sensation of being captured by him, her blood pounding as Thomas arched over her. With each stroke of his lips he turned his head, and with his hand turned her face so that that she matched his movements. For a moment the kiss slowed, and Hope's hand slipped further toward her. She shivered as his fingers brushed the skin of her neck, his thumb tugging at her earlobe; and then those fingers were tangled in her hair, and he was taking her bottom lip between his own.

All the while moving slowly, with great intent and concentration. His touch was sure but soft. She drank deeply, her belly turning over at his passion; hers, too.

Being kissed was wholly different, and God above so much better, than she'd imagined it would be. But even Sophia in her ignorance knew this was no mere kiss, not the kind a debutante would share with a beau. This kiss was too honest and bold. It spoke of forbidden things. Attraction. Desire. A curiosity to push further, and know more.

Through the pounding of her heart and lips, Sophia heard Princess Caroline making an odd, high-pitched sound. Her blood leapt in dismay at the realization her kiss with Thomas would end.

He slid his hand back to cup her jaw. He tugged at her lips one last time, his teeth lingering on her bottom lip before he pulled away altogether.

Sophia opened her eyes, chest heaving in an attempt to catch her breath. Thomas was looking at her, his blue eyes probing and full of concern.

As if he had anything to be concerned about. The kiss—*his* kiss—it was so deucedly good it left her all but shaking.

For a moment she was overcome by a sense of wonder. Where had Mr. Hope learned such sensual skill? And how did she get so lucky as to experience it?

Regardless, Sophia knew one thing for certain.

She was ruined. Not the kind of ruin that got everyone in the upper ten thousand, her mother especially, so excited. No.

She was ruined for whichever poor marquess or earl's son whom she (hopefully) married. For there was no way on God's green earth that anyone could possibly kiss as well as Mr. Thomas Hope, that any man could thrill her with his lips alone as he had done.

She wanted to throttle him for giving her a taste of something that could never be hers.

Looking into his eyes, she also wanted to beg him to do it again, right here in front of the princess, that diamond be damned. Beg him to kiss her again, and show her everything that came after.

She blinked, a small smile creeping to her lips.

Thomas let out a sigh of relief and returned her smile, the creases at the edges of his eyes deepening with laughter.

Why had Sophia never noticed how handsome he was until now?

Together they turned to face Princess Caroline, who was weeping noisily into the bowl of her hands.

Sophia handed Her Majesty the handkerchief Hope had given her moments earlier.

Caroline took it and blew her nose into it, making a very unladylike honking sound as she did so. Sophia bit her lip to keep from laughing.

"Oh, lovers, don't mind me." The princess waved the sodden handkerchief at no one in particular. "That kiss, God save me! I can see the love you bear one another. It is a—a"—here her voice faltered—"a beautiful thing!"

She collapsed into sobs. Mr. Hope wasted no time. He stood and patted the princess on the shoulder, whispering assurances in her ear—something about love, and life's journey, and the prince regent coming around.

Caroline gazed upon him with a watery smile, and thanked him for his kind words. She looked to Sophia, blotting her red eyes with the handkerchief, and sniffled.

"How lucky you are, dear girl, to be loved by a man like Hope," she said. She paused to blow her nose again. "In this world romance is all but dead. But in his eyes, I see it is alive. Oh, lovers!"

Again the sobs; again, Mr. Hope whispering kind words in her ear. The princess wiped at her eyes, smudging one of her eyebrows so that it appeared a slightly askew comma, hung high in the middle of her forehead.

Mr. Hope met Sophia's gaze over the princess's head as he patted her gently on the shoulder. He shrugged, and mouthed *I'm sorry* with a roll of his eyes. He tried, and failed, to repress the boyish grin twitching at the sides of his mouth.

Sophia looked into her lap and held back her own smile.

How many times she'd smiled this evening—well, considering the circumstances, diamond and deception and all that, more than was proper, surely.

It was all Hope's fault. He made her feel giddy, and alive, and safe, as if nothing she did or said would be the *wrong* thing. And what a relief that was.

At last, when the princess cried her eyes to slits, she called for her maids to put her to bed. Bowing his thanks, Mr. Hope held out his hand to Sophia and helped her rise from the settee, the box containing the French Blue tucked into the crook of his arm.

They left the princess with Gunter and Frederick in the puce-colored room, keeping their steps slow and even lest they be consumed by a newborn eagerness to know what, exactly, *did* come after the kiss they shared.

Sophia had known Mr. Hope for years now—in a professional capacity, of course. Most, if not all, of her family's meager fortune was invested in Hope & Co. stock; Mr. Hope had come to their shabby house in Grosvenor Square once a week to meet with Cousin Violet and discuss—well, Sophia didn't quite know what they discussed, though she was relatively certain it wasn't nearly as interesting as the conversations she'd had with Mr. Hope tonight.

But now that Sophia knew him on more *intimate* terms, she suddenly found it difficult to meet his eyes, training her own on her feet. They sat opposite each other in the swaying coach, the French Blue in its shiny box on the seat beside Mr. Hope.

While they both burst into laughter the moment the coach pulled away from Montague House, after they wiped their eyes a charged silence settled between them. Outside, the night was still and humid, holding its breath for the rain that would come at any moment.

Sophia bit her lip to keep from squirming, the lip that was still tingling from Mr. Hope's ardent attentions. In her chest her heart was giddy, her every sense aware of his presence an arm's length away. Her eyes traveled from his boots, dull from tonight's adventures, up the length of his long, shapely legs, to his square knees, set just apart. His thighs were impossibly long and well muscled, filling his fine breeches to great effect.

Really, she must've been blind all these years not to see what a very fine specimen Mr. Hope was. Very fine indeed.

Of its own volition her gaze kept moving up, passing over a suspicious bulge protruding from the place where his legs met his hips; up past the narrow waist to land on his broad, finely wrought chest, rising and falling in long, steady strokes.

She swallowed. It was more than a little impolite to stare as she was, but *my God* Sophia felt as if she were living in one of La Reinette's thrilling tales. And if this was her only chance to know, even for a night, romance and adventure and dangerous, good-looking men, then manners be damned, she was going to know them, and know them thoroughly.

Her gaze traveled up his neck to his face. Her breath caught in her throat when she caught him looking at her, and she burned beneath the intensity of his stare.

"Awful quiet in there! Any casualties?"

Mr. Lake's jolly, muffled voice startled Sophia and Hope into motion, Sophia jolting forward in her seat, and Mr. Hope jolting forward in his to catch her.

Hope groaned and rolled his eyes. "That man is a plague," he muttered. He reached up and pounded the ceiling with his fist. "No casualties!"

Mr. Lake chuckled. "We'll see about that, you devil."

Holding Sophia's elbows in his palms, Mr. Hope shook his head. "Some cheek that man has, calling *me* the devil."

Sophia smiled, doing her best to ignore the heat that pulsed through her at Hope's touch. "I think he means it as a compliment, Mr. Hope."

"Mr. Hope?" He cocked his head to the side, eyes sparking with mischief. "Sounds like a stodgy fellow, old and boring, doesn't he?"

"Thomas." Sophia's smile grew. "I suppose having shared a closet and a kiss, we are to be friends now."

"Friends, yes." Mr. Hope slid his palms down the length of her forearms to clasp her hands. He looked down at her fingers and ran his thumb along the edge of her palm.

That touch.

A shiver of anticipation sparked up her spine.

"I hope you'll forgive me—" He paused, as if deciding what to say next. At last he looked up. His eyes, very blue, seemed to glow in the darkness, earnest with an edge of daring. He scoffed. "There's no decent way to phrase this, I'm afraid. And what I'm about to say—I mean it as a compliment, I do, so I hope you will take no offense. But you are not at all what—whom—I expected. Where has Sophia been hiding all these years? Under Miss Blaise's bed?"

It was Sophia's turn to scoff. She looked down at their clasped hands, trying in vain to ignore the skittish pounding of her pulse. After a moment she looked up and smiled. "And what of Thomas? Does Mr. Hope stash him in the brandy board of his study?"

"Nowhere else to keep a scoundrel like Thomas. The fellow's liable to drink me out of house and home before summer's out. He's got dashedly expensive taste, you know."

Sophia nodded at the box on the seat beside Hope. "So I'm learning."

"But Sophia," Thomas said, leaning closer. "Sophia, I rather like."

Again she looked down at their hands, only to realize that she, too, leaned close to Thomas, so close the tops of their heads nearly touched. "Me, too. But I'm afraid the *ton* would disagree. And my mother—I daresay Sophia would send her into a fit of apoplexy. I can hear her now: 'The *horror,* oh, the *horror*! How my daughter doth deceive me! Jesus, I am ready, take me now!'

"No," she sighed. "Sophia will not do. She may be an adventurer—"

"And quite the actress, might I add."

Sophia grinned, a bittersweet thing that faded as quickly as it appeared. "Flatterer. Any debutante worth her salt knows how to make a scene. I've yet to master the swoon, but I can wail with the best of them."

He lightly squeezed her hands, imploring her to meet his eyes. They were narrowed, his head cocked to the side in curiosity. He was looking at her in that way again, his handsome face glowing with unabashed interest. Sophia didn't know what she'd done, exactly, to garner such attention; there had been none of the batting eyelashes or forced laughter or meaningless flattery she usually employed at Almack's.

Not that such things had proven effective in snaring suitors, anyway.

But still. Sophia did nothing to earn Hope's attention, save tear through the night at his side with giddy abandon.

And any debutante worth her salt knew giddy abandon was not the sort of sentiment that attracted a well-connected viscount or duke's son.

"Besides." Sophia made to drop Thomas's hands, but he held her fast. "No man in his right mind would risk life and limb on an attachment to an adventurer and an actress."

"The *horror*!" Thomas grinned, shaking his head. "No, Sophia, I must disagree. Men and their right minds aside—really, are we even in possession of such things?—some of us prefer adventurers far and away to debutantes."

Sophia looked away, face burning even before she said the words. "Not the sort of gentleman I hope to marry. That I need to marry."

Hope paused. She felt the heat of his gaze as a stifling silence filled the carriage. She hadn't meant to insult him; heavens, he'd shown her a grand time, and a goodly bit of his rather delectable body besides. It wasn't as if Hope had any intentions toward her, the interest in his eyes and the warmth of his touch notwithstanding.

So why did Sophia feel as if she'd just delivered a ringing blow to his handsome cheek? That she'd hurt him in some unknown, but still visceral, way?

"The sort of gentleman you *need* to marry?" Hope carefully released her hands. He sat back and placed his palms on his knees.

Sophia shifted uncomfortably in her seat. "You know my family's circumstances. I don't have much choice. A good marriage will go far to repair our fortunes, and our reputation."

"But you do have a choice. Your family is in the care of Lady Violet's capable hands. She is a savvy investor, Sophia, and sees to your family's fortunes most ably."

Sophia looked out the window. She swallowed. "It's not that I don't trust Violet. It's just—"

The words caught at a sudden, ominous swell in her throat. Good Lord, how many times was she going to weep tonight?

Only this time she wasn't trying to make a scene.

"It's just?" Thomas said softly.

Sophia waved a hand through the air. "Nothing." She pulled a long breath through her nose, hoping to still her wildly beating heart. Across the carriage she met Hope's eyes and managed a tight smile. "I'm sorry, Thomas. I don't mean to burden you with my. Ahem. Dramatics. Most unseemly of me, isn't it?"

To her very great relief, a smile broke out on Mr. Hope's face. "Let us not forget it was your dramatics that saved our arses tonight. Begging your pardon, Sophia." He patted the lacquered box beside him.

Sophia nodded in the French Blue's direction. "So. What's next for you and Mr. Lake?"

"Well." Mr. Hope sighed, an exhausted sound. "London is crawling with old Boney's spies, so it shouldn't be difficult to turn him on to our scent. The more people who learn of the diamond's discovery, the better chance we'll have of getting the highest price from that blackhearted scrum."

"Perhaps you should host one of your balls." Sophia tapped a finger to her lips. "They are the most famous event of the season. Last year's was one of the few events mama allowed me to attend, and I'll never forget the crush. Or how ridiculous you looked dressed up as that Borgia pope. Almost as ridiculous as Violet in the guise of Lucrezia. She drank so much wine that night she fell down the stairs, do you remember?"

They laughed at that, Hope slowly shaking his head. "How could I forget? If I hadn't been there to catch her, I daresay she'd have a very different nose than the one she has now." He took the box from the seat and held it in his lap. "But I do believe you're on to something, Sophia. Perhaps this year's theme could be 'Great Jewels of the World.' " He paused, a small smile creeping across his lips. "Though there might be some confusion as to what sort of jewels I'm referring to."

With startling clarity, Sophia recalled the scratch of her quill against a half-empty page, recording in badly translated English La Reinette's tale of a smuggler's jewels. Their great size, a "treasure trove the likes of which she'd never seen."

Sophia suddenly understood the madam was not talking about rubies or emeralds.

Her face flooded with a violent rush of heat, and she was grateful for the blurring darkness that hung between her and Thomas.

"Yes. Well." Sophia swallowed. "I'm sure you'll think of something."

She turned her head and nearly started. Familiar stuccoed facades filled the window, slumbering Mayfair mansions rising on either side of a wide, well-kept lane. The smells of London—close air, smoke, and a vague, medieval sort of stench—filled her nostrils.

She blinked as a wave of displeasure spread through her.

Tonight's adventure, it seemed, was over.

It was all she could do not to curse aloud. But she wasn't ready for it to end! Not now. There was more to be done. More to know and discover. More danger, and touching, and kissing—

Her gaze darted back to Mr. Hope, who was pressing his beaver hat onto his mess of curls.

"If you are in agreement, I thought Lake might drop us behind the mews," he said. "I dare not imagine what your poor mama would think if the horses jolted her awake to a face like his."

Sophia grinned. "I don't think she would ever recover."

Hope pounded twice on the roof; Mr. Lake coaxed the horses to stop. Hope removed the diamond from its lacquered box and carefully tucked it into his waistcoat pocket before disembarking. He turned and helped Sophia out onto the street, pulling up her hood against the drizzle that had begun to fall.

Lake looked over his shoulder, his one eye glinting in the dark. "Shall I wait?"

Thomas held out an elbow to Sophia. "No. Good evening, Lake."

Lake's eye narrowed. "Are you sure? I don't mind, really—"

"Lake." Thomas pulled Sophia against him. "*Good evening.*"

Lake sighed, shaking his head. "Very well. Until tomorrow, then. Miss Blaise, it's been a pleasure."

With a low whistle, he jostled the horses into motion and was gone.

Together, Sophia and Thomas turned left and made their way down a dark, narrow alley. Hope held her fast, their legs brushing with every step they took. Neither of them spoke, Sophia's thoughts scattered by the heady thumping of her heart.

Ahead, the familiar grim facade of her family's London house loomed where the alley came out onto the lane. If it weren't for Thomas's close—very close—presence, she would've buckled under the full weight of her disappointment.

It really was over. The adventure, her interlude with Thomas, the kissing and the intrigue, the *kissing*—

Hope suddenly turned to her. He tugged none too gently on her arm so that she faced him and stepped forward, pressing his body to hers. She fell back against the wall, her simmering blood at last ignited by the impatience of his movements.

"Sophia." His voice was barely above a whisper; she felt his breath on her face. Even in the darkness she could see the intent in his eyes. They were serious. Warm.

"What were you doing at The Glossy?"

She looked up at him, too terrified, too enthralled, to reply.

"Sophia. I'll have an answer. La Reinette is not the sort of company a lady like you should keep, adventurer or no. She is alluring, certainly. But dangerous, too. Any deal you have made with her will only come back to haunt you."

Sophia swallowed, hard. "I. Well. I. I'm not at liberty to say."

Hope stared at her. Again he stepped forward, pressing his arm to the wall beside her head, and leaned down so that his face was half an inch from hers.

He surrounded her, his enormous shoulders blocking the night from view. Around them came the growing patter of rain.

"Sophia." His voice was little more than a growl. "A debutante in search of a brilliant match doesn't dally about in whorehouses. Tell me. What business do you have at The Glossy?"

The rain was coming down with great intent, rolling off the brim of Hope's hat into her face. In a swift, impulsive movement, Hope pulled his hat from his head, his curls falling rakishly across his forehead.

Sophia let out a breath. If Hope wasn't holding her up with

his weight, her knees would have *definitely* buckled. Good God, never did a man look so delicious in his looming as Mr. Thomas Hope.

"Sophia," he repeated.

She ran her tongue along her bottom lip, suddenly alive with sensation.

The words came before she could stop them, a defense against his questions; a plea of desire.

"Do it again."

Thomas paused. "I beg your pardon?"

"Kiss me. Like you did for the princess. Do it again."

His eyes searched hers, moving from one to the other. With every sense she implored him to action, tilting her chin so that her lips waited just beneath the soft curve of his own. The air between them tightened, pulling them slowly toward one another.

Sophia vaguely heard Thomas's hat dropping to the ground beside her; and then his hand was cupping her face and his hair was falling into her eyes and his skin brushed against hers. He took her lips with his own, an urgent but luxuriously careful caress that drew a moan from the back of her throat.

He moved ardently over her now; no time, no need for introductions or assurances, just desire, sure and swift, beating between them.

Taking her bottom lip in his teeth, he opened her mouth to him, his tongue sliding along the slick insides of her lips. In her veins her blood pounded.

For the second time that night she surrendered to the ruin of Hope's expert touch, his hands and his shoulders, and dear God, this *kiss*.

Seven

It was her curiosity that did it, the challenge that sparked in her eyes.

That, and her damnably luscious lips. While Miss Sophia Blaise wasn't entirely guileless—she had, after all, helped him swindle the French Blue from Caroline's grasp—the debutante-cum-actress hadn't the slightest idea how alluring she could be.

Especially with that bottom lip caught between her teeth.

Then there was her sudden, impulsive request. *Do it again. Kiss me.*

Good Lord. What was a decent man to do but oblige the lady, and oblige her most thoroughly?

As for his fear that he'd forgotten how to kiss—it boded well, didn't it, if Sophia asked for another?

Somewhere in the back of his mind he knew she was using the kiss as a weapon against him, a way of avoiding questions she quite clearly did not wish to answer. Her presence in La Reinette's chamber was, to be fair, none of his business.

But when it came to Sophia, Hope did not feel like being fair. Fair was for business, for money, for duels. For cards and the races. For ledgers and war and the shops on Bond Street, the grocer, the steward. Fair was predictable and dull.

No. There was certainly nothing fair about Sophia; her egregious loveliness, her scent. There was nothing fair about the way she stoked his growing desire for her with every word she said, her unexpected bravado and the full, honest sound of her laughter.

He would find out what she was up to with La Reinette, come hell or high water.

Just after he kissed Miss Blaise senseless. Yes. He would find out then.

This time he held nothing back. He kissed her with a passion that was at once foreign and intoxicating, driving deeper, softer; the more of her he possessed and discovered, the more of her he wanted. He felt wild, his body and his heart pushing him forward, his hands cupping her face as he coaxed her lips apart with his tongue.

He'd forgotten just how lovely kissing could be.

Sophia yielded to his caresses, parting her lips. Their kiss deepened, slowed for a moment as he gently explored her warmth. Beneath him she shifted, running her palms up over his chest to land on his shoulders. She slid a hand up the side of his throat, and he groaned when she buried her fingers in the curls at the back of his neck, pulling him closer. With her thumb she gently stroked the cut on his cheek; her touch was featherlight, soothing the wound's sting.

He sensed his own fingers tingling for the feel of her bodice as her breasts pressed far too invitingly against his chest. The impulse—it was nearly impossible to resist. He hadn't expected her to be so willing, so curious, so passionate.

If he didn't stop soon, he knew he'd devour her whole. And while he knew the adventurer in her would very much like to be devoured, the debutante had a reputation to protect, and a certain sort of gentleman to marry.

With one last, lingering stroke of his tongue, he pressed his lips, hard, to hers. And then he pulled away.

For several beats they stood, foreheads touching, his hands still on her face as they gasped for air. Her breath was hot on his face; he slid his last finger down to her throat and felt the ecstatic screaming of her pulse. Her skin was scalding. An invitation for his lips to finish what his hands had started.

He did not want to let her go.

The rain began to fall in earnest, fat, insistent drops that fell straight from a low sky. It was a summer rain, and yet not quite. Not yet. The water was calm but cold.

Not yet.

He slid a wet ribbon of hair from her brow. "You are as a nymph, Sophia. So lovely. So tempting."

Hope dropped his hands from her face. He shut his eyes

against the shouting of his blood to kiss her, touch her, take her, and stepped back, releasing the tension between their bodies.

"I am writing her memoirs."

Hope's eyes flew open at the sound of Sophia's voice. Through the rain he could see the gleam of her eyes, her breast rising and falling as she caught her breath.

Out of all the things she could've said, Hope was certainly not expecting her to say *that.*

"You're a writer?"

Sophia shrugged. "I am no Lord Byron—"

"Thank heaven for that."

"But when I was young, I lived in books. They were an escape." She looked down at her hands. "An escape from my family, the chaos of our house. It wasn't long before I began to write. Stories at first, small things, always in secret. I wrote about romance, adventure, pirates of course. When I was seventeen, my governess discovered one of my pirate melodramas I'd foolishly hidden beneath my pillow. Imagine my shock when, rather than rapping my knuckles with her stick, she asked me to pen her memoirs."

Hope blinked as understanding dawned on him. "Your governess wasn't—"

"Yes."

"Not that Miss Entwhistle, surely—"

"Yes. *That* Miss Entwhistle."

"Dear God. I remember those memoirs caused quite the stir that year." Hope tugged a hand through his curls. "Surely your pirate melodramas were less, er, *explicit* than Miss Entwhistle's tales."

"Not really, no."

Forget his curls. Hope gave his cravat a ruthless tug and cleared his throat. "Well, then. How did you come to work for La Reinette?"

"Miss Entwhistle wrote me some weeks ago, said a friend of hers sought a writer for her memoirs. I had every intention of refusing, I did. But from the moment we met, La Reinette enthralled me. I couldn't say no. The stories she tells! Sometimes I feel *I* ought to be paying *her.*"

Thomas furrowed his brow, swiping back his curls with

his hand. La Reinette was his friend and, a decade ago, more than that; she was enthralling, yes, all too aware of the hypnotic power of her beauty.

"Does she mean to publish these memoirs?"

Sophia pushed back her sodden hood. "You know how popular memoirs are these days. The more scandalous, the better."

Thomas stepped forward. He hooked his thumb beneath her chin and lifted her face. Her eyes met his.

"Take care, Sophia. La Reinette may be glamorous, but she resides in a world much different from your own."

Sophia grinned. "If I'm old enough to make my debut, then certainly I'm old enough to look after myself, Thomas."

"I hope you recognize the irony of that statement."

"Please." She placed her palms on his chest. Beneath her touch his heart leapt. "You mustn't tell a soul. I am sworn to secrecy. I shall take care, I promise. Besides, La Reinette guaranteed discretion, protection, too."

"Did she." Thomas frowned. He covered her hands on his chest with his own and sighed. "Very well. But remember what you promised me. And should you find yourself in trouble, you must come to me straightaway."

Pleasure pulsed through him as her grin deepened. "Hm. I think Mr. Lake, with that vicious little eye patch of his, might be better at protecting my prized virtue than a scoundrel like you."

If they weren't standing pressed knee to navel in an alley in Mayfair well past midnight, Hope would've thrown back his head and laughed.

"I've been called many things, Sophia, but never a scoundrel. Though I suppose it *is* scoundrelly to kiss debutantes in dark alleys."

"Scoundrelly, yes. But only in the best of ways."

Her grin was saucy now, playful; her eyes gleamed with pleasure even as drops of rain rolled down the smooth planes of her cheeks.

In the very center of Hope's chest, a puzzling lightness took shape. A lightness he recognized, vaguely, but could not name.

He sighed, biting back the impulse to lean in and proceed with the devouring he'd reluctantly halted a few heartbeats ago. Instead he stooped to pick up his hat and, holding it above Sophia's head, held out his elbow.

Hope sensed her reluctance as she looped her arm through his.

So. She was no more eager for the night to end than he. Hope smiled. He'd done his job, and done it well.

Together they skipped across the lane, the rain mercifully obscuring the sound of their boots on the cobblestones. Sophia led him down the sloping walk that ran along the side of the house, and drew up at last before the kitchen door.

She released his arm and stepped up onto the stoop, turning to face him.

"Well." She clasped her hands. "Thank you, Mr. Hope, for a marvelous evening."

"Thomas. You must call me Thomas."

His name on her lips came out in a soft whisper. "Thomas."

They looked at each other. The lightness in his chest threatened to burst through his entire being. Around them the rain pattered noisily, an opaque curtain that hid this moment from the rest of the world.

Without thinking, Hope leapt forward onto the stoop. With his hand he cupped her face and, drawing close, pressed his lips to her cheek. It was a simple kiss, quick and tender; he couldn't help but kiss her with feeling.

Sophia inhaled, holding her breath as he looked down at her.

"Good night, Sophia." His voice was foreign to him, soft and rough all at once.

Beneath his hand he felt the working of her throat as she swallowed, her eyes never leaving his. "Good night, Thomas," she breathed.

And then, as if waking from a dream, she blinked; she turned and noiselessly scurried into the house.

In her haste, she'd left the door open a crack. He reached for the handle and for a moment allowed his hand to linger there, the metal alive with the memory of her touch. Bowing his head, he closed the door softly behind her. Then he turned and stalked into the darkness.

He took the familiar route in long, hard strides, heart thudding, throat suddenly tight, the pouring rain a welcome antidote to the heat that pulsed beneath his skin.

Thomas.

It had been so long. So very long since he'd been anyone but Mr. Hope, creditor, investor, banker, businessman. Casual acquaintance, trusted but distant friend. This *Thomas*, this man on the lips of a lovely woman, this adventurer—he couldn't possibly exist beside the likes of Mr. Hope. There wasn't time enough in the day, and too many memories besides. Memories he'd spent more than a decade trying to forget.

Hope had left that man behind for a reason. And thus far, forgetting Thomas had served him well.

But now.

He closed his eyes and took a long, deep breath through his nose.

Now all he could smell was the clean, fresh scent of Sophia's skin, the sweet hint of wine on her lips. All he could see were her green-gold eyes, the way they slanted so invitingly as she teased him. He could feel nothing but the warmth of her skin, the opening of her lips, her fingers tangling in his hair.

Could hear nothing but the soft breathlessness of her voice as she said his name.

Thomas.

Nymph indeed.

City of London
Fleet Street
Three days later

Mr. Hope held the diamond up to the thick, golden afternoon light that streamed through his office window. He turned the French Blue over in his fingers, wincing as the jewel blinded him with a particularly vicious spark of radiance.

He was thinking of her again. With a smile he recalled Sophia's theatrical sobs, and her wonder at seeing the diamond for the first time. Afterward he'd kissed her, right there in front of Princess Caroline—

"Forbidden fruit, old friend."

Hope started at the sound of the voice, grappling after the diamond as it tumbled from his grasp.

"Dear. *God!*" He caught the French Blue and held it fast in his palm. He looked up and met Mr. Lake's narrowed eye. "Damn you, Lake, how'd you get past my men? This sneaking about has gone on long enough. You're lucky someone hasn't shot you yet."

"Trust me, they've tried. No one's come close, of course—"

Hope rolled his eyes. "Of course."

"But I'm deadly good at this 'sneaking about,' as you well know by now. And besides. I like the challenge. Front doors are for ninnies," Lake said, setting a familiar black lacquer box before Hope on the desk.

"If by ninnies you mean normal people, then yes, I concur." Hope carefully placed the diamond back in Princess Caroline's box and shut the lid with an agitated *thwack.* He put his elbows on his desk and clasped his hands. "So. Assuming you haven't come to mock my *History of the World's Greatest Diamond* yet *again*—"

"That's not what I was talking about." Lake crossed his bulging arms and from his considerable height stared down at Hope.

Hope blinked, furrowing his brow. "I don't understand."

Lake continued to stare. "Oh, I think you do."

"Actually, I don't." Hope blinked again. *Forbidden fruit.* What the devil was Lake talking abou—

Ah.

Lake was talking about Sophia.

His face rushed hot, and Hope snapped his gaze to the lacquered box on his desk. Lake was a man of many skills; Hope didn't know until now that mindreading was one of them.

"Sophi—Miss Blaise is none of your business," Hope growled. "Nor is she any of mine, for that matter."

Lake's eyes went as round as his mouth. "Oh. Oh no. I wasn't talking about *her*! I was talking about the diamond." He nodded at the box. "Haha! A telling mistake. Well, then. You've made my point for me—best to stay away from them both, before—well, you know why."

Hope's head hit the back of his chair with a bang. "I hate this game."

"Neither of them belong to you, Hope. Not only is your desire for them useless, it's downright dangerous. Deadly, even.

The French Blue will go to Napoleon,"—Lake pounded the desk with his first finger—"and Miss Blaise will go to a nice marquess with a castle and ten thousand a year. Understood?"

Hope scoffed to cover the sharp, unexpected sting of fury that washed over him at the sound of Sophia's name on Lake's lips. "Perhaps I'll understand when I get back that twenty thousand I loaned you. Deadly my arse." He nodded at a neat stack of correspondence on the far end of his desk, each letter meticulously sealed in Hope's signature blue wax. "The invitations to my ball go out today. 'An Evening at Versailles: the Jewels of the Sun King.' A theme, if I don't say so myself, that is also a decent piece of diplomatic bait. Napoleon will be knocking on your door before the evening is out, make no mistake. And then our assignment is done. What's so deadly about all that?"

Lake glowered. "I didn't come to scold you about keeping your breeches buttoned—"

"You didn't? Really? Because it sure as hell feels like you did."

Lake's face softened into grimness. When he spoke his voice was quiet, serious. "There's a leak. Word has gotten out about our . . ." He looked away. "Ah. *Activities* last Wednesday night."

"What?" For the second time that afternoon, Hope started, fearful his heart might leap from his chest. At once he thought of Sophia, imploring him and Mr. Lake to silence on the side of the road in Blackheath. He'd sworn to keep her secrets safe, that no one would ever learn of her arrangement with La Reinette or involvement in Lake's plot.

Hope knew as well as anyone the *ton* was all too eager to tear apart and shun its own. A debutante who snuck out under cover of darkness to pen an infamous courtesan's memoirs was the stuff of dreams for dour dowagers and their miserable ilk. The gossip and censure would be unbearable; not only would it ruin Sophia, it'd likely destroy her family as well.

Never mind all that Hope had at stake. His reputation, his business, and the countless employees and clients who depended on him. His brothers, Adrian and Henry—though they'd been estranged since, well, since as long as Hope could remember—those wastrels remained his dependents. With the rest of the family gone, Adrian and Henry had no one else to whom to turn.

Lake held up his hand. "Whisperings only. Nothing to condemn us; nothing tantamount to blackmail. Not yet, anyway. But someone knows that we were together last Wednesday evening. And that we were up to something. Whoever he is, he's asking all the right questions."

It was Hope's turn to glower. "So what are we going to do? I made clear to you last time we spoke, it's imperative no one know I am involved."

"Trust me." Lake's eye gleamed with malice. Hope swallowed. "We'll find our rat. And when we do, he'll be *very* sorry he ever opened his mouth But you must take care, Hope. Keep your eyes and ears open. Guard the French Blue with your life. And for God's sake, stay away from that girl. If this rat hasn't already figured out Miss Blaise was involved in our plot, he certainly will if she's seen—er—*associating* with you."

Hope let out a long, hot breath and smiled tightly. "It's always the worst-case scenario with you, isn't it, Lake? If we don't end up dead or ruined or both, I'll do my best to help. But I make no promises."

"All right." Lake cocked a brow before he turned and limped toward the window. With a grunt he heaved it open. "But don't say I didn't warn you. Stay away from that girl."

Hope watched in mute shock as Mr. Lake, pushing aside the damask drapes, grasped either side of the window frame and swung his legs through it. Looking back over his shoulder, he nodded. "I'll see you at the ball. Don't forget, it's important everyone is talking about that bloody jewel. See to it that they do."

With another grunt, he launched his bulk through the window and was gone.

One bad leg.

One good eye.

Really, how the devil did Lake do it?

After Hope managed to retrieve his jaw from the floor, he stood and made his way to the stack of invitations on the edge of his desk. He grasped the letter at the top of the pile, the paper pleasantly smooth and heavy in his hands, and read the address scrawled in looping calligraphy across the page.

His Grace the Duke of Sommer
Her Ladyship Violet Rutledge
Her Ladyship the Dowager Baroness Blaise
Miss Sophia Blaise

Hope looked out the open window. A glorious spring day; the fashionable hour approached. No doubt her ladyship the dowager baroness would be chaperoning Sophia's stroll through Hyde Park. Perhaps they would stop to admire the fine horseflesh—and finer fortuned bachelors—on Rotten Row.

His fingers clenched around the invitation in his hand. He glanced at the gleaming malachite clock on the mantel behind his desk.

Quarter past three. He still had time before the beau monde poured out into the park.

He looked at the pile of pages, bills and wills and all matter of business, that cluttered his desk. An afternoon—and evening's—worth of work, at least.

He looked again at the sunlight streaming through the window.

The invitation had to get there *somehow*. He had a bit of business besides to discuss with Lady Violet.

Yes. Business. *Urgent* business. Business that had absolutely nothing at all to do with Miss Blaise.

But if he should perhaps run into her while conducting said business—well. Such things could not be helped. One *must* be polite, after all.

Calling to his man, Hope tucked the invitation into his waistcoat and made for the door.

Eight

It had been three days since her adventure with Mr. Hope. *Thomas.*

Three days since he'd pressed his body to hers as they ducked into a closet to avoid deadly assassins. It was so delicious as to be absurd.

Three days since he'd pressed that last kiss into her cheek, searing her flesh with his eager, knowing lips.

And three days since Sophia had seen or heard from Hope last.

She brought her hand to her face, the skin still burning with the memory of those lips. Truth be told, she'd thought of little else but Hope and his diamond since she'd left him standing in the rain outside the kitchen door.

The more she thought, the more she felt. Confused, certainly; she did not understand the first thing about Hope, who was chasing him and why he was involved with that one-eyed monster of a man Mr. Lake.

But even more certainly than that, she felt intrigued. Despite having spent the entire night at his side, Sophia wanted to see him again. Were his eyes as blue and daring as she remembered? Did he laugh as much during the day as he did at night?

And what was it about him, exactly, that made her belly turn over in the most marvelous of ways?

Having drunk deeply his presence, Sophia was thirstier than ever for more.

Who wouldn't be, after that kiss—

"Sophia!"

She nearly fell from her chair. Sophia blinked, the image of

Thomas's night-darkened face leaning in for the kiss replaced far too suddenly by Lady Blaise's look of horror.

"I'm terribly sorry," Sophia said, straightening her spine. "What was that?"

"The *marquess* was just *asking* if you *enjoy* the *theater*."

Sophia turned to the Marquess of Withington, baring her teeth in what she hoped was more smile than grimace. "Oh, oh yes, my lord. More than you could possibly imagine."

When the marquess had unexpectedly swept into their drawing room a half hour before, boots shining and sideburns trimmed, Sophia had nearly fallen out of her chair for the *first* time that day.

To have the Marquess of Withington call upon one was no small matter. Indeed, to see his gleaming phaeton and pair of matching blacks pulled up before the house had sent a pulse of excitement through her.

And now here he was, patiently wading through what was obviously an excruciating conversation with Lady Blaise and Sophia. She had to give him credit: he was trying very hard not to look at her breasts, and for the most part was succeeding.

Even so. Sophia kept waiting for her initial excitement to return; for the conversation to become enjoyable, or at least easier; for a jest, a joke, a roll of the eyes that would prove the marquess was not the mindless pink he appeared to be.

Thus far, however, he'd proven himself to be exactly that.

"Capital!" Withington's face lit up. "Perhaps you and your mama could join me in my box at Drury Lane. I am partial to Shakespeare—the comedies, of course—but do so love a good opera."

"That would be lovely," Lady Blaise cut in before Sophia could reply. "Perhaps next week?"

"Capital!"

Sophia's smile began to hurt. "I very much look forward to it."

The marquess rose, apparently satisfied. Sophia and Lady Blaise followed him to their feet. "Well, ladies, duty calls; her ladyship my mother is expecting me for tea. It has been a capital afternoon."

He turned to Sophia. To her very great surprise took her hand in his and, jerking into a rather enthusiastic bow, brushed his lips against her knuckles. For a moment his gaze lingered on her bosom before he reluctantly looked up to her face. "Miss Blaise, I do so hope to see you at the theater—"

Over the plane of the marquess's bowed back, a quick, blurred movement in the gallery beyond the drawing room door caught Sophia's eye. A figure, dressed in somber shades of blue and black; she watched as the tail of a jacket disappeared round the edge of the door.

Her heart beat a loud and unsteady rhythm. It couldn't be him. Not at this hour, not today.

Yet. Her heart would not be still.

"Yes, yes, of course, thank you," she murmured as Withington drew up before her.

It seemed an eternity between the time he dropped her hand and his final bow at the door. As soon as the marquess departed, Sophia was moving past her mother, murmuring apologies as she slipped through the door.

Darting into the gallery, she made for the back of the house, where Violet kept her study. Just ahead she heard footsteps, unhurried but firm.

A man's footsteps.

Sophia quickened her pace, walking as fast as her legs would allow without breaking into a run.

She turned the corner, breathless.

There, standing with his back to her in front of the study door, was a familiar figure. With no small appreciation she took in his long, powerful legs, broad shoulders, and the mop of dark, unruly curls that just brushed his collar.

At the sound of her steps he turned his head, right fist raised as if he were about to knock.

In the shadowy light of the hall their gazes collided.

Oh, yes. His eyes were *definitely* as blue as she remembered, and just as piercing. A breathless warmth washed over her, coaxing her lips into an open smile she couldn't have suppressed if she'd wanted to.

A smile that certainly didn't hurt.

"Miss Blaise!" He turned so sharply he lost his footing, falling into an ungainly bow. A wide, flat packet fell from his breast pocket onto the floor.

At once they both dashed forward to retrieve it, their heads nearly bumping as Sophia picked up the packet. Swiping back his hair with one hand, Hope helped her to her feet with the other.

He cleared his throat, his cheeks pink with embarrassment as he attempted to straighten his person. Sophia thought he appeared adorably disheveled; she struggled to resist the temptation to reach out and tuck an errant curl behind his ear.

"Thomas," she said softly. She held out the packet to him. "I did not intend to startle you. Aren't men of your—er—*experience* supposed to be immune to surprise? A sixth sense and all that."

Hope took the packet and looked down at it. While he did not smile, she could tell he was amused. "Seems the only sixth sense I've got is a knack for finding trouble."

"And diamonds. Very *big* diamonds. Besides, what you call trouble others might call—dare I say it?—adventure."

He laughed, looking up at her at last. His eyes were laughing, too, the skin around them crinkling pleasantly.

A beat of silence passed. The color in Hope's cheeks deepened, giving him the look of a shy—albeit devilishly handsome—boy.

She became acutely aware of it then, the tug of desire that moved between them. Bodily desire, of course; but also a desire to *stay*, to ask questions, know more, to understand and be understood.

She recognized the sensation from that night three days ago. But today it felt stronger than it did then. More immediate, a hungrier feeling.

Thomas must have felt it, too. He stepped forward, keeping his voice low. "I wanted—" He paused, embarrassed. "I wanted to write, I did—but I. Well. No, no, that doesn't sound at all right; let me try again. I have thought. Thought about this—er, often. Thought about *you*—"

Sophia waited on the tips of her toes as Mr. Hope tugged a hand through his hair, cheeks flaring with a huff of frustration.

"I'm dismal at this, aren't I?"

"Yes." Sophia offered a small, entranced nod. "But do go on."

"What I meant to say is, I care for—"

Suddenly the study door creaked open, and together they turned to see Cousin Violet, brow furrowed, step into the hall, a ledger cradled in the crook of her left arm. Her blue eyes slid from Hope to Sophia and back again, narrowing with suspicion.

"Did I," she raised a brow, "interrupt something? I wasn't expecting to see you, Mr. Hope, until Tuesday."

They both rushed to speak at once.

"No."

"No!"

"No, most certainly not, no interruption *what*soever!" Thomas looked down at the packet in his hand. He started, as if seeing it for the first time; after half a beat he thrust it forward, offering it to Sophia. "I was just delivering an invitation to my annual ball. Friday next; I do hope you and your family will be able to attend."

"Your ball!" Violet slammed her ledger shut, eyes alight with excitement. "Of course we'll be there. It's the only event of the season that's actually any fun. And your liquor! I promise not to drink as much of it as last year."

She wedged herself between Sophia and Thomas and grabbed the invitation, turning the packet over in her hands and breaking the seal. Sophia peered over her shoulder as she read it.

" 'The Jewels of the Sun King!' " Violet looked up in amazement. "I daresay it's even better than last year's theme! Wherever did you get the idea?"

Over her head, Hope met Sophia's eyes, a smile playing at the corners of his lips. "Come to the ball and perhaps you'll find out."

"You may count on it." Violet folded the page and playfully tapped him on the shoulder. "Are you to be the Sun King?"

"I should think so, yes."

"And your queen? Who is to play her?"

For a split second Hope's eyes widened with panic. A charged silence settled over them; Sophia winced as the floorboards creaked beneath her feet. Violet couldn't possibly know—could she?

Hope cleared his throat and brushed back his curls with his first two fingers. The color in his cheeks rose. "Well. No one at the moment, I'm afraid."

"Are you ill?" Violet drew close. "I've never seen you blush like that."

Again Hope met Sophia's eyes, a plea. "Yes, well . . . no, I mean no. . . ."

Sophia swept between them, looping her arm through Violet's. "After your inquisition, you're lucky Mr. Hope does not rescind his lovely invitation. Besides, we must change if we're to make it to the park on time."

Violet hesitated, searching her cousin's face with those narrowed eyes of hers. Sophia felt herself growing warm beneath Violet's scrutiny, waiting for her to call her and Hope out, question them on the palpably charged air that crackled between them.

Violet was no fool, but Sophia was no witless debutante, either. And so she returned her cousin's gaze levelly, coaxing the heat from her face with every passing heartbeat.

"Very well." Violet turned to Hope. "You're keeping something from me, I can feel it. But I suppose I can wait until the ball to squeeze it out of you. Until Thursday, then."

Mr. Hope bowed. Watching from half a step away, Sophia swallowed in appreciation. Like his person, Thomas's bow was elegant, earnest, and just singular enough to intrigue, rather than intimidate.

He rose. "Until Thursday, Lady Violet." Turning to Sophia, he said, "Miss Blaise. I look forward to seeing you at the ball. It is my sincerest wish that you find it as enjoyable as does your cousin."

She met his eyes one last time, heart thudding in her chest as she read the relief there, and the promise.

A promise, she liked to think, for another go at that kissing business.

"But I don't understand." Violet turned, peering over her shoulder at her reflection in the mirror. "What's a nymph to do with Louis XIV and his jewels? I still think my idea is better. Madame de Montespan makes for a far more intriguing character than a wood nymph. A more dramatic entrance, too."

Sophia glanced in the mirror and, furrowing her brow, bent to smooth the gauze of Violet's train. "My mother would drop dead if you paraded in public as the king's infamously nubile mistress, and you know it. The gauze is scandalous enough, don't you think?"

Violet tugged the neckline of her costume so low the threat of a rogue nipple was very real indeed. She puckered her lips in satisfaction before turning to her cousin. "I suppose. Here, sit; your curls have fallen."

Sophia watched in the mirror as Violet, pins clenched between her teeth, went to work on her hair, fingers featherlight as they tucked and twisted.

Her bravado notwithstanding, Violet would drop dead surely as Lady Blaise if she knew the *real* reason why Sophia so ardently insisted they costume themselves as nymphs for Mr. Hope's ball.

Even now a shiver ran down her spine at the memory of Hope's murmured words, the low, smooth rumble of his voice as he said them.

You are as a nymph, Sophia. So lovely. So tempting.

Would he remember? And more importantly, would he notice her amid the beautiful, perfumed masses that crowded his house?

"There. Lovely." Violet stood back to admire her handiwork. She caught Sophia's eye in the mirror. "Are you nervous? You look nervous. Is it that marquess again, Wart-what's-his-name?"

Sophia blinked, the pleasant reverie of Hope's voice and his lips and the rain dropping from the tip of his nose disappearing in the space of half a heartbeat.

"You know his name, Violet." She sighed. "Withington *is* handsome, isn't he?"

Violet wrinkled her nose. "If fops are your type, then yes, he's very handsome indeed. You always were ambitious, cousin."

"It's no surprise, considering I was raised on Debrett's." She scoffed, but in the mirror her eyes were serious. "I understand that marrying a marquess with ten thousand a year isn't the only dream there is. But my world is very small, Violet. *Our* world is small. What else am I to do? How else can I improve my lot, raise myself, than to marry a man like the marquess? I couldn't very well start a bank, or run a business, like Th—like Mr. Hope. There *is* no other dream for a girl like me, poor and nameless, than to seek a title and live in a great house. A house that doesn't leak when it rains."

Violet rolled her eyes.

"What?" Sophia pouted. "I thought that was a very good speech."

"The house doesn't leak *that* much." Violet playfully tugged on a loose curl at Sophia's ear. "Besides, you're young. Perhaps it's a blessing your first season is . . ." She paused, searching for the right word. "Off to a slow start. Perhaps it's a sign you should take the time to discover what other dreams, as you call them, exist. There's got to be others besides marrying that marquess of yours."

Sophia placed her hands on the vanity and rose, sighing. "You're an heiress with a fondness for books and brandy. Not all of us are so inclined to ignore the opposite sex."

Especially, Sophia thought, when said opposite sex kissed one as if the world were about to end.

Violet took one last look in the mirror, patting her hair. "I don't ignore them, cousin, I mock them. And you forget whatever meager fortune I am meant to inherit is in peril." She turned and looped her arm through Sophia's. "But enough of this boring talk of our troubles. Hope asked we arrive early—"

"He did?"

Violet paused, eyeing her cousin. "Yes. Though I haven't a clue why. Do you?"

Sophia's shoulders shot to her ears. "Why would I know? He's your acquaintance, Violet. Not mine."

But even as she said the words, a new wave of excitement rippled through her. They were to be guests of honor, then. Perhaps Hope *did* remember.

"Hm. A mystery, then. How so like him! Clever man."

Violet led Sophia down to the front hall, where Mr. Freeman, the butler, waited with a letter on a small tray.

"For you, Miss Blaise."

Sophia furrowed her brow. "For me? That's silly. A letter, and at this hour? No one ever writes to me."

It was addressed simply as *M. Blaise* in a gnarled, unfamiliar script. She freed her arm from Violet's grasp and opened the letter somewhat clumsily with her gloved fingers.

"What is it?" Violet asked casually as she straightened the embroidered edge of her own glove.

Sophia inhaled sharply as she read for a second time the

letter's three uneven lines. Her heart began to pound thickly in her chest, a rush of panic prickling at her temples.

For a moment she froze, throat closing with fear.

"Sophia?" Violet was looking at her now. "Is everything all right?"

With hands that trembled, Sophia folded the letter. "Do you know who sent this, Mr. Freeman?"

"I'm afraid I do not, Miss. Found it tucked into the kitchen door. I asked the maids, but they did not see or hear any visitors. Curious."

Sophia swallowed. "Curious, yes."

"What does it say?" Violet asked.

"Nothing important." Sophia managed a tight smile.

Lady Blaise scurried into the hall then, her face and gown a matching shade of pink as she struggled to catch her breath.

Sophia had never in all her years been so relieved to see her mother. She slipped the note into the elbow of her glove and turned to greet her.

"Good heavens, Mama, whatever is the matter?"

"My," she huffed, "gown. It's a bit. *Tighter* than I remember."

Violet raised a brow. "A bit?"

"Oh, hush, you. I can't wait until you get old; we'll see who is laughing then." She padded to the front door, waving her fan. "Come along, we mustn't keep Mr. Hope waiting. I hear from Lady Dubblestone that Withington is to attend. Oh! And rumor has it that wastrel Beau Brummell is to make an appearance, though everyone knows he is falling out of favor with the regent, and did you know he soiled himself at the race this past week . . ."

Sophia settled stiffly into the carriage beside Violet, who, as annoyed as she was at Mama's endless tittering, seemed to have all but forgotten about the mysterious letter.

Good. This sort of trouble was above and beyond even Violet's expertise. The sort of trouble that Sophia had hoped to avoid all along.

Nine

"I look ridiculous."

Mr. Lake shrugged at Hope's grimace. "But I thought you liked costumes? In France you were all too eager to don a disguise. Remember the time you played a one-armed butcher—"

"*This,*" Hope pointed to the towering wig of black curls that wobbled on his head, "is a rather different scenario, don't you think? The wig, the shoes—it's a bit much, even for me. And dear *God* my head hurts."

Lake waved away his words. "Small price to pay for king and country, my friend. Though it does make you wonder how old Louis managed it. Fellow must've been bald as a bat to want to wear a wig like that."

"He was a glutton for punishment, no two ways about it." Hope took a deep breath, resisting the urge to itch his head. "Actually, I'm beginning to think we have quite a lot in common."

They were on the terrace, an open bottle of French cognac, smuggled into London not two days ago, resting on the stone balustrade between them. Over the tops of neighboring houses a cloudless sky faded to dusk, the edges of the horizon glowing faintly with the last of the day's sun. A curving peel of moon swam noiselessly through the blue above their heads.

Sounds of last-minute preparations floated through the open ballroom doors. The hurried steps of a dozen footmen; the famous opera soprano he'd hired, practicing her aria; the clink of crystal; the murmuring of kitchen maids as they laid out the refreshment tables.

The sounds pleased him. Nearly five years ago to the day he'd hosted his first costumed ball with the intention of attracting wealthy—and well-known—clientele. A generation before, the Hopes were among the most prominent families in Amsterdam, bankers to and social equals of princes, dukes, even sultans. Their home in Groenendaal Park was one of the finest in the city, its rooms alive with a never-ending progression of teas, soirees, balls, and exhibitions.

It had all ended abruptly, one tragedy after the next. But the memory of his family, their home, and the people whom they had welcomed and entertained there, had kept Hope warm throughout the years of misadventure that followed. When he at last landed on his feet in London, he set about resurrecting the glamorous heyday of the family he so sorely missed.

The ball was an absolute triumph. By the third year, Hope counted among his clients the greatest and wealthiest titles of the *ton*. Though some of the more stalwart members of society refused to socialize with one who (God forbid) *worked* for a living, an invitation to Hope's costumed soirees was nonetheless a coveted one.

This year was no different; he'd done everything in his power to ensure its success. Hell, Hope had even convinced that infamously slippery rake the Earl of Harclay to attend. Tonight's ball was, Hope knew, going to be the biggest and best he'd ever hosted.

Surely there was no greater stage on which to play out Lake's plot to snare Napoleon with the French Blue.

Lake lifted the bottle of cognac to his lips and took a short, ruthless swig. He wiped his mouth with the back of his hand and, as if reading Hope's thoughts, said, "When Bonaparte's men make contact, send for me straightaway. And don't lose sight of that diamond."

Hope reached out and swiped the bottle from Lake's hand. "And you. Don't drink all my cognac. It's bloody impossible to get these days." He took a pull and, retrieving the cork from his waistcoat pocket, pounded it back into place with the heel of his hand. "Who do you think is going to steal the French Blue, anyway? Everyone who's coming tonight can buy their own damned jewels. If I were to peg anyone, it'd be you. Besides, I hired twenty extra men to patrol the ballroom, just in case. Trust me, Lake. *Nothing* is going to happen."

"I don't have to remind you there are no more famous last words than those."

Hope rolled his eyes, deciding a change of subject would best keep him from throttling his unwelcome guest. "Speaking of words. Any word on our leak?"

"No. But I can't shake th—"

They both turned at the sound of female voices coming from inside the ballroom.

"Ah," Lake said softly. "Appears your first guests have arrived."

"Indeed." Hope strained for a look inside, but straightened before the weight of his wig toppled him to the ground.

"Be careful, Hope. And good luck."

"Same to you. I'll be in touch in the morn—"

Turning back, the words caught in his throat. Lake was gone, nothing but the cool evening air in his place.

Hope peered over the edge of the balustrade and sighed. "One of these days you're going to hurt yourself, old man," he murmured.

Taking the bottle in his hand, he turned and made his way through the doors into a gallery, narrowly avoiding disaster when with his gilt-tipped walking stick he tripped a footman carrying a tray of petit fours. Hope apologized profusely, rolling his eyes in the direction of his wig as if that should explain everything.

He handed off the cognac to another passing footman with instructions to decant it so that Hope and his most important clients might enjoy it later that evening. Straightening his person as best he could with a two-stone wig on his head, Hope strode into the ballroom to welcome his first guests.

Three ladies stood in the center of the room, heads tilted back as they admired the spectacle of his very own Versailles. Lady Blaise, behind whose ample figure her wards were hidden, took a step forward, revealing a young woman with elegant posture, her gown a diaphanous creation of ivory gauze. Pale rosebuds, the same blush that now rose on her cheeks, were tucked into the swirl of her dark hair.

For a moment he stood watching, wonderstruck at her beauty, her daring.

So she *did* remember.

You are as a nymph, Sophia. So lovely. So tempting.

Did she think of that night as often as did he? These past weeks had been an exercise in frustration; without fail, his thoughts would wander from rents and markets to the slope of Sophia's cheek, the curious innocence of her touch. In the midst of appointments—important appointments, during which the fate of hundreds of thousands of pounds was decided—Hope would miss entire swaths of debate, enraptured as he was by the memory of their time together, the tantalizing possibility there would be more to come.

And now here she was, more lovely, impossibly, than he remembered. His heart tightened in his chest; his pulse took off at a gallop.

From across the ballroom she turned her wide hazel eyes to him. He saw his own anticipation mirrored in their gleam; but there was something else there, a worry, a fear.

A desire to know what troubled her overwhelmed him. He crossed the ballroom in three long, purposeful strides, a smile on his lips as he welcomed them to his ball.

Their conversation was brief but merry. Hope's admittedly excessive praise of Sophia's costume—"A nymph, I presume? What a marvelous conceit. A goddess of the wood, and of the hunt. The Sun King was a great hunter, and would have delighted in such a creature. We go together, you and I"—drew a look of consternation from Lady Violet, but he couldn't help himself.

Sophia said very little but kept her gaze trained on Mr. Hope, as if she were trying to tell him something. He nodded in reply. When the crowd thickened, it would be easy enough to pull her aside without being seen.

The ladies continued to gawk; when Hope waved over the men he'd hired as guards, one of them bearing Princess Caroline's black lacquered box, he thought Violet's eyes might pop out of her head.

It was a rather clever idea if Hope didn't say so himself. Mr. Lake was right to suggest that advertising the French Blue's discovery would only increase its value: the greater number of people who saw it, the greater number who would want it, speak of it, inflate its size and beauty. And what better way to advertise the beauty of the jewel than to display it slung about a beautiful woman's neck?

Better yet that said beautiful woman did and said as she pleased without a care for what others thought. Lady Violet was certainly one of a kind; Hope had yet to meet another woman with a taste for brandy and high-stakes gambling. She'd have everyone and their mother talking of the French Blue well before the night was out.

Hope laced the diamond onto a collar of gems he'd borrowed from a client's wife and carefully lifted the brilliant garland onto Violet's neck, the French Blue glittering from her breast. When he clasped the garland, his fingers grazing the nape of her neck, he felt her shiver.

"Are you all right, Lady Violet?"

"Yes, quite. What a thrill to wear the Sun King's diamond, truly," she said, and shivered again.

Hope's idea worked. As the ball began in earnest, dancers stomping and men laughing and women gossiping behind gossamer fans, it seemed no one spoke of anything but the Sun King's fifty-carat blue-gray diamond. It would only be a matter of time before Napoleon would knock on his door, begging for the jewel.

Assured the job was done and nothing, indeed, could possibly go wrong, Mr. Hope set out for Sophia. He hoped and prayed that whatever burdened her had nothing to do with their shared adventure.

His every sense told him otherwise.

Hope stopped once to accost the Earl of Harclay, that rakehell, who in turn was accosting Lady Violet, ogling her bosom as if he'd like to eat it. Only after Lady Violet assured Hope, in so many words, that she could look after herself, thank you very much, did he move on.

He found Sophia at last bobbing about in a cotillion. Hope smiled at her obvious awkwardness as she twirled clumsily around the Marquess of Withington, who, in his satin breeches and azure-velvet coat, cut an annoyingly dashing figure.

Hope's smile faded as his head began to pound with an unfamiliar urgency. It was the wig, yes, the bloody thing; but he recognized the prick of jealousy, too. It felt at once silly and terribly serious, more serious than silly as he remembered Sophia's halting speech about a brilliant match, Lake's admonition that Sophia would marry a titled gentleman with ten thousand a year.

His fingers clenched around the smooth, rounded finial of his walking stick. The metal felt hot against his skin, a welcome distraction from the entirely unwelcome feelings holding him captive. He breathed deeply, fighting back with every rational thought he could muster.

He was a man of business, first and foremost. He could not forget the hard work that had seen him to this moment; nor could he forget the work that had yet to be done. He was the bank. The bank was his life, a living tribute to the family fate had left behind.

And with Lake's plot in play, Hope had more to lose than ever. These feelings, the attraction he felt for Sophia, were dangerous. He'd dedicated his life to Hope & Co.; and in that life there was no place for a lovely, witty, beautifully terrible dancer like her—

Hope found himself at her side just as the dance was ending. When she turned to him, color high, lips parted in a half smile, he knew he'd made the right decision.

Or perhaps the worst decision ever.

"Miss Blaise." He reveled in the satisfaction of knowing her eyes were upon him, taking in his bow with no little appreciation. "The next dance. Might I have it?"

She eyed the wig towering over his person. "Are you sure you're able to dance with that—that *thing* on your head? It might pose a hazard to the other guests."

Damn it, Hope had forgotten about the wig. It was liable to cause a good bit of damage staying right where it was; should it move, the destruction could be catastrophic.

He pulled the monstrosity from his head, sighing with relief as he did so. "Forget about the wig. Dance with me."

Sophia glanced at the marquess, hovering just out of earshot. "We're in the middle of a set, you see, and I couldn't very well abandon his lordshi—"

As if on cue the dashing marquess stepped forward, wiping his brow with his sleeve. He smiled ebulliently at Hope. It was all Thomas could do not to sock him in his dashing jaw.

"Mr. Hope! Capital ball, good man, capital ball! And your costume!"

Hope smiled tightly. "Let me guess. Capital?"

The marquess threw his head back and laughed as if Hope had cracked the funniest joke he'd ever heard. "Capital, yes, how ever did you know?"

"A lucky guess. Listen, my lord." Hope pulled him close. "You must tell no one. But I've a stash of cognac in my study, smuggled in from France not two days ago. It's reserved for my best clients only—you included, of course."

"Capital!" Again the marquess wiped his brow, looking with some reluctance at Sophia. "After Miss Blaise's spirited dancing, I find that I *am* rather parched, though we're only halfway through the set . . ."

"Have no fear. I shall merely take your place and join you when the set is through."

"Are you quite sure? I wouldn't want to take you away from your cognac. And Miss Blaise, I couldn't very well leave her—could I, Miss Blaise?"

Sophia looked levelly at Hope, her lips curling into a grin. "Please, my lord, go find your refreshment. It won't do to have you parched."

Hope shoved the marquess off the ballroom floor as gently as could be managed, tucking the wig and cane into his hands as he went. "If you don't mind giving these to a footman, I'd be much obliged."

He turned back to Sophia.

Dear God she was beautiful.

And now, finally, she was his. At least for a little while.

"Well then, now that that's all sorted out—shall we dance?"

Sophia stepped forward. "Yes. Though you may regret asking me—I'm not very good at it."

"So I noticed."

Hope turned at the sound of commotion near the orchestra. That cad the Earl of Harclay—really, the man was far more trouble than he was worth—was tossing a reticule heavy with coin into the lap of the first-chair violinist. Hope couldn't make out what he was saying, but suddenly the ballroom was erupting with gasps and shouts as the master of the dance called for a waltz.

Hope looked at Sophia. They both rushed to speak at once. "A waltz?"

"That's impossible!" Sophia's eyes were wide. "A debutante can't be seen *dancing* the *waltz*! I don't even think I know how."

But the music was already starting; despite the risks to Hope's sanity and Sophia's reputation, he wrapped an arm around her waist and tugged her to him. With his other hand he drew out her opposite arm and together they moved—or, rather, stumbled—through the first steps of the waltz.

"Let me go!" she hissed. "I'll dance the next set with you."

Hope looked down at her with a smile. "Too late, Miss Blaise. Follow my steps—yes, that's—no, no, the *other* foot—no, the other *other* foot!"

He tripped over her misplaced foot and together they lurched forward, nearly toppling Lord Harclay and Lady Violet before Hope in his terror turned and righted his and Sophia's bodies.

"Dear God," Hope gasped. "If I'd been wearing my wig I daresay we'd both be dead!"

To his very great pleasure he watched as, despite her protests, Sophia dissolved into breathless laughter, closing her eyes against the force of it.

When she opened them she met his gaze, a small smile lingering on her lips as her steps, praise heaven, fell in time with his. He held her to him and they danced together, the music so loud, so insistent in its rhythm, Hope lost himself for a moment. He had cognac in his blood and the most beautiful woman at the ball in his arms; the plot was in play and business could only get better.

But something was not quite right. That fearful gleam had returned to Sophia's green eyes, and a shallow crease now appeared between her brows—though, to be fair, it *did* seem to require enormous concentration on her part to land the three steps of the waltz.

"What is it?" He turned, pulling her close enough so that he might murmur in her ear. "My promise remains the same, Sophia. I gave you my word then, the same as I give it to you now. Anything you say shall remain between us."

Beneath his hand on her back she stiffened. As they turned once, twice, three times, she glanced over her shoulder, watching with wide eyes the couples that twirled around them.

He pressed his lips to her ear. "I will know what it is that's bothering you. Tell me, Sophia, so that I might help you. You've my word."

"That's just it, Thomas." She looked up at him. "You may have given me your word, but someone knows. Knows about *us*. About what happened that night."

A clammy sweat broke out along his collar as he pulled her close, imploring her with his eyes. Just as he'd suspected. "Who threatened you?"

"I don't know. It—it was a letter. I didn't recognize the seal, or the script. It said something—" She paused, eyes wet. "Something like, 'two queens, the ace of diamonds, soon you will have a royal flush.' I've got it in my glove; it arrived this evening, just as we were leaving to come here."

"Well." Hope's throat tightened ominously. "Whoever wrote it has a terrible sense of humor."

He turned course sharply, making for the gallery at the far side of the ballroom. He saw nothing, felt nothing save the desire to get Sophia alone, to make sure she was safe, to talk and together tease out the source of these threats.

As he sped through the tangle of couples, Hope cursed himself for ever allowing her to join them in the first place. Yes, it had been mostly Lake's doing, but in his lust-filled haze Hope had done little to stop it. Sophia was intelligent, certainly, but she was also innocent. She hadn't a clue about the enormity and depth of the cesspool into which she'd dipped her pretty toe.

If Hope didn't put a stop to her adventuring, it would swallow Miss Sophia Blaise whole.

The music was reaching a crescendo, the ballroom a whirl of white satin and kerseymere coattails. There was laughter and whispered conversation, couples flush-faced from the heady thrill of such unexpected privacy in the midst of an epic crush.

Surely, Hope reasoned, no one would notice if he whisked Sophia away for a few moments? And even if someone did, he could pass it off as business—

His heart went to his throat at the enormous, shimmering crash that sounded just above their heads. In one swift, sure movement, he tucked Sophia into his chest, covering her head as shards of glass rained down on them.

He watched in mute horror as three lithe, shadowy figures catapulted through the gallery windows into the ballroom. They swung through the air and landed on the trio of enormous chandeliers that illuminated the crush. Handling the daggers held fast in their teeth, the intruders began sawing at the silken ropes from which the crystal monstrosities hung.

Panic, wild and hot, pounded through Hope. *My God, my God, what the devil is happening?*

The music came to a jarring halt as stunned silence settled over the ballroom. A beat later the crowd erupted in screams, shouts, swoons. Hope watched, trembling with fury, as the sinister-looking men he'd hired to guard the French Blue suddenly turned on his guests, waving their pistols as if they'd very much like to use them.

Traitors.

He'd been betrayed. The *why* was obvious enough: King Louis XIV's plum-sized diamond was no small prize.

But the *who* was more difficult. Had Napoleon's men foiled their plan? Was it one of Lake's own, working against his master? Or was it a band of ambitious petty bandits, hoping to make the theft of a lifetime?

A shot sounded; more screams. Against his chest Sophia was shaking. He did not answer her whispered questions.

"Who is it? Are you all right? What's happening, Thomas, please!"

He held her fast against him, pressing his back against the gallery wall. The crush roiled with chaos, bodies climbing over one another in attempts at escape.

From above came an ominous groan. The first chandelier now hung from a thread, the bandit hard at work severing the last bit of rope.

"Move aside!" he screamed, gesturing wildly with his free arm. "Move, quickly, everyone must *move*!"

With a thrumming *snap* the chandelier broke free. The thief somersaulted away, landing with inhuman lightness in a far corner.

The chandelier landed with a piercing crash, sending shards of crystal and gilt across the ballroom. People dashed about, streaming out of windows and doors like water in a flood.

Thomas, please, I must find my mother, and Violet—

"Not yet." It was all he could manage. He held her fast; in his confusion, his terror and his rage, she kept his head—just barely—above the water.

The second chandelier came thundering down, followed in quick succession by the third. Plunged into darkness, the ballroom descended into a pit of writhing shadows. The roar of panic was unbearable.

Under cover of blackness, Hope began to move, Sophia held close in the crook of his arm. Against his ribs he felt the furious working of her heart, her breath hot and fast on his collar.

Together they waded into the dark, Hope offering a hand to those he could reach. To his very great relief it appeared no one was seriously injured.

Across the ballroom came another shot, more screams; running footsteps.

The thieves. It would only be a matter of time before they found the diamond, and then, he knew, all hell would break loose; no doubt they'd shoot anyone who blocked their path to escape.

She couldn't stay, not with everything at stake. Her life most of all.

And Hope. He couldn't leave for the same reason.

He released Sophia, grasping her by the shoulders so that he might see her face. Pale, eyes wide and wet. No tears, but she did not meet his gaze. She opened her mouth as if to speak, but he shook his head, bending his neck so that their noses nearly brushed.

"Look at me, Sophia. *Look at me*. Go find your mother and get out of here. Do you understand? If you stay you'll end up hurt or worse. There's a hidden door the servants use toward the front of the ballroom. Use that, it will take you out to the street."

She swallowed, searching his eyes. "And what will you do?"

"Don't worry about me. Go. Now. Watch you don't trip over the chandeliers!"

Taking her by the arm, he pushed her toward the door,

watching as she haltingly made her way across the ballroom. A strange twist in his chest left him momentarily breathless.

But he wouldn't make the same mistake twice. Her reputation—never mind her life—was now in peril after she'd played a role in their plot. He would not stoke that fire by courting her involvement once more.

Just as Sophia was fading into black, he saw her loop her arm through that of a portly woman wearing a drooping feather headdress.

Her mother. Thank God, she'd found her mother. He watched as, making for the servants' entrance, they disintegrated into the darkened chaos of the ballroom.

He took a deep breath, closing his eyes against the impulse to follow them out, to see to their safety.

The diamond, he reminded himself. He had to secure the diamond, or all would be lost.

Hope turned to the ballroom, screams and shouts echoing off its tall-coffered ceiling.

And then there was a scream—well, a voice, really—that he recognized.

Lady Violet.

The French Blue.

He took off at a sprint, dodging his way to the center of the ballroom. From a knot of heads and legs Violet rose, the Earl of Harclay holding her by the elbow. Beyond came the sound of running footsteps—the thieves, Hope knew, making a run for it.

Violet's hand was at her neck.

A neck that was bare.

"The diamond! Lord Harclay, the diamond—it's gone!" Violet shouted, before promptly turning to the earl and vomiting on his very fine shoes.

Serves him right, Hope thought, for all the trouble he's caused tonight.

Hope turned, waving his arms in the direction of the intruders' fading footsteps. "Stop them! They're making off with the French Blue! Wait, you bastards, I'll have you hanged!"

But even as the words left his lips, Hope knew it was too late.

The French Blue was gone.

Ten

Sophia swung through the kitchen door into the stable yard, her mother huffing two steps behind. Above them they heard the cacophony of Hope's ballroom: muffled shouts, the crack of pistols, shattering glass.

"Sophia," she panted. "What in. God's name. Happened up. There?"

"I don't know," Sophia replied, before saying, more softly, "but I do mean to find out."

Across the yard, the mews were just as dark and disordered as the ballroom. Guests flung themselves into any carriage they could find; grooms scurried about helplessly as a great knot of traffic blocked the lane that led out into the street.

Sophia scanned the mess but, praise heaven, did not see the Rutledge family's dusty old coach among those vehicles trapped by the crush.

"Come, Mama, this way. Only a bit longer, I promise."

She tugged her mother around toward the street, Lady Blaise all the while moaning in staccato sentences about her poor nerves, and poor Hope, and where in God's name was Violet? They'd all better hope she was not with that handsome libertine the Earl of Harclay, or they would be ruined, the whole family . . .

Sophia tugged harder, mind racing all the while. The French Blue had been stolen, that much she knew, and by thieves with a flair for acrobatics. Whoever plotted the theft was no tenderfoot; he was one to make an entrance, and did not shy away from drama.

Then there was the mysterious note tucked into the crook of her glove.

Sophia's life, up until now a dull study in decorum and Debrett's, was suddenly full of excitement.

Not that a heady dose of fear didn't accompany said excitement. It was with shaking hands that Sophia led her mother round the dark corner and out onto the graveled half-crescent drive in front of Thomas's house.

There were people everywhere, crisscrossing the drive with cries for the constable, the mayor, smelling salts. Her mother was beginning to limp with the effort of keeping pace. Sophia had no doubt whatsoever that Lady Blaise would topple to the ground in an appropriately dramatic swoon if they didn't find shelter, and quick.

Over the din Sophia heard her name. She turned.

Relief flooded through her at the sight of her family's scuffed-up old carriage, the scuffed-up old coachman waving to her from the street.

As they sidled up to the vehicle, Sophia told him the story in so many breathless words. Together she and the coachman lifted Lady Blaise into the carriage, where at last she succumbed to that swoon she'd been saving all night.

Sophia collapsed against the coach, drawing deep, hungry breaths of the cool evening air.

The coachman held out his hand. "Best be goin', miss, before the real trouble begins."

Sophia looked at the man, swung her head to look back at the house. It was ablaze with light and life, guests still pouring out the front door. She wondered where Thomas was, and if he'd managed to stop the thieves before they could escape with the diamond.

The diamond that she'd helped him win from Princess Caroline. Her chest swelled with pride and something else—something softer—as she remembered how well they'd played that game together, she and Thomas. He never wanted to involve her in his plotting, she knew that, but she knew also that he was grateful for her presence, and that she played no small part in the success of his scheme.

Perhaps, she thought, eyeing her mother as she moaned softly in her stupor, she might again come to the rescue tonight. Surely Hope would need all the help he could get if those scalawags the acrobats had indeed made off with the French Blue. The more bodies involved, the more ground they could cover in their search.

La Reinette would surely dive in headfirst, wouldn't she, and seduce those she encountered along the way?

Surely indeed.

Besides. While she still trembled, heart in her throat, after so much action, the last thing Sophia desired was to go home to a quiet house for a quiet evening in. With her pulse racing as it was, she knew sleep would elude her. And there were her mother's hysterics with which to contend . . .

"Miss?"

Sophia blinked, turning to the coachman.

No. She was not ready for tonight to end just yet.

She smiled as she reached between them to gently shut the carriage door. When he tried to protest, brow furrowed with concern, she merely held a finger to her lips and shook her head.

"Very well," he said softly. "But the scene ov a crime ain't no place for a lady. You've only to send for me, miss, and I'll come straightaway."

She placed a hand on his shoulder in gratitude. Dipping her head, she stepped out into the fray.

It was like fighting against a monstrous tide. With no small effort she mounted the front steps, the press of the crush pushing her backward so that with every two steps she lost twice as many.

She tried slithering between bodies—she was an adventurer now, after all, and slithering seemed the adventurous thing to do—but her attempt was only met with sharp elbows and panicked feet, driving her ever backward until she stumbled down the same steps she'd spent precious minutes climbing.

Letting out a hiss of frustration, Sophia followed the crush out onto the drive. She veered to the left, retracing her steps back to the mews. If Hope and his men had made it out of the ballroom yet, they would be running for their horses to begin the chase.

A chase. She felt ridiculous even thinking the word.

Sophia ran to the mews as fast as her feet would carry her, pushing her way into the stables, where dozens of coaches and four times as many horses and grooms were still tangled in an impossible knot.

"Thomas!" she called. She turned this way and that, narrowly avoiding a run-in with an enormous black horse and its equally enormous rider.

The rider heaved expertly at the reins, jerking the horse onto its hind legs. Sophia gasped, cowering with her hands held out above her head.

"Christ, Sophia, is that you?"

She peeked between her splayed fingers to find none other than Thomas Hope glaring down at her, blue eyes cold, nostrils flaring with anger.

"I told you to go home. This—all of this—it is none of your affair." Though his voice was deadly calm, quiet even, she felt his simmering wrath as surely as if he'd howled the words.

She put down her hands, struggling beneath the weight of his gaze to remember why, exactly, she'd chosen to stay. Something about adventure, and what La Reinette would do, and oh, yes, the role she played in coaxing the jewel from Caroline's grasp—

"It is as much my affair as it is yours." Sophia would win this fight, come hell or high water. She was *staying*. "I daresay without my help, none of us would be in this mess in the first place."

Thomas peered at her, looking as though he could not decide whether her words amused or dismayed him.

She wrinkled her nose as she reconsidered the words. "Wait. No. No, that didn't come out at all right. What I meant to say is, you and I work well together, Thomas. Our success at Montague House proved that. Neither of us is nearly as good without the other. So let me help you. Whatever it is that you need, let me help you."

Thomas put a hand on his thigh, tugging his skittish mount into stillness as he ran a hand through his tangle of curls. He sighed. "I don't have time for this, Sophia. The thieves got away. The French Blue is gone. I am out twenty thousand pounds, never mind my debt to England. I'll not ask you again." He leaned forward in his saddle. "Go *home*."

"And I'll not ask *you* again." She stepped in front of his horse, hands on her hips. "Let me help. And don't think for a moment I wouldn't let you run me over. I'm not going anywhere until you accept my offer."

"Don't you have your mother to see to? And what of your cousin?"

"You know as well as I do that Violet can take care of herself. And my mother—well, suffice it to say she won't get out of bed until day after next, at the earliest."

Sophia watched as Hope's fingers tightened around his thigh. She bit back a smile of triumph.

She was staying.

A handful of horsemen rode up behind Thomas.

Thomas held up a hand in greeting. "The lot of you head east, toward the Thames. The thieves are nimble and likely faster than we'll ever be on horseback or even on foot. Tell no one what has occurred this night. Godspeed, gentlemen."

Sophia looked up at Hope. "And what about us? Where are we headed?"

"To where this whole mess began," he said grimly. He reached for her and, wrapping his fingers around her right arm, pulled her none too gently onto the horse. He settled her into the saddle in front of him, turning her so that her back was to his chest.

She heard a muted tear as he pried her legs apart, pressing his body against her so that she now rode astride the horse, the backs of her thighs resting against his knees.

So much for the nymph costume. No doubt the damage was beyond repair.

Never mind her dignity. That, along with her composure, had gone out the window long ago.

It was terribly uncomfortable, not to mention awkward, to be situated upon a horse with a fuming gentleman pressed far too invitingly against one's backside. Perhaps Sophia should have thought this whole staying business through. Then there was the very real threat of injury or death or, even worse, ruin to consider. What would the Marquess of Withington think, really, if he knew she'd run off into the night with Mr. Thomas Hope—and not for the first time?

This was not the wisest decision she'd ever made.

But as Hope wordlessly urged the horse into motion, holding Sophia tight between his arms as he handled the reins, it suddenly didn't seem so terribly unwise. While her head swam with all manner of things—panic, the waltz, just where on earth were they going, and would they find the diamond there?—she felt safe pressed against the warm firmness of Hope's chest, the long, lithe muscles of his legs.

Perhaps, while not the wisest decision, it *had* been the right one.

And so Sophia held on for dear life as Hope guided them through the darkened city streets. Her heart pounded in time to the horse's forward thrust, Thomas's body colliding with hers with each giddy leap.

The night was cool and clear and wide open. Sophia saw where they were headed long before Hope reined in the horse's frantic pace. Just past a familiar facade, its blue shutters glittering in the light of a vivid moon, Thomas veered left down a shadowy pathway.

They rode into The Glossy's small but neat mews. A groom, trying very hard not to gape at the breathless couple before him, held the reins while Thomas dismounted. The horse grunted with relief.

Hope turned to Sophia, his movements precise and ruthless as he hooked his hands around her waist and brought her to the ground. Glaring at the curious groom, Thomas whipped back his shoulders and removed his jacket.

He shrouded Sophia in the fine folds of its fabric, tugging at the collar so as to hide the better half of her face. Pressing a coin into the groom's palm, Hope murmured his thanks and guided Sophia into The Glossy.

Sophia was glad to have Hope's jacket. Stepping foot into the house's palatial hall, a chill ran through her, strong and visceral, as if she'd plunged through ice into a frozen lake.

For the first time Sophia did not feel welcome here.

She had not returned since that night she ran breathless out the door, struggling to keep pace with Hope as he sprinted toward the street. Nor had she yet worked up the courage to write La Reinette who, for obvious reasons, could not send a letter to Sophia at her uncle's house.

This much Sophia knew: the events of that night forever altered the rules of their arrangement. Both she and Madame had bared parts of themselves that were very much at odds with what each wanted from the other. Could Sophia trust La Reinette to provide the discretion and safety she'd promised?

And could Madame, in turn, trust her memoirs to a debutante possessed of a real terror for her reputation while, impossibly, exhibiting a taste for less than wholesome nighttime activity?

The arrangement couldn't possibly continue. Not as it had before—well, before *this* happened.

And then there was Madame's relationship with Mr. Hope to consider. Were they in business together? Master and servant? Friends? Allies? Or were they—

No. It was none of her business. She and Thomas were on the hunt for the stolen French Blue—nothing more, nothing less—though what La Reinette had to do with any of that, Sophia hadn't a clue.

Hope charged into the madam's room without knocking.

"What do you know?"

Sophia started at Hope's growl. He stalked to the far end of the room as if it were his own, pacing behind La Reinette as she sat before her painted vanity.

With exaggerated slowness the Little Queen dabbed the edge of her mouth with a handkerchief, patting back an errant curl. In the mirror her color was high; Sophia noticed the bed was unmade, its coverlet curled invitingly around rumpled sheets.

It shouldn't have surprised Sophia, this still-warm evidence of the skill that made La Reinette famous. Still, she looked away, training her eyes on something, *anything*, other than the bed; embarrassed, as if she'd interrupted the act itself.

Madame rose and turned to face them, the diaphanous robe tied about her trim person revealing as much as it concealed. She looked, Sophia thought, as effortlessly lovely as she always did.

What was it about Frenchwomen and their effortless everything? Really, it wasn't fair.

La Reinette's black eyes, inscrutable, took in her visitors' disheveled appearance, Hope's white satin breeches and red-heeled shoes; her gaze lingered a moment on the jagged rent that split Sophia's skirts. Sophia, face burning, was overwhelmed by a sense of guilt. As if she'd somehow committed a crime against the madam in her own house.

Sophia gathered the loose edges of her costume in her hands and looked to the floor.

"Your diamond." Madame turned to Hope. "Someone stole it, yes?"

He returned her gaze levelly. "The time for playing coy with me is long passed, Marie. I know well enough that London's secrets—the ones worth knowing, anyway—pass through this room. So." He clasped his hands behind his back. "*Tell me what you know.*"

She stepped forward and took him by the shoulders, halting him midstride. "Look at me, *mon chéri*, I do not play coy. That is the lucky guess I had, that the diamond, it is stolen. You should be wiser in these things. You display this beautiful jewel before all the world, *oui*? And what, you think no one will want it for themselves?"

"I cannot afford to lose the French Blue. Either tell me what you know—"

Madame scoffed. "Or what?"

In the beat of silence that followed, Sophia sensed something dark moving between La Reinette and Hope. Something heavy and well worn.

More secrets. So many deuced secrets.

At last La Reinette released Hope, making for Sophia. She took her burning face in her palms. "And you, *ma bichette*, more adventure for you! Soon you will write your own memoirs." Her thumb grazed the rib of Sophia's cheek. "Tell me. When it was taken, this diamond of *monsieur's*. Tell me what you saw. Were you together with him?"

Sophia swallowed. An odd question, yes. But clearly La Reinette knew something they did not. She glanced at Thomas, his blue eyes glowing in the dim light of the room. He nodded. *Go on.*

"Well." Sophia returned Madame's gaze. "Mr. Hope and I were dancing the waltz—"

Madame arched a brow. "A waltz? But then, did you intend to kill off all the nice ladies in your ballroom? I imagine many of them hit their heads, yes, when they swooned? That dance, for you English it is too much. Too much of the *passion*."

"Not amused." Hope closed his eyes and sighed, pinching the bridge of his nose. "Not amused, Marie, not one bit. See here, Miss Blaise and I were dancing, and then all of the sudden . . ."

Hope told his story, about the acrobats flying through the windows, his treacherous guards; he told her about Violet screaming, *It's gone, the diamond, it's gone!*, and then added, strangely, an anecdote about her losing her dinner on the Earl of Harclay's shoes.

Like that rapscallion had anything to do with the French Blue and its sudden disappearance from Hope's ballroom. Sophia hoped Violet had managed to escape that wicked man's presence. Though heaven knew he was handsome enough to slay even the most upright of the female sex. Perhaps Sophia *shouldn't* have left Violet to her own defense. For there was no defense, really, against a face like Harclay's.

La Reinette listened to Hope's tale closely, all the while holding Sophia's hands in the warm comfort of her own.

"It is unfortunate, this thing that has happened to you tonight," she said when Hope had finished. She held a finger in the air and made for her escritoire. "But the fear, let it leave you. These devils steal from you, yes, but we will take their own trick and use it for us. I will make inquiries, discreet of course. *Le bleu de France* will be yours again, *monsieur*."

Madame sat at the desk and took out a fresh sheet of paper, dabbing a swan feather quill in a pot of blue ink. Sophia bent her arm, intent to brush away a stray eyelash, when a small but succinct *crack* sounded from the crook of her elbow.

The note.

Of course.

If La Reinette was mistress of secrets, as Thomas implied, then who better to untangle the mystery of Sophia's note?

"There's something else," Sophia blurted. Hope's gaze snapped toward her, a warning; but she ignored it, drawing from her glove the tiny square of paper. "A note. It came to my house this evening—someone stuck it in the kitchen door. Do you think it has anything to do with the theft?"

Madame frowned as she unfolded the note, smoothing it over the blank page on her escritoire. "That night you came to me, here in this room. Who knows of it, besides us? I do not ask from you an explanation of why those men were after you. But you must tell me this."

"Virtually no one." Hope spoke before Sophia could reply, warning her off with narrowed eyes. "You, an associate of mine, one or two others. And then, of course, the men who chased us. As far as I know, no one has seen or heard from them since."

Madame nodded absently, her attention fixed on the note. "I have been watching for them, but they have disappeared—*poof!*—into the air. Let us hope they have gone back to the hole they came from, yes?"

"What of the note?" Sophia asked. "D'you think they wrote it?"

"Perhaps." Madame pursed her lips. "Perhaps not. I do not recognize the hand. But now, those men who chased you—they are the first suspects. Perhaps all this"—she waved a hand among the three of them—"is connected. We shall find out, yes?"

Thomas leaned in to grasp the note, which he tucked into the lapel of his jacket. "Thank you, Marie. As always I appreciate your. Er. *Expertise* in these matters."

La Reinette offered Hope a small but meaningful smile. So meaningful that Sophia felt as if she were eavesdropping on a private conversation.

"As always, *monsieur*, it is a pleasure to help you."

Hope was offering an arm to Sophia when La Reinette suddenly turned, finger to her chin. "Oh yes! I cannot forget. You, Hope, must watch over our dear friend the *mademoiselle*. The two of you, you were close, yes, in those last moments before the theft? The thieves, they may try to use her against you. Forget this chase tonight; you will find nothing. Go home, keep her safe. That note, I do not like it."

Sophia started, a pulse of fear racing through her. Dear God, just what did La Reinette mean by that?

"Thank you, Marie," he repeated, voice edged with impatience as he tugged Sophia out of the room. It was obvious, as head of his own bank, Thomas was rather more used to giving orders than receiving them.

"And do take care!" La Reinette called after them as they made their way out of the room. "These devils may want more than your diamonds, *monsieur*!"

Eleven

City of London
Hope & Co. Offices, Fleet Street

Hope shoved aside the detritus on his desk, setting in its place two heavy-bottomed crystal glasses and the only bottle of port he'd managed to rummage from his sideboard, crowded as it was with brown liquors of every shape and stripe.

From the stricken look on Sophia's face, he could tell the last thing the girl needed was a kick in the arse from an especially potent Scotch. Port, surely, was a better bet. Ladies drank port, didn't they?

And even if they didn't, Hope sure as hell did. He needed libation.

Several libations, in fact.

And even then he wasn't sure he'd be able to erase the fact that the French Blue—*the French Blue*, the Sun King's fifty-carat diamond, and quite possibly England's ticket to victory on the Continent—was stolen, right from under his nose.

The weight of his anger, his helplessness and his guilt, was suffocating.

The port. Yes. That would help.

At least a little.

Hope watched Sophia watching him as with swift hands he twisted the corkscrew into the mouth of the bottle, tugging the cork free with an airless *pop*.

In the soft glow of the lamp her eyes were enormous,

depthless; he could practically see thoughts cross her mind as she thought them, brow furrowed.

Part of his anger was directed at her. Why didn't she listen to him when he told her to run, to seek safety with her family? He had a stolen diamond to find, God damn it, and she would only slow him down. As La Reinette had so eloquently reminded him, whoever was after Hope was deadly, a very real threat. If those men dared take his diamond, perhaps they would not hesitate to take his life, too.

And now that Sophia was with him, she was also in danger. That bloody note proved nothing good came of her involvement in his plots; that nothing good came of her involvement with *him*.

Even so. Now that the damage was done and the night was darkest, Hope found he was relieved, glad even, to have her with him, to share a drink—many drinks, on his part—with her in the cool quiet of his office at Hope & Co.

He would take her home after the first glass. At least that's what he told himself as he helped her dismount in the mews behind the building. La Reinette was right to say Sophia was in danger; nevertheless, she *was* an unmarried debutante of gentle birth, and such creatures usually shied away from staying out all hours of the night with tradesmen like himself.

Hope poured each of them a glass and passed one to Sophia. She straightened, grasping the glass eagerly in her gloved hand.

He was, apparently, not the only one in need of a drink.

He held up his glass but could not think of a toast. Sophia waited impatiently, biting her bottom lip against an exhausted smile.

"Forget it," she said at last. "I can't wait any longer."

"Praise God. Me neither."

Over the rim of his own glass Hope watched Sophia take one, two long, luxurious pulls, wincing a bit as she guided the glass into her lap.

"That's good." Again she brought the cup to her lips. "That's very good, Thomas."

She set the empty glass on the desk and fell back into the chair with a contented sigh. With her hair and costume askew, a milky white thigh peeking through the makeshift slit in her skirts and lips purple-red from the port, Sophia appeared more nymph than debutante.

"More?" he asked, grasping the bottle.

She nodded. He poured.

They drank in silence. At once he felt the port working its magic way through him, the ache in his shoulders and neck easing with every sip he took.

After his second glass he grew courageous enough to step round the desk, trailing his hip along its edge until he drew up beside Sophia's chair. He refilled both their glasses and, setting the bottle on the desk behind him, leaned the backs of his thighs against the desk, facing her, and crossed his arms.

"I bet you wish you were at home, in bed. Don't you, Sophia?"

Sophia blinked, as if he'd just insulted her. She crinkled her nose. "No. Why? Do you?"

"What, home in bed? Your bed? My bed? What?" he scoffed, suddenly flustered. "No-o?"

So much for the debonair adventurer. After a glass or three of port he was no smoother than a randy fifteen-year-old boy.

He gulped his port. Yes, it could only make things worse, but what else was he supposed to do when she was looking at him like *that*, with those eyes and that hair and that goddamned thigh . . .

Hope cleared his throat. "What I meant to say is, don't you wish you'd kept dancing with that marquess of yours? Stayed safe and sound in your family's house? Seems the moment I step in, a whole heap of trouble follows."

He nearly winced as the words left his lips. Where the devil had *that* come from? Speaking of randy fifteen-year-old boys: the marquess was a perfect example, yes, but that hardly signified. He and Sophia had shared a dance; and if they shared more than that, well.

It was none of Hope's business.

Still. Even in his own ears the words smacked of jealousy. It was an unfamiliar feeling; Hope was not a jealous man. Especially when it came to women.

So why the sudden, hot tug in his belly at the memory of Sophia stumbling through the steps of a reel at the Marquess of Withington's side?

You know my family's circumstances. I don't have much choice. A good marriage will go far to repair our fortunes, and our reputation.

Hope recalled Sophia's words, her dreams of a brilliant match.

A match with a titled, fortuned man like the marquess. A man who couldn't be more different, in family, history, circumstances, than Hope.

Well, except for the fortune part. Hope trumped the marquess there.

Nevertheless.

Sophia, praise God, had the grace to ignore Hope's comment, but not without a small smile.

"I like your kind of trouble." She looked down into her glass. "I wish you'd stop feeling guilty, Thomas. You didn't drag me into this; I joined you willingly. Whatever trouble I'm in has been of my own doing. I daresay if I hadn't run into you my first season would prove awfully dull."

"I suppose," Hope said carefully, "I should take that as a compliment?"

Sophia raised her glass and clinked it against his own. "You should. Cheers."

She finished her port with a hiss, and waved away Hope's attempts to refill her glass. Her color was high; she shifted in her chair, crossing her legs invitingly so he could see just enough skin to drive him wild, imagining the vision of more skin, more leg.

Her eyes, gold in the low light of the room, caught on an array of pages that hung precariously off the edge of his desk. Brow furrowed with curiosity, she bent forward in her chair. Before he could stop her she reached for them, lips curling into a grin as she read the first line.

"*A History of the World's Greatest Diamond*, by Thomas Hope." Her eyes danced as she met his own. "I did not know you were a writer!"

He tried again to take the pages from her, but she snatched them from his grasp. "Yes, well. It's not quite finished, you see . . ."

Hope waited with bated breath as Sophia read one page after another, her smile at times fading, others growing, as her lips moved silently in time to the words. By the time she set her empty glass on the desk and gathered the pages in a neat pile, Hope's heart was racing.

"Well?" he asked weakly.

Sophia cleared her throat, setting the *History* on the desk. "Well."

Her gaze met his. She let out a sound—a sob, a sigh?—and only when Hope felt the rise in his own belly did he recognize it as laughter.

And then they were laughing together, tears gathering at the edges of Sophia's lovely eyes as she recited that bit about forbidden fruit, and Hope nodding yes, yes, it *is* terrible, isn't it?

"Not all of us, *Miss Blaise*, can be bestselling authors!"

"Bah!" Sophia wiped her eyes with her first finger. "Hardly signifies, when I am merely a vessel; the stories aren't my own. I only wonder why you wrote such a history? Why the French Blue? Aside, of course, from your interest in all things extravagant."

Hope sucked a breath through his teeth and rocked back on his heels. The laughter faded from his belly. He closed his eyes for a moment, willing his voice to remain even. This was nothing, a story. He could, his apparent lack of narrative prowess aside, tell a damned *story*.

"Before I was born, my father traveled to the court of Louis XVI. He'd gone on business, a meeting with the minister of finance; but he was taken by the beauty of the court, the allure of such excess. He was especially enamored of the jewels; jewels, he said, like he'd never seen before. When I was little he would tell me stories of the French Blue, the whisperings he'd heard at court of its curse, its journey across the seas. My father saw him wear it once, Louis, on a brooch hung from a ribbon slung about his chest. He never forgot that, my father."

"Incredible," Sophia whispered, shaking her head. "To have been witness to the spectacle."

Hope looked down into his glass. "I had hoped to make the journey myself someday. I wanted to see King Louis wearing *le bleu de France*, just as my father had. He promised, my father, to take me; and I promised to accompany him. We were to go together, he and I.

"Of course." Hope swallowed, hard. "Of course we never

went. But when I heard the Blue was in England, and in Princess Caroline's possession, I knew I'd been given a second chance. At last I would know the diamond as my father knew it, albeit without poor old Louis in the picture."

He sighed. "And now the French Blue is gone."

"I am sorry." Sophia's voice was soft.

"No. *I* am sorry to have ruined our merrymaking with yet *another* terrible tale." He held up the bottle. "More port?"

Despite her protests he refilled her glass.

"Are you sure you're all right?" she asked.

He held out the glass and met her eyes. "Very much so, thank you, Sophia."

She looked at him for a beat; satisfied, she took the glass in her hand and tossed back her head to look at the room. "Quite the office you've got. Looks more like a museum. Or an art gallery."

Glad for the change of subject, Hope swept his eyes over the priceless antiques, the Turkish carpets and Italian masterworks that decorated the space. "Do you have a favorite?"

"Yes." She rose to her feet, the port in her glass sloshing a bit as she made her way to stand in front of the fireplace. Pointing to the gilt-framed painting that hung above the mantel, she said, "This one. It's beautiful."

Hope joined her in front of the fireplace. Together they admired the painting, its vivid colors, the ethereal luminescence of the two figures reclining across the expanse of the work. It was beautiful, yes.

Beautiful in that sensual, explicit sort of way that made the old masters of the Renaissance so famous. Mars, in all his well-muscled glory, was naked, asleep after the rigors of physical love; Venus, curvy and luscious, lounged beside him in a diaphanous gown not dissimilar to the one Sophia now wore.

Hope blinked at the familiar twist of desire between his legs.

"Botticelli is among my own favorites," he said. "This is his *Venus and Mars*. Do you know the tale?"

Sophia cocked her head to the side, her purple-stained lips pouty in concentration.

Dear God. Was she trying to kill him?

More port.

"Star-crossed lovers, yes?" she said.

"Yes," he replied. "An ancient Romeo and Juliet, if you will. Venus is married to Vulcan, the king of the gods. He's powerful but—if you'll excuse my crudeness—impotent. It's no surprise, then, that our fair Venus falls in love with Mars, who, as you can see, is a rather handsome fellow, flowing locks and all that."

Sophia turned to Hope with a smile. "If his were a bit darker, they'd look just like yours."

Hope cleared his throat for what felt like the hundredth time that night. He was glad the glow of the fire was dim, for beneath the cover of semidarkness he felt himself blushing.

"You can see here"—Hope pointed to a trio of satyrs making off with Mars's spear—"that the artist is suggesting Venus's love for Mars disarms him. That his love for her in turn is so great, so powerful, that it leaves him defenseless."

Sophia turned to him. "That love," she said softly, "conquers all."

"Yes." Hope looked at her, his belly turning over at the soft slant of her eyes. "That love conquers all. Even, it seems, the matchless god of war."

For several breathless moments they looked at one another. Beside them the fire sputtered and cracked. Sophia's face, in shadow one moment, dancing light the next, was lovely, those lips of hers parted slightly. An invitation.

No. No. Not tonight. There was too much to do, and the French Blue, it was gone, stolen at his own ball—he had to keep a clear mind, focus on the task at hand—

More port. While it was making him forget everything good and right, his manners and his decorum and his sense of duty, it also helped him to forget his grief. The diamond, his father—they disappeared in the presence of Miss Sophia Blaise.

Sophia blinked, a look of—was that disappointment?—darkening her features. She placed her empty glass on the mantel and began to wrangle free of Hope's jacket.

"Too warm?" Hope asked, setting aside his glass to help.

In reply Sophia shot him a smoldering look over her shoulder.

That twist between his legs pulsed to a full-on rush of heat.

Warm? Dear *God*. A drop in the old proverbial bucket.

Hope stepped back, holding the jacket awkwardly in his hands, unsure what his next move should be.

Again that look in Sophia's eyes.

Harry, England, and Saint George. The diamond, and Napoleon; the twenty thousand pounds he'd put down to set the plot in motion, the bank and all the lives at stake, keeping her safe from the men after her—

It all went out the door when Sophia stepped forward and took the jacket from his arms, spreading it out on the carpet before the fire. She took her glass from the mantel and held out her hand.

"I like it here," she said. "Let's sit."

Hope, embarrassingly, let out a groan. "Just one—" He loosened his cravat. "Just one moment, Sophia."

He dashed to the desk, grabbing the bottle of port; turning back to the fireplace, he took his own cup from the mantel and held it between the fingers of one hand along with the bottle. With the other hand he took Sophia's, and together they began to sink to the floor when she stumbled over her dress, caught beneath her foot. She pitched backward; Hope's arm darted out just in time, grasping her by the arm.

"Oh," she gasped. "Oh, dear. That port's strong, isn't it?"

He guided her to the floor beside him. "No stronger than usual. Are you all right?"

Sophia stretched out her legs toward the fire, propping her weight on her free hand. Hope followed suit, her mirror image. Her slippered toes grazed the tip of his boot, once, before she moved her foot.

"Yes." Sophia held out her glass. In the moving light of the fire her color was high, eyes wet and willing.

He swallowed. And filled her glass.

He held the bottle up to the fire. Damn it. Almost empty.

"Did we finish the whole bottle?"

Hope splashed what was left into his glass, and looked up at Sophia with a smile. "Just did."

"Goodness." She brought the glass to her lips and took a long pull. "We should probably slow down, shouldn't we?"

He laughed, and she laughed along with him.

Again that heated silence. Propped on his hand, he was close enough to reach out and touch her, swallow her in a kiss.

Just as he was leaning in, she surprised him by speaking up.

"Might I ask you a question, Thomas?"

He pulled back slightly, praying she did not sense the foolish thing he'd been about to do. Putting aside his glass, he ran a hand through his hair and grinned. "Since when have you asked my permission to do anything, Miss Blaise? Go on, then."

"You and La Reinette. How—how do you know her? And why go to her about the French Blue before anyone else? I did not realize she was a woman of such great. Er. Importance."

Well. Out of all the things she could've asked, Hope wasn't expecting *that*.

He narrowed his eyes. Was that a reflection of his own jealousy he heard in her words? More likely Sophia was merely trying to piece together the details of the plot.

Still. Though it shamed him to admit it, some small part of him was pleased she might be jealous. Perhaps—*perhaps*—he intrigued her as much as she intrigued him.

Perhaps a small part of *her* cared for him, even.

He did not dare follow that thought any further.

"Ah, La Reinette." Hope wondered how much he should tell Sophia about his long, and often complicated, relationship with the mercurial Frenchwoman. "How much do you know?"

"Only that she's got a taste for pirates, and has a habit of attracting dangerous—albeit handsome—men."

"Well, then." Hope pulled back a curl with his fingers. "I shall begin at the—er, beginning, then.

"Marie and I are very old friends. We first met ten—no, twelve years ago, in Paris. I was working with Lake at the time, doing—well, it doesn't matter. Suffice it to say my line of work brought me into contact with Marie around the time Napoleon overthrew the Directory."

"Who is she?"

Hope sighed. "No one knows, really. She keeps her own secrets even better than she keeps everyone else's. I *do* know she rose to prominence during the Revolution, when it was rumored she—how do I put this?—*befriended* several high-ranking nobles. It wasn't long before she was the *maîtresse-en-titre* to the likes of royal dukes and German princes.

"More than that, she was their confidant throughout the bloodshed that was to come. Marie became involved in all sorts of intrigue to save her lovers. She was discreet, intelligent, too. But even she was not immune to the danger of those times. Back then France was a fearful place, you see; *madame guillotine* exacted terrible justice. Everyone was afraid.

"And so when the danger grew too great, I helped La Reinette escape to England. Together we found asylum in London. I loaned her the funds to establish The Glossy; she in turn became my first client and an advocate of Hope and Company besides. It wasn't long before I could count all of her high-ranking clients as my own. She operates, you see, in perhaps the most rarefied circle in all of England."

Sophia nodded. "Rubbing elbows with London's finest, La Reinette would be the first to hear of any plot against you."

"I wouldn't call what she does 'rubbing elbows,' exactly," Hope said, tugging at his cravat. "But yes. If anyone of any importance had designs to steal the diamond, she would be the first to know about it."

"And the note," Sophia said. "I know the diamond is of utmost importance, Thomas. But I do hope La Reinette can help us uncover who wrote that letter. Not only does he threaten us, he threatens my family, too."

Hope met her eyes. For the first time, she appeared frightened. "We'll find him, Sophia. I'll do everything I can to keep your family safe in the meantime."

Sophia looked down at her glass, shaking her head. "And here I thought myself an adventurer. My God! She wouldn't be afraid. Not after the things La Reinette must've seen, and the people she's known."

"So now you understand, Sophia," Hope said, finishing what was left of his port, "it is no small thing that she chose you to write her memoirs. If—when—they are ever published, they will be a sensation. You must be possessed of great talent."

Sophia scoffed. "Indeed, I beat out several other applicants for the assignment. Zero, to be exact."

"Marie wouldn't have taken you on if she didn't see something in you she liked."

"Well." Sophia tipped her head back, draining the last drop of her port. "We'll see if La Reinette still likes me enough to finish what we've started. Everything's—" Her voice softened. "Everything's changed, you know."

Hope turned his head to look at her. The words left his lips before he could stop them. "Yes. But some things, I hope, for the better."

A beat of charged silence settled between them, long enough that Hope would've squirmed if it weren't for the goodly amount of port hard at work in his blood.

Her face was open as she looked back, lips slightly parted as she waited. Willing. Curious.

Christ. He needed the port now more than ever. Up until this moment it had kept his hands and his mouth busy.

But now. Now they were left idle, set ablaze by the not insignificant amount of said port he'd imbibed in the last few hours.

He didn't like how much he liked not thinking about the diamond, or the bank, or the world outside. How much he liked thinking about Miss Sophia Blaise instead.

The silence grew unbearable.

And then, embarrassed—terrified, in Hope's case; terrified that he would do something he'd regret, that would compromise everything for which he'd worked so hard, but dear *God* he'd never wanted anything so badly—they both moved to stand at once.

Sophia bent her knees, the whole of her bare leg exposed as Hope took her by the arm and hauled her up beside him.

A lovely, lithe, impossibly shapely leg.

For some inexplicable reason, both Hope and Sophia were breathless as they stood, not daring to touch, before the fire. Hope trained his eyes on Botticelli's masterwork above the mantel, balling his hands into fists to keep from reaching out for Sophia, indulging the desire that pounded unabated through his body.

But staring at Venus only made his struggle worse. Had she always been this sensual, the goddess, her legs so visible through the transparent gauze of her gown?

If those damned Frenchmen, those acrobats, or the diamond's thief—heaven above, Hope was a wanted man—didn't kill him first, then this Venus at his side, brought to startling, sensual life, would certainly be the death of him.

Sophia turned her head and met his eyes, her breast working as she struggled to catch her breath. "Thomas," she said, her voice barely above a whisper. "We should—I should—"

In one swift, ruthless movement he reached for her, curling his hand around the back of her neck as he pulled her to him, lowering his lips onto her own.

Knowing as he did that, once he'd started, he would not be able to stop.

Twelve

Thank God Thomas kissed Sophia first, before whatever she was about to say slipped from her tongue. *I should go. I should stay. We should kiss, and keep kissing until whatever happens after that happens.*

No, it would not do at all; she did not trust herself with a bellyful of port and Mr. Thomas Hope looking at her like *that.*

Like he was racked with thirst that could only be slaked by swallowing her whole.

Sophia had only known Thomas—truly *known* him—for a week or two. But in those two weeks they'd each shared more of themselves than either of them ever had with anyone else. He knew her secrets, and she knew his. Well, a goodly amount of them, anyway. Together they'd shared adventure, cheated death, and outwitted villains, touching and talking and *kissing* along the way.

She felt as if she knew him better than she knew even her dearest friends.

Even so. One did not discuss the goddess of love over a bottle of wine with a frightfully unmarried member of the opposite sex. Never, never, *never.*

And yet.

It could've been the port—no, it was most *definitely* the port—but the memory of Hope's kiss, his touch, pounded through her with every breath she took. The longer they talked and drank, drank and talked, the press of the evening's events faded. In their place rose a dizzying—oh, that *deuced port*!—fire, its embers bursting to flame when he'd looked at her for several long, silent heartbeats, his eyes darkened by pain, struggle, something heavy with which he was grappling.

When they'd stood, chests heaving, before the fire, Sophia wasn't sure if Thomas would lean in or turn away.

When he'd leaned in—well.

Whatever reservations she had dissolved into desire when his lips met hers. This was no innocent kiss; his deadly intent was as palpable as the heat that radiated from his body.

Beneath the knowing gaze of Botticelli's Venus, Hope opened Sophia to him. His hand slid from her neck to her cheek, and together with his other hand cradled her face, turning her head in time to the strokes of his kiss.

When she matched him, caress for caress, he let out a deep, contented moan and stepped closer, pressing his body against hers. His flesh felt at once familiar and frightening. The warmth of his emotion, the terrific hunger of his desire—she recognized these things in her own response to the kiss, yes.

But if they were both flooded with longing, who would stop them from sinking into one another, from giving in and giving up everything that they wanted, that they were?

Hope's lips were traveling across her jaw now, pressing into the exquisitely tender skin of her neck. She inhaled his scent, clean lemon, spicy sandalwood. So lovely, so inviting . . .

No. Stop. The words were there, the debutante still alive somewhere inside the tangle of her limbs.

Thomas kissed her neck, teasing her with his teeth, his tongue, sending bolts of white-hot pleasure through her.

The words were lost. Her eyes rolled shut as she tilted her head back, surrendering to Hope's desire for her, the sensation of his mouth moving over her as if he knew where she wanted to be touched before she knew it herself.

So this—this was *it*. What came after kissing. The *it* Sophia had been warned against since she was old enough to listen.

But no one warned her *it* was going to feel like *this*.

As Thomas touched her, explored her with tender fingers and urgent lips, she felt her body unfurling beneath his hands. Her shoulders relaxed; the tension between her eyes and along her spine loosened.

Thoughts of her family, her fears for them, scattered like

shadows from a struck match. Here it was only Sophia and Thomas and the gasped breaths between them.

Here there was no war to wage, no marriage to make. The rules were what she made them. Here she was flesh and blood and heart, nothing else, nothing to pretend or force.

She suddenly felt light, alive. *Honest.* As if the walls of her pretending and forcing and worry had fallen, at least for a little while, to her feet.

The release was intoxicating. Coupled with the port—or, perhaps, in spite of it—Sophia felt as if her feet might leave the ground.

Hope's hands adored her, slow caresses as they moved down from her face to her shoulders. She inhaled when his hands slowly, oh, *slowly* traveled the length of her ribs, his thumb grazing her breast before dipping to her belly, tugging her further against him as he held her by the hips.

His lips were on the neckline of her gown. Sophia arched back, digging her hands into the inviting mass of his dark curls. She let out a long, hot breath, willing herself to remember this moment.

It would never be like this again. It couldn't.

Thomas raised his head, straightening so that he loomed over her, his eyes ablaze. He dragged his hands back up over her hips, hooking his thumbs beneath her ribs.

"Hold on to me," he growled. Without waiting for a reply he lifted her, a familiar, guttural tear sounding between them as her skirts—what little was left of them, anyway—were rent into a dozen pieces. He pressed her back against the wall beside the fireplace, holding her with one arm while coaxing her legs about his hips with the other.

Lightning shot through her at the feel of Thomas nestled between her legs. She felt open and vulnerable.

She felt like *more*.

Pulling his face close, she covered her mouth with his, and he moaned again, this one so deep and strong she felt the vibration of his chest in her own. She followed his example and moved her lips to his cheek, his chin, the place where jaw sloped to ear and neck.

She sensed the tension coiling inside him; vaguely she wondered if she was hurting him, if she should stop—

Sliding his hands along the backs of her thighs, he gathered her backside in his palms and lifted her away from the wall. She gasped as he took one, two unhurried strides across the room, setting her at last on the edge of his enormous, gleaming desk.

Sophia looked up at him, wondering what could possibly come next. There was a wicked gleam in his eye she'd never seen before. Thomas, it seemed, knew *exactly* what came next.

He leaned in, and she closed her eyes and surrendered to the rush of his lips against her. He ran his hands down her bare legs, the scrape of skin against skin sending a shiver up her spine; he pulled back his hands, allowed them to linger on her hips a moment before trailing them up her sides, over her breasts. She released his mouth, sucking in a breath at the exquisite sensation that rushed through her as he buried the fingers of his right hand into the neckline of her bodice.

With his teeth he nipped at her bottom lip. And then he was tugging at her bodice, pulling it up and over her skin, baring her breast to his touch.

Sophia gasped. "Thomas! Thomas—"

He put his first finger to her lips, pulling open her mouth as he met her eyes and lowered his head, kept lowering it.

She watched in breathless wonder as he took the hardened knot of her nipple into his mouth, sucking in a breath at the pleasure that pulsed between her legs.

As if under a spell her body arched further against him, her fingers tangling in his hair, encouraging him as he licked, then teased, scraping his teeth against her nipple with excruciating finesse.

In her veins she felt her blood rising, pooling between her legs. It felt good to have Thomas pressed against her there; good, and not nearly enough.

He went to work on the other side of her bodice, coaxing her breast free. While he moved his lips to this unexplored skin, he worked the other with his fingers, rolling her nipple between his thumb and forefinger.

Sophia's breath caught in her throat. She threw back her head, biting her lip against crying out. The more he touched and pulled, the more unbearable it became.

When she lifted her head, her gaze landed for a moment

on Botticelli's Venus, watching the scene impassively from across the room. How did she appear so calm, Sophia wondered, after Mars had done *this* to her moments before?

There was no shame or regret in Venus's eyes; only knowledge, a breathlessness in the pose of her head as if she would nod her assent. *Go on, go on, explore so that you might know.*

Hope's finger traced a line of fire along the inside of Sophia's bottom lip. In her mounting frustration she bit the tip of his finger, crying out as he returned the favor on her nipple.

She was pulling at his hair now, the silken curls catching on her fingers. Thomas released his mouth, feathering kisses across her breast. He lowered his hand to her hip, meeting her eyes.

Sophia should shake her head, push him away, end the encounter as a lady of good manners ought. Through the pounding of the port and of her desire, she knew this could only end badly. She was only as good as her virginity, at least in the eyes of those who mattered.

But here, now, blessed by Venus and drunk on wine, that lady of good manners felt as far away as the moon. Here and now under Hope's spell she was only Sophia, filled for the first time with the will to follow her own desires, rather than everyone else's.

Yes, she breathed, and ran her thumb along the ridge of Thomas's brow.

He did not waste any time. Grasping her hips in his hands, thumbs grazing the inside of her thighs, he got down on his knees. She watched with bated breath as he reached up with one hand, placing it squarely over her heart.

"Lie down." His voice was barely above a whisper. He gently pushed back her torso, guiding her down, and bent her knees so that her feet rested on the edge of the desk.

"Is this," she panted, "the sort of work you usually do at your desk?"

From his perch between her legs he scoffed. "Oh, this, and every now and again the odd bit of paperwork."

Sophia laughed, his humor alleviating her shyness at opening herself to him so freely, so wholly.

He tugged her skirts aside, revealing the length of her legs. One at a time he removed her slippers, then her stockings and the ribboned garters that held them in place. His touch was light, deliberate, a thrilling foil to the hard expanse of the desk pressing up against her spine.

Thus having untangled Sophia from the intricacies of her footwear, Thomas moved farther up her legs, over her thighs and hips to her belly. He hooked his fingers into the waistband of her drawers, and, grinning at Sophia's gasp, ripped them off, dropping them to the floor beside her slippers and stockings.

She was completely naked. Well, save for the scraps of gauze wrapped about her middle that were all that was left of her costume.

Not only that. Hope's face was mere inches from that most private place between her legs, the place she'd been taught to simultaneously ignore and worship as the source of all her worth.

He pressed on the inside of her thighs, inching her legs wider. She closed her eyes, unable to bear the thought that he didn't like what he saw.

"Sophia." The word was kind but spoken firmly. "Open your eyes. I want you to see how beautiful I think you are."

Her eyes flew open. "Beautiful?" She lifted her head as if to look herself. "Really?"

His hands crept closer to her center, his thumbs grazing her dark, slick curls. "Oh, God," he groaned. "You've not the slightest clue, Sophia."

Between her legs she felt a tug, at once painful and intensely pleasurable.

And then, just when she thought it couldn't get any better, that she might explode or die or swoon or all three, Thomas touched her.

It was his first finger, brushing lightly the very tip of her sex—the place that she quickly discovered was the center of all this delicious, maddening sensation.

She cried out, the agony of her pleasure at his touch overwhelming. He splayed his other hand palm-down over her belly, willing her to be still as he touched, and kept touching. The hand slid forward, caressing her breast, plucking at her nipple. A sharp stab of pleasure shot through her. She was on fire, every inch of her burning; her hips now worked against him, pressing harder, wanting more.

"Easy, Sophia," he purred. "Easy."

His finger slid from the top of her sex down to its middle where it gently, slowly, began to ease its way inside her.

She shot upright, eyes wide.

"No." Thomas pushed her back down. "Soon, soon. Patience, darling."

Patience. How was she supposed to have patience when he tortured her like this?

Pressure mounted around his finger as it delved deeper yet. His other hand slid back down her belly to rest where her legs met; and then with his thumb he began stroking that *place* again, the place that hurt and thrummed and sang the most.

In and out, he was inside her, over her, in her, all at once. A hard, tight sensation rolled through her, so poignant she gritted her teeth against it.

And then he was lowering his head, brushing his lips to the inside of one thigh, then the other, moving closer, closer, so very close . . .

Her eyes fluttered shut at the featherlight touch of his mouth on her sex. A new wave of pleasure coursed through her, potent but different somehow; it was forbidden, erotic, the idea of it alone enough to make her moan aloud.

His lips, his tongue, were moving faster now, circling again and again that bit of flesh. His teeth nicked her, gently pulling, caressing to the point of pain.

She watched his head moving between her legs, earnestly, slowly, her fingers once again finding purchase in his silken curls, now damp with sweat. He groaned against her; her desire spiked at the vibration of his lips, the vibration of her own.

The rising tide of heat inside her—it was impossible to escape.

It was coming now, whatever it was that came next; she felt the muscles in her legs tense, her shoulders flatten against the desk. She took a shallow breath in, closing her eyes as she searched in vain for something, anything to hold on to.

Her eyes flew open as the rush came, a tumbling, pounding thing. She cried out as pulse after pulse of sensation rounded through her, the ripples of pleasure slowly fading into a satisfaction so immense she felt limp beneath its weight.

Sophia sputtered for breath, pushing aside wisps of hair from her slick forehead with shaking fingers.

Dear God. Even La Reinette's stories hadn't prepared her for *that.*

Thomas's eyes appeared over the ridge of her sex, blue and serious; his mouth came next, not quite a smile; his lips glistened with her arousal. He waited for her verdict.

When her gaze met his, a warm happiness rolled through her. She longed to reach out, to touch him and hold him to her. But while his eyes were serious they were wild, too; she recognized the rising tide in him, those excruciating last moments before the crash.

She did not trust her touch. His hands and his lips were knowledgeable and fast. Hers would be clumsy. Where to even begin? Perhaps it was best to defer to Thomas. *He* would know what to do next.

And so she grinned, palms held fast to the desk. "Yes." She breathed. "Yes!"

He returned her grin. His eyes gleamed wickedly; and then he was sinking down again, moving toward her.

Sophia started at the feel of his fingers on her sex. She fought the urge to squirm; but as his hands began to move in earnest, she relaxed, the spark of her desire ignited again.

There was more? But how? Could she possibly do that *again—*

Just as she felt herself swelling against him, Hope suddenly froze, his thumb poised just below the jointure of all this delicious sensation.

Sophia did not dare to breathe, listening instead to the racket that reverberated just beyond the office door. Grunts, heavy footsteps, a shout or two for good measure.

Christ in heaven. Not this again.

Their gazes locked, eyes wide as the racket drew nearer.

In the space of a single heartbeat Hope was on his feet, gathering her slippers and stockings and undergarments in the crook of his elbow. With an efficient tug at the scraps of her costume he covered her breasts, her legs, wincing as that curious hardness between his hips brushed against her.

"I'm terribly sorry, Sophia." His voice was hushed. He met her eyes, holding out his free hand. "Seems we've become fast favorites of thugs and thieves and the like. I wonder who it could be this time."

Sophia blinked, virtually blinded by the haze of desire that hung between them. With no small effort she swung her legs over the back of the desk and with Hope's help ducked into the alcove occupied by his tall-backed leather chair.

"Please, *please* do as I say for once and stay here," Thomas said, handing her the misshapen bulk of her unmentionables. "There's a pistol in the top drawer there." He paused. "Though, on second thought, you may want to leave the shooting to me."

If Sophia's thoughts weren't still storm-tossed she would've stuck out her tongue at his jest. Her heart worked furiously as alternating waves of disappointment and relief and fear crashed through her.

Disappointment that she and Thomas could not finish what they had started. It seemed with every new sensation his body wrought she always yearned for more, and more yet. What heavenly part of him came after his fingers and his mouth?

Relief that she did not, in fact, experience said part. She was not entirely ruined. Not yet.

And fear—well, fear for the obvious reasons. Thugs, thieves, the revelation of her carefully guarded secrets.

Secrets that now included a rather heady, half-naked interlude on Mr. Thomas Hope's desk.

"Sophia."

She met his eyes once more. Licking his port-stained lips, Thomas's face momentarily softened, his eyes very full as he struggled to find the right words. "Sophia, I—"

She jumped at the slam of the door. Thomas darted upright; she saw him yank at the crotch of his breeches before stepping in front of the desk.

A familiar voice rang out across the chamber.

Thirteen

"We found them." Lake shoved a short, broad-shouldered figure into the room, the man's face blackened with soot. "Acrobats from a traveling troupe playing at Vauxhall. Ran 'em down in a tavern in Cheapside."

Hope carefully arranged the knot of his hands in front of his legs and tried to think of anything, *anything* but Sophia.

"And you're sure these are the men who attacked my house?"

Lake stepped forward, waving his pistol at the perpetrator's enormously calloused hands, his thick, corded neck. He pulled back the sleeves of the man's shirt, revealing the bulge of his forearms that were nicked with dozens of small, oozing cuts.

"I've never been wrong." Lake winked. Hope bit the inside of his cheek to keep from throttling him. "We've a few of his friends waiting outside."

"Good." Hope turned and made for the sideboard. All the better to hide the rather alarming condition of his breeches, a condition he could not subdue no matter how hard he tried. "We cannot interrogate them here; no one at the bank can know of this, not yet. Though I'm sure the gossip will be rife by morning. Take them to my house and wake the kitchens. I'm going to need coffee. A *lot* of coffee."

"Consider it done. I assume you've all the accouterments available there—pliers, hot pokers, an axe?"

Hope tried not to smile at the acrobat's high-pitched squeak of terror.

"No pliers, I'm afraid, but Cook does keep a rather interesting collection of paring knives. Might we experiment with those?"

"Oh, yes, let's do." Lake shoved the man back into the hall outside the office where the rest of his officers waited.

"Well?" he said after a moment, waiting for Hope at the door.

Hope waved him away. "I'll meet you back at my house. I've a few. Ah. Matters to which to attend here first." He pretended to busy himself at the sideboard. For the first time in his life—well, no, that wasn't true, exactly—suffice it to say he could not remember the last time he went green at the very sight of liquor.

Of course today would be that day.

As if on cue, the clock on the mantel struck five o'clock. Hope glanced out the window to see darkness fading to gray dawn.

The night—this night, spent in the half-naked company of Miss Sophia Blaise—was over.

But his troubles. *They* were just beginning.

Hope looked over his shoulder to see Mr. Lake backtracking into the room, moving too noiselessly, and with far too much finesse, than his injury should allow. His eyes took in Hope's coat, laid out before the crackling fire, lingering a moment too long on the Botticelli above the mantel. At last his gaze landed on the massive expanse of Hope's desk.

"I say." Lake furrowed his brow and bent over to retrieve something from the floor. "What's this?"

Hope watched in horror as Lake dangled a satin garter between his thumb and forefinger.

The banker reached out and snatched the garter before Lake could get a better look. "It's mine."

"It's yours? What the devil do you mean to do with it, *Miss* Hope? Use it to tie up those b*eau*teous curls of yours?"

Hope cleared his throat as he shoved the garter into his waistcoat. "Jealous, are you, of my flowing locks?"

"Ha!" Lake snorted. "I may be ginger-haired, old friend, but the ladies certainly don't seem to mind." He leaned over the desk, eyes narrowed, nose in the air. He was a bully, yes, but Lake was no fool. If Hope did not stop him, he would sniff out Sophia. And when he discovered her pink-cheeked, her costume in telling shreds, she would surely die of shame and embarrassment.

And, lest Hope ever forget, there was Lake's wrath to consider.

There was no telling what the man would do once he discovered Hope was further jeopardizing an already complicated plot.

"Well, then," Hope said briskly. He took Lake by the shoulder and turned him away from the desk. "Remember the coffee. And have those little bastards brought down to the kitchens; I don't need to tell you that no one must know they are in my house." Lake opened his mouth, but Hope pushed him out the door before he could speak. "Oh, and send for Lady Violet. What with the diamond being stolen from about her neck, she might shed some light on our proceedings. I shall join you directly, *old friend*."

Hope shut the door and leaned against it, clamping his fist around the knob. He waited, heart thudding, until he heard Lake's staccato shuffling down the stair.

He let out a long breath. "The coast is clear," he called out softly, making his way to Sophia. "You may come out now."

Hope helped her to her feet, trying all the while not to stare at her adorably disheveled appearance. Her hair was askew, lips bright red. Attempting to straighten her costume, Sophia only made the damage worse and revealed, to Hope's delight, far more bosom than was polite.

"That was close," she said, stepping into her slippers. "We're off to your house, then?"

Hope looked at her. She blushed. Adorably, of course.

His shoulders sagged. "I don't suppose I could convince you to end our adventure here, could I?"

She leaned in, a small, suggestive smile on those damnably alluring lips. "Not if you want to keep that garter as a souvenir. Besides, we've already come this far. The more ears you have to the ground, the better chance you have of recovering the French Blue."

Hope sighed. He couldn't say no, not when she stood before him in the gown he'd torn to shreds. Not when she smiled at him like that.

"All right. I've got to write a few letters to my friends at the papers. Buy us some time before word gets out of the theft. Once my clients hear of it—those who weren't at the ball, anyway—they'll panic. Then we'll send for your mother and meet at my house."

Only as he sat down to pen said letters did Hope realize

he'd said *us*—"Buy *us* time"—as if he and Sophia were true partners in crime.

It seemed Sophia was now an integral part of the plot, whether Hope wished it or not.

Despite Lake's supposed expertise in such matters, the interrogation of the acrobats proved a failure.

Until, that is, Lady Violet strutted into the room. A fuming Lord Harclay—what was *he* doing here?—at her side, she trailed perfume and the promise of forbidden things in her wake. The baby-faced men, their hands bound behind their backs, sat up straight in their chairs. With a strategic batting of the eyes, Violet squeezed the story out of them in five minutes flat.

Interestingly, while the acrobats admitted to crashing Hope's ball, they knew nothing about the French Blue.

"We was down the pub, yeah?, when a man wiv a fake-like beard, teeth rottin' out ov his head, yeah?, sat down," the lead man said. "Said he'd give fi'ty pounds to the each ov us for making a right nice mess of your fancy-pants party. Twen'y-five before, twen'y-five after."

"And what of the other twenty-five pounds the man owes you?" Violet asked. "Have you received it yet?"

The acrobat shook his head. "Nah. Seein' as we been caught, we ain't expectin' to see the rest. Though that ain't exactly fair now, is it?"

But when Violet asked them about the diamond, the man responded to her question with a blank stare; his companions, impossibly, appeared even more puzzled. And unless they were better actors than they were acrobats, Hope could tell they spoke the truth.

Across the room he met Lake's gaze.

So now they were looking for a man disguised in a strap-on beard and, from the sound of it, ill-fitting wooden dentures.

A description that encompassed a solid half of the inhabitants of London during the bustling months of the season.

Splendid.

"Discover any further information about this man," Hope said, knowing all the while his offer would come to naught, "and I will gladly pay you the twenty-five guineas he still owes you."

Head throbbing and heart sunk, Hope charged from the room.

"Keep them in your custody," he growled over his shoulder as Lake followed him out into the servants' hall. "In the extreme unlikelihood that we find this bearded, gap-toothed son of a bitch, those acrobats of yours might help us untangle his plot."

Without waiting for a reply, he mounted the stairs two at a time. He needed more coffee and a bath; as it was Friday, a goodly amount of paperwork awaited him at the bank before the start of the weekend.

Mr. Hope sighed. He wasn't used to dreading the day like this. His work was difficult and often frustrating, but he enjoyed it nonetheless. It was what he did, and who he was. He rarely, if ever, desired to be anywhere but the offices of Hope & Co. on Fleet Street.

And so the tug to remain at his house, and take his coffee in the upstairs drawing room where Sophia now waited, shocked him.

That he imagined taking more than his coffee, even with her mother there in the room—well, it quite frankly *petrified* him.

In his rational mind he knew there was no time for such things, and besides, his relationship with Sophia had progressed far enough. Too far, even.

As much as Hope loathed Lake's habit of barging in uninvited, thank God he interrupted Hope's interlude with Sophia before they'd done something they would both regret. Hope knew he would have done it, and done it again and again and again. And where would that leave the two of them today?

He dare not imagine the possibilities.

And so off to his study he went, nodding at a footman along the way for a pot—no, make it two pots of coffee and whatever potion Cook had on hand for a headache.

Slipping into the quiet, tobacco-scented calm of his study, Hope was about to close the door behind him when a sudden, inelegant movement at the desk caught his eye.

The Marquess of Withington sprang to his feet and dipped

his dark head in a single, elbowy jolt. He held his hat in his hands.

Hope's mouth went dry as he ran a hand through his curls. A visit from one of his largest investors and clients before nine o'clock on a Friday morning was *not* a good sign.

That said client was also courting Miss Sophia Blaise, procurer of impeccably timed sobs, temptress of Hope's restless dreams, had nothing to do with Hope's rising ire.

No, absolutely nothing at all.

At least that was what Hope told himself as he attempted a smile.

"My lord! Welcome. What an—*unexpected* pleasure. You must forgive my mess; it's been a busy morning, as you might imagine." Hope made for his desk. "Please, do sit."

Withington nervously eyed the leather-backed chair, but did not move. "My apologies for visiting you unannounced, and at so ungodly an hour. Thank you for seeing me, Mr. Hope. I shall make quick work of the business I have come to discuss, though I confess it—well, I'm afraid it's rather. Um. Unpleasant."

"Rather the opposite of capital, then?"

Missing the jibe, Withington furrowed his brow. "Capital? Heavens, no."

"Go on, then."

Withington jerked his cravat into disarray; his face burned pink. "The events of last night were. Um. Rather terrifying, actually. My mother lost her wig and her dignity and was up half the night howling like a madwoman because of it."

Good Lord. As if Hope didn't feel bad enough. "I do apologize for any grief her ladyship has suffered on my behalf. I understand it is no comfort, but I take full responsibility for last night's events. My clients—" He swallowed. "My clients are very important to me, my lord. You've my word I will do everything in my power to see that justice is done, and her ladyship compensated for any trouble I may have caused."

Withington passed his hat from one hand to the other. He looked as if he would burst into tears at any moment. "You don't know my mother, Mr. Hope. There is no compensating her. Not when she's. Er. In *this* sort of state."

Hope stood awkwardly beside his desk and cast a longing

glance toward the sideboard. "Well." He cleared his throat. "I've been on the hunt for the stolen jewel since the moment it was taken from me. Make no mistake, Lord Withington, I *will* find the French Blue. It's only a matter of time now. And you will be glad to know this whole—er, series of *unfortunate* events will have no impact on your funds."

Well. At least he could *hope* there'd be no impact. But if he and Lake didn't find the jewel, and soon, all hell would break loose—

"I'm sorry!" Withington blurted. "You have always done right by my family, Mr. Hope. If I had it my way—well, I'd have a different mother, I tell you that much. But I'm afraid I've no choice in the matter. I must." Oh, God, the man was going to faint. "I must move my accounts to—er—a different bank. I'm terribly sorry, Mr. Hope, *terribly* sorry."

Hope bit back his panic. At least one hundred thousand pounds were in those accounts.

This did not bode well for the hours and days ahead. At this rate, Hope & Co. would shutter its doors in a week or two, maybe less.

"I'm sorry," Withington repeated. He looked up to the ceiling, as if trying to recall a memorized bit of Chaucer. "Everyone knows that Hope and Company is only as great—no, that's not it. Only as *good* as its reputation. And I'm afraid your reputation will suffer on account of this. Um. Unfortunate incident. I cannot risk it, Mr. Hope. I've three sisters, you see . . . and my mother, of course, the old bat just refuses to die . . ."

Hope could hardly breathe for the sudden swelling of his throat. Those were his mother's words, probably hurled at the poor marquess over breakfast this morning. Hope would've felt sorry for the fellow if Withington wasn't pushing him to the brink of ruin.

If Withington wasn't after the woman Hope held in his arms mere hours ago. The woman who set his mind, his body, alight with desire.

"I told you," Hope said, trying not to grit his teeth. This jealousy, it made him feel wild, and he did not like it. "I will sort out this diamond business. Your funds shall not suffer, my lord. Do not forget how well I have safeguarded your family's fortune for years now. I've made you thousands, tens of thousands—"

"I know. And I appreciate your efforts; they have not gone unnoticed. It pains me to say this." Withington looked away; the fingers that held his hat were white. "But I must sell my Hope and Company shares and withdraw my deposits. I've already visited Fleet Street, and the transfer is under way as we speak."

Hope's breath shook as he tried to calm the panic, the rage, too, that rose in his belly. It took considerable effort not to leap across the desk and take his lordship's close-shaven neck in his hands.

The marquess was not being rude, nor unkind; this was a matter of business, and Hope never lost his head over business. So why this sudden urge to do violence to a kind, if odd, fellow whose only crime was harboring a *tendre* for Miss Sophia Blaise?

Hope swallowed the answer to his question and straightened. He had to get the marquess out of here before bad things—things Hope would forever regret—happened.

"Very well. I will see to the transfer straightaway, my lord."

Withington's shoulders fell back from his ears, and a breath of relief escaped from his open mouth. Thanking Hope, he jammed his hat on his head and hesitated, as if he would bow; remembering himself, he thumbed his hat in that abrupt way of his and exited the room.

Standing behind his desk, Hope fingered a heavy crystal paperweight as his fury burned to new heights. The Marquess of Withington was a client, an investor, no more than that; he couldn't possibly know of Hope's acquaintance with Sophia.

His desire for the woman Withington courted in earnest. The woman his lordship would in all likelihood take for his wife.

Even so. His presence this morning was like salt in a wound; nothing like adding insult to injury, and at so early an hour.

He took the paperweight in his hand just as Mr. Daltrey poked his head into the room, bearing coffee and biscuits.

Hope dropped the crystal with a dull thud onto the desk.

He sighed. "Your timing, Mr. Daltrey, is, as always, impeccable. Come in."

He sat at his desk, staring out the window at a brightening day, and drained cup after cup of coffee. It was bitter and hot but slowly burned away the knot in his throat. As he drank he found himself thinking about his father, a man who'd always occupied the shadows of his thoughts but rarely appeared center stage.

The elder Hope was brilliant beyond imagination: philosopher, inventor, theologian, and collector. How he'd managed to find the time to grow the family's smallish business into a world-renowned banking house, and be a husband and father besides, Thomas hadn't a clue.

He remembered when he was five, his brother Henry had been born sometime in the night, and the house was in a tizzy over a beautiful new baby. Forgotten by his governess (and everyone else), Thomas had hidden behind the drapes in his nursery and cried himself into a stupor, whimpering for his mummy.

It had been his father who discovered him. With a smile the elder Hope had taken his son in his arms and kissed his cheeks.

He'd clucked his tongue and said, "But my dear Thomas, surely you know by now it's best to leave the crying to babies! Besides, they cannot eat chocolate."

Thomas's sobs halted at the mention of *chocolate*. "They can't?"

"Absolutely not! If they do, their lips turn green and fall off. Ghastly, I know. But you and me, we can visit the chocolatier as often as we like."

"And still keep our lips?"

His father had laughed. "Yes. And still keep our lips."

Later that night, with a bellyache from eating far too many of Monsieur Cormier's truffles, Thomas held his father's hand as he met Henry for the first time. Though he wished he'd wake so that they might properly be introduced, Thomas kissed him anyway, and hugged his mummy with a smile.

"You naughty boy." His mother grinned and wiped a smear of chocolate from his face with her thumb. She met her husband's gaze. "Someone's been to visit the monsieur."

His father shrugged, then turned to wink at Thomas. "I don't know what you're talking about, darling."

Hope closed his eyes against the hot press of tears, dropping his cup onto its saucer with a clatter. God, how he missed them; how he wished his father were with him now. What would John Hope do? How would he seek out the diamond while assuring investors and keeping the bank afloat?

And what would he say to his son, still half-drunk on Miss Sophia Blaise's touch, about the choice between duty and following one's own desire?

Part of Hope believed his father would call him a fool. He'd remind him of all he'd sacrificed, and everything he'd been through, to make his dream come true of seeing Hope & Co. flourish once more.

But another part of Thomas, the part that recalled with startling clarity the sound of his father's laugh, believed his answer might be more complicated than that.

Hope rose abruptly, pushing the thought from his mind. The day was in full force now; there was much work to be done.

He dressed and made for Fleet Street.

Fourteen

Heart pounding, Sophia set down the paper. She reached for her cup and saucer, which—*drat!*—made a terrible clatter in the grip of her shaking fingers.

"Dearest," her mother said, looking up from her needlepoint. "Are you unwell?"

Sophia set the tea back on its tray and arranged her features into what she hoped was a smile. "I am quite well, Mama, thank you. Just a bit—"

"Tired? Regretful? Plagued by guilt? Yes, well, that *does* tend to happen when one leaves one's unconscious mother in a carriage to run about *unchaperoned* in the dead of night."

"Mama," Sophia sighed, too exhausted to resist the impulse to roll her eyes, "I already told you, Mr. Hope needed my help—"

"Regardless," Lady Blaise sniffed, returning to her embroidery hoop, "that does not excuse what you have done. We had better pray the marquess makes an offer before word gets out of your *nocturnal activities*."

With her bottom lip Lady Blaise blew a lock of hair from her forehead. "If I survive your first season, I daresay I shall fill the bathtub with champagne and drink it. Every"—a furious tug on the thread—"last"—another tug—"*drop*. No one appreciates how difficult it all is for the poor mamas. Debutantes these days! If I behaved as you did last night, my father would've locked me in the cellar and thrown away the key. Mark my words, it is the end—the *end* I say!—of my sanity and my soul. And your cousin—I cannot even *begin* to speak on *that* subject . . ."

Lost as Lady Blaise was in the heat of her diatribe, Sophia hoped she would not notice her daughter slipping the gossip sheets into the folds of her skirt. God forbid Mama discover the news. Sophia would be spending the rest of her life in that cellar of Grandfather's.

The lines of text glared in her memory. She'd run her thumb over the words, smearing the ink as if she might erase them.

Like any debutante worth her salt, Sophia devoured the gossip pages first thing every morning, always before she tucked into breakfast but never after her first cup of tea. And like any debutante, she shamelessly enjoyed the faux pas and *affaires de coeur* of London's most fashionable, if indiscreet, aristocrats.

That is, until the indiscretion was her own.

It has been revealed by Mr. C. that a certain debutante S. has been ghostwriting the memoirs of a royal more accustomed to the company of men.

Fear bolted through her, clouding her belly with dread. Sophia understood the entry for what it was: a threat. While readers would glance over the lines, thinking them nothing short of a riddle, Sophia knew that the advertisement was the first of many. Doubtless more would be revealed with each new entry—*S.* would become Miss Sophia Blaise of No. 8 Grosvenor Square; *royal* La Reinette, notorious madam of The Glossy in Mayfair.

The clock was ticking. Sophia did not know how much time she had, or who this Mr. C. was, but she would try her damnedest to stop him.

Besides. The devil hadn't a clue whom he'd crossed. The indiscretions that made Sophia the target of his wrath also worked to her advantage. She hadn't outrun caped assassins and outwitted a Princess of Wales on accident. If anything, her adventures at Mr. Hope's side had taught her she had more to offer than her pretty manners and mediocre dancing.

Courage. Cunning. A way with strategically timed sobs.

Oh yes. Mr. C. would be sorry he ever threatened Miss Sophia Blaise.

Still, that did not mean the burden of discovery weighed

upon her any less. The threat of losing everything that mattered was greater than ever. Her reputation, the glamorous match, the brilliant life she'd wanted for as long as she could remember—if she didn't move quickly, it would all be lost.

"The marquess." Sophia looked to her mother. "I believe we should accept the invitation to his box at Drury Lane. This evening, perhaps?"

Later that evening, Mr. Hope was at his desk at Hope & Co., when a breathless groom delivered the note.

Found thief. At Duchess Street, come as soon as you get this.

It was unsigned, but Hope recognized the wild scrawl of Violet's hand. He leapt to his feet, nearly toppling the chair as he grabbed his coat and raced down the stairs.

"To my house," he called to the coachman, "and quickly!"

Hope stared unseeing out the carriage window, his only awareness of the Friday evening traffic outside an occasional jerk this way and that as the driver careened onto backstreets.

His mind raced. Violet had found the thief. How? Who was he? What evidence did she have? A confession, perhaps. Or, even better, the diamond itself.

But Hope knew better. Violet would have mentioned such a thing in her note. And besides, it was too easy; he had the distinct feeling this chase would be long and messy. A fitting end, as it were, to his *History of the French Blue*.

The carriage had hardly come to a stop before Hope leapt onto the drive and up the wide stone steps of his house.

Mr. Daltrey, his butler, greeted him at the door. "In the library, sir."

Hope darted down the hall. "We shall require shackles, Daltrey, and a bottle of champagne!" he called over his shoulder.

Charging through the library's mahogany doors, Hope stared in dismay. Lady Violet was pacing before the fire, hands clasped at the small of her back. Mr. Lake, wet hair plastered to his skull, sat nearby, his bare shoulders wrapped in the thick folds of a blanket.

There was no one else in the room.

Violet raised her head at the sound of his entry. "You may cut the acrobats free. For I've reason to believe I've found our thief."

Hope removed his hat and watched Lake and Violet exchange glances.

"Pour us a drink, Hope," Lake said, nodding at the sideboard.

"I don't want a drink."

"Yes"—Lake looked him in the eye—"you do."

Hope sighed in exasperation. Truth be told, he was still recovering from last night's port, and needed a nip like he needed a hole in his head.

Nevertheless. Something was afoot, and the dull gleam in Lake's eye told Hope he wasn't going to like it. Not one bit.

"What the devil happened to you, Lake?" he asked over his shoulder as he poured three glasses of American whiskey. "You look like you fell—well, like you fell into a lake."

"Very funny." Lake took his glass. "As a matter of fact, it was the Serpentine."

Violet laughed. "And at the fashionable hour, too. Poor Lady Caroline, I don't know if she'll ever recover!"

"Lady Caroline." Hope thought for a moment. "Lord Harclay's sister?"

Violet ignored Lake's glower. "She was chaperoning Lord Harclay and me as we took our turn about Hyde Park this afternoon. Halfway through our stroll, Mr. Lake mysteriously appeared from behind a tree, and next thing I knew Lady Caroline was careening into the Serpentine. The two of them get on splendidly. If I didn't know any better, I would think they were very old friends indeed."

Hope glanced at Lake. Good God, was the man actually *blushing*? "You forget, Lady Violet, that Mr. Lake doesn't *have* any friends. Especially friends of the female variety."

"My friends are none of your business," Lake suddenly snarled. "Lady Caroline had the misfortune to fall into the river; I jumped in after her. No one was harmed. End of story."

Hope bit back his laughter; he'd never seen Lake so uncomfortable. Clearly that was not the end of the story.

"I am sorry to have missed this stroll of yours," Hope said

with a grin. "Apparently it was quite eventful. You didn't find our thief, too, in the midst of all your adventures?"

Lady Violet took a deep breath. She met Lake's eyes one last time before settling her gaze on Hope. "Actually—"

"You did?" He wrinkled his brow. "You *did*."

"I did indeed. You see, Mr. Hope, I've good reason to believe that William Townshend, the Earl of Harclay, stole your diamond."

Mr. Hope choked on his brandy. "Really, Lady Violet, now is not the time to jest. Why, Harclay is not only an *earl*, and one of the most powerful peers at that; he is also one of my largest and most faithful clients. Tread carefully."

Violet resumed her pacing. "I would not dare make such an accusation if I wasn't convinced it were true. Just as you would not dare forget my entire inheritance is invested in Hope and Company stock. I understand, Mr. Hope, how much you have at stake; I, too, risk everything in this."

"But how?" Hope gulped at his whiskey. "And, more importantly, *why*? I know for a fact the man's got more money than all the pharaohs of Egypt. Combined."

"It makes perfect sense," Violet replied. "Only a man of Lord Harclay's hubris is bold and brash enough to thieve a diamond in the midst of a ball. Don't you see? The man is desperate for a thrill. Look at how he gambles, wagering small fortunes on this trifle and that. It's only money to him; he's got plenty of it, and is willing to spend thousands in the pursuit of excitement. Harclay is rich, he is clever, and he is bored. A more potent combination for a crime such as this does not exist."

Hope stared down into his empty glass. Bloody hell, she was right; it *did* make perfect sense.

A gentleman jewel thief, moving in plain sight for all the world to see, risking the gallows in his search for a thrill.

Hope remembered the earl ogling Lady Violet at the ball, the French Blue glittering invitingly from her breast. Arm in arm, the two of them had waded through the crush, bodies pressed close as Harclay called for that fateful waltz.

And then all hell had broken loose, the ballroom plunged into darkness as the acrobats and Hope's traitorous guards harassed the perfumed masses.

It was genius, really. In the midst of the chaos, the earl

could've easily swiped the diamond from Lady Violet's neck, and her none the wiser.

That *bastard*.

Hope resisted the urge to hurl his glass across the room. He would have to take his own advice and tread carefully. As yet there was no proof; and besides, Hope couldn't risk running off yet another client, never mind the infamously rakish Earl of Harclay.

"I pray you're wrong, Lady Violet." Hope leaned against the mantel and looked into the fire, draining the last drop of his whiskey. "But if Lord Harclay is indeed our man, we need to find out where he's hiding the diamond. And we mustn't forget the diamond collar; I borrowed it from a . . . friend who misses it very much."

Indeed, a cousin of the Tsar's had loaned Hope the collar; and the last thing he needed was batty old Alexander coming after him with all the might of the Russian army.

Lake nodded his agreement. "There's no negotiating with a man who wants for nothing. If what you're saying is true, Lady Violet, the only way to get back the French Blue is to take it. I can canvass his house; and Hope, you might search his records for any mention of a recent acquisition . . ."

Violet swallowed her whiskey in two long gulps and winced. "No. I'll do it."

"Are you sure that's wise?" Hope turned to face her. "You just said you've got quite a bit at stake here."

"I said I'll do it. Lord Harclay and I—" She stopped and looked away. "Trust me. I've a much better chance of finding the French Blue than the two of you."

"Are you and—" Hope cleared his throat. "The earl—er—fond of each other, or courting, perh—"

"No."

The vehemence of her reply startled Hope. He met Lake's gaze. This was a bad idea and they both knew it, but what else could they do?

"Very well," Lake said, rising. "Don't say we didn't warn you. The earl is a dangerous man, my lady, and you could very well be harmed—or worse—on the hunt for the jewel."

Violet looked at Hope levelly. "I'm the one who lost the French Blue. And I'm the one who's going to get it back."

Fifteen

Sophia smoothed the pale silk of her skirts and wondered how much earsplitting opera, exactly, one could endure without losing one's hearing.

The marquess's box, while of prime location and excellent prominence, only made matters worse; they were so close to the stage Sophia heard every footstep, every murmured endearment, and, of course, every agonizing aria.

Beside her, the marquess raised his glass of claret and tried not to wince as the prima donna screeched a crescendo. "Capital, isn't it?"

Sophia nodded enthusiastically, unsure whether he was referring to the opera or the claret. "The best I've had—seen! Do you come often to Drury Lane?"

"Oh, yes," the marquess shouted above the din. "I am rather fond of Shakespeare's comedies. The operas—they are good, too. And you, Miss Blaise. Do you enjoy the theater?"

Sophia sighed, realizing they'd had this *exact* conversation in her uncle's drawing room some weeks ago. "Yes. Yes I do."

Even with actors yelling declarations of love at one another on the stage, the silence that settled between Sophia and the marquess was painful. A pulse of longing shot through her at the memory of her conversations with Mr. Hope; how easily words and thoughts flowed between them. There was no pretense, no desire to impress. She could be honest with him, and much to her surprise, she was fond of her honest self; Hope's, too.

Sophia wished, for a moment, that Hope were her escort tonight.

And felt ashamed as soon as the wish was made. She shouldn't feel this way about a man like Thomas Hope. She didn't want to *want* him like this, especially when the season's greatest catch sat in a chair mere inches from her own.

The marquess had kindly invited her to his box so that they might become acquainted—and, with any luck, more than that. It was an invitation for which her fellow debutantes would gladly sell their souls, surely. And the marquess—he wasn't such bad company. Not as bad, at least, as tonight's opera.

Sophia turned and caught Withington looking at her, a soft gleam in his dark eyes she recognized but could not place. His gaze was not lascivious or lustful, though she could tell the poor chap struggled not to look at her breasts. Rather she saw in his eyes curiosity, a steady declaration of interest that belied his boyish exclamations.

Understanding rolled through her, swift and startling.

He *liked* her!

The Marquess of Withington actually *liked* her.

All along, Sophia assumed the marquess hunted her for the same reasons she hunted him; practical, if not cynical, reasons. After all, what sort of fool believed affection, much less love, had anything at all to do with marriage?

While she claimed no great fortune, her uncle *was* a duke, and she supposed her face qualified as passably pretty. Withington would bring his fortune, and she would bring her hazel eyes and that greatest inheritance of all, her goodly-sized bosom.

But to her very great surprise, the marquess was proving far more honorable in his courtship. He called on Sophia, and strolled with Sophia, and invited Sophia because he genuinely *enjoyed* Sophia, no matter the subject of their conversation.

Withington looked away, blushing as he sipped nervously at his claret. His movements were ungainly, severe, as if he were a puppet and his strings were jerked too taught by an overeager master. While certainly odd, his lordship's awkwardness was also endearing; proof, perhaps, of the goodness of the heart that beat beneath his expensively clothed breast.

Sophia sipped her own claret, though it was shame, rather than embarrassment, that flushed her cheeks.

She had to salvage the evening. Not only because it would serve her well in obtaining that brilliant match—a match she needed to make, now more than ever—but also because Withington deserved kind company; wit, too. He was a gentle man, and right now she was making a mess of his good intentions.

The marquess deserved better. He deserved her honest self.

"I've recently acquired a predilection for port," Sophia said, ignoring her mother's gasp from the row behind. "Perhaps it might be amusing to arrange a tasting of sorts?"

Withington grinned so widely Sophia thought his face might split in two. "Well, Miss Blaise, I did not know ladies drank port! Capital news, I say, capital indeed! We shall arrange the tasting straightaway. We might have it on the terrace at my house, if it please you? The weather seems to have taken a turn for the better."

"Yes," Sophia said, smiling. "That would please me very much, my lord."

"Capital! It shall be a great pleasure to have you at *my* home for a change. Begging your pardon, Lady Blaise." He winked at Sophia before turning to her mama. "Of course I find your *salon* a most capital affair. The tea, it is so very. Yes, so very good."

Sophia bit her lip to keep from laughing. She was going to like this Withington fellow; and could only hope he would like the honest Sophia in turn.

One week later

Sophia tapped her slippered foot on the floor of the carriage, glancing out the window at a darkening sky.

"Where the devil is she?"

Lady Blaise clucked in disapproval. "Heavens, mind your tongue! I don't know where you learn these things—"

"Cousin Violet," she answered matter-of-factly. "We've an invitation to dine at the *Earl* of *Harclay's* house, and we're going to miss it, all because of her. If I've got to wait another minute—"

"I hardly doubt the marquess would approve, especially

after that dreadful comment of yours about having a taste for port. Really, where *do* you—"

"Cousin *Violet*," Sophia repeated through gritted teeth. "She's never late. Nor does she ever take such care in her toilet. Poor Fitzhugh dressed her in every gown we own between the two of us. I don't care what Violet says about searching the earl's house for the missing jewel. She is fond of him, I can see it in her eyes—oh, oh thank *heaven*, there she is!"

Violet appeared at the front door, her satin gown shimmering in the light of the gas lamps. She was coiffed and perfumed and pulled within an inch of her life, pink rose blooms tucked into the gleaming mass of her dark hair.

She looked dazzling.

And Violet did not dazzle for nothing.

"Well, aren't you coming, Violet?" Sophia poked her head out the coach window. "We're going to be late!"

Violet waved away Sophia's words. "Mr. Hope always arrives at a fashionably tardy hour. You won't miss a minute of his company, I promise."

Sophia resisted the urge to stick her tongue out at her cousin.

Alas, the urge proved too strong.

"So*phia*!" Lady Blaise rapped her none too gently with an ivory-handled fan.

Sophia fell back into the coach, a familiar fire in her cheeks.

"What's this about Mr. Hope?"

"Nothing." Sophia kept her eyes trained on her lap. "He's to be a guest of Lord Harclay's, that's all. Violet seems to think I've set my cap at him."

Lady Blaise tensed, her eyes widening before she could stop them. "Well. Have you?"

"No!" The force of Sophia's response surprised both of them. She cleared her throat and tried again. "What I meant to say is, it is a joke, mother *dear*est, nothing more. What foolishness! Dearest Cousin Violet has perhaps been at her flask again." Sophia's laugh was flat and grating. "Hope is a *banker*, for God's sake."

Even as the words escaped her lips, she hated herself for

saying them, thinking them, *believing* them at one point or another.

This snobbery, this heartless betrayal of all she'd shared with Hope—these things were at odds with the woman she was now. It wasn't her. Not anymore.

And yet, cowed by her mother, she did not deny them.

Lady Blaise relaxed into her seat and sighed with relief, hand on her breast. "Thank heaven, Sophia, you had me worried with all this talk of caps and tradesmen. And here you've managed to snare a marquess. Not just any marquess, either. *The* marquess. Ha! Now *that* is a good joke."

"Yes, the most amusing thing I've heard all day," Sophia said, watching through the window as Violet kissed her father on the cheek. He offered in turn an unsteady salute. Poor Uncle Sommer; he had not been himself for years now, and his condition was only getting worse. Violet certainly had her hands full. She was good, her cousin, for all her eccentricities.

Good, because she had chosen to stay with the family, while Sophia longed for nothing more than to escape it.

Sophia's pulse leapt as the old family carriage pulled onto Brook Street. Truth be told, Violet wasn't the only one sent into a tizzy by the arrival of Lord Harclay's invitation three days ago. Sophia smiled as she recalled Violet turning bright red whilst reading the note—something about money and champagne and settling their accounts.

All the ingredients for an appropriately scandalous evening out. Whatever her intentions, Violet had most *definitely* set her cap at that libertine the earl.

Over Violet's shoulder Sophia had managed to catch one last line—"*others of our mutual acquaintance shall join us*"—and knew, *knew*, that Mr. Hope would be among them.

Even now her heart danced in her chest at the thought of seeing him again. She had not heard from him since leaving his house the morning after the theft; that was nearly a week ago. Much to her disappointment he had not come to say good-bye after interrogating the acrobats with Violet and Lord

Harclay; Sophia in turn did not write him following her harrowing debut in the gossip sheets, perhaps out of spite, perhaps because she knew there was nothing either of them could do.

The French Blue, of course, remained at large.

Besides, the marquess kept her busy, calling most afternoons, offering invitations for the evening. While talk of an offer was assiduously avoided, Sophia saw in Withington's eyes he meant to do right by her. And what did one cryptic entry in the gossip rags matter when she was engaged to be married to a marquess?

Still. She often found herself thinking about Thomas. She wondered what occupied his time, what he did and whom he saw. Had he had much success in his search for the French Blue? What of La Reinette, the cloaked riders, Sophia's mysterious note?

And then there was the memory of his touch, his mouth and hands on her body in ways that made her ache when she thought of them.

Some days the longing to hear from him—a letter, a call, a stroll, *anything*—was unbearable.

And so it was no surprise that Sophia's entire being thrummed in anticipation as the carriage drew to a stop before the immaculate facade of Lord Harclay's residence in fashionable Hanover Square.

Even in the midst of her own excitement, Violet noticed her cousin's distress. As they dismounted, she took Sophia's hands and pulled her close.

"Do not worry, cousin," she said quietly, her blue eyes gleaming. "Tonight shall be great fun. Mr. Hope was asking about you today."

Sophia's heart skipped a beat. "He was?"

"Oh, yes." Together they mounted the front steps. "It was actually rather adorable. At the end of our meeting he tied his tongue in knots trying to ask, without asking, if you were to attend tonight's dinner. He had a certain spring in his step after I assured him you were."

The butler, a young, handsome man by the name of Mr. Avery, led them into the drawing room. He held the door open and motioned them inside.

Sophia swallowed, hard, to keep her heart from leaping

into her mouth. Violet patted the top of her hand and smiled. They were here at last.

At last.

Stepping over the threshold, Sophia blinked, turning her head; and there he was across the room, shifting his weight from one foot to the other, coupe held carelessly in his right hand, the left grazing a well-sculpted thigh.

In her veins her blood rushed as Mr. Hope met her eyes. His were bluer than she remembered, soft and serious and so lovely she could hardly bear to look. There was a tug, vaguely familiar, in the knot of her belly—the tug between their bodies, at once sweet and terribly overwhelming.

His lips were parted, face taut as if he, too, suffered from stolen breath. And still he did not look away; for a moment his eyes flashed with hunger, and she remembered his hands between her legs, the intoxicating tenderness of his fingers.

Hope set down his glass, eyes never leaving hers, and made to move in her direction.

"Miss Blaise? Begging your pardon, Miss—"

Sophia started, turning to face the footman at her side. He held aloft a tray of delicate coupes.

"Would you care for some champagne? An excellent vintage from his lordship's cellars."

"Oh, yes please." She took a coupe and smiled tightly. "Don't go too far."

Drinking deeply, Sophia let out a long breath. She squared her shoulders in a failed attempt to gather her wits, knowing she had to face Thomas whether or not she possessed the power of speech.

She turned, expecting Mr. Hope's fine form to be revealed to her in new detail, but met instead with her mother's round, radish-red face. Lady Blaise's eyes slid from Sophia to Hope and back again, lips pursed. Her gaze settled on Sophia, displeasure evident in the sharp, single swivel of her head.

No.

Lady Blaise blinked, a smile appearing as if by magic on her lips. She turned to the woman at her elbow, who wore her exotic looks—tall, taller than Sophia by a head or two, and very thin—as one would a tiara of diamonds: elegantly, confidently, as if she owned them and not the other way around.

Mama introduced her as Lady Caroline, the Dowager Countess of Berry and the Earl of Harclay's elder sister.

"A pleasure to make your acquaintance, Miss Blaise." Lady Caroline returned her bow, nearly mauling the champagne-bearing footman as she tripped over the hem of her gown.

Sophia grabbed Lady Caroline by the arm, catching her just in time before Lord Harclay's excellent vintage ended up on the rug.

"Oh, goodness, how clumsy of me! I wish I could say it was the first mishap of the day. My brother, the dear, wouldn't even let me dance after my coming out. He was worried I'd kill someone. Can't say that I blame him—I'm all thumbs, you see, and I can hardly walk without slaying either myself or my neighbor."

Sophia smiled. Lady Caroline certainly *looked* elegant, but was, apparently, anything but.

She liked her straightaway.

"I'm afraid I can relate." Sophia sipped her champagne. "I'm not much of a dancer myself. I dare not imagine how many poor gentlemen's toes I've broken this week alone. It's a wonder Almack's hasn't banned me for life."

"Oh, but Sophia, she is good at other things." Lady Blaise cast a warning glance her way. "Like. Er. Conversation! Yes. She's very good at that."

"Splendid!" Lady Caroline clapped her hands together. "I made your cousin's acquaintance the morning after Mr. Hope's ball. That Lady Violet, she's got pluck! And a rather wicked way about her. Perhaps the three of us might take tea together? I'm just out of mourning, you see, and would love the company."

The dinner gong sounded, and Mr. Avery stood by the door as he made his announcement. With a bow he motioned for the guests to follow him to the dining room.

Mr. Lake's hulking figure suddenly appeared at Lady Caroline's side. While he was smoothly sinister as always, more so, perhaps, dressed in fine eveningwear, an uncertain softness took captive his features as he looked upon her.

Sophia watched the working of Lady Caroline's throat as he grazed the bare skin of her arm with his fingers. Sophia looked away, face burning. She didn't know what she just saw, but she certainly knew she wasn't supposed to have seen it.

Wordlessly Lake moved past them, holding his arm out to Cousin Violet.

Sophia blinked, running through the calculation in her head. If Lake escorted Violet to dinner, and Lord Harclay his sister the dowager countess, that left Mr. Hope for Sophia and Lady Blaise.

That also meant she and Mama would be seated on either side of Mr. Hope at the dinner table. The three of them, stuck together for the length of the meal.

Thank God the earl had a well-stocked cellar.

She felt the heat of Hope's gaze as he moved across the room toward her. Anticipation, prickly and fast, shot up her spine, and for a moment she closed her eyes, reveling in the sensation as much as it pained her.

And then Thomas was at her side, bowing his greeting before holding an elbow out to Lady Blaise. She shot Sophia another look of warning over her shoulder—as if one were not enough—and took Hope's arm with a lukewarm smile.

"Miss Blaise." His eyes swept the length of her pale lavender gown, the strands of tiny pearls that hung from her neck. Even as she looked away, a grin rose unbidden to her lips. "You look lovely."

"And you." She took his arm. "You look like you haven't slept since we saw you last."

He scoffed as he led them down the corridor, the sounds of swishing skirts and murmured conversation echoing around them.

"That bad, eh? I was hoping my youthful good looks might compensate for the hell I've put myself through these past days—begging your pardon, Lady Blaise." Thomas sighed. "I suppose I'm not as youthful as I once was."

"Or good-looking."

Mr. Hope smiled. "Yes, that, too."

Lord Harclay's dining room was lit to full splendor, great chandeliers sparkling upon an enormous table set with the earl's family silver, the century-old gilt china. Sophia was relieved to see several footmen hovering in the perimeter of the room, each man wielding an uncorked bottle of wine.

Settling Lady Blaise in her seat, Hope turned to Sophia.

He pinned her in place with those deucedly blue eyes of his, offering his hand as a footman shuffled her chair into place.

She took it so that she might steady herself, the warmth of his palm seeping through the fine kidskin of her glove. She inhaled sharply at the firmness of his touch, the familiarity of it. Desire sliced through her.

Mr. Hope took his seat beside her, the heat between them so palpable Sophia was surprised the table linens didn't catch fire.

The food was splendid, the wine, delicious. Sophia spent the better part of the meal chatting with Lady Caroline, who sat at the head of the table to her left, while Mr. Lake sat in uncharacteristic silence across from them.

It pleased Sophia to hear her mother's laugh as Mr. Hope shared some jest or another. He *was* charming, and even in the midst of all his troubles appeared to be in good spirits. While he and Sophia did not so much as meet eyes during the meal, Sophia was aware of his every movement, every word, hypnotized from the corner of her eye by his handsomeness, the beauty of his manners, and his happy way with the other guests.

He was putting on a show, certainly; testing out Cousin Violet's theory that Lord Harclay was the thief. From what little she knew of the earl, Sophia had no doubt he was guilty. A more notorious rake in all England there was not; he was a gambler and a drinker besides, and it was rumored he'd fought more duels than could be counted on hands *and* toes.

It was obvious the man was far too intelligent for his own good, and doubtless at the age of one-and-thirty he'd drunk London dry of its every amusement and vice. Perhaps he'd thieved the diamond out of boredom, perhaps for a thrill. No matter his motive, Sophia was convinced he'd done it.

But Mr. Hope, she knew, must proceed with great care; he stood to lose everything on such an accusation. Violet had explained that Lord Harclay was Hope's wealthiest client, with well over a hundred thousand pounds in deposits at Hope & Co. The loss of such a client would be nothing short of catastrophic.

While the proceedings at dinner were delicate, the amount of wine consumed at the table was not. Each course brought with it its own French varietal, and by the end of dinner Sophia's head was swimming, her awareness of and desire for Thomas scorching through her unimpeded.

She was at once disappointed and relieved when Lady Caroline stood and invited the ladies to retire. The gentlemen rose to their feet, chairs scraping hoarsely across the floor. Sophia followed, determined not to look in Mr. Hope's direction lest he deliver the knockout blow.

Too late.

She met his eyes, which flicked for a moment to her lips before settling on her own. Sophia sensed the energy coiling inside him. He was struggling not to reach out, pull her to him, finish what he'd started in the room where Mars and Venus lay.

Head swimming, Sophia abruptly turned, catching her hip on the edge of the table. A beautiful cut-glass pitcher of lemonade—full, because no one had touched it—tumbled off the table and landed with a terrific clatter on the floor.

"Oh dear." Sophia's hand went to her throat. "I'm terribly sorry, Lord Harclay, I don't know what happened—how terribly embarrassing—"

Harclay waved away her words. "Think nothing of it, my dear."

Face burning, Sophia made for the door, followed by her mother.

"No more wine for you!" Lady Blaise hissed.

Violet swooped to the rescue, looping her arm through Sophia's as they scurried through the gallery. "We're all foxed, no shame in admitting it."

Sophia managed to smile in thanks, her thoughts a riot as Lady Caroline led them to a drawing room done up in bottle green velvet. She took a deep breath, trying with all her might to think of anything, *anything* but Mr. Hope, his blue eyes, the desire that simmered between their bodies.

It would not do; no, it would not do at *all*. If Sophia wanted to make it out of Lord Harclay's house alive, she would have to focus her attention on something else.

Like the marquess.

Yes. Yes, Lord Withington would do. They had arranged to meet up in his box at Vauxhall Gardens tomorrow night, and Cousin Violet caught wind the marquess spoke of nothing but their port tasting.

Port. That bottle she and Hope had shared beneath Venus's benevolent gaze, the sweetness of his lips as they'd plundered her own. Had it really been only a week since he'd kissed her? It felt like an eternity. No, longer than that . . .

Sophia jumped at the pinch on her arm, turning to see her mother glowering at her side.

She swallowed for what felt like the hundredth time that evening.

And knew that whatever trouble she'd already caused tonight, there would be more of it.

Much, much more.

Sixteen

Having lit his cigar, Hope waved the match between his thumb and forefinger and took a long pull. Smoke whirled over his head, the earthy reek of tobacco filling Lord Harclay's dining room.

"So." The earl's eyes glittered through the haze. "Lady Violet tells me you've made progress in your search for the diamond."

Hope exchanged a glance with Mr. Lake, who sat brooding at the far corner of the table, his face obscured by smoke. What in hell was wrong with *him*? He hadn't been himself all evening.

No matter. Hope had bigger problems, one of which was sitting just to his right, chomping merrily on his cigar.

Man had a set of stones on him, Hope would give him that. The earl, he knew, was baiting him, testing Hope's limits. It was all part of his deception, a deception that, judging from the smug look on his face, he was enjoying immensely.

Hope gulped what little brandy was left in his balloon and flopped further into his chair, running a hand through his hair so that it hung haphazardly across his face.

Two could play this game.

"Great progress, yes." Hope pulled on his cigar. "Lady Violet has proven quite wily, though I cannot say I condone her methods. Alas, I think you'll agree"—he winked—"ladies often have the upper hand in these sorts of . . . What shall we call them? *Situations*."

Hope bit back his smile as Lord Harclay's face darkened. The earl took one, two long pulls on his cigar, narrowing his eyes against the column of smoke that rose from his lips.

"Now now, Mr. Hope. I agree we must give credit where credit is due. But we must also acknowledge the fact that Lady Violet could run circles around any of us, even on the best of days. She is"—he paused, a small, secret smile unfurling across his lips—"most unusual and invigorating company."

Ah. So Hope's suspicion that Violet was—er, *fraternizing*, to put it kindly—with the enemy proved true. While she was indeed more intelligent, and more daring, than most anyone he'd known, could Hope trust her to choose the diamond and their livelihoods over her affection, whatever its nature, for the Earl of Harclay?

Hope brought his cigar between his thumb and forefinger and examined it, smoke curling languidly into the air. "Make no mistake, my lord, I'll find the French Blue—and our thief. And when I do, I have no doubt he'll be very, *very* sorry he ever crossed me."

Lord Harclay's lips twitched, but he had the grace not to scoff. "My offer of aid stands, Hope. The news bodes ill for my fortunes as it does for yours. I've men and money at my disposal. You need only ask."

"We've men and money of our own." Lake pounded his cigar into the ashtray, making what was left of the silver and the crystal jump on the table. "Besides. I rather enjoy the hunt. Not as much as I enjoy the kill, of course. The kill is my true skill."

Hope grinned tightly. Whatever was wrong with Lake, he was going to get to the bottom of it. "Let us hope more so than your poetry, Mr. Lake."

"Ah! My poetry." Lake smiled at him from across the table, a mirthless thing. "*That* I learned from you, old friend."

Hope tugged a hand through his hair to keep from reaching for Lake's neck.

The earl, eyes glittering with triumph, put out his cigar and stood. "Let's join the ladies, shall we? My new billiards table has just arrived. It's proven quite amusing; even Caroline likes to play. Perhaps we might teach Lady Violet and Miss Blaise? If Miss Blaise is anything alike to Violet, I daresay it shall make for great sport."

Hope tensed at the sound of Sophia's name on Lord Harclay's lips. While the earl did not insult her—his words were,

Hope knew, meant as a compliment—Hope was overwhelmed by the fierce urge to protect her. Possess her, even; Hope longed for nothing more than to take the earl by the throat and tell him in no uncertain terms that Sophia was his, damn it, and that a thieving prick like him had no right to even think her name, much less speak it.

Biting the inside of his lip, Hope took a deep breath through his nose. *Tread lightly. Harclay is your largest depositor. Think of the bank, all you've dreamed and accomplished in its name.*

"Let's do." Hope set down his cigar and rose. "I've yet to see one of these new-fashioned tables. Is it still lined with felt? And the pockets, I've heard they're all the rage now."

Lake slid to his feet with the speed and grace of a tiger on the prowl—had he always moved like this, like a healthy man, a whole man not crippled by injury?—and together with Hope followed the earl out of the room, Hope all the while resisting the urge to slip the pocketknife from his waistcoat and sink it between Harclay's proud, well-formed shoulders.

The earl's billiards room was as tastefully appointed as the rest of his home. Nearly as long and wide as a town coach, the billiards table occupied the majority of the space, while an equally enormous brandy board took up the rest.

Across the room, Lady Violet was arm in arm with Harclay's windswept sister, Lady Caroline, their heads bent in deep conversation. As soon as he entered, Violet halted midstride and met his eyes. He replied with a quick, grim shake of his head.

Nothing. The earl revealed nothing.

Though that didn't mean Hope absolved Harclay of all guilt. Quite the opposite, as a matter of fact: Harclay's assiduous hospitality, his offer of aid, and his fawning over the ladies present were suspicious for a selfish man such as he. In all their years as banker and client, the earl had never extended Hope an invitation to his home in Hanover Square. Until now, of course.

Hope had yet to untangle the intricacies of Lord Harclay's plot; but a plot there certainly was, Hope had no doubt. He merely needed proof, and then he would be free to make his move.

Violet nodded, slipping her arm from Lady Caroline's and making to walk toward him, when the earl stopped her in her tracks. He murmured something in her ear; she flushed pink.

Dear God. If Hope didn't know any better, he would say they were well acquainted indeed. Perhaps even more than that.

He resisted the urge to separate them, to warn Lady Violet off lest the earl do her irreparable harm. But if anyone could snare Harclay at his own game, it was Violet; she was smart and witty and could hold her liquor better than any man this side of the Channel.

Besides, Hope knew the lady would take offense at the intrusion. Violet wanted to prove she was capable of remedying the mess she believed she'd caused. And while Hope knew she was not guilty in the slightest, she *did* stand to lose everything on the outcome of their hunt for the jewel. Who was Hope to question her methods, or dictate instruction? He would have to trust her, whether or not he understood what in *hell* she was doing.

He balled his fingers into fists.

Tread lightly.

He turned, his pulse leaping at the knowledge that she would be there. *She.* The one he'd wanted to claim. Still wanted.

The one for whom he'd nearly thrown it all away.

Sophia sat on a far settee, color high as her mother sat purse-lipped beside her. Lady Blaise had two eyes and a brain; doubtless she'd witnessed Hope's interlude with Sophia in the drawing room earlier, their shameless ogling of one another. And doubtless she was displeased. For what lady in her right mind wanted a man like Hope—tradesman, orphan, foreigner—for her only daughter?

He felt her disappointment as his own. He knew it; Lady Blaise did, too: Sophia deserved better.

And yet he couldn't stay away from her.

In the golden light of the candelabra, Sophia looked lovely. Her lips were stained plum from French wine; the long strands of pearls at her neck gleamed a shade paler than her cheeks. Her eyes, wide and wet, reflected the fire's flame. When she turned them to him, his blood rushed with heat.

"Ladies." He nodded his head in greeting. "I hope I did not bore you overmuch with my company at dinner."

Sophia grinned. "No more than usual, Mr. Hope. Oh, look, Violet and Lord Harclay are pairing up for a go at this billiards nonsense. Shall we join them?"

Without waiting for a response she held out her hand. He took it, ignoring Lady Blaise's bland smile of dismay, and tucked her arm into the crook of his own.

Alone, at last! If they weren't in polite company he would've danced a jig. Hope was not prepared for the force of his happiness at having Sophia by his side; he'd missed her more than was proper or good. Much more, indeed, than he cared to admit.

He had told himself to keep his distance. It would not do to further embroil her in the worsening crises that now dominated his every waking hour. While the matter of the jewel thief was being resolved, that of Sophia's mysterious note and the bastard who threatened her and her family was not.

Still. To draw her to him was akin to the beating of his heart: an impulse, an inexplicable necessity over which he had no control.

There were four, maybe five steps from the settee to the billiards table. Hope had no time to waste.

"Sophia." God, what to say to her? There was so much, he felt about to burst. "I. Er. I want you to know that just because I haven't—haven't been in contact doesn't mean I don't think of you. Often." *All the time.*

He watched the working of her throat. "That is kind of you to say, Thomas. And how goes the hunt for the French Blue?"

"Fine. Awful. I don't want to talk about that bloody diamond anymore. Not when I'm with you."

Sophia turned to him, bottom lip between her teeth. "So what *do* you want to talk about?"

Hope swallowed. Truth be told, what he wanted had nothing at all to do with talking.

He lowered his voice. "What I'm doing—I do to protect you, Sophia. Every time I enter your life I make a mess of things. If I'm not careful I could very well ruin that brilliant match you've always wanted. I hear"—he swallowed again—"your courtship with the Marquess of Withington progresses apace."

Her eyes snapped to meet his. "Where did you hear that?"

"I am banker to the most prominent arbiters of the fashionable world, Sophia. That you have captured the attention of this season's most eligible bachelor has not gone unnoticed. I daresay you've sent every debutante and her mama into fits of rage and jealousy. The marquess is no small prize—as his banker, I would know."

Sophia drew to a stop, pulling Hope to her side. She looked at him, eyes narrowing as if she fought back tears. She opened her mouth, but thought better of it; quickly she looked away and resumed their stroll.

"Any word from La Reinette?" Her voice was barely above a whisper. "Whomever is after me tightens the noose; there was a short but direct attack printed in the gossip pages a few days ago. It's only a matter of time before he reveals that I am the author of a courtesan's salacious memoirs."

Hope's grip on Sophia tightened. "I'll get to the bottom of this, Sophia, you have my word. If you should come to any harm on my account—" He looked at her. "I won't let them touch you."

She returned his gaze levelly. "Then let me help you. We can smoke these men out together, you and I—"

Sophia jumped at a sudden, deafening *thud*. Hope turned just in time to see Lady Caroline, cue poised above the billiards table, launch a cue ball smack-dab into the middle of Lady Blaise's forehead. With a strangled cry, Lady Blaise toppled over on the settee; her arms flailed as she landed none too gently on the floor, and was inundated in the foaming lace of her petticoats.

It all happened so quickly Hope could hardly keep pace. The earl, that son of a bitch, was at Lady Blaise's side in an instant, cradling her head in his hands as he cooed soothing words.

"Bring water," he called to the footmen, "and smelling salts. Lots of smelling salts!"

Across the room, Hope met Mr. Lake's gaze. Was Harclay's sudden tenderness all part of the act? Over brandy and cigars the man was rotten, callous, vainglorious in the extreme. And yet here he was, gently whispering sweet nothings into a wounded old woman's ear.

The man was a paradox.

Sophia, her attempts to help having been shooed away by the gentleman, watched the proceedings in mute horror, letting out a small sigh of relief only when the earl helped Lady Blaise to sit upright. Her gaze landed on Hope and Sophia, still arm in arm before her. While her eyes rolled a bit in her head, her mouth settled into a tight, colorless line.

Waving away Harclay's offer of a bed and rest, she allowed him to haul her to her feet. "That is most kind of you, Lord Harclay, most kind indeed, but I would hate to put you out. No, I believe I'll be quite all right, if you'll just help me to my carriage. Come, Sophia, it's time to leave."

Hope reached out to help one second too late. As if he were King Arthur and she the Lady Guinevere, Harclay swooped Lady Blaise into his arms and without so much as a grunt carried her from the room.

If Hope hadn't wanted to strangle the earl before, he certainly was possessed of the urge now.

The rest of the party followed, Lady Caroline wailing her apologies, Sophia trotting behind in breathless silence.

As if by magic, Sophia's family coach was brought round the front of the house. With great care, Harclay deposited Lady Blaise onto the carriage's cushioned seat. Together they laughed at some private joke, Lady Blaise's eyes twinkling despite being hit in the head by a cue ball.

And then everyone was shrugging into his jacket or her pelisse. As they made their way out the door, Hope noticed Lake and Lady Caroline hanging back in the entry hall. They glared at one another, hungrily.

The earl and Violet, meanwhile, were staring drunkenly into one another's eyes as he helped Violet into the carriage; the horses shuffled and huffed.

Hope's heart hardened at the knowledge the night was over. For a moment he pressed Sophia to him, as if to say, *I am not ready to let you go.* She met his eyes, and from the flickering heat he saw there, Hope could tell Sophia was not ready to let him go, either.

How was it the hours he spent in her presence passed as minutes, seconds, even? He'd been looking forward to this evening for days; and now, in the space of half a heartbeat, it was over.

"Good night, Miss Blaise." He did not dare say more: that

he wanted to see her again, tonight, tomorrow, and the day after that, and the day after that, too. When it came to Miss Sophia Blaise, it was never enough.

Her hand lingered in his as he helped her into the carriage. The sound of Lady Blaise's snoring broke the silence; Sophia bit her lip to keep from laughing.

"Good night, Mr. Hope."

They met eyes one last time. He knew he was grinning like a fool, but he didn't care. Sophia was happy, and he was, too.

A poignant, bittersweet sort of happiness. He could not bear to see her go; the torture, it was singular and far too painful to witness, especially with brandy in his belly and a gallon of wine besides.

Hope pressed a yellow boy into the groom's palm with instructions that his coach be sent back to his house—yes, yes, he was quite sure he wanted to walk, the night being as fine as it was.

He turned his back and stalked into the darkness.

Seventeen

Sophia watched Mr. Hope's shoulders disappear into the shadows of Brook Street. Beneath the layers of satin and lace and wine her blood thrummed, skin burning from his touch. She'd never wanted anything more in her life than to follow him down the lane, allow him to swallow her in his arms, put his hands on her as he had that night on the shining expanse of his desk.

Beside her, Mama snored softly, the trauma of tonight's events apparently too much to bear.

Across the coach Sophia met eyes with her cousin; Violet pressed her first fingers to her lips and reached for the latch.

Heaven above, she was going back in!—back to the Earl of Harclay's lair.

If Violet was going, then Sophia was, too. Perhaps it wasn't too late to catch up with Mr. Hope.

"You wouldn't dare. And if you go, I want to come with you," Sophia hissed.

Violet returned Sophia's gaze; her dark eyes were pleading. "Next time, Sophia, I promise. I'll be home before dawn."

Before Sophia could protest, Violet bolted from the carriage.

Mama snorted in her sleep. The coach creaked into motion.

Sophia collapsed against the squabs in defeat. Violet and her deuced theories about Harclay being the jewel thief. Seemed more like an excuse to have all the fun, and stay out all hours of the night.

Next time indeed. Next time Sophia would escape first and never look back.

* * *

It was well past midnight when they arrived home. Together with the driver, Sophia brought Lady Blaise to her room. She and Fitzhugh undressed Mama and tended to her injury, which, as one might imagine, was no small task.

An hour after Sophia fell into bed, exhausted, she lay awake, unblinking in the darkness, thoughts and body alive with the memory of Mr. Thomas Hope.

She'd been about to confess everything to him in that moment he'd brought up the marquess. Yes, their courtship proceeded apace, and yes, they had become friends, good friends. She liked to think she and Withington genuinely enjoyed one another's company.

In an *innocent*, companionable sort of way. Though their acquaintance was awkward at first, it had blossomed into friendship; and while that friendship was lovely and good, it was certainly no romance.

Sophia did not feel for the marquess the heat, the desire, the longing to know and do and say more that she did for Mr. Thomas Hope. Tonight made her realize that while she felt affection for Withington, her feelings for him would never go beyond that.

Because whatever was *beyond that*—well, she felt it for Thomas. Dear God, merely occupying the same *room* as Hope made her heart soar and blood rush.

She couldn't explain it. All Sophia knew was she'd never felt this way for anyone else—including, it seemed, the Marquess of Withington.

Sophia threw off the covers. It was suddenly stifling in her chamber, her sheets and night rail damp with sweat. She hobbled to her feet, exhaustion ringing in her every limb, and made for the window.

With no small effort she hauled it open. She closed her eyes and took a deep, contented pull of fresh air.

And was then promptly hit in the nose by something cold, hard.

Her eyes flew open, landing on the narrow alley below. There in the shadows stood a figure, its hooded face turned toward Sophia.

"Mademoiselle." La Reinette's accent was immediately recognizable, even in a whisper. She dropped the rocks she held in her hands and motioned for Sophia to join her. "Your timing is very good. Come, quickly, we hurry."

Sophia blinked, meeting with mixed success as she attempted to clear Thomas and his fingers from her thoughts.

"Is everything all right?"

"Yes!" Madame hissed. "Come, quickly! They will see me."

Sophia nodded, darting through her chamber as she tossed whatever she found—morning gown, spencer—over her head.

The routine came back to her in a heady rush. She tucked her boots into the crook of her arm; then she listened at the door, sliding into the hall when she was satisfied the house was abed. Down the stair, and down again, tiptoeing through the servants' hall to the kitchen's back entrance.

La Reinette waited just beyond the stoop, hood pulled low. When Sophia appeared the madam looked up, her dark eyes reflecting the shallow light of the night sky above.

They moved through the darkness in silence, Sophia's heart alight as they traced the familiar route. She'd missed this: the clean night air, the gas lamps flickering silently as Sophia's thoughts swirled with scenes from Madame's latest adventure.

The Glossy blazed with light and laughter, a glowing star amid the sea of stony silence that was Mayfair past midnight. La Reinette led her past the back rooms, crowded with men in embroidered waistcoats and the beautiful, butterfly-like ladies who attended them, to a study at the front of the house.

"Come in, *mademoiselle*, we are safe to talk here."

Pulling back her hood, Sophia stepped over the threshold. Her eyes fell on a familiar figure seated in the slight wing-back chair by the fire. He rose to his feet and turned, running a hand through the dark coils of his hair.

"Tho—Mr. Hope!"

He fell into a brief, unsteady bow. The light in the room was low, but Sophia thought she saw his cheeks flush pink.

"Miss Blaise." His gaze slid accusingly to La Reinette. "I did not know you would be here."

The madam closed the door and swept into the room, waving away his words. "The news I have, it concerns the both of you. Miss Blaise, she has as much right as you, *mon chéri*, to know these things I have learned. You are naïve, yes, to think you keep her safe by not sharing your secrets."

She slid into the cane-backed chair behind a small desk. "Do not forget, *Monsieur* Hope. She is smarter than you."

"Bah! Of course she is. Smarter than me, and most everyone else." Hope met Sophia's gaze. Her face grew warm when she saw that yes, yes he *was* blushing, and rather adorably at that. "That doesn't make the danger we're in any less real."

"And so I must help you fight against it." Sophia held up her hand to keep him from interrupting and turned to La Reinette. "What news do you have, Madame?"

The Little Queen unclasped the round golden locket that hung from her neck, a tiny key falling into her outstretched palm. With the key she opened the first drawer in the desk and retrieved a square of rough paper.

She placed the letter on the desk and slid it toward Sophia and Thomas.

"S'ouvrez-le."

Open it.

Sophia met Hope's gaze.

"Go on, then." He nodded at the desk. "*Plus de secrets, mademoiselle.*"

Her blood leapt at the effortless confidence of his French. *No more secrets.*

Sophia reached for the note and unfolded it. She recognized the bold, shaky hand at once; the same hand that penned the threatening letter she'd received some days ago.

She stepped toward the fire, holding the page with trembling hands before the light. Like the previous note, this one was written in flowery, well-formed French.

To the Little Queen of my heart,

My dearest, how long it has been since we saw each other last! You left us so suddenly—even now I burn when I think of you leaving my bed before I had finished—it is a terrible crime to leave a man thus. How thirsty I was then—I swore I would have you again—these years in Paris, they have been cold. But I never forgot your little trick, sweet dove. I never forgot what you did to me. I do not think you have, either.

But fear not, my queen, for at last I am delivered of my suffering—I am in London now—and I would have you finish what you started a decade ago. How old we grow! I think you will agree that life—it is sometimes not worth living at such an age.

I shall come for you. Soon. Do not be afraid—it will be quick, and I hope you will feel no pain, sweet dove.

In Good Friendship,
G. Cassin.

Sophia looked up from the letter. "Who is Cassin? And why does he wish . . . wish you harm?"

Her query was met with silence. She looked from La Reinette to Mr. Hope, a chill creeping in her limbs as she took in his expressionless pallor. His eyes were trained on the madam; she returned his gaze steadily, but from the pucker of her lips, Sophia could tell she was afraid.

Slowly Sophia folded the note in her hands. "No more secrets, remember?"

"Guillaume Cassin." Hope's voice was quiet, ominous. "A name I never thought I'd hear again."

"Why? Who is he?"

"He is a man I knew a long time ago. In a different life, before I came to England."

He took the letter from Sophia, read it; swallowed its contents in the space of a single heartbeat.

He looked up, crumpling the paper in his palm before tossing it into the fire. "We've got to leave. Now."

"Wait." Sophia stepped toward him. "A name you never thought you'd hear again? Why?"

Hope's face was grim. "Because he's dead. That's why."

Eighteen

La Reinette leapt to her feet. "But it is safe here, *monsieur*, I have paid extra men to guard the house—"

"We're leaving. *Now*."

Without waiting for a reply, Hope grasped Sophia by the elbow and blew through the door. She trotted to keep pace with his enormous stride as he led her out into the mews, the madam a few breathless paces behind.

He whistled to the coachman sitting atop a waiting carriage. Though the vehicle was unmarked, its gleaming sides were lacquered a deep shade of red that spoke of discreet luxury.

Hope opened the door and all but lifted Sophia into the coach, helping La Reinette inside before settling into the seat beside Sophia. He pounded twice on the roof and they tore off the drive and into the night.

"We were perfectly safe, yes, back in my study," Madame sniffed, smoothing her ruffled skirts. "What, do you think I would let that animal make a mess of my house, scare off the clients? Never."

"He did before." Hope stared at her. "It was him, wasn't it, that night you shoved Sophia and I into the closet? Cassin, and whatever fools he's paid to do his bidding—they were the riders who gave us chase. How did you not recognize him?"

La Reinette's eyes widened in disbelief. "He wore the—the—" She made a tying motion at the back of her head.

"He wore a mask," Sophia said, trying not to smile at the quaint gesture. "Makes sense to me."

Hope dug a hand through his hair. "How did I miss it? I knew I recognized that voice."

"It has been a long while," Madame said. "A long while for the both of us. He is back from the dead."

"*He*. Would someone please tell me who *he* is?"

The carriage bolted left, and Sophia careened across the bench. Thomas grabbed her by the wrist and righted her, his fingers leaving traces of fire on her bare skin.

His touch, it seemed, electrified her no matter the circumstance. Heavens, even in the midst of an escape from an enemy risen from the dead, Hope's hands set her entire being alight. He could with his fingers alone make her forget everything, *every*thing, her good sense and her manners and all that she'd hoped and wished and dreamed for her whole life.

She wished he'd touch her again.

This time with his lips.

La Reinette and Hope met eyes across the coach. For a long moment they looked at one another without speaking. Sophia sensed tension between them, as if this were a subject neither party wished to broach.

"Guillaume Cassin, he was my admirer a long time ago," La Reinette began. "He inherits a very old banking house, yes, the best in all France. First he loans money to the king. Then he loans money to the emperor. Until I killed him."

Sophia's breath left her body. She stared at La Reinette as if seeing her for the first time. "You *killed* him? As in. *Shot* him through the *heart* killed him? Or just. Er. *Metaphorically* killed him. With your. Er. Eyes or wiles or whatnot?"

La Reinette smiled, a hard, rueful thing. "Ah, it is a bit of both. He fell in love with me. But I," she gestured at Hope, "I was working for *monsieur*. And *monsieur* wanted Cassin dead. So, yes. I killed his heart and then I killed the body. *Monsieur* was there, weren't you?"

Hope shifted uncomfortably in his seat, looking out the window as if he might leap from it. "Yes. Yes, I was. Not my favorite memory; thank you, Marie, for the kind reminder.

"It is quite simple." Hope sighed. "I worked for the British. Cassin worked for the Empire, as banker and as spy. His hands are stained with the deaths of hundreds, thousands of men. I won. Except I didn't, apparently."

"I slit his throat," Madame said without blinking. "The blood, it was everywhere. It is an impossible thing to survive."

Sophia closed her eyes against the well of tears. *I slit his throat.* As if that explained everything. As if the words were not at all connected to the horrific act itself.

No, no. Contrary to Hope's belief, this didn't feel simple at all; as a matter of fact it was deucedly complex, especially in the small hours of the morning. Something didn't make sense; there were missing pieces to this puzzle, *big* pieces, though Sophia couldn't begin to guess what they were.

"But what's this Cassin got to do with us?" she said. "He can't be the thief, the man who stole the French Blue. Could he? But we've pegged the earl . . ."

La Reinette shrugged. "Perhaps. Perhaps no. Cassin has come to settle the score, take blood for blood. The French, we have vengeful hearts. First he will kill me. And then he will come for you, *monsieur.* Already he threatens your woman."

"But how?" Hope burst. "How the hell does Cassin know about Soph—about Miss Blaise? We—she—we do not belong to one another."

Sophia's heart twisted at the words he left unspoken.

Miss Blaise belongs to someone else.

"I said before," Madame continued. "Cassin is a smart man. He will ruin those you care about, yes, and you, you watch in agony. Only then will he come for you."

Hope drew a long breath through his nose. The stubbly skin along his jaw twitched as silence stretched between them; at his sides his hands were balled into fists.

When he spoke at last his voice was low and mean. "I want you out of London, Marie. Tonight. It isn't safe for you here; it will only be a week, maybe two, before I get my hands on Cassin. I think it best you travel in disguise."

La Reinette turned her head to look out the window. Outside the coach the night was black.

"These wild days," she said. "I thought they were past."

"Yes," Hope replied. "Me, too. And they will be, once I take care of Cassin. Promise me you'll leave tonight. Do you need money, horses?"

The madam turned back to him and shook her head. "What do you think me, an imbecile? I will not leave a penny for that man to steal. My coach, it is unmarked, like yours."

"But where will you go?" Sophia asked. "Surely the roads cannot be safe."

"You will go to my house in Surrey," Hope replied briskly, "and wait there for further instruction. Do you understand?"

La Reinette raised a brow. "You do not give me an order, do you, *monsieur*?"

"Christ have mercy." Hope let out a hot breath, tugging a hand through his hair. "You women shall be the end of me, mark my words. Go where you want, then, but keep out of sight. I don't need to tell you Cassin is a dangerous man, and cunning besides. If you are not careful he will find you. Do I have your word?"

Madame stared back at him, her black eyes expressionless. Sophia wondered what she was thinking, how she stayed so calm in the face of all this danger. Heavens, she'd *slit* a man's *throat*, only to face him yet again after he'd come back from the dead. Just the thought of it made Sophia want to howl with terror.

"Yes," La Reinette said at last, gaze never leaving Hope's. "You have my word. Take me back home, yes, for I must pack my things."

They rode in silence as the coach backtracked to The Glossy. Sophia's thoughts were a riot, a hundred questions forming as she replayed all that happened, and all she'd learned, in the past few hours.

More than anything she longed to know what would become of them after it was all said and done; what their lives would be like, and would she ever see either La Reinette or Mr. Hope again?

When at last they reached the corner closest to Madame's establishment, she called for the driver to stop. Placing a hand on the latch, she looked back upon Sophia and Hope, and was about to make her exit, when Sophia reached out, impulsively, and placed a hand upon her arm.

"Madame, it has been a great pleasure making your acquaintance these past months. There are few things I enjoyed so much as visiting with you, listening to your stories, the things and people you have known. What an honor it has been"—Sophia swallowed—"to have put those stories to paper. I am better, and happier, for having known you. Thank you."

La Reinette ducked back into the carriage. She took Sophia's hands in her own and smiled, eyes shining. "No, *mademoiselle*, I am to be the one giving you thanks. Perhaps one day, when this is all done, we might meet again, yes, so we might finish what we started. Go safely, *ma bichette*." Madame's gaze flicked to Mr. Hope. "And do not let him order you about very much, yes?"

Hope groaned. "That's quite enough of that. Good *evening*, Marie."

Madame's smile deepened as she winked at Sophia. Squeezing her hands one last time, La Reinette slipped from the coach.

The driver nodded at Hope's murmured instructions, closing the door softly against the snorts and sighs of the horses as they struggled to catch their breath.

Once the door was shut and she was alone with Thomas, Sophia collapsed against her seat, blinking slowly as wide, hot tears coursed down her face and neck.

Perhaps it was saying good-bye, letting go of all she and La Reinette had accomplished; perhaps it was the awful circumstance in which Sophia found herself, the threat of ruin and death very real indeed; or perhaps it was her exhaustion, coupled with her thrumming desire for the man who sat so close beside her she could smell the heat of the valet's iron on his shirt. Whatever it was, Sophia could not swallow her tears.

She inhaled, a shaky, embarrassingly pitiful sound, and wiped her nose with the corner of her hood.

Mr. Hope took her bare hand in his, holding it as he lightly ran his thumb over the ridge of her knuckles.

"Sophia." He sighed. "Sophia, please. I can bear your domineering and your complete and utter disrespect for everything I say and do, but please, Sophia, I cannot bear to see you weep. It's as you say—neither of us is nearly as good without the other. We are an unbeatable pair. It's going to be all right."

She scoffed. "You don't really believe that, do you?"

"Well, no. But you must agree we've great luck when we're

together. Please, Sophia, don't cry. Here." He held out a handkerchief. "I promise it's been washed since you used it last."

Sophia blotted her eyes. "I"—sniffle—"am never one"—sniffle—"to weep. Too much"—sniffle—"work to be done."

"Never? Not once during your first season?"

"Not"—sniffle—"once. I have yet to meet a gentleman at Almack's worth"—sniffle—"crying about."

Thomas smiled. "For one who never weeps, you put on a hell of a show for the Princess of Wales. Those sobs of yours were most convincing."

"I learned from the best."

He arched a brow. "Your dear mama?"

"My mother would give Mrs. Jordan a run for her money."

Sophia leaned her head against the cushion and took a deep breath, steadier this time. A beat of silence passed between them. From the corner of her eye she caught Hope's gaze.

"No secrets," she said at last. "Tell me."

His eyes were transparent pools of blue in the dim light of the coach. They were clear, honest; devoid of his usual struggle over what he should and should not share with her.

Thomas looked down at their clasped hands and Sophia looked down, too. His enormous hand swallowed hers; the warmth of his calloused skin soothed as much as it inflamed her.

"I haven't told anyone this story." His voice was low, soft. "Even Lake doesn't know the whole of it."

Sophia swallowed. It was no small thing, what she now asked of him. London knew very little of Mr. Thomas Hope, and he'd worked hard to keep it that way; the mystery surrounding his name served him well.

But now he volunteered that information to her freely. Her, and her alone. It was an admission of trust and friendship; it was a gesture of goodwill.

No one had trusted Sophia with so much as a schoolroom secret in all her life. And here was Thomas, one of the richest and most important men in England, sharing with her things he'd never told anyone else.

She felt the smart of tears begin anew at his faith in her.

As if reading her thoughts, Hope squeezed her hand. With

his free fist he reached up to pound the roof, calling for the coachman to drive until he told him to stop.

Thomas turned to her, using the knuckle of his first finger to wipe away what was left of her tears.

For a moment his gaze flicked to her lips. She knocked her shoulder against his, shaking her head. "No. After, perhaps. But tell me your story first."

Nineteen

Thomas looked down at their joined hands, tilting his head as he considered her proposal. The sharp angle of his smooth-shaven jaw caught an edge of moonlight and gleamed blue; the muscle there jumped, rippling beneath the skin.

"We—my family and I—we were to flee Amsterdam before the French arrived," Hope said. "But we were too late. I was the only one to escape; I left my family behind. Later my brothers, Adrian and Henry, would follow me to London. But the terror—it changed them. We aren't close, my brothers and I."

Sophia swallowed. "I'm sorry."

"My family, my city." Hope squeezed her hand. "I left them behind, and was lost for years. Henry Lake found me, and offered me asylum in London."

"And in return?"

The sides of his mouth kicked up. "And in return, I gave him the name of the banking house that supplied Boney with funds for the invasion of England."

"The invasion of England?" Sophia started. "You knew about that?"

"Only the bank that was lending Napoleon the money to do it. Cassin & Sons, based in Paris. I knew of Cassin through my father's connections back in Amsterdam."

She drew back. "So you and Lake, with La Reinette's aid, went after Cassin, and in so doing saved England from Napoleon?"

Hope shrugged, as if during that fateful night in Paris he'd been a mere tourist, out for a merry jaunt about town, rather than savior of king and country. "Perhaps. Perhaps not. I doubt the invasion would have happened whether we took out Cassin or not. But it was a great victory for England, and for Lake."

Sophia looked from Thomas's face to their hands, clasped in her lap. She wanted to ask about his family—who they were, *how* they were, how he'd lost them—but she remained silent, holding his fingers tightly so that he might feel her warmth.

"We boarded a ship bound for London in Calais. The storm took us at the first glimpse of English coastline. Lake saved me from a fallen mainmast. That's why he walks with a limp now."

Sophia nodded. "He must love you, to have risked his rather enormous neck to save your own."

"He left his family, too, not long before I did. We were as brothers then."

"And now?"

Thomas's grin deepened. "I could loathe someone so much only if I loved him, much as it pains me to admit it. When he appeared in my study after all these years—it was more loathing than loving, yes. But now? Now I'm glad he's back, though I cannot say the same for my accounts at the bank. He's the only family I've got left. The only family with whom I'm in contact, anyway."

Thomas at last looked up to meet her eyes. "I came to London for them, you know," he said. "For my family. So that their dreams might not die with them."

"You've done well by them, Thomas."

He scoffed. "Hardly. They deserve better."

"And you. You deserve to be happy. Your parents, your family—they would want you to be happy."

"What does my happiness matter, when they will never know life, how it is to breathe summer's fine air? And my brothers!" Thomas harrumphed, though she saw his eyes flash with hurt. "It's a miracle their debauchery hasn't led them to an early grave."

"They are grown men, Thomas. Adrian and Henry can look after themselves."

"That's just the thing." He turned to look at her. "They

can't. All things aside, they are my blood. My responsibility. Without me they would be out on the street."

Sophia looked away. She understood the heavy burden of his guilt, and why Hope cared as much as he did for the bank. It was not a matter of fortune, or prestige; for Thomas, it was a matter of *family*. He worked so long and so hard out of love for those he'd lost.

At heart, she realized, Thomas was a family man. Which was a tragedy, in a way, because in his dedication to the bank, the family he left behind, the brothers from whom he was estranged, he would never start one of his own. Looking at him, Sophia knew he would make a wonderful father, fiercely loving, patient, kind.

She ached for him in ways she didn't know she could ache. This struggle of his, it was no small thing. And his story, the past he'd longed to forget—it was bloody, full of heartbreak and loss.

"You've done well by them," she repeated. "Better than I've done by my family. All my life I wanted to escape them, to leave. Leave behind the terrible mess of our lives and start over."

He released her hand. "You'll get your chance, Sophia."

Sophia shifted in her seat, clasping and unclasping her hands before finally clasping them again, squeezing her fingers so tightly it hurt.

"It's probably best if you leave London, too," Hope said at last. "It's not safe for you, either, now that Cassin has connected you to me and knows who you are."

Sophia was glad for the change of subject. She swallowed and her throat loosened. "Don't be ridiculous. I cannot leave London, not in the middle of the season. And besides, Violet won't let us go anywhere before we find the French Blue."

"Ah, yes, I'd forgotten about Lady Violet and your mother. Well, then." Hope ran a hand through his hair, the curls falling rakishly across his forehead, and sighed. "You must take extra precautions. I'll send men to your house."

She looked up to meet his eyes. They glimmered preternaturally in the low light of the vehicle; the skin around them crinkled, as if Hope was holding something in, keeping whatever it was he felt to himself.

"You don't need to do that, Thomas—"

"Of course I do." Thomas said briskly. He sat up, straightening his jacket, and gave his cravat a vicious tug. "I'll do everything in my power to keep you safe."

Again they met eyes. Again that same, guarded expression of his. He could reach out, shove the door open, tell her to leave and never come back; he could reach out and take her face in his hands and ravage her lips until they bled.

Sophia held her breath and waited.

Twenty

Hope couldn't stop staring. With her dark hair loose about her shoulders, the gentle curves of her body just visible beneath the flowing mass of her cloak, Sophia was unbearably lovely. She appeared as he imagined she would after a long, ardent tumble between the sheets of his bed.

Good Lord.

He swallowed the impulse to invite her back to Duchess Street to enjoy exactly that.

Hope shifted in his seat, tugging discreetly at his breeches lest she be exposed to his indecency.

He'd just told her what he never meant to tell anyone. He should run for the hills—or she should, now that he thought about it—especially after that confessional bit about not deserving much besides success at Hope & Co., the regret that plagued him over his strained relationship with Adrian and Henry.

Telling her all he had was a confession in itself. Sophia deserved to know; as La Reinette said, it was pompous of Hope to think he could keep Sophia safe by hoarding his secrets.

But more than that, he told her because he *wanted* to. Because, despite his every effort to focus on the bank, the missing diamond, his falling fortunes, it was Sophia who occupied his thoughts day and night.

In confessing his past, he'd also confessed his affection for her.

They rode the few blocks to her house in silence. He did not dare touch her again—if he did, that tumble between the sheets would occur in no uncertain terms—though he was acutely aware of her presence, the scent of her skin, as she swayed in time to the carriage beside him.

Exhaustion weighed him down besides. In the space of a single night, Hope had experienced every emotion under the sun and then some. He remembered the biting anger that washed through him over port with Lord Harclay; the despair that plagued him as he told Sophia of his past; the desire that tugged between their bodies in Harclay's billiards room.

It was enough to drive a man mad.

The coach stopped a block from the house. Hope helped Sophia to the ground and walked beside her the rest of the way, until they reached the familiar stoop at the back kitchen door.

Hope tapped the stoop with the toe of his boot as Sophia stepped up, turning to face him as she had the night they'd coaxed the French Blue from Princess Caroline's grasp.

"And so we find ourselves here yet again," he said, eyes trained on his boot.

"Doesn't feel at all the same, does it?"

He met her eyes. "No. It feels—" He paused, searching for the right word. At last he spread his arms. "It feels *more.* Everything we—I—felt then, but more of it. Good God if I don't burst."

Her lips parted, her eyes suddenly serious. "Yes," she said quietly. "That's exactly it. I feel as if I might burst."

Her bottom lip trembled, and for a moment Hope feared she might weep again. How he longed to fold her in his arms and comfort her, tell her it would be all right.

"Sophia—"

Before he could say anything further, she pressed a kiss into his cheek. "Good night, Mr. Hope."

She pulled back, meeting his eyes one last time.

Turning, she was about to open the door, when he grabbed her by the wrist.

"I'm not that man anymore, Sophia," he said quietly, impulsively. "That man I told you about, back in France. That isn't who I am."

She looked at him, her face inscrutable. "Thank you, Thomas. For telling me your story."

And then, as she had that night those weeks and weeks ago, she turned and disappeared into the house.

And just as he had that night, Hope reached for the doorknob. Only this time he stopped short of grasping it.

The memory of her touch—it was too much to bear.

Mr. Daltrey poked his head through the breakfast room door the next morning, eyes wide as saucers.

"Is something amiss, sir? I just heard—well, I dare not repeat what I heard, but it sounded like someone was shouting."

Hope clutched the paper in his hands as if he might tear it in two. "My apologies, Mr. Daltrey, but I couldn't help shouting after reading *this*."

He tossed the wrinkled paper across the table and pulled his spectacles from his ears, clutching the bridge of his nose between his thumb and forefinger.

"'Rare jewel snatched at banking scion's ball,'" Daltrey read, his voice as chipper as a springtime swallow's.

And then, upon having considered the words: "Begging your pardon, sir, but Holy Christ in heaven! The news—it's made its way to the papers, then!"

"Yes," Hope said without looking up. "The news has made it to the papers. I held them off for as long as I could. But a story this juicy couldn't be kept secret forever."

"Begging your pardon again, sir, but what the devil do you suppose you'll do now that everyone knows? Can't be good for the bank."

Hope met the man's gray eyes at last, a tight smile on his lips. "I suppose we'll just have to hunt down the thief, won't we?"

He sighed. "And no. The news is certainly *not* good for the bank. In fact"—Hope sighed again—"it's entirely possible there will be a run on Hope and Company this very morning. Once my clients—those who don't already know, that is—discover I cannot safeguard my own fortune, I daresay they won't trust me to safeguard theirs."

Mr. Daltrey went pale as a sheet, and seemed to waver

a bit on his feet before straightening. "Will the bank fail, sir?"

Hope threw back what was left of his coffee and stood. "Let's hope not, old man, or the both of us will be out of a job. Have my horse saddled—I haven't the time to wait for the coach."

He stalked across the room, and was about to make his exit when he stopped suddenly, turning to Mr. Daltrey. "One more thing. If I happen to make it back alive tonight, please have my best cognac decanted. The '73, I think it is. In the off chance my clients don't beat me to a pulp, I've a mind to do it myself."

Collapsing into one of a pair of wingback leather chairs before the fire in his study, Hope gulped all four fingers of his cognac in a single swig.

On the mantel, the clock struck half past three in the morning. He'd been at Hope & Co. all day, putting out fires when he could, solemnly watching them burn when he couldn't.

By his last calculation (somewhere around one o'clock, after the last investor left carrying a two-stone sack of guineas), Hope & Co. had suffered losses in the *hundreds* of *thousands* of pounds.

Another week like this one and Hope would be bankrupt. The run on Hope & Co. was coming—it was, at this point, only a matter of time.

He let his head fall back on the chair, the cognac setting alight the tightness in his throat.

This was bad. Worse than he thought it'd be. If he didn't find the French Blue, and soon, he could lose everything—

"That's dashed good, old man, very good indeed!"

Hope leapt from his chair, his gaze landing on the enormous shadow that lurked just beyond the brandy board.

Mr. Lake stood with a balloon in his hand, swirling the priceless cognac as he held it up to his nose. "What is it, an '87?"

"God *damn* you, Lake! Really, I don't understand your aversion to the front door. My reputation's already in shreds—" Hope threw up his arms in defeat. "Bah! Never mind."

"So it's not an '87, then?"

Hope glared at him. "No. '73."

"'73! Good God, man, who'd you have to kill to get your hands on such a treasure?" Lake took a pull, smacking his lips in appreciation. "Going out with a bang, eh?"

Hope refilled his glass, then turned and slumped back into his chair with a sigh. After a long pause, during which he drained said glass, he said, "Today was a bloodbath. All but a handful of my investors pulled out their money; the deposits fared better, but not by much. D'you happen to have an extra hammock on your pirate ship? I might need a place to sleep."

Lake stepped into the light of the fire, taking a seat in the chair opposite Hope's. "We're all of the same mind, old friend, that the Earl of Harclay is our man. Violet's getting close now; it will only be a matter of time before she digs up the diamond from wherever that bastard is hiding it."

"Even so." Hope brought the empty balloon to his lips and tilted it back, draining the last drop. "There's a very real chance my reputation never recovers from this debacle."

"Oh, believe me, it will. Especially when everyone knows you as the hero who saved England and her brave soldiers from Napoleon's clutches."

Hope's eyes darted to Lake. "Old Boney's contacted you, hasn't he?"

"Turns out word of your 'Jewels of the Sun King' soiree was slow to reach Bonaparte, on account of his location somewhere in the wilds of Russia. Which happens to work to our advantage, you see, for the little shit has yet to learn of the diamond's disappearance."

Hope sat up in his chair. "What did he say? Has he offered terms in exchange for the jewel?"

"Not yet." Lake yawned, stretching his feet toward the fire. "I can't share all the details. But suffice it to say I was privy to a conversation this evening, during which France's 'best wishes for the prince regent's continued good health,' and something or other about forging a friendship out of the 'ashes of our enmity' was discussed."

"So at the very least Napoleon's willing to negotiate. Excellent news, Lake. The best news I've had all day. Except, of course, we *don't have the damned diamond*."

In the light of the fire, Lake's eye glittered. "For one whose name is Hope, you keep very little faith."

"The irony is not lost on me."

"Of course not. You're a poet. A very bad poet; but a poet nonetheless."

Hope's grip tightened on his balloon. "You've done something, haven't you? What is it this time? Blackmail? Poison? Mistaken identity?"

"Mistaken identity! Now that's one I haven't used in a while. No, no, a bit of blackmail, perhaps. Relatively harmless, of course, but rather effective, at least in my experience. I've no doubt the earl will hand over the French Blue by week's end."

Hope sighed and stared into his empty glass. "Let's pray Hope and Company can make it that long. Anything I might help with?"

Lake shook his head. "Just trust that I know what I'm doing. And keep away from Miss Blaise. I saw the way you looked at her at Harclay's dinner; we don't have time for such distractions. Like I told you before, you're only placing her in harm's way."

Anger, hot and sudden, boiled in Hope's belly. "That's rich, coming from you! I saw the way *you* looked at Harclay's sister, Lady Caroline. You were sullen all evening. What," Hope said, mocking, "is she the one that got away?"

Lake froze, humor draining from his features in the space of a single heartbeat.

Christ above. Lake, in love? How had Hope not known?

"Oh." Hope paused. "So Lady Caroline *is* the one that got away. I did not mean to make light—"

"I know what you meant." Lake stood. "Lady Caroline is none of your concern. We are—we *were*—"

"Let's leave the ladies to one another, shall we? I shall not concern myself with Caroline if you do the same with Miss Blaise. Do we have an agreement?"

It was Lake's turn to glare. Hope had never seen him like this; clearly he'd struck a nerve. Lake must have known Caroline in the years before he left London and met Hope. He was intrigued—were they enemies? Lovers, betrothed even?

Hope pushed the thoughts from his mind. Too much going on in there as it was; there wasn't time to become involved in yet another plot, another tangle, another mystery to be solved.

"Agreed," Lake said darkly. And then, after a beat: "Your box at Vauxhall Gardens. Do you still keep it?"

Hope started at the sudden change in subject. "Yes, though I can't say I've had much time for amusement these past weeks. Usually I fill the seats with my more daring clients. Why do you ask?"

"Those acrobats we captured after the theft—the ones Harclay hired to distract your guests while he thieved the French Blue? They're performing at Vauxhall tomorrow—well, I guess now it's *this* evening. Send invitations to Harclay and Lady Violet and whomever else you see fit to attend."

Hope arched a brow as he put the pieces together. He recalled Lake's interrogation of the acrobats the morning after the theft, and the troupe leader's words about the man who hired them.

Said he'd give fi'ty pounds to the each ov us for making a right nice mess of your fancy-pants party. Twen'y-five before, twen'y-five after. We's still waitin' on that last payment, yeah?, if any of yous know where I can find tha bugger.

"Ah." Hope smiled. "So you plan to put the acrobats face-to-face with the fellow who still owes them money. But Harclay was in disguise when he went to them. How are they going to recognize him?"

Lake winked, his good humor reappearing as if it'd never been gone. "Leave that to me, old man."

Hope sighed, cupping his face in his hand as if he were considering the proposal.

Of course he'd say yes. Not only did he have next to nothing to lose at this point; he knew also that if he invited Lady Violet to his box, perhaps her cousin Miss Blaise might accompany her.

Even in the midst of his exhaustion, Hope's blood leapt at the prospect. He couldn't, he shouldn't, but dear *God* he longed to be near her again. Even for an hour, an evening. What harm, really, could come of that?

"Very well. I suppose I'll just skip bed altogether and send the invitations out first thing." Hope yawned and ran a hand through his hair. Good Lord, even his *hair* felt tired.

"We'll find the French Blue, Hope, mark my words. And when we do I will set everything to rights. You'll see."

"I pray you're right."

"I'm always right."

Silence settled between them. Hope yawned again, near delirious with lack of sleep. Though he longed for bed, there was one more matter to discuss with Lake.

The matter that would sink them both if they did not address it, and soon.

Best get it over with as quickly as possible.

"There's something else we need to discuss." Hope cast a longing glance at the brandy board and swallowed. "It appears Guillaume Cassin has returned from the dead. He knows it was us, Lake. He knows we were behind the plot to have him killed. And now he's come back to kill *us*. And, quite possibly, Miss Blaise."

Lake bolted upright, his crippled leg bending curiously at the knee Hope knew to be forever stiff, and choked on his brandy. "*Guillaume Cassin*—back from the dead? But that's impossible!"

"Apparently Madame did not sink her dagger deep enough."

Hope & Co. fared little better the next day. The offices on Fleet Street were a riot of shouts, queues, curses, and wishes for death. Hope's meeting with Viscount Richards had nearly come to blows; the viscount's person grew so red Hope feared his heart might burst forth from his mouth.

It was not, needless to say, a pleasant day at the office.

At last—dear God, *at last*—the hour arrived. Hope had grabbed his things and was in his coach before the clock reached its eighth and final strike.

Hope watched through the window of the coach as familiar sights passed. Westminster Bridge; the muscling, muddy waters of the Thames; and, finally, Vauxhall Gardens.

The lanterns that lined the walkways and pavilions were already lit, blinking through the trees like so many fireflies.

Hope emerged from the carriage and breathed deeply. It was a lovely summer night, the chill of spring gone at last. The sky was wide and fading, though the light from the sun would linger for some hours yet.

He paid the entrance fee, wondering vaguely if he could even afford the three shillings it cost for the evening's entertainment.

Once in his box, he took a seat closest to the stage and ordered food and drink from a liveried waiter. Knowing he was on display before the *haute ton*, Hope took pains to appear relaxed and happy, smiling as he sipped his arrack punch and tried not to gag on its bitter, biting taste.

His gaze landed on a supper box across the stage from his own. There, seated side by side, faces wide as if they'd been laughing, were Sophia and the Marquess of Withington.

Hope's heart lurched, veins flooding with heat. It was none of his business, their acquaintance; Sophia had been nothing but honest when it came to her intentions and the marquess.

Still. The facts of the matter did nothing to assuage Hope's wildly pounding pulse, the possessiveness that took captive his every sense.

Thomas watched as Withington passed her a tiny coupe of punch in that strange, halting manner of his. She brought it to her lips, sharing a witticism as she did so; Withington erupted into laughter, jerking an arm around to slap his knee; she smiled, satisfied.

Sophia looked beautiful, dark hair coiled fashionably about her head, the low neckline of her ivory gown trimmed in an alluring, wispy sort of gauze that emphasized her eager bosom.

A bosom that even the well-mannered marquess could not resist, try though he might.

Across the expanse Sophia met Hope's eyes. For a moment she hesitated, her smile fading. He was desperate to know what she was thinking, what Withington made her feel.

She raised her hand and waved. Hope's heart twisted in his chest. He waved back, smiling tightly; and promptly directed his attention elsewhere.

As if this day could get any, *any* worse.

He felt the stares as the beautiful half of London filled Vauxhall's supper boxes. Their curiosity was sharp and shameless. Everyone, it appeared, had heard of the French Blue being thieved from right out under his nose.

Was he bankrupt? Would he lose everything? Perhaps his house in Duchess Street would go up for auction . . . a lovely pile, yes, and of prime location, but those antiques of his, they are rather odd . . .

But Thomas Hope had not become a banking tycoon on his good looks—ha!—alone; a decade in the business had shaped his heart and head accordingly.

And so he slapped a jolly smile on his face and threw back punch as if he had not a care in the world. He nodded at acquaintances and flirted with old women; he tipped the waiters generously and complimented the food.

Mr. Lake joined him not long after and was all too happy to join the act, especially the arrack-punch bit.

Only when Lady Violet burst into the room, Lady Blaise and Sophia on her heels, did Hope's facade waver. His blood thrummed at the knowledge that Sophia was near, and would be his for the next hour or two; and yet some small part of him was angry with her.

Angry, perhaps, for sharing her company with that marquess. The idiot fellow didn't deserve her. Neither did Hope, but that was beside the point.

The small party exchanged greetings. Thomas came at last to Sophia. All thoughts of bankruptcies and auctions and stolen jewels flew from his mind as she met his gaze, lips parted, eyes full.

She was so damned beautiful.

But when he said, "Hello, Miss Blaise," her beautiful face fell, as if she was expecting more. He furrowed his brow, searching for any clues as to what *more*, exactly, might be.

"Thank you, Mr. Hope, for your lovely invitation."

Hope bowed, the words leaving his lips before he could stop them. "You are most welcome. It is my sincerest wish that you find it more enjoyable than the marquess's. Rather dull fellow, isn't he? Overly fond of the word 'capital.' "

For a moment she looked at him, too stunned to speak; he couldn't tell if it was pain or pleasure that flooded her dark eyes.

"Well," he hastened to add, "in my humble opinion, at least. 'Capital' *is* a popular word these days . . ."

He prayed it wasn't pain. After all she'd been through on his account, the weight he'd placed upon her shoulders, he couldn't bear to see her cry. Not again.

Hope stepped forward, lowering his voice. "Sophia, I—"

He turned at the sudden commotion toward the back of the box. Lord Harclay and his sister the Dowager Countess of Berry had arrived; already the earl was stalking toward Lady Violet, a smug grin on his infuriatingly handsome face; while Lake and Lady Blaise pounced on the dowager countess at the same time, as if she were the last especially well-frosted crumpet on a plate.

Hope turned back to Sophia. They exchanged a meaningful glance, Hope reining in the impulse to accost her with his lips.

But he couldn't, he shouldn't. The weight of his worry returned with crushing force: if he didn't move, and quickly, Hope could very well lose everything by dinnertime tomorrow. He needed to find the diamond so that he might stanch the bleeding at Hope & Co.

And he couldn't accomplish that by spending his time with Sophia, no matter how alluring, how lovely she was.

"I'm sorry," he said, and turned to the Earl of Harclay. Turned his back on her.

Twenty-one

Disappointment rushed through Sophia as she watched the outline of Thomas's broad, sloping shoulders move across the box. The gleaming velvet of his coat, black and well cut, stretched over the expanse of his back as he bowed before Lord Harclay. His face was hardened into a smile, blue eyes studiously vacant of the emotion that occupied them mere heartbeats before.

Hope and the earl exchanged words; and while they appeared friendly enough, Sophia sensed a predatory sort of energy between them, two lions circling one another, sizing up strength, weakness, willingness to charge.

And here men thought *women* were the catty sex. Not so, at least not tonight. Hope's biting comment about the Marquess of Withington's invitation was the perfect example: a mean-spirited admission of envy cloaked in wit and anger. How unlike him, brilliant, levelheaded businessman that he was, to exhibit such raging emotion.

And good Lord, it had thrilled her to no end. It was shameful, she knew, to take pleasure in Thomas's pain; but the fact that he was *jealous* of the marquess was no small thing. It meant Hope, despite his recent chilliness toward her, desired her as much as she desired him. It meant he adored her more than he cared to admit.

Not that they had time to indulge said desire. Cousin Violet was in a tizzy over the failing fortunes of Hope & Co. and, by extension, their family. With the bulk of their money invested in the bank, the sudden plummet in the prices of its shares had hit them hard. Though Violet was never one to air her worries, Sophia could tell she was under great duress. That Violet harbored a not-so-secret fondness for the source of said duress—the earl *was* a terribly handsome fellow—certainly didn't help matters.

And then, of course, there was this Cassin fellow intent upon the murder of Sophia's reputation and Thomas's person. There had been yet another attack in this morning's gossip pages; only by the grace of God had Sophia managed to conveniently misplace the paper before Lady Blaise could read it.

A certain S.B. of which we wrote some days ago is in possession of a most naughty pen. Perhaps the scandals of which she writes are those she has been witness to herself. For a debutante, she is proving a worldly creature.

Sophia glanced across the gardens to the Marquess of Withington's box. She didn't have much time now before her great secret was revealed, and in the worst manner possible. If she meant to marry the marquess, she'd better do it, and do it quickly, before all the world knew of the delicious perversions of her pen.

Scattershot applause broke out in the supper boxes. Sophia started when a troupe of acrobats, their squat faces sickeningly familiar, took the stage.

They were the acrobats that crashed through the windows at Hope's ball; the same acrobats hired by the thief to distract Thomas's guests while he went to work stealing the French Blue.

Her eyes darted to the Earl of Harclay. He stood frozen at the front of the box with Cousin Violet at his side, their clasped hands tucked discreetly into Violet's skirts. The acrobats were waving to the crowd now, their gazes lingering at last on the earl as if they knew, they *knew*, he was their man.

The breath left her body as Sophia watched the scene unfold. It was like something out of La Reinette's tales; all they needed was a pirate and a half-naked governess to complete the drama.

Harclay dropped Violet's hand and tucked her behind him,

away from the acrobats' glares. Across the box, Lake was biting back a snicker while Thomas watched in stony silence; Lady Blaise frantically fanned herself and Lady Caroline sat very still in her chair at the table.

Sophia's thoughts raced. Lake and Hope must've revealed to the acrobats that the Earl of Harclay was the man in disguise who hired them—and still owed them money. Doubtless the acrobats, knowing they had the wealthiest earl in London in their pockets, would blackmail him or worse. Sophia's belly turned over at the possibility that Violet, having been seen by the acrobats in the earl's company, would somehow be involved in the plot.

She understood why Lake, and Hope, too, set these events in motion. They thought by exerting pressure on Harclay in the form of blackmail and potential ignominy, they might coax the earl to return the French Blue. But it was a gamble, certainly, that nothing would go awry in the meantime. What if the acrobats took the twenty or so pounds the earl owed them and went on their merry way? And what if, God forbid, Violet were to be harmed, blackmailed herself, or worse, held by the acrobats for ransom?

Sophia closed her eyes against the panic that took wing in her chest. When she opened them she found Thomas staring at her, his face hard as ever but his eyes pleading.

Pleading for patience, perhaps; forgiveness, understanding.

A spot of softness in his strengthening resolve to keep them apart.

Another sleepless night. Sophia tossed and turned, the darkness stifling as her thoughts drifted time and time again to Thomas and those hauntingly beautiful eyes of his. Her body ached for him; it felt like an eternity since he'd put his hands on her last.

Sophia stumbled to the window, half hoping La Reinette would be waiting in the shadows below, and slid it open.

The night was warm and quiet.

Quiet, save for the strange rustling noise off a bit to the right.

Blinking, Sophia poked her head out the window just in time to see the Earl of Harclay launch headlong into Cousin Violet's window, one down from her own.

Sophia blinked again, catching the tip of the earl's shiny Hessian boot before it disappeared into the house. She heard Violet whispering some curse or another before closing the window behind her midnight visitor.

Ducking into her chamber, Sophia listened as several telling *thuds* reverberated through the wall between her chamber and Cousin Violet's. Whatever Lord Harclay was doing, he was doing thoroughly.

Well, then.

An interesting development, to be sure.

Sophia flung herself upon the bed and with a sigh of frustration tugged a pillow over her head. It was to no avail; she still heard Violet's fluttering sighs and Harclay's groans of pleasure. It was a miracle their ardent—er, *affections* did not wake the whole house.

She should be scandalized, should knock on Violet's door and warn her against fraternizing with the enemy. Then again, Sophia was guilty of walking a fine line herself; wasn't she the one courting the attentions of a well-fortuned marquess while dreaming at night of a different dark-haired gentleman, one with eager hands?

A gentleman she wished would climb through *her* window, and do to her whatever it was that Harclay was doing to Cousin Violet.

Clutching the pillow over her ears, Sophia closed her eyes. She and the marquess were to attend Almack's tomorrow; yes, she would think of that. They'd become friends, she and Withington. Even his notoriously sharp-tongued sisters had taken a liking to Sophia. All was going well, and could only get better.

Perhaps, *perhaps* he would propose by the end of the summer—or, at least, before she was outed as the author of La Reinette's memoirs—and all her dreams would come true: the extravagant engagement ball, the envious tittering of the *ton*, the titles and the castle and the fortune. The things she'd dreamed of all these years would at last be hers.

Sophia closed her eyes, willing herself to sleep.

And woke that morning with a start when she realized she'd dreamt not at all of a glamorous turn at Almack's on the arm of the Marquess of Withington.

No.

It had been Thomas Hope who'd taken captive her dream, whispering into her ear all the things he wanted to show her.

All the things he had yet to make her feel.

Twenty-two

City of London
Fleet Street

Standing with both hands on the desk, Hope stared at the open ledger and swallowed the panic that threatened to choke him.

Five more investors had sold their Hope & Co. shares, causing the price to plummet; a dozen or more depositors had pulled their funds from the bank, leaving his liquid assets dangerously low.

Another week like this, and he'd be through by month's end. The bank for which he'd sacrificed everything would no longer be solvent; he'd be as poor and disheartened as he was when he first arrived in London nearly a decade ago.

Hope glanced at the pile of newspapers beside the ledger. The news certainly didn't help. No matter his entreaties, the bribes he offered, Hope's friends at the papers printed headline after headline about the disappearance of the French Blue. The public, they said, couldn't get enough of the story: a cursed jewel, thieved in the midst of the season's most lavish ball—for an editor, it was the stuff of dreams.

Hope pushed aside the papers, tugged the spectacles from his head. He had to find the diamond, now more than ever. The Earl of Harclay was the thief, of that he had no doubt; but Lake's scheme to take back the stone, whatever it was, didn't seem to be working. If only Hope could get his hands on that bastard the earl—

Hope's head snapped to attention as the doors at the far end of the room were flung open, revealing the tall, broad figure of none other than Lord William Townshend, the Earl of Harclay.

Speak of the devil, Hope thought wryly, and he doth appear.

The earl's face was hard; Hope could tell the man's immaculate sense of self-control was on the verge of breaking.

Neither man made any pretense of greeting the other; Hope did not bow, and without so much as a how do you do, Harclay began speaking.

"I need to make a withdrawal. And quickly."

A withdrawal? For what? Perhaps Lake's scheme *was* working.

Though that didn't make Harclay's demand sting any less.

Rage, hot and sudden, burned through Hope. He rose, his eyes never leaving the earl's. His voice, when he spoke, was deadly quiet. "I assume you've seen the papers?"

The earl's face darkened. "I don't have time for this. I don't mean to be rude, Hope—"

"Eight days. I've been in the headlines for eight days straight. Each headline worse than the last; by now all of London must think me a brainless buffoon. Never mind the success of my business before the French Blue incident. Now I am being judged on one bloody night of theatrics; a drop in the proverbial bucket, as they say. And my business—it has suffered greatly, Harclay." Hope balled his hands into fists. "Greatly indeed."

To Hope's very great satisfaction, he saw the earl's dark eyes flash with pain. "I understand your frustration, Hope."

His rage pulsed hotter. "I don't think you do. You see, when Lady Violet came to me with her little theory about you being the thief, I very nearly dismissed her out of hand. Why would Lord Harclay do such a thing, I thought, and to me of all people? I've guarded his investment, shown him generous returns."

Hope knew this was his chance; his chance to pressure the earl into giving up the diamond. If he froze Harclay's accounts at the bank—accounts that held virtually all the Townshend family fortune—perhaps the earl, unable to pay so much as the grocer's bill, might be convinced to hand over the French Blue.

It was the only card Hope had to play.

And he wasn't about to pass up his chance to play it.

"But we've no other suspects, you see," he continued. "And as I've watched my clients vanish, scared off by my seeming incompetence, as I've watched the value of my company plummet—well, I need someone to blame. And I'm afraid that someone is you."

Understanding, swift and terrible, raced across the earl's expression. Hope could tell the man had begun to panic.

Good. Let the son of a bitch suffer.

Now he knows how I have felt all this time.

The earl made no move to deny the accusation. Lady Violet had been right all along.

The Earl of Harclay was the thief.

"Please, Hope, listen to me. I'll give you anything, anything at all, but it is imperative that I make this withdrawal, or Vio—"

"No."

The Earl drew back in shock. Now this—*this* was good sport. Watching Harclay flail about in distress was the best bit of theater Hope had seen in years.

"No? What do you mean, *no*? I've well over a hundred thousand at this bank, and I demand access to those funds!"

"I've frozen your accounts until the French Blue is returned to me. You'll not see a bloody penny before, mark my words. And if you did not steal my diamond yourself, as you claim, then this shall certainly prove motivation for you to help us find the man who did."

Harclay drew back, eyes wide. For a moment Hope wondered why the earl needed the money, and what he intended to do with it; clearly the man was desperate. Had it been Violet's name on his tongue before Hope had interrupted him?

Hope shook the thoughts from his head. He had no sympathy for this miscreant or his troubles. Hope had plenty enough of his own.

The earl was shouting now, red-faced, eyes murderous. "I need that money. Seventy-five pounds, and I swear I shan't ask for more until the diamond is found. I'm in trouble, and so is Lady—"

"That's your problem." Hope felt his limbs begin to shake with anger. "Now get out of my bank before I summon my men."

Harclay crossed the room in two impatient strides. Hope

did not draw back; he met the earl face-to-face, so close he thought for a moment Harclay might butt him in the head.

"If you do this, Hope, you'll have blood on your hands."

Hope called for his men, who materialized out of the shadows at Harclay's side. A man reached for his arm, but the earl flung him off, violence in his every movement.

He jabbed his finger into Hope's chest. "You'll regret this, Hope."

The poet in Hope had a feeling blood would be spilled this night. Watching a yellow moon rise high over the sprawling expanse of London, that vaguely familiar spider of suspicion had crawled up his back as he stood out on his terrace.

Since that night he sent La Reinette from London, he had no word from her. Cassin, it seemed, disappeared just as quickly as he arrived; Hope wondered what that bastard was waiting for, what tricks he kept hidden up his sleeve. The thought of him ever hurting Sophia, of ruining her and her family, made Hope's blood rush with rage.

What if Cassin planned to make his move tonight?

What if that move meant taking Sophia, holding her hostage, revealing her secrets, going so far as to bodily harm her or her family?

His rage burned so hot for a moment it blinded him.

It was Wednesday, which meant that Sophia and her family would be at Almack's.

Gah, Hope hated Almack's.

But not as much as he hated Cassin; hated the thought of Sophia tangled in his web of treachery, of violence.

In a rather Shakespearean state of mind, what with the blood and the spider and the moon, Hope stalked through the French doors into his office. He slipped the bejeweled Italian dagger into his waistcoat pocket and called for his coach.

Twenty-three

Having secured the affections of this season's most eligible bachelor, Sophia thought she might loathe attending Almack's a little less. Perhaps—dare she even hope such a thing!—she might even begin to *enjoy* it. The marquess, in all his sideburned, shiny-booted glory, showered her with attention, and filled her dance card with his name.

And truth be told, she did enjoy his company. He was as charming as ever, introducing her to family and friends as they trolled arm in arm through the crush. It was half past nine and already the Assembly Rooms were humid with laughter, sweat, and swearing; the marquess navigated it all with an ease peculiar to those with blessed births and noble blood.

In that moment, Sophia was possessed of everything she'd ever wanted. A marquess on her arm, a new gossamer gown on her shoulders; the promise of a glittering future and a fortune to go with it.

But the jealous stares and whispers of her fellow debutantes left her feeling hollow and vaguely embarrassed; it was not at all the satisfaction she'd been craving since she was old enough to know what a season was. And while her affection for the marquess grew, it was a companionable, rather than romantic, sort of affection. The kind she felt for Cousin Violet and Fitzhugh; the kind indulged over tea and charades and gossip.

The kind that had nothing at all to do with love.

The dancing was about to begin. Across the ballroom, Violet and that devil the earl were already paired up, her color high as he brushed his lips to her ear. A wave of longing washed through Sophia as she watched them. The earl touched

Violet confidently, adoringly, as if he understood her inside and out. Violet appeared at once flattered and flabbergasted by his affection.

If Sophia didn't know any better, she would say her cousin was in love.

She bit the inside of her lip, smiling tightly as the marquess introduced her to yet another of his classmates from Oxford.

She wished Hope were here, so that he might touch her like the earl touched Violet. Because Thomas's touch was confident and adoring, too. The best kind of touch.

And then, over the Oxford classmate's spindly shoulder, Violet caught sight of a familiar head of dark, unruly curls.

It can't be, not now, not tonight. What the devil is he doing at Almack's?

As if in answer to her wish, Thomas Hope appeared. Something unfurled inside her as she looked into those blue eyes of his. Her heart began to pound, and without willing it her smile grew.

The master of the dance was calling for a cotillion; Withington abruptly turned to Sophia, jerking out his arm.

"A cotillion!" he beamed. "Capital! This one you're rather good at, Miss Blaise."

Sophia swallowed, eyes flicking for a moment back to Thomas. "I make no promises, my lord. How many pairs of your shoes have I ruined thus far?"

The marquess laughed good-naturedly as he led her into the ballroom. "Two. Let's make it three, just for good measure."

"Yes, let's do."

They elbowed their way onto the dance floor. Standing across from one another, they bowed as the master called for the music to begin. Sophia returned the marquess's grin, and almost missed the strange gleam in his gray eyes.

Almost.

She recognized that gleam. It was the same gleam in the earl's eyes as he'd looked upon Violet heartbeats before.

Sophia's pulse took off at a sprint.

The dance began. Sophia moved through the steps haltingly at first, mind racing as she whirled once, twice, clapped and clasped hands with the marquess. What did Withington mean looking at her like that? Did it mean—dear God, it couldn't, it was too soon, didn't these things take more time?—what she thought it meant?

Withington set her out to the edge of the floor; she turned slowly, as if on air, and for a breathless moment her gaze landed on Thomas.

Of course. Out of all the hundreds and thousands of beautiful people pressed into Almack's, it had to be him. He had to be standing there, just so, in a place where she might find him.

Thomas was looking at her, his face tight, eyes full. Even from here she sensed the heat, the longing that radiated from him. There was a flicker in his eye, sharp and clear as glass, different somehow from Withington's; or perhaps it was Sophia's response to it, the way it made her feel, that was different.

She saw something else in Thomas. Something she recognized in her own heart.

Desire. Regret, too.

The music moved and Sophia moved reluctantly with it. She turned to face the marquess, and he was stepping forward the same moment as she was stepping back. She lost her footing, ankles crossing at the wrong moment, and she felt herself falling.

Withington caught her just in time, his grin deepening.

"I'm sorry, my lord—"

"Enough with this 'my lord' business." The marquess took her hand and together they turned. For one whose movements were awkward and severe, he was a rather fine dancer, as if in the crush of the ballroom he might at last, at last, be himself. "I'd prefer it if you called me Withington, like the rest of my family."

Sophia bit back her surprise.

It was no small thing, that she should call him so familiar a name. If their fellow dancers heard his request, they would assume the two of them were good as engaged. Only his lordship's mother—and, eventually, his *wife*—would ever refer to him as 'Withington.'

"You don't think 'Withington' is a bit too familiar?"

"Miss Blaise." He pulled her close, his hand slipping to the small of her back. His touch felt foreign, firm enough but not at all electric. Not the way Hope's touch felt. "You and I, we do not have the opportunity to be alone very often. You must," he spun her about again, "forgive me for saying these things, and at Almack's of all places."

"What," Sophia clapped, "things?"

They turned to face each other. Withington was blushing, bashful little lines forming around his mouth. "I hope you do not think me forward, Miss Blaise, but surely you must know by now how I—how I feel about you."

Oh dear.

"I've very much enjoyed the time we've spent together, however brief. That idea of yours, the port tasting, it was the most capital event I've attended. Ever. I—I mean this as a compliment, I do, Miss Blaise, but I never expected to enjoy a woman's company as much as I enjoy yours."

Sophia closed her eyes against the lump in her throat. "That is kind of you to say, my lord."

"Withington. Please, Miss Blaise. It would mean a great deal if you'd call me Withington."

But I shouldn't mean a great deal. Not to you.

"Of course." She smiled tightly. "If we are to be friends, then I must be Sophia to you."

Out of the corner of her eye, Sophia saw Violet twirling about the Earl of Harclay, both grinning like loons. For a brief, wild moment, she wondered what her cousin would do, what she would say to Withington's heartfelt confession.

Truth be told, Violet would likely duck and run.

But then again, Violet was not possessed of the ambition to make the match of the season. She didn't want to make *any* match, period.

"Sophia." The marquess smiled, stepping back, then forward. "I know we've only recently become acquainted, but I—well I—I'd like to think we get on well, and enjoy each other's company."

She glided past him, narrowly avoiding his left foot. "We get along splendidly, you and I. And I cannot deny I *do* enjoy your company, very much."

And that was true. After showing him her honest self, Sophia *did* enjoy the time she spent with Withington, more than she enjoyed the company of her fellow debutantes, her supposed friends.

Then why did saying so feel so wrong?

Sophia turned and had her answer.

Mr. Hope's eyes were steady as he watched her. The moment their gazes met, she lost all sense of time and place. This yearning, it was unlike anything she'd ever known; strange, for as yet she didn't understand what it was, exactly, she wanted from him, *needed* as surely as the air she breathed.

With all this bosom-heaving breathlessness and longing, it was a wonder Sophia hadn't fallen flat on her face in the midst of the dance. Blessedly it drew to a close, the music climbing to a stupefying crescendo before ending on a clipped, joyful note.

Sophia let out a breath she didn't know she'd been holding. Curtsying before the marquess, she rose to find him standing very close. His face was serious even as his color was high.

"What I meant to say, Sophia, is this." He kept his voice low, even as the crowd around them erupted in applause. "It is my wish my intentions toward you become public. My affection for you only grows; my family, they adore you. *I* adore you. If you'll have me, I'd—"

There was a sudden, vicious tug on her arm. Sophia spun about to see Mr. Hope, his dark face completely transformed from moments ago. Her belly dropped to her knees as the hair at the back of her neck pricked to life. Something had happened.

Something was wrong.

"What?" she panted. "What is it?"

His head dipped toward her, his lips brushing her ear as he murmured a single, devastating word.

"Violet."

Twenty-four

"Violet?"

"There isn't time," Hope murmured in Sophia's ear. "Come with me."

Over her shoulder, Sophia nodded her apologies to the marquess, who looked as if she'd just stabbed him in the heart. Hope felt a twinge of guilt at the smirk that rose to his lips.

A *twinge*.

His hand on the small of her back, Hope gathered Sophia against him. Together they shoved their way through the crowd, gulping fresh air as they tumbled out onto the street.

Farther down the lane, Hope watched the vague outline of a lone rider disappear into the darkness, the tails of his coat waving behind him like a standard.

It was the earl, in hot pursuit of whoever had taken Violet.

Hope turned to see Harclay's gleaming carriage loom just down the lane; its team of matching Andalusians was short one horse—the horse Harclay now rode to God knows where.

"What happened?" Hope caught the man lingering beside the coach. "Where is the earl going?"

The man turned; Hope recognized him as Harclay's butler, Mr. Avery. Beneath Hope's touch Avery stiffened, but his eyes gleamed with recognition; after a moment he nodded.

"Mr. Hope, I am glad to have found you. I don't know exactly what happened, only that the Lady Violet was taken from the ball by a man, perhaps two, and shoved inside a waiting hack that took off before I could stop it."

"Taken?" Sophia gulped. "As in—as in *kidnapped*?"

Avery looked to Hope before replying. “Yes, Miss Blaise. I'm afraid so.”

“Oh, for God's sake!” For a moment she went limp against him. Though she made no sound, Hope felt her shoulders moving in time to her sobs.

He glanced across the street; there were too many people about, too many prying eyes.

“It isn't safe here. I shall see Miss Blaise and her mother home”—Hope squeezed Sophia when he felt her stiffen in protest—“and we shall await word from you or your master. Or, for that matter, Lady Violet's return.”

“Excellent, Mr. Hope. Godspeed, then.”

Avery turned and made his way down the lane. Hope watched his sturdy figure disappear into the riot of horseflesh and hackneys.

That spider of suspicion—it had just bitten Hope in the neck.

Twenty-five

When at last, after spending the better part of three hours sobbing, Lady Blaise fainted—or fell asleep, Hope couldn't quite tell—he got up from his chair by the fire and stretched his arms.

"Are you sure you don't want to sleep?" he asked Sophia. "I'm happy to keep watch."

She hadn't moved since they'd returned to the house hours ago, and sat hunched over on a nearby settee, staring into the fire with her chin propped upon her fist.

"No, no. It is you who should be sleeping. Violet said you haven't seen your bed in days."

Hope felt the color rise to his cheeks at those words on her lips. His bed. God, how he missed it. God, how he longed to take her there now, and touch her in ways that would help ease her worry.

"Bah! Who needs sleep? I feel fresh as a daisy."

"Liar." Sophia grinned, meeting his eyes.

"Well. Nothing a few pots of coffee can't fix, at least."

Hope sat down and held out his hand. Sophia glanced over her shoulder; and, certain her mama and uncle had indeed gone up to bed, quietly placed her fingers in his palm.

"Thank you. For staying. I know you've seen enough trouble these past weeks—and now, ha!" She laughed mirthlessly. "Now Violet has been kidnapped. It's like something out of a play, isn't it?"

Hope scoffed, digging into his pocket to retrieve the ridiculous dagger he'd hidden there. "Try me."

This time her laugh was genuine.

Silence, at once tense and exhausted, settled between them as they gazed into the fire, the hiss of dying embers suddenly too loud to bear.

"I—I assume you've no word of—of that man, Cassin?"

Hope squeezed her hand, gently this time. He looked down at his feet and shook his head. "No. Nothing. I did see the gossip pages, though. I'm terribly sorry, Sophia. Know I'm doing everything possible to keep you safe."

He swallowed. "I want nothing more than to keep you safe."

Sophia made a choking sound. He snapped to attention, only to see her tears begin anew.

"Oh, dear." He ran a hand through his hair. "Did I say something? What is it, Sophia? Please. Please tell me. Seeing you cry makes me want to—to—"

He looked down at the dagger he held in his hand.

"It makes me want to pry out my eyes with this dagger. I'll do it, I will!"

"I'm not," she snorted, weeping with greater vigor, "*crying*. It's just—just—put that thing away, Thomas."

Sophia took a great pull of air, letting it out slowly as she closed her eyes in an apparent attempt to calm herself. She dropped his hand.

"I'm sorry."

Hope leaned back into the chair. "Don't be. Violet will come home, Sophia. Harclay knows what he's doing. He wouldn't let her come to any harm. Besides, he's an earl, for God's sake. No one crosses an earl. It's tantamount to being God, or at the very least Jesus—"

"That's not—" She looked down at her hands, thinking better of what she was about to say. "Thank you, Thomas, for your words of comfort. She'll come back, I know she will. She's *Violet*. Very much like being God, as you say."

The fire before them was dying; its merry crackling had subsided to small, silent licks of flame.

Silence stretched between Hope and Sophia. A silence filled with all the things he should say. All the things he *wanted* to say.

He pulled his thumb and forefinger across his closed eyes.

This waiting, it was terrible; he felt Sophia's pain as if it were his own. He'd lost more than his share of loved ones.

And he did not wish that kind of suffocating grief on anyone.

Least of all the lovely creature on the settee beside him.

Hope felt as if they were wasting precious time. They were alone, they were close, they had nowhere to be. Such moments were fleeting; he knew in the coming days and weeks there would be fewer and fewer of them.

And like the fool he was, he opened his mouth and spoke the first words that came to mind.

Sophia, too, moved to speak, their words tangling as each of them stopped, only to start at the same time yet again.

"So, the marquess—"

"Do you usually attend Almack's—"

A clap of thunder sounded outside, rattling the windowpanes. Sophia leapt to her feet, eyes wide; when the pounding became louder, halting abruptly seconds later, she dashed through the drawing room door. Hope followed a few steps behind; he wanted to be close enough for comfort, but not too close so as to intrude upon a moment between cousins.

He was relieved to hear, just before he stepped into the front hall, a muffled cry of relief, followed by a curse as Sophia squeezed the air out of Violet's lungs in a tight embrace.

Hope closed his eyes and sighed. Thank God.

Violet was back. She was back, and in one, foulmouthed piece.

Thank God.

Lady Blaise held Violet's face in her hands one last time, smiling tearfully as she pinched her niece's cheeks. Mr. Hope had long since left, wishing them good evening; now the ladies were free to touch and prod and tease one another as they pleased.

"I hope this means we'll never have to attend Almack's again," Violet said, grimacing after a particularly poignant pinch.

"Once Sophia makes her match," Lady Blaise winked at her daughter, "we shan't step *foot* in those dreadful rooms. Shouldn't be too long now."

Violet arched a brow. "You're really going to do this, then? Marry that marquess—Worcestershire? Withering?"

"Withington. You *know* it's the Marquess of Withington, Violet. And no. Yes. Nothing is as yet set in stone. We haven't talked much of our intentions, much less an *engagement*."

"Haven't talked *much*?" Violet said. "That means you have talked about it. What did he say?"

"Yes, what did he say?" Lady Blaise dropped her hands from Violet's face and turned to Sophia. "I saw him speaking to you during the cotillion. Poor man, he blushed so furiously I feared blood might spurt from his ears!"

Violet and Mama crowded round her, their faces upturned as they waited for a reply. Sophia swallowed, feeling stifled as the ladies drew yet nearer, the air between them thrumming with anticipation.

"Well." Sophia cleared her throat. "It was nothing, really. A few words about feelings—"

"Feelings! Gah."

Sophia's shoulders slumped. "That's lovely of you, Violet, really *lovely*—"

"Oh, come here, you silly goose." Violet laid a hand on Sophia's cheek. "I don't mean to make light of your *feelings*, dearest. It is your feelings that concern me most. I know you've always been a snob about whom you want to marry—"

"Violet," Lady Blaise warned.

"Let her finish, Mama. Violet offends everyone; we must not take it personally. You may proceed."

"Thank you, Cousin." Violet all but rolled her eyes. "As I was saying. I know you've always dreamed of making a splash, and marrying your marquess at St. George's before the queen and all that. But I've seen you with Mr. Hope—"

"Violet!" Lady Blaise sputtered in disbelief. "Really, now you go too far—"

"All right, all right," Violet demurred. "But I do wonder, Cousin, if having known Mr. Hope hasn't changed those dreams of yours."

Sophia drew a shaking breath. Was it anger that now rose in her chest, or something else—something akin to pain? Her throat suddenly felt tight; she wondered if she had any tears left. First Hope, now Violet—honestly, how many people would make her weep tonight?

She felt exquisitely tender, and very tired. Weary, as if her heart might give out beneath the great burden of all she'd felt and witnessed these past hours.

Sophia narrowed her eyes at Violet. "Did your captors steal your soul, too? Since when is Lady Violet Rutledge, cardsharp and self-declared spinster, a *romantic*?"

Violet returned her gaze steadily. Sophia had never seen her blue eyes so soft, so full of—dear God—was that *love*?

It shocked Sophia to see Violet thus altered. Shocked her, because she recognized that look in her cousin's eyes.

Sophia had seen it in her own, glancing in the mirror as Fitzhugh had dressed her earlier that evening.

The words left her lips before she could stop them, hand flying to her throat. "*Good heavens*!"

"What?" Lady Blaise's eyes went wide. "Tell me, Sophia, what is it?"

Sophia looked to Violet. A small, knowing smile crept across Violet's lips. She turned to Lady Blaise, looping arms. "Come, Auntie George, it's been one hell of a day. Let's to bed, shall we?"

"We shall." Lady Blaise looked pointedly at her daughter. "Cousin Violet's nerves are on edge, Sophia, after a traumatic event. Tomorrow she won't remember a thing she's said, and neither should you. Like the ravings of a deranged lunatic, Violet's words are nothing but meaningless jumble."

Violet scoffed, leading Mama up the stairs. "Deranged lunatic. Such an imagination you have, Auntie George! Come along, now."

With one last, piercing look at Sophia, Lady Blaise turned and followed her niece upstairs.

For several minutes Sophia stood unmoving in the front hall. In the center of her being her heart worked furiously, sending waves of sensation to every corner of her body. The weariness she'd felt earlier dissipated as readily as a summer storm, replaced by a fierce restlessness that demanded action.

She needed to see him. Now. Tonight.

Before decisions were made and futures decided, she needed to see him.

Him, the man she loved.

Door, stairs, cloak, boots.

Sophia stole out into the darkness, working through the route to Duchess Street in her head. She moved quickly, breathless with impatience as she ducked in and out of shadow. Worried her courage would desert her, she moved yet faster, all but oblivious to the sights and sounds of the night around her as Thomas took captive her every sense.

So consumed was she by rather explicit imaginings of a half-naked Hope that she nearly missed the patter of footsteps just off to her right.

Sophia plastered herself against a nearby wall, waiting with bated breath as the footsteps drew nearer. A shadow passed not six inches from where she stood, so close she thought it certain she'd be found out; but the shadow moved on, quickening its pace as it drew out into the street. The scent of tuberose hung in its wake.

Out of the darkness another shadow approached, this one vaguely familiar: tall and broad, with a loping gait and confident, almost cocky, swing of his arms.

Was that?—no, it couldn't be.

Could it?

Sophia watched wide-eyed as Cousin Violet flung herself into the Earl of Harclay's outstretched arms. For several heartbeats they clung to one another, heads moving rapturously as they kissed the sort of kiss to end all kisses.

Sophia drew back against the wall, heart pounding. Violet was doing more than fraternizing with the enemy; and by the way she kissed him, she was doing more even than *that*, too.

How like Violet to be in love with the man she hunted. Sophia rolled her eyes. They stood to lose everything, all of them, and here was Cousin Violet, assaulting the thief's lips as if they, and they alone, were responsible for the crime.

Perhaps it was all part of Violet's plan. Perhaps she was drawing the earl close so as to better aim her dagger.

Violet was, after all, far more cunning than even the devious Harclay.

Perhaps.

Besides. Sophia was in no position to judge. Wasn't she the one courting the attentions of a marquess while stealing into a banker's bed at night?

That deuced diamond had thrown them all into a state of chaos. Sophia hadn't felt like her status-obsessed self since she first laid eyes on the French Blue that night in Princess Caroline's drawing room. Perhaps there was truth to Thomas's *History*; perhaps the diamond *was* cursed, and they were all doomed to suffer poetically gruesome deaths.

When at last Cousin Violet and Lord Harclay came up for air, he tucked her into the crook of his arm and together they stalked down the street. Doubtless he would take her to his pile in Hanover Square and ravage her thoroughly in the comfort of his enormous four-poster bed.

Which brought Sophia back to her own intentions to ravage and be ravaged in turn. If Violet and Harclay were to indulge in a doomed affair, then by God Sophia would not be left behind. She had her own hopeless, foolish, irresistible liaison to see to.

By the time she reached Duchess Street, she thought she might burst with anticipation. If she had known how thrilling illicit love affairs would be, Sophia would've dreamt of them rather than miraculous matches with viscounts. It was too late for that. Too late.

But she had one last chance. Here, just for tonight, she would forget all that. Just for tonight, she would give in wholly, indulge every whim and fantasy.

And then tomorrow she would return to said miraculous matches, her mama, the marquess and his affections, his proposal, which she knew would come any day now.

Tonight, however, she would be Hope's. Her body, her heart, her every wish and desire—she'd surrender everything she had. Just this once.

Just tonight.

If, that is, Sophia could actually *get* to Hope.

She should've known the house would be a fortress following the theft. Surveying the property from a nearby corner off

Duchess Street, Sophia picked out at least a dozen men patrolling the crescent-shaped front drive. The tall iron gates on either side of the house were closed; toward the back of the building, Sophia picked out two windows glowing with low light. Otherwise, the house was dark.

Moving with as much care as her screaming pulse would allow, Sophia stole across the street, hiding in the shadow of a stone pillar that marked the corner of Hope's property.

She was about to turn and make for the mews, when she was grabbed from behind. Her assailant spun her around with such force it knocked the wind from her lungs, her hood falling back from her face.

"Please," she managed, panic filling her chest as her eyes fell on a familiar face.

"Miss Blaise!" Daltrey whispered, his white hair glinting in the moonlight. "What are you doing here, and at this time of night!"

Relief rushed through Sophia at the sound of his voice, even as she wondered why Thomas's butler was playing sentry in the wee hours of the morning.

"I don't trust these fellows," he said, reading Sophia's thoughts. "Not after those men betrayed Mr. Hope at his ball. I keep watch on them while they keep watch on the house. Come, let's get you inside. Mr. Hope will be pleased to see you."

Daltrey ushered her through the servants' entrance at the back of the house. He led her up a narrow set of stairs to a small drawing room on the second floor. Aside from the fire in the grate, there was no light.

"I'm not waking him, am I?"

"Psh!" Daltrey removed Sophia's cloak and carefully draped it over his forearm. "I think Mr. Hope's forgotten how to sleep, poor fellow. He will be curious, however, as to the purpose of your visit. It isn't safe to be about, and *without chaperone*, so late."

Sophia swallowed, her clasped fingers coiling over and through one another. She couldn't very well tell Daltrey the *true* reason for her visit; she could just imagine him fainting from horror as she said, "I have come to seduce his lordship, Mr. Daltrey. Might you point me in the direction of his bedchamber?"

And so, recalling with no small fondness the evening she'd spent in the Princess of Wales's drawing room, Sophia scrunched her face and stuck out her lip and let out the most pitiful sounding sob she could muster.

"Oh. Oh, heavens, Miss Blaise, I did not intend to upset you." Daltrey took a step forward, holding his arms awkwardly out before him as if he would embrace her. "There, there, Miss Blaise, there, there."

"It's just"—sob, along with a hysterical heaving of her bosom—"it's been so. So very difficult. My delicate sensibilities have been *assaulted*, yes, assaulted, and I—oh, dear, I feel a fainting spell coming on!"

Mr. Daltrey tapped her lightly on the shoulder, prodding as if to make sure she were still breathing. "Well. Er. I am terribly sorry, Miss Blaise, for whatever distress I have caused you. I shall lead you to Mr. Hope straightaway so that he might—er, address whatever it is that. Um. *Assaults* you so. There, there, come with me."

Sophia held up a hand to hide her smile of triumph as Mr. Daltrey steered her from the drawing room and up another flight of stairs.

At the end of a wide paneled gallery, Daltrey paused before a door. He leaned his ear against it, listening for a moment before pulling away in a huff.

"He's not here. Wait inside, Miss Blaise, and I shall locate the master of the house directly."

Daltrey held open the door. With a nod of thanks, Sophia slipped into the room, the door closing behind her with a small, quiet click.

For a moment she stood at the threshold, marveling at the room around her. Wiping a tear from the corner of her eye, she nearly laughed at the exquisite beauty of Hope's bedchamber.

On the near wall, a dying fire burned in a stone fireplace as high and wide as Sophia was tall. The small circle of light it emitted was bruised red, almost purple. Beyond that was utter, complete darkness.

Even so, she could make out the shape of the room's sumptuous appointments: the biggest bed she had ever seen, its pristine coverlet ironed and fluffed to a most welcoming proportion; Persian rugs of every color and shape; carefully curated paintings, hung from silken tassels to cover every square inch of the walls.

Sophia took a step forward, her heart soaring as the audacity of her actions settled upon her for the first time.

She swallowed her fear. She'd come this far. She was not about to go back. Not when she felt like this.

She swam to the darkest corner of the room, running her hand along the smooth, hard surface of a bedpost, the stack of leather-bound volumes on a bedside table.

"Sophia."

She started at the voice, nearly knocking the volumes to the floor. Turning, she saw nothing but darkness.

"You shouldn't be here. You shouldn't have come."

His voice was low, strained; as if something strong, something he wanted to repress, coiled inside him; as if he were a bowstring pulled taut, waiting for release.

She took a step toward him; he made no sound. Though she could not see him, she felt the stirring between their bodies, that familiar anticipation rushing through her with blinding force.

"I came for you," she said.

"It is foolish of you to be out alone, and at this hour."

"I don't care, Thomas." She paused. "I came for you."

"Please, Sophia—"

"No." She wished he would come forward so that she might see him. She wanted nothing more than to *see* him. "Please, Thomas. I did not come to talk."

She heard his sharp intake of air, sensed his mind racing under cover of darkness. For a moment she hesitated. Would he refuse her? He would be right to do so, of course; this was a bad idea, a dangerous idea, and he knew it.

Sophia waited for what seemed like an eternity, her limbs beginning to tremble as if she'd bared to him her body as well as her soul.

There was a rush off to her right, the air suddenly alive with his scent; and then his hands were on her shoulders, brushing her skin as they moved up her neck. She nearly cried out at the tide of sensation that slid through her, his touch firm and impatient as if he owned her.

As if she were his and no one else's.

Twenty-six

As soon as Thomas drew near, his impatient hands drawing her close, he disappeared, leaving her reeling in the darkness.

She turned this way and that, looking for any sign of where he might be. "Thomas, please—"

"I thought you did not come to talk." That voice of his; a growl that at once frightened and titillated her.

A wave of heat pulsed between her legs. Dear God, why wouldn't he touch her again, where was he, why was he *hiding* like this—

There was a tug at the back of her head as Thomas gathered her hair in his hand and pulled. She could not see much of anything, but she could smell him, sandalwood and a bit of lemon as he reared over her, pulling back her head and sinking his teeth into the soft flesh of her throat.

This time Sophia *did* cry out, her eyes wide as they searched the blackness. Nothing, nothing. Nothing save the sensation of his lips moving over her skin, his fingers tugging the pins from her hair. He buried his hand in her loosened waves, pulling, and pulling yet harder, arching her against him.

Beneath her skin her blood pulsed hot and wild. He'd never touched her like this, had never been as wildly possessive. There would be no going back from this place; no time for second thoughts or the heavy lives that awaited them outside these walls. He would have her, and she him, and in so doing they would forget everything but each other, and the desire that stretched between them.

At least for tonight.

Thomas's lips found hers, and Sophia's eyes fluttered shut in an agony of pleasure as he kissed her. It was forceful, this kiss, forceful and tender all at once. She felt the darkness falling in on them as the kiss deepened, blocking out everything but the sensation of his nearness. The backs of her knees relaxed; the tug between her legs was deliciously poignant.

Her body, her mind—the surrender was coming.

He took her bottom lip between his teeth, letting out a hiss of satisfaction at her moan. For a moment he released her mouth, resting his forehead against her own. His breath was warm and hard on her skin, coming in deep, long draws. She felt the flutter of his eyelashes on her eyelids, moving slowly, softly; she reached up and thumbed the scar on his cheek, no more than a slight ridge now. How long ago that night in Madame's closet seemed.

And then his hand was cupping her face, and he was kissing her again, moving over her with exquisite concentration. Her pulse rushed in her ears as he tugged at her hair. She could stay here, kissing him like this, forever, her mind blank except for the sensation of her body tangling with his.

Sophia's eyes flew open when Thomas pulled away, his hands leaving traces of fire where he'd touched her. She gasped for air, trembling in the darkness as she waited. What little light there had been from the fire was now gone; the room was a river of black, the only sound a small rustling somewhere in the dark.

She gasped at the sudden, vicious tug at the back of her gown. He was pulling at the laces with impatient fingers, pressing his body against hers. A shiver ran the length of her spine when his lips found the tender skin at the back of her neck, caressing her with his lips and tongue.

Her laces sighed softly as he pulled them free, working his way from her neck to the small of her back. Thomas slipped his hands inside her gown and coaxed it apart, pulling it over her shoulders and hips. It fell in a gust of chill air to her feet.

Thomas wasted no time. His lips moved from the ball of her shoulder to her collarbone and neck as he spun her to face him.

She reached for him, her fingers tangling in the fine rumpled linen of his shirt. She drew it upward and he stepped back from her body, allowing her to pull it over his head.

The sound of her palms scraping over the expanse of his bare chest filled the air between them. Sophia could see nothing, nothing but the dim outline of his person; but beneath her fingers his heart was warm, beating hard and healthy, the feel of skin on skin wildly thrilling. She ran her hands through the wiry hair at the center of his chest, over the smooth, turgid flesh of his neck, down the thick, lean expanse of his belly.

Thomas growled the lower she went, a low sound of warning. He hooked his thumbs into the neck of her chemise and drew it over one shoulder, then the other, moving with brutal straightforwardness that left her breathless.

He set both his hands on her hips, pushing down her pantalets along with the chemise; the air felt tantalizingly cold against her burning skin.

And then he was running his palms up the sides of her ribs, sending waves of exquisite longing through her. Her blood leapt as his thumbs moved over her belly and up to her breasts, scraping her hardened nipples once, twice, three times, taking them between his thumb and forefinger and pulling, *my God, my God, please—*

He dug a hand into her hair, bringing his lips to hers as he pulled her naked body against his own. She moaned into the kiss, her hands drinking him in, memorizing every slope, every muscle and sinew, for this would be the only time—the last time—she would ever have him like this.

Sophia curled her fingers into the waistband of his breeches. He bit her bottom lip, as if to say *yes*; she worked the buttons free one at a time, Thomas's mouth deepening its assault with each button she managed to undo.

She freed the last button; and then with a violence of which she didn't know she was capable, tugged them over the bulge between his legs, down, down the length of his enormous, hardened thighs.

For a moment he broke the kiss, stepping out of the breeches one leg at a time before kicking them to some unknown corner of the room.

And then he stood before her; she sensed the working of his chest, the air moving out of his lungs and into her own. Though she could not see him, she knew he was as naked as the day he was born.

As naked as she was, their bodies warm with desire.

He made no move, allowing that desire to burn to new heights between them. He was waiting, she knew, for her answer to his unspoken question.

Sophia stood very still, her breathing the only noise in the room. She would not turn back, not now, not when she felt so full she might burst. Never mind her conflicted desires outside this darkness; here, now, she felt wild with certainty.

She wanted Thomas. She wanted to surrender to him, to say *yes* to all the things she'd forbidden herself to feel and know these past weeks.

Sophia took a deep, shaking breath. This was her chance. Her chance to let him fill her being, her every sense. Her chance to forget the French Blue, the marquess, villainous Frenchmen, and La Reinette. Cousin Violet, *her family*, her writing, and her fellow debutantes at Almack's.

As she exhaled, it all fell away, the armor of her ambition disappearing in the darkness. In its place rose a bursting relief, a lightness she'd never experienced.

Yes. Dear God, yes.

Sophia stepped forward, her bare skin brushing against his for the first time. Fire shot through her, her entire being pounding with a craving so complete, so overwhelming, she could think of nothing and no one but *him*. Nothing but what was to come, what he would make her feel.

So *this* is what La Reinette was talking about in her memoirs. This thunderous feeling, this warm, wondrous taking of breaths, of confidences, of innocence. Being *taken*, and taking in turn—yes, this would be Sophia's greatest adventure yet.

Thomas gathered her against him, bending his enormous arms to cradle her in the curve of his body. One of his hands slid to the small of her back, his fingers clutching her skin; the other found its way to her face, guiding her lips to his.

Slipping his tongue between her lips, Thomas pulled her against him. She felt the leap of his cock against her belly, his pubic hair brushing the angle of her hip. The flesh between her legs throbbed, going from warm to hot to fiery in the space of a single breath.

His lips moved from her mouth to her jaw, working their

way down her throat to her collarbones and finally across her—

Oh God. Her eyes slammed shut as his teeth nicked her right nipple, then her left, his lips moving over her hungrily. His hand slid from her cheek down to her breast, running his thumb over the hardened point of each nipple. She arched back, digging her hands into the tumble of his curls, pulling against him, crying out for more.

His other hand moved from the small of her back down the slope of her backside, his fingers slipping between her buttocks to find the source of all this sensation.

Sophia gasped as he moved to cup her with his palm, his fourth finger finding its way inside her as his first two fingers worked that heady place at the tip of her sex. His fingers traced lines of fire, parting her folds with an expert touch while with his mouth he teased her nipples, pulling and biting, stoking her desire to breathless heights.

She felt herself tightening against him, that rolling tide of screaming pleasure very close, *heavens*, very close, if he'd just touch her one more time—

Thomas's hand slid away from her sex, moving down the backs of her legs, the other scraping up the length of her spine. In one swift movement, he lifted her into his arms. She opened her mouth to protest, but in the space of a single heartbeat he was tossing her onto the bed, the coverlet sighing contentedly as she landed on its surface. She searched the darkness for Thomas, but she saw a blackness so complete she wondered for a moment if his expert ministrations had blinded her.

But then she heard him at the foot of the bed; he was pulling at her boots, dropping them one at a time to the floor with a dull *thud*. His fingers moved up her legs, carefully sliding her silk stockings off her feet and onto the floor.

He grasped her by the ankles and tugged her toward him. Sophia felt the bed bow beneath his weight as he reared over her, trailing kisses along the length of her body as he made his way up: one for each knee, the inside of her thigh, her hips and belly, the left breast and right nipple, the place where her collarbones met.

She gasped as he bit into the flesh of her throat, her body screaming for release as he at last took her mouth with a force that knocked the breath from her lungs.

Of their own volition, her legs snaked around his hips; she felt the nudge of his cock against her sex, its slick warmth begging for more, *more*. She closed her eyes, allowing her need to swallow her whole.

Thomas placed his elbows on either side of her head; his curls fell into her face and eyes as he worked her mouth with his lips and teeth and tongue. Still he made no move between her legs. She wondered what he was waiting for; she felt as if she might lose her soul if he did not release her from this agony, this lovely, breathless moment of unbearable anticipation. He felt warm and impossibly enormous against her flesh. She wanted to know what it felt like *after* this forbidden moment passed; what it felt like *after* he was inside her.

Sophia bucked her hips against him, forcing his hand; above her, he froze.

In response he grabbed both her hands in one of his and thrust them above her head, pinning her to the bed. She cried out, writhing against him; but he held her fast, his other hand moving over the plane of her belly to rest between her legs.

Holding her hostage with the bulk of his body, he opened her, his fingers gliding through her wetness with ease. He slipped one, two fingers inside her, moving as if to ease the tightness he felt there. With his thumb he circled the tip of her sex, slowly at first, faster and faster as she pressed against him, her cries turning to whimpers as her legs went rigid with the approach of her climax.

His fingers worked feverishly now. The tide, it was coming, so powerful she felt as if she were falling through the darkness that surrounded her. She opened her eyes to see flashes of light and color, her back arching against the weight of her rising pleasure.

Thomas broke the kiss, his head moving down, down to her breast. He took her nipple in his mouth, circling it with his tongue in time to his touch between her legs. Her entire body clenched tight as a fist; and then—

Then.

A rush of blood, a thundering wave that pounded through her. Sophia let out a gasping breath, her limbs throbbing with the impact of her release. Her head fell back between her arms as her body reverberated with the fading pulse of her orgasm, her muscles loosening bit by bit in time to the slowing of her heart.

Thomas released her hands, gathering her against his chest as the throbbing subsided. She breathed in the scent of his skin, the wiry hair of his chest tickling her nose as she placed her hands inside his shoulders. His skin felt warm, firm but yielding; his heart was pounding so furiously she wondered if it had worked its way through his breastbone to lie right here beneath her palm.

Sophia curled into Thomas's embrace, finding comfort in his strength, his steadiness, after the riot that rolled through her moments before. He pressed his lips to her forehead, smoothing her long waves down the length of her back. His touch sent a shiver down her spine, and he pulled her closer, kissing her nose, her closed eyelids, and finally her mouth.

The kiss was gentle at first, a question; when she responded with rising vigor he pressed back in kind, running the length of her outline with his hand. He cupped her breast, lightly teasing her nipple with his thumb, and she felt that familiar twist of desire flame back to life low in her belly.

She couldn't, it seemed, get enough of Thomas; couldn't draw him close enough. She breathed him in, lemons, soap, that familiar spice. Her thirst for him was without depth.

He slipped his tongue between her lips. Gently he laid her on her back, rolling on top of her to rest on his elbows. His breath was warm on her cheek; she shivered at the expanse of their contact, his flesh pressed to hers from knee to nose.

Thomas dipped his head, trailing his lips along the edges of her mouth, her jaw, her neck. She closed her eyes and willed herself to remember this moment. What his mouth felt like on her skin, the heady trail of fire ignited by his lips. She'd never, not in all her life, felt something so poignant—a sensation that reverberated on both sides of her skin.

Above her he shifted, moving his leg to rest between her own. He paused, waiting for her answer. Sophia put her lips to the hollow between his earlobe and jaw; he tensed, sucking in a breath; and then with his knee he was coaxing apart her legs, settling himself between them.

Reaching back one hand at a time, he bent her legs so that he might fit more snugly against her. Again she felt his cock prodding her flesh, the tip warm and eager and far too large for its own good.

Without thinking, she reached down, curious to know how large, exactly, he was. Thomas let out a hiss as she wrapped her hand around his shaft, drawing a breath of surprise at the smooth, hard feel of him, the pulsing energy of his desire for her.

Carefully Thomas pried her fingers from his manhood, guiding her hand instead to the tip of her sex.

"Here," he said. Placing his hand over her own, he moved their fingers together over her slick flesh. Sophia gasped again at the unexpectedly intimate feel of her own body. This—this didn't feel at all shameful.

No. This felt dashedly *good.*

Thomas's hand moved down, sliding his cock down the length of her womanhood to rest just beneath where her hand worked. With his first two fingers he gently opened her, nudging himself inside her.

He kissed her mouth. She kissed him back, lips fervently working over and through each other.

She drew a breath, easing the tingle of nerves in her belly, and surrendered.

Twenty-seven

Hope closed his eyes, breathing in the feel of her flesh, ripe and willing, against his own. His body hummed with a passion that radiated from the very center of his chest; he wanted to be gentle and fervent with her all at once; he wanted to make love to her well, thoroughly, for this would be his only chance.

She was very wet, the curls of her sex slick and soft as he brushed them with his fingers, wet and very tight. He would have to go slowly, and with great care. The idea of hurting her—

Well. He would never forgive himself.

Slowly, very slowly, he slid inside her. For a moment her fingers stilled above the joining of their bodies. She breathed in short, shallow gasps; for a moment he worried she was afraid, but then thought better of it.

Sophia wouldn't have to come to him if she were afraid. Not like this.

His kiss softened, and she moaned into his mouth. Her fingers resumed their meandering, and with his hand Hope guided himself further inside her.

Breath by breath, inch by inch he moved forward. Her flesh tightened around him as her climax approached, and he sucked in a breath for what felt like the hundredth time that night.

Dear God she felt lovely; if he wasn't careful, he'd spill his seed in the space of the next heartbeat—and lest Sophia think him some randy adolescent, he was determined to make this last as long as he could.

He couldn't see a thing, not with the fire burning so low,

but the darkness only sharpened his desire; for what he could not sense with his eyes he did with his hands, his mouth, his skin. She was *here*; she was *his*.

Sophia's kiss grew messy, and she moved her lips over his jaw to his ear and throat. He winced at the shock of pleasure that ran through him, meeting the barrier inside her at that same moment.

He felt wild with the need to possess her, to make her his, at least for this moment.

At least for tonight.

Thomas gently bucked his hips, sinking to the root. Beneath him Sophia pulled back, sucking a breath between her teeth; he sensed her flesh tightening with pain. He bent his neck so that his nose grazed hers. In the dark he could make out the gleam in her eyes, wide with uncertainty.

Where their bodies were joined he grasped her hand and together their thumbs moved over her flesh. Her eyes fluttered shut, a moan of pleasure in her throat.

He pressed his lips to hers and began to move, slowly at first, soft, languorous strokes; Sophia rose to meet his caress. She did not hesitate; her movements matched his own, her hips riding against his as their hands tangled in her sex between them.

She sighed, a happy, luxurious sound, almost a laugh, and Hope felt in the midst of his merciless desire for her a tightening in his belly and his throat. She was impossibly beautiful, this woman, and he wanted nothing more than to make her laugh. To make her happy.

Sophia bucked against him, arching her back and baring her breasts to him. He devoured one nipple, moved to the other; and then he saw stars as her sex clenched around his cock, a series of viselike pulses that drew him to the point of his own orgasm.

Thomas pulled out just in time, gritting his teeth against the strangled cry in his throat as he spilled his seed on the smooth edge of her hip. Sophia was gasping beneath him, clawing at the skin of his chest as her legs gathered around his buttocks. Her hands slid over his shoulders to his back, pulling him to her.

He let out an exhausted sigh, and together they fell into the warm cocoon of his bed, their bodies slick with sweat. The scent of their lovemaking hung heavy between them.

They lay tangled, his leg crossed protectively above her own. As he struggled to catch his breath, his chest brushing the hardened points of her nipples—*Christ*, was she trying to kill him?—a sensation, loud, overwhelming, rushed through him, as if a flood had broken through the levee at the very center of his being. He closed his eyes, wrapping his arms about Sophia so that she might help him bear it; and found that having her so close, her head tucked into the curve of his neck, only made the sensation pulse brighter, the flood rush faster.

In his chest his heart felt enormous, painfully so; it was working double as Sophia's breath tickled the skin of his chest. Pressing a kiss into her hair, he rested his chin on the top of her head.

He was in love with her.

And now that he had the courage to admit it to himself at last, it was too late.

Not that he ever had a chance in the first place. This was, after all, the same Miss Sophia Blaise who dreamed of earls and castles and crests.

And while Thomas was in possession of none of these things, he was, at the moment, in possession of something—some*one*—he wanted more than he'd ever wanted the bank, the fortune, the paintings, and the titled investors.

This desire, *this* love—he felt it in his bones.

Even if she was never his to have.

Pain sliced through him, hot, wild, leaving him breathless. The thought of letting her go, of releasing her from his bed so that she might end up in that of the Marquess of Withington—

He bit back the angry surge of his blood. Sophia was his for tonight and tonight alone—that much Thomas understood. And he wasn't about to waste the precious few hours they had together burning with jealousy.

And so he quietly gathered her to him, trailing his lips along her forehead. He pulled back the coverlet, wiggling both their bodies beneath its warmth. His pain was matched only by the contentment of curling his body around hers, their limbs coiled in sheets damp from their exertions.

The contentment of knowing, though they spoke not a word, that Sophia loved him in turn.

Thomas leapt from the bed at the pounding on his door. Light, gray and watery, filled the room; it was almost dawn. He started, as if seeing the contents of his bedchamber for the first time. In the complete blackness of the disappearing night Sophia had taken captive of his every sense; nothing but her sighs, her rising body, and the beating of her heart had filled this room.

There were her clothes, puddled on the rug; a stray silk stocking hung from the back of a nearby chair. His breeches and shirt were scattered in a far off corner.

Well, then. The maids were in for a treat when they made their rounds later that morning.

Beside Thomas, Sophia bolted upright in bed, the sheets falling from her bare chest to reveal her breasts.

Hope swallowed. They were just as lovely, perhaps even more so, than he'd imagined last night in the dark. Her long, wavy hair was loose about her shoulders, tousled just enough to indicate he'd made quite thorough love to her.

He swallowed again at the familiar tightening between his legs.

"Come back later," he called, watching Sophia's cheeks flush pink as she covered herself with the sheet. "I'm afraid I'm indisposed at the moment."

Daltrey's voice was heavy. "I am sorry to wake you, sir, but I've just received news I believe you and Mi—*you* might want to hear straightaway."

Hope ran a hand through his hair with a groan. "All right, give me a moment."

He put his hands on the bed and leaned forward, grazing her nose with the tip of his own.

There was too much and yet nothing at all to say. Sophia had come to purge them both of the affection they bore one another by indulging it wholly, passionately; to slake her thirst by drowning in him for one night, and one night only. One night to forget the terrors that tightened the noose around each of their necks, the worries that bound them to fortunes and futures they did not choose.

And now that the night was past, Sophia would go back to her life, and her marquess; and Thomas to his bank and the missing French Blue and the memory of a family long gone; they would go back without regret.

Or so was the intention.

Before he could stop himself, Hope dipped his head and pressed his lips to hers, taking her bottom lip between his teeth. Good God she was delicious. Perhaps they had time for one more—

"Mr. Hope!"

Hope dropped his head and groaned. "I am very sorry," he said, meeting her eyes. He saw in them his own confusion; sadness and desire clouding the irises, turning them a darker shade of green. Christ, how he wanted to hold her face in his hand and kiss her until it was only desire he saw in her eyes. Desire for him and no one else.

Sophia slid under the sheets, pulling them over her head. Shrugging into a robe, Hope stalked to the door and wrenched it open.

"Well?"

Daltrey stood on his toes, peering for a moment over Hope's shoulder. Hope pulled the door shut behind him with a look of consternation. "Out with it, Daltrey. I'd like to get back to bed."

The butler cleared his throat, proffering a scrap of paper in his gloved hand. "It's the Lady Violet, sir. She's been shot in a duel."

Duchess Street

Hope stretched out his legs before the fire, the exquisite heat helping to calm the dull chill of horror, of rage and of sadness, that plagued him all day and into the night.

Lady Violet had not been dueling herself, though it wouldn't have surprised Hope if she had. Feisty, that one, with a mouth on her that would make a sailor weep. What a breath of fresh air she'd been after all the dour dowagers and witless heiresses he'd encountered over the years; Hope had liked her straightaway, even more so after he discovered her passion for brown liquor rivaled his own.

No, it was the Earl of Harclay and Mr. Lake who'd exchanged insults, and then bullets, that morning. Violet had the misfortune of trying to end such foolishness at the very moment both parties discharged their Manton dueling pistols. Apparently it was Harclay's bullet that lodged between her ribs, though the details on this were vague at best.

Sophia had burst into tears when she'd heard the news. They'd arrived at her house just as Violet's body was being brought in by the surgeon; already she was unconscious, her wound vicious-looking and black with blood.

His belly clenched at the memory of it. Though the surgeon reassured Sophia her cousin would be fine, just fine, his face was grim. Even Lady Blaise in the midst of her hysterics knew better than to believe him. Violet's condition was serious.

Hope had resisted the urge to throttle Lake, bloody idiot, then and there. He'd crossed the wrong man this time; Harclay was one of the few who could go toe to toe with Lake and best him at his own game. Lake had, after all, given up the earl to those beastly acrobats, which led to that business of Lady Violet being kidnapped; the earl couldn't have been pleased about that.

Then, of course, there was Lake's odd relationship with Lady Caroline, the Dowager Countess of Berry and the earl's sister, to consider.

Really, just what the devil was Lake up to? He had some explaining to do.

And so Hope waited in his study for Lake to appear through a window, or perhaps through the chimney this time; he would know Hope wanted to see him.

He did not have to wait long. As the clock on the mantel struck eleven o'clock, Lake silently moved from the darkness into the half-moon of light put off by the fire.

For a long moment Hope stared him down. His face was drawn, his skin pale; dark circles ringed his eyes, red from lack of sleep. While he longed to throttle the man, yes, Hope felt pity for him, too. He was selfless, Lake, and savagely loyal; but even such a creature as he had his weak moments, his bouts of extreme and utter stupidity.

He *was* a man, after all.

And this was one such bout.

"What happened?" Hope said quietly.

Lake sank into the chair opposite Hope's. He put his elbows on his knees and hung his head. "I went to visit Lady Caroline last night at her brother's house. It was foolish of me to have been there, but I will not say it was a mistake. I was climbing down from her window—"

"Really, your aversion to *front doors* borders on the insane."

"And the earl, he and Lady Violet, they were—well, you know. They were leaving the house just as I was; an hour or two before dawn. We met in the drive. He was insulted I would dare visit his sister, and she just out of mourning. He was *especially* insulted that Lady Violet was kidnapped after I sold him out to the acrobats."

"And so he challenged you to a duel. Why didn't you refuse him?"

Lake shook his head and scoffed. "I may not play the part, old friend, but I am the son of a baron. I cannot refuse a challenge when my honor is at stake."

"Honor?" Hope arched a brow. "You were climbing through a widow's window in the middle of the night. Somehow I doubt you and the dowager countess spent the wee hours of the morning brushing up on the Bible."

The sides of Lake's mouth twitched. "It isn't what you think. Well, it *is*, but Caroline and I, we—"

"Unless the two of you are secretly married, whatever you are or aren't doing is an insult to her honor as well as her brother's."

Above the ball of his enormous shoulder, Lake met Hope's eyes.

Hope sank further into his chair. "Oh God. You are secretly married, aren't you? But how—"

"That's beside the point."

"I hardly think you being secretly married to a *countess* is beside the point."

Lake pushed himself upright with a groan, wincing as he twisted his arms about his torso. "I'm getting too old for this dueling nonsense."

"Your *nonsense* has placed us further away from the French Blue than ever. I hardly think the earl will be inclined to hand over the jewel after shooting his—his—bah! After shooting Lady Violet in the ribs."

Lake groaned again. "He doesn't have it. Not anymore."

Hope pitched forward in his chair. "Doesn't have it? The French Blue? Christ above, Lake, what the devil do you mean by that?"

"That's an awful lot of religion in one sentence."

"I swear to God, I'll—"

"All right, all right." Lake held up his hands in surrender. "Lady Caroline knew where her brother was hiding the diamond."

Hope nearly choked. "But how? He could be hiding it anywhere!"

"Says when he was younger he used to hide all his naughty bits in a drawer with his socks. As a boy he'd keep rocks and bugs and even a pigeon in that drawer of his to safeguard them from his governess. When he got older the bits were less innocent, of course—a well-thumbed copy of *Fanny Hill*, a few fashion plates of girls without the fashion—but it was always the same. He hid his secrets in that drawer."

"My God." Hope ran a hand through his hair. "All this time, and that damned diamond was in his *sock drawer*."

"Last night Caroline took me to his dressing room, and together we rummaged through his socks. She swore we'd find it."

"But it wasn't there."

"Exactly, it wasn't there. At first Caroline and I were perplexed; she swore there was nowhere else he'd keep the jewel. You mustn't forget Harclay stole a fifty-carat diamond in the midst of the season's most well attended ball for the mere thrill of it. He could care less about money. Makes sense a careless daredevil like him would keep his prize in his sock drawer."

"But the diamond *wasn't there*."

Lake held up a finger. "Right. And Caroline was convinced it wouldn't be anywhere else, so I ran through the possibilities. He came to you after the kidnapping, didn't he, to ask for money?"

"Yes." Hope furrowed his brow. His eyes went wide as

understanding, swift and startling, smacked him square in the forehead. "The acrobats must've blackmailed him. Asked him for more money. But after I'd frozen his accounts, he didn't have access to nary a penny. So he traded the diamond for Violet's safety. Christ!"

"I don't believe Jesus has anything to do with it, but yes, I've every reason to believe Harclay traded away the diamond."

Hope fell back in his chair. "Christ," he repeated. "That means we're back to where we started, doesn't it? The diamond could be anywhere by now. Anywhere. This is bad news, Lake, very bad news indeed. If only I had known!—well. Too late for that. But I don't know how much longer Hope and Company can hold out. I need a good headline, Lake. I need good news so the bank might be saved. We've got to find the French Blue."

"I know," Lake said quietly. A vein jumped in his temple. "You aren't the only one with something to lose, old man. The French have grown impatient. They know something is not right; they are demanding the diamond, and soon, or they will go elsewhere in their search. So yes. We *must* find the French Blue. I am doing everything in my power, Hope, to set it all to rights."

Hope let the back of his head fall against his chair and stared at the ceiling. "Just when I thought it couldn't get any worse. Let us not forget our friend Cassin."

Lake scoffed. "At this point I'm tempted to let him kill us so that we might be put out of our misery."

"Ha! Wishful thinking."

"Wishful indeed."

For several moments they sat in silence. Hope contemplated the shadows on the ceiling, flickering in time to the beat of the fire. He was surprised he was possessed of enough energy to sense the sinking in his belly so keenly.

"Sophia," Lake said. "How is she?"

Hope cast him a sideways glance. "Forbidden fruit. Your words, not mine."

"Perhaps I've changed my tune. Forbidden fruit is, after all, the best kind."

Twenty-eight

Two weeks later
Grosvenor Square

Hope fingered the limp daffodils in the cut glass vase by the library window. They were a gift from the Marquess of Withington; Hope remembered him sweeping awkwardly into the house some days ago, flowers tucked under his arm. He'd jerked to his knee like a knight-errant and gravely offered them to Sophia. Hope hadn't even tried to keep from rolling his eyes. They were a hell of a way from Camelot, and he had no patience for King Arthur or his silly pantomime of courtly love.

Hope ran his thumb along the inside of a yellowing stem and sighed. Born and raised in the city made famous by its ruinous fervor for tulips, Hope was well versed in the language of flowers. The daffodils were an interesting choice; popularly known to embody rebirth, new beginnings, they were also a symbol of unrequited love.

Which meaning had the marquess meant to convey? By all accounts Sophia returned Withington's favor; when the fashionable half of London wasn't discussing the theft of the French Blue, it was whispering behind gilded fans and half-closed doors about the marquess's imminent proposal. *Why her?* they wondered. And: *What a fool he is, to pick her when he could have any other!*

Hope, of course, begged to differ.

Without thinking he snapped the sagging flower from its

wilted stem with his thumbnail. Its petals loosened into his palm, releasing an earthy scent, water and green and air.

Sophia's scent.

He gathered the petals into a fist, inhaling deeply, before releasing them onto the windowsill. The afternoon light was waning; she would be down soon, and he wanted to be ready.

Settling into a settee by the empty fireplace, he tucked the bottle of port into his coat and waited for what felt like an eternity. He listened to the sounds of the house, the crunch of gravel as vehicles passed below the open window. Summer had arrived at long last; and while the air was warm, Hope had been plagued by a chill these past days. The port—yes, that would help.

On the back wall the clock sprang into action, six strokes before it fell silent again. His heart skipped a beat at the sound of footsteps on the stair. He sat up, smoothing the dark kerseymere of his breeches.

He heard the whisper of her skirts at the threshold, followed by the click of the door as she closed it behind her. She sighed, a low, defeated sound; her steps were light on the carpet.

Blood thrumming, Hope shot to his feet and turned to face her.

Sophia started, her hazel eyes blinking wide in surprise. "Mr. Hope!"

Ah, that stung. The banker's name on her lips.

"Miss Blaise." He fell into a bow.

"I did not know you were here. Violet received your letters; when she is well enough she would like to thank you for your kindness in person."

Hope rose, meeting her eyes. The knot in his belly tightened. Though her eyes were red and wet, the sleeves of her print-cotton gown pulled up about her elbows, she looked beautiful. The light from the window set fire to the wisps of dark hair that framed her face; her lips were parted just enough to reveal the rosy-pink forbidden flesh of her mouth.

Nymph. He remembered her dressed in that diaphanous gown the night of the ball, the peek of a milky-white thigh through the fabric.

Hope cleared his throat. "I sent them as soon as I received word she'd woken. I cannot imagine your relief at knowing the Lady Violet would." He searched for the right words. "Would be all right."

"Yes." She looked down at her clasped hands and scoffed. "I knew she'd come back to us, if only to return the earl's favor and shoot *him* in the ribs. Though I must give credit where credit is due. Harclay didn't leave her side, not even to change clothes. At last my mother, bless her, convinced him to bathe. He left only after Violet sent him away."

Hope raised a brow. "Duel notwithstanding, I thought they were getting along rather swimmingly, the earl and Violet."

"Apparently not. The diamond is still missing; our fortunes continue to fall. Though Violet hasn't slept or ate since he left." Sophia looked up, a tight smile on her lips. "But now you have come to call. I usually take port at this hour, though I'm afraid our supplies are rather low, what with the earl having plundered the cellar these past weeks. That man has a *deuced* thirst."

Hope untangled the bottle from his jacket and held it aloft. "I thought that might be the case, so I brought this. Might I interest you in a nip?"

Sophia met his eyes. "How did you know?" she said.

Because I know you.

"Because I've been keeping my own vigil. Over Violet." He set the bottle on a round table near the far window and went to work with a corkscrew he pulled from his waistcoat pocket. "Over you."

"Over me?" she scoffed.

"Yes," he replied smoothly, though his heart beat a loud and unrelenting rhythm in his chest. "I pass your house every evening on my way home from the bank. These windows, they face the street. I see you standing there by the window, glass in hand. Always at six o'clock."

"Well." Sophia swallowed and took the tiny crystal coupe he offered her. "I cannot say if I am more flattered or terrified that you know the schedule of our days here. But I am willing to give you the benefit of the doubt."

"How kind of you."

She smiled. "I do try, Soph—Miss Blaise."

Hope looked into her eyes as he held his coupe out before him. "To Lady Violet, that she may be recovered. I've missed her, you know."

Sophia touched her coupe to his and together they downed the port. Hope's eyes nearly rolled to the back of his head with pleasure at the familiar burn in his throat. It helped loosen the tightness there; loosen the tangle of his thoughts.

"I've missed *you*." His voice was low, more intimate than he'd intended. But there it was: the truth.

Sophia's eyes flashed with uncertainty. After a beat she held out her coupe. "Another, if it please you."

"It would please me very much." Hope went to the table and refilled their glasses to the brim. He turned and motioned to the sill by the open window. "Please, let's sit."

Sophia sidled onto the ledge, pushing aside the gauzy curtain as it billowed in the breeze. She took the coupe from him, their fingers brushing, and stared down at it.

Hope lifted his knee onto the sill and leaned into it. An errant curl swirled about her forehead, her skin glistening in the yellow light of the dying sun. He reached out, intent to brush back the curl, but stopped himself.

"Sophia," he said.

She met his gaze; her eyes were wet. "Please, Thomas . . ."

"It was your wish that we not go on as we had. After the night in my room I understood what you wanted. *Why* you wanted it. And I had every intention of respecting that, Sophia, I did. I had told myself it was better for the both of us. You have your season, and your match to which to see; and I of course have the bank and that bloody diamond. I am sorry to break the vow we took that night—the vow that we should leave everything we felt in that bed, in those hours. But despite my best efforts I cannot leave it there."

"Thomas, you cannot . . . *we* cannot . . ."

Thomas looked out the window, looked back at Sophia. She bit her bottom lip to still its trembling.

He ran a hand through his hair and sighed. The breeze felt cool on his skin, suddenly warm on account of the workings of his heart.

"I only mean to ask how you have been, Sophia."

Sophia turned her head to look out the window, bearing the soft flesh of her throat. Thomas watched the jump of her pulse there; it matched his own. It took his every effort not to cradle her neck in his palm, not to hook his hand along her jaw and ear, to tangle his fingers in her hair.

"I am well." Again that tight smile. "Now that Violet is back, the house is less lonely, and the weather, it's been lovely."

"After our meeting. After that night. I . . . I didn't hurt you, did I?"

She turned and met his eyes. For a beat his words hung between them.

"No, Thomas. You didn't hurt me. I confess," here her cheeks burned pink, "I was a bit sore the next day. Hardly mattered, what with Violet bleeding from her chest."

"No." The word came suddenly, more vicious than he intended. "It matters to me. I wanted to make you feel as well pleasured as you made *me* feel that night. I wanted you to have everything you came for and more." *I wanted to be your first, your last, your only.*

Again she looked down at her glass, still full, and let out a sound somewhere between a scoff and a sob. "If you have any doubts as to your . . . your *pleasuring* that night, Thomas, allow me to put them to rest. Well pleasured. Well touched. Well lov—it was all done well. Better than that."

He let out a sigh of relief. "Good."

"I haven't had the chance to thank you for what you did. You didn't have to see me that night. I know what I asked was rather . . . unconventional. Not to say unexpected." She raised her glass and looked at him. "Thank you, Thomas."

His pulse leapt. As he pressed his glass to hers he felt the familiar tug between their bodies, that irresistible pull that moved in the center of his being.

"Thank *you*, Sophia, for blessing me with your friendship. I will not forget that kindness."

She smiled. Her eyes welled but she did not weep. "I am not leaving for the moon, you know. We might still be friends after all this," she waved her hand, "is over."

"Yes." He swallowed. The sun was waning now; evening had set in. The light reflecting off Sophia's skin burned gold to yellow to blue.

"And everything else." His eyes flicked to her midsection,

hidden beneath the tiny pleats of her gown. "It is well? I took the appropriate precaution, of course, but no plan is foolproof."

Sophia's cheeks went from pink to red. "Yes, all is well."

"You're sure of it? It's early yet."

"Yes, Mr. Hope, I'm sure of it. Yesterday I . . . well. Needless to say I received all the proof I needed, praise God."

Hope tipped back his coupe. "Yes, yes indeed. Praise God."

The breeze tickled a loose curl at his temple. He brushed it back. Looking at Sophia, her lips stained red from the port, a swift pulse of desire curled through him. Desire for her body, desire to *possess* her.

For a moment he selfishly wished all *wasn't* well. That in the darkness that night, as he'd joined his flesh to hers, they'd created something bigger than themselves. Miss Sophia Blaise, carrying his child. He knew they'd make a beautiful baby; her dark hair, her shapely lips, his eyes, perhaps, his long fingers and unruly curls. With his child in her belly, Sophia would be *his* and his alone. He'd have an excuse to take her under his protection, and give her his name.

Mrs. Sophia Hope.

He ached for it to be true. For her to confess, so that he might have an excuse to whisk her away to the altar and then, with any luck, to Italy for an extended honeymoon. Or would she like Greece better? She *did* have a soft spot for pirates, so perhaps Morocco was the ticket . . .

Impulsively he reached for her, taking her face in his hand. In the dying light of the window, something glinted at her breast. He looked closer to see a thin gold chain, from which hung a ring bearing a small but exquisite yellow diamond in the shape of a heart.

Which was ironic, as at that moment Hope's own heart seemed to lose its shape as it exploded in his chest. He felt bits of bloody flesh settle on the shelf of his ribs, his breath dying in his lugs.

Sophia's gaze flicked from the diamond to his eyes, her features loosening as if they might collapse.

"I believe congratulations are in order," Hope said, trying his damnedest to keep from choking on the words. "The Marquess of Withington is a lucky man. A good man. When did the happy event occur?"

Sophia drew back, taking the ring between her thumb and forefinger and pulling it across the length of the chain. "He proposed just this morning. I . . . I confess I did not know what to say. He was so lovely, and kind . . ." She looked away, her throat working as her eyes fluttered shut.

"Anyway," she shook her head, "he insisted I keep the ring while I considered his offer."

"How very chivalrous of him." Hope's gaze wandered to the sagging dandelions across the room. Unrequited love—bah! Nothing more than wishful thinking. What lady in her right mind wouldn't love ten thousand a year and a castle in the country?

He swallowed what was left of his port. "When you do say yes, the papers will be aflutter with the news. Perhaps my old friends won't run another headline about the French Blue for a day or two. God knows I could use the break."

"*If* I say yes."

"*When* you say yes. Your family stands to lose as much as I do if we don't find that blasted diamond and prove to my rather unadoring public that I can indeed safeguard the bank's assets. Your marriage to the marquess may be your family's only hope."

Sophia threw back her port with a wince. The sadness in her eyes evaporated, replaced by a gleaming mischief. " 'My family's only hope'—why, that's awfully grim stuff. You've been reading Shakespeare again, haven't you?"

Hope stiffened. "Perhaps."

"The tragedies? I bet you've been penning a poem or two as well. Something about that forbidden fruit you and Lake are always talking about."

Hope, suddenly warm, tugged at his collar and cleared his throat. "As you can imagine, the tragedies *have* suited my mood these past weeks. But what with the bank so far under water, I've hardly had time to pen poetry. *Poetry*. Bah! I gave that up long ago."

Even Hope wasn't convinced by his denial. Judging from Sophia's arched brow, she wasn't, either; she was grinning, the pallor of her sadness disappearing, her old colors—trouble, beauty, earnestness—rising in its place.

"I'd like to read it," she said softly. "You aren't the only one to have visited the tragedies so recently. My dearest mama has been nothing short of a nervous wreck and, as you can see, her antics have driven me to drink. I've found particular solace in the sufferings of Tybalt."

"Ah, yes. Jolly fun fellow, that Tybalt, if not a bit . . . oh, I think bloodthirsty's the right word. *Italians.*" Hope shook his head. "Never fear, Miss Blaise, the murderous rage shall pass in a few weeks' time. You must refrain from using any sharp objects in the interim, letter openers and the like, lest your dearest mama end up like poor Mercutio."

Sophia laughed, the kind of laugh that made the skin at the edges of her eyes crease with pleasure. "And *we* must take care, lest God smite us for plotting my mother's demise."

"Bah! God hath smote us already. Smite away, I say. Smite away."

For several heartbeats, Hope watched as Sophia's shoulders moved in time to her laughter. He knew without asking it was the first time she'd laughed in weeks, since Violet's accident that terrible morning at Farrow Field. He saw the tension in her neck relax, the sinews of her sloping shoulders loosen with her delight; her surrender, if only for a moment, to him.

He remembered with startling clarity the feel of those muscles and sinews beneath his hands as he worked his way across every inch of her body, the sensation of her sinking beneath him into the warm softness of his feather bed. How sweet it had been then, her surrender; how he'd reveled in it, worshipped it, while drowning in his own.

A breeze tickled his skin; the light from the window was softening now, burning the silken strands of Sophia's hair a fiery white. She caught him watching her; their eyes met for a long moment. She was so beautiful it made his belly hurt; he was lost in her gleaming skin and wild hair and almond-shaped eyes.

And then they were leaning toward each other, her lips parted just enough for Thomas to make out the white gleam of her pearlescent teeth. Her scent invaded his every sense, clean air with a hint of soap, his eyes fluttering shut as he inhaled whatever parts of her he could. He couldn't, they shouldn't, but . . .

They both jumped back at the sudden racket at the door.

Sophia managed to spill what was left of her port on her cotton dress, a very unladylike curse escaping the mouth he'd been about to kiss as she brushed at the stain with the back of her hand.

"Hello?" came Violet's voice, thin and tired. She was at the door in the arms of a rather diminutive footman, who sputtered and panted as he wove his way into the room beneath the weight of his burden. "Is that port I see on your dress, cousin? Damn you both, why didn't you wait for me?"

"Forgive me, Lady Violet, I was about to take my leave . . ."

". . . was in the library, looking for a book . . . Shakespeare, you know the one, star-cross'd . . ."

"I didn't know you'd be down . . . I was just visiting, er, the house . . ."

". . . dreadful headache after listening to Mama complain for an hour about the roads . . . terrible this time of year . . ."

Gasping with pain, Violet unwrapped her arms from about the poor footman's neck as he settled her on the nearby settee. She surveyed Hope and Sophia, her eyes narrowed with suspicion or pain, he couldn't quite tell.

"You're up to something," she said. "What is it?"

Hope cleared his throat, as if to speak, but Sophia interjected before he could begin.

"Mr. Hope was calling to ensure you received all the letters he'd sent you. He heard you had woken and was merely concerned for your well-being. Ah, the letters, there they are!"

The footman, poor chap, panted as he bent down to place a neat stack of correspondence on Violet's lap. Lady Violet blanched a whiter shade of—well, white as she looked down at the pile.

Mr. Hope took that as his cue to leave. "Miss Blaise," he bowed to Sophia, "I do so hope you enjoy the gift. Remember what I said about sharp objects. Good evening. Lady Violet."

He stalked from the room, Violet clutching the back of the settee as she turned to watch him go. "Sharp objects?" he heard her say. "What the devil does he mean by that? Sophia!"

Hope took his hat and gloves from the footman and charged through the front door, the blood marching in his ears so loudly he did not notice the Earl of Harclay bounding up the steps until it was too late.

They ran headfirst into one another, the earl drawing back as Hope muttered his apologies.

"Hope! Just the man I was . . . er . . . hoping to see! Do you have a moment, old man?"

Hope cleared his throat for what felt like the hundredth time and pulled at the wrists of his gloves. He had no patience for the earl this afternoon; he was as liable to ram his fist into Harclay's face as he was to give him a moment.

"I'm afraid not, my lord."

"Trust me." Harclay slung an arm about Hope's shoulder and pulled him close. "You're going to want to hear this news."

Hope went stiff, arching a brow. "News?"

"I've found it!" the earl whispered. "The French Blue. I've found it. Not only that—I've devised a plan, rather ingenious in my humble estimation, to have it back in your pocket by week's end."

Twenty-nine

Sophia had every intention of keeping her distance from Thomas. No matter her dreams of him at night, the delicious wanderings of her thoughts by day; no matter the ache in her heart or the heavy weight of the diamond ring about her neck. Sophia swore to focus her affections, and her thoughts, on the Marquess of Withington, and to do so required removing Mr. Hope from her heart and her head.

With the French Blue lost, the family's fortune dwindled; her uncle was in debt to the tune of thousands of pounds. First they lost their credit with the grocer, the fishmonger, the shops on Bond Street. Next, they would lose the house.

Guillaume Cassin was still at large. The threat of exposure, and subsequent ruin, was very real indeed.

If ever there was an opportune time in which to agree to an opportune offer of marriage, this would certainly be it.

Sophia had every intention of doing right by her family, she did. But fate, in the form of an unexpected visit from that scalawag Earl of Harclay, had other plans.

He'd found the diamond, or so he claimed. And his scheme to get it back—well, it was nothing short of absurd, as it involved multiple steps, multiple disguises, and crimes that were punishable by medieval sorts of death. Like his plan, the earl was either cracked or utterly brilliant; Sophia could not yet say which it would be.

"I was at White's, a few evenings ago," Harclay panted. He paced before the grate in the drawing room, Cousin Violet laid out upon the sofa, Sophia perched at her feet.

"As I was drinking myself into a stupor I happened to

overhear King Louis—yes, *that* King Louis, the one who's been living so high on the hog in exile, here in England—and his brother the Comte d'Artois discussing payment for *le bleu de France*. Seems we're not the only ones on the hunt for the diamond."

Of course Sophia knew of the French royals; they were in the papers often enough, tales of their enormous stipends and even more enormous appetites providing endless fodder for London's gossips. Brothers to the fallen Louis XVI, they lived in exile in the hopes that the new King Louis—he styled himself Louis XVIII—might one day reclaim the throne of France.

Seeing as Napoleon had no intention of ceding said throne; seeing as Louis and Artois were so fat they would sink any ship that attempted to bear them across the Channel; well, such ambitions were laughable at best.

Harclay's news did little to further their cause.

"They said a man by the name of Daniel Eliason, a jewel merchant, is in possession of the French Blue. This week they are to meet on Eliason's ship in the Docklands, and pay him thirty thousand pounds for the jewel."

Sophia swallowed, let out a breath.

"I propose—hear me out, before you object—I propose we lure the king into our possession, and force him to take us to his brother, who at this very moment is working to procure a loan for the thirty thousand. We take the money, have the royals lead us to Eliason, and—*Huzzah!*—buy the diamond for ourselves." He caught Sophia's eye and had the grace to flush pink. "For Mr. Hope, I mean. Of course the French Blue belongs to him."

Sophia furrowed her brow. "How do we set the plot in motion, then? What bait do we have to lure the king to our cause?"

"Ah!" Here the earl and Cousin Violet exchanged a knowing glance. "It's quite simple. The king likes whores. Begging your pardon, Miss Blaise, no other way to say it. I propose we—all of us, you and Hope and that one-eyed monster of his—lure old King Louis to my house under the premise it is a palace of pleasure or some such nonsense. Once he's inside, we get him drunk, very drunk, or . . . yes, or we give him a goodly dose of laudanum, just enough to make him docile.

Then he leads us to his brother, the money, and, at last, the diamond."

Sophia looked from the Earl of Harclay to Violet and back again.

Dear God, they were serious.

This senseless, dangerous, convoluted plot—they meant to put it in play.

But the plot *did* involve Mr. Hope; and before her better sense took hold, Sophia blurted, "I'm in! Count me in. Which part shall I take?"

Several days later
The Earl of Harclay's Residence
Brook Street, Hanover Square

A courtesan, as it turned out; Sophia was one of many half-naked goddesses inhabiting Aphrodite's Temple, a labyrinthine set that transformed the Earl of Harclay's well-appointed drawing room into a house of ill repute, complete with swaths of red satin and nude statues of Greek immortals in suggestive poses.

All was going to plan—Harclay and Cousin Violet managed to lure the king into the Temple, and His Highness King Louis XVIII appeared to be enjoying himself most thoroughly in his chair beside the earl—until Harclay, having sipped from a balloon of brandy proffered moments before by Sophia, suddenly pitched forward.

His eyes welled; his face matched the swaths of satin above his head.

Sophia looked down at the empty tray she held in her hands, and looked back up at the king. He appeared healthy as an ox, if not a bit perplexed by Harclay's sudden, violent movements.

She'd poisoned the wrong man.

She'd poisoned Harclay.

Across the room, Sophia met eyes with Mr. Hope, who up until that moment had been waiting in the wings. Her belly sinking, she watched his face unfurl with understanding, and then he was dashing forward, falling to his knees beside Mr. Lake as Avery, the earl's butler, held his master's head in his hands.

Sophia placed the tray on the edge of the stage and lurched toward the small knot of men, throat thick with tears. Violet was calling for a doctor; Lake, more menacing than ever in his gravity, called for mustard seed and water.

The earl's face was now a frightening shade of blue. His body was limp, devoid of any movement. Mr. Hope was shouting now, binding King Louis' hands and feet; the room pulsed into action around her.

Dear God. She'd *poisoned* the *earl*. And not just any earl. Violet's earl, the earl that was to lead them to the diamond, to sanity and salvation. What if he never woke? What if she'd killed him, killed him with her carelessness?

Sophia checked, and checked again, that the balloon with the chipped foot—the poisoned brandy—would go to His Highness King Louis. But then she'd caught Mr. Hope watching her, his blue eyes following her every movement, lingering on her every curve.

So much for keeping her distance. Such a thing wasn't possible, not when he looked at her like that; not when she felt her heart rising beneath his gaze, her heart and blood and the longing that plagued her day and night.

Sophia remembered her hands shaking as she offered the balloons to Harclay and Louis, her thoughts a riotous tangle. It was entirely possible she offered the wrong drink to the wrong man.

Her vision blurred by tears, she stood over Mr. Lake as he held a potion to Harclay's lips. The earl drank it in short, hot sputters; but time and time again his eyes fluttered shut.

He was dying.

Panic rose in her throat. Sophia swallowed it, willing herself to remain calm. She'd written scandalous memoirs, deceived a princess, dueled with sinister Frenchmen.

Surely she could bring a man back to life.

Sophia elbowed Lake aside and sank to her knees. "Allow me."

She wound up her arm and, squeezing shut her eyes, brought down her hand, hard, on Harclay's cheek.

Violet was crying out, holding the earl's head in her lap.

Sophia watched as his lips broke into a small smile; and then he was opening his eyes and turning over and emptying the contents of his stomach onto Violet's costume.

"I'm sorry," he sputtered, wiping his lips, "for ruining your toga."

An audible sigh of relief coursed through the room.

Sophia sat back on her haunches. "I'm so very sorry. I don't know how it happened—"

With a wince, William drew himself up. "Think nothing of it, Sophia. Just promise me you'll never again raise your hand to another man—you seem to enjoy it a tad too much. Bloody hurt, too."

Thank God he wasn't dead. Thank God. Through her tears she felt herself smile.

"I promise."

There was a tickle at the back of her neck. Sophia looked up to see Mr. Hope looming above her, his fingers moving to grasp her arm. Wordlessly he lifted her to her feet, branding her with the heat of his touch, his palm to her bare skin.

They stood very close. His eyes—oh, those *eyes*—searched her face. She grew warm beneath his scrutiny; when she tried to look away he pulled her closer, his fingers pressing into the flesh of her arm.

"Are you all right?" His voice was low, barely above a whisper.

"Yes." Sophia glanced across the room. The earl stumbled; Mr. Lake caught him just before he fell face-first to the floor. "Though I cannot say the same for his lordship. Poor Harclay."

"An accident." Hope squeezed her arm. "Nothing Lake and a little mustard seed couldn't fix."

"But I almost killed him! What if he's—what if he's crippled forever?"

"Darling." Sophia tried to ignore the thrill that sparked in her chest at his endearment. "If brandy could cripple a man, I daresay I'd be gnarled and stooped as an apple tree. That thieving rogue will recover, make no mistake. In the meantime, we must see to tonight's adventure."

Sophia swallowed, squaring her shoulders. Their last adventure; one last wild night. "Yes. Yes, you're right."

"Excellent." Hope smiled. He released her arm, running

his palm over her bare shoulder. "Here, let me get your shawl. It'll be chilly by the river."

She tried not to shiver at his touch. She didn't want to feel like this, not now, not when the fate of her family, of Hope and the bank, hung in the balance.

She did not want to feel this desire for him pulse through her being with every heartbeat, every breath, more potent than ever.

She did not want to feel like this.

But then she met his eyes as she ducked into the frayed cashmere shawl he held open for her. He was looking at her the way girls dreamed of being looked at; adoringly, intently, his eyes at once soft with affection, hard with desire.

No matter what she wanted, what was good and what was proper, there was no helping the way Thomas made Sophia feel.

The gentlemen, who, in their attempts to push King Louis through the doorway, had gotten him stuck, were calling for Thomas's aid; Cousin Violet was twittering about time, they didn't have much time now.

Hope reached for Sophia's hand, took it in his own. By now the gesture was familiar, but that familiarity was thrilling in its own way. It made her feel confident, and warm, as if she might count on his presence at her side no matter tonight's events. As if he would protect her no matter what happened.

He turned and made for the king, who was howling some French obscenity or another. For a moment Sophia stood, watching the roll of Hope's shoulders through the tunic of his Achilles costume.

"Sophia! Sophia," Violet snapped. "Oh, come, enough of this wallowing in self-pity. Harclay's alive, and with any luck he'll stay that way. We've got to go, or we'll miss our rendezvous with Artois!"

Sophia blinked, breaking the spell, and followed her cousin out of the room.

Their party piled into two hackneys. With a bit of cajoling, King Louis was at last persuaded to lead them to his brother, the Comte d'Artois, who waited like a sitting duck in his carriage on King Street, a thirty-thousand-pound note tucked into his tasseled pocket.

Sophia watched the proceedings in mute fascination. At gunpoint, the king and Artois agreed to accompany Hope's motley crew to the Docklands, where Mr. Daniel Eliason, that shadowy jeweler, awaited their arrival, the French Blue in the strongbox aboard his ship.

Thomas sat across from her as the hackney rumbled through the darkened streets toward the Docklands. Outside, the night was black, complete; this side of town had no gas lamps of which to speak, and the thoroughfares were narrow and mean, bordered on either side by shuttered tenements.

Sophia swallowed, and kept her gaze studiously focused on her lap. Not only was she terrified of what was to come—this adventure, it was dangerous, it was stupid, and it would likely get them all killed—she feared meeting Thomas's eyes. She couldn't bear to see him look at her like that again. Not when she would leave him behind after tonight. Leave him behind, and all that he had made her feel, all that she had seen and known at his side.

At last the hackney creaked to a stop. The gentlemen dismounted first. Hope held out his hand, guiding Sophia out of the vehicle. Her fingers shook in the warmth of his palm; he tucked her arm into the crook of his elbow and held her close against him.

She did not protest.

The stench of the Docklands reached out to them in the humid silence. Now that summer had at last arrived the River Thames was as fragrant as ever; Sophia pressed her nose into her elbow and tried not to breathe too deeply.

So this is where it's all going to end, she thought. This is where we shall find our salvation, mine and Violet's, England's and Mr. Hope's. This is where he shall take back what is his, and restore his good name.

His body felt warm against hers as they made their way to the hackney parked in front of their own. The king and Artois were leaning against the vehicle, panting in unison like two enormous, slobbering bulldogs. Mr. Lake, menacing as ever, was pointing a pistol at the royals.

She felt Hope hesitate; he reluctantly released her from his grasp, and with his free hand he adjusted the front of his breeches, much as he'd done that night in his study at Hope & Co.

With a wince, Lord Harclay drew to his full height before King Louis and the *comte*. "You know where this man Daniel Eliason keeps his ship?"

Artois sniffed, turning up his nose. Though he was hopelessly shorter than his lordship the earl, he would not, it appeared, be looked down upon.

When neither Artois nor his brother responded, Harclay waved the thirty-thousand-pound note before them, the paper flapping in a sour breeze.

"I've already got your money. Don't make me take your manhood, too. Do you *know* where this man *Eliason* keeps his ship?"

Artois huffed. "*Oui*."

"And you will get us to him?"

King Louis lurched forward in a huff that rivaled his brother's, and waved his curiously tiny arm at the circle of shadows gathered around him: Lake and Caroline, Sophia and Hope, Harclay, Violet. "Yes. But we cannot take all of you. Eliason is not a fool. If he sees so many coming, he will turn up his tail and run."

"Yes, he will run," Artois added. "We will only take two."

Hope stepped forward, pressing Sophia behind him. "It's a trap, Harclay. If these two won't lead us to Eliason, to the diamond, then we'll find him ourselves."

Cousin Violet, who until that moment had been unusually quiet, stepped forward and placed a hand on Hope's shoulder.

"No. Lord Harclay and I will go with the king."

Hope made a choking noise; Sophia saw his face flush pink. "The French Blue belongs to *me*, Lady Violet. I'll be damned if I make the same mistake I did that night in the ballroom. We cannot trust Harclay; not with the diamond, and especially not with your life."

He was not the only member of their party to object: Lake said something about the earl being liable to faint, to which his lordship replied he was fine, just fine, before turning to vomit quietly at Artois' feet.

"You have my word, Hope," Violet said. "I will return the French Blue to you."

His eyes flicked to the earl. "You understand why I question your motives, Violet."

"I do." Sophia watched above the ball of Hope's shoulder as her cousin looked up at him, her blue eyes wide, serious. "But you've got to trust me. Trust us. Harclay's the one who started all this—let us, together, finish it. Lake is—well, it's obvious what he is, too big, too mean—and liable to scare Eliason witless. And you, Hope."

Violet met Sophia's eyes. "You have other matters to attend to."

Hope opened his mouth to protest. Impulsively Sophia reached out, gathering his sleeve in her fingers. She looked at him with all the calm and steadiness she could muster. Though he remained flush, she sensed his surrender to her touch, his anger, his worry fading.

With a long, rather dramatic sigh, Hope stepped back. "Very well. But make no mistake, Lady Violet. If you're not back here in half an hour with diamond in hand, I'll search for you myself and have the two of you thrown in gaol. Do I make myself clear?"

Harclay nodded, and spoke some nonsense about being the one who fooled them all, the one who stole the French Blue from under their noses at the ball.

Hope was silent as they watched the stooped outline of the earl's figure disappear into the night beside Lady Violet's. Ahead of them, the king and Artois panted rather colorful obscenities at one another.

And then they were gone, lost to the night.

Sophia and Hope, Lake and Lady Caroline had only to wait.

Thirty

Everything, *everything* Hope had ever wanted, everything he'd worked for, all that he'd done for the family he loved and missed—it all hung in the balance. What happened tonight, in the minutes and hours ahead, would determine the course of the rest of his life. His failure or success—whether he would win back the diamond or not—now rested on the outcome of his enemy's foray into the great darkness spread before them. By dawn he would either have the diamond . . . or he wouldn't.

Hope should be terrified. He should be going with them. He should be ill with anticipation, or at the very least, drowning his sorrows with the flask of whiskey he'd stuffed into his breastplate.

Instead he was staring at the lithe figure beside him, electrifying his skin with the gentle probing of her fingers.

Sophia shivered in the breeze. Without thinking, he gathered her shawl in his hands and drew it tighter about her shoulders, her hand grazing his thigh as it fell from his arm.

In his belly desire curled, heady, fully formed in the space of half a heartbeat.

Not now. He must focus, concentrate what little energy he had left on the French Blue, his plans to save Hope & Co. from the brink of failure.

And the marquess's diamond ring. Sophia wore it about her neck, and soon she'd wear it on her fourth finger, where it would leave its narrow mark on the pale, tender skin of her hand.

It was useless, this desire. That night they swore they'd

leave these inconvenient longings in his room, and in his bed. Leave behind each other.

And yet he found leaving her behind more difficult than he could have ever imagined. The desire inside him was, despite his efforts, impossible to ignore.

Sophia gasped as he pulled her closer, fisting the fine fabric of her shawl in his hands. Gasped, but did not protest.

Beside him, Lake cleared his throat, rocking back on his heels. "Well, then. Jolly good of Harclay to do the heavy lifting for us, eh? Come, let's have a nip in the hack while we wait."

Grasping Sophia's shawl in one hand, Hope reached for the flask inside his breastplate with the other, and wordlessly passed it to Mr. Lake.

Lake cleared this throat. "Well, then," he repeated. "We'll just, er, meet you . . . there. Do take your time, we have all night. Half an hour, at least."

Placing his hand on the small of Lady Caroline's back, Lake led her into the darkness. Hope heard Caroline giggle, and Lake snort with laughter, before they disappeared altogether.

Lake, in love! Hope thought he'd never see the day.

Forbidden fruit indeed.

He turned back to Sophia. He should send her after them to wait in the safety of the hack. He should not move from this spot until the Earl of Harclay returned, French Blue in hand.

He should.

But he wouldn't.

Sophia looked at him, her hazel eyes gold in the half-light of the moon. He slid his hand into the inviting curve of her jaw, his fingers brushing the baby-fine hairs of her neck. She shivered again.

He ducked his head, lips brushing her ear. "Let's go."

Hope led Sophia down the quayside, bowing in and out of shadow as they passed bawdy houses, bawdier taverns, and the dark, nameless facades of weathered warehouses. The gaping blackness of the Docklands yawned over Hope's right shoulder. He held her closer.

"D'you think they're all right?" Sophia whispered. "I trust

Harclay to keep Violet safe, but seeing as I poisoned him an hour ago . . ."

"He's recovered. They'll come back to us in no time at all. Besides. With Artois' thirty thousand in their pockets, I hardly think this Eliason fellow will refuse them."

Even as he said the words, Hope winced. Though the Docklands were mostly deserted, the devil knew what characters trolled about this time of night: pickpockets, cutthroats, lightskirts. King Louis' beringed fingers and Artois' gilt costume certainly did their party no favors.

If Sophia saw Hope wince, she said nothing.

"Ah, here we are."

He drew up before a whitewashed warehouse, its facade covered in bold, black letters: HOPE & CO.

"Here? Really?" Sophia wrinkled her nose.

"No," Hope said, pointing toward the river. "There."

Her gaze followed his outstretched arm to the bulkhead at their right; a sturdy ramp led from the quayside down to the water, where a dozen gleaming, full-rigged ships bobbed silently in their berths.

He felt her stiffen. "Those are yours?"

Thomas scoffed. "Depends on the outcome of tonight's events. They may be heading for the auction block first thing in the morning, so I figure we may as well enjoy them while we have the chance."

He looked down and met her eyes. They were open, storm-tossed, moving from his gaze to his lips and back again.

"Please," he said. "Please, Sophia, come with me."

His heart drummed an erratic rhythm in his chest as he waited for her reply.

"Thomas, we shouldn't. I cannot—" She swallowed, hard, and looked down at their clasped hands. "I promised myself I wouldn't. I've made every attempt to keep my distance, I have, but I—"

"But you can't." The words came out in a rush of relief. "Neither can I, Sophia. I cannot keep away from you."

She looked at him, pleading. "We shouldn't."

"If you tell me to stop," he said, sliding his hand up her arm to rest on her neck, "I'll stop."

"Please." Her voice was barely above a whisper. "Please don't ask that of me, Thomas."

"Tell me," he pressed a kiss to the place where ear met jaw, "to stop."

He trailed his lips along the slope of her neck, breathing in her scent: water, soap, air. Each kiss was soft, lingering, sweet. It was madness, this embrace; it went against every rational thought, everything he could and should be doing.

But once his lips touched her skin he couldn't help himself.

Sophia arched against him, head lilting back in offering. "Thomas," she breathed. "Oh, Thomas."

"Do you want me"—another kiss—"to stop?"

She met his gaze with heavy-lidded eyes. "No. No, don't stop."

"Good," he said, pulling back. "Come with me. We shall have to be quick; half an hour, remember."

One side of her mouth curled into a grin. "Let's not waste a moment, then."

He tugged her down the ramp to the water; she let out a breathless laugh. Their bodies collided at the sway of the dock beneath their feet; Hope caught Sophia and held her against him. She looked up, lips half-open; her shawl fell, revealing the ball of her bare shoulder.

Hope took a deep breath, let it out. The river sighed with him, the dock rolling beneath them: raising them up as a wave crested, sending them down as it ebbed.

Planting his feet on either side of Sophia's, Hope bent his neck and gently pressed his lips to her shoulder. She tasted clean.

Sophia sucked in a breath, her body rising to meet his caress. He wasted no time; he moved his mouth along the ridge of her collarbone, nipping the tender flesh at the base of her throat. Beneath his lips her pulse took flight, an insistent fluttering like the wings of a bird.

His desire flared, filling every fiber, every thought and every space of his being. If he wasn't careful he'd take her here, now, against the bulkhead, hard and fast and rough. Not at all what he wanted for her; not at all what he wanted for this, their last night together. Even if they only had twenty minutes to themselves, he wouldn't take her like that.

He prayed the others—Hope and Violet, most of all—didn't come back, catch him and Sophia. He prayed they took the full half an hour he'd given them.

"Thomas," Sophia repeated. "Please. *Don't stop.*"

Above them loomed one of Hope's triple-masted merchant ships. From a cursory glance, Hope gathered it was vacant; the windows in the aft cabin were dark.

Or at least he hoped it was. Somehow he very much doubted Sophia would yield to his touch while a dozen toothless sailors looked on.

There was no ramp of which to speak, only a series of slatted indentions carved into the side of the vessel.

Hope pulled away. Sophia's pretty features creased in confusion. Pressing a kiss between her brows, he murmured, "Not here. Follow me."

Together they made for the ship. Nestling Sophia in the circle of his arms, he climbed up the ladder one rung behind her; he winced as the curve of her backside brushed far too invitingly against the bulge in his breeches. Again his desire flared, burning a hole in whatever logic he had left; whatever worry he had over being caught.

That Sophia was here with him; that she would again be his, after he thought he'd never get a second chance—his chest welled with gratitude.

She heaved herself over the banister onto the ship. She turned, wiping her palms together in satisfaction, and held out a hand; Hope took it, her grip firm as she helped him onboard.

He leaned back against the banister, catching his breath. Sophia placed her elbows on the railing beside him, her arm brushing his. He listened to her quiet panting; they did not meet eyes, but he sensed her every movement, the curling of her hair about her head in the breeze.

The ship undulated slowly beneath his feet, the river plunking against its bow some feet below. As far as Hope could tell, the ship was deserted. The deck had been recently swept, and appeared to be vacant of any cargo, empty save for a coil of rope and a pile of carefully folded canvas tarpaulins.

Relief washed through him. Catching his breath, he turned around and placed his elbows on the banister beside Sophia's. The River Thames stretched out before them, the moon setting alight a wide blue ribbon of radiance on the water's surface; the city glowed dimly at its banks.

How many pairs of eyes, he wondered, had filled hearts to bursting at this very sight. A hundred, a thousand years ago, had the Romans looked upon the Thames in the dead of night and found in its quiet, insistent rush, the glow of the moon upon its surface, solace or sorrow? How many hearts were broken in this place, how many healed? Generations of love lost, love thwarted, love quiet and dangerous; so many stories begun and ended here, at the edge of the River Thames.

Hope turned to find Sophia looking at him, her eyes soft about the edges. He wondered what she was thinking, if she felt her own heart, full and swollen, beginning to crack.

"Are you all right?" His voice was quiet.

Sophia reached out and tucked an errant curl behind his ear. "No. Not in the slightest."

He rose to his feet, running his palms up the length of her arms as he turned her to him. "Good." He tucked his hand against her cheek as he leaned in. "Neither am I."

His lips found hers, full and warm and yielding. She tilted her head to better match his movements, her arms rising to circle his neck as together they fell into the kiss. He slipped his tongue between her lips; she let him in, moaning as he pulled back, taking her bottom lip between his teeth.

He cupped her face in his hands and pressed his mouth to hers, harder this time. He felt her body rising to meet him, running her tongue along the slick seam of his lips. His blood ignited as she dug her fingers into the hair at his neck, his cock pulsing between his legs, painfully enormous.

Hope ducked, deepening the kiss. Her tongue was warm and deliciously wet tangled with his; her eyelashes fluttered against his cheek, featherlight. Her hands were on his face now, pulling him closer, closer, as if she might swallow him whole.

Please, he prayed silently. *Please.*

The breeze moved around them, tickling the hair on Hope's bare arms. He wrapped them around her, trailing his hands from her face down the slope of her back to rest on the rise of her buttocks. Her pert flesh yielded to the press of his palms; she gasped into his mouth and he nipped at her lip, a low growl in her throat as she bit back. He tasted blood and grinned; she was wicked, more rascal and seducer than painfully proper debutante.

Sophia began to attack the straps of his breastplate with her fingers; his body went up in flames at her impatience. He covered her hand in his and loosened the strap, breaking their kiss to quickly shrug out of the costume. Dropping it with a *thud* at her feet, he darted forward and crushed his mouth against hers. The tips of her hardened nipples pressed against the thin fabric of his tunic as the kiss became messy, urgent.

The pressure between his legs became too great to bear. He needed her here, now, before he was obliterated by the weight of his desire.

Hope pulled away, and as he stood to catch his breath, Sophia tucked her head into the curve of his neck.

His heart swelled against his ribcage as if it might expand through sinew and bone to meet her caress. It killed him, the tenderness of her gesture. How vulnerable she felt in his arms; and he—he was defenseless, holding her to his heart, the both of them knowing all the while that in the end they would betray one another.

He lowered his lips to the top of her head and left them there as he led her across the deck. With the toe of his ridiculous gladiator-style sandal, he coaxed the tarpaulin to unfold into a nestlike circle and guided Sophia to its edge. She was breathing hard; even in the darkness he could make out the luscious curve of her swollen lips, the prick of her nipples against the gauzy fabric of her costume.

Hope swallowed, gritting his teeth at the anticipation that coursed through him. He grasped the edges of his tunic and made to pull it off; in his haste it got stuck on his head, and no matter how he tugged, he couldn't untangle himself.

Sophia laughed softly; he felt her hands on his tunic, gently removing his hands from the fabric before pulling it over his head.

"Thank God," Hope breathed. He shook out his curls, wiping them back from his forehead, and lowered his gaze to see Sophia staring openmouthed at his naked chest. He felt himself harden even further—really, how was that even *possible*?—as her eyes traveled to the front of his drawers.

He made to cover himself with his hands, lest he frighten her away, but Sophia snatched his wrist.

"No," she said. She stepped forward and slipped her first finger into the waistband of his drawers. "Let me, Thomas."

Before he could stop her, Sophia dropped to her knees, digging the fingers of both hands into the waistband. With her thumbs she caressed the jutting points of his hip bones, slowly, *oh God*, so very slowly pulling down his drawers.

She coaxed them over the bulge; his cock pounced free, the drawers dropping silently to his feet. For a moment she drew back, her eyes widening as she took in his length, the enormity of his desire for her.

"Really, Sophia, you don't have—"

"Shh." Splaying her palms over the hardened flesh just above his groin, she drew up on her knees. "I *want* to."

He thought he might scream at the feel of her hands scraping down, down, *down* the length of his groin. She encircled the root of his cock in one hand, the shaft in the other; and then she was bending forward, pressing her lips to the head, kissing him as she looked up, curiosity sparking in those wicked, *wicked* eyes of hers.

He let out a long, slow hiss, drawing his thumb across her forehead.

"You feel so lovely," he breathed. "So goddamn lovely, Sophia."

Sophia did not hesitate, sliding open her lips instead, slick with the first show of his seed. Carefully, very carefully, she took his head into her mouth, one engorged inch at a time.

Hope sucked in a breath at the feel of her tongue on the very tip of his manhood, languorously, slowly caressing him. He watched as her lips stretched to accept him, digging a hand into her hair. He saw God, he saw stars, he had to hold on, she was so lovely, so beautiful, he wanted to remember every moment, every caress . . .

Her mouth felt hot and gloriously wet against him, tightening as she began to move, taking him deeper and deeper. He covered her hand at his root with his own, tightening her grip on his shaft, and together they moved, an easy, back-and-forth motion that had him growling with pleasure.

Sophia's rhythm increased, her eyes fluttered shut; he

watched as she lost herself in him, her toga slipping from her shoulder. That *shoulder.* There was something distinctly erotic about her bare shoulder, the way her skin glistened in the gray-blue light of the moon.

He felt himself coiling with pleasure inside her mouth, the familiar tightening almost unbearable as he watched himself disappear past the silken caress of her lips. He was tugging at her hair now, the braids wound about her head falling free under the ministrations of his fingers.

Wave after wave of sensation washed through him, each more potent than the last. She was here, she was *his*, for a little while, anyway, and she was giving herself to him without reservation, without regret. Again his heart swelled. How he ached for her; how he would ache after all was said and done, when he belonged to the bank and she, to another.

He bit his lip, the stirrings of his climax becoming more insistent with each stroke of Sophia's tongue. He cupped her face in his hand, her eyes flying open as he guided himself out of her mouth.

His eyes on hers, he sank to his knees before her. His blood jumped at her heavy-lidded gaze, her swollen lips parted to reveal the tiniest sliver of white teeth. She looked beautiful. She looked . . . aroused.

He kissed her lips; he could taste the tanginess of his body in her mouth and on her tongue.

That tongue. He caressed it with his own, great, sloping circles that had her moaning into his mouth. She arched against him, wild with need; he felt the insistent press of her hips against his cock.

Hope released her lips, trailing his own down to her shoulder. His fingers brushing her skin, he coaxed the toga off her arm and down her chest, his hands on her breasts as they surged free above the bodice of her toga. For a moment he held their heaviness in his hands, pressing his fingers into the silken skin; her nipples pleaded against the center of his palms.

"Thomas," she whispered. "Please."

He slid his left hand to the back of her neck and gently led her down onto the tarpaulin, leaning on his elbow above her as he rolled her nipple between his thumb and forefinger. They landed softly on the deck, the tarpaulin sighing around them in the breeze.

Sophia arched against him, moaning softly into the darkness. She was clawing his chest with her fingertips, her nipples brushing against his skin as he brought his mouth down on hers. The kiss was savage and hard, mindless as they lost themselves to their pleasure.

He reached down, drawing up the skirts of her toga. He parted her legs and found the slit between her drawers; his fingers first encountered the curls of her sex, silken and slick.

And then.

And *then*.

Hope groaned, his desire spiking. She was very wet, her flesh swollen with need; she gasped as his fingers grazed the apex of her sex, the nub engorged and hard.

His cock throbbed against her leg; his blood was screaming.

He bolted upright, grabbing Sophia by the waist and settling her on her knees above him, her hair swirling around them in the breeze. Her legs were spread just above the tip of his hardened prick, so aroused, the anticipation so great it hurt.

"Thomas," she was breathing, her fingers finding purchase on his naked shoulders. He placed his hands on her thighs and squeezed her flesh.

"It's all right," he whispered in her ear, his lips catching on the sloped ridge of her jaw. She tasted of sweat, salt. *"I want you, Sophia. Let me have you."*

He took his cock in his hand and held it upright. With his other hand he coaxed her legs wider, guiding her down.

She reached down and covered his hand with her own, nestling the tip of his cock into the cleftlike opening of her lips. He cursed aloud, pressing his forehead against hers as they fought for the air between them.

Slowly, with excruciating tenderness, she sank onto his length. She felt exquisitely tight, stretching to take in the enormity of his desire. She sucked a breath through her teeth, but before he could ask if she was in pain she threw back her head and thrust downward, swallowing him to the hilt.

For a moment they sat motionless; he didn't want to hurt her, didn't want to ruin these last moments together, and so he waited to take her lead. When at last she brought her head up to look at him, her eyes were dark and wet. He saw a bit of pain there, pain that quickly faded to wild desire.

"Are you all right?" he asked, breathless.

Sophia dug her hands into the hair at his neck and rested her forehead against his. "Never all right. Never, never. Please, Thomas, don't stop."

Hope slid his hands up her thighs and placed them on her hips. He gently coaxed them up and down, up and down, small motions at first that had him gritting his teeth to keep from climaxing then and there.

With his thumb he brushed the engorged space at the tip of her sex, now spread wide to accommodate his girth. As if he'd lit her body on fire, Sophia began to move on her own, rocking her hips against him.

He saw stars as he slid in and out, *in* and out of her slick warmth. His heart was beating so hard, felt so big in his chest, he thought he might explode. He dug his hand into her hair, fingering her loose curls down the length of her back.

Sophia arched against him, her head falling back as she bared her body to the night. Her breasts moved in time to her hips, and he bent his head to catch a pink nipple between his teeth. She moaned; he pulled back and swallowed.

Heavens, but she was beautiful. The way her skin shone beneath the light of the moon, the abandon in her dark eyes; her hair and her passion and the musky scent of her desire. He wanted her, he wanted her more than he'd ever wanted anything. He wanted her now and he wanted her after, he wanted her tomorrow, next week, next year.

Hope wanted her with him always.

His throat tightened. It was all too much; he couldn't breathe against the force of his emotion, the force of his body as Sophia swallowed him whole.

Hope was no fool. She was not his, never had been his. All he had was this moment, and their joined flesh. The exquisite sensations thrumming through him.

He felt her tightening around him, the first signs of her release. His pulse drummed in his ears. The tarpaulin fluttered in the breeze beneath their bodies.

He closed his eyes, willing her rising pleasure to blot out his grief.

Thirty-one

Head thrown back, Sophia gazed at the night sky above through the heavy-lidded haze of her desire. She felt so full, so completely lost in Thomas and the rising beat between her legs, she imagined herself bursting into a white-hot spatter of stars, the force of her climax banishing her to the far reaches of the blue-velvet sky.

His hand was at her neck, pulling him toward her. She smelled his desire, sweat mingled with sandalwood, lemons. She tugged at his hair with her fingers, her hips rolling of their own volition over and through and with him.

Thomas was so large with desire it had hurt at first to take him inside her; even now her pleasure was tinged with pain, each stroke a lesson in patience. But with this thumb working her sex where their bodies joined, the pain only increased her desire.

And now he was trailing his lips down her throat, skipping to her shoulder before taking her nipple in his mouth. He ran his tongue over its hardened tip, scraping it with his teeth, *oh God, oh my God, I can't, I can't wait much—*

Pleasure, blinding, complete, ripped through her, her legs bucking against the hardened plane of Hope's thighs. Sophia cried out, and cried out again, her blood rushing through her in a frenzied explosion of poignant sensation. Her limbs pulsed, painfully rigid against the force of her climax.

Vaguely she sensed herself pulsing around the length of Thomas inside her. He bit back a cry, as if she'd hurt him; and then he was lifting her off of him, his movements quick but gentle as he withdrew. She watched as he covered his manhood with both hands. He winced, face screwed tight with pain as he was overcome by his completion.

His seed pulsed through his fingers; she felt its warmth on the exposed flesh of her thigh.

"I'm sorry," Thomas whispered, wiping it away with the edge of the tarpaulin. He was breathing hard, his massive chest rising and falling rapidly, the dark, curly hair sprinkled across its expanse tickling the tips of her breasts.

Sophia let out a breath, her heart suddenly heavy in her chest. She reached out, brushing a curl from his temple before taking his chin between her fingers.

"Look at me, Thomas."

He looked at her from under his dark lashes. She saw her own pain reflected in the translucent depths of his blue eyes. Already she felt her desire rising again, her body's thirst for him only heightened by their coming together. She'd never known pleasure and happiness like she had with Thomas inside and around and with her. The completeness of it, the sheer expanse of it was terrifying. With his arms wrapped around her and his mouth on hers, she succumbed to who she was, whom she wanted. The worries of the world, the marquess and her family's falling fortunes, dissipated into the evening breeze. In those moments there was nothing and no one but she and Thomas and the love they shared between them.

Love.

Sophia blinked at the jagged pain that sliced through her chest; her eyes pricked with tears.

"Thomas, I—"

"Don't." He held a finger to her lips. "Please, don't."

And then he was taking her in his arms again, pulling the tarpaulin over them as he lay atop her. The canvas rippled above their heads in the breeze, blocking out the night sky.

Sophia stretched out her legs, stiff from exertion, as Thomas pulled her body against his. He pressed a kiss into her cheek, her chin, her forehead; he pried her lips open with his own, a depthless kiss, a desperate kiss, as if he knew it would be their last.

She melted beneath the weight of his body, the fleshy warmth of it. She closed her eyes and ran her palms over his shoulders down to his chest, memorizing every inch of his skin, every muscle and curlicue of hair. A tear escaped from the corner of her closed eye, trailing into her hair.

Sophia broke the kiss, pressing her cheek against Hope's as he wound his arms about her.

"I love you, Thomas," she whispered.

Thomas started, drawing back to look in her eyes. His were wide and full, gleaming as if they might be wet. His eyes, they were so beautiful; so beautiful it made her ache.

He parted his lips, swollen from kissing her.

"Fire!"

The cry rent the silent night air, a strangled thing that echoed through the endless expanse of the Docklands. Hope's eyes widened; he threw back the canvas and sniffed the air. Sophia inhaled, the crisp odor of burning wood invading her nostrils; above Hope's head she saw the dim outline of smoke curling into the night sky.

Thomas snapped upright and was already shrugging into that ridiculous tunic of his.

"Bring water, quick! Fire!"

Sophia's heart turned over in her chest. If the night's previous mishaps were any indication, then this fire had everything, *everything* to do with their plot; she could only pray that Cousin Violet and the earl were far from it, though her every sense told her otherwise.

With trembling fingers, she tried to set her costume to rights, dropping the sleeve of her toga once, twice, damning it to hell on the third try.

Thomas reached over and tugged the sleeve back into place; Sophia barely managed to tuck her breasts into her bodice before Hope was lifting her to her feet. Together they scanned the horizon, the smoke growing thicker now.

"There." Sophia pointed to an ember of color at the far edge of the void. Plumes of smoke rose to meet the sky; the back of her throat burned just looking at it. She could discern the dim outline of a ship, the tall shadows of its masts strangely angled, as if they were tilting into the water.

Thomas met her eyes.

They didn't have much time.

Scrambling down the makeshift ladder, Sophia leapt into Hope's outstretched arms. He caught her effortlessly, his thick arms holding her close for one breathless moment before he set her on her feet.

They took off at a sprint, Sophia working double to keep up with Thomas's enormous stride. She followed the outline of his shoulders through the maze of the Docklands, both of them slowing as their lungs filled with smoke.

For what felt like the hundredth time that night, Sophia panicked. She could hardly see on account of the darkness, and as the smoke thickened she worried she would be lost, and would never get to Violet, and Violet would be caught on a burning ship with no one but that bounder the earl to save her.

"Are we," she coughed, "getting close?"

"Yes!" Thomas called over his shoulder. Seeing her distress, he slowed his pace and wrapped an arm about her shoulders. "Stay close, Sophia. I don't want to lose you."

Shouts rang out around them; the crackle and snap of burning wood filled the summer air, the once-cool breeze now humid with sweat and smoke. Sophia struggled to breathe, her eyes watering as the haze surrounded them. It was too painful to keep them open, and she stumbled blindly at Hope's side, leaning further and further against him the more her lungs burned.

"Sophia." Hope drew to a stop. Choking, he took her hands in his face. "Open your eyes. Are you all right?"

"I can't," she panted. The smoke was suffocating; she felt faint. "Leave. I won't leave Violet."

"No." Despite the thickness of the air, his reply was savage, sure. "I'm taking. You back."

"You can't. Leave the diamond. And what. Of Violet!"

Sophia stumbled back as something—someone—ran headfirst into her chest, knocking what little wind was left from her lungs. She let out a strangled cry; an eerily similar cry rang out at her feet.

Violet. "Violet!"

A stroke of implausible luck at last.

Sophia bent and helped her cousin to her feet, doing her best to wave the smoke from Violet's face as she coughed and sputtered.

Thomas was at her side in a moment, wrapping an arm about Violet's waist as she swayed dangerously close to the edge of the dock. "Are you. All right?"

Violet met Sophia's eyes through the increasingly opaque haze. "We've got. To go." She waved a limp arm in the direction of—well, Sophia frankly couldn't tell up from down, left from right, so Lord knew where Violet was pointing—but she knew it was *away* from the French Blue.

Sophia looked at Hope. "But the. Diamond," she panted.

Violet was shaking her head. "No, no. The ship. Is in flames. And sinking. With William—"

She collapsed against Hope, head lolling on the broad expanse of his shoulder. Violet, who only abhorred swooning ladies more than swooning itself, had *actually swooned*.

Sophia's panic returned full force. This was serious. More so because Cousin Violet had referred to the Earl of Harclay by his given name, a name even his sister Lady Caroline did not use in public.

Really, what the *devil* had happened in the hour since they parted company on the quayside?

Sophia moved to help Mr. Hope carry Cousin Violet, but he waved her away, scooping her into his arms instead.

"But the. Diamond," Sophia said again.

Thomas shook his head. "Later. Let's. Go."

They retraced their steps along the dock, Sophia keeping her eyes trained on Hope's bare heels lest she lose him in the thickening smoke. She could tell by his sagging shoulders that he was exhausted, but he trudged forward, their pace slowing to a mere crawl by the time they miraculously reached the quay. Sophia's eyes blurred even further with tears of gratitude. Only a few more feet, a few more steps, and then they could collapse into the hack, and after that it was only a few miles to home, to bed . . .

"The hacks." Hope's head snapped left, snapped right. "They're gone."

The breath left Sophia's body as she took in the empty lane before them. She dashed about in the darkness, peering past the warehouses into alleys and hidden alcoves. Nothing. She glanced over her shoulder; the burning ship was now fully visible, the flames licking the top of its mainmast as smoke billowed into the sky, obscuring the moon and stars. Somewhere in the darkness she heard the wailing of a siren; the fire brigade was on its way.

Behind Sophia, Hope cursed none too gently in a language Sophia was grateful she didn't quite understand. Something about pigs, and Mr. Lake's—was that *bones* or *stones*?

"Wait here," she whispered, trolling further into the darkness.

"Don't you dare move, Sophia, it's not safe. Anyone could be about, what with those ruffians the king and Artois at large . . ."

Sophia ducked through an oiled canvas door that hung between two weathered clapboard buildings, finding herself in a dim, damp alley. Wading into the darkness, Sophia held her hands out before her.

Was that a muffled giggle? A beat later she heard a noise that sounded suspiciously like a man's playful growl of pleasure.

"Hello?" she called out weakly, coughing. "I don't want to, er, interrupt . . . whichever activity in which you are engaged . . . but I'm looking for my friends, you see . . ."

Sophia's outstretched hands encountered a hard, smooth surface, and a moment later the looming shadow of a hack came into view.

"Oh. Oh, thank God." Sophia went to open the door. "Mr. Lake, I—*Mr. Lake*!"

He tugged his buckskins over his bare behind, clamoring to the edge of the bench inside the hack. His hair, usually clubbed back in an immaculate queue, was disheveled, sticking straight up around his head like a halo; though he shrugged into his coat, Sophia could see the smooth skin of a well-muscled chest peeking through the lapels.

"I'm sorry to, er, disturb you, but we need to go. Violet is ill—"

Lady Caroline glanced over the slope of Lake's enormous shoulder. Her hair looked even worse for the wear than her paramour's. "Is she all right?"

"Yes, I'll explain everything, but we *need* to *go,* now."

"Right-ho." Lake held out his hand, sniffing the air. "I say, what's that dreadful smell?"

By the time they reached Thomas and Cousin Violet, Lady Caroline was hopelessly tangled in her toga after Sophia's attempts to get her dressed; across from the cacophony of the makeshift dressing room, Lake fumed silently, his forehead gleaming with perspiration in the light of a passing lantern.

"Where the devil did you go?" Hope spat, handing Violet's limp body inside the hack. "What if we'd been tailed, and attacked on the quay? Don't tell me—" Hope's eyes slid from Caroline to Lake and back again, narrowing with suspicion. "Never mind. I don't want to know."

Hope squeezed onto the bench beside Lake, called for the driver to keep moving. "No word of the diamond?"

Thomas shook his head. "The ship will sink, if it hasn't already. Violet told us virtually nothing; for all we know, Artois could've run off with the diamond before the fire started, or that Eliason chap could've jumped ship with it in his pocket. The French Blue could be anywhere by now."

Lake pounded the wall with his ham-sized fist, and called for the driver to make haste. "Bloody perfect. We came so close. So *bloody close*."

An enormous crack, round and deep as thunder, reverberated through the vehicle, the horses screaming as the cobblestones shook beneath their hooves.

Hope flung out his arm, pinning Sophia to her seat; in her lap, Violet's head lolled openmouthed, limp. The hack drew to a sudden, violent stop, and in a flurry of movement Lake was leaping from the hack, his voice hoarse as he called to the driver.

What the devil? What happened? What the devil was that?

Sophia shook in her seat at the driver's reply as the acrid odors of smoke and splintered wood filled the hack.

"Can' rightly say, sir, but all ov a sudden I seen a big explosion like, out there in th' river."

She looked down at Violet, smoothing the hair from her face, and blinked at the unexpected prick of tears. The ship on which Cousin Violet and the earl had hoped to reclaim the French Blue was sunk, or, at the very least, had erupted into a ball of fiery flames.

Sophia reached across the bench and took Lady Caroline's hand. Her brother was on that ship, as was Sophia's family's fortune, their future, too. The dowager duchess sat still as a statue, her long, swanlike neck bent toward the window. Lake and Hope stood outside, hands on their hips, their heads turned toward the black pit of the Docklands.

Sophia wanted to offer Caroline words of comfort, declare

her brother was, surely, far too wily to be caught flat-footed on an exploding ship. But in her mouth her tongue felt thick and dry as ash. There would be no comfort for Caroline, not until she knew her brother the earl was in one piece, and in her arms.

And so Sophia merely squeezed her hand. How many times Violet had done the same for Sophia before stepping into Almack's, or a wedding breakfast attended by far too many eligible dukes, she could not count; but the small gesture had always calmed Sophia's nerves. An unspoken promise of support, a pledge to gossip shamelessly about said dukes' foibles and follies when the breakfast was done; it was hope and faith when Sophia needed it most.

Lady Caroline squeezed back. *Thank you.*

Sophia watched out the window as Hope pressed a handful of guineas into the driver's palm; a moment later he was at the door of the hack, his blue eyes hard.

"I've given the driver instructions to take you home," Hope held up a hand as Sophia leaned forward to protest, "under pain of death. Lake and I will see to things here. Go home, Sophia, and take care of your cousin. If—*when. When* Harclay returns, he will come to the house for Violet. You'll do that for me, won't you, Sophia? Keep watch?"

Sophia bit her lip. He was right, of course. Thomas was *always* right.

But as she was *always* wont to do, Sophia longed to stay. And though she usually longed to stay for the promise of adventure and port, tonight she wished to say for an altogether different reason.

She wanted to stay with *him*. Her heart ached with it, with the knowledge that this would be their last night together, before they won or they lost and went their separate ways. It would end here, tonight. And she didn't want to let him go.

"Sophia." Thomas's voice was soft now, his eyes, too. "You must do this."

Falling back against the seat, Sophia swallowed the lump in her throat. "Yes. I'll do it."

"Thank you."

A beat of silence passed as their eyes met. Behind Hope, Sophia was vaguely aware of Lake's rather vile curses, something about bloody time and not having bloody enough of it.

But Thomas, all but oblivious, leaned into the hackney, opening his mouth as if he might speak.

Sophia, too, was leaning forward in rising anticipation. Would he confess undying love? Pledge his heart and soul to her honor? Say he could not bear to be away from her for more than a moment, reach for her and fling her over his shoulder and begin their grandest, most daring adventure yet?

Instead Thomas fell away, looking over his shoulder to shout, "All right, you cranky old goat, I'm *coming*!", before meeting Sophia's gaze one last time.

Sophia's belly turned over, and turned over again, at the smoldering desire burning his eyes a darker shade of blue.

With a stiff bow he closed the door, banging his fist against the side of the hack to signal the driver.

The horses jerked into motion. In Sophia's lap, Violet moaned; Lady Caroline bumped and jolted in silence beside her.

And then Thomas was gone.

Thirty-two

Two weeks later
The Residence of the Marquess of Withington
St. James's Square

Sophia toyed with the thin strand of matching yellow diamonds that snaked about her wrist. The bracelet was lovely, understated yet glamorous, and of the latest fashion; yellow diamonds were, it seemed, all the rage this season. Considering feathered turbans and a ghastly shade of puce were also a la mode, Sophia had good reason to be wary of such a gift; but it *was* a gift, and from a marquess at that.

Even so, Sophia could not summon the gasps of gratitude and virgin blush with which any debutante worth her salt would accept such a gift. She was no virgin—a fact that, conversely, *did* made her blush—but more importantly, the diamonds, *of course*, made her think of Hope.

Mr. Hope, and the extravagant diamond they together filched from the Princess of Wales. Sophia remembered the silence that settled over Caroline's puce-painted drawing room (really, that dreadful color was *everywhere*!) as Her Royal Highness opened the lacquered box. She remembered the way the French Blue glittered in its puddle of white silk velvet, its watery transparency taking captive Sophia's imagination.

She remembered being afraid to touch it; foolishly she believed it cursed, the apple in the Garden of Eden. Surely something so beautiful, so transcendently indulgent, was not meant to be plied by mere mortals. She wondered at its story, the first stirrings of a tale coming to life as she'd looked upon it, Hope at her side.

And his history! How they'd laughed that night in his study. An adventure to end all adventures, surely, if not a bit overzealous in its style and sense of doom.

"Sophia, my dear." Withington flushed pink, twitching nervously on the settee beside her. "May I call you 'my dear'?"

Sophia swallowed. "Of course you may."

He jerked his head to the side, brow furrowed as he looked at her. "Do you not like it? We might bring it back to Rundell and Bridge, if you'd like, and exchange it for something better suited to your tastes?"

Sophia looked up from the bracelet, and tried again to swallow the tightness in her throat. Here was a marquess, offering a diamond bracelet to match the diamond *ring* he'd given her. Very earnest, very expensive tokens of his affection.

Here, sitting anxiously with his hands on his knees, was exactly the sort of man, offering exactly the sort of match, for which mere months ago she would've sold her soul.

Sophia stiffened her spine, and tried to ignore the throb of pain in her chest. *Remember who you are. Remember what you want, all that you've fought for.*

"It's lovely," she said, extending her arm. "Would you put it on?"

Withington brushed the sliver of exposed skin at her wrist as he took the tiny gold clasp in his fingers. After several failed attempts, he slid the clasp into place and pulled away with a sudden jerk, as if she'd burned him. His blush went from pink to purple, rising from his clean-shaven neck up to his cheeks and, impossibly, to his forehead.

"I'm . . . er, terribly sorry, Sophia."

She wiggled her arm so that the bracelet caught a beam of late afternoon sunlight, blinding them both as the diamonds flashed and winked, throwing a spray of translucent shadows about the walls. "You've nothing to be sorry for. They're beautiful, Withington. A beautiful gift."

From the far corner of the drawing room, Lady Blaise exclaimed her pleasure, the dowager marchioness cooing a reply. Withington glanced over his shoulder as if to admonish his mother, and Sophia watched with a smile as the ladies returned to their tea with suspect scrupulousness, Lady Blaise going so far as to compliment the biscuits around a mouthful of said confection.

Withington let out a long sigh, turning back and smiling at Sophia with a roll of his dark eyes. "Shameless, aren't they?"

"Terribly. I've had your cook's biscuits, and I mean no offense when I say they are anything *but* deliriously delicious. My mother, you see—she has a flair for the dramatic."

"*Your* mother? Your mother's a warm, fuzzy puppy compared to my own."

Sophia's grin deepened. "I sympathize, I do."

A beat of silence stretched between them as the marquess's gaze wandered to the base of her throat, where his diamond ring rested in the small cleft between her collarbones.

"I thought I might take a page from my mother's book and be a bit shameless myself." He looked down at his hands, clenched over the balls of his knees. "I was hoping the bracelet might convince you to wear my ring on your finger at last. They will look better together, after all."

Sophia's heart turned over. By now Withington's face was the color of an eggplant.

His willingness to bare his heart to her, to be honest and kind and good, was lovely, and more than a little endearing. So much so the lump in Sophia's throat grew until it was large as the moon, her heart in her chest so swollen with affection for this new companion she could hardly breathe; with affection, and a special kind of self-loathing that she would drag *his* heart, as honest and kind and good as it was, through the mud of her own indecision.

Withington deserved better than a woman who loved another. She wanted more for him; she wanted him to know the wild, senseless love she knew for Thomas. Withington deserved to be the *one*. He deserved to love fully, and *be* loved fully in return.

He deserved better than what Sophia had to offer him.

Even now, with her family on the brink of bankruptcy—the diamond was still missing, as was the Earl of Harclay and his butler, Mr. Avery—even as Violet quietly dismissed their household servants and sold off their possessions; even as she debated putting the house up for auction; even then, Sophia could not deceive her admirer the marquess.

Not like this. Not with his pride, his future, his heart in the balance.

She brought her fingers to her neck, tangling them in the fine gold chain. With a gentle tug she pulled it from her throat, folding the ring in the palm of her hand.

The marquess, brow furrowed, watched Sophia reach for his wrist, pulling out his hand. She unfurled her fingers and dropped the ring into his palm, curling his fingers around it. As the chain wrinkled into his grasp, Sophia felt her heart gasp for air as the great weight of her indecision was lifted from it.

She was nameless and even poorer than when the season began some months ago.

She'd never felt more free, more sure, or more frightened than she did at this moment.

"But." Withington's eyes flicked from his hand to Sophia and back again. "I don't understand."

Sophia held his fist in the cradle of her hand. She leaned forward, ignoring her mother's pointed look of warning over the slope of Withington's shoulder. "You honor me with your proposal, Withington, and your friendship. I hold you dear in my heart. I adore that you love port. I adore your easy laugh and the kindness you show your family. I adore our conversation and your good nature. I adore you, but—"

"But," he repeated.

"But," she said thickly, "not like you deserve to be adored. Whomever's heart you capture—it won't be long for you—she will love you as you should be loved, and you will understand me then."

Withington scoffed, meeting her eyes. "But I want you."

Sophia's face pulsed with heat. She blinked at the sting of tears. "One day, very soon, you'll be glad it *wasn't* me. It was a close scrape, our courtship. A scrape with disaster, unhappiness. You must believe I am saving you from these things."

For a moment Withington was very still. At last he began to nod slowly, his shoulders sagging. Behind him, the matrons gave up all pretense of tea and conversation *about* tea, and were watching Withington and Sophia with naked interest.

"Sophia. Sophia!" Lady Blaise's voice rose with panic. "Is

everything all right? I hate to see his lordship distressed thus—"

Withington turned abruptly and offered a tight smile over his shoulder. "Quite all right, Lady Blaise, *thank* you."

Sophia's mother flushed and turned back to the dowager marchioness, applying herself with great care to her teacup.

"Hardly fair, that my mother listens to you," Sophia whispered. "Tell me, how do you manage it? Witchcraft? Deals with the devil?"

The marquess's smile loosened. "I would gladly trade my soul if it meant mother dearest kept her pretty nose out of my affairs. Alas, I do not think my soul would prove sufficient payment. It *is* a lot to ask."

Together they scoffed; and then that terrible silence again. Withington's fingers flexed and unfolded around the ring in his hand.

"My only wish is that you find happiness, Sophia." Withington kept his voice low. "If I am not the man with whom you find it, so be it. As long as you are content—that is all that matters to me."

For a moment, Sophia was speechless. He was a good man, Withington, and a better friend.

Friend. Sophia wanted to laugh at the absurdity of it. No self-respecting debutante made *friends* with the season's most eligible bachelor; it was akin to the spider befriending the fly before ensnaring him in her web and eating him for supper. Women and men were not *friends.*

Not in England, anyway.

But here they were, Sophia and the marquess, laughing mean-spiritedly at their mamas, confessing wishes for each other's happiness, reminiscing over their shared love of port.

It was enough to make a girl cry.

And that's exactly what Sophia did.

"Thank you." She grasped his hand and squeezed. "I wish the same for you, Withington. And I have no doubt you will find great happiness. I can think of at least a dozen debutantes who would gladly consider—"

Withington held up a hand and laughed. "Please, for the love of God, spare me! There's a reason I chose you, Sophia. A reason I chose you above all the others."

He made to rise, jerking to his feet, but Sophia pulled him by his sleeve back onto the settee. "If I may be so bold—why *did* you pick me?"

Withington sighed, running a hand through his close-cropped hair as his blush crept back up his neck. "It's rather simple, actually. You are . . . different from all the rest. I knew the moment I met you that you were not cut from the same cloth as the fortune hunters, the heiresses. You wanted so badly to be ambitious, Sophia, to make the same match that all the others wanted. But you are too honest. Too passionate. I like that about you, very much."

He scoffed, shaking his head in that abrupt, nervous way of his. "I suppose those are the same reasons why you *won't* wear my ring. But that doesn't . . . doesn't mean I admire you any less, Sophia. To do the honorable thing, the hard thing, is no small feat. You could very well be the best friend I've got, considering the scalawags and seducers that populate the clubs these days."

By now, tears fell so profusely from Sophia's eyes she could hardly see. Somewhere in the blurry dimness of the room, she heard Lady Blaise's cries for smelling salts and a snifter of brandy; none of it registered as she flung herself into Withington's chest.

"Thank you," she breathed. "Thank you for all that you've done, and all that you are."

Withington was stiff at first; but then he reached around and patted her gently on the shoulder. He stood, pulling her up with him. He stepped away, holding her by the arms, and smiled into her eyes.

"Save your tears for Lady Blaise." His gaze flicked to the tittering ladies across the room. "I think you're going to need them."

Sophia took a deep breath, returning his smile; and was about to gather what was left of her mother when the glint at her wrist stopped her short. "Oh. Oh, here, don't forget this."

She unclasped the bracelet and held it out to him.

"Keep it," he said, waving her away. "It is my gift to you."

Sophia rolled her eyes. "You know me better than that, Withington. I can't keep it."

"I insist."

"And I insist you take it back." She glanced over her shoulder. "Perhaps give it to the dowager marchioness; who knows, it might buy you a little luck. I think you're going to need it."

Withington smiled, taking the bracelet with a sigh of defeat. "Until next time, then."

Sophia reached out and squeezed his hand. "I look forward to meeting all those scalawag friends of yours."

"Scalawag. Such a diverting word."

"More so over a bottle of port. Let's skip the theater next time, shall we?"

Withington groaned with pleasure. "I thought you'd never ask."

Sophia released his hand. His brown eyes were kind but full; and not everything she saw there was joyful or relieved. Even so, he bowed low, tucking the jewelry into his waistcoat pocket; and when he rose, he leaned in and pressed a soft kiss into her cheek.

Behind them, Lady Blaise hit the floor with a dull *thud.* Withington pulled back, a secret smile on his lips.

"Told you to save those tears."

Lady Blaise made a miraculous recovery the moment the musty family coach pulled away from Withington's well-appointed pile.

Sophia sat very still against the squabs, waiting for the assault to begin. Mama opened and closed her mouth several times, her small, heart-shaped face white with anger; Sophia drew several deep breaths, though they did nothing to relieve the knot in her belly.

Lady Blaise focused her gaze on the street outside the grimy carriage window. When Sophia, unable to bear the silence any longer, moved to speak, Mama pinned her to the seat with an icy glare.

"I never pressed this dream upon you, Sophia," she said. "Whatever you desired, I desired, too. You are my only daughter, my only child, and I wished to give you the world. If that meant remaining a spinster like Violet, so be it; a match with a poor vicar, I would have supported you. But you came to desire this match all on your own; you became the creature you are on your own. I wanted what you wanted. And I still want this match, this title, whether you do or not."

Withington was right; the tears came. Sophia had no reply. She was not fool enough to believe her decision would come without consequence; still, the shame that washed through her, the guilt of disappointing her mother; these things were not easy to bear.

Still. She would have to bear them. And hope that in time her mother might forgive her.

Before the carriage drew to a full stop in the mews behind the house, Cousin Violet appeared breathless at the coach door. In her right fist she held a crumpled piece of paper; her cheeks were wet with tears.

"It's him!" she cried the moment Sophia swung to the ground. "It's *him*, Sophia, he's alive!"

Sophia's eyes widened as a fresh wave of weeping threatened to break. "Lord Harclay? The earl is alive?"

"Yes!" Violet thrust the page into Sophia's hand, choking on the words as she said them. "Look. Look what he—what he sent."

Sophia held Violet against her as she attempted to smooth the wrinkled surface of the paper. "What? What is it?"

But Violet had collapsed into noisy sobs, and could hardly breathe, much less speak.

Sophia glanced down at the page. It was smaller than standard letter paper, about the size of a flimsy; it brought to mind the banknote Mr. Hope had set down on Princess Caroline's marble-topped table the night they bought the French Blue.

But this couldn't be a banknote, certainly not one worth much money, anyway; it was wrinkled almost beyond recognition, and one corner appeared to be missing entirely. The paper itself felt coarse, and crumpled, as if it had come into unwanted contact with water.

Sophia scanned the first few lines.

Banco Giugliano di Firenze . . . 23 June 1812 . . . pay to the bearer . . .

"Thirty thousand pounds." Sophia's head snapped up. "*Thirty thousand pounds*! Good God, Violet, this is the Comte d'Artois' note, isn't it? The money he was going to use to buy the diamond?"

Violet merely nodded, and appeared ready to swoon for the second time in as many weeks.

Sophia felt a swoon coming on herself. "This means—does it mean—heavens, Violet, it's a gift! Harclay's giving you the money as a gift!"

The earl's invitation arrived the next morning:

To His Grace the Duke of Sommer
and all the Ladies of his house,
His Lordship the Earl of Harclay
requests your presence
At a Masquerade Ball
This evening, at half past eight o'clock.
A prize shall be awarded
To the jewel who shines brightest.

Thirty-three

Later that night
Brook Street, Hanover Square

Mr. Thomas Hope gave his hat a vicious tug, but to no avail; his curls were as wild as ever, and no matter his best efforts, the beaver hat atop his head would not stay put.

Not that he was surprised. The French Blue was still missing; by Hope's estimation it was lost forever, disappeared into the tumult of history as it did some twenty years ago, in Paris.

And because Hope had yet to miraculously recover the diamond, proving to his clients, investors, and those nasty editors at the papers that yes, he was a capable man of business, and yes, he would safeguard the wealth of those who depended upon him with his very life, he was seen as exactly opposite that: a careless, vulgar idiot.

As Hope's situation deteriorated and Hope & Co. slid further into debt, he'd spent the week at his desk mired in panic, tugging his hands through his hair as if he might pull it out by its very roots. By Friday his dark curls stood on end, lending him the appearance of a wide-eyed street urchin who'd been struck in the arse by lightning.

"Really, old chap, you should try to get some sleep," Mr. Lake had counseled. "We'll find the diamond. When that rascal the earl resurfaces, I'll take him by his—"

Hope had cut short that thought with the wickedest glare he could muster. *Sleep*. Ha! As if he could afford such luxury. Besides, whenever his exhausted eyes fluttered shut—even for a moment, a second, a heartbeat—he saw Sophia's face tensed with passion, screwed tight in pain. Her eyes full as he closed the door on whatever it was they had shared these past weeks.

Even now it stole his breath, the memory of that unspoken good-bye; regret pressed heavy on his chest. He'd never had the chance to tell her that he longed, more than anything, to hold her in the circle of his arms and make her his.

To tell her that he loved her.

The coach pitched to a sudden stop, nearly launching Hope headfirst into the opposite row of velvet squabs. He was going to miss this carriage, yes, but the driver? Not quite.

Hope let out a sigh. The time for regrets had passed. Tonight was his last chance to gain back all that he'd lost. If Harclay, as his invitation suggested, had indeed returned from the dead, then perhaps he'd managed to bring the French Blue back with him. And perhaps—though this was highly, *highly* unlikely—he might feel, after his trip to the underworld, the compulsion to atone for his sins and return the diamond to its rightful owner.

Perhaps.

He glanced out the window; the Earl of Harclay's house was ablaze, the twinkle of crystal and shine of satin-clad ladies peeking through the massive front doors, which were flung open to greet an impossibly long line of guests that snaked along the perimeter of the drive.

For a brief moment his heart rose with hope. Hope, not for the earl to give back what he'd taken, but for Sophia to be there, at the door, her gold eyes alight with mischief. Would she be wearing that pale pink gown of hers, the one with the rosettes embroidered about the neckline? Or, more daringly, the gauzy confection she wore to his own soiree? The invitation *had* said something about a masquerade . . .

Heart pounding, Hope tugged the strings of his white leather domino into some semblance of a knot at the back of his head, his fingers for a moment getting lost in the tangled nest of his curls.

Regret be damned. If he was going to see Sophia tonight, or win back the diamond—he wasn't stupid enough to hope for both—he could not afford to waste a single moment.

Mr. Hope waited rather less patiently than was polite in the receiving line. While he understood that this was the first ball the earl had hosted since he'd come into the title some years ago, it did not excuse the snail-like progression of introductions.

After waiting a lifetime—five minutes, actually, but who was counting?—Mr. Hope ducked into the shrubbery and strode through the front doors beside his grace the Duke of Devonshire, who, as the infamous bachelor duke, arrived alone, and started in that baffled, Labrador-like way curious to the English.

"Hope, old boy, out to avenge your honor?" The duke wagged his heavy brows. "I've been reading up on your diamond, ho ho!"

"My honor's been shot to hell, your grace."

The duke pulled back so violently he nearly fell down the stair, his face wide with horror. "Good God, but what will you do?"

Hope shrugged. "Die, I suppose."

The duke gaped at him as if his brain had just exploded inside his skull. Only after Hope slapped him, hard, on the back, did his good humor return. "Ho, ho, it can't be as bad as all that. You, without honor. Ho ho! What will you live for, old boy? What *will* you live for?"

Hope turned to glance up the stair. There, standing at the top of the landing as if God himself had sent her down from heaven to answer the duke's idiotic query, stood Miss Sophia Blaise.

She was wearing the gown of gauze; the nymph gown. Her dark curls were gathered loosely at the back of her head, a stray lock or two brushing her temples as she smiled at something Cousin Violet was saying.

Hope's gaze darted to the fingers of her left hand. Damnation; she was wearing gloves. But there was no hint of the ring through the fine satin, and he'd seen no mention of the engagement in the papers or gossip sheets.

Not that he'd been looking, of course . . .

Stop.

It took a special kind of idiot to believe a debutante as wicked, and as wickedly pretty, as Sophia would ever refuse the season's most eligible bachelor.

Bah. Even thinking the words *most eligible bachelor* made Hope recoil in distaste. Really, he had to stop reading the gossip sheets.

The Marquess of Withington was heir to a family that traced its lineage back to some hideously handsome medieval knight, who, after saving England from those devil-worshipping Yorkists at Bosworth Field, built the family's current rambling seat with his own two hands and the help of six strapping sons. His title was ancient and his fortune enormous; almost as enormous as his fashionably furry sideburns.

His was the name that every debutante whispered into her pillow at night. Sophia, with her dreams of a brilliant match, was no different. She'd be a fool to pass up the chance to marry the *Marquess* of *Withington.* What with the prince regent being more akin to a hippopotamus than King Arthur, a match with the marquess was even better than a match with royalty.

Hope climbed the stairs slowly, Devonshire breathing heavily beside him.

Sophia turned to him, her smile fading as if in his gaze she could read his dark thoughts. In the molten light of the chandeliers above her eyes burned a deep shade of amber, depthless pools of passion. Whatever she was feeling, she felt it acutely, wholly; she teetered on the edge of something nameless, and it bothered him that he could not assuage it.

His grace the duke bowed low, murmuring some nonsense about the weather and its effect on his delicate knees before excusing himself as one of his mistresses, this one decked out in head-to-toe peacock feathers, tickled him on the ear as she passed.

This left Hope flat-footed and openmouthed before Lady Violet, Sophia, and Lady Blaise. He felt Sophia's presence beside him as one might feel heat from standing too close to a fire. The urge to touch her, to look her shamelessly in the eye, overwhelmed him.

Stop.

Hope pulled off his ridiculous mask, attempting to quell the rapid beating of his heart with thoughts of the diamond, the earl, the bank. He was here to get back what Harclay had taken from him. He was here to protect all those who depended on him.

He was here to fight back in the name of his family.

He turned to Lady Violet.

"Our plot is still in play, yes?" he asked, a bit more breathlessly than he intended.

With no little impatience Violet replied that yes, the plot was still in play, and yes, if Harclay did not hand over the French Blue, she would have him arrested. From the way her eyes wandered toward the crush of the ballroom, looking for the earl, waiting for him to make his move, Hope didn't believe her, not for a second.

Especially not with the slip of paper held in the hand she clutched to her breast. It peeked out between her first and second fingers, a small sliver of fine, smooth-edged stationery. He peered closer, trying to make out the embossed seal half-hidden by her glove.

His weary eyes betrayed him; years spent poring over ledgers in the dark had ruined his sight. But he knew, he *knew*, it was a note from the earl.

Harclay was here.

Hope scanned the ballroom that thrummed beyond the arched threshold, parsing through the masked and feathered and bejeweled faces. Damn him, Harclay had done it on purpose; with everyone in disguise, that devil could move freely about without anyone the wiser.

Well. Two could play this game, Hope thought with a harrumph, and went about refastening the ties of his mask.

Only they kept getting tangled in the wild mass of his hair.

"Here," came a voice, soft, from beside him. "Let me help you, Mr. Hope."

He froze, casting a sidelong glance at Sophia as she raised her arms.

"Thank you." He let his arms fall to his sides as her fingers went to work.

"It is my pleasure."

Hope sucked in a small breath as her fingertips grazed his scalp; a wave of goose bumps broke out on his neck and arms.

The silence between them was broken by Lady Blaise's twittering about moving on, why, look, the dancing's begun, and is that the Dowager Baroness Hat-Wittlesby . . .

"There you are." Sophia patted him lightly on the shoulder. "Does the white suit me?"

"Not at all."

Sophia smiled. Hope's heart lurched.

"I thought I might stand out from all those would-be rogues in their dashing black leather." He sighed. "I suppose one can't win them all, Miss Blaise."

She blushed, her eyes never leaving his. "I suppose not."

For a moment they stood, eyes locked, at the top of the stairs, guests prodding and elbowing their way past them. The music had started; somewhere in the back of his mind, Hope registered the *one-two-three* of a waltz.

He felt desire welling up inside him, grief, too, a kind singular to the sort from which he'd suffered all these years for his family. His heart was full enough of mourning; he did not want to have to mourn Sophia, too.

Stop.

The French Blue.

The bank.

And that bloody bastard the earl.

When he opened his mouth to speak, Sophia rose with hope, eyes wide and willing. Pain ripped through him, pain and rage and the desire to throw her over his shoulder and leave this place forever, the rest be damned.

Stop.

He tore his eyes from her as he fell into an awkwardly stiff bow; and because he could not bear to see her disappointment, he turned and without another word stalked into the ballroom.

For a moment the edges of his vision blurred. Stop, stop, *stop* you bloody fool, stop; the words came in time to the savage pounding of his heart. The agony of leaving Sophia alone, of leaving her so rudely and abruptly to chase after that bloody jewel, left a bitter taste in his mouth.

Hope stole a coupe of champagne from a passing footman and downed it in a single gulp. There, that helped; the ballroom materialized around him, the lilting music, the scents of sweat and spilled wine, the honeyed light of twinkling chandeliers above. He returned the coupe to the gaping footman's tray and stepped into the crush.

The ballroom appeared to be evenly divided: half using the waltz as an excuse to grope one another, half yelling above the din that said dance would lead them all straight to hell. Yes, yes indeed, the waltz was the harbinger of the apocalypse, and did you see the way the Earl of Harclay swept into the ballroom, that dashing black leather mask of his . . .

"Pardon me, Lady Featherstone." Hope watched with no little satisfaction as *both* her chins flushed at his smile. "Did you say the earl has at last made his appearance?"

"Oh, Mr. Hope, yes, yes indeed!" Lady Featherstone leaned in, the wisps of her wig flying in the furious batting of her fan, and lowered her voice. "He's *dancing* with *Lady Violet Rutledge*! Out of all the girls in England, he picks a degenerate gambler, and did you know she openly professes her love for liquor! . . ."

"Thank you," Hope said, peering in the direction of her outstretched arm. Ah, yes, there they were; there was no missing them, pressed against one another as if these were their last moments on earth. The heat between them was palpable, even from here.

Indeed, a small circle of observers had gathered around them, staring incredulously. From the crowd there rose an audible gasp, loud enough to cause the musicians to falter. Hope's heart went to his throat; he pushed toward Violet, desperate to see what was happening, what would happen next.

The crush here was thick and stubborn. No one, it seemed, wished to relinquish their position at the forefront of what was sure to prove this season's greatest scandal.

Hope ducked; he leapt into the air; still he could see nothing.

At last, squeezing between two potbellies, Hope found himself inside the circle.

His eyes fell on Lady Violet.

There, strung from a collar of glittering white diamonds, was the French Blue, nestled just above the overeager rise of Lady Violet's bosom.

The French Blue.

Disbelief pulsed through him, along with a wave of panic so strong it made him nauseous. Without thinking he leapt into motion, pushing bodies out of the way as he made for Violet, the diamond, his salvation.

The Earl of Harclay was nowhere to be found; it seemed he'd vanished as quickly, as inexplicably, as he'd appeared some moments before.

The crush was terrible, and even with the advantage of his height and breadth he could make little headway. His heart raced. He was close, so close, he couldn't let the diamond out of his sight . . .

If only for Sophia. If only to save her family's meager fortune, her cousin, her mother, and her uncle. If only for Sophia, he would reclaim the diamond, make it his once more.

When at last he trampled his way to the middle of the room, Lord Harclay had, predictably, disappeared; Violet was nowhere to be found. He frantically searched the sea of faces that surrounded him on all sides, thousands and thousands of masked people he did not recognize. Was that the back of her head there? Or her skirts, was she wearing blue, or had it been white? No, no, he thought, ticking off faces as he looked, not her, not her, *definitely* not her . . .

But then he caught sight of a small ripple on the sea's surface, a parting of bodies as if someone were snaking between them. He followed the movement as it made its way across the ballroom and into the gallery beyond; as the figure rounded the corner, he caught the glimmer of a gauzy gown, followed by the flash of diamonds.

It was Violet. She was going after the earl, wherever he'd disappeared to.

Hope pushed and prodded his way after her, ignoring the cries and gasps of outrage as he went. He wasn't about to lose the French Blue, not after he'd come so far; not after all he'd lost, and still had to lose.

He stumbled into the gallery just as Lady Violet ducked through the narrow servants' door at the far end of the hallway. Hope paused, catching his breath, his mind racing with options, his chances, what his next move should be; and as he stood there, his eyes of their own volition settled on a shapely figure in an alcove to his right.

Sophia stood dutifully next to her mother as Lady Blaise

chatted with a circle of flush-faced matrons. Watching Sophia, face studiously blank as if she were about to weep, eyes darting over her mother's shoulder in search of him—he *knew* she was looking for him—something inside Hope broke and began to bleed. He felt the poison seeping into his lungs, weighing down his limbs and his will to move on.

But he had to move on. *Move*, but his feet remained planted on the parquet floor of Harclay's high-ceilinged hall.

Hope gritted his teeth. There would be time enough for grief. Right now he *had to move.*

Only with tremendous effort did he coax his body into motion. Down the gallery, through the door, he nearly fell down the darkened corridor of the servants' stair. His unexpected tumble lent him momentum, and the cacophony of the kitchens passed by in a whirl of scents and shouts and the clatter of pots.

He heard Violet's voice, soft and breathless, followed by the burly cook's booming reply: "He's thataway, my lady. Just missed 'im, you did. You'd best hurry!"

He followed Violet into the servants' quarters at the back of the house. Violet was calling for Harclay, *William, William, wait*, as her footsteps quickened on the cold stone floor.

Hope followed her through the back kitchen door and out into the night, skidding on the loose gravel of the drive. Lady Violet was several paces in front of him; she was cursing, something about damning said William to hell; in answer to her curses, an enormous coach silently materialized out of the darkness.

Hope plastered himself against the house's far outer wall, peering through a thorny tangle of a rosebush. The vehicle slowed but did not stop; the door flung open, and with a little yelp, Violet was swept from her feet and into the carriage, the door clicking quietly shut behind her.

His blood rushed as he bolted out into the drive. Had Lady Violet, with that fifty-carat diamond about her neck, been *kidnapped*? Hope was as tired of that plot as anyone, but it *did* make sense; it wouldn't be the first time the French Blue was thieved out from under his nose.

Or had the Earl of Harclay—*William*, Lord Townshend—

defied everyone's wildest expectations and actually done the honorable thing? Had he swept Lady Violet off her feet so that he might take her to the *altar*, the diamond aside?

And could Harclay even speak words like *honor* and *altar* without bursting into flames?

Only time would tell.

And Hope didn't have very much time at all.

He leapt out into the drive and burst into a sprint, his heart hammering as he gunned after the coach. The gravel slipped and skidded beneath the fine soles of his pumps; his chest and throat burned.

He was so close. So very, very close to getting back what was stolen from him those weeks and weeks ago. The diamond was within his grasp; he could feel its cold weight in the palm of his hand, the thrill of his triumph.

But it was slipping further and further away, the coach disappearing into the darkness as the pair of matching blacks was urged into a gallop.

The drive curved into the lane up ahead. Hope watched as the coach pulled into the evening traffic, disappearing into the seamless tangle of horseflesh and lacquer that heaved just beyond the gates of Harclay's property.

And then, as if it had never existed at all, the coach was gone.

His heart burst with pain and Hope doubled over, hands on his knees as he fought to breathe. He tried to curse the vilest curses he knew, in every language he spoke, but all he managed were a few pitiful wheezes.

The diamond was gone. That bloody jewel was gone *again*.

He felt sick at the finality of it, the irony of it. Hope knew better than anyone that the French Blue brought misfortune to those who owned it—first Shah Jehan, then that wily traveler Tavernier, the kings of France. And now it brought misfortune to Thomas Hope; a hideously classic example of mankind being doomed to repeat its terrible history.

Doom. Even the poet in Hope winced at the word. It was 1812, damn it, and no such thing as doom existed anymore. Everyone knew it died out with the Tudors, or, at the very least, with wart-faced Oliver Cromwell.

Even so. Watching the innocuous push and pull of traffic in the lane, the slow turning of the moon in the night sky above, Hope could not shake the sense of dread knotting in the pit of his belly.

He was about to collapse in defeat and, with any luck, roll into a ditch somewhere when a familiar hiss—*psst! Psst!*—sounded from over his shoulder.

Hope rose, chest releasing with relief at the sight of La Reinette leaning out a carriage door, her face obscured by a red satin domino.

"Venir, monsieur, vite!"

She waved him over to the coach in that singularly elegant way of hers, her eyes on his face as he trotted toward her.

"We've got," he wheezed, pointing in the direction of the lane. "To go."

La Reinette held out her hand. "*Oui, oui*, I know, come!"

Thank God.

Thank God she was here to save him. He still had a chance.

Hope fell heavily onto the fine velvet squabs. It was dark inside the coach, the lanterns having been extinguished; the better, he figured, to slip through London's streets unnoticed.

"Oh, Marie." He gasped. "I cannot tell you. What a relief. It is. To see you."

He saw the flash of her teeth as she smiled. In the dark they appeared small and sharp, like the talons of a falcon.

He paused. "Wait a. Moment. What are you. Doing back in London?"

"It was time," she replied. He waited for her to say more but she remained silent.

"Well then," he said uneasily. "Shall we be off?"

The voice that answered did not belong to La Reinette.

Or any woman, for that matter.

"*Oui*, we shall." The voice was like gravel; the accent heavy but clear, clipped.

Hope recognized it at once.

Beside him, Guillaume Cassin pounded the roof with his silver-topped cane. The carriage heaved into motion.

Hope jerked to life, leaping for the door; but the man who had indeed come back from the dead, whose neck La Reinette had sliced open in that sour-smelling room in Paris, stopped him short, using his cane to thwack Hope soundly in the head.

Hope fell face-first to the floor with a ringing *thump.*

In his head his blood rushed.

And then, nothing.

Thirty-four

Thankfully Lady Blaise had wept herself into a stupor over Cousin Violet's sudden disappearance at the ball, leaving Sophia to face the black evening ahead in blessed solitude.

After helping Fitzhugh, one of the few servants left at the house, carry Mama upstairs to her bed, Sophia pleaded exhaustion. With promises that she would wait up for any word of Violet's whereabouts, she ducked into her room and closed the door behind her.

She stripped off her pale satin gloves and loosened a particularly painful pin that had assaulted her right ear all night, allowing them to fall through her fingers to the floor.

And then she fell back against the door and let out the breath she'd been holding all night, tears welling as she sank slowly to the ground.

She wrapped her arms around her knees and allowed herself at last to cry, her hurt and her anger and her grief pouring from her eyes, the tears hot as they slid down the length of her neck.

It was the sort of cry reserved for prima donnas on stage and hapless heroines in novels.

But Sophia would not be thwarted; she had wronged, and been wronged in return, and hang it all if she wasn't going to get a good, solid, one-for-the-ages cry out of it.

Mr. Hope had looked handsomer than ever tonight; and while he would've looked better in black leather rather than white, her heart had skipped a beat at the blue of his eyes, the boyish curve of his lips. He'd excused himself so abruptly on the landing of the top of the stairs; as she watched him walk away, intent on seeking out the French Blue, her heart, so exultant moments before, sank into the depth of her disappointment and seemed to dissolve altogether.

It would be the last time. The last time he would bow over her hand and her blood would pulse with the knowledge that he was hers and hers alone. The last time she would look into his eyes and see her own desire, the love she bore him, reflected in the wide, startling blue irises.

On ne peut avoir le beurre et l'argent du beurre.

Sophia remembered the faraway look in La Reinette's eyes as she said the words.

One cannot have one's cake and eat it, too.

The madam had been talking about some lover or another, one who broke her heart; one she loved above all the others. Now Sophia understood La Reinette's pain, her regret. By setting her cap at London's most eligible—and often most lackluster—gentlemen, Sophia had neglected men like Thomas.

Passionate men, handsome men, men who made her feel alive, adored.

Men who loved her, and whom she loved in return.

What a fool she'd been! To even *think* of choosing the Marquess of Withington, sweet natured as he was, over Thomas Hope.

Thomas hadn't broken her heart; no, Sophia had done smart work of that herself.

And now she was alone in a crumbling house, no money or future of which to speak; it would only be a matter of time before that Cassin fellow, wherever he'd disappeared to, revealed her identity as the author of some of the most scandalous memoirs England had seen in decades. What little she had left—family, reputation—would be ruined.

Again the tears threatened; but even as Sophia was tempted to give in, and give up, and resign herself to a thankless and gray spinsterhood in some thankless, gray place like Scotland—for surely Mama's exhibitions of grief would force all of them into exile—she found herself wondering what La Reinette would do.

La Reinette. Yes, thinking of Madame always made Sophia feel better; and in the early, heady days of her courtship—if one could call it that—with Mr. Hope, the Little Queen's adventures occupied her thoughts often.

Sophia glanced toward her bed, the single taper on the table beside it. Its flame wavered sluggishly in the still air of the room.

Barely enough light by which to read.

But it was enough.

Sophia wiped her eyes with the heel of her hand and scampered to the side of the bed. Drawing up on her knees, she pushed aside the bedclothes and ducked to peer into the dark space below.

Admittedly not the cleverest of hiding spaces, but then again Lady Blaise was not the cleverest of mamas. Besides, if anyone needed watching, it was Cousin Violet; no one suspected Sophia of much beyond the usual sins of youth: vanity, a proclivity for gossip and flirtation.

Harmless things, really, when compared to her usual nighttime activities. If her mother only knew! Lady Blaise would be dead of apoplexy in five seconds flat.

The tattered hatbox scraped across the floor as Sophia drew it out into the small circle of light. She traced the familiar lettering, now faded, with her fingers: LOCK & CO HATTERS. 6 ST. JAMES'S ST. LONDON.

Carefully she placed the box on the bed and climbed up after it, her slippers falling to the floor with tiny, hollow *plunks*. Drawing near the taper, she opened the box, inhaling the animal scents of leather and fur that still clung to it so many years later.

Inside, a scattered pile of fine paper lay strewn about the box's silk-lined interior. Each page was covered in Sophia's careful copperplate handwriting, La Reinette's extraordinary life boiled down to a series of looping *p*'s and *g*'s, the grand arch of an *A*.

Sophia read the first line of script at the top page—*It had been a cold winter, a terrible winter, and I knew the duke's warm embrace could not last forever*—and only when the taper's light sputtered, the wick having burned down to a blackened nub, was La Reinette's spell broken.

Sophia looked up, blinking. She sat up, running a hand

along the stiffness in her neck, and set the pages down on her lap.

Goodness, but the memoir was good; Madame's stories were intoxicating; the romance and the bare-chested barons and long, naked nights spent before roaring fires made for some exquisite reading.

Sophia glanced out the window; outside the night was black, no sign yet of dawn or sleep.

Settling a few pillows against the headboard, Sophia leaned against them and bent her knees, propping the pages on her thighs. She still had a few minutes yet of light, and the story was just getting good . . .

The spy had no name but the bluest eyes I had ever seen in my short life. With his gaze alone he could fell any woman, rich or poor, royal or common . . .

Tonight he played the part of pirate, leaping from his ship on the Seine, his billowing shirt open, his eyes alive with danger. It took all my strength not to swoon at his feet. His dark hair was wild in the wind, the curls held back by a red handkerchief . . . I waited for him to touch me, for the stars in the blank sky above to answer my urgent prayers that he love me as I loved him . . .

Sophia pulled back, her thoughts sparking with a vague sense of recognition, of familiarity. Blue eyes, fallen woman, dark, curly hair.

Dread snaked up her spine; her body went stiff. It couldn't be; couldn't *possibly* be him. He and La Reinette were no more than strangers back then, two people brought together by a series of exciting, if unfortunate, events. She couldn't be in love with him, not after what they'd done together . . .

But Sophia knew better. She recalled her conversation with La Reinette the night Mr. Hope had interrupted their meeting at The Glossy:

I enjoyed this week's tales. Thoroughly. That spy you knew, back in France—the one with the curls, who could fell a girl with his gaze alone? He is my favorite gentleman yet.

La Reinette had smiled; a smile Sophia now understood to

be the secret sort, the malicious sort. *Yes. He is my favorite, too.*

Blue eyes, fallen woman, dark, curly hair.

It could only be one man.

It could only be Mr. Thomas Hope.

Sophia leapt to her bare feet, her mind racing as she tore into her armoire in search of her boots.

Of three things she was certain.

First, La Reinette was in love with Mr. Hope, had been since they'd first met nearly a decade ago.

Second, Hope was not in love with La Reinette, never had been.

And third, La Reinette was French. She said herself the French were possessed of vengeful hearts. As a woman spurned, Sophia had no doubt Madame would do everything in her power to destroy the object of her unrequited affections.

Everything, like colluding with Hope's enemy, Guillaume Cassin, to mastermind a plot to bring Hope to his knees.

A plot to bring the woman Hope *did* love to her knees, too.

It made perfect sense; Sophia was angry at herself for not seeing it sooner. La Reinette was the only one other than Thomas who knew Sophia was writing scandalous memoirs. The madam was the missing link; *she* was the one who sold Sophia out to the gossip sheets.

And now that La Reinette and Cassin had Sophia by the short hairs, they would turn their attention to Mr. Hope.

It was, ironically enough, just the sort of plot, of adventure, that populated the Little Queen's memoirs. Only now, the madam would use her cunning and wily nimbleness against Sophia; it was no longer an adventure but a duel, a race to ruin.

Sophia quickened her steps, and was about to scuttle down the stairs, when she caught sight of the narrow door that led to Uncle Rutledge's dressing room. She paused, but only for a moment; she darted into the room, emerging moments later wearing only her chemise, a ball of clothes tucked into the crook of her arm.

She skipped down the stair as she tugged one leg, then the other, into her uncle's rather voluminous breeches; she tugged a shirt over her head, tossing aside a musty waistcoat after tangling her arms in its armholes. Too much work, that, and no one would notice, anyway.

At least she *hoped* no one would notice.

Skidding out the kitchen door, Sophia shrugged into a jacket. She topped off her costume with a hat that was two sizes too big and twenty years out of fashion.

She tucked the last of her pilfered finds into her jacket and, tipping up her nose so that she might run without the hat falling into her eyes, Sophia took off at a sprint.

There wasn't much time. She had to stop La Reinette and that rat-faced Frenchman Cassin from getting to Thomas.

If they hadn't already.

Thirty-five

The Glossy was a far less pleasant place, Hope found, when one was bound and gagged and dragged none too gently down the stairs to a dark, smelly room behind the kitchens.

His senses returned slowly. He was vaguely aware of the murmured conversation between La Reinette and Cassin as they followed him into the basement; every word, spoken in crisp, clipped French, made the pain in his head pulse sharply.

When at last he opened his eyes, the darkened room swam languidly about him; he was suddenly aware of the chafe of rope against the skin of his wrists, his arms bound behind him to the rickety chair in which he sat. A handful of stray curls had fallen into his eyes, and the impulse to push them away made his fingers itch.

He managed a glance about the room. It was a pantry, its shelves lined with flour and turnips and cellars of salt; a trio of cured pig haunches hung listlessly from the ceiling, lilting back and forth, back and forth, as if they, too, were impatient to know what the *devil* this was about.

Aside from the pig haunches and turnips, the room was bare, illuminated by a single lamp La Reinette had placed on a nearby shelf.

Umberto, seemingly unscathed from his run-in with Hope's pursuers some weeks ago, was tying Hope's legs to those of the chair. Marie urged him *faster, faster*, then shooed him from the room when the task was done; quietly she closed the door behind him, turning to Hope.

Her eyes were alive, joyfully triumphant as if she'd wagered her last guinea on a no-count featherweight and won. Hope swallowed. He didn't like that look, not on La Reinette; it made her look wild, like she might do or say anything and Hope would be none the wiser.

From behind her, where Cassin moved in the darkness, there came ominous scraping sounds, metal against metal; he was sharpening something, a blade. Hope swallowed, his belly turning over. He did not care to know what Cassin was up to back there.

Not yet, anyway.

La Reinette sauntered toward him, crossing her arms over her chest. She wore a robe of watery Japanese silk that was so fine as to be transparent, showing every curve, every sinew, highlighting especially the hardened points of her nipples.

Hope looked away, annoyed. Had she come to slay or seduce him? How like her to confuse the two.

"Thomas, look at me."

His gaze snapped to meet hers. "Don't call me that. I am not Thomas to you."

The triumph in her eyes faded somewhat; she chewed the inside of her lip as she considered him. He gently tugged at his bindings, only to find they wouldn't budge. Umberto, it seemed, knew his way around tying innocent men to rather uncomfortable chairs.

Hope swallowed the panic that rose in his throat. He'd faced worse odds than these and had somehow managed to survive. Tonight will be no different, he told himself. Think. *Think*.

"So you and Cassin." Hope nodded at the figure that moved in the shadows behind La Reinette. "What an unlikely alliance, considering you killed him eight years ago. Tell me, Marie, how'd you manage such a feat? The mind boggles. Really, it does."

The madam twisted her lips into a sour smile. "I am perhaps a witch. That answer, does it satisfy you?"

Hope scoffed. "Don't insult me, Marie."

She tilted her head; after a moment she uncrossed her arms and pulled up her sleeve, fingering a ribbonlike scar that ran up the pale flesh of her inner arm.

"It was my blood on his throat. I went to Cassin before,

and told him you meant to kill him. And to myself I thought, let Hope think his enemy is dead; what a surprise it will be, yes, when he knows he is alive! And my friend Cassin. A very good actor he is."

Hope felt the damp break out beneath his arms and along the edge of his scalp; if he didn't feel ill before, he definitely did now. Though he knew the answer, he asked the question anyway.

"Why?"

Marie smiled. She let down her sleeve, resting her hands on the arms of his chair.

"And you." She bent over him and brushed her lips to his ear. "Do not play stupid. These things I do not want to say. Don't make me say them, *Thomas*."

He winced. It was all wrong, that name on her tongue. Thomas belonged to Miss Sophia Blaise.

Thomas was dead.

He looked La Reinette in the eye. "Answer the question, *Marie*."

The movement behind the madam stilled; she turned and murmured something soothing in French. After a beat, Cassin resumed his sinister doings, and Marie turned back to Hope.

He sensed her hesitate when she met his eyes; for a moment her own went blank, as if she were lost, under a spell.

"My God," he breathed. "You can't still—no. Not after all these years. Surely there have been others."

Marie blinked; her eyes went hard again. She rocked back on her heels, gaze trained on Hope's feet. "You. You I loved from that first time we met. There has only been you."

Understanding rolled hard and heavy through him. "Marie. I made clear to you my feelings—"

"Your feelings." She scoffed, meeting his eyes. "That is it, you see. You never had them for me. Not the feelings I had for you."

Hope swallowed. The bindings at his wrists and ankles felt unbearably tight. "I'm sorry, Marie. I am. We had a jolly bit of fun, you and I, I thought we were partners, friends, even. I gave you everything I could—"

Her eyes flashed with anger now; for the first time ever he

saw color rise to her cheeks. "What about that time, in the, how do you say? *Vignoble*."

"Oh, God, Marie, that was *one* time. We were drunk. I was drunk. I should have never—"

"Yes. You should have never. I will make you regret it, Thomas. Tonight. You will regret what you did to me."

Hope let his head fall back, closing his eyes. "It was a mistake. I apologized for it. I regret what I did, I do. Christ, Marie. Out of all the men who have loved you all these years. Kings and princes and tsars—you could've had any man you wanted, and still you wanted *me*?"

Again that wry twist of her mouth. "Ah, yes. I am always wanting what I cannot own. And you know the tsar, he was, how do you say it?" She made a pinching gesture with her first finger and thumb.

"Tiny."

"Ah, yes, tiny."

Hope swallowed for what felt like the hundredth time. He straightened, opening his eyes. "We could've never been together, you and I. We were partners. An entanglement . . . it would've gotten in the way. I had a job to do, Marie. You knew I was running for my life. Mr. Lake saved me, but only on the condition that I help him—"

"Mr. Lake. Do not use him as the excuse, Thomas. No. You used me, my brain, my body, as if I was nothing to you, the dirt under your boots. My heart, you broke it. And so I decide to make the score even, make you bleed the way I bleed."

Hope glanced over her shoulder. "So you went to Cassin. Allied with my enemy, plotted my demise in the most epic and medieval fashion you could think of, cursed my black soul. All the usual tomfoolery, yes? Except you didn't kill me. You could have, right then and there in that room in Paris, and been done with the whole business. Why wait until now?"

La Reinette's smile deepened. Turning to the shelf, she asked, "Wine?"

"Thank you, Madame." Hope rolled his eyes. "But my hands are, at the moment, otherwise occupied."

Madame shrugged, pouring red wine into a fine Murano glass tumbler. She brought it to her lips, her dark eyes dancing with glee. Damn her, she was enjoying this a tad too much.

"I wait all this time," she said, "because I believe in taking, what is the expression? Two eyeballs?"

Because it appeared he would not have them to roll much longer, Hope rolled his eyes again. "Eye for an eye."

"Ah, yes, eye for an eye! I have been waiting all this time for you to fall in love, to love someone as deep as I loved you these years. I bide my time so that I might take from you what you take from me."

Hope started, his vision blurring as rage engulfed his carefully practiced nonchalance. He gave his bindings a vicious tug, hardly feeling the rope as it scalded his ankles and wrists.

"Leave Sophia out of this," he growled. "She did nothing to deserve your wrath. She is innocent. Punish me if you must, but leave Sophia alone."

The viciousness of his defense of her, the wild pulse of his blood, the violent urge to do violent things to keep her safe—it shocked him. He loved Sophia, had loved her since he pressed her body against his in that dreadful closet; but now he suddenly, devastatingly knew just how much he *loved* her.

"She did nothing!" La Reinette threw back her head and laughed. "Nothing but steal the heart that was meant for me! No, Thomas. If I cannot have you, no one will. Especially not that silly girl Sophia."

At the sound of her name on La Reinette's poisoned tongue, Hope lurched forward, straining against his bindings with all his might. So wild was his assault that Hope would have toppled the chair if Marie had not reached out a hand to steady him.

"It all was so perfect, yes," she said. "Cassin at last was in London, here to seek his own revenge against you. And then you fall in love! It is too perfect. The missing diamond, I did not plan that, but it was, as you English say, the ice on the biscuit."

Hope didn't bother correcting her. "Cassin is a traitor and a murderer, Marie. When he has his way with me, what the devil do you think he'll do to you?"

As if on cue, Guillaume Cassin's unshaven face appeared over La Reinette's shoulder. His wolfish grin revealed slimy green teeth—really, did the French practice any sort of dental hygiene at all?—and when he spoke, his cigar-ravaged voice raised goose bumps on Hope's arms and the back of his neck.

It was *him*. Understanding unfurled as Hope thought back to that first night in Mayfair, the night he and Lake had gone out looking for the French Blue.

It had been Cassin who'd given Hope and Lake chase; Cassin, who'd followed Hope up to La Reinette's rooms in The Glossy. Hope recalled La Reinette distracting Cassin as he and Sophia escaped. Now Hope understood that Marie had merely told her partner in crime to hold back, be patient, wait for the right time to strike.

Cassin, who'd penned that nasty note to La Reinette to throw them off her scent. He imagined them, heads bent over the page, cackling gleefully at their *savoir-faire* as Cassin scrawled his filth.

"He-*llo, Mees*ter Hope." Cassin stepped forward around La Reinette. He was bigger than Hope remembered; his teeth blacker, skin sallow. "What I am going to do to you, I have been saving, for only you. It has been many long years, after all. Many years to plan your pain, *Mee*ster Hope. You kill me, you kill my man. And I now—haha! You know the rest."

He held something that glinted silver up to the low light, reverently fingering its surface as he would a woman's body. For a moment Hope was blinded by a metallic flash; blinking, he made out the long, pointy shape of a French-style rapier, complete with overly bejeweled handle that swooped out in a series of gilded loops and swirls.

Hope swallowed. Again. And somehow managed to muster a scoff. "Ah, *monsieur*, I admire your sense of humor! Does it have a name?"

Cassin swung the sword through the air in a high, dramatic arc; the weapon made an equally dramatic *whoosh whoosh!* noise as he did so. "Of course. In France, our weapons are like our women. Beautiful, lithe, very deadly. This one I have given the name Bernadette."

"Bernadette?" Hope wrinkled his nose. "You're really going to kill me with a sword named *Bernadette*? Surely you can do better than that."

Cassin pursed his lips, offended. "You insult her," he said, polishing the blade of the rapier with his cape, "and you insult me. *En garde!*"

The Frenchman squatted into a lunge, and before Hope knew what he was about, Cassin charged forward, bringing the blade down on his face so quickly he hardly felt it slice through his cheek.

Hope did, however, feel the sting of the cut a moment later, followed by the warm drip of blood down the slope of his face. He smelled its sickly sweet scent above the must of the pantry; it filled his nostrils, thick, nauseating.

Two cuts, in nearly the same place: first La Reinette's hedgerow, poking his cheek that night weeks and weeks ago; and now Bernadette, making mincemeat of his face.

Maybe Cassin would poke his eyeballs out next. Soon Hope and Lake would be twins.

He would've laughed at the thought if panic didn't slam through him. It struck him, suddenly, that he faced death; *he would die here, tonight.* Before it had been petty games and witty banter, trading barbs with La Reinette as she told her tale of woe.

But now.

Now the diversion was done, leaving only the vengeful hearts that beat in the bodies standing before him.

Hope was going to die, and by a *rapier* named *Bernadette*, no less. No honorable death for him; no battle-scarred sword to the neck. Cassin would kill him and throw his body in the Thames, and that would be that.

It was a rather sobering thought.

He closed his eyes against the rage, the regret, and the hurt that welled up inside him. All he could think of was Sophia; all he could see in the vast blackness behind his eyelids was her face, the tender indent in her bottom lip as she bit down on it. More than anything he wanted to see her one last time, to tell her that he loved her above all things, above the bank and his grief and the family he left behind.

To tell her that *she* was his family now. That they should start one of their own.

To tell her he should've never let her go. That he couldn't bear the thought of another man, no matter her dreams of a brilliant match, touching her, having her, marrying her.

God, what he would give to kiss her one last time. He remembered that first kiss in Princess Caroline's puce-colored drawing room, the way Sophia had yielded to him, invited his touch. Her sense of adventure, her wit, and her honesty.

While his heart was glad to have known her at all, to have loved her and held her when he did, he cursed himself for never telling her. For letting her go.

And then his brothers—why did he never apologize, try, and try again until things between them were right and good? They were the only family he had left, and Thomas had kept them at arm's length, virtual strangers.

He would go to his grave regretting these things.

Hope opened his eyes. Cassin was raising his rapier, his dark eyes gleaming with malice. He swung Bernadette in the air, winding up for the deathblow.

Sophia, he pleaded silently. *Sophia, I am sorry.*

Cassin brought down the blade. Hope flinched, his heart lurching in his chest.

Was it to be heaven or hell for his soul? Probably hell, all things considered; surely the devil enjoyed his liquor more than all the angels and saints . . .

"Stop!"

There was a great racket by the door; Hope's eyes flew to the threshold to see a disheveled lump of a man dart into the pantry, tossing his ridiculous feathered hat to the side as he launched himself at Cassin.

The Frenchman's eyes went wide; and then all Hope could see was a tussle of a black cape and long, shining curls, Cassin grunting and La Reinette screaming and Umberto falling face-first to the ground just inside the door.

Bernadette fell, too, with a scraping clatter that did not bode well for its bejeweled handle.

Cassin had somehow managed to take the man by his curls, tugging him viciously against his chest so that the intruder now faced Hope, his head caught in the crook of Cassin's rather massive arm.

"Sophia?" Hope breathed. "What the devil do you think you're doing?"

"Yes." Cassin panted. "Yes, what is she doing here?"

La Reinette swooped down and retrieved Bernadette, placing

her in Cassin's outstretched hand. "Guillaume, it is perfect. We will kill them both, and poof! All our problems, they are gone."

Hope's blood surged as he watch Cassin pull Sophia against him, holding the blade of the rapier at her throat.

"You foolish girl," Cassin murmured into her ear. "You think you might save him, all by yourself? Haha! You make us laugh."

Sophia's eyes were wide; she grasped Cassin's forearm as if that might keep him from slitting her throat. For a moment she met Hope's gaze; he could not tell what she was thinking. There was nothing she could do, nowhere she could go. They were done for, as good as dead.

Without warning, Sophia winked—at least he *thought* he saw her wink. And then she let out a hot, distraught sigh, her hand moving from Cassin's arm to her face before she crumpled against him, eyes rolling up into her head before they closed altogether.

Dear God. She'd *swooned.*

And she'd looked just like her mother as she'd done it. Learned from the best indeed!

Cassin froze; La Reinette drew back, brow furrowed.

It was just enough of a pause for Sophia to leap into action. Her eyes flew open as she slammed her elbows into Cassin's gut, and he doubled over with a shout of pain. His rapier once again clattered to the floor; at once Sophia and La Reinette dove after it.

With his heart in his throat, Hope watched the women wrestle each other to the ground, Sophia yelping as La Reinette tugged at her hair. His own limbs pricked to join the fight, to shield Sophia from the madam's wrath.

La Reinette got the better of Sophia, rolling on top of her as she drew back her fist and slammed it into Sophia's cheek. Hope burned with white-hot rage, tugging at his bindings with a viciousness that made his wrists bleed in sympathy with her bloody lip.

Cassin was still rolling on the floor, whining meekly in unintelligible French. Sophia continued to struggle, but La Reinette had the clear advantage. Pinning her to the ground between her knees, Marie reached over Sophia's head and snatched the rapier from the ground.

She climbed to her feet, breathless, and held the point of Bernadette to Sophia's throat.

"Don't," Hope snarled. "Leave her be, Marie."

Marie ignored him, using the rapier's tip to tilt Sophia's chin. "So pretty," she murmured. "So very, very pretty. I see why he loves you, *mademoiselle*. Your charms are many."

Sophia glanced toward Hope. She held her hands by her ears in surrender; but as he watched, she lowered her right hand slowly, very slowly, toward the waist of her suspiciously enormous black-satin breeches.

"Marie." Hope turned to face La Reinette. "Point your blade at me. I am the one deserving of your anger. Besides. Disposing of one body is one thing; but two bodies is a different matter altogether. Isn't that so, Cassin?"

Cassin moaned his consent.

La Reinette met Hope's gaze. "Before, yes, I to—"

Sophia pulled the gleamingly ornate pistol from her breeches and held it in her right hand, releasing the safety as she pointed it at La Reinette.

Hope's heart went to his throat. Out of all the things Sophia could have been hiding in those breeches, he never guessed she'd hide an antique dueling pistol that looked to be a relic of Queen Elizabeth's court; but the trick worked.

La Reinette stumbled back in horror, Sophia rising to stare down the barrel of the gun at Marie's pale face.

Sophia nodded at the rapier. "Drop it."

Marie did as she was told. Holding up her hands, she said, "*Mademoiselle*, listen to me. Listen, yes? I let you go. We let you go, forget the gossip sheets and the memoirs, we forget everything we did to you. Keep your honor, your reputation. Marry whatever lord you pick. I give you this if you give me *him*."

Hope's pulse stilled at her words. He glanced at Sophia; he could not tell what she was thinking. But La Reinette was offering her everything she ever wanted: the peace to pursue her marquess, and marry him without event, her reputation and her pride intact.

His throat tightened. At least he got to see her one last time.

It was too enticing an offer. Sophia should take it and run. She was on the verge of making her dreams come true; this one last push, and it would all fall into her lap.

Sophia should leave Thomas and never look back.

But she didn't.

Instead, she said, "Untie him."

"But, *mademoiselle*, I—"

"Un*tie* him," Sophia thrust the pistol against La Reinette's temple, "or so help me God I'll put a bullet through your head. I am not a soulless lightskirt like you; I won't leave Thomas. I can't leave him."

After a beat, Marie stooped before Hope, head down as she went to work at the ropes that bound his ankles.

Relief washed through Thomas as she untied one leg, then the other. Perhaps he would make it out of here alive; perhaps he and Sophia had a fighting chance.

He glanced up to meet Sophia's eyes. They were hard, still full of alligator tears, but hopeful.

Venturing a smile, Hope opened his mouth to speak when a flash of movement behind Sophia caught his eye.

Too late did he see Cassin rising to his feet, reaching through the gloom with his broad-fingered hand for Sophia's throat.

Thirty-six

It all happened so quickly Sophia hardly had time to think. She was pulled, hard, from behind, a hand wrapping around her neck and squeezing shut her windpipe. Cassin's warm, foul breath filled her nostrils as he tugged her around to face him.

With trembling hands she jabbed the pistol into his ribs, but he merely smiled down at her, tightening his grip on her throat.

"Do it," he hissed. "I remember your shot, it is not very good. I was there, remember, when you could not shoot me?"

Sophia swallowed. Of course she remembered. If only she had remembered to have Thomas teach her how to properly fire a pistol in the meantime. Damn him, she'd been too distracted by his body, his hands, specifically, to waste what precious time they had on so mundane a thing as *shooting*.

Still. Such knowledge would've come in handy at a moment like this.

Sophia fingered the trigger. Dear God, was the gun even loaded? She'd snatched it as an afterthought from a drawer in Uncle Rutledge's dressing room. For all she knew it could be a prop from Drury Lane, an ancient heirloom that hadn't been fired in two hundred years.

Well.

Whatever it was, Sophia was about to find out.

Screwing shut her eyes, she gritted her teeth in anticipation of the discharge and pulled the stiff trigger.

There was a great rushing sound in her ears as her heart

leapt to her throat. She opened her eyes, and Cassin was staring at her, his dark eyes inscrutable.

And then his face creased and the gruesome seam of his mouth opened and he laughed, a loud, triumphant sound. He let loose her throat and wrenched the pistol from her hands, tossing it to the floor where it landed with a decidedly hollow *clunk.*

Sophia glanced at Hope, eyes widening with panic.

This was bad.

He sat very still in his chair. Behind him La Reinette dropped his bound hands—*blast, his hands were still tied*—and slowly rose, her doe eyes brimming with triumph.

"I gave you the chance," she said, grinning. "I gave you the chance to go but you do not take it. So now, we will have the two bodies."

Sophia glanced at Hope, feeling the heat drain from her face. His blue eyes sparked; her heart skipped a beat.

Before she knew what he was about, he reached out and with his foot kicked the rapier up into the air. With bated breath Sophia watched it arc through the room; reflexively she reached up and managed to catch it, thoughtlessly, by the blade.

Ignoring the searing burn that burst across her palm, she took the sword by its rather ridiculous handle. This time she did not hesitate; she whirled about and, praying she was better with a rapier than she was with a pistol, slashed the weapon in the general direction of Cassin.

She sensed the blade finding purchase in the hardened flesh of his arm. He cried out, more a girlish scream than a shout, and fell back. She slashed again and again, so many times until she was breathless and sure Cassin would stay put crumpled there in the corner.

From behind her she heard a scuffle and a decidedly female groan. Sophia turned just in time to see Hope take La Reinette's legs between his own and haul her to the floor.

La Reinette screamed, *No, no!*; her head came down on the floor with a liquid *thud*; she was silent, suddenly.

A strange, heady sort of quiet descended upon the room as Sophia met Thomas's eyes. He was breathing hard, the muscled expanse of his chest straining against his shirt, stained with blood and sweat.

Sophia dropped the rapier.

It was just the two of them. The only ones left standing. Or sitting, in Thomas's case.

She began to shake, her eyes warming with tears.

"Thomas," she breathed, throat so tight with relief she could hardly breathe.

His blue eyes were soft as he spoke. "Don't cry, Sophia. You know how I feel about you crying. Untie me, and I shall see to the rest."

They remained in the shadows, stalking through the darkened streets of Mayfair much like they had done that first night those weeks and weeks ago.

Only this time, Thomas held Sophia's hand firmly in the warmth of his own, their arms brushing as they walked the familiar route side by side.

She felt as if she were walking on a cloud, or perhaps among the stars. Everything felt different; everything looked and smelled and *was* different with Thomas moving quietly beside her. He swallowed her whole in the great bulk of his shadow. Sophia felt safe here, warm, as if nothing and no one could touch her. Nothing and no one mattered, not when she was with Thomas.

It would hurt to let him go; she was no fool, and knew that despite their victory over La Reinette and Guillaume Cassin, the matter of the missing French Blue still remained. Thomas belonged to Hope & Co. He would need to see the matter through to its bitter end, and she knew there was not time enough in his days for her.

Still.

Still her heart hoped.

She squeezed his hand.

I love you.

Sophia waited for him to squeeze back, but he did not.

Her throat tightened with disappointment as they turned into the familiar alley that led to the lane on which her family resided. A chill ran up her spine at the memory of the kiss she shared with Thomas; yes, it was this very spot where he turned . . .

Sophia nearly tripped over his boots as Thomas drew to a sudden stop. With his body he pressed her, hard, against the wall, the scrape of the brick against her bare neck a welcome foil to her pounding heart.

She sucked in a breath as he pulled her against him, his touch rough and riotous and urgent. In the space of a single heartbeat her body went up in flames, the blood rushing hot and wild beneath her skin as he cupped her face in his hands.

And then he was kissing her, his lips gentle as they pulled and teased and stroked her own. His hands were in her hair and his nose was brushing hers and she surrendered to the inescapable tug between their hearts. He surrounded her, her legs nestled between the hardened mass of his thighs, his arms brushing her shoulders as with his hands he moved her face in time to his lips.

Sophia let out a moan; whether it was pleasure or distress, she could not say; but Thomas pulled away, his breath hot on her cheek as he touched his forehead to her own. His eyes were closed.

"Sophia," he breathed. "Sophia, I love you."

Despite herself, she felt the corners of her mouth edging up into a grin.

"What?" he whispered. "What's so amusing?"

"I thought I'd never hear you say it."

He pulled back, looking into her eyes. "And do you have anything to say in reply?"

"Perhaps," she teased. "Perhaps not."

"The anticipation is killing me."

Sophia glanced down to where their hips were pressed snugly against each other. "I know."

"Well?"

She looked up and met his eyes, face creasing with happiness. "You fool. Of *course* I love y—"

He captured the words with his mouth, his kiss in his excitement, his relief, adorably clumsy. Her heart turned over in her chest.

Lovers, let them love.

Thomas pulled back, his eyes serious. "Don't marry the marquess, Sophia. I beg you, don't do it."

"You don't have to beg." Her grin faded. "I couldn't."

"Couldn't? Couldn't do what?"

She looked down at her hands. "Withington is a fine fellow. Better than that. He is kind and generous, and deserving of greatness. I desire for him the love that I know for you. I refused his proposal. I gave back his ring."

"You did." Hope let out another breath. "But he's the season's greatest catch! Everyone wants to marry the marquess, including your mother."

Sophia scoffed. "Everyone, it seems, but me."

Hope couldn't help himself; he smiled. "Marry me, then. I don't have a title, nor do I have a castle; and my fortune—well, I don't have much of that left, either. But I love you. By God, Sophia, I love you more than is proper, more than I should. I love you, and I want you with me all the days of my life."

Sophia swallowed the ominous tightening in her throat even as her heart leapt. "But the bank—the diamond . . ."

Hope shook his head, brushing back a handful of rogue curls. "I was blinded by my grief. My greed. But I don't want to be blind anymore, Sophia. You've opened my eyes to a kind of happiness I never thought I deserved. That I never thought I'd know. And now that I know it, I cannot live without it. I want to do right by my brothers, and by you. Marry me, Sophia. Please do me the great honor of becoming my wife."

The tears were warm as they streamed from the corners of her eyes. "Yes," she said, wiping her cheeks with the lapels of his jacket. "Yes!"

Thomas kissed her long and hard after that, the sort of kiss that left her breathless, lips throbbing, her body alive with the desire for more, *more*. She tangled her hands in the wilds of his hair, pulling him closer; he could never be close enough.

"We're going to have to tell my mother, you know," Sophia said, when at last Thomas had released her, draping an arm about her shoulders as they strolled bonelessly toward the house.

"I know." Thomas pressed a kiss into her forehead. "I'm decently handsome, or so I've been told. Perhaps I might use my masculine charms to woo from her a blessing?"

"You're not *that* handsome," Sophia teased.

They turned out onto the lane, and Sophia looked up from

the scuffed tips of Hope's boots—her *betrothed's* boots!—to see her family's ramshackle house ablaze with light.

"What the devil?" Sophia quickened her pace, Thomas trotting in time beside her. "I hope everything's all right."

"Perhaps Lady Violet has returned?"

"Perhaps."

Together Thomas and Sophia flew through the front door. The hall was empty; the quiet was punctured by a distant chiming, or was that laughter she heard, a vaguely familiar trill?

Sophia tugged Thomas through a pair of French doors at the back of the house that opened onto a derelict rose garden. There, on the crumbling stoop, sat Lady Blaise and Uncle Rutledge, each of them puffing on the most enormous cigars Sophia had ever seen.

"Mama!" she gasped, blinking in disbelief. "What's happened?"

Lady Blaise waved away Sophia's words, chewing thoughtfully on her cigar.

"Your cousin," she said, releasing a plume of smoke from between her lips. "She's run off with the Earl of Harclay. Gretna Green, she told us. Can you imagine?"

Sophia glanced at Hope. "Oh, dear, Mama, I am so very sorry."

"Sorry?" Uncle Rutledge's hairy white brows shot up. "What's there to be sorry for, dear girl? We're celebrating!"

"Celebrating?"

"Yes," Lady Blaise said. "The circumstances of the marriage are not ideal, of course, but neither of us thought Violet would ever be wed, much less to the *Earl* of *Harclay*! Ha! To think she would be the one to tame that wicked rogue."

Lady Blaise turned to Thomas and started, as if seeing him for the first time. "Oh! Before I forget. Violet left something for you, Mr. Hope. The box is on the table inside, in the drawing room."

Thomas and Sophia exchanged a glance. A beat of breathless silence passed between them.

Then, without further ado, they skidded into the house and through the hall, their footfalls giddy as they echoed through the empty rooms.

There, on the round pedestal table in the center of the drawing room, rested a plain wooden box. It was small and square, its hinges oiled bronze.

"Dear God," Sophia breathed, eyes glued to Hope's fingers as they feathered across the lid, at last lifting it open. "Is it—"

"Yes." Thomas held the French Blue between his thumb and forefinger. It glinted in the light of the chandelier above, sparkling wildly as he turned it over in his hand. "Yes, Sophia, it is."

"Well." She took a step forward. "Perhaps you might woo mother dearest, after all."

Thomas lobbed the stone into the air and caught it in his palm. He met her gaze, his eyes alight with mischief as he took her hand, turning it over in his. Carefully he set the diamond in the middle of her palm, curling her fingers around it.

"It's for you. A necklace, perhaps. We'll call it the Hope Diamond." He traced his fingers lightly over the edges of her collarbones, his thumb grazing the edge of her bodice.

Sophia gaped. "But Thomas, I couldn't possibly . . . it's far too large, and precious . . ."

"What was it I said in Princess Caroline's drawing room? Oh yes: 'Only such a stone would be worthy of your beauty.' I meant what I said then, and I mean what I say now. It's yours."

Sophia blinked at the sudden prick of tears. Really, the weeping was getting a bit excessive; but she couldn't help it. This kind of happiness, it was unspeakably wonderful.

"What is it?" he said, brow furrowed with concern as he looked at her. "I know my poetry's terrible, but it's the thought that signifies, isn't it?"

"Yes," she said, burying her head in his chest. "Yes, Thomas, it is. Thank you."

Beneath her ear his heart beat a steady rhythm, strong and assured. "But we *are* going to have to work on your poetry."

"I thought you'd never ask." He grinned. "Might I inquire after your services? I've a memoir—well, a history, really—that needs. Er. Your professional touch. I have nary a penny to my name, you see, but I *am* able to pay you in diamonds."

Sophia smiled. "In that case, let us begin straightaway. I've a desk in my room, right beside the bed . . ."

Thomas swung Sophia into his arms, pressing his lips playfully to her throat as he carried her up the stairs.

Historical Note

The French Blue vanished from historical record following its theft in Paris from the Royal Warehouse in autumn 1792. It reappeared some two decades later in 1812 London, in association with French émigré and jeweler John Françillon; in his papers, Françillon described an enormous, and enormously unique, blue diamond that was at the time in the possession of another jeweler (you may recognize his name from the dockyard scene!)—Daniel Eliason.

There are a variety of scenarios that point to the French Blue's whereabouts between 1792 and 1812; according to Richard Kurin's excellent *Hope Diamond: The Legendary History of a Cursed Gem*, it's possible Caroline, Princess of Wales, inherited the stone from her father, the Duke of Brunswick. If this had indeed been the case, Kurin posits the duke—under duress while at war with Napoleon—had the stone recut sometime around 1805, before sending it to his daughter in London for safekeeping.

While it's impossible to know, exactly, how the French Blue crossed the Channel, I'd like to think this the most likely scenario. It was also a fabulous opportunity to incorporate Caroline into the story—she's an incredibly divisive, fascinating figure (if you haven't noticed yet, I adore having real-life historical giants make cameos in my books!).

That Thomas Hope and his paramour, Lady Sophia Blaise, purchased the French Blue from Princess Caroline under false pretenses—well, that was a delicious twist provided by my imagination.

The diamond disappeared again, mysteriously, for another two decades. It resurfaced in 1839, when it was recorded as being part of Henry Philip Hope's impressive collection of gems. The Hope who is the hero of this book is *Thomas* Hope, Henry's elder brother.

So why not Henry? For starters, I found Thomas a more compelling historical figure; as you learned reading this book, he was an intriguing, well-traveled member of London society, and an author in his own right.

I'd like to imagine that, as heirs to the immense Hope & Company banking empire and expatriates marooned together in London, Thomas and his brother Henry worked together to build their collections—art, books, *jewels*. Perhaps they even comingled their possessions; in *Hope: Adventures of a Diamond*, Marian Fowler suggests that Thomas's wife wore the French Blue to a ball in 1824.

Thomas was well-connected in royal circles and would likely be among the first to know when such a unique stone came up for sale. While no written records exist, it's possible Thomas was involved in the purchase, and perhaps at some point even the ownership, of the stone—after all, Thomas's sons would go on to inherit it.

The theft of the French Blue by a daring—and daringly handsome—earl, however, is entirely the product of my imagination (well, my agent's, too, but that's neither here nor there).

It is true King Louis XVIII and his brother, the Comte d'Artois, lived in exile in London following the Revolution. They would return to France in 1814 during the Bourbon Restoration. That they frequented White's—and had a penchant for nubile women—is, as far as my research tells me, purely fiction.

For more on the Hope Diamond, check out Richard Kurin's *Hope Diamond: The Legendary History of a Cursed Gem* and Ms. Fowler's *Hope: Adventures of a Diamond*, both of which proved indispensible to my research for this trilogy.

Turn the page for a preview of the next book in
Jessica Peterson's Hope Diamond Trilogy

The Undercover Scoundrel

Coming in June 2015 from Berkley Sensation!

Oxfordshire
Summer 1800

Their vows echoed off the chapel's mottled ceiling, rising and swooping like birds to surround the couple in soft whispers of faith and hope and love.

"Rings?" the Vicar said, arching a brow.

For a moment the groom's eyes went wide; and then he plucked the pale green ribbon from his queue, releasing a curtain of red hair about his shoulders. He used his teeth to cut the ribbon in two. Tying one length into a small circlet, he slid it onto the bride's fourth finger.

A sea of flickering candles held the darkness at bay as Lady Caroline Townshend was kissed for the first time by her husband. Joy welled up inside her and she smiled against the warm press of Henry Beaton Lake's lips.

He kissed her far less chastely than was proper at a wedding, even a secret one. He kissed her as if every stroke, every pull, every move of their lips roused, rather than satiated, a growing need inside him.

Henry held her face in his hands, guiding her toward him as he pressed a kiss to one corner of her mouth, then the other. Breathless, Caroline stood on the tips of her toes to meet his caresses, streaks of light and bursts of color illuminating the backs of her closed eyelids.

The Vicar, a rather less romantic fellow than Romeo and Juliet's priest, shut his ancient Bible with a censorial *thwunk*.

Blushing, Caroline fell back from Henry, their hands entwining between them.

Lips pursed, eyes wide, the Vicar glared at them. "God. Sees. *Everything.*"

In a whirl of black he turned and stalked down the aisle, shaking his head at young people these days and their carnal proclivities. Caroline's lady's maid, Nicks—the one and only witness—hurried after him.

Beside Caroline, Henry shook with repressed laughter.

"How much did you pay him?" she whispered.

"Clearly not enough."

"Will he tell our parents?"

Henry ran his thumb across the back of her hand. "In the morning, yes."

"Then we haven't much time."

"Do you mean to ravish me, Mrs. Lake?"

"I do indeed."

"Let's get on with it, then," he said, and swung her into his arms.

Caroline grasped the windowsill and, as Henry gave her a boost from below, somersaulted into his bed chamber. Inside the room it was warm and quite dark, save for a single lit taper on the bedside table.

"Really," she panted, wiping her hands on her skirts. "Why. Not use. The door? Your parents are. Still at my house for the. Ball."

Henry landed noiselessly on his feet, closing the window behind him. "Where's the challenge in that? Besides, I like all this sneaking about. Suits the secret marriage bit, don't you think?"

He took her outstretched hands and pulled her a smidge too enthusiastically to her feet. Her nose bumped against the hardened center of his chest.

"Oh," he said, thumbing her chin. "Oh, Caroline, I'm terribly sorry. Are you all right? I only meant to, um . . . I forget sometimes that you're so little, you see, I'm used to my brothers, as you know they're rather large . . ."

Caroline looked up at Henry. Large was an understatement;

like his older brothers, Henry was a broad-shouldered, ginger-haired giant with the wickedest cheekbones she had ever seen. His green eyes were even wicked*er* (if that was a word), so brightly suggestive, so darkly penetrating, Caroline feared she might burst into flames every time he looked at her.

"I'll have a devil of a time explaining that to my mother."

Henry angled his neck and brushed his lips to her injured nose. "Bloody business, marriage."

"Mm-hm," she said, burrowing further into the circle of his arms. Her ring of ribbon slipped from her finger—it was a tad too large—and she coaxed it back into place.

His hand slid from her cheek to cup the back of her neck. With his thumb he tilted her head and caught her mouth with his. He kissed her deeply, passionately, as if he were out to steal not only her heart but her soul, her body, her being.

Henry took her bottom lip between his teeth. She saw stars.

His hands were on her face now; Caroline clung to his wrists, fearful the rush in her knees might cause them to give out. She felt the scatter-shot beat of his pulse beneath her fingers, the jutting architecture of his bones. Strength rippled beneath the surface of his skin; strength she felt him struggling to restrain.

And yet he touched her with great care, gently, as awed by her shape as she was of his. His fingers tangled in the hair at her temples as his mouth moved to her neck, working the tender skin there with his lips.

Caroline let out a breath, desperate, suddenly, to be free of her stays and ridiculously ruffled muslin gown. She couldn't breathe, couldn't think; she was lost in the longing she'd felt for Henry from the moment they met eyes across the garden, three weeks before.

She was hardly seventeen, set to make her debut at St. James's the following spring. Even so, Caroline knew the intensity of her feelings for Henry was a rare thing; rare and fragile, as the world seemed fanatically intent to nip such reckless affection in the bud before it ever had a chance to bloom.

But Caroline was intent to bloom. Beneath Henry's careful, confident touch, his insistent caresses, she felt herself unravel and open, giving as Henry took, and took, and kept taking.

She slipped her hands beneath the lapels of his jacket. Henry rolled back his shoulders and shrugged free of the garment, tossing it aside. He began to move forward, pressing his body into hers as he guided her farther into the room. His fingers found purchase in a row of buttons between the blades of her shoulders, working them free one at a time.

"Hold up your arms, darling," he murmured against her mouth, and gently coaxed the gown over her head.

It fell with a rustling sigh to the floor. The night air felt coolly potent against the bare skin of her arms. She shivered.

Henry gathered her in his arms, surrounding her body with the heat of his own. She could smell his skin, the clean, citrusy spice of his soap. Her desire soared.

In a hushed frenzy of movement they unclothed one another: his waistcoat, her stays, his neckcloth; his head caught in his shirt, and after several futile attempts to remove it, Henry ripped it open. Buttons ricocheted about the room, landing with small *pings* as they rolled across the floor.

Caroline stared at his bare chest. She swallowed.

Henry took her hands and placed them on the center of his breastbone. She inhaled at the shock of warmth that met with her palms, the spring of wiry hair. She could feel his heart beating proudly within the cage of his ribs. Proudly, wildly, an echo of her own.

In the darkness she bent her neck, and pressed her lips to his chest. He inhaled sharply, his chest rising and falling beneath the working of her lips across his collarbone, up the corded slope of his neck.

Heavens, but she hoped his parents would not return for some hours yet; Caroline couldn't have kept quiet if she'd wanted.

His fingers tugged at the neckline of her chemise, taking her bare shoulder in his mouth. The heat between her legs burned hotter. Henry coaxed the garment down the length of her body, releasing one breast, then the other. Quickly his mouth moved to take her nipple between his teeth, rolling it in the velvet touch of his tongue. The sensation was so poignant it hurt.

"Henry," she breathed, tangling her fingers in his hair. "Please. Show me."

He raised his head, eyes luminescent, translucent; they were warm and soft and they were on her, gleaming with desire.

"I was hoping you'd show me," he replied.

"You've never? Never . . . you're almost twenty, I thought . . ."

"This is to be the first time for both of us, I'm afraid."

"Then I really *am* to ravage you."

He grinned. "If you don't mind terribly."

His mouth came down on hers, and he was digging at the pins in her hair with impatient fingers. She heard them fall, one by one, until at last her hair tumbled in soft waves about her shoulder blades. Henry drew his hands through its tangled mass to rest on the naked small of her back. He pulled her to him, skin to skin; the hardened knots of her nipples brushed against his chest, and she nearly cried out in agony, in desire.

The backs of Caroline's thighs met with the bed. Henry grasped her hips, and her breath caught in her throat as he tossed her lightly onto the mattress. The coverlet felt cool and deliciously soft against her bare skin.

Henry looked down upon her with narrowed eyes, his face suddenly tight.

"Caroline," he said roughly, slowly. "You are so . . . so very lovely. Beautiful."

He ran a hand up the side of her ribcage, cupping her breast; he thumbed her nipple and she arched into his touch.

And then both his hands moved to her legs, sliding off her stockings; his fingers were in the waistband of her pantalettes, tugging them over the smooth expanse of her belly, her knees.

Caroline was naked. She winced at the sudden rush of cool air against the beating throb of her sex. *Please*, she prayed. *Please let it be soon.*

Henry unbuttoned his breeches and swept them down to his ankles. He rose; Caroline stared at his cock, heavy with need, as unrepentantly enormous and thickly veined as the rest of his body. It jutted out from the sharp angle of his hips, unembarrassed, and she was at once hesitant and terribly curious.

"Caroline," he said.

She swallowed. "I'm all right."

"Caroline," he said again. "We don't have to do this. I couldn't bear it if I hurt you, if you weren't ready."

For a beat he did not move, as if waiting for her to change her mind; waiting for her to roll over and demand he escort her home, take back all they'd said and done this night.

"I want to," she said. "We're married now, remember? We get to do this at last."

Caroline sat up and reached for him. He drew a breath as her hand followed the narrowing trail of hair down his hardened belly; his whole body tensed when she wrapped her hand around his cock. He felt hard and soft all at once, the skin impatiently hot and silken. She put her mouth on his belly. One of his hands went to her hair while the other moved down to cover her own around his manhood.

"How?" she whispered.

"Like this," he said, and together their hands moved up and down the length of his cock, once, twice, until he groaned and pulled away, suddenly, as if she'd hurt him.

"Caroline," he said, his face in her hair. "I love you."

"I love you," she whispered.

"I can't wait much longer. I want—I need you. Badly. Here." He reached behind him, producing his rumpled shirt. "Lie down on this, love. I'm afraid you might bleed."

Bleed?

She swallowed for what felt like the hundredth time that night. He wasn't kidding about marriage being a bloody business.

Wedging the shirt beneath Caroline's bottom, Henry coaxed her back onto the bed. He took her knees in her hands and moved them apart, stepping forward so that he was wedged between her legs. She was wide open to him; she was afraid; she was overwhelmingly aroused.

Henry reached down and they both drew a breath when his first two fingers slipped between her slick curls, revealing a warmth, a wetness, that neither of them expected. Her desire soared; she ached for him to be inside her.

"You're," he swallowed, "ready?"

"Yes," she panted. "Please, Henry."

"Once we . . . I can't stop then."

"I don't want you to stop."

He stepped forward. The bed was set high, so high that, even while standing, Henry's hips were level with hers. He put his hands on the inside of her thighs, pushing her legs even wider.

"Bend your knees about me," he said.

Caroline did as she was told. He wrapped her bent legs about his hips, hooking her feet at his buttocks. She felt his fingers on her sex, holding her open as, with his other hand, he guided his cock into her folds. He nudged against her, wincing.

"Is it . . . are we going to work?" she asked.

"Yes," he breathed. "It's very small in there."

"Is it. Um. As it should be?"

He closed his eyes, lips curling into a pained half grin. "You're perfect."

She tried not to recoil as pressure mounted between her legs. She felt herself stretching. Her pleasure was edged with pain.

"Caroline," he said. He was looking at her now, eyes wide with concern. "Tell me how you're feeling, all right?"

"I'm all right."

He guided himself farther against her, using his fingers to keep her open to him. He moved his hips, pressing into her. He pressed harder, sucking in a breath as the first bit of him entered her.

The pleasant throb between her legs heightened to burning discomfort. Her eyes smarted. Henry was saying her name but she told him to keep going, and he did. Slowly he slid into her wet warmth; they both paused when he met the barrier inside her. He looked at her. She nodded, overwhelmed by the sting; by the sense of fullness he brought her.

I'm all right, Henry. Keep going.

He inhaled through his nose, and then he bucked his hips. In a single heartbeat he sunk to the hilt. A sound escaped Caroline's lips, something between a cry and a whimper.

He was bent over her then, taking her cry into his mouth as he set his forearms on either side of her head, surrounding her. His body was wound tightly; she could tell he wanted to move between her legs, but he waited.

He grit his teeth.

The sting began to subside, her pleasure—her heart—rising in its place. Oh, this felt lovely. A little full. But lovely.

Her hips began to circle against him, asking for more. Henry let out the breath he'd been holding and gently rocked his hips, withdrawing, entering again. Their skin, damp with sweat, slid and stuck.

She surrendered.

She surrendered to the pounding beat of her passion. To the heavy weight of her love for him.

She surrendered to Henry.

They moved against each other ardently, lost in a whirl of pain and limbs and pleasure. Her hands moved over his shoulders, marveling at the roping and bunching of his back muscles as he worked between her legs. His lips trailed over her jaw and throat.

He slowed, suddenly, and then his eyes fluttered shut; he stilled and she could feel his cock pulse inside her.

"Christ," he said when the pulsing subsided. His lips fluttered over her eyelashes. "I'm sorry, Caroline, I didn't mean . . . I meant to be more careful, but you felt so good, I couldn't stop. I wanted to stop."

"I didn't want you to stop," she whispered. "I don't want you to ever stop."

Slowly he withdrew from inside her; she felt his seed seeping warmly from between her legs.

He cursed again when he looked down at the shirt beneath her.

"What is it?" she said.

"Blood," he replied, mouth drawn into a line as he used the shirt to clean her. "A lot of it. Are you sure you're all right?"

Caroline flexed her stiff legs. She felt very sore between them. "All right. Sore. A little sore."

He crumpled the shirt between his hands and tossed it to the ground. He tugged the coverlet aside, holding it open for her. "Here, lie down. I'll get a towel."

She crawled between the bedclothes, smiling as she drew them up to her nose. They smelled like him. Like her husband.

He returned from the washstand with a damp towel, climbing into bed beside her. Thankfully he was still naked as the day he was born; he pressed his body against hers as he coaxed her legs apart, pressing the towel between them. It felt blessedly cool.

"I love you, Caroline," he murmured in her ear, nicking the lobe with his teeth. She felt him smiling against her skin. "*Wife*."

She smiled, too, a wide, irrepressible thing she felt in every corner of her being. Despite everything—despite how it appeared, her ten-thousand pound dowry and his lack of position—despite their youth, their parents' disapproval—despite all that, she knew this was where she was meant to be.

Caroline loved him. She felt loved by him. And wasn't that the end of everything?

Henry spun her around and tugged her against the hardened mass of his body, her back to his front. He pulled the sheets over their heads and she, giggling, yielded to his hands as he took her body again and again and again, until the sun burned away the darkness.

It happened the next afternoon. As she was wont to do when in need of solitude and space, Caroline disappeared into the garden. Henry—her *husband!*—had a habit of sneaking from his father's house to meet her there besides; she had half a mind to toss him beneath a bush and ravage him soundly, as she promised she would last night.

She was on her knees, digging at a half-dead holly, when she heard the telltale rustle in a nearby boxwood. Her chest lit up with excitement; she was smiling, hard, when she brushed back her hair and turned toward the noise.

Only it wasn't Henry. George Osbourne, Viscount Umberton, heir to the wildly wealthy Earl of Berry and Henry's very best friend, emerged from the hedgerow. Caroline's joy hardened in her throat at the sight of Osbourne's well formed, if slight, figure. His face was hard, his dark eyes soft.

A tendril of panic unfurled inside her belly. She didn't like that look; something was amiss.

"My Lord," she said hopefully, as if she might will good news with the tone of her voice. "What an unexpected surprise. Have you . . . er . . . come for tea?"

Osbourne bowed. "My Lady, I am sorry to meet you like this, but I came straightaway."

"What?" So much for the soothing tone of voice. "What is it?"

He wiped the sweat from his thick eyebrow with a trembling thumb. When he spoke his voice was low, hoarse.

"He's gone. Henry—Lake—he's gone. I—" Here Osbourne looked away. "I thought you should know. I understand the two of you have . . . become quite close this summer, and I—"

The brass-handled garden trowel fell from her gloved hand to the earth with a muted *thud* of protest. "Gone? Where? But how . . . I don't understand!"

Osbourne's face was tensed with pain as he looked down at her. He swallowed. "Emptied his drawers into a valise—there's nothing left, and he took the five pounds his older brother was hiding in his pillow. He left a note, something about duty, and not coming to look for him. He said he wouldn't come back. Lady Caroline, Henry is gone."

Caroline's vision blurred; tears burned her eyes, and she fell back on her haunches. "Perhaps it's a mistake," she said. "A misunderstanding with his father, or maybe it's a joke, or—or—"

"I know Henry," Osbourne said. "He's gone, Caroline. I don't know where, and I don't know why. But he's gone."

She was sobbing then, and George Osbourne fell to his knees beside her and held her to his chest. They sat like that, damp with the heat of one another's tears, until the garden was tawny with twilight.

That was the last Caroline heard of Henry Beaton Lake, her husband, before he disappeared from Oxfordshire, from England, from her life.

Before he disappeared forever.

In an era when ladies were demure and men courtly, one priceless treasure set England ablaze with scandal and passion—the Hope Diamond.

FROM

JESSICA PETERSON

The Gentleman Jewel Thief

The Hope Diamond Trilogy

Heir to an impressive title and fortune, Lord William Townshend, Earl of Harclay, is among the most disreputable rakes in England. Desperately bored by dull heiresses and tedious soirees, he seeks new excitement—starting with a dangerous scheme to steal the world's most legendary gemstone from its owner, Thomas Hope. To his surprise, it's not the robbery that sets his blood burning but the alluring lady he pilfers the gem from...

jessicapeterson.com
facebook.com/JessicaPetersonAuthor
facebook.com/LoveAlwaysBooks
penguin.com

M1534T0714

FROM AWARD-WINNING AUTHOR

ANNE GRACIE

THE *Autumn Bride*

A Chance Sisters Romance

Governess Abigail Chantry will do anything to save her sister and two dearest friends from destitution, even if it means breaking into an empty mansion. Which is how she encounters the neglected Lady Beatrice Davenham, who agrees that the four young ladies should become her "nieces," eliminating the threat of disaster for all. It's the perfect situation, until Lady Beatrice's dashing and arrogant nephew, Lord Davenham, returns from the Orient—and discovers an impostor running his household...

"I never miss an Anne Gracie book."

—Julia Quinn, *New York Times* bestselling author

"Treat yourself to some super reads from a most talented writer."

—*Romance Reviews Today*

annegracie.com
facebook.com/AnneGracieAuthor
facebook.com/LoveAlwaysBooks
penguin.com

M1389T1013

Enter the rich world of historical romance with Berkley Books . . .

Madeline Hunter

Jennifer Ashley

Joanna Bourne

Lynn Kurland

Jodi Thomas

Anne Gracie

Love is timeless.

berkleyjoveauthors.com

M9G0610

Be afraid of the dark.

From the corner of his eye, Tanner saw a shadow rushing toward him, saw the glint of moonlight on blue metal: *Gun.* He pulled the sap from his pocket and whirled. Ten feet away, the man skidded to a stop and raised the shotgun. Tanner took two bounding steps, slammed his foot down on the shotgun's barrel, trapped it against the floor, then lashed out with the sap, catching the man in the temple.

Tanner looked up. On the second-floor landing, a figure spun and disappeared down the hall. With Cahil on his heels, Tanner hurled up the steps. He reached the landing, looked left, saw nothing, looked right. A long hallway stretched before him. There were two open doors on each side, and one at the end. It was closed.

Tanner gestured to Cahil: *I'm gonna crash it. Cover my back.*

Cahil nodded.

Tanner took a deep breath and charged down the hall. . . . He hit the door and it crashed inward. To his right, a figure was trying to climb through the open window. Tanner ran over and jammed his heel in the man's Achilles tendon. The man squealed and fell back. Briggs grabbed his collar and turned him around.

"Good to see you again, Genoa."

THE WALL OF NIGHT

Grant Blackwood

JOVE BOOKS, NEW YORK

THE WALL OF NIGHT

A Jove Book / published by arrangement with the author

PRINTING HISTORY
Jove edition / April 2002

Visit our website at
www.penguinputnam.com

ISBN: 0-515-13278-0

A JOVE BOOK®
Jove Books are published by The Berkley Publishing Group, a division of Penguin Putnam Inc., 375 Hudson Street, New York, New York 10014.
JOVE and the "J" design are trademarks belonging to Penguin Putnam Inc.

PRINTED IN THE UNITED STATES OF AMERICA

10 9 8 7 6 5 4 3 2 1

ACKNOWLEDGMENTS

First, and most important, my heartfelt thanks to the many friends, family members, and strangers alike who not only embraced *The End of Enemies*, but who also helped make it a success. I am honored by your support. You were entertained and transported, and I'm glad.

To Jonathon, Christi, and the entire Lazear team. I'm a lucky man.

To my editor, Tom Colgan, and the folks at Penguin Putnam, thanks again for everything.

To Trent Fluegel, a fine friend indeed.

To Julie: I love sharing my life with you.

And finally, to Gus, who I forgot to mention last time. Thank you for choosing me as your friend. You stood by me every step of the way.

PROLOGUE

Lake Baikal, Russia, 1909

The last day Priscilla Hadin was to see her husband alive was breathtaking: the air crisp and fresh, the sky a cloudless blue. Beyond the pier, the lake was a perfect mirror for the reds and golds of the trees bordering the shoreline.

She watched her husband cajole the stevedores as they scurried up and down the boat's gangplank, carrying crates of all sizes and shapes. The pier thrummed with activity: throngs of natives, the babble of different languages, vendors hawking grilled meat and trinkets, the wail of boat whistles.

Something bumped Priscilla from behind and she turned. A goat was chewing at her fur boots; a gap-toothed woman tugged at the goat and kept walking. *A far cry from Long Island*, Priscilla thought.

"You there!" she heard her husband call. "Be careful, will you? Good man!"

Andrew Galbreth Hadin turned and flashed a grin at Priscilla. *So like a little boy*, she thought fondly. In many ways Andrew was a mystery to her. He had the courage of a lion and the dogged curiosity of a toddler who's just realized he's surrounded by a giant, fascinating world.

Known in the newspapers as "Dashing Andy" or "The Millionaire Buccaneer," Hadin was renowned for his wild, globe-hopping explorations. If it hadn't been mapped, braved, or—better yet—discovered, Hadin was game for it. During their marriage, Priscilla had seen him off on dozens of adventures: Arabia in search of Ubar, the Atlantis of the Sands; Turkey, for Noah's Ark; Tibet in search of the Yeti. . .

Wherever he went, however long he was gone, he always came back to her.

Why, then, couldn't she shake this gloom? It was silly. Andrew always came back. "Glorious day, eh?" he called to her, walking up.

"Yes, it is. These Russian folk are interesting."

"Hard workers, too. Wish I'd had them in the Congo. Wouldn't have been half as dicey."

"You don't suppose there are any of those Trotskyites around, do you?"

"No, dear, most of them are in Vienna. Some lake, eh? 'The Jewel of Siberia,' they call it."

"It's beautiful."

"The oldest lake in the world; the deepest, too. Did you know there are over three hundred rivers emptying into it, but only one going out—the Angara?"

"No, I didn't—"

"And over a third of its fish aren't found anywhere else in the world. Legend has it there's a tunnel at the bottom, a natural lava tube that leads all the way to the Pacific Ocean. Wouldn't that be something to see? Perhaps I could find one of those diving bells—"

Priscilla put her finger to his lips. "Dear, perhaps you should finish this adventure first?"

Hadin grinned. "Yes, of course."

"So tell me again, this place you're going to . . . Tonga—"

"Tunguska, darling."

"Tunguska. What's so special about it? Something landed there?"

"More like *slammed into*, Pris. Nobody's sure what happened. That's what we hope to find out. Some say it was a space rock; others think perhaps an alien ship—from Mars, perhaps!"

"Oh, good lord, Andrew!"

"Anyway whatever it is flattened hundreds of square miles of forest. Thousands and thousands of trees bowled over like toothpicks. Folks in Belgium could feel the impact. And we'll be the first to see it! The trick, of course, will be finding it. Moscow is being rather stingy with information—"

"Then how did you get permission?"

Hadin grinned and leaned closer. "They think I'm on an expedition for the Smithsonian. Not to worry, Pris. Nogoruk's the finest guide around; he could track a snowflake across Alaska! We'll follow the Selenga to the northeast, looking for clues as we go. It will be fantastic fun!"

The paddle wheel's horn blew, echoing over the lake. Standing on the bridge, a squat man in a fur hat waved at Hadin. "That's Nogoruk, Pris. We're ready to go."

Priscilla felt her eyes filling up with tears. "Must you?"

"I'm afraid so, darling. Chin up. Don't I always come back to you?"

"Yes, but . . ." *But what?* she wondered. *He did always come back.* "When will you be back?"

"Hard to say. Four months, perhaps. We don't want to get caught out when the snow flies. It's fearsome, they say. First chance, I'll send word." Hadin kissed her. "My love to the children."

He kissed her one last time, then started up the gangplank. At its head, he waved to her, then jumped onto the deck and began barking orders. Crewmen cast off the lines and slowly the boat began drifting away from the pier as the current took hold. The horn blew once more then the giant waterwheels started churning, froth and mist billowing around the stern.

A lone figure appeared on the afterdeck: tall and broad-shouldered, his cornstalk hair wild in the wind, beaming like a child on his first roller-coaster ride. Hadin raised his arms and waved at his wife.

She waved back.

PRISCILLA HADIN LATER DIED SEVENTY-FOUR YEARS TO THE DAY her husband left, never discovering what had become of him. Nor could she know what pivotal role his ill-fated expedition would play in saving the lives of four strangers carrying a secret that would decide the fate of hundreds of thousands of people.

Chengde, China, 1990

Set amid the peaks and wooded valleys 150 miles northeast of Beijing, the Imperial Summer Villa had for centuries been the summer home to emperors hoping to trade the heat of Beijing in favor of the cooler mountain air. Since the '70s it had been one of China's most famous parks.

In the two months he'd been in China, Briggs Tanner had spent many hours in Chengde, first posing as a Westerner taking in the sights, and then as a deep-cover operative reconnoitering the ground on which he hoped to pull off the most dramatic defection since the Cold War.

Four months earlier, chief of staff for the People's Liberation Army, General Han Soong, had secretly passed a note to an attache during a reception at the U.S. embassy. The missive was short and direct: Soong wanted out. The stunning request was hurriedly passed on to the CIA, who in turn immediately arranged to send a controller to oversee the operation.

Tanner had spent his first five weeks in-country running a small network of support agents and laying the groundwork for Soong's escape before turning his attention to the nuts-and-bolts of how he planned to spirit Soong from the country.

He chose Chengde for several reasons: its distance from Beijing and the city's ubiquitous police force; its popularity with not only tourists but with Beijingers as well; and lastly, its setting.

Encompassing some 1400 acres and surrounded by an ancient stone wall measuring six miles in circumference, Chengde is a warren of grasslands, wooded hills, blooming gardens, dozens of miles of landscaped paths, and over a hundred buildings, from traditional Chinese pavilions and temples to rustic longhouses that had once served as barracks for imperial guards.

Armed with a camera and a map, Tanner walked every corner of Chengde until the layout was embedded in his brain. He knew where every path began and ended, where they intersected with others, where the shortcuts and dead ends lay. He could stand at any section of the wall and know precisely what lay on the other side. Above all, he knew the best meeting places and the vantage points from which he could survey them.

The November day Tanner was to put Soong into the "pipeline" dawned crisp and cool. Chengde's trees blazed in a thousand shades of red and gold. Before first light fell over the park, Tanner was in position at an overlook near Gold Mountain Temple. The park was all but deserted, with only a few caretakers going about their business. Below him, a quarter mile distant, lay Ruyi and Jinghu lakes and beyond them, west of the Front Palace, Dehui Gate, the park's main entrance. Fifty yards down the central path lay the fountain at which he and Soong were to meet.

Tanner checked his watch. Forty minutes to go. He felt a flutter in his belly and took a deep breath. *Relax, Briggs,* he commanded himself. *Almost there.*

He aimed his camera's long lens on the gate and saw the day's first tourists entering the park. He scanned the paths and courtyards until he had a rough count of several dozen people, an even mix of Chinese families and Western sight-seers.

He got up and wandered the paths around the temple for twenty minutes, snapping the occasional photo and studying his map, all the while keeping one eye on the main gate. Five minutes before the meeting time, Briggs was scanning the Front Palace when something caught his eye.

A Chinese mother and father with a child were stopped beside the fountain feeding the ducks, when suddenly the toddler lost his balance and plunged into the water. The father rushed forward to help. As he stooped over to pick up the child, his coat swung open, revealing a shoulder holster.

Heart in his throat, Tanner tightened on the man and saw, trailing from his left ear, a nearly transparent wire that led down into his collar. *What the hell is this. . . .* He checked his watch: *Time.* He swiveled the lens to the main gate. As if on cue, General Han Soong stepped onto the path.

No, no, no. . . .

Briggs looked around. In a nearby garden bed, a caretaker knelt in the dirt with a trowel. The man looked up, caught Tanner's eye, then glanced away. Briggs felt his heart lurch. They were here, the *Guoanbu* was here. A dozen questions whirled in his brain, but he quashed them. The "how" of it didn't matter. He and Soong were standing in the middle of a trap.

Tanner's mind raced. This couldn't be happening—*shouldn't* be happening, but it was.

At the main gate, Soong was strolling toward the fountain. From his vantage point, Tanner could see them now, *Guoanbu* agents moving in, exiting nearby pavilions and walking along the trails on either side of Soong. Oblivious, Soong kept walking.

From the corner of his eye, Briggs saw the caretaker raise his wrist to his mouth and speak into the hidden microphone there. *Calling in backup,* Tanner realized. Having assumed Soong's controller would be close to the meeting site, they'd moved in too early, leaving Tanner outside their perimeter. He still had a chance. But what about Soong?

As he asked the question, he saw a pair of agents trot up behind Soong and grab his arms.

Tanner was torn. *Leave, Briggs, get away!* There was nothing to be done for Soong now.

Forcing an easy pace, he turned and began strolling back toward the temple; a hundred yards beyond it he could see the vine-draped wall. He mounted the temple's wooden walkway.

"You there! Stop!"

Tanner glanced over his shoulder. The caretaker was charging toward him. Tanner broke into a sprint, turned the temple corner, then stopped and flattened himself against the wall. The pounding of feet drew nearer. The caretaker barged around the corner, saw Tanner, tried to backpedal. Tanner grabbed him by the collar, pulled him close, and lashed out with a short jab to the man's kidney. The man gasped and arched backward. Tanner slammed his fist into his temple, knocking him unconscious.

He pulled back the man's sleeve, revealing the microphone. "I see him!" Tanner shouted in his best Mandarin. "Bifeng Temple! Hurry!"

He sprinted to the wall, took a bounding leap onto the vines, and started climbing. At the top, he stopped, turned back. He focused his camera on the main gate. There, being led away by a dozen men, was Han Soong. Just before he disappeared from view, Soong glanced over his shoulder.

Looking for me, Tanner thought in anguish. *God, I'm sorry Han.*

He tore his eyes away, rolled himself over the wall, and started running.

Central China, 1999

Though the deep, twisting gorges and towering rock spires of the highlands provided the ideal hiding place for the test facility, they did little for traveling comfort—especially in a Russian-built Hind-D attack helicopter designed more for durability than luxury.

Such is the price of secrecy, Kyung Xiang thought, and gripped the armrests a bit tighter.

As the head of China's *Guoanbu,* or Ministry of State Security, Xiang was charged with many secrets, but the facility they'd just left surpassed all of them—except for Rubicon itself, of course. That he'd been entrusted with such an operation was both exhilarating and daunting. If it succeeded—if *he* succeeded—China would become the world's premier superpower. As it should be.

But that was only part of it, Xiang knew. This was also his chance at redemption.

In his thirty-first year of government service, Xiang had seen firsthand the brutality of Chinese politics, but until the Soong affair he'd never felt it personally. That he'd thwarted what could have been a disaster for the People's Republic was never mentioned; in fact, the mere proximity of disaster had nearly sealed his fate. His superiors had painted him as the scapegoat with typical Mandarin efficiency. One day a promising *Guoanbu* chief, the next a mere agent. His rise to the top of the MSS had surprised many people, and truth be told had Rubicon not landed in his lap, he would be on his way out.

Everything hinged on Rubicon. Failure didn't bear thinking about.

Xiang felt himself mashed against the door as the pilot rolled the Hind onto its side. An outcropping of rock swept past the windshield, so close Xiang could have reached out and touched it.

He glanced over his shoulder. The two civilians in the back were slumped in their seats, their faces pasty. Hopefully they would recover. He wanted his passengers clearheaded when they reached their destination; nothing should blunt the impact of what they were going to see.

The gorge widened and the pilot descended, following the river until it opened into a lake. The village—little more than a cluster of huts surrounded by millet fields and forest—lay on the far shore.

"Land upwind of the lake," Xiang ordered the pilot.

They banked around the shoreline and set down on the outskirts of the village. As the rotors spooled down, Xiang got out and gestured for the passengers to do the same.

"What is this place?" asked the older man, the director of the facility.

"Just a village," Xiang said. "One village amid thousands. It doesn't have a name."

"Where is everyone?" the younger man, the director's assistant, asked.

"Good question. Come, I'll show you."

Xiang led them down the empty main road to the edge of the village. Ahead lay a berm of dirt almost twenty feet tall. Xiang started up the mound, the two men struggling to keep up. When they reached the top, Xiang pointed down the opposite slope.

At the base of the mound lay a pit, ten feet deep, ten feet wide, and some fifty yards long. Stacked to its rim were bodies—hundreds of them, all nude—ranging in age from six months to ninety years.

The older man sputtered, his eyes wide. "Oh. . . . Oh, my—"

"Your what?" Xiang said. "Your Buddha? This is not the work of your fat little God. This is your work."

"What do you mean?" said the assistant director. "What happened here?"

"Their water supply was contaminated by a type of radioactive isotope, I'm told. The test you performed at the facility last month not only failed, but some of the runoff found its way into the river, then into this lake. The villagers drank the water and fed it to their livestock. Now they're all dead."

"No, that can't be—"

"Not only has your mistake put us behind schedule, but now we have to cover it up before we have swarms of Western media digging around," Xiang said.

The older man found his voice. "Is that all you care about? Public relations? You heartless—"

"This goes beyond public relations! We're talking about the future of China. The deaths of a few peasants is inconsequential. In fact, it's so inconsequential that one more won't make any difference."

In one fluid motion, Xiang drew his side arm, pressed it to the director's forehead, and fired. The back of the man's head exploded. He crumpled to the ground. Xiang reholstered his pistol, then placed his foot on the corpse's hip and rolled the body down the slope.

Mouth agape, the younger man watched the body land in a heap atop those of the villagers.

"You've just been promoted," Xiang said. "See that you do better than your predecessor."

White House, Washington, D.C.

Ten months to retirement, thought President John Haverland, staring out the window of the Oval Office. Ten months left in a career that had spanned forty years. After November he'd serve out his last days as a lame duck, a glorified house sitter. Even now, his official duties were becoming fewer and fewer, which, truth be told, didn't bother him much. It gave him time to think.

In all, he decided, he'd done a fair job. He'd made his mistakes, but that was life. He'd learned from them, however, and worked hard to base his decisions in that wisdom. *Most of them, at least.*

His own vice president was such a case. He'd never liked Phillip Martin, not when they worked together in the Senate, and not when his campaign advisors had put his name at the top of the list for vice presidential running mates. He'd argued against it, but in the end the choice was simple: Martin's inclusion on the ticket would secure the votes Haverland needed to win. Of course, if the only issue had been victory, he would have told his advisors to shove it.

Quite simply, John Haverland believed in the power of service and he believed he could make a difference to the welfare of his country. Four years ago, Americans didn't trust such sentiments. They were tired and mistrustful. Even so, by the time the election entered the final stretch, Haverland had changed a lot of minds. It still wasn't going to be enough, his staff told him. Without Martin, we lose.

They had the statistics to support their claim. He reluctantly assented, and two months later he was elected president. Martin had played his role well enough, but the irony of their partnership was never lost on Haverland. He, the faithful, buck-stops-here president; and Martin, the polished, self-serving, chameleonlike vice president.

And now the son-of-a-bitch is making a run for the presidency.

"Not if I can help it," he muttered. He pressed his intercom button. "Joanne, please call Vice President Martin and tell him I need to see him."

"Yes, Mr. President."

Martin arrived ten minutes later. He flashed his plastic smile at Haverland and strode across the carpet. "John, how are you today?"

"Sit down, Phil."

Martin's smile never faltered, but Haverland saw a flash

of uncertainty in his VP's eyes. *The perfect political animal,* Haverland thought. *God help us. . . .*

"Phil, I'll come to the point: Your secretary has accused you of sexual harassment."

"What?" Martin cried. "Peggy Manahan? That's ridiculous, John. I would never—"

"In fact, Phil, what she describes sounds more like sexual assault."

Martin chuckled. "Oh, come on. . . ."

"She claims you had her pinned against the wall, that you were pulling up her skirt."

"That's not true."

"What part?"

"All of it, John. For God's sake—"

"It never happened?"

"No." Martin spread his hands. "She's confused, John. Perhaps she had ideas about us. . . ."

Oh good Christ, Haverland thought. "So it never happened and Peggy Manahan, a solid, faithful White House employee for eighteen years is either lying, or she's caught in the throes of an obsessive fantasy about you. Is that what you're telling me?"

Martin smoothed out his tie. "I'm not sure I like what you're insinuating."

"We're well beyond insinuation, Phil. I believe her. I believe every word of it. But the truth is, this is my fault. I knew what and who you were when I brought you aboard. I buried it, called a lesser evil to do a larger good. But that's crap. I put you where you are because I needed you to win. I put you in the running for the presidency."

"That's right! That's exactly right!" Martin shot back. "And whether you believe it or not, I've earned it. Now it's my turn. You've had your shot. Now I get mine!"

Haverland stared hard at Martin, gauging him, waiting.

Martin cleared his throat. "So where does this leave us? What are you going to do with this?"

"Nothing. I've spoken with Peggy. She's retiring. It was

her choice. She wants to get as far away from you as possible and forget it ever happened."

"Good. Good for her. Best we all put this behind us."

"Not quite, Phil." Haverland reached into his drawer and pulled out a spiral-bound address book. He plopped it onto the desk. "This is forty year's worth of names: CEOs, senators, ambassadors, PACs, jurists, lobbyists, newspaper editors, investment bankers. . . . Starting this afternoon, I'm calling in every marker I own. By this time next week, the tap on your campaign is going to start drying up."

"You can't do that!"

"Watch me."

"Come on, John. Can't we work this out—"

"No."

"Without that money I haven't got a chance in hell of winning!"

"Exactly. You don't deserve the office. More to the point, America deserves better than you."

Martin's face turned purple. "You bastard! This is not fair! What gives you the right—"

Haverland stood up, turned his back on Martin, and walked to the window. "We're done, Phil. Get out of my office. If there's any justice, you'll never see it again."

Bhubaneswar, India

Sunil Dhar enjoyed his work. Kashmiri by birth, Dhar was more sympathetic to his Indian customers, but beyond that he was an equal-opportunity agent. Such was the beauty of his vocation. As long as the customer paid, their nationality and cause were of no concern to him.

This would be his second meeting with the client, and he'd chosen the café for its many exits and open facade. If there were watchers, he would see them. Not that he expected problems. His client seemed genuine in his intention, if not in his presentation.

The client certainly looked Japanese, but Orientals all looked alike to him. Even so, Dhar had dealt with JRA terrorists before, and there was something wrong with this one. But what? The man wasn't with any police or intelligence agency; his network of contacts had told him that much.

If he's not JRA, who is he? There were two likely scenarios: a rival group looking to insulate themselves should the transaction fail; or a go-between trying to establish cover for a larger operation.

Wheels within wheels, Dhar thought. His line of work was much more satisfying—not to mention simple. Most of the time, that is. This job would require some delicacy. Sarin was the king of nerve agents, so toxic it could kill a theaterful of people. He idly wondered what they (whoever "they" were) wanted it for, but quickly pushed the question from his mind. Not his business.

His client appeared on the patio and walked to Dhar's table. "Welcome," Dhar said with a smile. "Sit down. Can I order you some tea, something stronger, perhaps?"

"No. Do you have an answer for me?"

Dhar nodded. "What you want will cost a lot of money, but it is obtainable."

"How much?"

"Seven hundred thousand, U.S."

"That's outrageous!"

"A bargain, I promise you. The product we're talking about is well guarded. We're talking about Russia, you realize. There are bribes, special transport requirements. . . ."

The client hesitated for a moment. "Yes, I can see that. But you can get it? You're certain."

"If I weren't, I wouldn't have brought you here. In my line of work, customer satisfaction is a matter of survival. So, what is your answer?"

"Go ahead. We will pay you."

Dhar slid a piece of paper across the table. "My bank and account number. Once you have deposited half my fee, I will start. I will call you in sixty days with an update. Only one thing remains. Where do you wish to take delivery?"

The man's answer was immediate. "Russia, the port of Nakhodka-Vostochny."

Dhar nodded. “Very well. I’ll begin.”

The man stood up and walked away.

Curious choice, Nakhodka, Dhar thought. *So much easier to take it out via truck or plane. Why choose a harbor?*

1

Washington, D.C.

Tonight was to be Jerome Morris's first solo duty shift in Rock Creek Park, and before it was over he would find himself questioning his decision to trade his post at Shenandoah National Forest for the urban sprawl of the capital's largest park.

A backwoods boy and third-generation cop from rural Georgia, Morris found the best of both worlds with the USPP: Not only did you get to catch bad guys, but you got to do it in some of the most beautiful places in the country.

Tonight, Morris was part of a two-officer team patrolling the West D-3 Station, which included the 1800 acres of Rock Creek, plus Meridian Hill, Fort Totten, and portions of the C&O Canal.

Morris's radio cracked to life. "Station to Three-One."

Morris keyed the handset. "Three-One."

"Head on over to Pierce Mill, will ya? Got a report of a car in the parking lot."

Probably kids making out, Morris thought. There were plenty of entrances and exits to the park and amorous teenagers rarely paid attention to signs. He'd give them a lecture and send them packing. "On my way."

It took him ten minutes to get there; the Suburban handled the park's occasionally rough roads well enough, but Morris was still unfamiliar with much of the terrain, so he took it slow. An accident on his first night wouldn't do much to impress his supervisor.

He swung into the mill's parking lot and his headlights immediately picked out a red Lumina sitting beside the waterwheel. Morris stopped, turned on his spotlight, and shined it on the car, expecting to see a pair of heads pop up from the backseat. Nothing happened.

Morris honked his horn. Still nothing.

"Three-One to Station, I'm ten-ninety-seven at the mill. I'm getting out to check."

"Roger."

Morris climbed out, clicked on his flashlight and unclipped his holster strap. He didn't like walking up on cars at night. No cop did. Too many things could go wrong—too easy to get ambushed.

Walking along the car's rear panel, he shined his beam over the interior. *Nothing in the backseat. . . .* There was a figure in the driver's seat, though: a male, with his head resting on the headrest. He extended his flashlight away from himself to misdirect a gunshot should it come, then shined it on the driver's face. "Sir, this is the Park Police."

No response. Behind the glare of the flashlight, the man remained still.

Morris tapped on the glass. "Sir . . ."

Again there was no response. Now Morris felt the cold sheen of sweat on his face. *Should he call backup? Maybe— Jesus, Jerome, just do it. . . .*

Very slowly, Morris reached out, lifted the handle, and opened the door. The stench of feces and urine washed over him.

Suddenly the man was moving, tipping toward him.

Morris backpedaled, fumbling for his gun. The flashlight clattered to the asphalt. The beam danced wildly over the car, then rolled to a stop, illuminating the man's head. Still buckled in his seat, the man lay half out of the car, his arms touching the ground.

The top of his skull was missing.

THE WATCH SUPERVISOR ARRIVED FOUR MINUTES LATER AND found Morris squatting a few feet from the Lumina. "Jerome? You okay?"

"Yeah, Sergeant, I think so. . . ."

"Just stay there, lemme take a look. You touch anything?"

"No . . . uhm, yeah, the door handle."

The supervisor shined his flashlight over the man's head and knew immediately it was a gunshot wound. The roof upholstery was covered with blood. A revolver lay on the floorboard below the man's right knee.

"He's been dead awhile, I guess," Morris called.

"Why's that?"

"No blood on the ground; any more recent and he would have bled when he tipped over. Plus, his ankles are fat."

"Yeah, probably. Well, whoever he is, he picked one hell of a place to kill himself."

"Why's that?"

"Because we're standing in the middle of a jurisdictional black hole, that's why."

WHILE ALL NATIONAL PARKS ARE OVERSEEN BY THE DEPARTMENT of the Interior and its law enforcement body, the Park Police, a homicide on federal property tends to wreak havoc with standard procedure.

Within an hour of Morris's initial call, the Lumina sat under the glare of five sets of headlights and was surrounded by the USPP Duty Commander, an investigator from the USPP's Criminal Investigations Branch, a Special Agent of the FBI, a city Medical Examiner and, because Rock Creek's roads and parking lots are regulated by metro traffic laws, a pair of patrol officers from the DCPD.

"The car's got a government parking sticker," the CIB investigator called to the FBI agent. "Commerce Department. Dead fed on fed property. Looking like yours, Steve."

"Yeah." The agent opened the glove compartment and extracted the registration. "Owner is a Larry Baker." He handed it to one of the cops. "You wanna—What's your name?"

"Johnson. My partner, Meade."

"You guys wanna check the house?"

Meade, the rookie of the pair, took it. "Jesus, you don't think he. . . ."

"Hope not," said the agent, "but it's best we check."

"Man drives away from home, parks his car, and blows his brains out. . . . God."

The agent understood Meade's trepidation. Either Baker had come here so his family wouldn't find him, or he'd come here because he'd done something at home he couldn't bear seeing.

The address took the officers to Parklawn Drive, a neighborhood in Randolph Hills, three miles from Rock Creek. The Baker home was a two-story Chesapeake with a pair of maple trees bracketing the driveway. A bug zapper glowed purple on the front porch.

"No lights on inside." said Meade. "Asleep, you think?"

"Yeah, probably," replied Johnson.

They got out and walked to the door. Meade raised his finger to press the doorbell. Johnson stopped him. "Wait," he whispered, then pressed his knuckle against the door and pushed. It swung open a few inches.

"Oh, shit," Meade whispered.

Johnson pushed the door open until it bumped against the wall. Inside, the marble foyer was dark; beyond it lay a T-turn hallway.

Johnson keyed his radio. "Two-nine to dispatch."

"Dispatch."

"We've got an open door at our location. Request you attempt contact via landline."

"Roger, standby."

Thirty seconds passed. In the distance, a dog barked once, then went silent. The bug zapper sizzled. Inside the house they heard the distant ringing of a phone. After a dozen rings, it stopped.

Johnson's radio crackled. "Dispatch, two-nine, no response landline."

"Yep, we heard it. We're going in."

Johnson looked over at Meade, gave him a reassuring nod, then drew his gun and clicked on his flashlight. Meade did the same, then followed.

They turned right at the T and walked through the kitchen, dining room, and living room. All were empty. A side door led from the living room into the garage. Johnson peeked out, pulled back, and shook his head.

They retraced their steps out of the kitchen, past the foyer, and followed the hall to a set of stairs leading upward. At the top they found another hallway: two doors on the right, balustrade on the left. At the far end lay another door. *Master bedroom,* Johnson thought.

Moving by hand gestures, they checked the first two rooms. Bedrooms: 'N Sync and Britney Spears posters, toys scattered on the floor, colorful wallpaper and curtains. . . . *Kid's rooms.*

They moved on. At the last door they stopped. They glanced at one another. *If there's anything to find,* Johnson thought, *it'll be here.* He gulped hard, looked over at Meade, and gave him another nod.

Johnson turned the knob and pushed open the door. The room was black. The air smelled stale. There was another odor as well, but Johnson couldn't quite place it. *Like metal,* he thought. *Coppery.* Even as his brain was identifying the odor, he tracked his flashlight across the floor to the bedpost, then upward.

What he saw made him freeze. "O sweet Jesus."

Burdette, Maryland

Charlie Latham jolted awake at the phone's first ring. Part habit, part instinctual consideration for his wife, he rarely let a phone ring more than twice. "Hello."

"Charlie, it's Harry." Harry Owens, a longtime friend of Latham's, had recently been promoted to assistant director of the FBI's National Security Division, which made him Latham's boss. "Did I wake you up?"

Latham smiled; the joke was old between them. "Nah. What's up?"

"Multiple murder. I think you're gonna want to see it. I'm there now."

Latham was wary. As head of the NSD's Counterespionage/Intelligence group, he had little business poaching on a homicide; his bailiwick was spies and terrorists. "What's going on, Harry?"

"Better you see it for yourself."

"Okay. Give me the address."

It took Latham twenty minutes to reach Randolph Hills. The driveway to the Baker home was filled with three DCPD patrol cars and a van from the medical examiner's office. Strung from tree to tree in the yard, yellow police tape fluttered in the breeze. Robe- and pajama-clad neighbors gawked from across the street.

A cop met Latham on the porch, handed him a pair of sterile booties, a gauze beanie for his head, and latex gloves, waited for him to don them and then led him inside and up the stairs. Owens was waiting; his face was pasty. "Hey, Charlie."

"Harry. Bad?"

"Pretty bad. Mother and two children."

Latham had known Owens for seventeen years and he could count on one hand the number of times he'd seen Owens so shaken. Still, that didn't answer why he was here. "What is it?" Latham asked.

"Just take a look. I don't want to put a spin on it. I need your eyes."

He led Latham down the hall to the bedroom door, gestured for Latham to wait, then poked his head inside and waved out the Crime Scene people. "Go ahead, Charlie."

Latham stepped through the door. And stopped.

The mother, an early forties redhead, sat in a hard-backed chair beside the bed. Her wrists were duct-taped to the chair's arms, her ankles to the rear legs, so her thighs were stretched tight. *Harder to rock the chair that way*, Latham thought. She'd been shot once in the forehead. Behind her, the yellow bedspread was splattered in blood and brain matter.

The children, both blond-haired girls under ten years of age, were sitting against the wall with their arms taped behind their backs. Their feet, similarly taped together around the calves, were secured to the bed's footing by nylon clothesline.

Both girls had been shot once in the crown of the skull. The shock wave from the bullets' passages had left each child's face rippled with bruises. The effect was known as "beehiving," named after the ringed appearance of beehives in cartoons.

Latham felt the room spinning; he felt hot. He took a deep breath. "What the hell happened here, Harry? Where's the—"

"He's in Rock Creek Park, shot once under the chin."

Latham felt a flash of anger. "Son-of-a-bitch. . . ."

"Maybe. Look at their ankles, Charlie."

Latham stepped over the children's legs and squatted down beside one of them. He pulled back a pajama cuff. There, beside the knob of the ankle bone, a tiny red pinprick on the vein.

Oh, no. . . . Latham grabbed the bed's footboard to steady himself.

Owens held up a clear, plastic, evidence bag. Inside was a hypodermic syringe. "We found it on the stairway. There's a little bit of blood on the tip."

Latham opened his mouth to ask the question, but Owens beat him to it. "We'll have to get the lab to confirm it, but the syringe looks empty. No residue, no liquid—nothing."

Nothing but air, thought Latham. They'd seen this before.

2

White House

"WHAT'S NEXT?" SAID PRESIDENT MARTIN, FLIPPING TO THE next page of the brief. "The Angola thing?"

"Yes, sir," replied Director of Central Intelligence Dick Mason. *The Angola thing. . . .*

Martin spoke as if the plight of thousands of refugees carried no more import than a photo op with the Boy Scouts. Since the start of the war in Angola, thousands had been driven from their homes in the capital and Luanda and into squalid tent camps.

"If we don't find a way to get the Red Cross in, disease is going to start hitting the camps."

"I see."

Do you? For the first time in his life, Mason found himself in the unenviable position of disliking his boss. It didn't help that his boss also happened to be the president of the United States. Not that it mattered, of course. He wasn't required to like the man—he just had to follow his orders.

Martin was what Mason called a "too much man." Too handsome; too polished; too poised—too everything but genuine. Not that he was a simpleton; in fact, he was well-educated and quick on his feet. The problem was, Martin cared for little else than Martin. He was a dangerous narcissist.

His smartest move had been hiring his chief of staff, Howard Bousikaris, his right hand since the early days of the Haverland administration. The third-generation Greek was loyal and adept at playing Martin's political hatchet man. Inside the Beltway, Bousikaris had been nicknamed "The Ninja": It was only after you were dead that you realized he was after you.

"What does State have to say about this?" Martin asked.

Bousikaris said, "Not much at this point, sir. We don't even know for sure who's running the government. The central news agency in Luanda has changed hands four times in the last week."

"Lord, what a mess. Okay, Dick, what's next?"

Moving on again, Mason thought. Martin was loath to make executive decisions. Fence riding, when skillfully done, was safer. From here, Angola would be dumped on Bousikaris, who would in turn dump it on either the National Security Council or the President's Foreign Advisory Council. Meanwhile, the situation in Angola would deteriorate and the death count would mount until Martin *had* to move lest he lose face. *You don't have to like the man,* Mason reminded himself.

"The elections in the Russian Federation. The issues are no different: the economy, agriculture, oblast autonomy—but it looks like the current president might have a real race on his hands."

"You're kidding," said Martin. "From this Bulganin fellow?"

"He's gaining ground fast."

"What do we know about him?" asked Bousikaris.

"Not as much as we would like," said Mason. *Not nearly enough, in fact.*

Vladimir Bulganin, a former factory foreman and local politician from Omsk, had founded the Russian Pride Party six years before and had been gnawing at the flanks of the major parties ever since.

On the surface, the RPP's platform seemed based on moderate nationalism, infrastructure improvement, a more centralized government, and, paradoxically, an emphasis on the democratic power of the people. That Bulganin had been able to dodge this apparent inconsistency was largely due, Mason felt, to his chief advisor, Ivan Nochenko.

A former colonel in the KGB, Nochenko was an expert at propaganda and disinformation. Before the fall of the Soviet Union, the First Directorate had toppled governments, swayed world opinion, and covered up disasters that would have been front-page news in the West.

Since his retirement in 1993, Nochenko had worked as a freelance PR consultant in Russia's always uncertain and often dangerous free market. Though no one on Madison Avenue would dare admit it, there was little appreciable difference between public relations and propaganda.

Lack of solid evidence notwithstanding, Mason suspected Nochenko was not only the driving force behind Bulganin's success, but also the reason why no one seemed to know much about this dark horse of the Russian political scene.

Mason said, "We don't think he's got enough backing to take the election, but a solid showing will give him clout in Moscow."

Martin nodded. "Leverage for the next go-around."

"Yes, sir. Maybe even some policy influence. Problem is, nobody's been able to nail down Bulganin's agenda. So far he's done little but echo the frustrations of the average Russian citizen."

"Dick, it's called politics. The man's building a constituency."

"In a country as volatile as Russia, sir, political ambiguity is dangerous."

"For who?"

"The world. The fact that Bulganin has gained so much support without tipping his hand is worrisome. There can be only two explanations: Either he's avoiding substance because he doesn't have any, or he's got an agenda he doesn't want to lay out until he's got the influence to make it stick."

Martin leaned toward Bousikaris and mock-whispered, "Dick sees a conspiracy in every bush."

Mason spread his hands. "It's what I'm paid to do, Mr. President."

As astute a politician as Martin was, he was naive when it came to the world scene. Though the concept of the "global village" was finally taking hold in the public consciousness, it was nothing new to the intelligence community. Nothing happens in a vacuum, Mason knew. With six billion people and hundreds of individual governments on the planet, there existed lines of interconnectedness that only God could fathom.

Some events—say, a farm county in Minnesota hit by flooding—take longer to exert influence. Others—such as a neophyte candidate in Russia gaining leverage in a national election—have an immediate and powerful effect on everything from world markets to foreign relations. The fact that Martin, arguably the most powerful man in the world, didn't understand this frustrated Mason.

"My point is," the DCI continued, "is that unless something changes in the next few weeks, Vladimir Bulganin is going to become a player in Russian politics. I'd feel better if we knew more about him."

"Understood," Martin said. "What do you propose?"

"I want to do some back-channel nudging of the networks—CNN, MSNBC, ABC. . . . We plant the seed and hopefully their Russian correspondents will start asking some tough questions of Bulganin. If we can get a snowball rolling, it may put some pressure on him."

Martin looked to Bousikaris. "Thoughts, Howard?"

"As long as it can't come back to bite us."

Mason shook his head. "It's a routine play. Once Bulganin starts talking more, we can start dissecting him, see where it takes us."

"Okay, get on it. Anything else?"

"Toothpick," said Mason. "Live-fire testing is scheduled for next month; I think it's time we consider briefing members of the Armed Forces Committee, but we need to choose carefully."

"Toothpick—the Star Wars thing?"

"Yes, sir."

Martin turned to Bousikaris. "Let's put some feelers out. Make sure whoever we brief is fully on board; I don't want any wafflers when it comes to funding."

"I'll handle it."

"Anything else, Dick?"

"No, sir."

"That'll be all, then."

Once Mason was gone, Martin sighed. "Howard, that man is a naysayer."

"As he said, Mr. President, that's what he's paid to do."

"I suppose."

"We could replace him."

"Better we wait until this Redmond thing dies down."

While the appointment of former-senator Tom Redmond to the directorship of the Defense Intelligence Agency had been politically necessary, Bousikaris had argued against making the change so soon after Martin took office. But Redmond had delivered California during the campaign, and that was the kind of favor you didn't want hanging over your head.

"How's the schedule today?" Martin asked.

"One addition: The ambassador to the People's Republic of China. He wants a few minutes. In person, in fact." Almost exclusively, the PRC communicated by formal letter. Bousikaris often joked that the dictionary entry for the word *taciturn* should simply contain a photo of a Chinese diplomat.

"Any idea what's on his mind?" Martin asked.

"His secretary declined to answer."

"Okay, give him ten minutes before lunch."

U.S. Embassy, Beijing, China

Though he had considered them worthless back then, Roger Brown found himself glad he'd paid attention during those mind-numbing economics courses he'd taken at Notre Dame; they'd given him the ability to look attentive while being bored out of his mind. However gifted they may be at diplomacy, government functionaries rarely made good conversationalists.

Ah, well, Brown thought. *Such is the price of success at the CIA.*

Working under the title of advisor to the secretary for economic affairs, Brown was in fact the embassy's new CIA station chief. Of course, the title was not designed to fool anyone (the *Guoanbu* was very good at keeping tabs on embassy personnel), but rather to give him diplomatic immunity should he get caught playing spy. Then again, he thought, the Chinese secret police wasn't known for its strict adherence to diplomatic rules.

Tonight was his first official embassy dinner, a meet-and-greet affair for members of China's Ministry of Agriculture. So far he'd had no trouble playing his part, discussing the impact of corn nematodes on world grain markets, but as the evening had worn on, the novelty had worn off.

His job was to listen for bits and pieces of information that he and his staff could hopefully fit into the great jigsaw puzzle called "intelligence gathering." Few civilians realized how tedious spying could be. Earth-shattering revelations were rare; most often, insights came from the patient collection and collation of random bits of information. That was especially true in the PRC, the most politically and culturally oppressive nation on earth. It was a shame. Brown found the Chinese people fascinating, their history and traditions stirring.

He looked up to see one of the Chinese agricultural attachés headed his way. During dinner the man had spent thirty minutes detailing why America was so decadent. *Not much of a recruiting prospect there,* Brown thought. He grabbed a glass of champagne from a waiter, made his way to the tall French doors, and stepped through onto the empty balcony.

Despite it being April, the air was warm, with none of D.C.'s spring chill. Plumeria bushes hung from the eaves and partially draped the rail. A block away he could see the lights bordering Ritan Park.

He let his gaze wander along the street, pausing at each parked car until he found the one he was looking for. Through the windshield he could see a pair of silhouetted figures. Guoanbu *watchers*, Brown thought. *Ninth Bureau boys*. They were good at their job, largely because they weren't overly concerned with citizen's rights. *Guoanbu* and PSB (People's Security Bureau) officials could arrest anyone, for anything, at any time; they could invade homes without warrant, and they could ship you off to a *laogi*, or government prison camp, without trial.

"Good evening," Brown heard from behind him. He turned. It was the bombastic attaché from dinner. The man was in his early fifties, with sad eyes and a wide mouth.

"Am I disturbing you?" the man said.

"No, not at all. I was just enjoying the night."

The man strode to the railing. "I don't believe we were properly introduced. My name is Chang-Moh Bian." The man made no move to shake hands, keeping them firmly on the railing.

Smart fella, Brown thought. Assuming they were being watched, Bian didn't want to complicate matters with even a perfunctory show of familiarity. As it was, Bian would likely be questioned about this interaction. "Roger Brown. Nice to meet you."

"I apologize for my earlier comments, Mr. Brown. Certain things are expected of us at these functions. I hope you understand."

Interesting. . . . "Of course."

"Well, I just wanted to say hello. I must be going."

"Good night."

As Bian turned, Brown heard something clatter on the balcony's flagstones. He looked down. Laying near his foot was a ballpoint pen. "Excuse me, I think you dropped something."

Bian turned; he frowned. "No, I don't think so. It belongs to you, I am sure."

Bian opened the doors and stepped back inside.

Brown waited another ten minutes, thinking hard, wondering if he'd misread the incident. There was only one way to find out.

He let the champagne glass slip from his hand. It shattered. He stepped back, angrily brushing at the front of his pants, then leaned down, grabbed the pen, and tucked it into his sleeve, then stood up with the broken glass in his hand.

Excusing himself with the ambassador in the main room, he headed downstairs to his office. He laid the pen on his desk, then picked up the phone. "Carl, it's Roger. Can you come down to my office?"

Carl Jones, the embassy's security manager, was there in five minutes. He listened carefully to Brown's story, then said, "He didn't say anything else? No pitch, not even a hint?"

"Nope."

"You're sure the pen wasn't already there?"

"I'm sure. Carl, I looked him in the eye. He knew what he was doing."

Jones considered this, then grinned. "So, what, you're afraid it's some kind of exploding pen?"

"Jesus, Carl."

"I say open it. Just hang on. . . . let me get behind something solid."

"Oh, for the love of—"

"Of course, your family will be well provided for if—"

Brown unscrewed the pen and tipped the contents onto his blotter.

Wrapped around the ink cartridge was a slip of onionskin paper.

White House

The Chinese ambassador arrived promptly at 11:45 and was shown into the Oval Office.

Martin stood up and walked over. "Mr. Ambassador, it's a pleasure to finally meet you."

"And you, President Martin." The ambassador was a portly man with bushy eyebrows and a surprisingly high-pitched voice. "Congratulations on your victory."

"Thank you. Please . . . sit. Can I offer you something to drink?"

"No, thank you."

They settled around the coffee table, Martin in a wingback chair, the ambassador on the couch. Bousikaris took his place at Martin's left shoulder.

"I understand this is your first spring in Washington," Martin said.

"Yes. It's lovely."

There were a few seconds of silence as each man regarded the other.

"You're surprised by my visit," said the ambassador.

"Surprised, but pleased nonetheless."

The ambassador nodded, as though weighing Martin's words. "Well, to the point of my visit: It is a rather delicate matter. I hope you will accept what I am going to say in the spirit it is offered."

What's this? Bousikaris thought.

"Please go on," said Martin.

"It has come to the attention of my government, President Martin, that during the last election you received some generous campaign contributions from a certain political committee. Some eighty million dollars, I believe."

Martin's smile never wavered. "All on public record."

"Of course. It has also come to our attention that your supporters may not have been completely candid. It seems the consortium in question was in fact backed by a group of industrialists from my country."

There was a long ten seconds of silence. Martin glanced up at Bousikaris, who kept his eyes on the ambassador. "That's not possible," said Bousikaris.

The ambassador reached into his coat pocket and withdrew a sheaf of papers, which he placed on the table. "Details of each contribution, the domestic accounts from which they were drawn, and routing information for each transaction, including authorization codes you can use to trace their origin. Though the source accounts are now closed, I think you'll find all the funds originated from banks in the People's Republic."

Bousikaris picked up the document and began paging through it.

"Howard?" said Martin.

"The information is here, but we have no way of—"

The ambassador said, "Of course. I would not ask you to take my word for this. By all means, look into it. In the meantime—"

"What do you want?" Martin growled, his smile gone. "What's your game?"

"No game, Mr. President. My government would be as embarrassed as you by this. We have no desire to see this information made public. The People's Republic is eager to take steps to ensure this information never becomes—"

Martin bolted upright. "You sons-of-bitches. You're . . . you're trying to blackmail me. *Me!*"

Bousikaris said, "Mr. President—"

"You heard the bastard, Howard—"

"What I heard," Bousikaris replied, "is the ambassador offering his country's help. Am I reading the situation clearly, Mr. Ambassador?"

"Very clearly," replied the ambassador.

Bousikaris knew they needed time. Of course it was blackmail, of course the Chinese wanted something, but to reject it capriciously would be disastrous. He doubted the PRC would think twice about revealing its complicity in sabotaging a U.S. election. Whatever their game, the stakes were high.

"However," Bousikaris said, "just so there's no misunderstanding. . . . Can we assume your government is looking for some kind of . . . reciprocation?"

"Yes. Reciprocation. Friends helping friends—that's what we have in mind."

Arms crossed, Martin glared at the ambassador.

Bousikaris said, "Mr. President, I think we've misunderstood the ambassador's intent."

"Exactly so," replied the ambassador.

Martin stared hard at Bousikaris and then, like the chameleon Bousikaris knew him to be, smiled. He carefully smoothed his tie. "My apologies, Mr. Ambassador. Sometimes my temper gets ahead of me. That's why Howard is so valuable; he keeps me from making a fool of myself. So, tell me: What is it you need help with?"

"Terrorists, Mr. President."

Rappahannock River, Virginia

"Uncle Briggs, why don't fish drown?"

Crouched down to rinse his hands in the surf, Briggs Tanner looked up and shielded his eyes from the setting sun. "What's that? Why don't what?"

With one tiny hand wrapped around her fishing pole, the girl pointed to the water. "They live underwater all the time, so there's no air, right? How come they don't get drownded?"

Uh-oh, Tanner thought. Lucy Cahil, five-year-old daughter of his best friend Ian Cahil, had finally asked the kind of question Tanner dreaded. As her adoptive uncle and godfather, Tanner loved Lucy as his own, but was never sure how to handle such queries. *Serious answer, or funny one?*

Lucy solved the problem for him. "And don't say 'cuz they've got tiny scuba things. My dad already tried that."

Tanner laughed. *Translation: I'm young, not stupid.* "Okay. Fish don't drown because they have gills. Gills absorb oxygen from the water, and the fish breathe that."

"So, if there's ox . . . oxi . . . air down there, how come *we* can't do it?"

"We're just not built that way, I guess."

Lucy considered this for a moment. "Okay." She returned her attention to her pole.

Tanner patted her on the shoulder and walked over to Cahil, who had been watching the exchange from his lounge chair. Behind him, up a set of long, winding stairs set into the wooded embankment, sat Tanner's home, an old spruce and oak lighthouse he'd purchased from the Virginia Historical Commission. The narrow-mouthed, tall-cliffed cove the lighthouse guarded sat well back from the Rappahannock's main channel. Tanner's closest neighbor was a mile away.

"See, that wasn't so bad, was it?" Cahil asked.

"No."

"I'm telling you, bud, you'd make a great father."

"I seem to recall getting the same pitch from your wife last week."

Cahil's bearded face split into a grin. "Maggie loves lost causes."

"There's still plenty of time for kids." Saying the words, Tanner suddenly realized it didn't sound so bad. On the other hand, how would he balance a family with what he did for a living? How did Bear do it? Until he figured that out, playing uncle would have to suffice. Truth was, he liked it.

"Briggs, you're forty."

"I plan to live to be a hundred and twenty."

Cahil laughed. "Oh, well, in that case. . . . How, may I ask, do you plan to do that?"

"Clean living and an apple a day."

"An apple a day keeps the grim reaper away?"

"That's the theory I'm going on."

Good ol' Bear, Tanner thought. He and Cahil had been friends for nearly fifteen years, having first survived Navy Special Warfare training together, and then ISAG, or Intelligence Support Activity Group selection. In those early days, Cahil's fiercely loyal and ever-reliable nature had won him the nickname "Mama Bear."

After ISAG's disbandment due to Pentagon politics, he and Cahil—who were only two of the sixty operators to survive ISAG training's 90 percent attrition rate—were recruited by former spymaster Leland Dutcher to join a Reagan-era experiment called Holystone Group.

In the intelligence community, Holystone was called a "fix-it-shop", a semiautonomous CIA-fronted organization that handled tasks that were deemed too delicate for direct government action. Since Holystone worked outside normal channels—or, "on the raw"—it was completely deniable. In short, if a Holystone employee got caught doing something he or she shouldn't be doing, somewhere he or she shouldn't be, they were on their own. As Dutcher was fond of saying, "It's a brutal necessity. Brutal for us, necessary for the job."

For all that, for all the ups and downs he'd seen since joining Holystone—including losing his wife, Elle, in a skiing accident—Tanner counted himself lucky to be working with people like Dutcher and Cahil. They were family.

"Speaking of wives and children and such," said Bear. "Have you heard from Camille lately?"

"We talked last week. She's in Haifa."

"You're kidding?"

"Nope. *Mossad* hired her as a security consultant."

Up until six months ago Camille had been a Mossad *katsa*, or case officer. Her career—and nearly her life—had been cut short when she bucked her superiors to save Tanner's life aboard a ship bound for Tel Aviv. Thanks to the intercession of then-President John Haverland, Camille had been allowed to retire with honor and impunity from Mossad service. That the Israelis had even allowed her back into the country was extraordinary: Mossad was not known for its magnanimity.

Though neither of them had said it aloud, Tanner knew he and Camille had reached the same conclusion about their relationship. Given their respective careers and given the fact that neither was ready to quit, the best they could hope for was an on-again off-again romance. *It could be worse,* Tanner realized. He could not have her in his life at all. Camille was a wonderful woman, and if the circumstances were different. . . . *Well.*

"Whoa!" Cahil called. "Looks like our girl's got a bite."

Tanner looked over his shoulder. Lucy Cahil was sitting on her haunches, feet dug into the sand, her fingers white around the jerking pole. She was losing the battle. Whatever was on the other end was more than a match for her—and still she wasn't calling for help. *Stubborn like her father.*

Cahil's cell phone started ringing; he tossed it to Tanner, then jogged over to Lucy. Tanner flipped open the phone. "Hello?"

"Briggs, its Leland."

"Evening, Leland."

"Have you got some time?"

"Sure, when?"

"Right now."

Tanner hesitated; there was an unaccustomed hardness in his boss's voice. "What's going on?"

"You remember Treble?" Dutcher asked.

Tanner remembered; for twelve years it had never been far from his mind. "I remember."

"We just got word: He may be alive, Briggs."

3

FBI Headquarters, Washington, D.C.

Though he would never admit it publicly, Special Agent Paul Randall revered his boss. Charlie Latham was a near legend, the Bureau's top CE&I expert since the early eighties, but that kind of blatant veneration didn't play well in J. Edgar's house. Besides, Latham himself would never stand for it. "Do your job, do it discreetly, and let glory worry about itself" was one of his favorite aphorisms.

Having followed Latham's career since he was a brick agent in Robbery, Randall knew his boss's CV backward and forward. He'd been involved in most of the big ones—Kocher, Pollard, Walker, and just six months ago, the capture of former-KGB illegal and fugitive Yuri Vorsalov. But what impressed Randall most when he finally got his long-awaited transfer was that Latham was a regular guy—a "stand-up guy" in FBI parlance.

Quiet, unassuming, and quick to share credit, Latham was not the Hollywood image of a spy hunter: medium height, wiry, and bald save a monkish fringe of salt-and-pepper hair. Latham was an "everyman." You could pass him on the street and never give him a second glance, which is exactly what so many of his targets had done.

This morning Latham was preoccupied. Randall knew he'd been called out the night before by Harry Owens, that it involved a homicide, but that was all—almost all, that is. "We're gonna get a hot one, Paul," Latham had said upon walking into his office. "Clear your plate."

If the "hot one" was in fact this homicide, there had to be a connection to his boss's past. *But what?* Randall wondered. What would draw them into the grisly murder-suicide of an entire family?

LATHAM WAS SIPPING HIS SECOND CUP OF COFFEE WHEN THE phone rang. "Charlie Latham."

"Charlie, it's Harry. Come on down, will ya?"

"On my way."

"Owens?" asked Randall. Latham nodded. "You planning to fill me in anytime soon?"

Latham looked at his partner; the eagerness was plain in his eyes. "Yeah. Later."

Latham walked to the elevator and took it up one floor. As he stepped off, a pair of men stepped aboard. Latham recognized both of them: the DCPD police commissioner and the Park Police district commander. Each man gave him a solemn nod.

Sympathy or anger? Latham wondered. *Or a little bit of both?*

They'd just come from Owens's office and knowing Harry, the turf fight over the Baker murders had likely been short and bloodless. Though each cop probably loathed having his territory invaded, each was probably breathing a sigh of relief as well. *If they only knew,* Charlie thought.

He stepped past them into Owens's office. Owens, a jowly man with bloodhound eyes, was on the phone; he pointed Latham to a chair and kept talking. "Yes, sir, I just met with them. We'll have their full cooperation. Yes, sir."

Owens hung up. "The director," he explained.

"Wow, Harry, two 'yes sirs' in one conversation."

"You only caught the tail end; I was already into the double digits. Wanna trade jobs?"

"Sorry, I couldn't admin my way out of a paper bag."

"And I couldn't spot a spy if he were in my bathtub. The Baker case is ours. DCPD and the Park Police signed off."

"How much do they know?"

"Not much. Truth is, I don't think they want to know."

"Any word from the medical examiner?"

"Tomorrow, probably. Crime scene should have things wrapped up by tonight."

"They won't find much."

"I know. Baker's home computer is already at the lab."

"I'm going over to Commerce, talk to Baker's boss. I want to know what he was working on. Can you put in a call—"

"Already did. They're expecting you."

"Expecting me, but not happy about it?"

"They probably thought they'd have a little more time to get their ducks in a row."

"I don't want their ducks in a row."

Either way it went, the murders were going to shine badly on Commerce. If Baker was simply a homicidal nut, the media would be asking why Commerce's screening missed it; if he turned out to be dirty and it had gotten him and his family killed, Commerce would be swarmed by investigators.

"If they start talking to the press," Latham said, "it could foul up our case."

"Then you'll have to put the fear of God into them."

"Yep. After Commerce I thought I'd drive up to Dannemora and see Cho."

Owens frowned. "He's a tough son-of-a-bitch, Charlie. You think he'll tell you anything?"

Latham shrugged. "I'll plant the seed and see where it takes us."

Moscow, the Russian Commonwealth of Independent States

"National destiny must not be decided by the few!" Vladimir Bulganin shouted, his amplified voice echoing through the square. "The purpose of an election is to make manifest the will of the people! *Your* will! And I tell you this, my friends: The bond between a public servant and his people is. . . ." Bulganin paused. "To break that bond—*that trust!*—is nothing short of betrayal!"

The crowd of ten thousand roared its approval, the cheers drowning out the sounds of the city around them. Spread throughout the crowd were dozens of Bulganin's security men—"The Guardians" of the Russian Pride Party—all wearing navy peacoats and crimson armbands. On nearby streets, traffic had ground to a halt and drivers stood beside their cars. At the edge of the square, local reporters filmed the event, and beyond them a line of Moscow Militia officers stood at parade rest.

Very good, thought Ivan Nochenko. *He hit it right this time.* Timing was as important as content—perhaps more so.

If not a perfect pupil, Bulganin had a natural feel for collective emotion. Unfortunately, the man often let passion override craft. Perception was everything; perception always conquered truth. Most people's decisions were guided by the heart, not by the mind. Win the heart and you can convince any public—especially an impassioned Russian public—to vote a chimp into office.

Nochenko knew his business. He'd spent twenty of his thirty years in the KGB weaving fiction into propaganda and truth into fiction. The art of propaganda was, after all, nothing more than the blue-collar cousin of public relations.

Nochenko had seen much in his time: Mine collapses in the Urals, nuclear submarine sinkings in the Chukchi, mini-Chernobyls in the wastes of Siberia, rocket explosions in Yavlosk. . . . Thousands of lives and hundreds of near disasters about which the world had never learned.

Nochenko had loved his work and occasionally, in moments of private self-indulgence, he understood why: influence. Kings rule countries, but the king who relies on truth is a king soon dethroned. Information is the true power and those who control information are the true kings. Nochenko's mentor, Sergei Simov, had said it best: "Truth is a lie, a tale told by men frightened by the vagaries of life. Get enough people to believe a lie and it becomes truth."

Days gone by, Nochenko thought, watching Bulganin conclude his speech. *The days before we started believing the tale told by NATO. . . .* Truth was, the Soviet died long before the wall came down; her death rattle began the day the Politburo started believing they were losing the great game.

He ached for those heady days, and for years after leaving the KGB he'd thought they were gone forever. Then he'd found Vladimir Bulganin. Bulganin would be his final triumph. Cover up the deaths of a hundred coal miners? Child's play. Erase from history a nuclear submarine lost to the icy waters of the Atlantic? Masturbation. But take a raw, unknown peasant—a goddamned shoe factory foreman!—from Omsk to the grandest seat of power in all of Russia. . . . That was a feat.

Bulganin was wrapping up: "And so my countrymen, we stand at a precipice. Your votes will decide whether the Motherland plummets over the edge, or she takes wing and soars. I know what I choose. I know what I'm prepared to do for the Motherland, but only you can decide on whom to bestow your faith. I promise you this, my friends: If that person is to be me, I will never tire of the burden, and *I will never betray your faith*!"

The crowd went wild, ten thousand voices cheering as one, caps flying into the air and scarves waving in the breeze. To Nochenko, the cacophony was a symphony, a perfect blending of frustration and hope. *They're turning,* Nochenko thought. *They're almost there.*

White House

To Bousikaris's surprise, it hadn't taken much to bring his boss around to his way of thinking. For all his flaws, President Phillip Martin had a well-honed sense of survival.

Despite the pleasant mask Martin had donned while listening to the ambassador's "proposal," Bousikaris had seen the signs: the pulsing jaw, the tapping finger on the chair's armrest. . . .

The explosion had come the instant the door closed: "Those sons-of-bitches! Who do they think they're dealing with? Terrorists, my ass. They're up to something, Howard! They're trying to screw me! Well, they're in for a surprise. . . ."

Bousikaris let him rant for a few minutes, then said. "Phil, we don't *know* anything."

"They're blackmailing—"

"They're leveraging. There's a difference." *Is there*? Bousikaris thought. In this case, not really, but the sooner he could get Martin on track, the sooner they could start thinking of a way out. "They're looking for help. They're worried we'll be less than enthusiastic about it."

"Bullshit," growled Martin.

"Look, it happens in Congress every day. You know that. This is the same thing, just on a larger scale." Bousikaris stepped forward, placed his fists on the desk, and stared hard at Martin. "Phil."

"What!"

"Listen to me: This is a game you know how to play. This is what you do best. Don't let anger put you off your game."

Martin stared back, then took a deep breath, and nodded. "Okay, right. What do we do?"

4

CIA Headquarters, Virginia

WITH A NOD FROM THEIR ESCORT, LELAND DUTCHER AND HIS deputy at Holystone, Walter Oaken, stepped off the elevator into Dick Mason's outer office. As Dutcher had expected, Mason's secretary, Ginny, was waiting. Ginny had been Dutcher's assistant when he'd served as DDI years before.

"Leland!" She gave him a hug. "I heard you were coming."

"Ginny, I doubt there's much you don't hear. Here's hoping you're never kidnapped."

"Oh, lord, who would want me? I'm a glorified typist."

"Sure you are. You remember Walt."

"Of course. Nice to see you again, Mr. Oaken."

"You, too, Ginny."

Tall and gangly and stoop-shouldered, Oaken was not only Holystone's second-in-command, but also its "chief scrounger and cobbler," as Dutcher was fond of saying. Whether it was information, equipment, or documentation, if somebody needed it, Oaken either had it or knew where to find it. A former division head at the State Department's Bureau of Intelligence Research, Oaken had been Dutcher's first recruitment for Holystone.

Dutcher nodded toward Mason's door. "Who's waiting for us in there?"

Ginny said, "Mr. Mason, Mr. Coates, and Ms. Albrecht."

"Ah, the big three."

George Coates and Sylvia Albrecht were Mason's Deputy Directors of Operations, and Intelligence, respectively. When Mason first came aboard as DCI, he'd done some housecleaning, which included the hiring and firing of two sets of

DDs until he'd found a pair that could set aside the intradepartmental infighting that had become endemic at Langley. Coates and Albrecht were a rare breed, content to let hard work and merit, rather than political acumen, decide their careers. It helped that Mason set a good example; the DCI had little stomach for politics and worked tirelessly to keep it out of Langley. Gruff and grizzled but always fair, Mason was the epitome of a CIA cold warrior: A good man to have on your side, a terrible man to have against you.

Mason's door swung open. "Dutch, Walt. Thought I heard your voices. Not trying to steal Ginny away, are you?"

"It's crossed my mind."

"Forget it. She's a company woman to the bone."

Ginny waved a dismissive hand. "Go, both of you. I've got work to do."

DUTCHER AND OAKEN TOOK THEIR SEATS IN A PAIR OF CHAIRS around the coffee table. Sunlight streamed through the window, casting shadows on the burgundy carpet. After greetings were exchanged and coffee poured, Mason came to the point. "Leland, how much do you remember about Ledger?"

"The defection of Chinese PLA General Han Soong. I was DDI then. We put together the assessment and background, but after it went to Operations, I lost track of it. Rumor was it was handed to ISAG for execution. I later learned Briggs was involved, but that was before Holystone."

ISAG, or Intelligence Support Activity Group, was a multiservice hybrid experiment that had gathered together SpecWar experts from the navy, army, air force, marines, and FBI, and put them through a course designed by the CIA. The goal was to create operators armed with superior military and intelligence training, a combination that had thus far been shunned by the military and the intelligence communities.

The training lasted two years and covered an astonishing range of skills: languages, agent handling, weapons, improvised demolitions, evasion and escape, communications, deep cover, surveillance and countersurveillance. . . . If there was even a remote chance of it coming up in the field, it was taught.

"As I understand it, the defection fell through," Dutcher continued. "Soong was arrested the day he was going into the pipeline. What I'd always wondered was why ISAG got the job."

"Soong requested a controller with military background; Tanner fit the profile. As it turned out, it was a good call. The *Guoanbu* and PSB were waiting at the meeting site. You and Briggs never talked about Ledger?"

"No. I don't think it's his favorite topic."

"Understandable," said Mason. "He was Soong's controller for three months. They got close."

And Briggs has been playing the what-if game ever since, Dutcher thought.

Dutcher knew and loved Tanner like a son. The same reasons that made Tanner good at what he did were the same reasons that got him in trouble. He was tenacious—occasionally to a fault—and in this business, the ability to detach yourself was often a necessity of survival. Tanner's "detachment instinct" was flawed—not dangerously so, but just enough to cause him heartache from time to time. *Of course,* Dutcher thought, *there was no formula.* In the end, pragmatism was perhaps the best measure. If it works, leave it alone.

And Tanner worked. He not only got the job done, but he could also sit alone in a room with himself afterward without going crazy. The best ones could. The ones who couldn't, or the ones that didn't let themselves, weren't long for the business—or this world, for that matter.

Dutcher said, "Why the history lesson, Dick?"

"Three days ago our station chief in Beijing was contacted by someone in China's Ministry of Agriculture—a mid-level bureaucrat named Bian. The pitch was subtle, ambiguous."

"Or so Brown thought," Coates added and slid the report across the table.

Dutcher picked it up and read it, then said, "Interesting trick with the pen. Very old school."

"Probably picked it up from a LeCarre novel," said Sylvia Albrecht. "Cliché or not, it works."

"There's nothing here about the message's content."

Coates slid over another folder. The message was short, written in small block letters:

GENERAL HAN SOONG ALIVE LAOGI.
REQUESTS DEFECTION.
CONDITION: SAME LAST CONTROLLER.
BIAN TO SERVE AS CONDUIT.

The laogi. . . . Dutcher suppressed a shiver.

Laogi was the Chinese word for the government prison system—or "reeducation centers"—but had come to describe any one of the hundreds of gulaglike camps spread throughout China. Once you went into a *laogi*, you either died there or you came out forever changed, a reconditioned zombie. Dutcher had once met a Brit who'd served two years in a *laogi*. By all accounts, the man had received decent treatment in comparison to his fellow Chinese inmates, but still he'd been a shell: unable to sleep more than an hour at a time, plagued with migraine headaches and permanently slurred speech, incapable of holding down a job or a relationship. . . . They'd killed him, but left him alive.

Oaken said, "If Soong is really alive, will he be the same man we dealt with twelve years ago?"

Mason nodded. "That's the rub."

"I don't like any of it," Coates said. "The demand for Tanner, the stipulation that Bian is our only conduit. . . . We have to consider this might be a ruse."

"To what end?" Albrecht countered. "To get Tanner back? I doubt it. Sure, he almost stole the PLA's best general, but all this for revenge? I don't see it."

"Then the other option: a plant. They've had twelve years to recondition Soong. We get him back, he starts planting disinformation. . . ."

"They'd have to know we'd put him under the microscope first."

"Twelve years, Sylvia," Coates repeated. "Hell, put me in a *laogi* that long and they could convince me my mother's a goddamned beach ball."

Dutcher agreed. Conviction and honesty were two sides of the same coin. The first created the appearance of the second. Believe a lie strongly enough and it becomes your truth. Still, in the end it wouldn't matter; they had no choice but to go back in for Soong. Until his defection attempt, he'd been China's premier military strategist for three decades; he was a potential gold mine.

As if reading Dutcher's mind, Mason said, "We speculate all we want, but the fact is, we can't ignore this. If there's any chance at all of getting Soong, we have to take it. Dutch?"

"I'll talk to Briggs." *And I know what he'll say,* Dutcher thought. In Briggs's mind, he'd failed Soong and his family. If there was even a remote chance to get them out, Tanner would take it.

Coates said, "Let's say Tanner's up for this. . . . That doesn't solve our biggest problem."

"What's that?" asked Sylvia Albrecht.

Dutcher answered. "We have to assume Soong gave the *Guoanbu* everything. Twelve years ago or twelve days ago, it doesn't matter: The *Guoanbu* has a long memory. Tanner is still a face in China. He may not even make it past the border."

Northern China

With the groaning of gears, the massive steel doors shut behind *Guoanbu* Chief Kyung Xiang.

There were several seconds of complete darkness before the generators kicked on and the lights flickered to life. Stretching into the distance along the walls, fluorescent lights cast pale shadows across the stone floor. From wall to wall the corridor was two hundred yards wide, the vaulted ceilings extending 30 feet above their heads.

"Amazing," murmured Xiang's deputy, Eng.

"Indeed," replied the base commander. "This tunnel extends two kilometers to the north. There are eight elevators, four on each side. Below us lay three sublevels, each three hundred meters wide. Crew quarters and support areas are on the lowermost level."

"How many men?"

"Six hundred."

Amazing indeed, thought Xiang. Ten years under construction, this base was the largest of its kind in the world. It was an unprecedented feat. Of course, compared to the Great Wall or the Three River Gorges Dam, the base's construction had been a straightforward engineering problem. What made this special was the fact that the outside world knew nothing about it.

All their satellites, all their spies, and still they couldn't see what was right in front of them.

Thousands of workers, all carefully screened and monitored, all transported in and out of the project area without ever knowing where they were. . . . And only a fraction of them—most of them specially trained PLA soldiers—had known what they were building.

What a surprise we will give them.

Before long, the world's intelligence agencies would be asking the same question: How did they do it? The answer was so simple it probably wouldn't occur to them: Patience and focus. Conditioned by thousands of years of history, the Chinese people did not think in the short term. The Great Wall took thousands of years to build; the Three River Gorges Dam over a decade. Americans complain if a megamall or high-rise apartment building takes more than six months to build. To the Chinese people, six months was but a flicker. True greatness is measured in generations, sometimes centuries.

And what of personal greatness? Xiang thought. That too can come and go in a flicker. After the Soong debacle Xiang had had to scrabble to merely survive. The *Guoanbu* did not suffer failure gladly. After those initial years, amazed to find himself alive, Xiang had begun the long climb up the MSS ladder: enemies to be eliminated, competition to be discredited, victories to be invented. Xiang often wondered if the defection attempt had been a blessing in disguise. It had made him a harder man, and that's what China needed: Hard men who could make hard choices.

Soong had cost him much. Of course, the good general was now paying the price: China's greatest general, now a rat in a cage, knowing every day he would never see the outside world again. But there were other debts outstanding, weren't there? The man who'd nearly stolen away Soong was alive and free. The insult was almost too much to bear. Thinking of it now, Xiang could feel that old familiar gnawing in his belly. . . .

He stopped himself. *Focus.* The past was done. The future. . . . Well, a large part of the future—both China's and his own—depended on this base and the role it would play in the coming months.

". . . we should be fully operational in four days," the base commander was saying. "The final tests will be completed tomorrow."

Xiang gazed down the length of the tunnel. "And the men?" he asked. "They are ready?"

"We conduct full drills three times a day. They're ready."

Eng's cell phone, whose frequency had been linked to the base's internal communication system, trilled. Eng answered, listened for a moment, then hung up. He walked over to Xiang and whispered, "Message from Qing. It's done."

"What about the family?"

"Them, too."

"Complications?"

"None," Eng replied. "It went flawlessly."

5

Washington, D.C.

LATHAM COLLECTED RANDALL AND THEN CALLED COMMERCE'S Office of Investigations to let them know he was on his way. Though it had no authority beyond itself, the COI was touchy about its turf; Latham didn't expect a warm greeting.

They were met in the lobby by the COI's director. "Morning, gentlemen," he said with a humorless smile. "If you'll follow me, the director is expecting you."

He led them to the elevators and up five floors to a corner office decorated with potted palms and Ansel Adams prints. The director and another man were waiting for them; both were standing.

Nervous boys, Latham thought. It was understandable.

The director strode over, hand outstretched. "Agent Latham, Frank Jenkins. This is—excuse me, *was*—Larry Baker's supervisor, Bud Knowlton."

Latham introduced Randall and everyone sat down.

"We were devastated to hear about Larry," Jenkins began. "He's going to be missed."

Straight from the Bureaucrat's Book of Platitudes, Latham thought. He absently wondered if Jenkins even knew Baker. Doubtful, he decided.

"You'll have our full cooperation," Jenkins concluded.

"Thank you," Latham said. "Before we get started, I want to make sure everyone understands the ground rules. We're investigating the deaths of a federal employee, his wife, and their two young children. It doesn't get any worse than that."

"Yes, of course—"

"If we get any leaks—even a trickle—out of your office, or if your PR people talk to the press, we're going to start handing out obstruction-of-justice charges."

Jenkins stiffened in his chair. "Agent Latham, there's no need to get—"

"I assume you've already called the Public Affairs director?"

"Well, of course. She needs to—"

"All she needs to know is this: No leaks, no talking to the press. She can use the standard 'can't jeopardize an ongoing investigation,' but beyond that, not one word."

"Obviously you don't understand our position. If the press suspects we're—"

"Dump it on us. Tell them you're cooperating fully, but the FBI has requested that you make no statements until the investigation is concluded."

Jenkins thought about that. "I suppose we could do that. Okay. How else can we help?"

"Tell us everything you know about Larry Baker and what he was working on."

AN HOUR LATER LATHAM AND RANDALL WALKED OUT OF COMmerce and got into their car.

"Well?" asked Randall.

"Either Baker had the most boring job in the world, or they've already circled the wagons."

According to Jenkins and Knowlton, the most controversial issue Baker had had on his plate was hearing-aid technology that a U.S. company was trying to sell to Ireland, an item which, according to Commerce's Office of the Inspector General could be considered an "Advanced Electronic Device." Until it was cleared, Knowlton explained, the hearing aid would remain on the NCTL, or National Critical Technologies List.

"Our tax dollars at work," Randall said.

"Yep," said Latham. "My guess is they're reviewing his files right now. Once they're satisfied there are no grenades laying around, they'll call us, apologize, then turn over the files."

"And if they find something? Into the shredder?"

"I doubt it. Better to lose it than find it later if they have to; they have no way of knowing Baker was making copies."

"We could subpoena them, the records—everything."

"We'll see. Let's check with the lab, see if they got anything from Baker's computer. After that, how do you feel about a trip to Dannemora?"

"As in the prison? What for?"

The fatherly part of Latham didn't want to bring Randall into this, but if he and Owens were right about where this case was going, Paul deserved to know. "I'll explain on the way."

THE LAB HAD NOTHING FOR THEM, SO THEY CAUGHT THE SHUTTLE to New York, then another north to Albany, where they rented a car and took 87 north toward Dannemora. Once Latham had the cruise control set, they both leaned back and enjoyed the scenery.

"So," Paul said. "The story."

"You remember the Callenato murders in New York about six years ago?"

"A city councilman and his family, right? There was almost another one, too, but a beat cop broke it up before it happened. Caught the guy, as I remember—some nutcase named . . ."

"Hong Cho."

"Right."

A naturalized citizen from Hong Kong, Cho had been hired by the Callenato crime family as a freelance enforcer. The councilman Cho had murdered had been under investigation by a joint FBI-NYPD Organized Crime Task Force for funneling work to Callenato-owned construction firms. The Callenatos, not only suspecting the councilman of cooperating with the police, but of helping himself to a larger percentage than they'd agreed upon, decided it was time to be rid of the man.

Late one August night, Cho broke into the councilman's home, tied up his wife and three children, then shot each of them execution style. Initially it had been ruled a robbery/

homicide, but the ME later determined several hours had elapsed between the time the family was tied up to the time they were killed.

"Both the cops and our people were baffled," Latham continued. "What had Cho been doing for those two hours? The house hadn't been tossed and there were no signs of torture. The mother and father's wrists were rubbed raw, though, almost to the bone."

"Like they were trying to get loose. Maybe Cho was putting the gun to the kid's heads."

"We had some profilers look at that. In most cases the parents—or whoever is being forced to watch it—don't struggle much. They're too busy pleading, trying to divert the attention away from their children. Struggling usually occurs when the parents are watching something being *done* to their kids."

"But what? You said—"

"They figured it out when Cho tried to pull his next job, another local politician. A beat cop heard a scream from an apartment, broke in, and caught Cho in the act. The mother and father had been duct-taped to chairs, the kids on the floor in front of them."

When the details of the crime finally reached the newspapers, Cho's method of torture had shocked an otherwise unflappable city. Under the horrified eyes of the parents, Cho had inserted an air-filled syringe into a vein of one of the children and then proceeded to question the parents with his thumb on the plunger. For each untruthful answer he got, Cho would pump another air bubble into the child's bloodstream, all the while describing to the parents what the accumulation of bubbles would eventually do to the child. Once he got the answers he wanted, Cho killed the family.

Randall stared openmouthed. "That's brutal."

"Cho was careful, too. He used a small-bore needle. The pinprick was almost invisible. The cops and agents involved were stunned—not just because of the cruelty of it, but because of the sophistication of the technique. Either he had a hell of an imagination, or he'd had some training."

"That's how you got involved?"

Latham nodded. "Harry was running the New York field office then; he called me, thought I might be able to help. With nowhere else to go, they started looking at terrorist groups and foreign organized crime."

It had taken six months, but slowly Cho's history began unraveling. The real Hong Cho had died of natural causes three years before in a Coral Gables, Florida, nursing home. Using sources from cases Latham had worked in the past, they soon suspected Cho was working for China's Ministry of State Security, or *Guoanbu*. Latham assumed Cho had learned his skills from them.

"At first we thought maybe the Callenatos and the *Guoanbu* were in bed together, but it turned out Cho was simply moonlighting."

"You're kidding."

"Nope. Of course, the PRC denied any knowledge of him. So Cho went away for the first murder and the attempted second. He got a hundred seventy years total."

"And this murder last night—"

"Same signature as Cho's work."

"Except for the father. So you're thinking the suicide was staged."

"That's my guess. If so, Baker was probably the target. The question is, What was so important the *Guoanbu* would slaughter an entire family?"

THEY SIGNED IN AT THE CLINTON CORRECTIONAL FACILITY'S front desk, turned over their guns, and followed an officer to a windowless interview room; it was painted light pink. The table and chairs were bolted the floor.

"So how's he done here?" asked Randall. "Cons don't care much for child killers."

"I heard his first month was tough, but nobody messes with him now. The first two inmates that moved on him got hurt pretty badly. The last one ended up with a broken collarbone, a ruptured kidney, and a glass eye. Now nobody comes near him."

"Wow."

"Wait till you see him."

As if on cue, the door opened. Two officers walked in. Waddling between them, shackled hand and foot, was a Chinese man in his mid-forties, slightly balding, with black, prison-issue glasses. Standing just a few inches over five feet, Hong Cho weighed no more than 120 pounds. His hands and wrists were small, almost delicate. He stared at the far wall, seemingly oblivious to their presence.

The guards sat him down, secured his ankles to the chair, his wrists to an eyelet bolted to the tabletop, then left.

"Hello, Hong," said Latham.

Cho's eyes flicked to him, then to Randall, then back to the wall.

Latham pulled out a chair and sat down across from Cho. "Hong, I'm not going to waste your time with small talk. There's been a murder in Washington that looks a lot like your work. We're onto the guy"—Cho's eyes narrowed briefly, then went blank again—"but we'd like to keep it from getting bloody. If you know of any places—"

"No."

"We've got him, Hong. He won't get out of the country. You could make it easier for him."

"You're lying."

"Why would I do that?"

"Why would you care about making it easier on anyone but yourself?"

"If we can pick him up without incident, there's less chance of civilians getting hurt."

Cho waved his hand dismissively: Collateral damage didn't concern him.

"That's okay," Latham said. "I didn't really expect you to help, but I had to give it a shot."

"Long drive for nothing."

"It happens." Latham stood. "By the way, how're they treating you?"

In response, Cho arched his head backward so his jumpsuit collar exposed his neck. Running diagonally across his larynx was a purple scar inlaid with black stitches. "Last week."

Latham suppressed a shiver. "Shank?"

Cho nodded. "Too dull. He wasn't fast enough."

"What happened to him?"

Cho returned his gaze to the wall. "He went away."

OUTSIDE IN THE HALLWAY, RANDALL WHISTLED BETWEEN HIS teeth. "Hard-ass."

"That he is."

Latham asked their escort to take them to the warden's office. Latham introduced himself and Randall. "Warden, we're working a case and we think Cho might have something. Problem is—"

"Problem is, he's a hard-ass."

"Right. We saw his latest scar. What happened to the other guy?"

"Cho took the shiv away from him, used it to cut off his ear, then stuffed it in his mouth."

"Very nice. Can we take a look at his visitor log? The last six months, maybe?"

"Sure." The warden swiveled in his chair, dug through one of the filing cabinets, and handed Latham a file. "Not much there. Two visitors—the same since he got here."

Latham scanned the log. "Stephen Yates?"

"His lawyer. Comes about once every six months."

"What about this one: Mary Tsang."

"Cho's pen pal. Sort of a nutcase if you ask me—a soul saver. She started writing him as soon as he got here, said she'd read about his trial, and didn't think he could have done what they accused him of—you know the rest."

Latham did. Ted Bundy got more marriage proposals than hate mail. There was always someone—usually a well-meaning but slightly off-kilter woman—who thought love could soften the hardest of hearts.

Randal asked, "What's their mail like?"

"Routine stuff."

"And the visits?"

"The same. You can tell he enjoys her visits, though. He even cracks a smile once in a while."

Latham said, "Could we get the particulars on her and the lawyer?"

"Sure."

WALKING OUT THE MAIN GATES, LATHAM READ THE INFORMATION on Mary Tsang. "Hmmph."

"What?"

"She lives in Washington. That's a long trip to make once a month."

"Unless she flies—which is speedy—it's a twelve-hour trip each way. Boy, that's love."

"Maybe. I think we should find out a little more about the dedicated Ms. Tsang."

6

Rappahannock River, Virginia

THIRTEEN MONTHS AFTER THE TIANANMEN SQUARE MASSACRE in Beijing, General Han Soong, chief of staff of the People's Liberation Army, slipped his fateful note to a U.S. defense attaché. The general's defection request sent shock waves through the CIA.

Already sickened by his government's ever-worsening treatment of its citizens, Tiananmen Square had pushed Soong over the edge. He had only one condition: His handler must be a military man; with a CIA case officer, he explained, he had no bond. A military man was a comrade in arms. Regardless of flag or anthem, a soldier could be trusted.

Realizing the golden opportunity they'd been handed, the CIA didn't argue and began looking for a controller. They found their man in the then–newly formed Intelligence Support Activity Group.

Tanner, a twenty-eight-year-old navy lieutenant commander not only had the skills and experience, but also the temperament to handle the environment. Tanner accepted the job and the preparations began. The operation was codenamed Ledger, Soong was Treble.

Two months later he was in China. Two months after that, on the day Tanner was to evacuate them, Soong and his family were arrested. Just minutes ahead of PSB and *Guoanbu* pursuers, Tanner went to ground. Eighteen days later he appeared in Taipei and was evacuated.

Later, Harve Brandt, one of the old-timers in ISAG and a former CIA handler, tried to give Tanner a short course on why the incident had so shaken him. "You liked the guy; you liked his family. That's natural, but it's a mistake. Better to see 'em for what they are: Product. Sometimes you deliver the product, sometimes you don't."

Tanner told Harve to stick his product up his ass.

So soon after China, it was still heavy in Tanner's heart: He'd screwed up. He didn't know how or where, but there was no other explanation. Eventually he managed to trade that conviction for the realization that no matter the cause—whether it was his fault or nobody's fault—Soong, his wife, and his daughter were either dead or rotting inside a *laogi*.

Lian Soong . . . She'd been twenty then, which made her thirty-two now—if she was even still alive, that is. *Laogi*s were especially hard on women, it was said. Maybe it would be better if she were—

No no no . . .

God, how he'd loved her. During the early days of the affair, that rational voice in the back of Tanner's mind had tried to warn him off, but it was too late. They were already caught up in each other.

Later, it was the not knowing that haunted him most. Had the affair distracted him from the job? If he'd stuck to business, would Soong and his wife be running a deli in Tallahassee or a nursery in Seattle? Would he and Lian have—

The telephone broke Tanner's reverie. He stared at it, then reached out and picked it up.

"Briggs, it's Leland. I'm back."

"And?"

"You may want to dust off your passport."

DUTCHER ARRIVED AN HOUR LATER. TANNER MADE COFFEE AND they sat on the deck overlooking the cove; beyond it, a rain squall was closing over the bay.

Dutcher recounted to Tanner his meeting at Langley. "Whether he's really still alive or not . . ."

"What do we know about the embassy's contact?"

"Chang-Moh Bian. Not much. Mason's going to ask his station chief to arrange a face-to-face. If Soong is still alive and Bian is in contact with him, he'll have some details."

My God, Tanner thought, *could he really be alive? After all this time, was it possible?*

"Here's the interesting part," Dutcher said. "Soong won't accept anyone else. Just you."

"Just like last time."

"Yep. It's got Mason nervous."

Tanner understood. However remote, all this could be a setup designed to lure him back into China. Though Kyung Xiang had managed to rise to the top of the *Guoanbu*, his career—and life, possibly—had hung in the balance for several years after the Soong affair. Could Xiang have been waiting all this time for a chance to get his hands on Tanner?

Briggs didn't think so. Xiang was a professional. It was unlikely he would hold a grudge this long—even more unlikely that he'd create this scenario to satisfy that grudge. Still, as the head of *Guoanbu*, Xiang had enormous power. If he wanted a little revenge, who would deny him?

The more likely scenario was that Soong himself was a plant. After this long they could have turned him into a marionette. The professional side of Tanner's brain couldn't discount the idea, but the emotional side—the side that still considered Soong a friend—refused to believe it.

"The truth is," Dutcher said, "whether this is genuine or fake isn't the issue."

"I know: Dick's a little worried about my head."

"He knows you've got the skills, but the environment . . . Hell, this is China. The *Guoanbu*, PSB, and PAP are forces unto themselves. Given what you went through last time. . . ."

The odds are against me, Tanner thought. Too much emotional investment; too much "preexposure" to the target country; too many triggers that might derail him. In the eyes of the CIA, he was a bad gamble. Problem was, if they wanted Soong, they had no choice but to use him.

"Leland, there's something else you should know. While I was there, Soong's daughter and I . . . There was something between us."

Dutcher stared at him. "Pardon me?"

"It was my first time on this kind of op; I was young . . . stupid. It shouldn't have happened—"

"Damn right it shouldn't—"

"—but it did."

Dutcher exhaled. "Christ, Briggs."

"I know." Like her father, Lian had probably broken and told the MSS everything; if Tanner went back into China, she could be used as leverage against him.

Dutcher asked, "Did this thing with her affect the outcome?"

"I don't think so," replied Tanner. *God, I hope not.*

Dutcher studied his face, then nodded. "We've still got a problem. I have to tell Mason."

"No, you don't."

"Briggs—"

"Leland, I can do this." Tanner suddenly felt slimy. Leland was more than a boss; he was like a second father. Was he trading on their relationship for a chance to ease his own conscience? *I can do this. . . .* Was he certain? "I can do the job."

Dutcher sighed and shook his head. "God almighty. . . . I must be getting soft in my old age. Okay: What Dick doesn't know can't hurt him. But I'll tell you this: If it goes wrong, they're gonna hang us both from the nearest lamppost."

Tanner smiled. "Then I'll just make sure it doesn't go wrong."

Washington, D.C.

Latham and Randall got back into town in the early evening and parted ways. When Charlie got home he found Bonnie standing at the kitchen counter. He kissed her, then looked down at the bowl she was stirring. "Is that that cold salsa soup stuff?"

"It's called 'gazpacho,' Charlie. You like it."

"I do?"

"You said you did last time I made it."

Uh-oh. "Oh, yeah . . . gazpacho. I was thinking of that other stuff."

Bonnie smiled. "Liar. Go shower. We'll eat when you get done."

An hour later, Latham decided he did in fact like gazpacho. How was it that Bonnie knew what he liked when he couldn't even remember if he'd had it before? *Ah, the joys of marriage. . . .* Bonnie was a wonderful wife and mother, and he made it a point to remind himself daily how lucky he was.

"Sammie called today," Bonnie said. Their oldest daughter, Samantha, was a sophomore majoring in economics at William and Mary College. "She said to say hi."

"Everything okay?"

"She's just a little homesick, I think. Finals are next month; she'll be home after that."

"Good. I kinda miss the patter of . . . young adult feet around here."

Bonnie gave him a sideways smile. "We could always—"

"Please tell me you're kidding."

"I'm kidding."

The phone rang and Bonnie picked it up, listened, then handed it to Latham. "Hello?"

"Charlie, it's Paul. The coroner's done with the Bakers. She may have something for us."

"I'll meet you there." He hung up and turned to Bonnie. "The Baker thing. Sorry."

"It's okay, go ahead. I've got paint swatches to look at."

"Paint swatches?"

"We're painting the kitchen, remember?" She shook her head and smiled. "Go, Charlie."

THE MEDICAL EXAMINER, A GANGLY WOMAN IN HER EARLY FIFties, was sitting in her office finishing the report. "Hello, Charlie. Been a while."

"Not long enough, Margaret," Latham replied. "No offense."

"None taken." She looked at Randall and mock-whispered, "Charlie doesn't much like morgues. I think he's got a phobia about stainless steel."

"Just one of his many quirks."

"Come on, I'll show what we found."

She led them into the examining room. The air was thick with the tang of disinfectant. The tile floor reflected the grayish glare of the overhead fluorescent lights. Each of the room's four stainless-steel tables were occupied: four sets of sheets—two adult-size, two child-size.

What used to be the Baker family, Charlie thought. He didn't know how coroners did it. Two weeks in this place and he'd be drinking his lunch every day.

"First, the routine stuff," said Margaret. "All were negative for narcotics or toxins. No signs of disease or degeneration in any of the major systems. Aside from bullet wounds in each of the victims and ligature marks on the extremities of the woman and the children, there were no gross injuries."

"Did you check the syringe?"

"Yep. No toxins, no narcotics. It was brand-new—fresh out of its blister pack, in fact. There were minute traces of adhesive residue on it: the manufacturer uses it to keep the syringe seated in the pack while it's going down the assembly line. If it had been handled any significant amount after opening, the residue would have been wiped off."

"The needle?"

"Blood only. Type A positive; we matched it to the youngest child."

Son of a bitch, Charlie thought. Part of him had been hoping against hope that he and Owens were wrong. Somewhere out there was at least one Second Bureau *Guoanbu* operative, perhaps more. But the question remained: Why kill Baker and his family?

"Did you recover the slugs?" Randall asked her.

"Yeah, but they're in bad shape; you might get some metallurgy and rifling info, but it's a toss-up. I sent them over to Quantico. My guess is nine millimeter. The mother's wound is starfished, but there're no powder burns or stippling."

In cases of contact or near-contact gunshot wounds, the entry point is almost always bordered by radial tears, hence the "starfish" appearance. The lack of gunpowder burns or graphite "tattooing" on the skin could only mean one thing: The weapon had been equipped with a noise suppressor that had absorbed both the gas and the powder. That would explain why none of the neighbors had reported hearing anything unusual during the night.

"In the case of each child," Margaret went on, "the bullets bisected the vertical axis of the skull, traveled down the neck, and lodged in the chest cavity."

"Any idea about time of death?" asked Latham.

"Between nine and midnight."

"What about the father?"

"He died after them, about an hour or so. Here's where it gets interesting. Take a look."

She drew down the sheet to reveal Larry Baker's head. Except for the bruised swelling from the gunshot under his chin, his face was snow white. Margaret had partially reconstructed the exit wound on top of the skull, but still it looked like a jigsaw puzzle of blood, matted hair, and jagged bone.

Margaret pointed. "See the spot just above the entry wound . . . that indentation?"

"Looks like a sight stamp?" Latham said.

"Right. It's from pressing the barrel hard against the skin. In suicides a stamp usually means the person wants to make sure they don't miss, or they're holding on tight so they don't lose their nerve."

"Okay . . ."

"Look to the right of the stamp. See the gouge in the skin? It's the same pattern as the indentation." She let it hang, looking from Randall to Latham.

"I don't get it," said Randall. "He moved the gun; he had second thoughts. So what?"

"No," Latham said. "If you have second thoughts you lower the gun, then put it back. You don't drag it around your skin. Think about it: You're parked in your car, sitting in the driver's seat. Someone's next to you, in the passenger seat. Suddenly they pull out a gun, reach over"—Latham mimicked his words—"and put it under your chin. You react by jerking away, to the side."

Now Randall caught on. "And if the gun's pressed tightly enough, the site drags across the skin."

Latham nodded. "Baker saw it coming. He tried to move, but wasn't quick enough."

IT TOOK SOME DELICACY TO MAKE THE INQUIRIES WITHOUT RAISing suspicion, but three days after the Chinese ambassador's visit to the Oval Office, Chief of Staff Howard Bousikaris had confirmed the source of Martin's eleventh-hour campaign contributions.

Though still unsure how China had done it, Bousikaris knew it didn't matter. If made public, the evidence would be irrefutable. More importantly, no one would believe Martin was an unwitting dupe. The American public had no more stomach for corruption.

Having satisfied himself they'd been checkmated, he focused on the next step: How to turn defeat into a victory. First, however, they had to find out exactly what the Chinese wanted.

To get that answer, Bousikaris had left his home at midnight, drove his car to the Eastern Market metrorail stop, boarded the train, and taken it to the last stop, Addison Road. The ambassador's instructions had been clear about the time and place of the meeting, if not the identity of his contact.

"Stand at the railing overlooking the parking lot on Adak," the ambassador had said. "You will be approached by a person who will identify himself as Qing."

The train squealed to a stop and Bousikaris stood up. There were only two other passengers in the car, a spiky-haired teenager and a businessman. Bousikaris resisted the impulse to pull up the collar of his trench coat. *Relax. You're just a man on a train, another late night commuter. . . .*

It was all very surrealistic, if not downright bizarre, Bousikaris thought. Here he was, chief of staff to the goddamned president of the United States, skulking around in the middle of the night like a character from an Ian Fleming novel. If not for the stakes, it might actually be amusing.

The doors opened. Bousikaris stepped out. The platform was deserted except for his two fellow riders, both of whom quickly disappeared down the steps to the street. The train's doors *whooshed* shut and the train started out again, trailing scraps of trash in its wake.

Bousikaris looked down the platform, saw no one. He checked his watch: 12:55. He walked to the railing. Across the street he could see the streetlights encircling the parking lot. Except for a dozen cars, the lot was empty. A minute passed. Then two. Suddenly, a figure was standing beside him.

"You were not followed, Mr. Bousikaris."

Bousikaris wasn't sure if it was a question or a statement. "No, I wasn't. You're Qing?"

"I am."

"I have to say, you're . . . You're not what I expected."

Qing shrugged. "It's unlikely we will meet again, but if it becomes necessary, I'll leave a message in the *Post*'s classifieds. It will read, "Adrian, I love you. Come back. Always, Harmon." Check the paper daily. If you see the ad, meet me here the following night at eleven p.m. Is that clear?"

"Yes."

"I understand you've been told about our problem." Qing handed across a 3.5-inch diskette. "On this are the details of what we want done, and how. Follow them precisely."

Bousikaris hesitated. *Very serious people.* Qing was so businesslike it was unnerving. "At least give me an idea of what you're asking."

Qing considered this for a moment, then shrugged. It took two minutes of explanation.

"God, you can't be serious," Bousikaris rasped. "Do you have any idea what you're asking?"

"Don't ask stupid questions, Mr. Bousikaris. Of course we know. Follow the instructions."

"That kind of operation you're talking about is . . . complex. If even one part of it goes wrong, we could find ourselves in a goddamned shooting war."

"Follow the instructions and nothing will go wrong."

7

FBI Headquarters

"So it's official," said Owens. "We can start worrying."

"Yep," replied Latham. "We've got at least two, maybe more, *Guoanbu* operatives out there. We're gonna have to be careful with the media."

"They're treating it like a murder-suicide. Until you're done that's going to be our party line."

"Good. Maybe these sons-of-bitches will let down their guard."

"Maybe. You doing okay with this?"

"Yeah. It's just . . . Christ, what they did to that family."

"I know. You said *two* operatives. Why two?"

"Part deduction, part instinct. We know they gained entry at the kitchen door because one of the glass panes had been tapped out. I'm guessing they'd probably been watching the house, waiting for the lights to go out before moving.

"Once they were inside, they went to the master bedroom, woke Baker and his wife, then took him into another room and held him there. The second intruder rounded up the family and gathered them in the master bedroom, where they were tied up. Once done, Baker was taken in to see them."

"Why?"

"To show him his family's in jeopardy. To show him there's nothing he can do about it. Here's where it gets sketchy, but I think it fits: Baker is taken away again. They question him for a while, get nowhere, then start describing what they're going to do to his family. He still balks. One of them takes him away again, this time in his car. They drive to Rock Creek Park."

"Before his family is killed?"

"Right. It's unlikely he would've been able to drive after seeing that. Once parked at Rock Creek, the intruder places a call to the Baker home."

"We've checked—"

"One incoming call at eleven-forty. It was from a cell phone; lasted seven minutes. We tracked the phone; it was stolen from a woman's car at a Bethesda shopping mall the day before the murder. We narrowed down the location to a cell that encompasses all of Rock Creek and about a mile beyond."

"Why make the call?"

"So Baker can listen to his family being tortured."

Owens's face went pale. "Jesus."

"At this point, Baker's already been told what will happen to his family. His imagination is working overtime. He's cut off from them, helpless, forced to listen as the other intruder works on them. . . . It would be devastating. A couple minutes of that and even the toughest SOB would talk."

"About what, though? What did he have they wanted? That's the big question."

"Exactly. So, hearing his wife and children screaming, Baker breaks. He tells the intruder everything he knows, or at least enough that the intruder is convinced they've wrung him out.

"Now, this is another guess, but at this point the intruder probably tells Baker it's all over, that his family will be released. Baker relaxes, lets down his guard. The intruder reaches over, puts the gun under Baker's chin, and pulls the trigger."

Owens picked it up: "Then, as arranged, the second intruder kills the wife and kids, then leaves the house and picks up his partner."

Latham nodded. The scenario contained a fair number of leaps, but it felt right.

"Where now?" Owens asked. As if on cue, his phone rang. He punched the speaker button. It was Randall: "Quantico's working with Baker's computer. They want us over there right away."

"Something good?" Latham asked.

"Depends on how you define 'good.' "

Moscow

Vladimir Bulganin was in one of his moods, Nochenko realized.

Bulganin stood up from his desk, clasped his hands behind his back, and strode to the window. He parted the curtains and peered out. A shaft of sunlight fell on Bulganin's face, and he lifted his chin and narrowed his eyes as though seeing something on the horizon.

Where are the cameras when you need them? Nochenko thought.

Bulganin looked like something out of a Cold War propaganda poster. All that was missing was a giant red sickle and hammer looming over his head. *The stalwart Russian proletariat, a peasant thrust into service by the needs of the Motherland. . . .*

Nochenko couldn't decide if these dramatic posturings of Bulganin's were genuine or an affectation. It didn't matter, really. Whatever the truth, Bulganin knew how to work a crowd—and *that* was why he was going to be the next president of the Federation.

"What's wrong, Vladimir?" asked Nochenko. "You seem troubled."

"You saw what happened last night. It was a debacle!"

The previous night's speech in Gorky Park had drawn nearly twenty thousand people. The cheers and applause had been thunderous. With each passing day more voters swung their way. Soon their momentum would be unstoppable.

"I don't understand," Nochenko said. "The speech was a rousing success."

"Yes, the speech was fine. I'm talking about the press conference. You were there, you saw!"

"What—"

"The questions! Those reporters . . . like dogs nipping at my heels. Always with details: gross domestic product, agricultural output, manufacturing infrastructure. . . . Where's their vision?"

"Vlad, that's their job."

"A country's greatness is built on vision, not details," Bulganin continued as though Nochenko hadn't spoken. "When the Motherland called, I did not ask questions, I obeyed."

Straight from Joseph Stalin's handbook, Nochenko thought. Bulganin was not only an admirer of the old ways, but of the old leaders as well, especially Koba Stalin. It was an idiosyncrasy Nochenko preferred the public did not see; luckily, his pupil had thus far cooperated.

"Vladimir, we've discussed this," Nochenko said. "As bothersome as it is, the media is powerful. It can shape the opinions of voters we can't reach—"

"Ah! But don't you see? The people who cast the votes decide nothing. The people who count the votes decide everything."

Another damned Stalinism. "Perhaps long ago, but not anymore. The Federation is—"

"Russia, Ivan. They can dress up the name as they wish, but to true patriots it will always be *Russia*. The Motherland."

"Yes, of course."

Bulganin's eyes narrowed. "You say the words, friend, but sometimes I wonder if you believe them. Do you, Ivan? Do you believe?"

Nochenko stared into Bulganin's inscrutable eyes and again marveled at the man's charisma; he could almost feel the power radiating from Bulganin like a wave. Another page from Koba's playbook: *An implacable gaze always enfeebles the blustering coward. . . .* There was only one response that would satisfy Bulganin when he got like this.

"You dare ask me that?" Nochenko snapped. "I *served* the Motherland! I toiled in her factories before you were born. Be very careful when you question my patriotism, Vladimir!"

There was a long silence as the two men stared at one another. Finally Bulganin's face cracked into a beaming smile. He clapped Nochenko on the arms. "There! That's what I like! Some fire from my compatriot! Well spoken, Ivan!"

Bulganin spun on his heel and strode back to his desk. "Back to work. We have much to do!"

White House

Mason's summons to the Oval Office had come directly from Bousikaris. When Mason arrived, the chairman of the joint chiefs, General Chuck Cathermeier, was already there. "You, too?"

"Yeah. Any clue?"

"None."

The secretary's phone buzzed. "General Cathermeier, Director Mason, you can go in."

They found President Martin seated behind his desk, Bousikaris at his shoulder. Sitting in one of the chairs before Martin's desk was Tom Redmond, the director of the Defense Intelligence Agency.

Interesting, thought Mason. Redmond was a recent political appointee, one of many Martin had brought aboard after his inauguration. As far as Mason was concerned, Redmond had about as much business running the DIA as a chimp had flying the space shuttle.

"Sit down, gentlemen," Martin said. "We have a situation. Go ahead, Howard."

"Director Redmond has uncovered some information regarding the sale of chemical weapons."

"Uncovered how?" Mason asked.

"HUMINT," answered Redmond, referring to human intelligence—eyeballs on the ground.

"Whose?"

"Ours."

Crap, Mason thought. The DIA's mandate did not include developing human assets. Redmond was either lying or he was spreading his wings. Either way, Mason was wary. It was no secret that Martin didn't much care for him, and the DCI recognized a knee shot when he saw it.

"What kind of agent?"

Bousikaris answered: "A stringer. One of yours from long ago, in fact: a Kashmiri named Sunil Dhar. He was approached about seven months ago by a broker for the Japanese Red Army. They were looking for some sarin nerve gas and knew Dhar had contacts in the Russian black arms market."

"By contacts, I assume you mean former military," said Cathermeier.

"Correct. Dhar hasn't given up a name, but it's probably someone in the rocket forces."

It took all of Mason's discipline to hold his tongue. A DIA controller handling a former CIA agent, who's brokering a deal for a terrorist group. . . . None of it fit.

"We're aware of Dhar," Mason said. "We've never taken any of his product at face value; he likes playing both ends against the middle. Without corroboration, I'd be skeptical of his information."

Martin smiled. "Dick, I know it stings a little that you missed this, but nobody's blaming—"

"Mr. President, with all due respect—"

"This is a team effort, Dick. Don't forget that."

"Sir, I'm not concerned about saving face. Sunil Dhar is—"

Bousikaris said, "We feel Dhar's information is solid. Now that we're aware of the problem, we need solutions. To that end, Director Redmond came up with a plan. Tom, if you would."

"According to Dhar, his contact will have the sarin at the delivery point within the next seventeen to twenty days," said Redmond. "He'll have a more exact time as it nears."

"That's where we'll need your help, Dick," Bousikaris said. "We want you to coordinate with the DIA and make sure this is the real deal."

"Where's the delivery point?" asked Cathermeier.

"Russia. The Bay of Vrangel, the port of Nakhodka-Vostochny. The cargo is to be transferred to a ship called the *Nahrut*. Once the cargo's aboard, the ship will be heading for Rumoi, Japan."

Martin said, "That ship cannot be allowed to leave port."

Suddenly Mason realized where this was going. "Why not take it while it's at sea? Board the ship, secure the cargo, detain Dhar and his crew."

"Too risky," said Bousikaris. "More to the point, the Russian's have been playing fast and loose too long with their weapons of mass destruction. It's time to send them a message."

"By sinking a ship in the middle of the Bay of Vrangel? It's an act of war, Howard."

"The target ship will be of Liberian registry. The Russian government won't—"

"They won't care if it's a rubber dinghy. If we attack it in Russian waters, they'll retaliate."

President Martin broke in. "They can't retaliate if they have no proof. The plan Tom has developed will get the job done without leaving any footprints."

Tom Redmond couldn't plan a sandwich, Mason wanted to say, but the spook inside him told him to shut up and listen. "Okay," he said, "Let's hear it."

Redmond spoke for ten minutes, outlining the plan from start to finish.

Cathermeier asked, "Who do you plan to put on the ground?"

Redmond told him. "It would be a small team. Four to six men."

"Insertion method?"

"Submarine."

There were a few seconds of silence as Cathermeier considered the plan. Finally he said, "Good plan, wrong scenario."

"That's a political issue," Bousikaris said. "Let us worry about that."

"You're talking about putting armed men onto the soil of another country," said Cathermeier. "Doing that under any circumstances is dicey, but doing it with shaky intell is—"

"General, what we need to know from you is, can you put it together? Is it feasible?"

"I need to run it by my J-3—"

"No. We're keeping the loop tight on the operation. What's your answer, General?"

"It's feasible, but I have to tell you, I have serious misgivings about this."

Mason said, "As do I."

"Goddamnit!" Martin roared. "What—"

Bousikaris stepped forward, placed a restraining hand on Martin's shoulder, and said, "Gentlemen, you're cautiousness is appreciated, but the time for debate is over. Your commander-in-chief has given an order. If you can't carry it out, say so now."

The gauntlet was down, Mason realized. Whatever was happening here, it was serious enough that Martin was willing to end careers to get it done. Cathermeier would obey because he was duty bound to do so. As for himself, if he refused to go along, he'd be out, and while that in itself didn't bother Mason, he wanted to know what Martin was up to. To do that, he had to stay.

"Mr. President, I've voiced my objections. That said, you give the order, I'll do my part."

Martin nodded, then looked to Cathermeier. "General?"

Cathermeier shrugged. "I'll start the ball rolling."

Holystone

Tanner found Oaken in his office. Lined with floor-to-ceiling bookcases, filing cabinets, a map wall, and three computer workstations, this was Oaken's second home, a fact to which his wife, Beverly, would readily attest.

Oblivious to Tanner's entrance, Oaken reclined in his chair doodling on a yellow legal pad.

"Let me guess," Tanner said, leaning on the doorjamb, "You're planning an expedition to K2."

Oaken looked up. "Huh?"

"Everest?"

"Very funny."

Of the thousands of interests that occupied Oaken's mind, outdoor adventure was not one of them. The closest he'd come to the wilderness in the past six months was watching *Wild Kingdom* reruns. "That Marlon Perkins guy has the right idea," he'd told Tanner. "Letting that Jim guy do all the work. He doesn't even wear shoes, did you know that? Talk about unsanitary. . . ." From there the discussion had deteriorated into his musings about tetanus boosters and parasitic infections.

For all Oaken's quirks and for their dissimilarities, Tanner considered himself lucky to not only have Walt on his side, but to also count him as a friend.

"Algebra," Oaken replied. "Polynomials, sequences. . . . It helps me clear my head."

"Algebra helps you clear your head."

"It's concrete. The answer's either right or wrong. It's . . . refreshing. So, what's up?"

"I'm wondering if you're up to a little research project."

Oaken's eyes twinkled. "Have you ever known me not to be? What's the topic?"

"Double agents."

SINCE HEARING ABOUT SOONG'S CONTACT, TANNER HAD BEEN looking at Ledger with fresh eyes. Of the dozens of things that might have caused its failure, he kept returning to the same theory: Someone in his network had been either a double or an informant.

He'd spent much of his time in Beijing running countersurveillance—following Soong before and after meetings, watching dead drops, staking out meeting places, setting up wave-off locations— Anything and everything that might force the hands of *Guoanbu* watchers. Nothing ever came of it.

That led him to two conclusions: One, Soong had in fact been under surveillance and he'd missed it; or two, someone was feeding the opposition, making surveillance unnecessary. Tanner realized there'd been only one agent in his network who could have given the *Guoanbu* that kind of information. Known only by his code name, Genoa had been what's called a "block cutout."

Unlike a "chain cutout"—a go-between who knows only the agent who recruited him—a block cutout knows not only the names of all the agents, but their meeting spots and dead drops as well. Moreover, Genoa had been a colleague of Soong's. In his excitement, had Soong told Genoa the time and place of his final meeting with Tanner?

It would explain much. How else was the *Guoanbu* able to roll up the entire network so efficiently? How else could they have covered the meeting place and escape routes so well?

Design meant planning, Briggs knew, and planning meant foreknowledge.

"What happened to Genoa?" Oaken asked after Tanner finished explaining his theory.

"He disappeared like the others. Problem is, that's an easy ruse. Plus, by that time, my picture was plastered all over the city; I was on the run."

"Is it possible you missed something in your countersurveillance?"

"It's possible, I knew it was going to be a weak spot. Beijing was—still is—crawling with PSB and PAP officers. All it would have taken was one slipup on an agent's part and the whole thing would have unraveled."

Oaken nodded. "I think your theory is solid. Didn't the CIA already check it out, though?"

"Not until a year after it happened. It might be worth another look."

"True. . . . What's all this about, Briggs? Curiosity or something more?"

"If I'm right about Genoa, *and* he's still alive, *and* he's still active—"

"That's a lot of 'ifs.' "

"*If* all those things are true, maybe we can use him."

Oaken smiled. "Assuming Mason is going to send you back in."

"Right." *Send me or not, I'm going back.* "What do you say? Want to give it try?"

Oaken chuckled. "Find one man amid a billion Chinese, who may or may not have been a double agent, who we only know by a code name? Damn right I want to give it try."

8

Quantico, Virginia

LATHAM AND RANDALL WERE MET IN THE COMPUTER LAB BY ONE of the department's experts, a young African American named James Washington. "You guys got here in a hurry," he said.

"We're hoping you've got something good for us," Latham said.

"Yeah, I think so."

James gestured to a pair of stools before a Formica counter on which sat Baker's computer, a top-of-the-line Hewlett Packard tower attached to a twenty-one-inch Sony monitor.

"This case, it's the Baker thing?" James asked. "The murdered guy from Commerce?"

"Right."

"Well, either he's a real computer geek, or he had some help. This system's got some gnarly security programs attached."

Latham chuckled. "By 'gnarly,' I assume you mean 'superior'?"

"Right. Anyway, his system's got all kinds of blocks on it—routines designed to keep the information from being backed up or routed to an exterior drive. Hell, if you even try to *print* the stuff without a password, the hard drive erases itself."

"This isn't stuff you can buy on the open market?" asked Randal.

"Like at Best Buy? No way. I'll know more once I tear it apart, but none of it looks familiar to me. I think I found a way through it, but there're no guarantees. If I'm wrong, the hard drive goes *poof*. Since it's your case, I wanted you to make the call."

"Gimme odds," Latham said.

"Fifty-fifty."

"Do it."

THE PROCESS WAS SIMPLE, JAMES TOLD THEM. THE ONE CON-tingency the security program could not guard against was regular system maintenance. Using a "slightly recoded" CD version of the computer's native antivirus software—in this case, Norton—James initiated a scan of the hard drive. Recognizing this as a routine event, the security program didn't interfere. However, instead of scanning files, proclaiming them clean, then passing them back to the drive, James's version of Norton copied each scanned file and transferred it to the CD before returning it to the hard drive. Since the security program cared only whether files were sent to an output device, it did not intervene.

There was an electronic *bong*. James removed the CD and rebooted the system. "Now we see if we raised any alarms," he said.

The desktop reappeared on the screen. James used the mouse to check the drive's directory. He smiled. "We're okay. Not even a hiccup."

"Good job, James," said Latham. "Let's take a look at the CD."

• • •

MOST OF THE DATA WAS USELESS—GAMES, LETTERS, RECIPES— but when they got to Baker's money-management program, they struck pay dirt. "Holy cow," said Randall. "Charlie, the balance in this checking account is almost three hundred grand. The account's routing number looks odd, though."

"Offshore probably," Latham said. "Let's see who he was paying."

Randall clicked the mouse a few times to filter the account by payee. There were dozens of transactions, but one stood out. "WalPol Expeditions," Randall murmured. "Here's a check for eighty thousand . . . another for a hundred twenty."

"How far back does it go?" asked Latham.

"Almost two years."

Bingo, Charlie thought. Whoever or whatever WalPol was, the late Larry Baker had paid them almost 250,000 dollars in the last eighteen months.

Beijing

Roger Brown had been expecting the order from Langley to arrange a face-to-face with Chang-Moh Bian. In the week it took them to make the decision, he'd made a decision of his own.

Brown believed in leading from the front, and he wasn't about to ask one of his people to do something he wasn't willing to do himself. Not to say he wasn't apprehensive. Playing controller to an agent who is in turn playing intermediary for an already famous defector was a daunting task at best.

Bian's "ballpoint message" had designated a marker drop that Brown could use to establish contact, which he did the following Sunday by strolling around the Forbidden City's 250 acres while performing a string of identifiers: his coat held a certain way, a newspaper folded and left on a bench, tying his shoe near a fountain. He passed several uniformed and plainclothes PSB and PAP officers, but none paid him any attention.

After two hours of this pageantry, Brown returned to the bench beside the Golden Water Stream and sat down. Two minutes later he saw Bian enter the courtyard.

The man's a wreck, Brown thought. Bian's hands were visibly shaking. Trying to cover the movement with a camera, he stopped and looked behind him every few seconds. *This is bad.* Best case, Bian was simply scared; worst case, he was bait. The sooner Brown could distance himself from Bian the better. He was about to give the wave-off signal when Bian turned, walked directly to the bench, and sat down. "You came."

Ah, shit. "You don't look well."

"I feel awful. My stomach—"

"Nerves."

"I suppose."

"You've got to relax. If you're being watched, they've already got us. If you're not being watched, then your jumpiness is going to get you caught. Me, too, for that matter." Brown forced some humor into his voice: "I'll tell ya, if I get thrown in prison, I'll have hell to pay with my wife."

"I'm sorry. I just . . . I'm . . ."

"I know. Just breathe. Enjoy the sun."

After a few seconds, Bian's posture eased. "Your people are interested in helping the general?"

"We are."

"What about his conditions? He was adamant about the man he mentioned."

"We're working on it. First off, though, I have to ask you some questions."

Brown spent fifteen minutes questioning Bian about himself: school, family, work, hobbies, and finally, his motivation for helping Soong. All the answers would later be dissected by the Intelligence Directorate, then compared to what they already knew about the man. If any inconsistencies appeared, the DO would have the option to either abort the operation, or order it forward with the knowledge that Bian may be damaged goods.

"Where is Soong right now?" Brown asked.

"I don't know."

"Pardon me?"

"He's in a *laogi* somewhere to the north, but I don't know its location."

"Then how are you in contact with him?"

"I'm sorry, the general was very specific. I can only give those details to the man he asked for . . . this Tanner person."

Alarms went off in Brown's head. "That's unacceptable."

"I know." Bian hesitated, started to speak, then stopped. "I . . ."

"What?"

"He'll be angry I gave you this information."

"Why? What information?"

"He desperately wants to get his family out of China with him."

"We assumed that," Brown said. "I don't understand—"

"That's why he wants Tanner to come *here*. Soong trusts him."

"So?"

"So, I may know a simpler way. You may be able to get him out without setting foot in China."

San Clemente Island, California

If not for the added conditions, tonight's exercise would have been a simple one, something Master Chief Robert Jurens and his team of three SEALs had done dozens of times. In this case, the "added conditions" involved a guided missile frigate lobbing three-inch shells onto the beach they were trying to reconnoiter.

Known to fellow operators as "Sconi" because of his proud Wisconsin upbringing (one of the only black dairy farming families in the state, he was fond of telling people), Jurens was a rail-thin black man with a goatee and an easy smile. Jurens had been on the teams for fourteen years, having gone from a lowly seaman during BUD/s training to one of the youngest master chiefs in the navy. Since navy SpecWar ran on the merit system, he was frequently put in command of platoons, often over the heads of commissioned officers. No one complained. Jurens knew his business and he knew how to lead.

Tonight's swim-in had been taxing, largely because the currents surrounding San Clemente Island were ferocious. In wartime they would have come here to map the shoals for obstacles, dangerous gradients, bed consistency—anything that might impede an amphibious force.

Through the murky water Jurens could hear the muffled *whoosh-crump* of the three-inch shells pounding the beach ahead of them. *Very close,* he thought. He could feel the impacts rumbling through the sand beneath him. *Hope the fire-control boys are on their game tonight.*

He reached out and gave the buddy-line a double tug, signaling the team to advance. His belly scraped the sand. As each wave crashed over his head and then receded he caught glimpses of sloped beach and—

Crump! A geyser of sand and flame erupted on the beach, then another.

Suddenly he saw a flicker of blue light in the corner of his eye. He rolled onto his back and poked his mask out of the water. High above, a flare arced into the sky, followed a moment later by a yellow. It was the "abort exercise" signal.

The other team members had also seen it, and one by one they waded ashore. Before anyone could ask questions, they heard the thump of helicopter rotors. A few seconds later a pair of strobe lights materialized out of the darkness. The helicopter—a Seahawk from the frigate, Jurens guessed—stopped in a hover over the beach, then landed in a storm of sand. The cabin door opened. The crewman inside pointed to Jurens and waved him over.

Jurens jogged over. "What's up?" he shouted.

"Orders for you, Master Chief!"

"Now? We're kinda in the middle of something, if you hadn't noticed."

"I'm just the messenger. They said *now,* so here we are."

Jurens took the message and trotted away as the Seahawk lifted off behind him and disappeared into the night. He opened the message and started reading.

"Bad news, Skip?" asked Smitty.

"I guess that depends on how you feel about Alaska," Sconi replied.

Pearl Harbor, Hawaii

Three thousand miles to the east, a man to whom Sconi Bob Jurens would soon owe his life was also receiving a message. Commander Archie Kinsock, skipper of the USS *Columbia*, was standing in the sub's Control Room when the radio-shack operator called on the intercom.

"Traffic for you, Skipper. Eyes only."

"On my way."

As *Columbia* was in port, only a skeleton crew remained aboard to perform housekeeping functions. Most of the crew was either on liberty or in one of Pearl's BEQs, or Base Enlisted Quarters, whose rooms, though far from luxurious, certainly seemed so to submariners.

Kinsock walked forward, punched the cipher keypad on Radio's door, and pushed through. "It's on the printer, Skipper," said the RM3.

"Thanks, Finn." Kinsock tore off the sheet and read.

"Bad news, sir?"

"Huh?"

"You're frowning."

"First thing they taught us in CO school, Finn. Go grab yourself a cup of coffee, will ya?"

"Yes, sir." Finn left.

Kinsock reached above his head, switched the intercom to the 1MC, or the boat-wide public address, and keyed the handset. "XO to Radio."

Jim McGregor, the boat's executive officer, appeared a minute later. "What's up, Skipper?"

"How many have we got ashore, Jim?"

"Eighty-two. Four on leave."

"Get 'em all back here," Kinsock said. "We've got a job."

9

Langley

"WE'VE HAD OUR FIRST MEETING WITH SOONG'S CONTACT," Mason said, then recapped Brown's report. "So far, Bian seems on the level. He's frazzled, though, and that's a worry. We don't think he's bait, but Brown said he stood out like a wooden leg at a beauty contest."

"A white crow," said Dutcher. "White Crow" was an old KGB term for an agent whose behavior tends to single him out in crowds.

Tanner asked, "Can Brown limit his contact with him?"

"Hopefully. If not, his risk goes up every time they meet."

"Do we know anything about his motivation?" asked Oaken.

George Coates answered. "Ideology. Admiration, from the sound of it."

Of the many reasons that spur agents to work for enemy services, personal motivation, or "feel goods," is the rarest. Admiration—unless it stems from a deeply personal relationship—will carry an agent only so far. Once things get dicey, admiration is almost always overpowered by fear.

"He's a Soong groupie, for lack of a better term. In the seventies and eighties Soong was a genuine hero. The people's nickname for him was *Jie,* which means both 'grandfather' and 'hero,' depending on the inflection. After Tiananmen, when Soong began speaking out, he made a lot of enemies in the government, but gained a real grassroots following."

And that was his downfall, thought Tanner. Knowing this, and being torn between loyalty for his country and fear for his family, Soong contacted the CIA. In the end, Soong's worst fears were realized.

"The good news is, we may have gotten a break. Soong is scheduled to leave the country."

"What?" said Tanner. "Where?"

"Jakarta, as a member of the PRC's delegation at the annual Asian Economic and Foreign Affairs Conference. If so, it'll be the first time Soong has been seen in twelve years. Best guess is they plan to have him speak about human rights."

"The poster child for a kinder, gentler PRC," said Dutcher.

Coates said, "It's unprecedented, really, for Beijing to let someone of his notoriety out of the country—especially after being so vocal against the government."

"If they've still got his family, it's no risk at all," Tanner said. "As long as they've got that leverage, they know he'll behave himself."

"That's the catch," said Mason. "If we manage to get him in Jakarta, will he go? And if he does, what happens to his family?"

"Maybe nothing," said Dutcher. "If we got him, Beijing would know they can't stop him from talking to us. What they can do is keep him from speaking out against their government."

"Blackmail," said Coates.

"But it works both ways: As long as Soong stays silent, his family is unharmed; as long as his family is unharmed, he stays silent."

Tanner said, "Either way, his family loses."

Mason turned to him. "That might be the price, Briggs."

"But will he pay it?" *And should we even be asking him to consider it?*

"We won't know that unless we ask."

They talked for a few more minutes before the meeting broke up. As everyone was filing out, Mason said, "Briggs, stay for few minutes, will you?"

• • •

THEY'D BEEN IN THIS POSITION BEFORE, MASON REALIZED: TANner being the right—hell, maybe the *only*—person for a tough job, while at the same time being the exactly *wrong* person for the job.

Nine months ago it had been the Beirut affair. Tanner had gone there to hunt down a friend-turned-terrorist. That relationship had been both Tanner's edge and his weakness. In the end, he'd managed to get the job done, saving thousands of lives in the process, but it had been a near thing.

Too near by far, Mason thought.

Tanner's recounting of the events in Beirut had been thorough, but reports don't let you look into a man's mind, especially a man like Tanner. Like any operator worth a damn, Tanner never gave much away. Good operators listened more than they talked, absorbed more than they observed, intuited more than they analyzed.

It was ironic, Mason thought. In this age of high technology, where satellites could tell him what some third-world despot had for breakfast and computers could predict down to a few bullets an enemy's war-making power, all he could do here was go with his instincts.

So, the question was, Despite his baggage, could Tanner get out of his own head, go in, grab Soong, and come back out? And, if necessary, could he leave Soong's family behind?

"Pain in the butt, isn't it?" Tanner said.

"What's that?"

"Nine months ago you didn't have much of a choice. I might have been the right guy for the job, but given the stakes, it would have been nice to have more options."

Mason chuckled. "You been reading my diary? Listen, if I had to choose somebody to put on the can't-be-done stuff, you'd be on every one of my short lists."

"Thanks. Do I hear a 'but' in there?"

"But . . . the day they were passing out consciences, you got a double dose. You get involved, and that's a liability in this business."

"So I've heard."

"Do I hear a 'but' in there?"

Tanner smiled, shrugged. "But I'm still around."

"Good point." After a moment, Mason said, "I won't be able to give you much support."

"I know."

"If you get caught—"

"If I get caught I better hope *laogis* aren't as bad as they say." Tanner turned to face him. "Go ahead and ask the question, Dick."

"Okay. Can you do it?"

"I can do it," Tanner said. "You send me in, I'll bring him out."

Mason stared at him for a long five seconds, studying his eyes; they never wavered.

The DCI nodded. "You leave in ten days."

Beijing

Xiang could hear nothing of the conversation through the oak doors of the Politburo room. It didn't matter; he knew the topic: Rubicon.

He could easily imagine the discussion: *This is simply Xiang's attempt to regain his lost glory. . . . The scope of the plan is too vast. . . . What if the Americans do not respond as he's planned?*

The nearer Rubicon's launch date came, the more heated the debate became. None of the members would openly disagree with the premier's decision to adopt the plan, but Xiang knew they were split on the subject. Thankfully, the premier had more vision than his colleagues. Like Xiang, he knew China's greatness had to be seized, not debated and pondered. The time for that was over.

Ten long years, thought Xiang. *And it was almost time.*

The doors swung open and the members began filing out. Befitting his status, Xiang stood up and nodded respectfully as each member passed. Their responses ranged from curiosity to open disdain. *Curious to see if I succeed and wondering what it will mean for them if I do; disdain because I have the premier's ear.*

Xiang straightened his tunic and strode through the doors. The room, cast in stripes of sunlight and shadow, was filled with gray cigarette smoke. The premier sat at the far end of the conference table. "Sit," he said, gesturing to the chair nearest him.

Xiang walked over, sat down.

"I'll tell you this, Kyung, this plan of yours certainly makes for interesting Politburo discussion."

"I can imagine, sir. Do they—"

"They'll do as I say. They may claim to represent the people, but *I* represent China. They will grumble, because that is what they do, and I will indulge them."

"Yes, sir."

"Besides, the time for debate is over. Truth be told, it was over many years ago; those who don't realize that soon will. I understand you visited one of the facilities. Are we ready?"

"Fully."

"An amazing feat. I wouldn't have thought it possible." The premier smiled and shook his head. "All of it happening right under their noses. Tell me about this business in America. This murder, it was necessary?"

"The man had outlived his usefulness; also, he was leaning toward extortion."

"How so?"

"He told Qing he'd withheld key components to the process. He wanted more money, or he would go to their federal police."

"And his family?"

"Also necessary. Their newspapers are treating it as a murder-suicide. If they had suspicions beyond that, we would have heard about it. Their media virtually runs the country. Don't worry, sir. Qing is one of my best. Their police will look, but they won't find anything. Even if they do, it will not lead them to us—not in time, at least. And even then, it will not matter."

"Why is that?"

"Because, sir, victors write the history."

10

Blanton Crossing, Virginia

LATHAM'S RESEARCH INTO HONG CHO'S PEN PAL, MARY TSANG, had so far turned up little.

Tsang was thirty-two, single, and worked as a legal secretary; as far as they could tell, she had few extracurricular interests except television. She drove a modest compact car, had a stellar credit history, no traffic tickets, and received few visitors.

In the spycraft jargon, Tsang was "gray." Whether this trait was contrived or natural, Latham didn't know, but he wanted to find out. Most important, she didn't strike him as the type to initiate a relationship with a multiple murderer. If Tsang turned out to be something other than she seemed, he was guessing it would be a conduit for Cho. But to whom, and for what purpose?

While Randall and a team of agents started digging deeper into Tsang, Latham drove south to Blanton Crossing, a small railroad town about seventy-five miles south of D.C., where he hoped to find the headquarters of WalPol Expeditions, the recipient of nearly a quarter-million dollars from Larry Baker.

WalPol was a sole proprietorship created six years ago by a man named Mike Soderberg. According to the IRS, WalPol—which billed itself as an "exotic vacation provider"—filed its taxes on time and had never shown more than sixty thousand dollars of revenue.

Fifteen minutes after turning onto Route 54, Latham entered Blanton Crossing's city limits. The address led him to a trailer park nestled between a set of railroad tracks and a sewage canal. Charlie stopped before a rundown mobile home painted the color of lemon sherbet. The driveway was empty.

He got out, walked up the steps, and knocked. Thirty seconds passed. No one appeared. He opened the screen and tried the knob. Locked.

"Can I help ya, mister?" a voice said.

Latham turned. Standing in the yard, his hands resting atop a rake handle, was a man in a John Deere baseball cap and a tank top that read, "If you can read this, you're standing too close."

"I'm looking for WalPol Expeditions."

"That's it, there."

Latham detected a Georgian accent. Redneck farmer, he guessed. The man had heavily corded forearms and hands that looked tough as leather. "Are you—"

"Nope."

"Have you seen—"

"Nope."

"Who are you?" Latham asked. "The local rake salesman?"

The man chuckled. "Nope, just the handyman. Name's Joe-Bob."

"You have any idea where I can find the owner?"

"Been gone a few days. Don't know where. You lookin' to go expeditionin' or somethin'?"

Latham nodded. "A buddy of mine recommended WalPol; said they do good canoe trips."

"Huh." Joe-Bob nodded to Latham's car. "Maryland. Long way to come."

"I'm retired. Got plenty of time on my hands."

Joe-Bob lifted his cap and scratched his head. "Gimme your name. I'll pass it on."

"That's okay. Maybe I'll drive down next week."

"Suit yourself."

On the way out, Latham found the trailer park's office. Inside, an old man stood at the counter watching a *Gunsmoke* rerun. "How's Sheriff Dillon doing?" Latham asked.

"*Marshall* Dillon," the old man grumbled. "Okay, I guess, but I'll tell you what: If I were him, I would've put a bullet in Festus by now. Annoying son-of-a-bitch. What can I do for you?"

"I'm looking for Mike Soderberg."

"Good luck. He keeps weird hours, that one. Haven't seen him for a couple days, but then again, I don't watch for him. You a friend of his?"

"Since we were kids." Latham leaned a little closer and said conspiratorially, "Here's the thing: His mom called me yesterday. She hasn't heard from him for about a month and she's worried. Problem is, Mike and his dad don't get along—"

"Sounds like my kid. Never calls, never writes—"

"Yeah, and if Mike's dad knew she was in touch with him, there'd be hell to pay, so she asked me to check up on him—quietly, if you know what I mean. If he's okay and he finds out his mom was trying to nursemaid him . . . well, you know."

"Gotcha. What d'ya want from me?"

"I got a buddy that's a state trooper. If I had a license plate number I could ask him to keep a look out, see if Mike's run into any trouble." The lie was thin, and Latham held his breath.

The old man frowned. "Sorry, my records ain't that good."

"Thanks anyway. It was worth a shot." Latham turned to leave.

"Twit!" the old man blurted.

"Pardon?"

"The plate number on his pickup—the first three digits: T-W-T. Reminds me of the word *twit*. Always worth a good chuckle."

Latham smiled back. "Yeah, that's a good one."

LATHAM WAS AN HOUR NORTH OF BLANTON CROSSING WHEN Qing received the phone call.

"You recognize my voice?" the caller asked.

"Yes. What is it?"

"There was somebody snooping around down here. He left about an hour ago."

"Describe him."

The caller did so, then added. "Got his plate number, if that helps."

Qing copied down the number. "Is there somewhere you can go for the next few days?"

"Yeah. I got some friends down south I can stay with before I leave."

"Go there," Qing said. "I'll take care of this."

Fort Greely, Alaska

Beyond the navalese language, Jurens's orders had been short and simple: *You and three men. Don't pack, don't talk to anyone. Just get on the plane and go.* No mention of gear, or of weapons, or even of what they were to do when they reached their destination.

He chose Schmidt, Gurtz, and Mendrick, who'd been dubbed "Dickie" by an inebriated team member who'd thought "Mendrick" had an anatomical ring to it. For similar reasons, Gurtz's handle had been truncated to "Zee." Schmidt was simply known as "Smitty." They were good men, and if Sconi's instincts about this mission proved right, he could think of no one else he'd rather have along.

He knew of Fort Greely, but having been a warm-water frog all his career, he'd never been there. Specializing in cold weather riverine and mountain operations, Greely was home to the Army's Northern Warfare School.

The C-141 touched down amid flurries on Greely's airstrip and taxied to a nearby Quonset hut. A Humvee was waiting at the bottom of the plane's steps. A corporal called, "Master Chief Jurens?"

"Yes."

"If you'd follow me, please."

THE CORPORAL DROVE THEM TO THE NORTHERN EDGE OF THE base, past obstacle courses, firing ranges, and jump towers, until they reached a lone Quonset hut near a lake. Scrub pine dotted the ice-rimmed shoreline. "This is it, gentlemen," said the corporal.

They piled out, then watched the Humvee turn around and disappear down the road. Aside from the wind whistling through the trees and an occasional *pop* as the lake's ice shifted, it was silent.

"Wonder how cold that water is," Dickie said.

"I have a feeling we're gonna find out," replied Zee.

"Come on," Jurens said.

They opened the door and walked inside.

"Welcome to Alaska, gentlemen," said General Cathermeier.

The rear third of the hut was stacked with crates and boxes. Jurens recognized the stencil on some of them: rebreather rigs; Heckler & Koch MP-10SD assault rifles; 9mm ammunition; wet suits. . . .

"Nice of them to pack for us," Smitty muttered.

Cathermeier sat at a card table atop which sat a slide projector. Four chairs were arranged in a semicircle before the table. Hanging from the wall was a white screen.

"Have a seat," said Cathermeier. "Master Chief, we've met, but why don't you introduce me."

Jurens did so, then said, "General, no disrespect intended, but what the hell is going on?"

Cathermeier's presence not only suggested they were about to drop into what operators called a "rabbit hole," but it also told Sconi their normal chain of command had been bypassed.

"You and your men are on temporarily assigned duty to my J-3 staff."

Dickie said, deadpan, "Excuse me, General, but when is your staff expected? If it's soon, we're gonna have to rustle up some more cots—"

"Dickie . . ." Jurens muttered.

"It's okay, Master Chief. For the next hour, we're just five soldiers in a room." Zee opened his mouth to speak, but Cathermeier beat him to it. "No, Mr. Gurtz, you may *not* call me Chuck."

There was laughter all around.

"Let's get to it." Cathermeier shut off the lights and turned on the slide projector. A black-and-white satellite image of a commercial harbor appeared on the screen. "We'll start from the top," Cathermeier began. "Penetration. . . ."

He spoke for twenty minutes, clicking through the slides as he covered every aspect of the area: terrain, weather, military, and civilian presence. . . . Everything save the location or why they were going.

Smitty broke in: "General, what's the job? Are we supposed to just render this mystery location safe for world democracy, or is there something specific you want us to do?"

Cathermeier laughed. "You'll get the specifics once you're en route, but in short, your mission is straightforward: Infiltrate a heavily guarded coastline via submarine lock-out, penetrate inland, lay up, reconnoiter the harbor, and finally, provide strike support as directed."

Provide strike support as directed, Jurens thought.

Translation: Something was gonna get bombed, and it would be their job to make it happen.

Holystone Office

Faced with steep odds against finding Genoa, Oaken had to make some assumptions.

The first was that Tanner's theory held water, which seemed the case. The timing and efficiency with which the *Guoanbu* had rolled up the Ledger network was telling. They'd known details that surveillance alone couldn't have provided.

What about Genoa himself? According to Tanner, the man had been a colleague of Soong's, which meant he worked in either the military or intelligence communities—or both. Therefore he was not an agent, but rather a professional spook. That certainly narrowed the field of candidates, but even so, Oaken knew it would be like looking for a piece of lint in a snowstorm.

With no where else to start, he went back to the beginning.

• • •

EIGHT HOURS LATER HE KNEW THE DETAILS OF LEDGER FROM start to finish, top to bottom. He'd read every intelligence report and every analysis he could get his hands on. He was looking for a nick in the onion's skin that would allow him to start peeling layers. It wasn't there. Ledger should have worked, but it didn't. No one knew why.

He stood up, stretched, then walked into the kitchen to make a pot of coffee. He was dumping water into the pot when an angle bubbled up from his subconscious. "Wang Trahn," he murmured.

IN 1997, WAN TRAHN WAS A THIRTY-NINE-YEAR-OLD CLERK IN the archives of the Ministry of State Security. Unmarried, lonely, and enticed by the sexy images flooding his country from the West, Trahn began to imagine America as the paradise so many immigrants believe it to be. The Coca-Cola was refreshingly sexy; the hamburgers were made "your way" by smiling beach bunnies; the automobiles were plentiful and luxurious. If you wanted it, you could have it and/or be it. You could work on Wall Street, or be a cigar chomping police detective, or even an actor in Hollywood.

Having heard rumors of how hard it was to get to America, and how so many of his countrymen arrived only to find themselves enslaved by the same people who transported them, Trahn started looking for a better way. It didn't take him long to realize his job was the key.

Every day he handled documents for which the Americans would pay handsomely. Not only would they get him out of China, but they would make him rich in the process.

Trahn spent the next year gathering thousands of documents, reducing them on the photocopier, then smuggling them out of the archive building. If it looked even remotely important, he took it. The crawl space in his basement soon overflowed with files, reports, and photos.

Once certain he'd collected enough, Trahn bought a backpack, stuffed it to the brim with his plunder, took a taxi to the U.S. embassy, then begged his way into the courtyard. He was met by the CIA's deputy station chief, who looked at Trahn's identification, then inside the backpack, and then promptly took him inside.

IT WAS JUST PAST DAWN WHEN TANNER, CAHIL, AND DUTCHER arrived at the office. They found Oaken asleep on his couch.

"I'll go make coffee," Cahil said. "You see if you can rouse him."

Ten minutes later they were sitting in the conference room. Red-eyed and hair askew, Oaken was sipping a cup and arranging notes. Despite his obvious exhaustion, the glint of excitement in his eyes was unmistakable.

He's in his element, Briggs thought. *Adventure, Oaken style*. "How long have you been here?"

Oaken glanced at his watch. "Thirteen—no, fourteen hours."

"Nothing spells fun like an all-night research session," Cahil said. "That's my motto."

"You have a motto?" asked Tanner.

"Several. Depending on the situation."

"So," Dutcher said, "Briggs told me about your project. I assume you found something?"

"I did," Oaken replied. "First, though, the story." Oaken took them through the Wan Trahn saga, ending with his evacuation to the United States and subsequent debriefing with the CIA. "Trahn was what they call a 'Hoover': he sucked up every bit of information in sight then dumped it on us. When Langley finished counting, he'd delivered four thousand pages of documents."

"Four *thousand*?" said Cahil.

"Yep. Since he worked in the archives, though, none of it was current. It gave us a lot of general info on how the MSS and PSB run their in-country stuff, but since most of it was still coded, we didn't get any nuts-and-bolts details. Plus, there was a lot of random stuff—bits that fit other puzzles, but not enough to build a picture—unless you know what some of the puzzle pieces look like, that is."

"Which you do?" Dutcher asked.

"Yep. I accessed the database where Langley keeps Trahn's dump, then ran a search using some of the dates and keywords from Ledger. They way I figured it, if Ledger *hadn't* been burned by someone inside the network, you wouldn't expect to see any of that info in the *Guoanbu* archives until *after* the network was rolled up. The only way they could have gotten the information was from the interrogation of agents, right?"

Tanner nodded. He had an idea where this was going, and he could feel his heart pumping a little harder. "Right."

"Well, surprise: I turned up over four hundred references that match Ledger criteria."

Cahil said, "So in plain English, the MSS was talking about Ledger *before* they rolled it up."

"Long before. The first reference was just ten days after you got in-country, Briggs."

My God, Tanner thought. Less than two weeks in, and they'd been onto him. He'd been certain he'd covered all the bases, but in truth the *Guoanbu* had been ahead of him every step of the way.

Dutcher said. "You know how lucky you are? By all rights, you shouldn't have gotten out."

Tanner managed a half-smile. "Glad I didn't know that then. What about Genoa, Oaks?"

"That's the kicker. You said everyone was arrested, right? No one got away?"

"No."

"In all of the *Guoanbu*'s references to Ledger, the name Genoa doesn't show up once. You met with him dozens of times, either in person or by brush pass, and he's not mentioned *once*."

"They didn't have to; they already knew who he was."

Oaken nodded. "You were right. Genoa was the double."

"Too bad I didn't figure it out twelve years ago."

"There was no way you could have," Dutcher said.

"I suppose. Okay, now that we know who we're looking for, the question is, can you find him?"

"I'll give it my best shot," Oaken said.

11

Washington, D.C.

RANDALL WAS WAITING WHEN LATHAM RETURNED TO THE OFFICE. "How was it?"

"I can't say much about Blanton Crossing proper," Latham replied, "but the local trailer park is a site to behold." He recounted his visit to WalPol's headquarters.

"We got a hit on that plate you called in. It's registered to a David Wallace Polson."

Latham thought for a moment. "WalPol. . . . His middle and last names. Have you got—"

Randall handed him a fax of Polson's DMV registration. "Photo's on page two."

Latham read the info, then flipped to the photo "You gotta be kidding me. . . ."

"What?"

"The bastard was standing right in front of me. Polson is Joe-Bob!"

"The handyman?"

"Yeah. He's a cool customer."

"Here's surprise number two: Just for kicks I fed the names Soderberg and Polson into the alias database. We got a hit—somebody named Michael Warren Skeldon."

"Skeldon. . . . Whatever he's got going on, he's layered himself pretty well," Latham said.

"It gets better. He's ex-military—army Rangers."

"Straight leg?"

"No, airborne. He's also got a rap sheet. One arrest for interstate arms, another for criminal facilitation of forgery. Both charges were dropped."

"What was the forgery about?"

"Passports down in Asheville. The indictment stated he was in possession of bogus entry stamps. It was thrown out on a bad warrant. I've got a call in to the Asheville PD and the North Carolina BCA."

What was going on? Latham wondered. What would a Commerce analyst be doing in cahoots with an army Ranger turned gunrunner and forger? Moreover, what did the *Guoanbu* want with either of them? The fact that Baker was dead and Skeldon was still alive suggested two possibilities: Either the *Guoanbu* didn't know about Skeldon, or they knew about him and were still using him.

"What do you want to do?" Randall asked.

"I hate to say it, but my visit probably sent Skeldon running. Let's see if we can get ahold of his service record. I want to see what he did for the Rangers."

Langley

Unsurprised, Mason found that the DIA's brief on Sunil Dhar and the sarin purchase seemed to hold water, but the story came from assets he couldn't probe without jeopardizing both the transaction and the players involved—or so said Tom Redmond. Mason didn't buy it; the whole affair was fishy.

The big question was, if the DIA didn't develop this, who did?

His intercom buzzed: "Sir, General Cathermeier is here."

"Send him in." Mason met him at the door. "Chuck, thanks for coming. Coffee?"

"No, thanks. I think I know why I'm here, Dick."

"I'd be surprised if you didn't. What're we going to do about this, Chuck?"

"I've already got the assets moving."

"That's not what I'm asking."

"I know what you're asking. I'm going to do what I've been ordered to do."

"Chuck, when was the last time a president got this hands-on with an operation?"

"This isn't the president's plan. The DIA is—"

"Tom Redmond doesn't know an M-16 from his asshole. This is Martin and Bousikaris."

"You don't know that."

"I'd put good money on it," said Mason. "Answer my first question."

Cathermeier shrugged. "Vietnam. LBJ."

"Right. And even then did Johnson decide unit composition and penetration plans?"

"No."

"And now, out of the blue, Martin wants to sink a goddamned ship in the middle of Nakhodka-Vostochny Harbor, and that doesn't worry you? And that nonsense about 'sending a message' . . . The only people who're going to get the message are the poor bastards who die on that ship—unless of course the Russian government is involved in the sale."

"According to the DIA, Dhar's Russian contact is freelance."

"Exactly. So the only way Moscow's going to get any message is if we tell them we sank the ship and why. What's the likelihood of that?"

"Low."

"Chuck, listen: I'm not asking you to *do* anything right now. Just think about what I'm saying. If this were your operation, how would you do it?"

"An at-sea boarding. SEAL team. Secure the cargo and the crew, turn the whole thing over to the Russians and stay on them through diplomatic channels."

"Right. And if you *had* to sink her. How would you do it?"

"Open sea. Surface-to-surface missile—Harpoon, probably."

"That's what I'm getting at. This business of putting men on the ground is bad business."

"Dammit, Dick, you're still treating this like it's some pet project of Martin's. The intell came from the DIA, the plan came from the DIA, and unless you've got proof to the contrary, I'm not gonna assume otherwise."

"Why put men on the ground? Who in their right mind would advise Martin to do it?"

"I have no idea."

"But you agree it's a bad idea."

Cathermeier shrugged. "The plan is workable."

"That's not an answer."

"Dick, I'm a soldier. My job description is simple: I follow the orders of the commander-in-chief and defend my country. That's what I'm doing. Love him or hate him, Martin is the president of the United States and—"

"I know that, Chuck."

"—and if you've got an agenda with him or Bousikaris or Redmond, that's fine. Just don't try to enlist me. I haven't got the stomach or the patience for it."

Mason was silent for a few seconds. "Chuck, do you really think that's what this is about?"

Cathermeier met his gaze, then shook his head. "No. Sorry. Either way, though, we're back where we started: I've got my orders and I'm going to carry them out." Cathermeier stood, walked to the door, then turned. "You're not going to let this go, are you?"

"No. This thing stinks, and I'm telling you right now, we're not getting the whole story."

"You know where to find me."

Yuyuan Lake, Beijing

Langley's interest in Bian's latest news came as no surprise to Roger Brown.

If they could avoid sending someone into China—especially a "face" like Tanner—they had to take the chance. Brown was under no illusion, however: Even Jakarta wouldn't be a cakewalk. Soong would be surrounded by *Guoanbu* security guards day and night. Whatever Tanner planned, he'd have to be in and out before Soong's watchers realized he was gone. If not, Tanner would find himself on a very small island with nowhere to hide.

Not my problem, Brown reminded himself. He had his hands full with Bian. Whenever they met, the man's body language shouted, "Arrest me and this Anglo-Saxon fella sitting next to me." The sooner they could sever contact, the sooner Brown could get a good night's sleep.

For today's meeting he'd chosen what was known as a "pointer pass," a cross between a "brush pass"—where a controller and agent bump into one another for a hand-to-hand exchange—and a "drop flag," a physical signal indicating a package was waiting at a drop.

Brown paused by the railing to photograph the lake. A few feet away, ducks quacked and pecked the water for insects. Across the lake he could see a line of people waiting to enter the Zhongguo Military Museum. He checked his watch: *Time*.

He took one more picture then walked on. A hundred yards down the path he spotted Bian walking toward him. Brown angled himself so Bian would pass on his right, then slung his camera over his left shoulder and shoved his hands in his pockets, leaving his right pinky finger outside the pocket. *Just a glance, buddy. . . . A casual glance and walk on. . . .*

To Brown's surprise, Bian did just that.

RESISTING THE IMPULSE TO GLANCE BACK AT THE CIA MAN, BIAN kept walking. *That went well*, he thought, trying to swallow the lump in his throat. *Friendly but perfunctory, just like Roger explained. . . .*

What did the signal mean? One finger outside the pocket was the pointer for the northeast—no, southeast—drop—the hollow railing along Xisanhuanzhong Lane. Yes, that was it. The hard part was over. Now he just had to wait a few minutes to let Roger get away, then retrieve the message.

WALKING TWENTY YARDS BEHIND BIAN, OFFICER MYUNG NIU of the People's Security Bureau saw the pass, but failed to recognize it for what it was. Though Chang Moh-Bian and Roger Brown would never know it, Niu's presence was one of those rare coincidences that ends up snowballing into catastrophe.

It was Niu's day off—one of the few that PSB officers get—and he was doing what many single men do during their spare time: trying to meet a woman. A few months ago a fellow officer had met his fiancée at this very lake. Hoping it held some special charm, Niu had been walking around the lake every chance he got.

He passed several attractive women and even exchanged a few promising smiles. But as his grandfather was fond of saying, "A smile is not a woman, boy. Gotta talk to them."

The path began to curve around the shoreline toward Xisanhuanzhong Lane. Niu stopped at the rail and gazed across the water. He suddenly felt silly: Strolling around this lake, hoping the perfect woman would jump into his arms, or fall into the water and need saving—

What is this?

Farther down the path, the man ahead of him had also stopped. Hands raised to block the sun's glare, the man looked left, then right, then walked to the railing. He then removed the top from the post, dipped his hand inside, replaced the top, and walked on.

Niu wasn't sure what he'd just seen, but his curiosity was piqued. He let the man get a hundred yards ahead, then followed.

NINETY MINUTES AND THREE BUS CHANGES LATER, NIU'S QUARRY disembarked near the Agricultural Exhibition Center in the Chaoyang District. Niu followed him three blocks to an apartment building.

Niu crossed the street to a bench and sat down. After an hour, the man had not reappeared. Satisfied he'd located the man's home, Niu got up and started searching for the nearest phone booth.

12

Washington, D.C.

NOTHING'S EVER AS SIMPLE AS YOU WANT IT TO BE. **BOUSIKARIS** had no idea who'd coined the aphorism, but the older he got the truer it seemed to become—which was why he wasn't surprised when he picked up Sunday's *Post* and saw the ad: *Adrian, I love you. Come back. Always, Harmon.*

Qing wanted another meeting. Bousikaris considered ignoring the summons, but decided against it. Qing didn't strike him as someone to be antagonized, and until he and Martin could find a way out of this mess, it was better to not poke the dragon.

As before, the Addison Road metrorail stop was nearly deserted. Bousikaris stepped off the train, paused at a pay phone, and pretended to make a call until the last passengers had disappeared, then walked to the railing. He heard footsteps behind him. Qing walked up. "Who were you calling?"

"No one. I was waiting for the platform to clear."

"Very well."

"What do you want?" Bousikaris said.

"Tell me about the plans. Are there any problems?"

"The whole damned thing is a problem. You don't just order the chairman of the JCS and the director of the CIA to put on this kind of operation and expect them to not ask questions."

"What kind of questions?"

"Nuts and bolts stuff." Bousikaris noted Feng's confused expression: "Tactical details. It's highly unusual for a president to dictate those. The background we put together is solid enough, but the rest of it . . . They're both nervous."

"They answer to the president, do they not?"

"Yes, but—"

"Then they'll do as they're ordered. Is the operation moving forward?"

Bousikaris nodded. "If anything goes wrong, though, there *will* be investigations. Mason is a cold warrior at heart. He sees conspiracy behind every bush."

"That's his job. Nothing will go wrong and Mason will find other things to worry about. There's another matter that requires your attention. The FBI is investigating an . . . associate of ours. If it goes any further, it could endanger our arrangement."

"How so?"

"That's not your concern. We want the investigation stopped."

"Christ, we don't have that kind of power. You don't just call the FBI and—"

"Then don't use power," Qing replied. "Reach out, plant the seed. Let others do the work."

"What's the case?"

Qing told him.

"That was you? You did that?"

"Of course not. We're not stupid. Our connection to the man is accidental. According to our associate, the man had a gambling problem. He owed many thousands of dollars to . . . what's the word?"

"Loan sharks? Are you saying he and his family were—"

"I'm not saying anything. I'm merely stating facts. Somehow he got the name of our associate and contacted him hoping to buy several kilos of cocaine, which he hoped to turn into a profit. The FBI must have come across our associate's name in their investigation, and now they're interested in him."

"How does this person relate to our arrangement?"

"That's not your worry. We want the investigation stopped. How you choose to do it is up to you, but you *will* do it."

Though Qing didn't bother saying "or else," Bousikaris knew it was there. *What* would *happen?* he wondered. The country had had a bellyful of scandal. How would the public react if it realized China had funded the lion's share of Martin's campaign? They'd be lucky to escape prison.

They'd worked too hard and too long to get here. Whatever China's game, that was their business. He and Martin would play their part, then move on. If they had to get their hands a little dirty for the greater good, so be it. A little dirt never hurt anyone. "I'll handle it," he told Qing.

Moscow

Vladimir Bulganin stared out the car window. "Two weeks until the election, Ivan," he said. "We have them. We're so close."

Nochenko felt the same, but wasn't ready to celebrate yet. "The polls may be in our favor, but now is the time we must push even harder."

"Yes, yes, whatever you decide." Something outside the window caught Bulganin's attention. "Driver, pull over!"

"Vlad, what are you doing? We're expected at the Duma. We cannot keep them—"

"The Duma can wait," Bulganin replied, then grinned. "After all, in a few weeks, they'll have no choice but to wait on me—hand and foot!" Bulganin laughed uproariously and opened the car door. Nochenko followed.

They'd stopped on Kuybyshev Street. To their right stood St. Basil's Cathedral—or, as Bulganin demanded it be called—the Cathedral of the Intercession; to their left lay Red Square.

As Bulganin stepped out, his security detail formed a ring around them. "Pyotr," Bulganin called to his security chief, "I feel like a stroll. I'll sign a few autographs, but no more."

"Yes, sir."

Nochenko said, "Vladimir, we don't have time—"

Bulganin clapped his shoulder, "Perhaps in public, Ivan, it might be best we avoid familiarities."

He must be joking, Nochenko thought. "Pardon me?"

"Mr. Bulganin will do, I think. Of course, in private, we're just two comrades having a chat. All right, Pyotr! Lead on."

Bulganin was immediately recognized. Within minutes he and Nochenko were surrounded by well-wishers and autograph seekers. Pyotr and the other bodyguards cut a path through the crowd, occasionally letting an admirer through for Bulganin to greet and dismiss. Nochenko felt himself jostled from all sides; the cacophony of voices was almost deafening.

After a few minutes, Bulganin nodded to Pyotr and the bodyguards spread out, pushing the crowd away until Bulganin and Nochenko had a circle in which they could stroll.

"How well do you know your Red Square history, Ivan?" Bulganin asked.

"Fairly well, I suppose."

"What about the very name—*Krasnaya Ploshchad*? In Old Slavonic, *Krasnaya* also means "beautiful." Too bad the West didn't pick up on that, eh? Instead of 'Reds,' perhaps they would have called us 'the beautiful ones.' Do you know where all that St. Basil's nonsense began?"

"No."

"St. Basil was nothing more than a delusional hobo. The truth is, the cathedral was built to commemorate Ivan the Terrible's capture of Kazan. Oh, what I would give to have been there—to see the expressions on their dirty Tartar faces when Ivan fired the city."

Ivan the Terrible had earned his moniker for good reason, Nochenko wanted to say. The man had been a butcher. How Bulganin could—

"And there!" Bulganin called, pointing to the GUM department store. "Moscow's first concession to capitalism right across from Lenin's Mausoleum. It's an insult! No, that's not the right word . . . betrayal is more like it."

Bulganin stopped before the Mausoleum. On either side of its heavy wooden doors stood a pair of stoic sentries. "Six times in the last year," Bulganin muttered.

"What's that?" Nochenko asked. "Six times for what?"

"To repaint the tomb's facade, Ivan. Just last week a pair of thugs pelted it with paint-filled balloons. Can you believe it? What's happening to our country?"

Knowing Bulganin didn't want an answer, Nochenko remained silent.

"And this," Bulganin murmured, "this is where it happened. The worst crime of all."

"What are you talking about?"

"The removal of Koba's body. Until that backstabbing dog Khrushchev removed it, he was resting in his rightful place: next to Lenin, next to his friend and mentor, the founder of the Soviet."

Nochenko suddenly realized that Bulganin was weeping.

"Wrested from eternal peace, shoved into a pine box, and buried under the mausoleum wall like some commoner. It makes my blood boil, Ivan, it truly does."

Nochenko didn't know what to say. In all the years he'd known Bulganin, this was the first moment of unguarded sentiment he'd seen from the man; that he was crying over the corpse of Russia's greatest mass murderer chilled Nochenko. Was all Bulganin's talk of the great Koba Stalin more than just historical musings? Was there something more to it?

"Did I ever tell you where I was born?" Bulganin asked.

"No, you didn't."

Bulganin turned to him. "They call it the Valley of the Blossoming Orchards."

The nickname sounded vaguely familiar. "Gori," Nochenko said. "Kartli, Georgia, correct?"

"That's right. And why else is it remarkable? Do you know, Ivan?"

"No."

"Gori, my friend, was also the birthplace of the great Koba."

They walked in silence for a few minutes, Bulganin virtually marching, his hands clasped behind his back. "So, Ivan, you were saying. . . ."

"Pardon me?"

"In the car—about the polls."

"Oh, yes. The election is nearing. Now, more than ever, we must stay focused. The greater the pressure on the current administration, the greater the likelihood they will make a mistake. When that time comes, we must be ready to exploit it."

"A chink in the armor, is that what you mean?"

"I suppose you could call it that."

"Yes, yes. An Achilles' Heel. We must expose the opponents' true colors. Of course!"

If nothing else, Nochenko thought, *Bulganin certainly knew how to string together clichés.* "Yes, Vladimir, I see that, but we must be careful not to . . ."

Bulganin didn't seem to hear the question. He continued pacing, muttering to himself.

Holystone Office

Still working under the assumption that Genoa had not only been a colleague of Soong's, but also a career spook, Oaken returned to the Wan Trahn database, this time looking for a face.

Using both open and classified sources, he and Tanner constructed a "yearbook" of every officer that had served with Soong in the years prior to Ledger. It took Tanner an hour before he was able to narrow the field to half a dozen candidates. "It's tough," he said. "It's been twelve years."

"Don't think too hard," Oaken replied. "Go with your gut."

Tanner leaned back, closed his eyes, and tried to recall his meetings with the man known as Genoa. He let the images flow. *Don't think, just look. . . .*

He leaned over the photos again, scanning faces—

"That's him," Briggs whispered, tapping a photo. "Jesus, that's him."

"You're sure?"

Tanner nodded. "I'm sure."

Oaken turned over the photo and read: "Commander Moh Yen Fong, People's Liberation Army Navy. He was Soong's personal aide."

Tanner nodded. "Let's find him."

13

Washington, D.C.

LATHAM HAD MET THE CURRENT DIRECTOR OF THE FBI SEVERAL times, either at formal functions or in passing at the Hoover Building, but had never had reason to speak with him at length. Until now.

With a nod from the secretary, Charlie knocked once, then opened the door and walked through. Owens was already there. The director stood to shake hands. "Special Agent Latham. Thanks for coming. Please sit down. It's Charlie, isn't it?"

"Yes, sir."

"Charlie, I'm going to get to the point. The Baker case is being put on hold for a while."

"Pardon me? Why?"

"I'm not at liberty to say."

"Sir, this is my case. If it's being jerked out from under me, I deserve to know why."

"The decision's been made, Special Agent Latham."

The hell with it, Charlie thought. "That's unacceptable, sir."

"Charlie. . . ." Owens said.

Latham pushed on: "This is an active case; it's moving forward. If the decision's been made, fine, I'll deal with it, but I'll say it again: I deserve to know why."

The director stared at him and then, to Latham's surprise, he smiled. "You know what? You're right. You *have* earned the right."

Well, I'll be damned. . . .

"Surprised?" the director asked.

"Frankly, yes."

The director chuckled. "I know my strengths, Charlie, and telling agents how to do their jobs ain't one of them. Here's the short answer to your question: The Justice Department has asked us to back off. Certain sections of the Commerce Department are under investigation for corruption, and Baker was one of the employees under the microscope."

"What kind of corruption?"

"The JD believes that several U.S. computer manufacturers were bribing Commerce employees to approve overseas sales of restricted processor components."

"These components are on the NCTL?"

"They are."

"How much money are we talking about?"

"Perhaps millions. If so, that might explain Baker's bank account."

But not the slaughter of his family, Latham thought. "And the murders?"

"Hard to say. Maybe Baker broke. Stress, remorse, guilt. . . ."

Latham didn't buy it; he knew who was responsible. "We've still got a lot of holes," he said.

"I know. And you'll get your chance, but for now I've agreed to put our investigation on hold until Justice can wrap up theirs. I don't like it either, Charlie, but that's where we stand."

Latham nodded. "Okay."

The director stood and extended his hand. "Thanks, Charlie. Harry."

Latham and Owens headed for the door.

"You know," the director called, "it just occurred to me: Too bad there's not a way to keep our plate warm while Justice does it's thing."

Latham smiled at him. "Yes, sir."

"Loose ends . . . background stuff—that sort of thing."

"Yes, sir."

The director shrugged, gave a dismissive wave of his hand. "Oh well, just thinking out loud."

• • •

Back in Owens's office, Charlie said, "What the hell was that?"

"That," Owens replied, "was everything and nothing."

Translation: Dig if you want to, but stay away from Commerce. "What do you think?"

"Your case, Charlie. It's got to be your choice. I can run some interference, but not for long."

"I know."

"On the other hand, we shouldn't count on Justice to wrap up any time soon. If we're right about the *Guoanbu*—and I know we are—every day that passes, the colder the trail gets."

"I keep thinking about those little girls—taped up, tortured, watching their mother shot dead. . . . My own girls were that age once. I want to get the sons-of-bitches, Harry."

"When was the last time you took a vacation?"

"Last year, I guess."

"Might be nice to get away for a while."

"It might at that," Latham replied.

Three hours later, Latham was sitting on his patio grilling some chicken when Bonnie poked her head out the screen door. "You've got a visitor."

"Oh?"

Paul Randall stepped through the door. "Nice apron, boss."

Latham looked down at his "Kiss the Cook" apron. "Bonnie's mother gave it to me. It's sort of grown on me."

"Where's your chef's hat?"

"At the cleaners. Can I get you a drink?"

"I'll take a beer if you've got one."

Latham dug into a cooler and handed across a plain, brown bottle. Eyes narrowed, Randall removed the top, sniffed, then took a sip. "Not bad."

"It's straight from the Latham Basement Brewery."

"I like it. So, what's going on with the Baker case? We're off it?"

"For the time being."

"And suddenly you're on vacation."

Latham shrugged, said nothing.

"Want some company?"

"No, Paul."

"Too late," Randall replied with a grin. "Harry's already signed off on it."

Latham stared at him. *It would be nice to have some backup*. . . . "Should I bother arguing?"

"I wouldn't."

Latham reached over and clinked Randall's bottle with his own. "Welcome to the club. Now we just have to figure out where to start."

"I think I've got that covered. I got an abstract of Skeldon's service record."

"And?"

"About half of it was blacked out, but I know what he did for the army: He was a Lurp."

"A what?" Latham asked.

"LRRP—Long Range Reconnaissance Patrol. The name is different now, but Skeldon was a Lurp through and through. Sixteen years' worth."

"Which means?"

"He's got some pretty scary talents. Lurps are trained to go deep into enemy territory, stay hidden for months at a time, gather intell, then get back out again."

"I guess that makes sense," Latham said. "I doubt Baker was paying him for his raking skills. The question is, Why did Baker and the *Guoanbu* need a former U.S. Army commando?"

College of William and Mary, Williamsburg, Virginia

It was almost eleven p.m. when Samantha Latham left Swem Library and began walking toward her dorm. She had an early morning study group and another hour of reading before she could go to bed. She stifled a yawn and kept walking.

Dew was forming on the grass and she could feel the dampness seeping through her canvas sneakers. In the distance she could see the lighted windows in Rogers Hall. What she wouldn't give to have a room in Rogers; instead of having to trudge all the way back to Chandler, she'd already be in bed. *Well, maybe next year. . . .*

She reached the path bordering Rogers, followed it to the end, then around the corner to Landrum Road. To her right, a couple hundred yards away, she could see the lights of Chandler.

Almost home.

She looked down the road, saw no cars coming, and started across.

Samantha would never remember which sensation registered in her brain first, the sound of the engine revving, or the glare of headlights washing over her, but in those last few seconds, as she saw the dark shape rushing toward her, she thought, *He doesn't see you. Run, Sammie, quick. . . .*

She was taking her first running step when the front bumper touched her.

14

Fort Greely, Alaska

Even before they set foot in the water, Smitty dubbed it Lake Shriveljewels in anticipation of the effect the water was going to have on their anatomy. If not for their dry suits, he'd be right, Jurens decided. Even so, he could feel the cold pressing in on him, a watery glove encasing his body.

The goal of tonight's exercise was to simply get past the guards waiting for them and wreak some benign havoc. The coming nights would bring increasingly difficult exercises that more closely matched the mission's goals.

Jurens checked his depth gauge: twelve feet. One of the drawbacks of their LAR VII rebreathers was that it fed them pure oxygen, which quickly turned toxic at pressures below twenty feet. The beauty of LAR was that it created no bubble stream for enemy eyes to spot.

Jurens depressed the chin button inside his mask, then called, "Everybody with me?"

He got three double *clicks* in return.

Jurens resisted the impulse to glance back. The water was pitch black, visibility less than four feet. Under such conditions it was all too easy to lose someone. Here it was forgivable, but in real life, when one man made up a quarter of your team, it could be disastrous.

He checked his compass against the map on his diveboard. "Rally on my chemlite."

He plucked the tube off his harness, crushed it to release the phosphorus, then dropped it. One by one the rest of the team swam forward out of the murk. They formed a ring and clasped forearms for what was jokingly called the "dead check": *If you were there, you weren't dead.*

"Going up," Jurens said. "Standby."

He clipped his diveboard to his harness, peeled back the glove covering his index finger, then flicked his fins until he felt his finger break the surface. The relatively cold air felt like an electric charge on his skin. He gave another flick of his fins. The top of his mask came clear.

The ice-rimmed shoreline lay fifteen feet away; beyond that, fifty yards inland, lay their Quonset hut and the three storage sheds, all illuminated by pole-mounted spotlights. Jurens knew the sentries were there, but not where and how many.

A flicker of movement near the corner of the Quonset caught his eye: A darker shadow against the blackness. *There's one.* Sconi hovered still for the next five minutes, until sure he'd spotted all of them. There were eight guards—five on roving patrol and three hunkered down in the shadows.

Jurens let himself sink, then finned down to the team.

"How's it look, Boss?" Dickie asked.

Jurens explained what he'd seen. "Let's go play a little hide-and-seek."

• • •

Loosening the ice along the shoreline was the easy part, since all they needed was a gap through which they could squeeze. The hard part was moving each chunk aside then replacing it behind them without making any noise. As it was, the roving guards periodically strolled along the shore, shining their flashlights into the water as Jurens and his team waited, mere shadows beneath the ice.

Once onto the beach, Jurens led them inland, following the shore to the tree line, where they slipped into the underbrush.

Sconi pulled out his binoculars and scanned the beach. All guards were accounted for. He watched for a few more minutes until sure the rovers hadn't altered their routes, then set out again.

Giving the huts a wide berth, they slipped east through the trees along the ridge then across a field to the main road, where they found an irrigation ditch overgrown with scrub brush.

Jurens felt a tap on his shoulder. Smitty pointed toward their three o'clock: A hundred yards away, a Humvee sat blocking the road. Smitty gestured: *Two inside, two outside.*

That's a mistake, Jurens thought. *Better to sit back in the trees and wait for us to stumble onto them.* He keyed his headset. "Anybody feel like taking a ride?"

Twenty minutes later they pulled the Humvee to a stop in front of the Fort's administration building. A pair of soldiers armed with M-16s stood on either side of the entrance. Jurens climbed out, followed by Smitty, Zee, and Dickie. One of the guards stepped forward, his gun coming up slightly.

Jurens flashed his temporary ID. "Son, go get your duty officer."

The soldier eyed the ID. His eyes went wide. "Uh, yes, sir. Hold on."

He trotted inside. Sixty seconds later he returned with a sleepy-eyed major wearing pajama bottoms and slippers. "What the hell is going on here?"

"Just wanted to return your property, Major," Jurens said, then walked to the rear of the Humvee and opened the hatch. Inside, bound and gagged, were the four soldiers.

"Christ," the Major muttered. "Are they—"

"They're fine, Major. A little embarrassed, probably a lot pissed off, but fine. Now, if you don't mind, could you point us to the chow hall? We've got some thawing out to do."

Beijing

Guoanbu director Xiang was enjoying his first cup of tea of the day and scanning the overnight reports when he came across a flagged message. He punched the intercom button. "Eng, come in here."

His aide, Eng, was there in seconds. "Yes, sir?"

"This is a routine contact report," Xiang said. "Why is this flagged?"

"Check the name, sir."

Xiang scanned the message. "Officer Myung Niu—"

"The contact's name, sir."

"Chang Moh-Bian. So?"

"Bian's an official at the Ministry of Agriculture. He's on a watch list."

Well, that doesn't narrow the field much, Xiang thought. At any given time, the *Guoanbu*'s watch list contained thousands of names. "Regarding what?"

"General Han Soong. We've long suspected Bian of being an underground supporter of his."

That got Xiang's attention. "And what is he suspected of now. . . . Fiddling with a fence post?"

"The next day the PSB checked it. It looked like it had been hollowed out. Could be a dead-letter drop. Add to that Bian's demeanor and history, and I thought it might be worth your attention."

Xiang considered this. It was probably nothing, but still, anything to do with Soong warranted caution. "Assign a detail to watch him. Might as well give it to this . . . Officer Niu."

Williamsburg, Virginia

Two hours after a jogger found Samantha lying in the street, the phone rang in the Latham home. Whether from mother's instinct or simply coincidence, Bonnie answered instead of Charlie. Hovering on the edge of sleep, he heard her say, "Oh, God. Where? Okay . . . yes, we're on our way."

He sat up. "Bonnie, what?"

She turned to him; her face was pale. "Charlie, it's Samantha. . . . She's hurt."

One call to Owens was all it took to get a helicopter dispatched to the Germantown airstrip near Latham's home. As they were boarding the helicopter and heading south, Owens placed another call that cleared them for landing at the Newport News/Williamsburg airport, where a James City county sheriff was waiting to take them to Williamsburg Community Hospital Trauma Center.

They were met by the ER's attending physician. "Agent Latham, Mrs. Latham, she's still unconscious, but aside from a concussion, we haven't found any head trauma. The CAT scan looked good, and she's showing all the reactions we would hope to see—"

"You said she was unconscious," Bonnie said. "What does that mean?"

"Her pupils are equal and reactive, and she's reacting to pain stimulus. Those are all good signs. Her legs, however, worry us. Both of her femurs were fractured—the left one pretty badly."

"Oh, God," Bonnie cried. Charlie put his arms around her.

"Define 'bad,' " Charlie said.

"We're concerned about her distal pulse—the one farthest from the point of injury, in this case, the ankle. It's weak, which might suggest artery damage. She'll be heading to surgery shortly. We'll know more in a couple hours."

"And if there's artery damage?" Bonnie asked.

"Let's just cross that bridge if we come to it."

Irreparable artery damage, Latham thought. *Amputation.*

Bonnie asked, "Can we see her?"

"Sure, I'll take you to her."

Latham felt like he was in a fog. *Somebody hurt my girl . . . my God, somebody hurt my child.*

15

Williamsburg, Virginia

OAKEN PUSHED THROUGH THE ER DOORS AND IMMEDIATELY SAW Paul Randall. "Hey, Walt."

"How is she?"

"Still in surgery." Randall explained Samantha's injuries. "They've got a good vascular department here. If it's fixable, they'll do it."

"Where are they?"

"Upstairs in the lounge. Come on."

Oaken found a bleary-eyed Charlie Latham pacing the hallway near the elevators. He saw Oaken and walked over. They embraced. "Thanks for coming, Walt."

"How's Bonnie?"

"She's okay."

"What happened?"

"The cops are saying hit-and-run. They're still canvassing, but so far there are no witnesses."

"What can I do?" Oaken asked. "Tell me how I can help."

"When she gets out of surgery, we'll talk. I'm going to need a favor, Walt. A big one."

• • •

Oaken and Latham had met nearly ten years before during an antiterrorism conference, Oaken from the State Department's INR, Latham from the FBI, and had been friends ever since, having lunch and coffee as their schedules permitted. Oaken always assumed Latham knew Holystone's role with the CIA went beyond mere consultation, but Charlie had never pressed the issue.

Until now, Oaken thought. He felt certain Latham had called him in search of more than moral support. It would have something to do with Samantha, but what?

She got out of surgery three hours later. Though severe, the damage to the artery had been repaired. She would be hospitalized for another week, in double leg casts for three months, and in physical rehabilitation for six months after that, but by this time next year she would be as good as new.

Oaken and Randall left Charlie and Bonnie to be with their daughter and wandered down to the cafeteria. An hour later, Latham joined them. His eyes were red rimmed, but he was smiling. "She's okay, she's gonna be okay."

Randall clapped him on the shoulder and Oaken said, "Thank God."

Latham poured himself a cup of coffee. "Walt, this wasn't an accident."

"Why do you say that?"

"Samantha's awake; we talked. Now she's remembering she'd seen the car that hit her around campus the last few days. It stuck with her because it had Maryland plates and the hood ornament was missing; an older model, light blue Cadillac. The more she thought about it, the more she remembered seeing it. She would come out of a class, and there it was; after lunch, there it was."

"An old boyfriend maybe?"

"No. I've got nothing to back this up, but. . . . you heard about the Baker murders?"

"Just what I read in the papers."

Latham spent the next twenty minutes taking Oaken through the case: the murders, their suspicions about the

Guoanbu, Baker's secret bank account, the former LRRP Mike Skeldon, and finally his suspension from the case. "I know it's a big leap, but I can't help feeling like somebody wants me to drop this—or at least get sidetracked."

A very big leap, Oaken thought. Though he knew better than to discount Charlie's instincts, Oaken was skeptical. Latham's little girl had nearly been killed; that was enough to cloud anyone's thinking. "Supposing that's true, why go after Samantha? You were already off the case."

Randall answered: "Look at it this way: If somebody kills or kidnaps the child of a cop or FBI agent, the weight of the whole U.S. law enforcement system crashes down on them. On the other hand, if the child is hurt, say in a random accident, all you get is a distraught mother or father. The last thing that agent is thinking about is his or her caseload."

Oaken spread his hands. "Charlie, I'm not unsympathetic, but this is a real stretch."

"Humor me. A Commerce Department employee is murdered; he's involved with a foreign intelligence agency; he's paying an Army commando hundreds of thousands of dollars; and just as I'm starting to make headway, I'm jerked off the case."

"You think the Justice investigation is bogus?"

"I think it's too convenient. If I'm wrong, I'm wrong. No harm done. Walt, somebody ran down my little girl. I can't afford to assume anything—not until I'm sure."

Looking into Latham's eyes, Oaken found himself thinking of his own daughters. If there was even a chance—even one in a million—that someone was trying to hurt them, how would he react?

Oaken nodded. "Tell me what you need."

Irkutsk, Republic of Sakha, Siberia, Russian Federation

Lieutenant General Vasily Basnin stared at the peeling yellow paint on the ceiling and thought, *An old library for a headquarters building . . . what's the army coming to?* Of course, he admitted, it could be worse. The city of Irkutsk was nearly 350 years old, and some parts of it looked older still. From that perspective, this place was brand-new.

Founded as an *ostrog,* or fortress, in 1661 at the confluence of the Irkut and Angara rivers, Irkutsk was known locally as the "Jewel of Siberia," a nickname that had never quite caught on. If not for its proximity to gorgeous Lake Baikal, Basnin thought, Irkutsk would be all but worthless.

Born and raised in St. Petersburg, Basnin's assignment as the Irkutsk Army Garrison's commandant felt like a slap in the face. This was the most reviled command slot in the Far East District, and yet here he was, servant of the Motherland, protecting this backwater village from . . . what, exactly? Protesting fur traders? Surly lumberjacks?

Though the population of Sakha—which the locals called Yakutia—was predominantly Russian, the formerly indigenous population of Buryats, Dolgans, and Yukagirs, emboldened by *glasnost*, had begun to protest discrimination on the part of their Russian masters. With the rolls of the Sakhan government dominated by Russians, little had changed for Yakuts since the Federation's birth—or since the birth of the Soviet, for that matter.

At least one thing has changed, Basnin thought. *Unionization.* All the downtrodden natives had banded together into unions. A goddamned coalition of horse breeders, lumberjacks, and fur traders! Of course, it might pay to coddle the hunters, Basnin thought. With Moscow cutting the army's funding at every turn, he'd been forced to supplement his garrison's rations with local game. And what of the fur traders and horse breeders? If the money continued to dwindle, would his men be wearing beaver coats and riding around on horses instead of in armored personnel carriers?

With any luck the upcoming elections in Moscow would bring some relief. If the polls were correct, that Bulganin fellow might soon be the Federation's new president, which might be good for the army—if, that was, Bulganin kept his promise to resume the military restructuring Putin had abandoned the previous year.

Basnin checked his watch. Almost supper time. A quick bite, then back to his quarters for some television. At least tonight we would have some peace. Thus far, the unionists had been cooperative enough to register their protest plans with the city. Tonight they were taking a break, which in turn meant a break for his troops.

BASNIN HAD JUST DRIFTED OFF TO SLEEP WHEN THE KNOCK CAME at his door. He rolled over and looked at the clock: Almost midnight. He got up, threw on his robe, shuffled to the door, and opened it.

"Apologies for disturbing you, General," a soldier said. "The duty officer sent me—"

"What is it?" Basnin growled. "What's the problem?"

"The protesters, sir. They're back."

So much for the niceties of schedules. "Where? How many?"

"At the Railway Monument. Several hundred. It looks like they're preparing to march."

"They're probably headed for city admin building. Wait in the truck. I'll get dressed."

Goddamned natives, Basnin thought. *Just one night of peace. . . .*

THEY WERE NEARING THE CORNER OF KARL MARX STREET WHEN Basnin saw it: Flickering flames on the street bordering the river. "What is that?" Basnin asked.

"Torches, sir. They're carrying torches."

"You're kidding."

"No, sir," the soldier replied, then laughed. "Just like Frankenstein, eh, sir?"

"What?"

"The angry villagers in Frankenstein. You know—"

"Yes, Corporal, just like Frankenstein. Turn around. Circle up Gagarina; no sense trying to drive through the mob."

Five minutes later they were driving along the river's edge. Two hundred meters from the monument, Basnin ordered the driver to stop, then got out.

At least three hundred strong, the protesters milled around the base of the monument. At their center, the monument's red granite obelisk rose into the night sky, reflecting the light from the torches. Amid the cacophony of voices, Basin could hear the occasional bark of a soldier's voice as troops hurried to set up a perimeter "Where are the riot control troops?" he asked his driver.

"On the other side of the crowd, posted at the Okhiopkov Theater. The IFVs are—"

"IFVs?" An Infantry Fighting Vehicle was essentially a light reconnaissance tank. But Basnin knew in the eyes of civilians, a tank was a tank. Disorganized mobs tended to run from them; well-organized mobs tended to challenge them. "Who ordered IFVs deployed?" he demanded.

"All our trucks are down for maintenance, sir. The duty officer decided—"

Now Basnin saw them: Two BRT-70s parked on the museum lawn, their 14.5 mm cannons pointing toward the mob. "Get the unit commander on the radio," he barked. "I want those BRTs pulled back immediately! And for God's sake, get those turrets turned away from the crowd! If—"

From the trees around the library Basnin saw a flash of light, followed by what looked like a smoke trail streaking through the darkness. A half-second later one of the BRTs rocked sideways and burst into flames.

The crowd broke, half of the protesters running up Gagarina and Karl Marx Streets, the rest fleeing toward the trees along the Okhiopkov Theatre—toward the surviving BRT.

No, no, no. . . . Basnin thought, praying the BRT commander was seasoned enough to show restraint. *Please, God, don't—*

The rapid, overlapping boom of the 14.5 mm cannon cut through the night. The cannon's shells—each larger than a man's thumb and traveling at twice the speed of sound—raked through the crowd. Bodies began to drop. People stumbled about, some missing limbs, some torn open by shards of flying stone and concrete, still others falling under the crush of the stampede.

Behind him, Basnin could hear his driver yelling into the radio, "Cease fire, cease fire!"

The cannon stopped firing.

The square fell into silence. In the distance Basnin could hear screaming. A pall of smoke drifted over the square. In the distance came screaming. Basnin could see bodies writhing on the ground. A man in a fur hat struggled to his knees. Eyes wide, he reached across his body, feeling for an arm that was now just a bloody stump. A young girl's voice called, "Mother . . . Mother. . . ."

Basnin stared at the scene, stunned and momentarily confused. *Oh God, what have we done . . . ?* He turned to the driver. "Call the hospital! Tell them to send ambulances! Quickly!"

16

New Zealand

If he hadn't known better, Tanner might have mistaken the view for a scene straight from a Norwegian postcard. He now knew why this region of New Zealand was called the "Fjordlands."

Carved by glaciers during the last ice age, the southwestern flank of New Zealand is crosscut with towering mountains, ice blue lakes, tumbling waterfalls, and alpine forests, all of which made the thirty-five-mile-long Milford Track one of the country's biggest attractions.

After some haggling, they found a guide in Sandfly Point who was willing to drive them up the mountain to where they now stood, Giant's Gate Falls overlooking Lake Ada. Together they stepped to the edge and looked down. Beneath them the mountain dropped away to the lake's surface nearly four thousand feet below. "Wow," Cahil murmured.

"Amen," Tanner whispered.

According to Maori folklore, the Fjordlands were created millions of years ago by a giant who, after a particularly long day of world walking, had unwittingly dragged the tip of his spear across land, allowing the ocean to rush into the gouges.

Cahil said, “Almost makes me want to sing *The Sound of Music.*”

Tanner laughed. “The hills are alive with elusive *Guoanbu* spies?”

“It does have a nice ring to it.”

“Sing on. I promise not to tell Julie Andrews.”

“Oaks is sure about this? It doesn’t strike me as a likely hangout for a retired Chinese spook. Not that I’m complaining, mind you. Given Walt’s track record, it could be worse.”

The last two “vacations” Oaken had planned for them had involved a sinking ship in Alaska and a deserted island in the middle of the Pacific Ocean. By comparison, this looked suspiciously pleasant.

“He swears this is it,” Tanner replied and pointed across the lake to the snowcapped peak of Mount Ada. “Fong’s ranch should be in the valley on the other side.”

“How do we get there?”

Tanner looked south toward McKay Falls until he spotted the winding trail that led down to the shore. “Down there,” Briggs said. “We can catch the ferry. After that, we’re off the map.”

THE FINAL PHASE OF OAKEN’S SEARCH FOR MOH YEN FONG, THE *Guoanbu* agent known as Genoa, turned out to be the easiest. Armed with Fong’s true identity, Oaken had again turned to the Kyung database but, unsurprisingly, found little help there. It was unlikely the *Guoanbu* would either mention Moh Yen Fong by name or continue to use his code name after Ledger was finished.

Oaken turned to ECHELON. Cloaked in equal parts myth, suspicion, and secrecy, ECHELON is a National Security Agency project created to monitor millions of e-mails, faxes, telexes, and, unbeknownst to most, capture phone calls and radio transmissions.

If, for example, a DEA informant reports to his controllers that a Columbian judge has been targeted for assassination by a drug cartel, the NSA can program ECHELON to scan its captures for word convergences such as the judge's name, "kill," and "bomb," then flag them for attention.

Though ECHELON rarely produces ready-to-wear or even earth-shattering intelligence, it does give the U.S. and British intelligence communities an unequalled view of the world's ever-changing communications puzzle.

With a little horsepower from Dick Mason, Oaken's request went straight to the NSA's director of archives, who punched in Oaken's search string.

It took ECHELON thirty-eight hours to search the twelve years' worth of data it had accumulated since Ledger's demise, but in the end Oaken owed his breakthrough not to a painstaking review of the output, but to the meticulous record keeping of the People's Liberation Army's Bureau of Personnel.

Guoanbu operative or not, Moh Yen Fong was first and foremost a military man; consequently, every detail of his life, from doctor's visits to performance evaluations was meticulously recorded.

With the help of further searches to narrow the field, Oaken finally found a telex from the Bureau of Personnel to Fong's last command posting. An NSA translator quickly recognized it as a separation of service report. "Basically it's a DD-two-fourteen form—what our people get when they retire or are discharged," the translator told him.

The report listed Fong's home address, his phone number, next of kin, and most importantly Oaken would soon learn, his e-mail address.

Oaken returned to the ECHELON output, this time using only Fong's e-mail address. He got over two-hundred matches, which he further filtered by frequently repeated words and phrases. Time and again, the same ones kept appearing: "Te Anu," "Ada," "great-grandfather," and "sheep."

Knowing "Te Anu" and "Ada" were both geographical names found only in New Zealand, Oaken hacked his way into Auckland's Ministry of Immigration's computer system and started hunting. It took less than two hours. "Believe it or not," Oaken told Tanner, "New Zealand has had a sizable Chinese diaspora community since the mid-1880s. They farm, fish, herd sheep—"

"And this is where Fong ran off to?"

"Yep. He probably had a hell of a time convincing the *Guoanbu* to let him out of the country, but that's where he went. His family has owned sheep land there for nearly a hundred years."

"So, he traded in spying for sheep ranching," Cahil said. "Talk about a career change."

"There's a downside, though," Oaken said. "The *Guoanbu* has had a security detail assigned to Fong since he moved. At least eight men, living on the ranch full-time with him; they probably work as laborers."

"Chinese cowboys," Tanner said. "This should be interesting."

IT WAS MIDMORNING BY THE TIME THEY REACHED THE FERRY landing.

They walked to the end of the deserted jetty, where they found a log-and-plank ferry bumping lazily against the moorings. A man in a red parka lay on a chaise lounge on the deck.

"Morning," Tanner called.

"Morning. Wanna cross?"

"If you can squeeze us in."

The man chuckled. "I think I can manage it." He nodded at their backpacks. "You're going the wrong way if you're looking for Milford Track."

Tanner smiled. "We're on the economy tour."

Thirty minutes later they were standing on the eastern shore of Lake Ada and staring up at the mountainside as the ferry chugged its way back across the lake. "Please tell me we don't have to climb that thing," Cahil murmured.

"Not unless the map is wrong. We follow the ridge for about five miles; once there we should find a pass that'll take us through to the high meadows where Fong's ranch is."

Washington, D.C.

"Do we have any casualty figures yet?" asked President Martin.

"Initial estimates say fifty-four," replied Mason. "Including six children. That figure may change as more information comes in, but not by much."

News of the "Irkutsk Massacre" had spread quickly, which Mason found particularly surprising given the remoteness of the location. During the Cold War news of this kind of incident may have never reached the West. Nowadays, CNN, Reuters, and API had it on the wire within hours.

"What do we know?" asked Bousikaris.

"Not much. There were over three hundred protesters. Some reports say there were Federation tanks present, others say just scout vehicles—like BRTs or BMPs. One of them exploded, cause unknown, and the mob bolted. The surviving vehicle's commander opened fire."

"God almighty," Bousikaris said. "What kind of armament are we talking about?"

"Heavy machine gun. Reports say the shooting lasted less than ten seconds. Judging by the number of casualties, it was probably a 14.5 millimeter—essentially a sixty-caliber machine gun."

"What's happening now?" asked President Martin.

"Both the Red Cross and the UN are offering aid, but so far no reply from Moscow."

"Typical Russian mentality," Martin said.

"Maybe yes, maybe no. Right now they're trying to figure out what happened. Irkutsk is seven hours from Moscow. Until they get the right people on the scene, they're smart to keep quiet."

"Especially if you're trying to cover something up," Bousikaris said.

Mason didn't respond. Even he, a Cold Warrior to the core, knew that no government—communist, socialist, or otherwise—was either purely good or purely evil. He was surprised Martin and Bousikaris had jumped to that conclusion; reactionism was a dangerous quality for a president—

especially one like Martin, whose ego rarely let him admit mistakes. As far as Mason was concerned, imprudence, conceit, and obstinacy had caused more wars than anything else.

"Only time will tell whether they'll try to gloss it over," Mason said. "The question is, how is this going to affect the presidential elections? If Bulganin's smart, he'll use Irkutsk."

"How so?" asked Martin.

"Polarization. Within hours we'll probably see him speaking out: 'Are these the actions of a caring, responsive government? A government that guns down citizens who simply want fair treatment?'—that sort of thing. If he can get the voters whipped up, it'll work to his advantage."

"Vote their hearts, not their minds," said Martin. "No room in the polling booth for both."

"Exactly."

"We need to start thinking about a response. The world is going to be watching which way we go. We'll need all the facts, Dick. I assume you'll keep Howard informed."

Mason read between the lines: *Let's see which way the political wind is blowing before we commit ourselves.* If Bulganin was able to turn this incident to his advantage, he might soon be the next president of the Russian Federation—in which case Martin would want to be on the winning side.

Damn the issues, full speed ahead, thought Mason.

Holystone Office

Latham's plea to Oaken was straightforward: *Help me get my family to safety, then give me the backup I need to finish the Baker investigation.*

Straightforward but fraught with danger, Leland Dutcher thought when Oaken approached him. Dutcher knew Latham well enough to take seriously his suspicions, but as had Oaken, he wondered whether Charlie's thinking was governed more by the father in him, or by the FBI agent in him.

If he agreed to help, he would be pitting Holystone against both the FBI and the Department of Justice—and given the nature of Holystone's work, that was the kind of exposure they couldn't afford.

• • •

LATHAM ACCEPTED A CUP OF COFFEE FROM DUTCHER AND LEANED back in one of the overstuffed chairs in Holystone's conference room. "How is she?" said Dutcher.

"Better," said Latham. "She's gonna be okay."

"I'm glad, Charlie. I understand they found the car."

Latham nodded. "It belongs to an elderly woman in Chevy Chase; she hadn't driven it in two months. She didn't even know it was missing. They found it abandoned twenty miles outside Williamsburg, full of cigarette butts and empty beer bottles."

"Window dressing?" Oaken said.

"That's my guess. Somebody's trying to make it look like a stalker or a joyride gone bad."

"Smart," said Dutcher.

"And damned frightening," Oaken added. "It means whoever took it knew the car's lack of use would buy them time; same thing with the butts and bottles. It would send the police in the wrong direction. Unless it *was* random, that is."

"It wasn't," Latham said. "The *Guoanbu* is methodical. Whether they planned to go after Samantha from the start, I don't know, but you can be sure they didn't do this on a whim. It was insurance. Truth is, I doubt they were trying to kill her. Something like that. . . . It would be bad, but after a few weeks I'd be back at work. This way . . . it was designed to tie me up."

"When will it be safe to move her?"

Latham sat forward. "You're going to help me?"

Dutcher nodded. "You have to understand, though: Our way of doing things may be a little more . . . gray than you're used to."

"I'm okay with that. The people we're up against don't give a damn about the law. If we have to play a little dirty to get them, so be it."

"Let's hope it doesn't go that far," Dutcher said. "First things first: We need to get Bonnie and your girls someplace safe. Once that's done, we start hunting."

17

New Zealand

It took most of the afternoon for Tanner and Cahil to traverse Mount Ada's southern spine and reach the pass. The trees along the path suddenly fell away to reveal a meadow of knee-high grass and wildflowers that curved out of sight around the mountain's lower slopes.

"Seems almost a shame to walk on it," Tanner said.

"I think somebody beat us to it." Cahil pointed at a wide groove in the center of the meadow.

"Horses."

"Yeah. This high up, it's probably the preferred method of travel. The only question is, are they from Fong's watchers or not."

Tanner sat down on his haunches, pulled out the map, and made a few quick calculations. "The ranch is in the next valley—seven miles, give or take. If they're patrolling this far out, it's a sure sign they're on the ball."

The closer they could get to the ranch before having to go to ground, the easier time they'd have planning what Bear had come to call "The Great Kiwi Fong Snatch."

"Any preference?" Tanner asked Cahil. "Lost hikers or daring botanists?"

"Lost hikers. I couldn't tell a daisy from a sunflower."

A light wind swirled down the valley, making the meadow's chest-high grass sway like waves. They were less than two miles into the meadow when Tanner heard the distant clomp of hoofbeats over the swishing of the grass. "Company," he whispered over his shoulder.

They both peered ahead, gazing over the top of the grass.

Closer now, the whinny of a horse. Thirty feet to their right, two horses materialized out of the grass. Sitting atop them were a pair of grim-faced Chinese men.

"Smile," Tanner whispered. "Wave."

Cahil broke into a grin and waved. "Hello, there."

Neither man wore cowboy gear, Tanner saw, but they did look cowboy tough, with ruddy, weathered faces. Each was dressed in khaki BDUs. Hanging from each saddle was what looked like an oversized fanny pack. Tanner knew better: *Fastpacks*. Inside the pouches would be guns, probably H&K or Grenoir compact assault rifles.

"You are on private property," one of the men said.

"Really?" Tanner said. "We thought this was the Medford Track."

"You mean Milford—Milford Track."

"Oh, right, sorry."

"The track is that way, across the lake."

"Are you sure?" Tanner pulled out his map. "I mean, it's right here." Pointing at the map, he started walking toward them. The second rider eased his horse left and dropped his hand to the fastpack. *Very cool,* Tanner thought. "See. We're right here."

The man didn't look at the map. "It is across the lake. You are on private property."

Tanner and Cahil exchanged glances. Briggs walked over to him and they leaned over the map.

"Ideas?" Cahil whispered.

"I doubt we can take them. They'd have their guns out before we got two steps."

"I agree," Cahil said. "We might get one, but not the other."

"Plus, who knows what'll happen if they don't check in." Tanner turned back to the riders. "You're sure this isn't the Minifred Track?"

"Mil*ford* Track. Yes, I am sure. You must leave now."

Tanner shrugged. "Okay. Sorry for the trouble."

He and Cahil shouldered their packs, turned around, and started walking.

• • •

AN HOUR LATER THEY WERE CROUCHED IN THE TREES AT THE mouth of the pass, watching the riders retreat across the meadow until they disappeared from view. The wind had picked up and dark clouds roiled along the upper slopes as the sun dropped toward the horizon.

"Well, that answers a few questions," Cahil said.

Tanner checked his watch. "We'll lay low and wait a few hours."

"And then?"

"And then we find out just how good Fong's watcher's are."

WITH NIGHTFALL CAME THE RAIN, A STEADY DOWNPOUR THAT soaked their clothes and chilled them to the bone. Lightning flashed along the foothills, casting the valley in strobe light.

They followed the trail south, skirting the meadow until the reached the opposite ridge, where they started climbing. The forest closed in around them until they were picking their way from trunk to trunk, wet branches swiping their faces as they went.

Tanner stayed parallel to the meadow, moving southeast until they reached the ridge overlooking Fong's valley. Below them he could see half a dozen yellow dots that he assumed were flashlights. Between claps of thunder he could hear the mewling of sheep.

"His men are probably trying to gather the sheep before the storm gets any worse," Cahil said.

The weather could work in their favor, Tanner realized. In addition to masking their approach, Fong's men would be cold and tired by the time they finished gathering the flock. Hopefully, the last thing on their minds would be patrolling.

As if reading his mind, Bear said, "Nasty job in this weather."

"Not as nasty as it could be."

"What've you got in mind?"

Tanner briefly outlined his plan, then said, "With the storm, it should be quite a sight."

Cahil broke into a grin. "Ah, yes, The Great Kiwi Fong Sheep Stampede."

It took Fong's men another hour to corral the flock. As they headed to the barn to put up the horses, Tanner and Cahil crawling down the slope, moving from tree to tree until they reached the valley floor. They found a cluster of pines and settled down to watch.

To their right, two hundred yards away, lay Fong's home, a multilevel log cabin with dormer windows and gambrel roofing; to their right, the corral and barn. The barn's doors were open, revealing lantern light and shadowed figures moving about.

Finally the men walked out of the barn, shut the door, and started toward the cabin. One by one they mounted the porch and disappeared inside. Moments later lights glowed to life in three downstairs windows.

"What do you think?" Cahil whispered. "Six men, two to a room?"

"Makes sense." If so, Fong's bedroom was probably on the second floor. That could either help or hurt them; while it isolated Fong, it also meant that unless they could find an outside route to the second floor, they'd have to walk past the guard's rooms.

"The big question is whether they post a watch at night," Tanner said.

"How long has Fong been here?"

"Four years."

"How many kidnap plots, you think?"

Tanner smiled. "We're probably the first." Cahil's point was well-taken. After four years the guards had probably gotten comfortable. "Okay, we'll sit tight for a few hours, then move."

They spent the next three hours lying perfectly still under the boughs of the pines as the rain pattered the leaves around them. One by one the cabin's windows went dark. Nothing moved except for the sheep milling about in the corral. They saw no roving patrols, no silhouettes in the windows, nothing to suggest a posted watch.

With a mutual nod, they parted ways and got to work.

FORTY MINUTES LATER THEY MET BACK UNDER THE PINES. "Change of plans," Cahil said. "I found a garage on the other side of the cabin; there are two Range Rovers inside. There's a road—and I use that term loosely—leading to the southeast."

"Fuel?"

"Both tanks are full. I trashed the distributor cap on one of them; it's dead."

"A Range Rover is better than a horse," Tanner said. "The corral gate's ready."

"Shall we?"

"Let the exodus begin."

While Cahil made his way to the corral, Tanner sprinted to the cabin wall and crawled forward until he reached the edge of the porch. He pulled out his red-bulbed penlight, aimed it toward the corral, and blinked twice.

A moment later he saw Cahil climb over the fence. Almost immediately the sheep began mewling. Cahil ran to the gate, swung it open, and then charged into the herd, waving his arms. Lightning crashed. Two of the sheep squealed and trotted out the gate, followed by three more. The remainder of the herd broke and scattered into the meadow. Cahil climbed back over the fence and sprinted over to Tanner.

Above their heads, light burst from the bedroom windows. They heard muffled shouting. The front door crashed open and one by one men ran out, shrugging on coats as they ran for the barn.

"I counted four," Cahil whispered. "That should leave two inside."

With Cahil in the lead, they crawled onto the porch, stood up, and charged for the open door. A shadow blocked his path. He barely had time to lower his shoulder before he and the man collided and tumbled inside. Tanner was one step behind, scanning left and right for movement.

From the corner of his eye he saw a shadow rushing toward him, saw the glint of moonlight on blue metal: *Gun.* He pulled the sap from his pocket and whirled. Ten feet to his right, a guard skidded to a stop, shotgun dangling by his side. He started to raise it. Tanner took two bounding steps, slammed his foot down on the shotgun's barrel before it came level, trapping it against the floor, then lashed out with the sap, catching the man in the temple.

As the man dropped unconscious, Tanner snatched up the shotgun. Cahil was rising to his feet with a pistol in his hand. "Little guy tried to shoot—stairs, Briggs!"

Tanner looked up. On the second-floor landing, a figure spun and disappeared down the hall.

With Cahil on his heels, Tanner hurdled up the steps. He reached the landing, looked left, saw nothing, looked right. A long hallway stretched before him. There were two open doors on each side, and one at the end. It was closed.

Tanner gestured to Bear: *I'm gonna crash it. Cover my back.*

Cahil nodded.

Tanner took a breath and charged down the hall, forcing himself to concentrate on the closed door rushing toward him. If anyone was in either of the side rooms waiting for him to pass . . .

Bear's got you, keep going. . . .

He hit the door and it crashed inward. Already stumbling, he dropped to one knee and spun.

To his right, a figure was trying to climb through the open window. Tanner ran over and jammed his heel into the man's Achilles' tendon. The man squealed and fell back. Briggs grabbed his collar and turned him around. "Clear, Bear!"

Cahil came through the door. "Is that him?"

Tanner pulled out his penlight, and shined it in the man's face. He was older, of course, but there was no mistake. Briggs said, "Good to see you again, Genoa."

18

Moscow

Nochenko knew Bulganin to be an early riser, so he wasn't surprised to see his boss's entourage already posted at the entrance to the RPP's headquarters when he arrived. As he passed the receptionist, she gestured him over. "He's been here all night."

"What's happening?" Nochenko asked.

"No idea. Everyone's been racing around like the world's on fire."

"Okay, thanks." Nochenko walked to Bulganin's door and knocked. He got an "enter" and walked inside. Bulganin was staring out the window. Uncharacteristically, he had the drapes drawn back and the room was flooded with sunlight. "Vladimir?" Nochenko said.

Bulganin turned. "Ivan! Ivan, my friend, have you heard?"

"What? What's happened?"

"See for yourself!" Arrayed across Bulganin's desk were half a dozen newspapers. Nochenko scanned the headlines: IRKUTSK MASSACRE. . . . PROTEST TURNS BLOODY. . . . SLAUGHTER IN SIBERIA. . . .

Nochenko grabbed a copy of *Izvestia* and scanned the story. "Good God! This is awful."

"What? This is wonderful!" Bulganin countered. "It couldn't be more perfect. This . . . fracas in Irkutsk is perfect! *It* will be our watershed—just as you said!"

"Vladimir, people are dead!"

"Yes, of course, it's a tragedy. But, Ivan, think what it means for us!"

It couldn't be, Nochenko thought. From a corner of his subconscious, another thought: *Coincidence is the mother of deception*. . . . It had been one of his mentor's favorite maxims, embodying the essence of successful propaganda. *And what is coincidence,* Nochenko thought, *but the favorable confluence of timing and events*?

Could Bulganin have anything to do with this? No, of course not. How could he?

Vladimir was right: Tragedy though it was, the incident could turn the election for them. They must be very careful, though. All of Russia would be waiting to see how Bulganin reacted. One hint that he was anything but devastated and it could all backfire.

"You see, don't you?" Bulganin said. "You see the momentous opportunity before us."

"Yes, Vladimir, but golden opportunity or not, we can't afford to come off as opportunists. Nearly sixty people are dead—sixty fellow Russians, including children—"

"Yes, yes," Bulganin droned. "Citizens who simply wanted fair treatment, a better life for their children . . . and what do they get for their trouble? A rain of bullets."

He's already rehearsed the speech. "Vladimir, when did you hear of this?"

"Late last night."

"From where?"

"Pyotr. He happened to be in Ulan Ude."

Ulan Ude was less than fifty miles from Irkutsk. "What was he doing there?"

The phone buzzed and Bulganin picked up, listened, then said, "Put him through." He hung up and turned to Nochenko. "The dogs come to beg for scraps, Ivan."

"Pardon me?"

"They're panicked, Ivan. Watch and learn."

The phone rang and Bulganin picked it up. "Bulganin here . . . yes, good morning. Certainly, but be quick, if you would. I have a brunch engagement." Bulganin listened for a few seconds then said, "Very well. I can make time for you . . . this afternoon at four. Please be prompt." Bulganin hung up.

Nochenko asked, "What is it?"

"The president's domestic affairs advisor is paying us a visit."

Now Nochenko understood. Aware of Bulganin's growing influence with voters, the president was hoping to blunt the RPP's attack before it began. "Irkutsk," he murmured.

"Yes, Irkutsk! We have them, Ivan!"

Holystone

Within hours of Samantha Latham's accident, every member of Charlie's team had pledged their support. As Oaken arranged a safe house for Latham's family, agents shuttled between Washington and Williamsburg to help any way they could.

Hesitant to involve them in an endeavor that could easily end their careers, Latham ordered everyone back to work. Janet Paschel and Tom Wuhlford, the two that had been with him the longest, refused, and along with Randall they began rotating guard shifts at the hospital.

Latham was spending his days in Williamsburg and his nights in Washington, brainstorming with Dutcher and Oaken. The cornerstone of their plan was Latham's conviction that Baker had been killed by the *Guoanbu*. Everything flowed from that. Accordingly, their approach would be three pronged.

Oaken searched for a motive behind the murders. What was the connection between Baker and the *Guoanbu*? If he'd been working for them, what had he been supplying?

Next, Latham and Randall would pursue the Mary Tsang and Hong Cho angle. However obliquely, Cho's methods in New York tied the Baker murders to the *Guoanbu*; similarly, unless she was in fact nothing more than a pen pal, Tsang was Cho's link to the outside world.

And lastly, upon his return, Cahil would begin hunting for Mike Skeldon. To understand the whole picture, they had to know why Baker had hired him.

Somehow this disparate group of people were connected to a larger whole—something so important to the Chinese government that it had ordered the slaughter of an entire family.

• • •

OAKEN FELT CERTAIN BAKER HAD HAD MORE ON HIS PLATE AT Commerce than a simple hearing aid. To confirm this, he proposed a scheme that got an enthusiastic smile from Latham.

The next day Charlie returned to Commerce for another meeting with Baker's supervisor and the department's director. "So what brings you back, Agent Latham?" asked Jenkins.

"How common is it for your employees to take home classified work?"

"It's against regulations," Jenkins replied.

"Closely monitored, I assume?"

"Of course."

"Then maybe you can tell me why Baker's computer was full of Commerce material."

"That can't be," Knowlton said. "There's got to be a mistake."

"At last count, Baker had material from twenty-three case files on his hard drive."

"Do you have the case numbers?" asked Jenkins.

"They're being transferred to a warrant as we speak. If I don't start getting some cooperation, that warrant will be on the desk of the U.S. attorney within the hour. After that, I'm coming back with a couple dozen agents and start digging through your documents vault."

"You can't—"

"Depending on what we find, I may start looking into obstruction charges."

"Agent Latham, this is unnecessary—"

Latham stood up and started toward the door. "I'm done being nice, Mr. Jenkins. You've just bought yourself and your department a world of heartache."

Jenkins bolted out of his seat. "Wait! Wait, please!"

"What?"

"You have to understand: This is very difficult."

Time to let them breathe. "Look, if Baker was up to no good, that's on him. Unless you were aiding and abetting him, the worst you'll face is some embarrassment. Be smart."

Jenkins looked at him for a few seconds, then nodded. "I'll have what you need in ten minutes."

An hour later Latham was back at Holystone with four large boxes of manila folders.

"Wow," Oaken said, helping him carry them into his office.

"Baker was a workhorse," Latham agreed.

"No, that's not what I meant. I figured it was a toss-up whether they'd fall for the bluff. I half expected him to pick up the phone to the Bureau. I was trying to figure out how we were going to post bail for you."

"Very funny, Walt. Jenkins is a bureaucrat down to his socks. I just spoke his language."

"Well, whatever you did, it worked." Oaken reached into one of the boxes and pulled out a file. "Now, get outta here—I've got some reading to do. Time to see what the late Mr. Baker was up to."

19

New Zealand

Fong blinked his eyes against the glare of Tanner's flashlight. "Who are you?"

"You don't remember me? Twelve years ago . . . Beijing?"

"No, I don't. What do you want?"

"You're sure? Ledger—General Han Soong was Treble; you were Genoa."

Fong's eyes widened. "You! They told me you were—"

"They were wrong," Tanner said. "Not by much, but enough."

Here's the answer, Tanner thought. Twelve years of wondering what had gone wrong with Ledger, and here, huddled on the floor before him, was the answer: a frightened old man.

Briggs wanted to hate Fong, but instead he felt nothing. The *why* of it didn't matter. Whatever the reason, whoever was to blame, he'd made a promise to Soong and his family, then failed them. He was alive and free and they were still in China, their lives draining away inside a *laogi*.

"How did you find me?" asked Fong.

"Three years and a lot of hard work," Tanner lied. "You're the last agent in the Ledger network. I've already visited the rest. Truth be told, I hadn't expected to find you."

"Last agent? What does that mean?"

"You're going on a trip."

"Where? What for—"

"Bear, give me the duct tape."

They stood Fong up, had him bend forward slightly, then taped his wrists to his thighs.

"This is uncomfortable," Fong whined.

"We'll make you some hot cocoa later," Tanner said, then pressed a piece of tape over his mouth. "Bear, tie up the two downstairs, stash one, and bring the other up here. We'll make him a sleep-in for Fong."

"Gotcha."

Bear took two steps toward the door, then stopped. He tapped his ear and pointed downward: *Noise*. Briggs crept down the hall and peeked around the corner. On the first floor, a pair of guards were kneeling over the two he and Cahil had incapacitated. What they did next told Tanner much about their training: Instead of racing up the stairs to check on their charge, the two men backed slowly out the door and disappeared. *Going to get reinforcements,* Tanner thought.

He returned to the room, told Cahil what was happening, then knelt beside Fong. "Listen closely. You have two choices: You can cooperate and live to see this place again; or you can die here."

Despite the threat, Tanner had no intention of killing Fong. Twelve years ago he'd been serving his country; now he was just an old man trying to live in peace and herd sheep.

Fong stared into Tanner's eyes for a long five seconds, then nodded.

From the first floor Tanner heard the scuff of a shoe on wood, followed by murmured voices.

Hurrying now, Briggs climbed out the window onto the roof. The rain was falling heavily, and steam rose from the still-warm shingles. With a shove from inside, Fong came out the window, followed by Cahil.

Tanner crept to the edge of the roof. He handed Cahil the shotgun, then eased himself forward until he could peek over the eaves trough. He froze.

Directly below him a man crouched in the shadows along the wall.

Behind them, voices from Fong's window.

Out of time, Briggs thought. He looked at Cahil and got a nod.

Tanner turned himself around so he was squatting backward over the edge, then dropped.

He landed in front of the crouching guard, who hesitated a half-second too long. Tanner clamped his hand over the guard's mouth, drew back his leg, and slammed his knee squarely into the man's solar plexus. The guard let out an explosive grunt and went slack. Tanner snatched up his rifle, a Norinco SKS-D.

Cahil and Fong, who Bear had lowered by his collar, were already on the ground and moving through the mist toward the garage. Tanner sprinted to a nearby bush and dropped to his belly. Nothing moved. To the west, he could see a hint of orange on the horizon. He waited until Bear and Fong were inside the garage, then followed.

From the cabin came the first shout of alarm. Voices called back in Chinese. Rusty though his Mandarin was, Tanner caught a few words: "Gone," "Intruders," and "Horses."

In the garage, Bear was swinging open the doors. Fong lay in the backseat of the Range Rover. Tanner jumped into the driver's seat, Cahil into the passenger seat. "I think we've worn out our welcome," Bear said.

"You're assuming we were welcome in the first place."

Briggs turned the ignition, floored the gas pedal, and the Rover lurched forward.

From the left, two figures were running toward them, muzzles flashing. Bullets peppered the Rover's rear quarter panel. Tanner spun the wheel hard, fishtailed, then accelerated, spewing a geyser of mud. The headlights swept over a gap in the trees. Tanner steered for it.

Bullets thunked into the Rover's tailgate. The rear window shattered. Fong screamed.

"Whoa," Cahil shouted. "Unfriendly!"

That answered one question for them: Whether Fong knew it or not, the guards were here not only for his protection, but for the *Guoanbu*'s as well: Rather than risk Fong's capture, they were to ensure his silence.

Tanner called, "Bear, I think our passenger has something to say."

Cahil reached back and peeled the tape from Fong's mouth.

"—shooting at us! Don't they know I'm in here?"

"They know," Tanner said.

"Then why . . . oh . . . I see now."

"I'm sure it's nothing personal," Cahil replied.

"I can never go back there again, you know."

"Not necessarily," Tanner replied. "Once we get out of this, I'll explain."

"*If* we get out of this, don't you mean?"

"Think positively."

The trees closed in around them until branches scraped the Rover's sides. Mist swirled over the ground. Rain splattered the windshield. Tanner tightened his grip on the wheel. "Any company, Bear?"

Cahil leaned his head out the window. "Nope, I don't see any— Whoa!"

Tanner saw headlights in the rearview mirror. They were a hundred yards back, but rapidly closing the distance. "I see them! I thought you disabled—"

"I did. Those aren't truck headlights."

Fong said, "They're four-wheel ATVs."

"What?" said Cahil. "From where?"

"There's an old hay bin under the barn."

"Oops," Tanner said.

"The entrance is disguised," Fong said. "You weren't meant to find it."

"I'll say this much, your watchers are good."

"Let us hope you're better."

Tanner floored the accelerator, opening the gap between them and the pursuers. As long as there were more straightaways than curves, they might be able to lose the ATVs. He wasn't confident, however. This high in the mountains, winding roads were more likely.

"Bear, how's our—"

"Already on it," Cahil called and began checking their weapons. "Seven rounds in the shotgun; Beretta's got fourteen, SKS's got a full magazine. What say I try to create a little gridlock?"

"Good idea. Hang on, there's a corner coming up."

Cahil climbed into the backseat, shoved Fong to the floor, and propped the SKS on the seat.

Tanner skidded around the corner, punched the accelerator for fifty yards, then braked hard and doused the headlights. Seconds later the lead ATV came around the corner. Cahil opened fire. The ATV swerved right, then left, then plunged into the trees along the road. Tanner floored the gas pedal and took off.

In seconds the Rover was back up to speed. Branches whipped past the windshield.

"Dawn's coming," Cahil said.

To the east the sun's upper rim was rising over the mountains.

Tanner said, "We should only be about ten miles from the highway. If we can—"

"Briggs, watch it!" Cahil called.

Through the fog, the headlights picked out a tree lying across the road. Beyond it stood half a dozen horses and riders. Tanner slammed on the brakes. The Rover slewed broadside. He spun the wheel, straightened out, and the Rover shuddered to a stop.

"Your men?" Tanner asked Fong.

"Yes. They must have gone overland. There's a game trail that parallels the road."

"Now what?" Cahil muttered.

"Now," Tanner said, jamming the shift lever into reverse, "we take the road less traveled."

The Rover lurched backward, the transmission whining as they picked up speed. Behind them, the three remaining ATVs skidded around the corner. "Briggs. . . ."

"I see them."

Tanner spun the wheel, slammed on the brakes.

"What do you think, Bear?" Tanner said, pointing through the windshield at a gap in the trees. Mostly overgrown with brush, the trail sloped away from the road and disappeared. "Wide enough?"

Fong shouted, "No, wait! It—"

"Pretty steep," Cahil said. "But, given the alternative. . . ."

"My thoughts exactly," Tanner replied.

He slammed the Rover into gear, aimed the hood for the gap, and floored the accelerator.

20

THE ROVER LEAPT OVER THE DITCH AND SLAMMED ONTO THE trail, shearing off a pair of saplings as it passed. Tanner and Cahil were thrown against their seat belts. In the backseat, Fong tried to sit up, but lost his balance and fell back again.

"This is *not* a trail!" he yelled.

"What?" Cahil shouted.

"It's not a trail! It used to be part of a launch."

"A what?"

The Rover hit a rut, veered right, and clipped a tree trunk.

Fong yelled, "A *boat* launch!"

Even before Fong said the words, Tanner saw the trees thinning ahead and caught a glint of sun on water. *The Joe River*, he thought.

"Aw, shit," Cahil moaned.

"How deep is it, Fong?"

"I have no idea!"

Cahil glanced over his shoulder. "Well, at least they're not following us anymore."

"That's a plus," Tanner replied. "Hold tight!"

He turned the wheel, trying to catch the bumper on a passing tree. It wouldn't budge. He wrenched on it. Nothing. Cahil poked his head out the side window, then pulled back. "We're stuck in the ruts."

Suddenly the trees disappeared, giving way to a short beach.

"We're gonna get wet!" Tanner shouted.

A WAVE CURLED OVER THE HOOD AND CRASHED AGAINST THE windshield.

Tanner flicked on the wipers. They drummed and squeaked across the glass.

Aside from the beach they'd just left, most of the river's shoreline was surrounded by sheer rock walls and scrub pine.

Cahil peeked out the window. "Water's up to the wheel wells."

Tanner pressed the accelerator. The wheels slipped, then took hold, grinding gravel.

"We're moving!" Cahil called.

"Good!"

"No, Briggs, we're *moving*!"

Tanner looked out and saw the opposite shore drifting laterally across the windshield. "Climb in back, Bear, give me some weight!"

Cahil scrambled over the seat. Fong let out a yelp.

Tanner pressed on the accelerator. For a moment there was nothing, then came the crunch of gravel as the wheels found purchase. The Rover lurched backward.

"You've got it!" Cahil yelled.

Come on, come on, come on. . . . Inch by inch they began backing toward the shore. Tanner looked in the mirror. The beach was sliding out of view. *Running out of room. . . .*

He felt the wheels slip, grab again, then he heard them whine as the Rover's tail end floated free. He floored the accelerator. A rooster tail of water arced behind the Rover. He let up on the pedal. The Rover began wallowing in the current. Water lapped at the doors. Cahil climbed back into the front.

Tanner asked Fong, "Any idea where this heads?"

"Which way are we going now?"

"Roughly east."

Fong thought for a moment. "I'm not sure how far, but eventually we should end up parallel to Highway Ninety-four."

"We'll sink long before that," Cahil said, rolling up his window.

Tanner did the same. The water was three inches below the window frame.

The gorge was narrowing now, the bottom becoming rockier. The water began to churn. Froth broke over the hood. Slowly at first, and then with growing speed, the Rover began spinning.

"I think I'm going to be sick," Fong groaned.

Cahil patted him on the head. "It's okay—it's your car."

"Can you swim?" Tanner asked him.

"Badly."

With a groan, the Rover's engine-heavy nose began tipping into the water. The front tires touched bottom, and the tail spun around until they were traveling backward.

"Time to abandon ship," Tanner said.

They climbed into the backseat. Tanner cut away the tape from Fong's wrists and Cahil helped him into the cargo area. Cahil was climbing through the rear window when he stopped suddenly.

"What is it, Bear?"

"Shhh . . . ! Falls! There're falls ahead!"

"Oh, God!" Fong murmured.

Tanner ducked down and looked out the half-submerged windshield. Fifty yards downstream, a cloud of spray billowed above the river. Through the mist he caught glimpses of car-size boulders lining the shore. "Go, Bear, get out!"

Tanner knew if they were inside the Rover when it went over, they wouldn't survive: If the undertow didn't trap them, the current would knock them around the interior like marbles in a tin can.

"Try for the boulders!" Tanner called. "I'm right behind you!"

The driver's window shattered. Water gushed through and engulfed the front seats. The Rover's tail continued to rise until Briggs was standing on the backseats.

With one arm wrapped around Fong, Cahil climbed out the back window and stood on the bumper. Tanner followed. Now he could hear the roar of the falls. Mist swirled around them.

Briggs glanced at Fong; his eyes were bulging. "You okay?"

"Yes!"

Tanner felt a twinge of admiration for the man. He was old, frail, and terrified, but was doing his best to hold himself together. "Ready, Bear?"

With Fong between them, they slipped into the water. They kicked off the Rover's bumper and started swimming for the nearest boulder. Immediately Tanner felt the current grip him. White water and froth boiled around them.

Don't look, just swim, he ordered himself.

Legs thrashing, they paddled toward the shore.

Twenty feet . . . not gonna make it. For every foot they gained laterally, they were losing three to the current. On impulse, Tanner glanced left just in time to see the Rover tumble over the falls.

As they drew closer to the shore, Briggs suddenly realized all the boulders were as slick as glass. Sitting at the water's edge for thousands of years, they'd been polished smooth.

"We got a problem!" Cahil called.

"I see it. Keep swimming!"

Cahil grabbed at a boulder, but his fingers simply trailed over the surface.

Tanner felt something solid beneath his feet. *Rock!* He tried to stand up, slipped, then tried again. Cahil continued to slip downstream. Tanner tightened his grip on Fong's collar. Fong's head slipped beneath the surface. Cahil pulled him up.

"I'm going over, Briggs!"

"Hold on!"

Tanner tried to stand again, but the current was too strong. He felt himself being dragged under. He grabbed at the rocks. *Not going to make it,* he thought. He looked at Bear and saw the same realization in his eyes. Tanner reached toward him and they locked hands, sandwiching Fong between them.

"Take a deep breath!"

Tanner felt himself pushed up and out. For a moment he floated. The roar of the falls seemed to fade. And then the world tipped upside down.

Tanner's vision became a blur of white water and boulders. Everything went black. He felt the icy water envelop him, squeezing his chest like a vice. He opened his eyes. He could feel the pound of the water above him.

Fong's face materialized out of the murk. Tanner grabbed him, held on, then groped for Cahil. He felt a hand close over his own, and a moment later they struck bottom. Tanner heard a *pop-crunch.* Fong's mouth opened in a silent scream.

With Fong pressed between them, Tanner and Cahil kicked for surface and broke into the air.

Five minutes later and fifty yards downstream, they crawled ashore and collapsed.

"Fong, are you alright?" Tanner called.

"My foot. Ahhhh. God, it hurts!"

He crawled over. Fong's foot was wrenched almost completely backward. The toe of his shoe pointed into the sand. Briggs patted him on the chest. "You're going to be okay."

"It could be worse," Cahil said with a smile.

Tanner grinned back; the joke was an old one between them "Could be dead."

• • •

An hour later they had a makeshift camp set up and Fong was resting with Tanner's cold, water-soaked anorak wrapped around his foot. He and Cahil had faired better. Aside from some scrapes and bruises, they were unscathed.

Cahil left to scout their location and returned forty minutes later. "Highway Ninety-four's about two miles to the east; from there it's about five miles to the Homer Tunnel."

"Now what?" asked Fong.

"Now we make a deal," Tanner replied.

"What kind of deal?"

Tanner couldn't risk telling Fong the real reason they'd come lest they be forced to smuggle him out of the country and keep him incommunicado, in which case Fong could never come back here without facing a lengthy, and perhaps fatal, *Guoanbu* debriefing. If Tanner could get what he needed without destroying Fong's life, all the better. Of course, that depended on how well he told his story.

During Ledger, Briggs began, he met and fell in love with a young Chinese woman, a poet named Siylin. Soon after the failure of Ledger, Tanner learned the government had labeled her poetry "ideologically impure." She was sent to a reeducation camp. A few months ago, she'd been released.

"I want to get her out," he concluded.

"This has nothing to do with Soong?"

Tanner shook his head. "I doubt he or his family survived a year in the *laogi*."

"Then why are you here? I don't understand."

"I want the names of a few . . . untrustworthy *Guoanbu* informants I can use."

"Why?"

"Getting in and finding Siylin is going to be the easy part. Getting out could be tricky. If I run into trouble with the *Guoanbu,* I want to have some misdirection up my sleeve."

Fong frowned. "I see. And if I refuse?"

"Then you'll have to come with us."

"Which means I can never come back here."

Tanner nodded. "Our way, you get to stay."

"Explain."

"You'll be found along the edge of the highway, having jumped from the moving car of your kidnappers. Scraped and battered, you crawled into the underbrush and hid before the kidnappers had a chance to turn around. Scared off by passing cars, the kidnappers fled."

"Kidnappers, eh?" Fong mused.

"Two hours after we drop you off, the police will receive a tip giving them your location."

"How do you know the names I give you won't be false, or that I won't contact the *Guoanbu*?"

"Two reasons. One, if you burn me, they'll want to know where you got the information. They'll doubt your kidnap story, and you'll find yourself back in Beijing."

"And the other reason?"

"If I don't get out of China, my friend here will be paying you another visit."

Fong glanced at Cahil, who smiled and gave him a short wave.

"I see," said Fong.

Tanner said, "I'm hoping none of that will be necessary."

"As do I. If I give you these names, can you promise me they won't be hurt?"

"I can promise I won't knowingly put them in harm's way. That's the best I can do."

"Why not just take me until you're done? Easier still, why not get the names, then kill me? I would've thought I'd given you reason enough."

"Maybe I'm getting soft in my old age," Tanner replied. "You did what you did in Beijing because it was your duty. Providing you hold up your end of the bargain, I don't see any reason why you shouldn't be allowed to live in peace."

Fong considered this for a moment, then nodded. "You have a deal."

21

Holystone

Driving straight in from the airport, Tanner and Cahil reached the office in midmorning and were greeted by Dutcher, Oaken and, to their surprise, Charlie Latham. "Welcome home," Dutcher said.

"New recruit?" Tanner said, smiling at Latham.

"Temporarily," Dutcher replied. "I'll fill you in later."

"Good to see you again, Charlie."

"You, too."

Dutcher led the group into the conference room. Tanner and Cahil, whose body clocks were still on New Zealand time, gladly accepted coffee.

"I assume you found Genoa?" asked Oaken.

"Your directions took us to his front door," Cahil said. "I have a new respect for sheep."

Dutcher said, "Tell us."

Tanner recounted their trip, starting with their crossing of Lake Ada and ending with their tumble over the falls. "Alternating piggybacking duties, we hiked overland to the Homer Tunnel, then stashed Fong in the underbrush and flagged down a tour bus to Dunedin. We called the police, boarded a charter to Auckland, then here."

"It's a gamble you're taking with Fong," said Dutcher.

"He's got more to lose than we do. Plus, he knows it could have been worse."

"Give the names to Walt; we'll start gathering some background on them. As it stands, you've got a date in Jakarta in two days. That brings us to the reason Charlie's here. Do you think you can get along without Ian?"

"I don't know . . . he does read to me at night."

"He's a difficult child," Bear said.

Dutcher smiled. "I'll take that as a yes." He brought them up to speed on the Baker case, from the murders to Samantha's accident just days before. "We're going to lend a hand."

"How's she doing, Charlie?" asked Tanner.

"We're moving her, Bonnie and Caroline to the safehouse tomorrow. Tom and Janet are there now. Once we get that done, I'll sleep a little better."

"You've got some pretty good folks on your team."

"Don't I know it. Here, too."

Dutcher said, "We're approaching it from three directions. Walt's digging into Baker's cases."

"Anything there?" Cahil asked.

"Nothing yet," Oaken said. "He was with the BXA—the Bureau of Export Administration—so he had a pretty full plate: Everything from computer chips to precision lathing equipment for artillery barrels. It's gonna take a while."

Dutcher continued: "Charlie and his people are going to try to shake the tree with Hong Cho and Mary Tsang."

"What are you looking for, Charlie?"

"The *Guoanbu* is partial to using bridge agents—in-country sleepers assigned to help their controllers—I doubt they've written off Hong Cho entirely. If this Tsang woman is a bridge, it would explain her visits."

"The home office staying in touch."

"Exactly. Unless they've bolted, Baker's contacts are probably still in the area. If we push Tsang, maybe she'll lead us to them."

Cahil said, "Leland, you said three approaches. I'm the third, I assume?"

"Yes. Baker paid Mike Skeldon a lot of money. We need to know what he was doing for them. Latham's got some leads on him. You'll be following those."

Latham added, "From what little we were able to gather, he's got connections in Asheville."

"Makes sense," said Cahil. "There's a big underground mercenary community in North Carolina. They're pretty tight-knit."

"Is that a problem?" asked Dutcher.

"No, but there're a lot of wannabes down there, too. I'll just have to find the right group."

Dutcher nodded. "Anybody have any questions?"

Tanner said, "Just one: Charlie, if you're right about the Justice probe being bogus, where did the order really come from? Who jerked the rug out from under you, and why?"

"Both good questions, and I don't have any answers. One thing's for sure, though: Whoever it is, they've got the power to make the Justice Department dance. And that's pretty damned scary."

TANNER'S HOME WAS A MULTISTORY, RAISED CABIN ATTACHED to a two hundred-year-old lighthouse he'd rescued from condemnation with the help of the Virginia Historical Commission. Overlooking the cove below, the lighthouse had never been much of a navigation aid, but it had delighted the original builder, an eccentric mill owner who, according to legend, loved lighthouses, but hated the ocean.

Briggs parked in the detached garage, walked along the wraparound deck to the back door, and stepped inside. Sitting on the kitchen table was a strawberry-kiwi pie and a note:

> FOR WHEN YOU GET HOME. . . . CALL WHEN YOU GET A CHANCE.
> LOVE, MOM AND DAD.
> P.S. THANKS FOR THE WATCHAMACALLIT. I USE IT EVERY DAY!

Tanner laughed. The "watchamacallit" in question was one of those machines designed to suck the air out of a storage bag then hermetically seal it, forever imprisoning whatever food item happened to be inside. In the case of his mother, that meant everything she could get her hands on. According to his father, she'd sealed everything from rump roast to creamed corn. He claimed he was afraid to sit in the same place for more than a few minutes at a time.

Briggs had no idea how long the pie had been here, but it looked oven fresh.

He took a potpie out of the freezer, stuck it into the oven, then took the stairs to a loft that held his bedroom and the bathroom. Once showered, he went into the bedroom and walked to the closet. It took a few minutes to find what he was looking for: an old shoe box of mementos.

The thumb-size chunk of jade was there; carved into its surface where three Chinese characters.

The day before Tanner was to take Soong and his family out of China, they'd had their last meeting. "There's something I want you to have," Soong had said, and handed him the stone. "Like everything Chinese, it is a metaphor. Do you see it?"

Tanner shook his head. "My character recognition still needs work."

"We'll have plenty of time for that once we're out. The characters represent the sun, the earth, and friendship. It means, Wherever you are under the sun, you are my friend, and I am yours."

Tanner sat down on the edge of the bed and stared at the carving.

Who was Han Soong? The man who'd tearfully given him this gift, or the willing participant in a disinformation campaign? As much as Briggs wished otherwise, he wasn't sure, but whatever it took he was going to find out.

USS *O'Kane*, DDG-77

What a change a day and three thousand miles can make, Sconi Bob Jurens thought.

Twenty-four hours ago he and his team had been emerging from Lake Shriveljewels, cold, wet, and tired. Now they were warm and rested aboard a ship in the middle of the Pacific, soaking in the sun.

Beyond the railing, Jurens could hear the *swoosh-hiss* of the water skimming along the hull, and the faint whirring of *O'Kane*'s gas-turbine engines. He shaded his eyes and looked over the water. Somewhere out there was their ride, submerged and waiting for *O'Kane*'s signal.

Almost time to get down to business. They were ready, but still there remained the nagging question of their destination. Much like the real estate business, the success or failure of an operation often depended upon three things: location, location, location. Until he knew that, they were in limbo.

"Any guesses, boss?" asked Smitty.

"Nah. Guessing will drive you crazy. I just realized: You know who this ship is named after?"

"Nope."

"Dick O'Kane. He was a sub driver in World War Two. You've heard of the *Tang*, I'll bet."

"Sounds familiar."

"*Tang* was O'Kane's last command. Five patrols, thirty-one ships sank. That's over a quarter-million tons worth of steel sent to the bottom."

"You said *last* command."

"On her last patrol *Tang* sank thirteen ships before she got mixed up in a surface brawl. One of her own torpedoes malfunctioned, circled back, and blew off her stern. O'Kane and those lucky enough to get off were picked up by the Japanese and held prisoner until the end of the war."

Smitty groaned. "So here we are, aboard a ship named after a sub driver, headed for another sub that's going to take us God-knows-where. If I were a superstitious man, I'd be nervous."

Whether they will admit it or not, most operators did in fact tend to be superstitious to some degree. For anyone who'd seen the capriciousness of combat, it was hard not to believe in dumb luck.

A crewman poked his head out of the deck hatch. "Master Chief, we've just made contact with your ride. We're fifteen miles out."

"Thanks. Smitty, go round up Zee and Dickie. Time to start earning our pay."

• • •

FIVE MILES FROM THE SUB, *O'KANE*'S CAPTAIN ORDERED THE ship to Security Alert to keep gawkers out of the passageways and off the decks as Jurens and his team went about their business. Aside from themselves, the only people on the fantail were the ship's XO and her chief boatswain's mate, who would operate the hand winch that would lower the team's gear over the side.

"Breech, four o'clock!" the XO called, pointing.

A quarter mile off the starboard quarter, a submarine's fairwater broke the surface, followed by the foredeck and tail fin, all trailing white water and froth.

"Your chariot, gentlemen," said the boatswain's mate.

Ten minutes later they were sitting in their IBS raft, unhooking the last piece of gear from the winch. Once done, Smitty planted a boot against the hull and pushed off. Standing on the starboard bridge wing, *O'Kane*'s skipper gave them a half salute. Jurens returned it. Zee fired up the motor, revved the throttle, and aimed them toward the sub.

Five minutes later they were alongside. The forward escape trunk, just a few feet behind the fairwater, was already open. A sailor wearing a baseball cap poked his head out and said, "Howdy."

"You our working party?" Jurens asked.

"Me and five guys below. We'll stow your gear; you can sort it out later."

Once on deck, they deflated the IBS, set up an assembly line, and began handing gear down the hatch. When everything was aboard, they climbed into the trunk. Jurens entered last, closed the hatch behind him, spun the wheel tight, and descended the ladder.

A short man with red hair and startling blue eyes was waiting for them. "Archie Kinsock, skipper of *Columbia*."

"Good to meet you, Captain," said Jurens, then introduced his team.

Kinsock gave each man a handshake. "We'll get you and your men situated, Master Chief, then I think you and I have some orders to open."

• • •

JURENS KNOCKED ON KINSOCK'S STATEROOM, GOT AN "ENTER" in reply, and walked in. The space was roughly ten feet square, carpeted, with two chairs bracketing a desk that doubled as a fold-down bunk.

"Have a seat," Kinsock said. "Get settled?"

"Yep. Feel bad about taking over the Goat Locker, though."

"Don't worry about it. A little hot bunking won't hurt them."

Though the name's origin had been long ago forgotten, the Goat Locker was where the boat's chief petty officers lived while at sea. With their intrusion, the displaced chiefs would have to share racks, one sleeping while the other was on duty.

"This isn't your first time aboard an LA, I assume," Kinsock asked.

"Nope. Good boats—quiet."

"They are that. I understand you didn't want the clamshell. Mind telling me why?"

Clamshell is the nickname for the chamber affixed to a submarine's deck to transport a team's Swimmer Deliver Vehicle, or SDV. Using a clamshell allows a team to begin its penetration far from an enemy's shore, thereby reducing its chance of being detected.

"Personal preference," Jurens answered. "Locking out is a pain in the ass. Plus, I'm kinda old school: I like to swim in. Is that a problem?"

"Nope. I'll get you so close you can wade in, if you want. Besides, I've never liked having those damned things stuck to my boat. They remind me of ticks."

Jurens laughed. He liked Kinsock; they would get along fine.

Kinsock walked to his wall safe, dialed the combination, opened the door, and pulled out a red-bordered manila folder. He handed it to Jurens. Already aware of the "whats" of the mission, Jurens scanned to the section outlining the navigation plan. "You've got to be kidding me," he murmured.

"What?" Kinsock asked.

Jurens handed the folder across. "Russia. We're going to Russia."

22

Blanton Crossing, Virginia

THOUGH CAHIL DIDN'T EXPECT TO FIND SKELDON LOITERING around WalPol's headquarters, it seemed the logical place to start. Ninety minutes after leaving Washington, he pulled into the trailer's driveway.

He got out, hefted out a case of beer onto his shoulder, then walked to the door and knocked. Thirty seconds passed. He knocked again. Still no answer.

He looked around; the road was deserted. He set down the beer, opened the screen, and tapped the door. It was a hollow-core model. Using both hands he turned the knob counterclockwise, braced his shoulder against the door, and started pressing, letting his legs do the work. After ten seconds he heard a muffled *pop*. The door swung inward. He grabbed the beer and walked inside.

"Hey, Ernie! Hey, you sumbitch, where are ya?"

Nothing moved.

"I got some suds! Get yer ass out here!"

Silence.

The trailer's bed-sheet curtains were drawn closed. The interior was empty except for a cot, four battleship gray filing cabinets against one wall, and a homemade sawhorse-and-plank desk.

He made a quick search of the remaining rooms. All were empty.

"Time to check Mike's housekeeping," Cahil muttered, and set to work.

An hour later he was done. Skeldon had covered himself well. Aside from a roll of toilet paper in the bathroom and a pillowcase on the bedroom floor, the man had left nothing behind.

His job had just gotten harder. Though Skeldon had ties to North Carolina, it was a big state. Trolling around asking random questions would be not only time consuming, but could be dangerous if he came across the wrong people.

He was opening the door to leave when something caught his eye. He walked to the table and knelt. Tucked beneath one of the sawhorse's legs was a matchbook cover. Cahil pulled it out and read.

BUD'S GUN SHOP AND FIRING RANGE
ASHEVILLE, NORTH CAROLINA

Cahil smiled. "Bingo."

THE DRIVE TOOK MOST OF THE NIGHT. THE SUN WAS RISING above the shadowed foothills when he spotted a billboard for a Denny's and pulled into the parking lot. Inside, he found a booth and sat down. The waitress, a fiftyish bottle blond wearing bright pink lipstick, walked up. "Morning. What can I getchya?"

"Coffee, two scrambled eggs, whole wheat toast, and orange juice."

"Comin' up."

Cahil liked Asheville. He and Maggie had stayed in a nearby bed-and-breakfast years before. Nestled between the Great Smokey and Blue Ridge Mountain ranges, it was a quiet city of two hundred thousand, and like many Southern cities, it was steeped in the architecture of antebellum South, with wide, tree-lined boulevards and colonnaded plantation houses perfect for lazy summer evenings.

The waitress returned with the food, flashed a nicotine-yellow smile at him, and left.

As he ate, Cahil thought about Skeldon. The former Ranger had been discharged for medical reasons in 1993 after sixteen years of service. Latham's transcript hadn't listed the cause of Skeldon's medical condition, an omission Cahil found curious. After sixteen years—most of them spent in an elite unit—it was unlikely Skeldon had volunteered to opt out. That left forced retirement, which begged the same question: What had happened to drive Skeldon out of the army four years shy of retirement?

Cahil had two more cups of coffee, paid the bill, then walked outside to a phone. He found the listing for Bud's Gun Shop and Firing Range and dialed.

"Bud's," the voice drawled.

"Howdy," Cahil said. "Wondering about your hours."

"Open from six p.m. to midnight, Monday through Saturday."

"You got a combat course?"

"Yep. Forty targets, plus two buildings for CQB."

CQB was short for Close Quarters Combat. "Thanks." Cahil hung up.

Six o'clock. He had some time to kill.

HE CHECKED INTO A MOTEL AND NAPPED FOR THREE HOURS, THEN made a list of local gun shops in the area and started driving. Because of zoning laws, most of the shops were located outside city limits.

The first four shops didn't have what he needed. The fifth, run from a shed beside the owner's ranch-style home, was tucked between an apple orchard and a horse pasture west of the city. As Cahil got out of the car, a pair of Labrador retrievers trotted over, sniffed his legs, then wandered away.

"Afternoon." A potbellied man in denim overalls walked toward him. "Help ya?"

"You Hersh?"

"Jim Hersh. Who're you?"

"John Malvin. I'm looking for something a little unusual. Heard you might be able to help."

Hersh pulled a rag from his pocket and wiped his hands. "Come on in."

The shed had a concrete floor and unpainted Sheetrock walls. Floor-to-ceiling shelves loaded with guns and boxes of ammunition lined the walls. The shed's only window was crisscrossed with steel rebar. A pair of box fans hung from the corners, churning the dusty air.

Hersh opened a mini-fridge. "Grape soda?"

"Sure."

Hersh tossed him one. "What kind of unusual?"

"Heckler & Koch USC forty-five."

Hersh took a gulp of his soda. "Trojan." The gun had gained the nickname from the University of Southern California's football team. "Government just put a moratorium on 'em. That's one step away from being banned."

"That's why I'd like to get one before it's too late."

"Still don't change nothing. I can't sell 'em."

Cahil looked around at the gun displays. "Nice collection. How long've you been in business?"

"Fourteen years."

"Ex-military?"

"Marines. You?"

"Army Rangers."

"Airborne?"

Cahil shook his head. "Straight leg."

"Me, too."

"Why fly when you can march."

"Damn right."

They sat in silence for a few minutes. Outside the dogs barked a few times, then went silent. Hersh was mulling it over, Cahil guessed. As far as the police were concerned, selling a moratorium weapon was the same as selling a banned weapon. He could lose his license and go to jail.

"Why the Trojan?" asked Hersh.

"I'd rather have a tommy-gun, but so far I'm not having much luck. Till then, I'd settle for the USC. I got a buddy who can attach a box magazine on it."

"No shit. How many rounds?"

"Hundred."

"Whatchya gonna use it for?"

"Quail hunting."

Hersh was in the middle of taking a sip; he choked, then started laughing. "A .45 round ain't gonna leave much bird to eat. No, really, what for?"

"I like to run combat courses."

Hersh finished his soda, tossed it into a nearby garbage pail. "I've got a Trojan, but it ain't registered. That a problem?"

"Not for me. What about the serial number?"

"Somebody spilled some acid on it. Can't read it for shit. Three grand."

They haggled for a few minutes and Cahil got him down to $2800 with ten boxes of ammunition and a Browning 9mm pistol thrown in. As they walked to Cahil's car, Hersh said, "There's a good course south of here."

"Bud's?" Hersh nodded. "I'm headed there tonight." Cahil stuck out his hand. "Thanks."

Hersh shook it. "Pleasure. Just so we understand each other, I don't sell many of those. If it comes back on me, I'm gonna be unhappy."

"I hear ya," Bear said.

CAHIL WAITED UNTIL THE SUN WENT DOWN, THEN FOLLOWED Highway 240/74 out of the city to Minehole Gap, where he turned north, following the signs for Bud's. After another seven miles the road took him into a clearing where he found a ten-foot-high fence made of rusted corrugated steel. Above the razor wire, he could see the glare of stadium lights. He heard the staccato popping of semiautomatic gunfire.

Parked along the fence was an assortment of pickup trucks and muscle cars, most sporting a mix of Confederate flags, pro-NRA bumper stickers, and naked lady mud flaps.

Rebel heaven, Cahil thought.

The men inside would likely be stereotypical "good 'ol Southern boys": patriotic, bigoted, and full of "aw-shucks" charm masking mean streaks ten-miles wide. Cahil suddenly realized how far from civilization he was. If he got into trouble out here, he would be on his own.

He got out, locked the H&K in the trunk, and walked through the gate. He found himself standing beneath a lean-to porch attached to an open-ended WWI-style barracks; inside were several dozen men sitting at tables, drinking and laughing. To his right, spread out over a quarter mile, lay the grass shooting lanes. Three or four men, each armed with some version of a banned assault weapon, were shooting at man silhouette targets.

"Evening," a man called from the counter.

"Evening," Cahil said and walked over.

The man was in his early sixties, wearing a yellow "Prowl Herbicide" baseball cap. Tacked to the collar of his flannel shirt was an American flag pin with a gold "II" superimposed on it.

That told Cahil much. The pin was the symbol of the militia group known as America Secundus, or Second America. Believing the government was tainted by corruption, cultural decay, and racial impurity, America Secundus was dedicated to the foundation of a new United States built on the ashes—metaphorical or literal, no one knew—of the old.

Was Skeldon a member? Cahil wondered. And if so, did his affiliation have anything to do with his business with Baker and the *Guoanbu*? "Are you Bud?" he asked.

"I am. You're John Malvin."

Uh-oh. "That's a helluva guess."

"Hersh called, said you might be stopping by."

"Nice of him. Listen, if I'm not welcome, I understand."

"Nobody said that. We're kinda family out here, that's all. Hersh said you seemed okay, asked me to make you welcome."

Cahil was guessing Bud's was not only the headquarters for Secundus's North Carolina chapter, but also the Southern version of a mafia social club. "Then I guess you know about our transaction."

"Yep. Nice rig."

"Mind if I give it a whirl?"

"Go ahead," Bud replied, then grinned. "Just don't shoot no quail."

Looking better. "Deal."

Cahil gathered the Trojan and chose a shooting lane. He shot a few dozen rounds, getting a feel for the gun, then set to work sighting it in, starting first at twenty-five yards, then moving back to the fifty and one hundred marks.

He heard voices behind him. He turned. Twenty or so of Bud's patrons were standing on the porch watching him. As he'd hoped, the Trojan had attracted some attention.

"Not bad for standing still," one of the men called.

"You volunteering to stand-in?" Cahil replied.

There was general laughter.

"What I mean is, try it on the run." The man was nearly six and a half feet, with a long beard and heavily tattooed forearms. Cahil mentally named him "Beard."

"If I'm gonna tire myself out like that, I'd like it to be worth my time," he said.

Beard sauntered over. The rest of the pack followed at a distance, forming a semicircle around the lane. All of them were wearing either belt or shoulder holsters.

"Hundred bucks says you can't put two in the head of each target at a full sprint," said Beard.

Obviously, Hersh's courtesy call hadn't quite given him a full pass. Beard was either the de facto leader here, or the enforcer. To back down now could be disastrous.

"I've got a better idea," Cahil replied. "Turn off the lights, and for two hundred I'll put three in each head."

"Bullshit."

Cahil shrugged. "If you don't have the cash. . . ."

His eyes locked on Cahil's, Beard called, "Bud, turn 'em off."

A few moments later Cahil heard a double *thunk,* and the range went dark except for what little light filtered out from the barracks windows.

"Wanna flashlight?" somebody called. There was laughter.

Cahil turned to face the lane. Working by feel, he changed the Trojan's magazine, then stood still, letting his eyes adjust. After a few seconds, the outline of the twenty-five-yard silhouette came into focus. He brought the Trojan to his shoulder in the ready-low position.

Nice and easy . . . get the sight picture, then squeeze.

He started running.

Thirty seconds later he was done. As he returned to the head of the lane, Bud flipped the lights back on. There was a few seconds of silence, then a lone, "I'll be damned," followed by murmuring.

Each of the target's foreheads was punctured by a near-perfect triad of shots.

"Not bad," said Beard.

Time to back him down a little bit, Cahil thought. He took a step forward, pushing the man's space. "Better than 'not bad,' I'd say."

Beard's eyes narrowed, then he grinned. "Come inside. I'll get your money, buy you a beer."

THEY DRANK BEER AND TALKED FOR AN HOUR BEFORE BEARD asked, "What brings you down here?"

"Looking for an old army buddy. I heard he'd been spending some time here."

"What's his name?"

"Mike Skeldon."

As Cahil had expected, Beard quizzed him for several minutes about the army. Finally Cahil said, "You know Mike?"

"Maybe, maybe not."

"Hey, forget it. If he don't wanna be found, no problem. I know how it goes."

Beard took a gulp of beer. "Why wouldn't he wanna be found?"

"Forget it."

"No. Why wouldn't he wanna be found?"

Cahil shrugged. "Couple months before the army booted him, we were bullshitting—talking about work on the outside. Mike figured his experience oughta be worth something to somebody."

"Damn right it should. Why'd they discharge him?"

Cahil put his mug on the counter, slid it away, and stood to leave. "I'm done getting quizzed. If you don't know why Mike got out, it ain't my business to be telling you."

Beard put a hand on his shoulder. "Okay, relax. Nobody's seen Mike for a few weeks. There's a woman, though—she might know. She's a stripper at Rhino's downtown."

"Is she working tonight?"

"Every night. She's got a habit to feed. Name's Candy something . . . Candy Kane, that's it."

Cahil nodded. "Thanks, maybe I'll look her up."

23

Jakarta, Island of Java, Indonesia

The plane's approach to Soekarno-Hatta International Airport gave Tanner a breathtaking view of the Pulau Seribu, or the Thousand Islands, an archipelago that stretches from Jakarta into the Java Sea. From this altitude the islands were mere emerald dots against the blue ocean.

Protected by Indonesia's Ministry of Conservation, the 250 islands of the Pulau Seribu are mostly uninhabited except for a handful of resorts, ecological preserves, and tourist attractions such as old pirate fortresses and diving caves. Those islands that are privately owned serve as luxury retreats for Indonesia's rich and famous.

The plane banked again, revealing Jakarta proper and the Kota, or the Old Batavia quarter. All cobblestone, canals, and Dutch architecture, the Kota was a throwback to Java's imperialist period when the English, Portuguese, and Dutch all fought for control of the Orient's trade routes.

To most, the name Jakarta conjures up images of colonial empires, Oriental warlords, and pirates, not an urban sprawl with nearly twelve million inhabitants rivaling that of New York City's.

Tanner had three days. Whatever plan he settled on, he wanted to be ready as soon as the delegation arrived. That's when Soong's security detail would be at its most vulnerable: Unfamiliar territory, arrangements to be finalized or adjusted, local authorities to deal with. . . . Surprise was going to be his greatest, and perhaps only, advantage.

The twenty-mile taxi ride into the city took nearly an hour as the driver negotiated traffic on the congested expressway. Every few minutes he would turn and offer a sheepish smile. "So sorry. Traffic bad this time of day."

"Is there a time when it's not bad?"

"Truly, no. Many people on Java. Almost one hundred twenty million." His "million" came out "mellon." "Which hotel, sir?"

"I haven't decided yet," Tanner lied. In fact, Oaken had rented him a bungalow in the foothills below Bongor outside Jakarta. "You can just drop me in the Kota."

"You will have trouble finding lodgings. Big conference soon."

"I have friends I can stay with in Kebayoran if I need to." Kebayoran, also known as Bloc M, was home to Jakarta's mostly British expatriate community. It was another lie, of course, borne of old habit. However unlikely the possibility, he didn't want to leave a trail for anyone to follow.

The driver stopped outside the Fatahillah Cafe. Tanner climbed out, waited for the taxi to disappear down the street, then walked four blocks to a Hertz office where he rented an old VW bus for a week and asked the agent to leave it parked at the Tanah Abang Railway Station.

Next he caught a taxi to the harbor and made another rental, this one an old Honda Express moped. He stuffed his duffle into the rear basket then took off down Martadinata, following the coastline east out of the city. He drove for fifteen minutes until Jakarta proper was behind him. To his left lay the Java Sea; to his right, the island's mist-shrouded jungles.

After another ten minutes he turned off the highway onto a narrow gravel road. A few more turns took him to a bungalow with a red, tiled roof and hibiscus bushes shading the porch. As advertised, he found a key under the mat.

The interior was all white stucco and wicker. He dropped his duffle onto the couch and wandered into the kitchen. On the table was a note: "Mate: Bungalow's yours as long as you need it. Fridge is stocked. Enjoy."

Tanner smiled: *Just another friendly contact in the Walter Oaken Secret Friends Network.* Judging from the salutation, the owner was probably a Brit or Aussie expat.

He opened the fridge, found a beer, then headed for the shower.

FREE OF THE SWEAT AND GRIME OF THE FLIGHT, HE CLIMBED aboard the Honda and headed back into Jakarta, where he pulled off Martadinata and drove until he found the Batavia Café. He locked the Honda to a bicycle rack and started walking.

His destination was the Sunda Kalepa, the city's old docks. A full-service harbor serving Java's outer islands, the Sunda Kalepa is also home to the Jakarta's fleet of Makassar schooners—or *pinisi*—with their brightly painted hulls and rainbow sails.

Briggs paid his entrance fee at the Bahari Museum and walked onto the docks.

The air was thick with the smell of tar. Old men in rowboats glided along the pier, waiting to be hailed by tourists, and children darted about, pointing at the *pinisi* and waving to the crewmen, many of whom displayed ancient Javanese tribal tattoos on their faces.

The Kalepa's piers were a maze of slips and turnarounds, so it took him several minutes to find the right path, then followed it away from the tourist area. At the end, he found a man coiling rope in the stern of a red-and-yellow skiff.

"What's the farthest you've been out?" Tanner asked.

The man squinted at him. "Eh?"

Tanner repeated the question.

The man frowned for a moment. "Oh . . . yes. Let's see. . . . I have tennis elbow; not very far."

Good answer. "You're Arroya?"

"I am. Do I dare ask your name?"

"Briggs." If Mason's people were wrong about this man, he had a lot more to worry about than using his real name.

Arroya stood up and hopped onto the dock, a surprising feat, Tanner thought, given his physique. Barely five feet tall and pushing two hundred pounds, Arroya looked like a Javanese version of the Buddha, right down to the wispy moustache and cherubic smile.

Arroya extended his hand. "Welcome to Java. Care for a tour of the Kalepa?"

HE ROWED THEM INTO THE HARBOR, THEN TOSSED A CINDER block anchor over the side. He handed Tanner a fishing pole, tied a sinker to the line, and plopped it into the water. "For cover," he explained.

"Do we need cover?"

"Better safe than sorry."

"Fair enough. How long have you been—"

"Working with your government?"

"Yes."

"Seven years. For the last decade the Chinese have grown stronger and stronger here. Many people—people who still consider themselves Javanese and not Indonesian—do not like it. Since my government seems only too happy to sell our country to the PRC, I long ago decided I must do what I can, so I made myself known in the British expat community here."

"You work for them as well?"

"So long as I'm not asked to do anything against my people, I am happy to help where I can."

"Which brings us to why I'm here."

Arroya smiled. "Indeed it does."

"I'll do my best to use you as little as possible, but I may need a few favors."

"Do not worry about that. I am very good at what I do. No one looks twice at me. Besides," Arroya said, patting his ample belly. "I've cultivated a rather harmless image."

Tanner laughed. "That you have."

"So, how can I help?"

Tanner had to make a decision: Tell Arroya everything, the partial truth, or a lie—or a mixture of all three? If he followed strict tradecraft it would be the latter, which would make it harder for anyone—Arroya included—to discern Tanner's purpose here. On the other hand, Arroya's knowledge of the islands would be invaluable. Tanner went with his gut.

"It's pretty simple," he said. "I'm here to help one of the Chinese delegation defect."

Arroya chortled. "Oh, yes, very simple."

"Perhaps 'straightforward' is a better word."

"Semantics won't help you here, my friend. What you're planning will be very difficult."

" 'Very difficult' doesn't worry me."

Arroya smiled. "Something tells me 'impossible' would worry you only a little more."

"What can you tell me about the delegation?"

"Security is very heavy. Rumor is that there is already an advance team here. The delegation will be staying at the Hotel Melia. I have a friend who is a busboy there. He's seen no less than two dozen Chinese security men in the hotel."

"Is everyone from the delegation staying there?" Briggs asked.

"Officially, yes, but there is another rumor. Earlier this week, the advance team rented a fishing boat; they've been out to Pulau Sekong several times."

"That's one of the Thousand Islands?"

"Yes. Privately owned. You have seen James Bond—*The Man with the Golden Gun*? You remember the villain's private island—the crescent beach, the jungle, the rock spires?"

"Yes."

"Rumor is, Pulau Sekong is where they filmed that."

"No kidding."

"No kidding. It is owned by Somon Trulau. Very rich importer, friendly with Beijing. I suspect he's offered them use of the island. The man you have come for . . . is he someone worth guarding?"

"Yes."

"Then Pulau Sekong would be a good place for him."

It made sense, Tanner decided. Letting Soong out of the country was a risk; separating him from the delegation and assigning him a private detail was one way to lessen that risk. Whether Soong was truly their prisoner or not, the less he was exposed, the better.

"First things first," Tanner said. "We need to confirm the man I've come for will be staying on Pulau Sekong, and how they plan to get back and forth."

"I can do that," said Arroya. "What else?"

"Find a boat. I want to see this island."

Arroya nodded. "I know just the man."

24

Asheville, North Carolina

Armed with Beard's description of Candy Kane's car—a white Trans Am with two candy-cane decals on the windshield—Cahil drove downtown and found Rhino's strip club. He walked inside, found a stool at the bar, and ordered a beer.

Candy, an early twenties platinum blond with impossibly large breasts, was in the process of removing her red-and-white striped cowboy boots. She strutted about the stage, robotically grinding her hips to a rock-a-billy version of "Baby Got Back." Her eyes were vacuous black holes. *Meth or crack,* Cahil thought.

The crowd cheered and waved bills at her, and she moved down the line.

"She's popular, huh?" Cahil said to the bartender.

"She'd be popular with a pumpkin on her head."

Cahil laughed. "How late is she here? I got a buddy from Durham who wants to see her act."

"She'll be here to close. After that, it depends on who's got the cash."

"That right?"

"Yep. You interested?"

"Nah, but maybe my friend. I'll be back."

Outside, he followed the alley behind Rhino's until he came to a small parking lot he assumed was for employees. Candy's car was parked in the far slot. He memorized the license plate, returned to his truck, and dialed his cell phone.

Oaken picked up on the second ring. "Hey, Bear, where are you?"

"Asheville, outside a bar called Rhino's."

"How nice for you. What's up?"

"I need a QMR." In police jargon, QMR stands for Query Motor Vehicle Registration. Cahil recited the plate number. "She's Sheldon's girlfriend, I think."

"Give me five minutes, I'll call you back."

Three minutes later Cahil's phone chirped. "Hello?"

"The plate belongs to a ninety-six Trans Am, owner is a Amanda Johnson," Oaken said.

"Also know as Candy Kane, exotic dancer at large."

"Very catchy. Please tell me the candy cane thing isn't part of her act."

"I didn't stay long enough to find out. You got an address?"

THE ADDRESS TOOK HIM TO A TRAILER PARK IN A TOWN NAMED Stony Knob, north of Asheville. The park was deserted except for five trailers, most of which looked abandoned. Darkened streetlights lined the dirt road. He found Candy/Amanda's trailer and got out.

Penlight in hand, he walked to the front door and repeated the procedure he'd used at Blanton Crossing. Once the door popped open, he stepped inside and shut it behind him. The smell of cigarettes and rotting food filled his nostrils.

"Anybody home?" he called. "Hey Mike, Amanda, you guys around?"

No answer.

He clicked on his penlight.

The trailer was a disaster: Clothes strewn about, empty pizza boxes and food cartons, garbage cans brimming with trash. The kitchen sink overflowed with dirty dishes, above which hovered a cloud of flies. Two recliners patched with duct tape and a rickety card table were the only furniture. On the bedroom floor he found a grimy mattress; beside it lay a half-empty twenty-four-pack of condoms.

"Christ Almighty," Cahil muttered, and got to work.

HIS SEARCH LEFT HIM WISHING FOR A DECONTAMINATION shower. Worse still, he'd turned up nothing he could connect to Skeldon. There were dozens of men's names and phone numbers scrawled on slips of paper and matchbook covers, but he assumed they were part of Candy's rolo-trick.

On impulse, he picked up the cordless phone and punched the Talk button. Instead of a steady dial tone, he got a punctuated one: She had voice mail. Doubting that Candy would have enough brain cells to remember her PIN, he rifled through the drawers, scanning notepads and scraps of paper until he found a Post-it note with "Phone: 9934" written on it. He punched in the code.

Candy had three messages. The first sounded like a former client trying to arrange a date; the second was her mother. The third, which had been left just an hour earlier, sounded promising:

> "Mike, this is Lamar. Hey, I left you a couple messages last week, don't know if you got 'em. . . . Wondering maybe, y'know, if you got my money yet. Gimme a call. You know the number."

"I don't," Cahil muttered. He punched star sixty-nine, retrieved Lamar's number, and jotted it down. He flipped open his cell phone and dialed the number. After five rings a voice said, "Yeah, what?"

"This Lamar?" Cahil said.

"Yeah, who's this?"

"My name's John. I'm a friend of Mike's; he asked me to give you a call."

Lamar coughed. "Yeah? Where's Mike? I mean, is there something—"

"Nothing's wrong. Mike's out of town. You guys have some business to clear up, he said. He asked me to float you some cash until he gets back."

"Oh, man, that would be great."

"Where are you?"

Lamar gave him directions to his house in southeast Asheville.

"Twenty minutes," Cahil said.

THE HOUSE WAS INDISTINGUISHABLE FROM ITS NEIGHBORS: A whitewashed box home with a postage-stamp yard fronted by a chain-link fence. Cahil parked beside the mailbox labeled, "L. Sampson," then pushed through the gate and walked to the porch.

Before he could knock, the door jerked open. He reached behind him, palm on the butt of the Browning. A man in a tattered gray robe stood in the doorway. He was in his early forties with receding brown hair and wide, red-rimmed eyes. His hand trembled on the doorjamb.

Alcoholic, Bear thought. Mike Skeldon certainly knew how to pick his friends.

"You Jim?" Sampson asked.

"John."

"Yeah, right. Umm . . . come on in."

The living room was carpeted in a pumpkin-orange shag that hurt Cahil's eyes. A black-and-white TV flickered in front of a lime green couch. Sampson plopped down. "So. . . ."

Up until this point, Cahil had been winging it, following the trail where it took him. Now he had to choose carefully. How much did Sampson know about Skeldon's work, and what was the best way to go at him? Judging from Lamar's demeanor, he was a timid drunk with an opportunistic streak a mile wide. "We got a problem, Lamar."

"What?" Sampson squeaked. "What problem?"

"Mike thinks you're holding back on him."

Sampson stood up. "That's crap! I did everything he asked! I gave him everything."

Cahil growled, "Sit down."

Lamar sat back down. "Hey, what about the other guy?"

"What other guy?"

"The other guy I hooked Mike up with! If anybody's holding out, maybe it's him."

"Give me his name."

"Stan Kycek!"

"Who is he, what's he do?"

"I used to work with him; he's a demolition guy—used to work mines."

What's this? Cahil wondered. "Lamar, what do you do for a living?"

"I work in a grocery store. I'm a bagger."

"Before that."

"I worked for the USGS."

USGS . . . ? It took a moment for Cahil to place the acronym: United States Geological Survey. "You're a geologist?"

"Was."

"And Kycek?"

"Him, too. Dammit, I gave Mike everything! Oh, man. . . ."

"You're sure you didn't keep a little something for insurance?"

Sampson looked at him, puzzled, and Cahil thought, *Wrong path.*

"He said that?" Sampson said.

"He wants to be sure. The people he's working for aren't exactly the forgiving sort."

"Hey, I did my part."

"Lamar, what do you say I tie you up, toss your place, and see what I find? If you've got something, you'd best tell me now. If you make me look for it, I'm not gonna be happy."

Sampson stared at his trembling hands. "Jesus, Jesus. . . ."

Cahil felt sorry for the man, but there was no other way to do this. "Time's up, Lamar."

"Okay, okay, listen, I wasn't gonna do nothing with it. I just wanted to make sure Mike paid me, that's all." Sampson got up and walked into the next room, where a light clicked on.

Cahil rested his hand on the Browning. "What're you doing, Lamar?"

"Just a second . . . hold on."

He returned carrying a shoe box. Cahil could see papers sticking out from under the lid. Sampson handed over the box. "I made copies of everything. But like I said, I wasn't gonna use it. Talk to Mike, huh? Make him understand?"

"Sure," Cahil said.

"Uh, you think maybe you could . . . you know. I need some groceries and stuff."

Cahil pulled a pair of hundred dollar bills from his wallet. "I'll talk to Mike about the rest."

Sampson smiled nervously. "Yeah?"

"We'll see." Cahil turned to leave, then stopped and nodded toward the box. "What is all this?"

"The survey data. You know . . . all the stuff we collected."

"You and Mike and this Kycek."

"Kycek wasn't there. I got no idea what Mike's doing with him."

"Survey of what? From where?"

Lamar barked out a laugh. "The asshole of the world, man: Siberia."

CAHIL GOT KYCEK'S ADDRESS FROM SAMPSON, THEN WARNED him to stay off the phone, and drove to Kycek's apartment on Olny Road. Deciding he'd worn out his "friend of Mike's" routine, Cahil walked to the front door and pounded on the door. "Open up!"

Thirty seconds later the door opened, revealing a man in his mid-forties with a beard, a potbelly, and sunken eyes. *Soft,* Cahil thought. Like Sampson, Kycek was another man beaten by life.

Cahil flashed a counterfeit FBI badge at him. "Stan Kycek?"

"Uh, yeah?"

"FBI, Mr. Kycek, we need to talk."

Wide-eyed, Kycek let him in. "What's . . . what's going on?"

"Do you know a man named Mike Skeldon?"

"Uh, no, I don't think so."

"That's lie number one, Mr. Kycek. One more and you're going to jail."

Kycek hesitated. "I know him through a friend."

"Lamar Sampson."

"Yeah. I've never actually met Skeldon."

"The man hired you, and you're telling me you've never met him?"

"He didn't hire—"

"Careful," Cahil warned.

"What I meant is, he hasn't paid me yet. What's going on? I don't want no trouble. Lamar said Skeldon needed a good blaster, and I'm . . . between work right now, so I figured, why not?"

"I'll tell you why not."

Speaking off the cuff, Cahil rattled off a bogus laundry list of Skeldon's crimes: illegal possession and transport of explosives; the manufacture of methamphetamine with intent to distribute; and finally, suspicion of conspiracy to commit murder. "Murder!" Kycek cried. "Christ almighty!"

"You hired on with the wrong guy, Stan."

"I told you, I haven't taken a dime from him. I've never even seen the guy."

"Then what's the plan? Where're you supposed to meet? What's he want you to do?"

"I have no idea. I'm supposed to sit by my phone. He said he'd call between Tuesday and Thursday next week with the details."

"That's it?"

"That's it, I swear. He told me to be ready to travel, but nothing else. Listen, I don't want no trouble. Whatever he's got going on, I'm out."

Cahil stared hard at him. "Problem is, you're already involved. I think we can help each other, though. Would you be willing to work with us?"

"Doing what?"

"Pack a bag," Bear ordered. "I'll explain on the way."

After I figure out what all this means, he thought.

25

Clinton Correctional Facility, New York

WITH HIS FAMILY TUCKED AWAY IN A SAFE HOUSE, LATHAM decided it was time to shake things up.

Armed with a little creative documentation from Oaken, he took the noon shuttle to New York, then drove north to Dannemora, where he was escorted to the interview room. Minutes later Hong Cho was escorted in.

As before, the diminutive Cho wore an orange jumpsuit and was manacled hand and foot. He shuffled forward, sat down, and stared impassively at Latham as the guard cuffed his hands to the table.

Once the guard was gone, Latham said, "Hong, have you ever wondered how we caught you?"

"You didn't catch me."

"I'll rephrase: Didn't you ever find it curious that a beat cop just happened to be walking by the apartment of the people you were trying to murder? Lucky timing, wasn't it?"

Cho said nothing.

"Or how quickly backup was on the scene? Didn't that ever make you think?"

Cho's eyes narrowed for a moment, then went blank again. "No."

"Sure it did," Latham said. "Since I know you're too proud to ask, I'll tell you. We caught you because we knew who we were looking for. We'd had you under surveillance for weeks."

"You're lying."

"We knew who you were, and how to look for you. We had profiles of where you were likely to hide, how you'd react to given situations, how you were trained—everything."

"That's impossible."

Latham opened his briefcase, pulled out a piece of paper, and slid it across to Cho. "Do you recognize the letterhead?" Charlie asked. "It's from the *Guoanbu*—your former colleagues. They burned you. All your moonlighting for mobsters. . . . You were an embarrassment."

As if handling a snake, Cho studied the letter. Latham could see his jaw bunching. Cho lashed out, shoving the paper off the table. "This is a trick!" he shouted.

"It's called politics, Hong. Your government found out about your side profession and they knew we'd eventually catch you, so they decided to cut their losses. Instead of facing the humiliation of having an active *Guoanbu* agent on trial for murder, they sacrificed you."

"They wouldn't do that."

"Why not? Are you really that naive? You were a liability, plain and simple; they did what was necessary. Unfortunately for you, that means you get to spend the rest of your life here."

With a growl, Cho tried to lunge to his feet, but the manacles jerked him back. "Get out!"

Latham collected the letter from the floor and walked to the door. "These are the people you're protecting, Hong. You're here because of them. Think about it."

"Get out!"

• • •

Back in his car, Latham dialed his cell phone. When Randall picked up, he said, "It's done."

"Did he buy it?"

"If he didn't, he's a hell of an actor. How's our girl?"

"She just got home from work. I'll let you know the minute she moves—if she moves, that is. Janet and Tommy are standing by if we need them."

"Keep your fingers crossed. If Hong's as pissed as I think he is, we won't have long to wait."

He spent the next ninety minutes parked in the prison parking lot listening to an oldies station before his cell phone trilled. "Latham."

"Agent Latham, it's Warden Fenstrom. Cho just asked to make a telephone call."

"Good. Put up a stink, tell him it's past telephone hours, then finally give in."

"Gotcha. I'll call you back." He called back fifteen minutes later: "You guessed it. His call went to the same woman. Mary—"

"Tsang."

"Right. We're not allowed to tape or listen in, but I had a guard keep an eye on Cho. The guard says he didn't look too happy. What the hell did you say to him?"

"I told him he'd just run out of friends," Latham replied. "Thanks, Warden, I appreciate it."

"My pleasure."

Latham hung up and called Randall. "He went for it. Keep your eyes peeled."

"Will do. You're coming back?"

"I'll be on the next flight."

Latham was sitting in the passenger lounge at Kennedy waiting for his boarding call when Randall called. "About an hour ago she went for a jog," he reported. "She went about a mile, then stopped at a Seven-Eleven and used the payphone."

"And?"

"I had Oaken get the dump from the phone. She called the *Post*, Charlie. The classifieds."

The Post*?* Latham thought. Then it hit him: "She's making contact," he said. "Have Walt start working on that ad. I want to see it."

AS LATHAM WAS LANDING IN D.C., OAKEN WAS PLACING HIS own call to the *Post*. He took out an innocuous ad—a lawn mower for sale—then jotted down the order number the clerk gave him, then hung up and nodded to Janet Paschel, who then placed her own call.

Posing as Tsang, she told the clerk she might have made a mistake in her ad and asked that it be read back to her. The clerk asked for her order number. Praying that only a few ads, if any, had been placed between Tsang's call and Oaken's, she recited a number a few digits lower than Oaken's.

"Sorry, but I'm not sure about the last couple digits," Janet said. "Sometimes I can't read my own writing."

"That's okay," the clerk said. "Let's see . . . here it is: 'Adrian, please accept my condolences on your loss. Thinking of you, Harmon.' Is that what you wanted?"

"It's perfect. How did you spell Harmon?" The clerk spelled it out. "Yeah, that's right. Thanks very much; I appreciate your help."

Paschel hung up and handed Oaken the note. "Mean anything to you?"

"Nope. Maybe it will to Charlie."

26

Jakarta

It took Arroya mere hours to probe his contacts and confirm that not only would Soong and his bodyguards be staying on Pulau Sekong, but that Trulau had loaned his yacht to the delegation for the week. "That didn't take long," Tanner said.

"I have many friends," Arroya replied and patted his belly. "Not to mention all the restaurateurs I keep in business."

Tanner laughed. "Now, let's see about Pulau Sekong." The man Arroya felt could help was a distant cousin named Sugeng. Sugeng, he said, was something of an adventurer—part smuggler, part charter captain, and part Robin Hood-esque pirate. "Can I trust him?" Briggs asked.

"Can you pay him?" Arroya countered.

"Yes."

"Then yes, you can trust him. But," he added, "you might want to put some fear into him. If he thinks he can take advantage of you, he will do so."

They found Sugeng at his slip in the Kalepa, polishing the handrails of his sixty-six-foot cabin cruiser. The *Tija* was sleek and white, with a sharp bow and a swept-back pyramidal superstructure covered in charcoal tinted glass.

The Indonesian smuggling trade must be lucrative, Tanner decided.

"Sugeng!" Arroya called.

Sugeng looked up. He was Arroya's complete opposite: tall and sinewy, with a full head of wavy black hair. "Ah, cousin, how are you! Come aboard!"

They stepped onto the afterdeck and Arroya introduced Tanner. "A good friend of mine, Sugeng. He'd like to hire you."

Sugeng grinned, displaying a gold tooth. "At your service. As luck would have it, I'm free."

"Glad to hear it. With a boat like this, I'm surprised you weren't hired by the Chinese."

"Ah, well, Trulau has his own yacht, you see, and he is the delegation's unofficial host during their stay. I considered sabotage, but decided against it."

Though he said it with a smile, Tanner got the impression he wasn't kidding. "Why's that?"

"Trulau is an unforgiving sort. If he found out I damaged that barge of his, my business might suffer. And business, my friend, is everything."

"If Trulau's yacht weren't available, yours would be the next logical choice?"

"Oh, yes. Next to his there is no finer vessel in Java than the *Tija*. So, how can I be of service?"

"How much for the day?"

Sugeng frowned. "Oh, is that all you want? One day? Perhaps you might be more comfortable with a more modest vessel."

"If I like what I see, I may want to hire you for the week."

"You have cash?"

"Yes."

"American?"

"If you prefer."

"Five hundred for the afternoon."

Tanner reached into his pocket, peeled off five one-hundred-dollar bills, and handed them across. "Since you're Arroya's cousin, I'll overlook the fact you're charging me double the going rate. If we continue to do business, I trust you'll rethink your fees."

Sugeng locked eyes with him, then grinned. "Of course. Anything for a friend."

ONCE THEY CLEARED THE HARBOR'S BREAKWATER AND WERE away from shore, the ocean became glassy and calm. The sky was an unblemished blue save for a few cotton ball clouds. After an hour's sailing, Sugeng called from the flying bridge, "Pulau Sekong dead off the starboard bow."

From his spot on the foredeck, Tanner raised his binoculars. Five miles distant he could see Solon Trulau's island, two great spires of jagged rock joined together by a saddle of rain forest. Nestled between the spires was a cove surrounded by the churned white line of a coral reef. Arroya was right: If this wasn't the island from the Bond movie, it was a close match. The only thing missing was Herve Villachez trotting down the beach carrying a martini on a silver platter.

Arroya said, "Trulau's estate is halfway up the slope, near the spire."

Briggs scanned up the mountainside until he spotted the white, plantation-style mansion. "That must have been quite a task to build," he said.

"He has the money. There's a helicopter pad at the top of the access road."

That could complicate things, Tanner thought. Timing and stealth were going to be vital. If he failed to grab Soong without being detected, their escape would be short-lived. Movie portrayals notwithstanding, trying to outrun a helicopter at sea was a losing proposition.

"Sugeng," Tanner called, "how close can we get without attracting attention?"

"A mile, no closer. Throw out a couple fishing lines. We'll troll for mahi."

They spent the next hour circling the shore as Tanner studied the terrain, picking out promising entry and exit points and working through scenarios until he had settled on a rough plan. Much would depend on what he saw when the delegation arrived, but he felt better now having a direction.

He ordered Sugeng to head for home.

Reeling in his line, Arroya asked, "What do you think? It can be done?"

It was feasible, Tanner knew, but as with most operations, the gap between feasibility and success was wide indeed. Everything can work flawlessly on paper, only to go to hell once you were on the ground. *Then again,* he thought, *there was something to be said for positive thinking.*

"It can be done," Tanner answered.

THE FIRST STEP WAS TO GET SUGENG HIRED. TRULAU'S YACHT had to become unavailable.

As the afternoon began to wind down, Tanner sat on the dock beside Arroya's rowboat, dangling his feet in the water and brainstorming. By dusk he'd settled on a plan. He jotted down a list of what he needed and gave it to Arroya, who looked it over. "I can have it within the hour."

"Thanks. After you're done, pick up Segung and go out to dinner. Make sure you're noticed."

"Why?"

"Alibi. Stay out until midnight, then meet me back here."

TRULAU'S YACHT WAS ANCHORED A HALF MILE SOUTH OF THE Sekunda Kalepa in the middle of the Ancol Marina. Tanner studied it through his binoculars until night had fully fallen and the marina's traffic tapered off. Light clouds had closed over Jakarta, partially obscuring the moon and dulling the reflection of the city's lights on the water.

He packed his materials into the watertight rucksack Arroya had purchased, donned the swim fins and mask, slipped into the water, and started stroking toward the marina.

WHEN HE WAS A HUNDRED YARDS OFF THE YACHT'S PORT SIDE, he stopped. Under the glow of the amber deck lights he counted two guards, one stationed on the fantail, the second roving between the forecastle and afterdeck. He watched for another ten minutes until certain the rover wasn't varying his route or timing, then took a breath, ducked under, and stroked toward the bow.

The white keel slowly emerged from the gloom before him. He groped until his fingers found the anchor chain, then surfaced beneath the bow. He went still and listened.

A few seconds passed before he heard the click of footsteps on the deck above. The footsteps grew louder, then stopped. Feet shuffling. He smelled cigarette smoke. After a minute, the guard turned and walked off.

Moving fast now, he shed his mask and fins, hooked them to the anchor chain, then shimmied up the chain, chinned himself level with the deck, and crawled under the railing. The deck was empty. From the ruck he withdrew a towel, dried himself off and mopped up any telltale puddles from the deck.

He sprinted across the forecastle to the cabin, opened the sliding-glass door, and slipped inside.

He was in the main salon: Furnished with walnut captain's chairs, leather couches, and thick shag carpet, the space oozed luxury. Everything was dark and quiet except for the hiss of the air-conditioning. Briggs felt goose bumps on his skin.

Outside, a guard strolled past the cabin windows and disappeared onto the foredeck.

Tanner crossed the cabin and trotted down the aft companionway steps.

Ahead lay five doors, two on each side of the passageway and one at the end. *Engine spaces,* Tanner guessed. As he neared the door he could hear the hum of machinery. He eased it open. The hum was louder now. A set of metal stairs led downward. At the bottom he found a long catwalk bordered by a pair of diesel engines. Tucked into the corner beside the starboard engine he found what he'd come for: the main generator.

He knelt down, unzipped the rucksack, and withdrew a wax ball about the size of an apricot. Filled with a mixture of common household cleaners, the ball was not only the fruition of Arroya's shopping list, but also a crude "binary bomb" designed to detonate when the fuel in the generator's tank eroded the wax and reached the core.

While the explosion would not be enough to sink the yacht, it would certainly destroy the generator and perhaps the starboard engine as well. With no mechanical bomb components to be found in the wake of the explosion, the yacht's demise would hopefully be written off as an act of God.

Tanner dropped the ball into the tank, then retraced his steps into the main salon, where he waited until the guard had passed by and disappeared from view. Briggs opened the door, sprinted to the bow, lowered himself over the side and back into the water.

ARROYA WAS SITTING IN HIS ROWBOAT UNDER THE GLOW OF A lantern when Tanner swam up. Startled, Arroya clicked on a flashlight and shined it in Tanner's face. "Oh, good lord, it's you."

"Give me a hand."

Arroya took his fins and mask then helped him aboard. "Everything went well?"

"So far. Now we find out how good my chemistry is. Where's Sugeng?"

"Out dancing. He met a woman. I doubt he'll be going home tonight." Arroya opened a cooler at his feet. "I thought you might be hungry, so I brought you leftovers: *Capi cai udang*."

"Pardon me?" Tanner said, accepting the carton.

"It's a mix of fried rice, vegetables, and shrimp. Very good. Cold beer, too."

Tanner took a gulp of beer and sighed. "Thanks."

They talked and ate until Tanner got drowsy. He settled back and drifted off to sleep.

Some time later they were jolted awake by what sounded like distant thunder echoing across the water. Tanner sat up and grabbed the binoculars and focused them on Trulau's yacht. Smoke was pouring through a jagged tear in the starboard side.

"Good lord," Arroya murmured. "Do you see the guards?"

"No, I—wait. There they are. They're okay."

Arroya chuckled. "Goodness, Briggs, you put a hole in Trulau's boat."

Tanner shrugged. "Too much pepper in the recipe."

"Indeed. Now what?"

"Now we wait and pray Sugeng gets a job offer tomorrow."

27

White House

"BOTTOM LINE, DICK: HOW'S IRKUTSK GOING TO AFFECT THE election?" asked President Martin.

Flip a coin, the DCI thought. When it came to elections in Russia, projection polls could be dead-on one day and out the window the next, which had as much to do with the multitude of pollsters in Moscow's circuslike political scene as it did with the vagaries of public opinion.

"It's still ten days away, Mr. President," Mason replied. "A lot can happen. Initially, however, this can only help Bulganin. He was speaking out before the Kremlin even acknowledged the incident. In fact, given Bulganin's tone, I wouldn't be surprised if he tries to ride this all the way to election day."

"How?"

"Speeches, news conferences, public rallies, special editions of the RPP newsletter."

"Anything from the Kremlin?"

"They're being drowned out. From a PR perspective, they're in the unenviable position of having to not only deal with the problem, but also refute Bulganin's accusations. The public is swarming to his version of events—true or not."

"I agree," said Bousikaris. "Regardless of why, Federation soldiers gunned down over fifty unarmed citizens. There's no making that disappear, and the current president is going to have a tough time taking the high ground away from Bulganin."

"Have we learned anything more about this guy? He can't be that big a mystery."

"Bulganin is an icon, Mr. President—a representation of what Russian voters think is missing from their government," Mason said. "That's Nochenko's touch; he knows what moves the people."

"Are you trying to tell us there's nothing to Bulganin?" Bousikaris asked. "I don't buy that."

"There's something to him—probably quite a lot, in fact. The rub is, what exactly?"

It was the same question many people had asked about Hitler in the 1930s, and compared to Bulganin, Hitler was downright chatty. By the time the Wehrmacht invaded Poland, Hitler had told so many lies his neighbors didn't know which way was up. If anything, Bulganin's PR skills were more in line with those of Stalin: Say nothing, and when pressed for details, say less.

"In fact, it's Bulganin's caginess that's making a lot of the Federation's neighbors nervous," Mason continued. "Every time he gains ground in the polls, the EC markets twitch."

Martin's intercom buzzed. Bousikaris picked it up, listened, then hung up. "Call for you, Dick."

Mason walked to the coffee table and picked up the phone. "Mason. Yes, Sylvia. . . ." Mason listened for several minutes, asked a few questions, then hung up.

"What is it?" asked Martin.

"There's been an accident in Russia. The cause is still unclear, but it sounds like the reactor in Chita vented some gas into the atmosphere."

"Where's Chita?"

"About nine hundred miles east of Irkutsk and three hundred miles north of the Chinese border."

"Any word on a cause or severity?"

"No. Same with casualty figures, but we should be ready for the worst. It was a MOX reactor."

Martin said, "Explain."

"MOX is short for mixed-oxide," Mason replied. "A lot of European and Asian countries are using it to dispose of old radioactive cores—called pits—from disassembled nuclear weapons. The process takes the cores, turns them into a powder, then mixes that with standard feedstock uranium.

"The stock burns efficiently, but the problem is, plutonium is just about the deadliest toxin on earth. A single grain inhaled into the lungs can cause cancer; worse still, the half-life of the stuff is twenty-four thousand years. If it gets into the high atmosphere. . . . Well, you can imagine."

"God almighty," Martin said.

"First thing's first, we need to confirm all this, then we need to find out what Moscow's doing. We'll want to put Energy on alert, have them prep some NEST teams," Mason said, referring to Nuclear Emergency Search Team. "Even if Moscow doesn't ask for help, we need to be ready to offer it—hell, *force* it on them, if necessary. This is not a time for piecemeal measures. It wouldn't take much of that stuff to kill a whole lot of people."

"Be specific, Dick."

"That's a question best answered by Energy. It's going to depend on the size of the leak, the type of gas vented, weather conditions. . . . We have very few facts right now."

"Then get some," Martin said. "Quick."

THE CHINESE EMBASSY'S REQUEST FOR AN AUDIENCE REACHED Bousikaris's desk just hours after Mason's news. As the PRC had already called for a meeting of the UN Security Council, Bousikaris was unsurprised by the request, but was nonetheless wary as the ambassador was escorted into the Oval Office. Their first and only meeting with the ambassador had proven—*was proving*—costly.

Ever the politician, Martin walked from behind his desk to greet the ambassador. "Mr. Ambassador, a pleasure to see you again. The circumstances are unfortunate, of course, but such is life."

"Indeed it is, Mr. President. I thought it important we talk before the Security Council meeting."

"Certainly. Please sit down. We're still gathering facts about the accident, so we don't have much more information than a few hours ago."

"Nor do we. Which brings me to the reason for my visit. As you may know, there is a significant Chinese diaspora in southern Russia, much of which is located in and around Chita. With the Federation's blessing, our people emigrate to the Siberian republics to live and work with the native Russians there.

"Early reports indicate there are Chinese citizens employed at the reactor site in question. We think it's safe to say they will be among the casualties."

"We're sorry to hear that, Mr. Ambassador," Martin said. "We'll keep them in our prayers."

"Very kind. If only prayers were enough. You see, this is the fourth accident in eighteen months in which Chinese lives have been lost."

"Mr. Ambassador we don't yet know if any lives were lost—Chinese or otherwise."

"Given the type of reactor, I think it likely."

"Perhaps. You mentioned three other accidents. . . ."

"Two mine cave-ins and an ammunition depot explosion. In all, nearly twelve hundred Chinese citizens have lost their lives on Russian soil in the last two years."

Martin glanced at Bousikaris, who said, "We know of those incidents, but we weren't aware any of your citizens were involved."

"The ever-efficient Russian propaganda machine at work. You see, our citizens have become a valuable part of their workforce, accepting many jobs native Russians don't want."

Where's this going? Bousikaris thought. The ambassador was clearly leading up to something, and he doubted it was a lesson in international labor issues. "Are you saying the Russian government has conspired to cover up the deaths of over a thousand Chinese citizens?" he asked.

"I am."

"That's a harsh accusation. I hope your government exercises discretion before making any formal charges."

"Whether we level formal charges or not will depend entirely on the Security Council meeting. Of course, we will be demanding the Federation take steps to ensure the safety of our citizens. In Moscow's eyes they may be immigrants, but to us they are family—regardless of where they live."

"What kind of steps do you have in mind?" asked Martin.

"We'll leave that to them. Too many Chinese have died because of Russian negligence, and it is high time Moscow address the issue."

Now it's negligence, Bousikaris thought. In a court of law, charges of death by negligence and conspiracy add up to murder. The ambassador had just taken a very dangerous leap. Bousikaris could see the trap looming before them.

"I'm sure the Federation will do everything it can to help," President Martin said. "But, I have to ask: If, for whatever reason, their response doesn't satisfy your concerns, what will you do?"

"We're hopeful the Federation will be properly responsive."

"With respect, sir, that doesn't answer my question."

"Mr. President, I can tell you this: The People's Republic is committed to ensuring the welfare of its citizens. To this end, we will do whatever is necessary."

"Are there any measures you will not consider?"

"Given the seriousness of the situation, we will consider every option."

In failing to rule out military action, the ambassador had just put the option on the table.

"Again," the ambassador said, "We hope this will be settled in a reasonable manner. We have no reason to think otherwise."

Ask the question, Phil. . . .

"I assume your counterparts in Great Britain and France have paid similar visits to those country's respective leaders?"

"No."

"Then why have you come to us?"

"I've been instructed by my premier to make clear his hope that China can count on your help should this situation escalate any further."

There it is, Bousikaris thought. *They're coming back for a second drink at the well.* Diplomatic niceties aside, this was another ultimatum.

Martin said, "Define what you mean by 'help.' "

Ignoring protocol, the ambassador stood up, ending the meeting. "We'll let tomorrow take care of tomorrow, Mr. President. If we need to talk again, I'll contact Mr. Bousikaris for an appointment."

USS *Columbia*

Three days out of Pearl Harbor, *Columbia* was nearing the Kent Seamount, four hundred miles northeast of Midway Island. Captain Archie Kinsock was standing beside one of the blue-lit plotting tables when Jurens walked into the control room. Kinsock waved him over.

"We lost?" Sconi said with a smile.

"Not so far."

Jurens had gotten to know Kinsock over the last few days. Though often gruff, Kinsock knew his job and didn't take himself too seriously, which showed in not only how smoothly the boat ran, but in the demeanor of the crew.

"Where are we, Captain?" Jurens asked.

"Make it Archie when we're alone?"

Jurens nodded. "Call me Sconi."

"Interesting name."

"Born and raised in Wisconsin. We're nearly famous—not a whole lotta black dairy farmers in Wisconsin."

Kinsock laughed. "I can imagine. To answer your question, we're near Midway. From here we'll keep heading northeast until we reach the Intersection."

"What's that?"

"It's the nickname for the point where the Emperor and Chinook troughs meet south of the Aleutians." Kinsock flipped through several layers of charts until he found one showing the ocean floor. He pointed to a groove nestled inside what looked to Jurens like the spiny back of a giant lizard. "From there we head north to the Aleutian Trench."

"The big deep."

"Four miles and twenty thousand feet worth. Of course, we'd be long dead before we saw the bottom of that. Red paste in a can."

"Thanks for the imagery."

"Don't worry about it—you'd never feel a thing."

"Is this why you wanted to see me, Archie? A navigation lesson?"

"No. It's our orders. I'm not trying to talk you into anything, but I've got a few concerns."

"Such as?"

"Such as why I'm being told exactly where to launch my missiles."

"What do you mean 'exactly'?"

"Down to a GPS lock—a few meters either way."

This *was* unusual, Jurens admitted. While submarine commanders were usually given a LZ, or launch zone, the precise launch point was traditionally left up to the captain. Given how close *Columbia* would be to the Russian coast, a tight LZ made sense, but to micromanage the launch point like that . . . He understood Kinsock's worry.

"Any explanation offered?" Jurens asked.

"None."

"What do you want to do? It's your boat."

Kinsock sighed. "Play it by ear. Hell, tight LZ or not, it won't matter. From periscope to missile launch, we can be in and out in two minutes. Ain't nobody gonna sneak up on us in that short a time."

28

Jakarta

TANNER WAS PULLING THE VW INTO THE AIRPORT'S PARKING lot when he heard the whine of a jet engine overhead. He looked up in time to see the broad belly of the 747 cross the terminal buildings and disappear toward the runway. When it passed, he caught a glimpse of Chinese tail markings.

As he got out and started across the loading lane, a convoy of three limousines and two charter buses surrounded by motorcyclists from the Jakarta Police *Satgasus* traffic squad roared around the corner and stopped beside the curb.

Tanner walked into the terminal and took the escalator up to the second level, where he found a seat in the lounge overlooking the runways. Four commercial aircraft were taxiing about, either waiting for a gate or waiting for clearance to lift off.

After five minutes the Chinese 747 rolled into view following the hand signals of a ground director, who steered it toward a trio of gate slots. Tanner walked down the concourse to a café near the gate area, ordered a beer, and sat back to watch.

There was no mistaking which gate belonged to the Chinese delegation. A dozen POLRI—or Indonesian National Police—in dress-white uniforms stood at attention along the lounge's perimeter, while nearer the gate a cluster of city politicians milled about.

First off the jetway was an elderly Chinese man who Tanner assumed was the delegation ambassador. He shook hands with the politicians, smiled through the introductions and photographs, then allowed himself to be led away by a phalanx of POLRI and Chinese security men.

The rest of the delegation began disembarking. Tanner scanned faces, looking for Soong's until the last passenger was off the jetway and the delegation began moving down the concourse. Briggs felt a jolt of panic in his chest. Soong wasn't aboard.

Tanner ran through the possibilities: bad information from the CIA's Beijing contact; a last minute cancellation from the *Guoanbu*; Soong was coming via another route . . . or a trap.

No, the chances of that were—

He heard voices from the jetway. He turned.

Two beefy-looking Chinese men in charcoal suits stepped off the jetway, paused a moment to survey the lounge, then turned and nodded to someone behind them.

The man that came out next was short and stooped, with silver hair and a heavily creased face. The eyes, though, were exactly as Briggs remembered: sad and wise, but somehow good-humored, like those of a grandfather who'd seen the worst of life and yet made peace with it.

Tanner felt like a stone was sitting on his chest. *Han. . . .*

He'd imagined this moment a hundred times, and suddenly here it was. He felt the sting of tears and suddenly realized how tightly he'd been holding on to the hope of seeing Soong alive again.

He forced himself to wait five minutes, then took the escalator down to the concourse. He wandered into a gift shop and started browsing while keeping one eye fixed on the windows. At the curb, the last of the delegation was boarding the buses.

When the lead vehicle started moving, Tanner started walking. By the time he hit the doors, the rear guard of *Satgasus* motorcycles was pulling away.

An hour later he pulled into the Grand Hyatt's parking lot. Across Kebon Street he could see the last of the limousines pulling to a stop beneath the Melia's canopied turnaround. Engines roaring, the *Satgasus* riders raced ahead to seal off both entrances. Traffic on the Kebon slowed to a crawl. Horns started honking.

The VW's side door opened and Arroya got in. "Everything okay?"

Tanner nodded. "He's in the third limousine."

"I have good news and bad news. First, the good: Sugeng's yacht has been chartered by the Chinese. They've ordered him to be at Ancol Marina at six o'clock for inspection. The bad: Trulau has demanded a kickback from Sugeng's charter fee. Sugeng is demanding that you pay—"

"That's fine."

"It will be three thousand U.S., Briggs—"

"Tell him he gets half now, half when it's over."

"Very well. I rented our boat; it's at the Kalepa."

"Good. What else?"

"My bellhop friend says there will be a welcoming ceremony for the delegates from four until six, then cocktails and dinner until nine. If your friend is going to the island, it will likely be after that."

Tanner nodded. "Tell Sugeng to be ready between midnight and two."

ARROYA RAN THE BOAT AT FULL POWER UNTIL HE WAS THREE miles from Pulau Sekong, then doused the navigation lights and turned off the engine. On the forecastle, Tanner listened to the waves lap at the hull. The sky was bright and clear, with stars sprinkled across the blackness.

"Anything?" Arroya whispered.

"No. If anyone's interested in us, we'll know soon enough." However unlikely, it was possible Trulau and/or the Chinese would have boats patrolling the coastline. "Take down the canopy; if they've got a navigation radar worth a damn, they'll spot it."

Arroya rolled back the bridge's cover and tied it off. "How long do we wait?"

"Another half-hour should do it."

The time passed without incident. Briggs waved to the flying bridge. Arroya fired up the engines and throttled up. "The north side of the island?" he called.

"Yes. With any luck, there'll be less chance of being spotted there. I'm going to check the gear. Call me when we're a mile out."

TWENTY MINUTES LATER HE HEARD A DOUBLE STOMP ON THE cabin ceiling and stepped onto the deck.

Arroya said, "Two miles."

"Okay, shut of the engines and let her drift."

Arroya did so, then joined him on the afterdeck. Tanner sat down on the gunwale and donned his fins as Arroya slipped the rucksack's straps over his shoulders. "What's in here?"

"Blankets and dry clothes." If in fact Soong had spent the last twelve years in a *laogi*, his immune system was probably shot. "By the time we reach the raft, he's going to be cold and wet. Spending the night like that could kill him."

"Yes, I see. You care very much for him, yes?"

Tanner nodded. "I do."

"He's lucky to have a friend like you."

We'll see, Tanner thought.

Arroya walked into the cabin and returned with the patched-over zodiac raft they'd purchased earlier in the day. The accompanying trolling motor had been absurdly expensive, but its noiseless engine would be invaluable. The downside was the battery: At its full output, it would last only five hours. They'd need every bit of that to get away before Soong's watchers discovered his absence.

"Long way to swim towing a raft," Arroya said. "I can get us closer, you know."

"This is close enough." Tanner spit into his mask, then dipped it into the water. "Besides, I want you far away from here by the time the *Tija* arrives."

"Briggs, I can help—"

"Thank you, but no."

Once this was over, Tanner knew, Arroya would still have to live here; the less involvement he had, the better. Tanner had come to like Arroya, and the last thing the Javan needed was the Chinese and Indonesian security agencies interested in him.

Arroya said, "You know, with my belly, I am probably a better swimmer than you."

Tanner smiled. "I believe it."

He checked his watch: Nine-twenty. The *Tija* would just be leaving Ancol Marina.

He turned around on the gunwale and lowered himself into the water. Arroya slid the raft overboard and handed him the painter line.

"I'll see you bright and early tomorrow morning," Arroya said. "Be safe."

"You, too. Don't forget to bring breakfast."

ONCE THE BOAT HAD DISAPPEARED INTO THE DARKNESS AND HE could no longer hear the engines, Tanner checked his wrist compass, then started toward the island in an easy, energy-saving sidestroke. The sea was calm, with only a slight chop, but he could feel the surge of the current beneath him.

Thirty minutes later the spires of Pulau Sekong emerged out of the darkness. Around the base of the cliffs Briggs could see foam breaking against the rocks. To his left, hidden by the curve of the headland, would be Trulau's private cove.

He picked up his stroke and before long he was treading water at the foot of the cliffs. The roar of the surf was thunderous; great plumes of spray crashed off the rocks. He turned parallel to the cliff and swam until he spotted a pocket of beach, then spent ten minutes negotiating the tide until he was able to drag himself ashore. He flipped the raft onto its back and pushed it into the shadows under the cliff.

Suddenly, from above, a beam of light swept over. He froze. The beam glided along the waterline and over the rocks, then blinked out. Briggs craned his head until he could see the top of the cliff and the silhouetted figure standing there. After a few minutes, the guard walked on.

Tanner began picking his way over the rocks, wriggling through nooks and crannies until finally the cove came into view.

Tija was already at anchor, and drifting gently around her chain. Her exterior lights were lit, and under their glow Tanner could see four figures: one each on the forecastle and afterdeck, and another two walking along the port and starboard railing. Inside the cabin, a single yellow light glowed.

Tanner checked his watch. *Come on, come on. . . .*

After a few minutes a lone figure stepped out of the cabin, strolled to the railing, and lit a cigarette. The figure smoked for a few minutes, then stooped to tie his shoe and returned inside. *Atta boy. . . .* Sugeng's signal told Tanner everything he needed to know: The guards were posted and Soong was asleep in his cabin.

Tanner began donning his fins. *Time to see an old friend again.*

29

Washington, D.C.

MARY TSANG'S AD RAN IN THE *POST*'S SATURDAY EDITION.

Paul Randall and Janet Paschel spent the morning sharing surveillance duty on her apartment. At noon, Tsang stepped out her door wearing sweatpants, sweatshirt, and running shoes, then got into her car and drove off. Paschel called Latham. "She's moving, Charlie. I'm passing Florida and Q. I don't know if it means anything, but it looks like she's dressed for a workout."

"Maybe something," Latham replied. In the ten days they'd been watching Tsang, the most exercise she'd performed was carrying grocery bags from her car. However subtle, this was a change in behavior. *Better safe than sorry,* Latham thought. "Where's Paul?" he asked.

"Went to grab some lunch."

"Call him and see if he can rustle up some sweatpants, then have him meet you."

AS IT HAPPENED, RANDALL WAS ONLY FIVE MINUTES FROM HIS own apartment when Paschel called. He changed clothes and began heading toward Paschel's location. "Passing the Spectrum Gallery on M Street," she reported. "Looks like she's trying to find a parking spot."

"Good luck," Randall replied. "I know that area. Finding a spot there on a Saturday morning is going to be a trick."

Latham asked. "Doesn't a jogging trail start around there—the one that goes to the zoo?"

"We're passing Thirty-first," Paschel announced.

"Yeah, you're right. It starts on Prospect."

"You may have called it," Paschel said, "She's turning toward Prospect . . . slowing down now . . . yep, she's looking for a spot."

"I'll be there in five minutes," Latham said. "Paul?"

"Less than that."

Whatever aversion Tsang had to exercise, it wasn't apparent as she parked her car and started jogging northeast toward Rock Creek Park and the National Zoo.

Following Paschel's directions, Randall took a few shortcuts and found a parking spot on P Street, then got out and started stretching. A few minutes later Tsang jogged past him.

"I've got her," Randall called over the cell phone. "Damn, she's moving fast."

"Stay with her," Latham said. "Dinner's on me if you do."

"I'll hold you to it."

Tsang headed down Q Street to where it crossed the jogging path bordering Rock Creek, then turned north, following the trail into the park's half-mile-wide forest of spruce and pine. She never once looked over her shoulder, Randall noted. In fact she seemed to be in a hurry, so focused was she on the path ahead.

A mile into the park she turned east onto a narrow path. The wooden sign at the intersection read "Steep trail—For experienced hikers and joggers only."

"Just great," Randall muttered, and pushed on.

Tsang began to slow as the grade increased. Randall adjusted his pace accordingly. The trees crowded the trail until branches brushed his arms and the canopy blotted out the sun. He took a bend in the trail and found himself on a straightaway. Fifty yards ahead, Tsang was rounding the next corner. Randall sprinted ahead and made the turn: another straightaway, this one downhill. . . .

What's this? He stopped and backpedaled out of sight.

Tsang, barely ten yards ahead of him, was emerging from the trees along the path.

Randall waited five seconds, then peeked around the corner. She was gone. He started out again, studying the underbrush as he passed it. He saw nothing.

TWENTY MINUTES LATER HE EMERGED FROM THE PARK AND turned onto Q Street. A hundred yards ahead of him, Tsang had slowed to a walk. He pulled out his cell phone, dialed Paschel, and gave her his location. "I see her," Paschel said. "She's passing me now."

"Thank God," he panted. "Damn, I'm outa shape."

"At least you earned your dinner. Hold on, I'll get Charlie conferenced in."

Latham came on the line. "You alive, Paul?"

"Barely. She's a dynamo. We may have something, though." He explained what had happened on the trail. "I didn't see anything, but it's worth a check."

"Okay. Janet, follow her home, make sure she's got nothing else on her itinerary. Paul, I'm headed your way. Let's see if we can figure out what she was up to."

HAD THEY NOT BEEN LOOKING FOR SOMETHING, THEY WOULD have never found it.

The pill bottle was tucked inside the knothole of a fallen tree about twenty feet off the trail. The white top had been smeared with mud, and a leaf was stuck to the plastic.

"Take a good look, Paul," Latham said. "Memorize it. When we put it back, I want everything just as it was." If Tsang had left any telltales—physical peculiarities designed to betray tampering—Latham wanted to make sure they recreated them perfectly.

Randall examined the knot from several angles. "The leaf's stem is pointing at twelve o' clock . . . hold it. . . ." Randall leaned closer. "There's a toothpick, Charlie. It's covered in mud; almost looks like a twig. It's wedged under the bottle."

Very smart, Latham thought. *Move the bottle and the toothpick falls.* "I thought you said she was only back here for ten seconds?"

"She was."

"Then she's been practicing. Anything else?"

"Nope."

Latham eased the bottle out and peered into the hole. It was empty. Next he pried off the leaf and set it aside. He examined the bottle for more telltales. There were none. He unscrewed the cap. Inside the bottle was a folded piece of white paper. Counting folds as he went, Latham opened it. Inside he found six characters in what he assumed was Mandarin Chinese.

"Damn, Charlie, you were right about her," Randall murmured.

"Looks that way."

The unremarkable Mary Tsang had just serviced a dead-letter drop.

"What do you want to do?"

"Copy down the characters as best you can. We'll see if Oaken can make sense of them."

When Randall was finished, Latham refolded the note and returned it the bottle, then slid it back into the knot and replaced the toothpick and leaf. Stepping carefully, they backed onto the trail, brushing leaves over their footprints as they went.

"Now what?" Randall asked.

"We're gonna have to stake it out."

Randall chuckled. "I've got a sleeping bag."

"Don't laugh, it might come to that. I'm guessing whoever's coming won't wait long."

"No problem. Take that to Walt. I'll get things set here."

"IT'S MANDARIN," OAKEN SAID. "HOW ACCURATE WAS PAUL IN his copying?"

"Looked good to me. Why?"

"Chinese dialects are tricky—both in the written and the verbal. You take two characters, both seemingly identical, but curl a brush stroke a certain way and you've got a different meaning. Chinese is a metaphorical language, so there are very few single word characters. Hell, I studied Mandarin for a year in college and I still had a hard time telling the difference between the characters for 'water running downhill' and 'eternal bliss.' "

"No wonder our governments are at odds," Latham said. "That kind of subtlety doesn't make for easy communication. They're abstract, we're more concrete."

"Exactly," Oaken said. "Okay, let's see what we can do with this."

He placed the note on a scanner, transferred it to his computer, then fed the file into a language database. After a few minutes, the computer chimed. Oaken looked at the screen, then tapped a few keys. "Done." He took the sheet out of the printer's tray and peered at it. "Now, remember, this is probably pretty close, but it's not exact." He handed Latham the translation and he read aloud:

" 'Opposition interested family; making connections; caution.' That answers a couple questions."

"Such as?"

"First, Hong Cho knows—at least in general terms—who killed the Bakers."

"And second?"

"He didn't buy the story we fed him."

"But he sent a message anyway."

"Which means he doesn't know we're onto Tsang. If he did, he wouldn't have let her service the drop."

"But he did," Oaken said, "They're still out there somewhere."

Latham nodded. *And up to God-knows-what,* he thought. What was keeping them here?

30

Jakarta

TANNER SLIPPED INTO THE WATER AND STARTED OUT IN A breaststroke, submerged except for the upper rim of his mask. He kept his eyes fixed on the *Tija*'s decks, watching the guards come and go. When he was fifty yards off the port beam, one of the guards stopped, leaned on the railing, and looked out.

Come on, keep walking. . . .

After ten seconds, the guard turned and walked aft.

Tanner turned and circled the boat until he was on the bow, then started swimming in. He got as close as he dared on the surface, then took a breath, ducked under, and started kicking.

Slowly the white curve of *Tija*'s bow appeared out of the gloom. He stretched out his hands. *Easy now, Briggs. . . .* Distances under water were exaggerated; similarly, sounds were amplified. Anything more than the lightest touch on the hull might draw unwanted attention. He felt the cold fiberglass under his fingertips, then kicked to the surface, snatched a quick breath, and dove again.

He arched his back and angled deeper, following the sweep of the keel. He pulled a chemlite off his belt and crushed it to life. He held the green glow against the keel and kept swimming aft.

Segung's directions had been specific: twenty-five feet behind the forefoot, just off the centerline. He almost missed it, so well was the hatch set into the keel.

Segung had called it his "dump door." On dicey smuggling runs, he explained, forbidden cargo was placed atop this hatch. If a customs official happened to get nosy, Segung would dump the cargo, then wait for nightfall and dive over the side to collect it.

Briggs tapped his knuckle against the hull. There were a few seconds of silence, then a responding tap. A crack of light appeared around the seam, then the hatch swung open. Tanner finned through until his fingers touched a metal grating. His head broke into the air.

Segung was kneeling on the catwalk above. "Welcome aboard," he whispered. "Any trouble?"

"None. Give me a hand."

Segung helped him onto the catwalk, then reached down, grabbed a knotted rope, and pulled the hatch shut. "Clever, yes?"

Tanner took off the rucksack and set it aside. "Very. Ever had to use it?"

"Once or twice."

"How many guards aboard?"

"Four, all on deck. There is a shift change coming from the island at four."

Tanner checked his watch; time was going to be tight. "How about Soong?" he said.

"He's in the master cabin—forward companionway, last door on the port side."

"There's no one else aboard?"

"No," replied Segung.

"Okay, wait here. I'll be back in five minutes."

"One moment. What about our arrangement? The other half of the money?"

"I told you: The other half when it's done."

"I would say we are done now. In a matter of minutes, you and your friend will be gone."

"In a matter of minutes, my friend and I will be in the water, in the middle of the Java Sea with only a few hours before the Chinese seal off the island."

"That's your problem. I will take my money now, thank you."

Tanner put an edge in his voice: "You'll get your money. I gave my word, and I'll keep it."

Segung raised his hands, smiling sheepishly. "Of course, whatever you say. Go find your friend."

TANNER CLIMBED TO THE TOP OF THE LADDER, SLIPPED THROUGH the door, and eased it shut.

The passageway was dark. What little moonlight that filtered through the skylights was absorbed by the earth-toned carpeting and wood paneling.

Walking on flat feet, he moved into the salon: cream carpet, sectional sofas, and wide, convex windows lining both bulkheads. He dropped to his belly and crawled across the carpet to the companionway steps. Once at the bottom, he stopped and listened. Outside, the click of footsteps came and went. Voices murmured.

Last door, port side. . . . As he neared the door, he could hear snoring. He could feel his heart pounding. A rivulet of sweat ran down his cheek; he wiped at it with his shoulder. He eased the door open and slipped through.

Fully-clothed, Han Soong lay in the fetal position on the bed's coverlet, the unused pillows pushed into the corner. He was tiny, all bones and sinew, his skin a pasty white.

Why wasn't he sleeping under the covers or with pillows? Tanner wondered. Then it struck him: There were no such amenities in the *laogi.* In that moment, Briggs knew in his gut that it was all true. Soong *had* been in prison for the last twelve years.

He knelt beside the bed and gently placed his hand over Soong's mouth.

Soong's eyes sprang open, but he didn't move. He blinked his eyes a few times, and then they settled on Tanner's face.

"Han, it's me. It's Briggs. Nod if you recognize me."

Soong nodded vigorously.

"I'm going to take my hand away. Don't make a sound."

Another nod. Tanner took his hand away.

"Briggs. . . ." Soong whispered. "Heavens, Briggs, it's you, it's really you. What are you doing here? What is happening—"

"We'll catch up later. Right now, I need you to come with me. Don't ask any questions. Okay?"

"Yes, of course."

As Soong put on his shoes he said, "I'm a little older than you remember me, eh?"

"We both are. You're alive—that's what counts."

Soong patted Tanner's face. "You've grown up. What are you now, thirty-eight?"

"Forty."

"I see a few silver hairs here and there."

Tanner smiled. "Don't remind me. Okay, time to go."

With Soong behind him, Tanner slipped out the door, up the steps, and into the salon. Once certain the way was clear, they crab-walked to the engine-room hatch. Tanner descended the ladder first, then helped Soong to the bottom.

Segung was waiting. "I was getting worried."

"Everything's fine," Tanner said. "Segung, this is Han Soong."

Soong gave him a bow, then shook his hand. "Thank you for your help."

Tanner led Soong to the hatch, then sat down and began donning his fins.

"Briggs, what is going on?" asked Soong.

"I'm getting you out of here."

"What?"

"I know I'm about a dozen years late, but better late than—"

"I can't go with you."

"What?"

"I can't go, Briggs. They still have Lian; if I don't go back, they'll kill her."

Another question answered. Thank God. "What happened to her? Where—"

"She's alive. That's all I know."

"What about Miou?"

"Miou got pneumonia and died the first year. They refused to treat her."

"I'm sorry, Han."

"I can't leave my child. She's the only family I have left. I won't abandon her."

"We can still get her. Once you're out, we'll have leverage. They'll release her."

"No they won't."

"Then I'll go back for her. Han, you have to come with me."

"No, Briggs, I—"

"Enough!" Segung barked. "Both of you shut up."

Tanner turned.

Segung was pointing a thirty-eight revolver at them. "General, you're staying. Briggs, you're leaving—but not the way you came in."

Tanner stood up and stepped in front of Soong. "Why are you doing this?"

"For the reward, you idiot. I've just broken up a plot to kidnap the general."

"Segung, they won't buy it. Listen to me: They'll arrest you, seize your boat, then—"

"I doubt that."

"You're making a mistake."

"There's a lesson in this for you: Never haggle with a man who holds your life in his hands."

Tanner knew his plan had just gone to hell. Regardless of whether the Chinese believed Segung's story, they'd whisk Soong back to Beijing and he would disappear into the *laogi*. There was only one way out of this. Briggs steeled himself for it.

"Segung, stick to our deal. There's a bonus in it for you—ten thousand U.S."

"And what am I supposed to do? Let you go and wait here for the money? I don't think so."

"I have the money here."

"You're lying. Where?"

Tanner reached down, picked up the rucksack, and extended it to Segung. "Here."

"No," Segung said. "Put it down and open it yourself. *Slowly*."

As he knelt, Tanner took a casual lean forward. He opened the zipper, reached inside, and pulled out a money belt. He showed it to Segung. "Ten thousand. It's all yours."

Segung barely heard him; his eyes were locked on the belt.

Tanner hefted the belt in his hands. "It's a lot of money. What do you say? Do we have a deal?"

"Give it to me."

"We have a deal?"

Segung nodded absently; his gun never wavered. "Of course, yes. Give it to me."

Easing his foot forward, Tanner pushed the belt toward Segung's right shoulder, the same side on which he held the gun. Instinctively Segung grabbed at it with his left hand. His torso followed the movement, pivoting left and drawing the gun along—across Tanner's body and slightly off target.

Even as Segung's fingers touched the belt, Tanner was moving. Sidestepping left to clear the gun, he clamped his hand around Segung's wrist—thumb pressed into the radial nerve—then lunged forward, jerking Segung off balance and jamming the revolver into the open rucksack. With a muffled cough, the revolver discharged into the blankets.

Before Segung could pull the trigger again, Tanner slapped his open palm hard across Segung's windpipe. Stunned and off balance, Segung fell backward, his head striking the catwalk railing with a dull crunch. He slumped to the deck.

Tanner knelt down and checked for a pulse; there was none. His skull was fractured.

"My lord, Briggs," Soong murmured. "What did you just do?"

"I just got very lucky, that's what. Wait here."

Tanner picked up the revolver, scaled the ladder, and opened the hatch. He listened for thirty seconds, heard nothing, then climbed back down. Soong was sitting on the catwalk, staring at Segung.

"Are you okay?" Briggs asked.

"It's been a while, that's all. Funny, no? All those years in the army, I never got used to it."

"Me neither. It's better that way."

"It seemed easy enough for you just then."

"That doesn't mean I enjoyed it. Han, come with me please."

"I told you, I can't. Please understand."

Tanner hesitated. "Then I'll come back for both of you. Do you know anything about the prison? Anything that might help me find it?"

"No, I'm sorry. It would be very dangerous for you, Briggs. If they catch you—"

"I'll figure something out. Just keep your bags packed."

Soong smiled. "I will. What are you going to do about Segung?"

"He'll have to disappear. When the guards can't find him, they'll wake you. You didn't see or hear anything, understood? You never woke up."

"Yes."

"Let's get you back to your cabin." He helped Soong to his feet.

"Briggs, how long before you come?"

"As soon as I can."

Soong placed a hand on his shoulder. "Make it very soon."

"Why?"

"I want you to take a message back. You can reach the CIA, I assume?"

"Yes."

"Give them this: Ming-Yau Ang and Night Wall."

"That's it? Nothing else?"

"They'll figure it out," Soong replied. "When they do, they'll understand."

31

Washington, D.C.

THOUGH JOKING WHEN HE MADE THE OFFER, RANDALL DID IN fact end up spending the night sleeping in the bushes of Rock Creek Park watching Tsang's dead drop. Given its location and the limitations of their three-person team, there'd been no other option. Aside from some rambunctious teenagers strolling the trails and drinking beer, Randall's night passed without incident.

At dawn, Latham and Janet called on the radio. "Morning, Paul, are you there?"

"I'm here. Cold, tired, and hungry, but here."

"Come on out," Latham said. "I'm at Q and Twenty-seventh. Janet's playing jogger on the main trail. I've got breakfast for you."

Randall was there in ten minutes. He climbed in the car—groaning as he felt the warmth hit him—and accepted a cup of coffee and Egg McMuffin. "Ah, Charlie, you're a good man."

"Sorry you had to play Rambo all night. Thanks, Paul."

"No problem. How's Bonnie and the kids?"

"Fine. I saw them last night. Samantha's already complaining about the casts being itchy."

"That's a good sign. Say, did you know there are mosquitoes out in April? You'd think it'd be too cold for them, but nope, they're out in swarms."

"I can tell."

"What?"

"Your face."

Randall pulled down the visor and looked in the mirror; his face was pimply. "Great."

"Finish your breakfast, then go home. We'll call you if there's any action."

JANET SPENT THE MORNING TRAVERSING THE TRAILS OF THE park, stopping occasionally to check her watch and write in a notebook, an affection they hoped would disguise her as a runner on a training schedule.

At noon, she called in: "Charlie, there's a tour bus pulling into the Adams Mill lot. The whole group is heading in the general direction of the drop. They're all Chinese."

"What?"

"There's not a Caucasian in the bunch."

What would a Chinese tour group be doing in Rock Creek Park? Latham wondered. It didn't make sense. Then he caught himself: Maybe it did.

Last year a female Olympic runner from Beijing came to Washington on a goodwill trip. While running in the park late one night, she was raped and murdered, her body dumped just off the trail. Her killer was never apprehended, and the woman became an icon in China.

"Janet, you remember that murder—the Chinese marathoner?"

There was few second's pause. "Damn, you think—"

"I wouldn't rule it out. Where are they now?"

"About a half mile from the drop; the guide is stopping to talk."

Probably retracing the woman's route. "Okay, stay back. If our target's in the group, he'll be watching. Also watch for late joiners. Any chance you could get a head count?"

"I'll try."

"I'm driving over to the lot and check the bus."

Latham started up Q, turned north on Connecticut near Dupont Circle, then east again on Columbia. Six more blocks and three more turns took him to Adams Mill Road. He parked away from the bus and sat watching for loiterers. There were none.

"Charlie, they're starting up the path east of the drop. I'm gonna circle to the other end of the trail and jog past the group."

"Okay. Head count?"

"I've got fifty-two."

Latham got out of the car and strolled past the bus to a bank of phones near the bathrooms. He made a fake call, then walked back to his car and got in. He flipped open his notebook and jotted down the bus's particulars: company name, plate number, and side number.

Fifteen minutes passed, and then, "Charlie, you there?"

"I'm here."

"The group's coming off the trail. I tell you, that girl must have been special; there's not a dry eye in the bunch. As far as I can tell, the count's the same."

"Good. Meet me at the drop."

THE AREA AROUND THE DROP WAS TRAMPLED BY OVERLAPPING footprints, and Latham assumed this was where the woman's body had been found. *Very smart,* he thought.

He knelt on the fallen log and leaned down. The knot was empty. The bottle was gone.

"Clever sons-of-bitches," Janet Paschel said.

"Yep."

But ingenuity could be a double-edged sword, Latham knew. While the tour group had given their target anonymity, it had also lumped him into a unique and hopefully identifiable group.

"What now?" Janet asked.

"We dive into the haystack and look for something shiny," Latham replied.

Moscow

The days following the Irkutsk Massacre became a whirlwind as Bulganin virtually uprooted his office and took to the countryside, leading an army of print and television reporters.

The campaign had reached critical mass, Nochenko realized. No longer did they have to contact the media to announce press conferences or rallies. Bulganin's calendar became increasingly jammed with interviewers clambering for his time. The grassroots network of RPP supporters was now a finely tuned machine. Bulganin and the RPP had become an ongoing news story.

And when exactly had they turned the corner? Nochenko wondered. *The day after Irkutsk.*

Try as he might, he was unable to dismiss the idea that Bulganin had been involved. The odds against the incident being anything but a tragic accident were enormous. More importantly, it would take a special kind of ruthlessness to arrange such a slaughter. Bulganin was eccentric, not homicidal.

Then why couldn't he put it out of his mind?

Nochenko was a logician at heart. The world turned according to physical laws; people behaved as they did because of the electrochemical impulses swirling in their brains; two plus two always equaled four. And suspicious hunches . . . they were for men of weak intellect.

And yet, Nochenko's suspicions persisted.

Two days after the incident at Chita, he began his own discreet investigation of Irkutsk. So far, he'd turned up nothing unusual—save one item.

Bulganin's chief bodyguard and leader of "The Guardians," Pyotr Stomanov, had gone missing two days before the Irkutsk incident then reappeared the day afterward. No one at RPP headquarters knew where he'd gone and Bulganin himself demurred when Nochenko put the question to him.

"Pyotr was running an errand for me. A personal matter."

"I would have been happy to handle it for you, Vlad."

Bulganin had waved his hand. "You? No, Ivan, this was gopher work. You're too important for that; I need you here. Especially now."

Typical of Bulganin, the conversation had ended with an abrupt subject change.

Unsatisfied with Bulganin's explanation, Nochenko turned his attention to Pyotr himself and called an acquaintance in the SVR's archives directorate.

Bulganin's chief bodyguard was a former *Spetsnaz* special forces soldier, discharged from the army six years before after being accused of killing a civilian during a nightclub fight. Nochenko's contact could find no details on what had become of the charges, nor could he get access to Stomanov's service record, neither of which were surprising. *Spetsnaz* activities had always been cloaked in shadow.

It was no wonder Bulganin had excused Stomanov and his men from Nochenko's background checks. What about the rest of the Guardians? Nochenko wondered. Like Stomanov, were they also ex-military? Why would Bulganin load his entourage with thugs?

Unless. . . .

Unless the man's fascination with "Koba" Stalin ran deeper than he had imagined. From what little he'd read of Stalin, Nochenko knew the man had been something of a thug in his youth, and that he'd shrewdly distanced himself from such activities as he gained power, instead delegating such chores to cronies he kept around for that very purpose.

Nochenko's desk phone rang. "Yes?"

"The Chief wants you."

"Very well. I'm on my way."

He found Bulganin standing at his desk, hands clasped behind his back. "Ivan, come in, sit."

Nochenko took one of the wingback chairs before the desk.

"Ivan, guess who I just got off the phone with."

"Vladimir, please. . . ."

"All right, all right." Grinning, Bulganin banged his fist on the desk. "Fedorin! The man himself! Can you believe it?"

"What? When?"

"Minutes ago. He would like to come over to 'pay his respects'. His words exactly."

"My God," Nochenko murmured. This was significant.

Sergei Fedorin was the head of the SVR, the successor to the KGB. Though much had changed in Russia over the last decade, one thing had not: By whatever name, the Committee for State Security was alive and well. Though now leaner and more circumspect in its methods, the SVR still wielded tremendous power.

Fedorin's visit could mean only one thing: Like the rest of Russia, the SVR had decided Bulganin's momentum was irresistible, and Fedorin wanted a head start on backing the winner. By day's end the media would have the story, and one by one other government organs—along with their own constituency and power base—would begin tacitly falling into place behind the SVR.

"We've done it, Ivan!" Bulganin roared. "We've won!"

He's right, Nochenko thought, still numb. *God almighty . . . just like that.* Of course, the formalities of the election would still take place, the votes would still be counted, but the outcome was virtually locked. In a few day's time, Vladimir Bulganin would be president of the Russian Federation.

Nochenko realized he had a decision to make. If he moved now, he might still be able to thwart Bulganin's victory. It would be dangerous, but it could be done. But that begged a question, didn't it? Were his suspicions enough to justify such action? What proof did he have of anything? True, Vladimir was something of an oddball, but perhaps that was his strength. Bulganin wasn't a cookie-cutter politician. Albeit a tad arcane at times, he had vision.

For Nochenko it came down to one question: Had all his work over the last six years been in vain? Had he taken a damned peasant from a shoe factory to the brink of the Russian presidency only to throw it away over a . . . spooky feeling in his belly?

No, Nochenko decided, *No.*

Bulganin clapped him on the shoulders. "Ivan, don't you see? Do you know what this means?"

Nochenko looked up at him, then smiled. "Yes, Vlad, I know. We're almost there."

32

White House

THE SPECIAL SESSION OF THE SECURITY COUNCIL ENDED WITH the Chinese delegation storming out an hour after it started. Two hours after that, Martin's own ambassador arrived with the transcripts.

Following a brief statement describing the reactor accident in Chita, then moving on to similar incidents in the past, China's normally circumspect ambassador proceeded to lambast the Russian representative, accusing the Federation of negligence, illegal labor practices, and racially biased safety standards toward Chinese citizens living in Siberia.

"Not very smart of the Chinese to come out swinging like that," Martin said as he read. "The Russians don't like being backed into a corner."

Maybe that's what they want, Bousikaris thought. The natural assumption was that China wanted a solution. True or not, nothing the PRC did was unconsidered. Every word spoken in that meeting had been decided in advance. "They're grandstanding," he said. "Jockeying for advantage."

Martin turned to his ambassador. "What's your take, Stephen?"

"I've been at the UN for eight years, and I've never seen a Security Council meeting go this badly this quickly. I don't think China is looking for a solution just yet. I wouldn't be surprised if we see a news conference at their embassy later today."

"I agree," Bousikaris said. "If so, I'm betting we're going to see a whole different tone."

"Explain," said Martin.

"Very solemn, very disappointed: 'We were hopeful the Federation would be appropriately responsive to our concerns, but it appears we were mistaken'—something along those lines."

The ambassador said, "Right or wrong, much of the world still sees Russia as the big hungry bear. It won't take much to paint China as the underdog."

"And everybody loves the underdog," Martin said.

"Especially when the victims are peasants just trying to scratch out a living in a foreign land. China's got the high road. By this time tomorrow, the Federation's position will be lost in the shuffle."

Martin considered this. "So where's all this headed? Howard?"

Where this is headed, thought Bousikaris, *is to another visit from the PRC ambassador.*

"Once China gets the leverage it's looking for, we'll see their real agenda, sir."

USS *Columbia*

One hundred twenty miles from Russia's coast, *Columbia* had its first close encounter.

"Conn, Sonar."

Kinsock keyed the intercom above his head. "Conn, aye."

"Contact, Skipper. Designate Sierra-four. Bearing zero-zero-five, close aboard—make it eight thousand yards. He was laying in the grass, Skipper."

Four miles off our beam, Kinsock thought. "What's he doing?"

"Bearing rate indicates a turn to the south; he's headed our way, but in no big hurry."

No chance he knows we're here. Still, better safe than sorry. "Diving officer, make your speed one-third for eight knots. Sonar, how soon can you get me an ID?"

"Twenty minutes, Skipper. Less if you can get me closer."

"Stay on it. Let's see what he does."

• • •

SIERRA-FOUR KEPT COMING, TURNING IN AN ARC THAT BROUGHT it three miles off *Columbia*'s starboard quarter. "We got an ID, Skipper. Need to refine it a bit, but it looks like an Akula."

Damn. An Akula was a Russian hunter-killer, fast and dangerous. More importantly, Akulas were prestigious billets in the Federation navy and reserved for its best skippers. "Conn, aye."

A few minutes passed. "He's turning again . . . coming north, but still heading generally west."

Jim MacGregor, *Columbia*'s exec, whispered, "He's hunting, Archie."

"Yep. Zigzagging to open up his passive sonar."

Kinsock felt the first tinge of wariness. He'd tangled with Akulas three times, the last incident lasting nearly fourteen hours before they'd been able to slip away. On this trip they couldn't afford such an encounter. Though currently ahead of schedule, the closer they got to the Russian coast, the greater their chances of running into more bad guys. Out here, a stray Akula was something of a fluke; inside the mouth of Vrangel Bay. . . . Well, it didn't bear thinking about.

"Sonar, Conn, how many turns has he done in the last half hour?"

"Four, Skipper."

MacGregor said, "About one every seven minutes. Pretty slow turn rate."

"Maybe we can use that."

Together they leaned over the chart table, jotting numbers and making calculations. Finally satisfied, Kinsock keyed the intercom. "Sonar, Conn, let me know the instant he starts his next zig."

"Aye, sir."

Two minutes later: "Bearing shift on Sierra-four. He's coming around."

"Conn, aye. Diving officer, all ahead two-thirds for twelve knots."

Kinsock felt the deck surge beneath his feet as *Columbia*'s engines sent more power to the screws. MacGregor clicked his stopwatch. "How long, Archie?"

"Make it forty seconds."

Kinsock was doing what's known as a "scoot-and-die" and its success depended on three things: the angle of the Akula's turning radius, her speed, and how well Kinsock had done his math. The theory was sound, if not exact: As the Akula turned to open its port sonar array, there would be a period during which it would have an "aural blind spot" on *Columbia*'s general bearing.

MacGregor counted off the seconds. "Thirty seconds . . . thirty-five . . . forty. . . . Archie?"

Kinsock shook his head, waiting.

"Forty-two . . . three. . . ."

Kinsock turned to the diving officer. "All stop."

"All stop, aye."

Columbia's deck shivered. She began slowing, drifting forward on her own momentum. There came a soft squeal from the pressure hull. They were scraping against the thermal layer; the temperature change was expanding the hull.

The diving officer whispered, "Might be losing our layer."

"Two degrees down plane, all ahead one-third for two knots."

"Two degrees down, one-third for two, aye, sir."

Ten seconds passed. Fifteen.

"Conn, Sonar, Sierra-four still opening, shaft rate decreasing. . . . He's slowing, Skipper."

All the better to hear us with, Kinsock thought.

MacGregor said, "You think he heard—"

"We'll know soon enough. Sonar, time to Akula's next turn?"

"At his new speed, nine minutes."

If the Akula had heard their hull squeal, its next turn would come sooner than its last. If the Akula's skipper was feeling frisky, he might go active on his sonar and try to get a bounce off something solid—in this case, *Columbia*'s hull.

The air in the control room grew thick with tension. Everyone's movements slowed, became more deliberate. Except for commands from Kinsock and the occasional soft chirp from consoles, everything was silent. Eyes not glued to consoles stared at the overhead.

"Conn, Sonar, two minutes to turn. No change on Sierra-four."

"Conn, aye. Jim, crunch the numbers again; we'll try another scoot when he turns."

"Right. . . . Make it thirty-two seconds. His slowing down gave him a tighter turn radius."

"Okay."

Without realizing it, the Akula's skipper had partially countered Kinsock's tactic. Unless the Akula changed course or slowed even more, *Columbia* would now gain only a few hundred yards on each scoot. It could take several hours to leave the Russian far enough behind to breathe easy again.

"Conn, Sonar. Sierra-four's time to turn in ten seconds. Nine . . . eight—"

MacGregor held up crossed fingers. Kinsock smiled.

"Mark! Listening . . . no change on shaft rate . . . no change on bearing rate or doppler. . . ."

Come on, buddy. . . .

"Wait! Here he comes, Skipper. Bearing rate indicates port turn—he's coming south again."

Kinsock ordered, "Diving Officer, all ahead two-thirds for twelve."

MacGregor clicked the stopwatch.

"Sonar, Conn, how's his speed?"

"No change. Up Doppler . . . bearing rate steady. . . ."

All good signs. Suspicious though he might be, the Akula's skipper wasn't sure of anything. So far, *Columbia* was still just a ghost on his screen.

THE NEXT FOUR HOURS PASSED WITH AGONIZING SLOWNESS: *Columbia* scooting forward a few hundred yards at a time, the Akula remaining doggedly astern, but slowly losing ground as it tried to gain contact.

"Conn, Sonar, Sierra-four is fading. Haven't had a bearing shift in twenty minutes. I make his range at twenty thousand plus."

Standing at the chart table, Kinsock replied, "Conn, aye. Good work."

"Stubborn SOB," MacGregor said.

"Yep, they usually are." Kinsock chuckled. "Like trying to scoop sand with a net."

"What's that?"

"That's how my first skipper described trying to hold contact on an LA boat."

"Thank God and pass the silence," MacGregor said.

"We're gonna need it."

"That bad, you think?"

" 'Fraid so. That game we just played was a preview. The closer we get to Nakhadka the more traffic we're gonna see. Add to that the hydrophone array outside the harbor—"

"Which may or may not be operational."

"Never rely on maybe, Jim—it'll get you killed. We assume it's operational. If we're wrong, fine, we're wrong *and* alive."

Dozens of things could go wrong between here and the coast. Dozens of chances to be picked up by a passing frigate or another attack sub. And once inside Russia's territorial waters, the rules changed from cat-and-mouse, to shoot first and ask questions later.

ONE HUNDRED EIGHTY MILES TO *COLUMBIA*'S SOUTH, ANOTHER submarine, this one a specially modified, Russian-built Kilo class, was heading north at a leisurely four knots, her captain unaware of *Columbia*'s close call with the Akula. Had he been, he would have fretted the situation as much as Kinsock himself. Everything depended upon the American sub reaching her destination.

The captain walked to the chart table, where the navigator was working. "On track and slightly ahead of schedule, Captain."

"How far ahead?"

"Two hours."

Have to adjust for that, the captain thought. *Timing will be critical.*

The navigator said, "Of course, we could improve that if we increased speed."

"This will do for now." Four knots was the Kilo's best, quiet speed. "Inform me when we're a hundred miles from the intercept point."

"Yes, sir."

The captain was under no illusion: His was a good boat, but it was no match for the American—not on an even playing field, at least. Of course, by the time they reached the intercept point, the field would be heavily canted in his favor.

33

Washington, D.C.

DUTCHER WAS WAITING WHEN TANNER STEPPED OFF THE JETway. "Welcome home."

"Good to be home," Briggs replied, meaning it. "I almost had him, Leland."

"I know. We'll talk in the car."

"Where's Bear?"

"Got back from Asheville last night. I told him to get some sleep and meet us in a couple hours. You and I have an appointment at Langley."

Once in the car, Tanner asked, "How much does Dick know?"

"Not much. I told him the op fell apart. How'd Soong look?"

Had the question come from any other man, Tanner may have read between the lines: *Have you figured out whether he's on the level?* But this wasn't any other man. Dutcher's question meant what it meant. "Old, tired. He was . . . frail. It broke my heart."

"I'm sorry, Briggs. I've got to ask: Is he on the level?"

"I think he is." He told Dutcher about Soong's sleeping habits.

" 'Sleep betrays all affectation,' " Dutcher said.

"What's that?"

"A quote from Jonas Barnaby—a British spymaster from World War One. He said sleep is the one thing even the best-trained men can't entirely control."

Tanner wondered how that theory would play with Mason. The CIA was already skeptical of Soong, and what had happened in Jakarta wasn't likely to improve that—unless, of course, Soong's message meant something to them.

THEY ARRIVED AT LANGLEY AND WERE ESCORTED TO MASON'S conference room. Mason, DDI Sylvia Albrecht, and DDO George Coates were waiting. The exchange of pleasantries was brief.

"Let's hear it," Mason said.

"One of my contacts got greedy." Tanner told them the story, starting with his arrival in Jakarta and ending with Arroya picking him up the morning after the incident aboard the *Tija*. "Segung decided to switch sides; he thought playing the hero for the Chinese would be worth more."

"You killed him?" Albrecht asked. Her tone was neutral: just a question.

"Yes. Extra money or not, he was going to kill me, maybe even shop Soong to the Chinese."

"What did you do with the body?"

"I took it out the hatch, weighted it, and dropped it."

Hearing the words come out of his mouth, Tanner felt a pang of guilt. The fact that he'd had no choice in the matter was cold comfort.

He'd dragged Segung's body back to the rocks, where he'd placed it in the raft, towed it past the continental shelf, and dumped it. He spent the rest of the night on a nearby island waiting for dawn. When Arroya arrived to pick him up, he asked the inevitable question.

"What happened, Briggs? Where's your friend?"

Tanner told him the whole story. "I'm sorry, Arroya."

Arroya frowned. "I should be the one apologizing. I should have seen this coming. Segung has always been greedy—even as a child. That he would betray a friend of mine is something I would have never imagined." With tearful eyes, Arroya clapped Tanner on the shoulder. "You had no choice, Briggs. I'm glad you're safe."

After reaching Jakarta's marina, Arroya had driven him to the airport, where they parted ways. Tanner had given him the rest of the money. "For the Save Java Fund." he explained.

As Tanner finished the story, Coates said, "Segung's disappearance had to worry the Chinese."

"There was no helping it," Tanner replied. "I stripped the body and left the clothes in his stateroom along with a half-empty bottle of gin. It's a leap, but they might've assumed he went for a swim and drowned. With nothing else to go on, and with Soong safe in his bed, it might fly."

Mason nodded. "It might at that. What about Soong's reason for not leaving—do you buy it?"

"His wife is dead; all he has left is his daughter. Plus, there's something else." He repeated the story about Soong's sleeping habits.

"Interesting," Coates said. "It tends to support the *laogi* angle, but it's not proof."

"I don't like it," Albrecht said. "If Soong had come along, we could've leveraged her free."

Dutcher said, "Soong knows his captors better than we do. Unless this was all theater for our benefit, we have to give some weight to what he says."

"You're begging the question, Leland. If Soong has been locked up for the last twelve years, it would take an extraordinary act of willpower to say no to freedom."

"Han Soong is an extraordinary man," Tanner replied.

"You're biased."

"You're right, I am. I know him. I know his character. Look at it from his perspective: He's the prize, not his daughter. Would you entrust the life of your child to strangers you've never met?"

"Good point," said Mason. "Okay, we've got some thinking to do. Anything else, Briggs?"

"One thing: Before I left, Soong gave me a message to bring back."

"What is it?"

"Ming-Yau Ang and Night Wall."

"That's it?"

Tanner nodded.

"It doesn't mean anything to me. George, Sylvia?"

Both deputies shook their heads. Coates muttered, "Christ, the man's baiting us."

"I agree," said Albrecht. "He's got us hooked, and he's playing—"

Mason held up a hand, silencing them. "Briggs, what—"

"That's all he gave me. His last words to me were, 'They will figure it out. When they do, they'll understand.' "

"Then I guess we better figure it out," Mason said. "But I'll tell you this: if he's playing a game, the good General Soong is on his own."

Holystone Office

When they walked into the office an hour later, Latham was in the kitchenette watching Cahil make a batch of his famous dill-tuna salad on rye. Bear saw Tanner, grinned broadly, and gave him a bear hug. "Glad to see you're in one piece."

"You, too. How was Dixieland?"

"Interesting."

"Charlie, how's Samantha?"

"Getting addicted to soap operas."

Dutcher asked, "Ian, where's Walt?"

"In his office. He had that far-off look on his face."

"Caught in the throes of the paper chase," Tanner said.

They gathered around the conference table. Cahil passed out sandwiches and iced tea, then sat down. Oaken arrived a few minutes later carrying a stack of manila folders in one arm, a shoe box in the other. He greeted Tanner, then began sorting paper. "Sorry, there's something I've gotta check."

Dutcher started the meeting by having Latham bring them up to speed. For Tanner's benefit, Charlie started with his visit to Hong Cho and Tsang's placing of the ad in the *Post*.

He ended with the incident at the Rock Creek drop. "We're working on the passenger list. The one thing we still don't know—the million-dollar question—is, What's so important that the Chinese would risk all this?"

Dutcher said, "Once we answer that, the rest will follow."

Out of nowhere, a question popped into Tanner's head: *And what's so important that Han Soong had to make contact now, after all these years? And why is he in such a hurry?*

Aside from the China connection, there was nothing to suggest a link between Soong's defection and the Baker murders. So why was his subconscious shouting at him?

Latham continued: "Who knows, maybe we'll get lucky with the bus."

Dutcher turned to Cahil. "Bear?"

Cahil recounted his hunt for Skeldon, starting with Blanton Crossing and ending with his discovery of Lamar Sampson and Stan Kycek. "I've got Kycek stashed at a motel," he said. "Once I told him who he was mixed up with, he turned about seven different shades of queasy and thanked me for rescuing him."

"What about Sampson?"

"He doesn't think much beyond his next bottle. Plus, he's terrified of Skeldon."

"What about the shoe box Sampson gave you—the stuff from Siberia."

Cahil nodded toward Oaken. "It's being fed into the hopper as we speak."

"Walt, anything interesting?"

Oaken gave a vague wave, muttered something, then went back to jotting notes.

Latham said to Cahil, "Both Sampson and Kycek were with the Geological Survey?"

"Yep. Lamar was a rock picker; Kycek a demolition guy. Kycek claims he and Skeldon never met face to face; everything was done by phone."

"Skeldon's no dummy," Tanner said. "Kycek can't ID him and he can't lead anybody to him."

"Okay, let's try to put the puzzle together," Dutcher said. "Last year Skeldon and Sampson are in Siberia, digging around for . . . God knows what—"

"Presumably funded by Baker, who in turn is funded by the Chinese," Latham added.

"And now Skeldon is traveling again—destination unknown, but probably still under contract by Baker—"

"Who Skeldon may or may not know is dead. . . ." Tanner added.

"Right again. Now he's getting ready to meet up with a demolition expert. The safe money is that Skeldon is heading back to, or already in, Siberia."

"Which brings us back to why."

From the end of the table, Oaken cleared his throat and said, "I think I can answer that."

Everyone turned to face him. There was ten seconds of silence as Oaken gathered his thoughts. "I spent most of last night reading every scrap of paper in Sampson's box. Most of it was far above my head—"

Cahil broke in. "I find that hard to believe."

"Believe it. Lamar's specialty wasn't just ordinary rocks. Time and again I came across some pretty specific terminology: kerogen, cylcofeeders, diluent, coking desulpherization. . . . Anyway, a couple hours ago it hit me: I'd seen a lot of those words before. Care to guess where?"

There were no takers.

"In Baker's case files," Oaken said. "I went back and found at least two-dozen terms shared by both Sampson's field notes and one of Baker's cases."

Dutcher leaned forward. "Which case?"

"Something called TASSOL. It dealt with a device called a 'recycling feed pump.' Guessing there was a link between TASSOL and Sampson's survey, I gave myself a crash course in geology. I'm still not positive what this pump does, but I can tell you what they were doing in Siberia."

"What?" said Cahil.

"Mapping shale oil deposits. Big ones."

"How big?" said Dutcher.

"Half of Siberia, give or take."

Tanner said, "If that's true, it means—"

"It means that, by proxy, China has been secretly hunting for oil in the middle of Russia."

34

COULD THIS BE WHY SOONG WAS IN SUCH A HURRY TO GET OUT? Tanner wondered. One glance at Dutcher told him they were thinking alike. Lack of solid connections aside, the timing was hard to ignore.

Dutcher said, "If you're right, Walt, we're in new territory. I assume you've got a theory?"

"A rough one."

"Let's hear it."

"I'll have to give you a short course in shale oil basics—"

"Oh boy," Cahil muttered.

Oaken gave him a sideways grin and kept going. "First of all, shale oil isn't shale at all, but something called organic marlstone—a mixture of clay, calcium carbonate, and kerogen—plants that have decayed into petroleum over a few million years. In essence, shale oil is a kind of crude oil."

"Which means it needs a lot of refinement," Latham said.

"Right, but first comes extraction. The most common method is called retort mining: A block of shale is bisected with shafts, then holes are drilled into the block and stuffed with explosives."

Tanner asked, "How big are these blocks?"

"The average size is one square mile and two thousand feet deep. After the charges are in place, the block is 'rubbled,' breaking the shale into smaller chunks. Think of it like a skyscraper that's blown to bits, but held upright by massive scaffolding; in the case of retort mining, that scaffolding happens to be the earth surrounding the block."

"How small do they make the . . . chunks?" asked Cahil.

Oaken paused for a moment. "Gravel sized."

"That's a lot of blasting."

"Yep. After the block is rubbled, it's ignited. The burn is controlled by either injecting or evacuating air into the block. Once the shale reaches about a thousand degrees, the kerogen separates out and trickles to the bottom shaft, where it's pumped into tanks for transport to a refinery."

"How much of this stuff is lying around, and why hasn't someone collected it?" asked Cahil.

"Rough estimates put worldwide deposits at about nearly three trillion barrels."

"Three *trillion*?"

Oaken nodded. "To answer your second question, no one's been able to come up with a recovery method that gets around shale oil's two biggest problems: cost and pollution. It's a balancing act. You can go low cost—strip mining, for instance—but the leftover pollution and hazardous waste is staggering. Some countries have even played with injecting radioactive isotopes during the heating process to increase the output, but the isotopes tend to leak into groundwater systems.

"Now, if you go the environmentally friendly route, it becomes a losing proposition."

"How so?" asked Dutcher.

"A couple years ago Atlantic-Richfield did a study. They estimated it would take twelve years of output to simply break even; until then, it was all money down the drain."

"So, let's suppose someone found an inexpensive, environmentally friendly way of recovering shale oil. What kind of money are we talking about?"

Oaken thought for a moment. "Hundreds of billions a year—pure profit. And that's not even including offshoot ventures like transportation agreements, sub licensing, intellectual property royalties. . . . The list goes on. Plus, whoever has the process would gain enormous political power. Virtually overnight, they'd be on par with the Saudis or the UAE. We're talking *real* power here."

"Enough power to warrant the slaughter of an innocent family?" Cahil asked.

"Worse has been done for less."

"That it has," Dutcher said. "I think it's time we learn more about TASSOL."

WHEN THE MEETING BROKE UP, DUTCHER LED TANNER TO HIS office. "Briggs, I'm not sure I like where this is going. If this Baker business has anything to do with Soong, it brings up a whole new set of questions."

"Such as, if he's been locked up all this time, where's he been getting his information?"

"Right. The carrot-and-stick game he's playing with the CIA doesn't help matters."

"As I told Dick, Soong would have to be a fool to assume the CIA is going to care about Lian. By doing it his way, he increases the chances of us rescuing both of them."

Dutcher sighed. "Wheels within wheels. You know what the worst part is?"

"What's that?"

"I keep getting the feeling we're still not seeing the whole picture."

Tanner nodded. *Like there's an ocean beneath us, just waiting to open up.*

White House

Mason walked into the Oval Office to find General Cathermeier sitting before the president's desk. Bousikaris, the ever-watchful sentinel, stood beside Martin's chair. "Dick, thanks for coming. I feel it's important you hear about this along with General Cathermeier. Please, sit down."

What now? Mason thought. Both Martin's and Bousikaris's expressions were grim.

"The Security Council went badly," Bousikaris announced.

"How bad?" Mason asked.

"The Chinese stormed out. The Russians are claiming the reactor leak was minor and that there were no deaths—Russian or Chinese. More importantly, they're denying the accusation that this is just another in a long line of accidents. They say it's all fiction."

"You mean they're downplaying them, or they're claiming they never happened?" said Mason.

"The latter," Martin said.

"When's the meeting going to reconvene?"

"It isn't. The Chinese are getting ready to release a statement. Unless the Russians fully admit their culpability, agree to reparations, and allow inspectors into all facilities employing Chinese citizens, Beijing will not return to the table."

"That's extreme. They're not giving the Russians anywhere to go."

Bousikaris said, "According to the Chinese, this isn't the first time they've voiced their concerns to Moscow. They've been batting this issue back and forth for years."

"What kind of proof do the Chinese have?"

"We don't know," Martin said. "They're claiming Moscow has been covering up the accidents."

"I'd be interested to know where the Chinese are getting their intell."

Cathermeier asked, "Why would the Russians be covering up accidents?"

"Over the last five years, a lot of Chinese citizens have moved into Siberia; they retain their original citizenship, but live and work in Russia, often taking jobs that Russians either don't want, or won't accept."

"Cheap labor."

"Exactly. The problem is—at least according to the Chinese—the Russians see them as second-class citizens. To the Russians they're just warm bodies."

"The solution is simple," Mason said. "We bring in the Red Cross, attach a small, neutral peacekeeping force, put them both under the aegis of the UN, then send them in to sort it out."

"The Chinese won't accept that," said Bousikaris.

"Why?"

Martin cleared his throat. "We had a visit from China's ambassador this morning. This afternoon they'll be holding simultaneous news conferences here and in Beijing. At the same time, China's ambassador in Moscow will be delivering a message to the Russian foreign minister."

Mason felt a flutter of fear in his chest. "Do we have any idea what this message will say?"

"Judging from the ambassador's tone, they're probably going to give Moscow an ultimatum."

"This is a mistake, Mr. President. They're moving too fast, too aggressively."

"That may be, Dick, but we don't set Chinese policy."

No, but you are the leader of the most powerful nation in the free world, Mason thought.

Right or wrong, America had fallen into the role of global policeman. The moment the Chinese ambassador left his office, Martin should have lit a fire under every state department official between here and Beijing and Moscow.

"Mr. President, we need to intervene—put a diplomatic buffer between Moscow and Beijing."

"I agree," said Cathermeier. "If we can slow things down a bit—"

Martin raised his hand, silencing them. "Gentlemen, you don't understand: This is *happening*. Of course we need to intervene; of course we need to buy some time for a diplomatic solution, but that's tomorrow. *Today*—in a matter of hours—China's ambassador will be sitting in front of the Russian foreign minister. We have to assume Moscow will react badly to the ultimatum. So, the question is, what's our response?"

We're running in goddamned circles, Mason thought.

"General, what kind of assets do we have in range of Russia's eastern coast?" asked Martin.

"Pardon me, sir?"

"Naval assets. What do we have and how long would it take?"

"You're talking about battle groups, Mr. President?"

"Yes."

Mason thought, *No, no, no. . . .*

"As far as ready assets, the *John Stennis* group is coming off an exercise in the Pacific."

Bousikaris asked, "Its composition?"

"One aircraft carrier, seven surface ships in escort, a handful of support ships, and two LA-class attack submarines. Mr. President, I have to advise against this. Parking that kind of firepower off the Russian coast is going to be seen as provocative. At best, it's premature."

"If diplomatic measures fall short and this thing escalates, I don't want to be caught playing catch-up. If it becomes necessary, that group might provide a stabilizing influence until we can cool things off."

Mason could no longer contain himself. "Or, more likely, it will piss off both the Russians and the Chinese and we'll find ourselves in a hell of a mess."

"Dick, you're here as a courtesy—to serve as my chief intelligence officer, not to set policy."

"For God's sake, Mr. President, these are superpowers we're talking about, not some banana republic we can frighten into submission. If we're not careful—"

"Watch your tone, Dick!"

"This is a mistake, I want it on the record—"

Cathermeier was at his side, whispering, "Dick, ease up. . . ."

Bousikaris barked, "That's enough!"

"I want it on record that I'm formally advising against this course of action."

Martin bolted from his seat. "That's it! Not another word, or I'll have you removed!" Bousikaris placed a restraining hand on Martin's shoulder. "Dick, you serve at my discretion! If you can't do your job, say so! I'll see that a change is made."

Mason's mouth was halfway to "Go ahead" before he caught himself. This was a fight he couldn't win. Martin wasn't bluffing; he would gladly fire him then install a bootlicker like Tom Redmond. *Don't hand it to him,* Mason thought. There was something very wrong going on, and the only way he could get to the bottom of it was to keep his job.

He forced a cowed expression onto his face. "Mr. President, I apologize. I'm out of line."

Martin glared at him. Bousikaris whispered something in his ear and he nodded vaguely and sat down. "Forget it, Dick," he said with a chuckle. "Truth is, I need a devil's advocate from time to time."

Nice try, Mason thought, *but no sale*. Martin had almost gotten what he wanted. Hell, he'd almost *given* Martin what he wanted. Perhaps the man wasn't such a dummy after all.

"Thank you, Mr. President."

"Well," Martin said, "back to business: General, how long before *Stennis* can be en route?"

35

Holystone

BY LATE AFTERNOON, LATHAM HAD A LIST OF THE BUS'S FIFTY-two passengers, which he faxed directly to Tom Whulford at FBI headquarters. As the day wore into evening, a trickle of passenger information began rolling off the Holystone fax machine.

Despite Latham's prayers to the contrary, it was soon evident that every passenger was in fact a Chinese citizen. However unlikely, he'd been hoping he'd find one that was either a U.S. citizen or a recent immigrant. If so, that person would have likely been Tsang's contact: A wolf among the sheep. Alas, it wasn't to be.

"Now what?" Randall asked, yawning.

"Where are we with pictures?"

"Tommy's working on it. If they'd been part of the same tour, we'd be done by now."

Despite sharing the same bus, most of the passengers were individual travelers, so instead of one entry point to check, there were dozens ranging between Atlanta to New York City. Tommy was slogging his way through Immigration's red tape, trying to nail down passport photos.

"Besides, what good are pictures going to do us?" Randall asked.

"I don't know, I like to have faces—it makes them more real."

"I hope so. Otherwise we're going to be visiting a lot of hotels."

Approaching nine-thirty, photos began spooling off the fax machine. They set up a system: Randall would pick up the photo, give it a quick look, then pass it to Latham, who would do the same, then clip it to the appropriate passenger's file.

The hours passed and the faces became a blur. The conference table grew ever more crowded with manila folders and photos. At eleven, the last one came off the fax.

"Nope," Randall muttered. "Of course, I don't think I'd recognize Jimmy Hoffa right now."

Latham looked at the photo, shook his head, then clipped it to the matching file. He plopped down into a chair. His head was buzzing. *Too much coffee, too much thinking.*

Randall sat down on the carpet, then lay back. "What d'ya think? Get some sleep and come back fresh in a few hours?"

"Sounds good."

Latham leaned his head back and closed his eyes. After ten minutes, his brain was still clicking over. *Something there. . . . something I'm overlooking. . . .* He got out of his chair and started pacing.

From the floor, Randall murmured, "What's up. . . ."

"Nothing." Latham circled the table, thinking, thinking. . . . Then, suddenly, it was there. "Paul!"

"Huh . . . what?"

Latham began flipping through the files, glancing at pictures. As Randall watched, Latham circled the table, checking a file, moving on, checking a file, moving on. . . . On the twenty-sixth one, he stopped. He picked up the passport photo and studied it.

"Something, Charlie?"

Latham turned the photo around. "This." He picked up the phone and called Wuhlford. "I need something: an old case of mine. . . ." Latham gave him the details and hung up.

Forty minutes later, Tommy called back. "Got it, Charlie."

"There should be two composite photos."

"Yep, I see them."

"Fax them to me."

Latham stood by the machine as they arrived. He glanced at the first one, laid it aside, then grabbed the next and laid it beside the passport photo. After a few seconds, he nodded. "Hot damn."

"What?" said Randall.

Latham slid the photo and the composite across the table to him. The composite depicted a Chinese woman in her mid-sixties with a round face and silver hair; the photo was an almost exact duplicate except for the age.

Randall read the file: "Siok Hui Zi. They're the same person. What's going on?"

"About six years ago," Latham began, "some executives at Raytheon suspected they had a spy ring in their fire control division. An employee had come forward, stating she'd been approached by a coworker who asked how she felt about the company . . . the way it treated the employees—basically stirring the pot. Finally she was asked if she wanted to make a little extra money.

"Raytheon called us and we started digging into it. The employee who'd been approached strung along her coworker. Slowly the pieces came together. There were three others in the ring, but we were having trouble pinning down the group's controller.

"Finally we got enough on the ringleader and confronted him. He broke down and gave us everything—including a composite picture of the controllers and their names. By the time we went to grab them, they'd disappeared."

Randall said, "You said controllers—plural."

"Right."

"You're telling me this old woman was one of them? Sweet-faced Grandma Siok Hui Zi?"

"Her name was different then, but yes."

"And her partner?"

Latham picked up the other composite. "Sweet-faced *Grandpa* Mihn Zi."

"Charlie, they've gotta be nearly seventy years old. . . . If you're right, that means these two. . . ." Randall stopped, shook his head as though to clear it.

"It means that Grandma and Grandpa Zi are the ones who broke into the Baker home, then tortured and slaughtered a husband, wife, and two children."

Like Randall, Latham found it hard to imagine a pair of wizened, cherubic-faced Chinese septuagenarians doing something so savage. Could he be wrong? Perhaps the Zis were just gophers, cogs in a larger network. "What hotel did she list on their entry visa?" Latham asked.

"They won't be there, Charlie. They—"

"It's a place to start. It's all we've got."

"What about Tsang?"

"What about her? I doubt she could lead us to them even if she wanted to."

"She listed her hotel as the Marriott in Bethesda—Pooks Hill. Checked in four days ago."

"Okay, that's where we start. Maybe we'll get lucky."

Latham's cell phone trilled. "Latham."

"Charlie . . . is that you?"

"Who is this?"

"Charlie, it's Mrs. Felton . . . from down the street."

His neighbor: spinster, six cats. . . . "Yes, Mrs. Felton, is there something wrong?"

"I'm not sure. That's why I'm calling. Bonnie called me earlier today—"

"Bonnie? When?"

"This morning. She was worried about her ficus and asked if I would water it. I was just over there. Charlie, there's water all over the basement floor."

Ah, shit. "Does it look like there's something running?"

Mrs. Felton paused. "Uh, well, I . . . yes, I heard water running. I was afraid to look."

"Okay, I'm on my way. Thanks, Mrs. Felton." He hung up.

"Problem?" asked Randall.

"I think my water heater finally gave up the ghost."

"The hotel's halfway to your place. I'll run home, feed my cat, then meet you."

LATHAM MADE GOOD TIME, TAKING 270 PAST BETHESDA THEN up to Burdette. Forty minutes after Mrs. Felton's call, he pulled into his driveway.

Aside from the amber light on the porch, the house was dark. Bonnie's flower baskets swung in the breeze. He punched the garage door opener. The door began rolling upward.

Gotta be some kind of unwritten law, he thought. *Minor home disasters only happen on holidays or late at night. . . .* He checked his watch. *Almost midnight, for God's sake.*

The garage door reached the top and stopped with a *clunk. Gotta replace that track spring.*

He pulled into the garage until the hanging tennis ball bounced against the windshield, then shut off the engine. *Almost midnight. . . .*

The overhead light clicked off, casting the garage in darkness except for what moonlight filtered through the open door.

Latham stopped. "Midnight?" he muttered. "It's almost *midnight.*" Mrs. Felton was eighty years old; she was lucky to make it past nine o'clock.

Even as the alarm went off in his head, he glanced at his review mirror and saw a shadowed figure enter the garage. Moving fast, hunched over, it came around the side—

Gun!

He rolled right, reached into his jacket for his holster. He heard three muffled thuds and thought, *noise suppressor.* His side window shattered. Glass peppered his face. He drew his gun, pointed it toward the window and pulled the trigger three times. Nearly blinded by the muzzle blast, he scrambled to the passenger door.

Thud.

The window above his head shattered. He extended his gun, pulled the trigger twice more, then yanked the door latch and tumbled onto the garage floor.

He took a deep breath. His heart pounded in his ears.

He heard feet shuffling on the other side of the car. He pressed his head to the concrete and peeked under the chassis. A pair of feet streaked past the front tire and disappeared from view. Latham pushed himself to his knees and laid his gun across the hood.

There was nothing.

The door to the laundry room banged shut.

They're in the house, he thought. *The sons-of-bitches are in my house . . . Gotta assume they're both here . . . that's how they work. . . . Mrs. Felton—God, let her be alive. . . .*

He leaned into the car and turned the ignition key. The engine roared to life. He scrambled back out and waited.

The laundry-room door flew open. Silhouetted in it was a small-framed figure with hunched shoulders. *Grandma Zi.* Her gun game up, pointing at the car's windshield. Latham adjusted his aim and opened fire. Lightning fast, she turned, snapped off a shot, and ducked back inside as Latham's bullets shattered the doorjamb.

Latham reached into the car and shut off the engine.

Silence. The engine ticked as it cooled.

He stood up, pressed himself against the wall, then reached out and pressed the garage-door button. As it clattered shut, he ducked down, gun pointed at the laundry-room door.

Five seconds passed. Nothing happened.

They're too smart for that, he thought. *And fast. God almighty, she was fast.*

It was decision time. Did he go in after them, or do the smart thing and go for help?

No, he thought. They'd invaded his home; they'd been looking for Bonnie and the kids.

"The hell with it," he muttered.

36

LATHAM PRAYED HE HAD THE ADVANTAGE. THOUGH THE ZIS HAD probably familiarized themselves with the layout of his house, he knew its feel, its nooks and crannies; he could walk it in his sleep. On the other hand, there were two of them and they'd obviously put some thought into the ambush.

He crouched down, pressed his palm against the door, and pushed it open. The doorway was empty. He peeked between the door hinges: Clear. He crept inside and eased the door shut behind him.

He stood still, waiting for his eyes to adjust. The air in the laundry room felt strangely cool on his skin, and it took him a moment to realize why: Bonnie usually had a load of laundry going in the dryer when he got home at night.

He removed his shoes and tested his socks on the linoleum: Too slick. He removed his socks.

He visualized the lower level of the house: The laundry room led into the breakfast nook and kitchen; to the right would be the small family room; to the left, a short hall leading to the foyer.

Gun extended, Latham paced into the nook, looked left, then right, saw nothing, and kept going. He peeked around the corner into the family room. It was empty. He skirted the breakfast table and he leaned over the center island. Again, nothing.

He heard a squeak and immediately recognized the sound. *Floorboard in the foyer hall.*

He spun.

A shadow dashed around the corner into the foyer. Then, more creaking: footsteps going up the stairs. Latham sprinted down the hall, moving fast, then stopped short. *No, Charlie!*

Even as he was ducking back, he heard a crack from the landing above like two heavy books being slammed together. He felt a sting of heat on his left forearm, but kept back-pedaling.

Stupid, stupid. . . .

They'd baited him, and it had almost worked. His forearm was slick with blood. He wriggled his fingers; no bones or ligaments hit. He backed into the kitchen, found a dish towel, then wrapped it around the wound. Wincing, he pressed his arm against chest.

They were upstairs. If they wanted to get out, they had to come past him.

Back in the hall, he turned sideways and leaned his head out for a peek at the landing. It was clear. *Okay, Charlie, second floor: bathroom at the top of the steps; hallway goes left and right. Master bedroom to the right; spare bedrooms to the left. . . .*

He backed into the foyer, his gun trained on the landing. The tiles felt cold under his feet. He sidestepped toward the stairs, hand groping until his fingers touched the banister. He started up the stairs. At the third step, he stopped. He tested the tread with his toes until he found the cracked floorboard.

Eyes fixed on the landing above, he put his weight on the tread. It creaked.

Suddenly, a figure was there, rushing from the bathroom door. Latham shifted his aim and pulled the trigger. The figure's gun winked back. Bullets ripped into the wall. Charlie dropped to one knee, fired two more shots. The figure kept coming. *Center mass, Charlie. . . .* He fired twice more.

The figure let out an explosive grunt, then doubled over and tumbled down the steps, landing in a heap on the tiles. Latham reached out with his foot, kicked the gun away, then rolled the body onto its back. *Grandpa Zi.* The old man had three wounds, two in his side, one in the sternum.

"Christ," Latham muttered. *Three shots and he'd kept coming.*

He stepped over the body and started up the stairs. *One more to go. Where was she?*

He imagined her hiding in the darkness, listening to the gunfire, waiting for him.

Check the spare bedrooms first, then move down the hall, clearing rooms as you go—

He felt a chill breeze on his back. He looked over his shoulder.

Standing in the center of the foyer, her gun leveled with his chest, was Grandma Zi.

The front door was open and Latham instantly realized what she'd done: From the laundry room she'd gone out the front door and waited for him to pass. With the moonlight at her back, her face was in shadow. She looked so tiny, almost comically so, with the too-large gun in her hand.

He was done. He might get off one shot, but not quickly enough. Even so, he wasn't going to make it easy for her. He tensed, readying himself.

"Freeze . . . FBI!"

Grandma Zi spun toward the kitchen hall. She raised her gun. There was a double *boom*. Her head snapped back. She pirouetted to the right, then fell crumpled in the open doorway.

"Charlie!" Randall shouted. "Charlie!"

"I'm here!" Latham's legs started trembling. With one hand on the banister, he sat down on the steps. He laid his gun beside his feet. "It's okay, come on through!"

Randall came around the corner, sidestepped to Grandma Zi, kicked the gun away, and checked her pulse. "She's alive, but not by much," Randall said. "Jesus, Charlie, are you okay?"

"I'm okay, it not bad. God, I'm shaking."

Randall let out an adrenaline chuckle. "Your car looks like hell, Charlie."

Latham let out his own laugh. "Nothing a little duct tape won't cure—Mrs. Felton!"

"What?"

"My neighbor!" Latham pointed at Grandma Zi. "Take her—Germantown Memorial . . . it's three miles down two-seventy. We need her alive, and I need to find their car before the police get here. You've gotta buy me a little time."

They quickly searched both bodies and found a set of car keys on Grandpa Zi.

"Go, Paul!"

Randall scooped up Grandma Zi and ran out the door. As he got in his car and squealed down the street, Latham sprinted across to Mrs. Felton's house. The front door was locked. He ran to the back door, turned the knob. It was open. "Mrs. Felton!" *God, let her be alive. . . .* "Mrs. Felton!"

Above his head he heard thumping. At the top of the stairs, he suddenly found himself surrounded by a cluster of mewling cats. He picked his way through them and rushed into the bedroom.

Mrs. Felton lay gagged and bound to her bed. Seeing him, her eyes rolled wildly. Latham removed the gag. "Oh, Charlie, I'm sorry, they made me—"

"Forget it, Mrs. Felton. Are you okay?"

"Yes, yes. My cats! Where are my cats?"

Latham smiled. "Your cats are fine."

There was no way to avoid it. The police had to be involved. One person was dead in his house, another was at the hospital with a bullet in her skull. Even if he were so inclined, Latham couldn't cover that up. Still, he wasn't about to let the case unravel. He flipped open his cell phone, called Dutcher, and recounted the incident.

"Paul's taken her to the hospital," he finished. "I've got to call the cops, and then my boss. I've got their keys; I'm guessing their car is nearby. Can you send Cahil or Tanner?"

"Charlie, it might be time to cut our losses—"

"If we get their car, we can track down where they're living. This could be the break we need, Leland. If we hand it to the police, we lose it all."

"You're sure the police aren't already on their way?"

"Aside from Mrs. Felton, my closest neighbor is a quarter mile away. Besides, the sheriff's station is two miles from here. If they'd gotten a call, they'd already be here."

"Okay, I'm sending Cahil—but I want him out of there before you start making calls."

"No problem. Tell him to hurry. I've got a dead man lying in my foyer."

37

USS *Columbia*, Bay of Vrangel, Russia

"CONN, SONAR: BOTTOM'S COMING UP. LOOKS LIKE WE'VE GOT the shelf, Skipper."

"How far, Sonar?" asked Kinsock.

"We still have three hundred feet under the keel."

"Conn, aye." Kinsock returned to the chart. Clustered around him were Jim MacGregor and Sconi Bob Jurens. "Gentlemen," he whispered, "now it starts getting dicey. Sconi, if you guys want your tour money back, ask now."

Jurens laughed. "How often does a man get a chance to invade Russia?"

"We're about to find out. Once we cross into their waters, it's the same thing as standing on their soil. So we're agreed: I'll put you two miles off the beach, you swim the rest."

"Suits us fine. How long?"

"Best case: four hours. That's without much traffic overhead. We're gonna take it slow and quiet. If they catch us close in-shore, we'll have no room to maneuver."

"How's the water temp?"

Kinsock glanced over his shoulder at the display. "Fifty-two degrees."

"Ouch," said MacGregor.

Kinsock replied, "Hell, that's warm for these parts."

"Maybe so," Jurens said, "but cold for *my* parts. Why don't you check into finding a tropical current for us, Archie.

I'm gonna go roust my guys. Gimme a call when we're two hours out."

JURENS AND HIS MEN HAULED THEIR GEAR FROM THE GOAT Locker to the Officer's Wardroom, where they began final equipment checks.

Jurens watched each man as he worked. *We're okay,* he thought. Everybody's head was where it needed to be: Focused on the job, running through mental checklists, working through contingencies.

It was a fine line, Sconi knew, this premission "what if" game: What if the insertion goes wrong? What if somebody gets hurt? What if we lose part of the equipment load? The list is endless, and it inevitably includes the more unnerving questions about capture and death, which is when rehearsal goes from being constructive to destructive.

There was something about the human brain—caveman wiring, perhaps—that drew it to doom-and-gloom. The defense against "caveman wiring" was to exercise that long-held voodoo to which most operators secretly subscribe: Talk about coming back to the real world and that's what'll happen. So far it had worked for Jurens.

Smitty caught Jurens's smile. "What's up, Skipper?"

"Thinking about a big vanilla milk shake and a cheeseburger."

"And about a pound of French fries."

Dickie chimed in: "The hell with that. I'm thinking, crash the Playboy mansion, fill a Jacuzzi with grape Jell-O, and—"

"Whoa. Grape? That's sick. Now, raspberry I could see, but grape?"

"Grape is good for you, Skipper Good for your urinary tract, or digestion, or something."

"I think they mean the real thing, Dickie—not Jell-O."

"Hey, don't mess with the fantasy."

From the other table, Zee broke in: "My kids."

Jurens looked at him. "What, Zee?"

"That's what I'm looking forward to: Seeing my kids again."

There was a moment of uncomfortable silence. Jurens clapped him on the shoulder. "Amen."

THREE HOURS LATER THE BULKHEAD PHONE TRILLED AND JURENS picked it up, said, "On my way," then hung up. "We're there," he announced. "Haul the gear to the escape trunk; I'll meet you."

Jurens followed the passageway aft, then climbed the ladder and walked into the Control Room. Kinsock was standing before the backlighted Plexiglas status board. The room was quiet except for a few muffled voices. "How're we doing?" Jurens asked.

"As good as can be expected for being parked on Ivan's doorstep. Might have a problem. The current's running pretty fast—almost six knots and parallel to shore. Add to that our speed. . . ."

"That's almost a riptide," Jurens said.

"Welcome to springtime in the Sea of Japan. Once you're out of the trunk, the slipstream from the fairwater is going to beat you like a rented mule."

Jurens considered this. Six knots didn't sound like much, but underwater, burdened with equipment, trying to keep the team together. . . . "Ideas?"

"I could stop us dead, but you'd still have the current to deal with when you release."

"Which escape trunk?"

"Your pick," said Kinsock. "Go out the forward trunk and you get bounced off the sail if you lose your grip; aft trunk means you have to dodge the vertical stabilizer."

"What about noise? At that speed, isn't the hatch going to cavitate when we open it?" Jurens asked, referring to the turbulence created by the current striking the hatch face. Such noise, however slight, might be detected by nearby sonar.

"We put dunce caps on them before we submerged. The current will slip right past 'em."

"How about this: Steer her into the current—say at about four knots—and we'll go out the aft trunk. You turn abeam of the current, then we release and get dragged clear."

"Sconi, even if we fast-fill the trunk, the first two guys out will have a two-minute wait. That's a long time in the slipstream."

Jurens grinned. "That's why they pay us the big money."

"Well, I'll say this much: You've got a pair of brass ones. Just don't go banging up my boat, hear me? You scratch the paint, I'll have your ass."

"Aye, Captain."

Kinsock extended his hand. "Good luck. We'll be back for you in three days."

"Glad to hear it. My Russian isn't good enough for an extended stay."

THEY STOOD TOGETHER AT THE FOOT OF THE TRUNK LADDER, checking one another's wet suits, making small adjustments, glancing at the overhead occasionally as each man went through his own premission ritual: Smitty plucking at the neoprene hood beside his left ear; Zee whistling silently and drumming his thighs; Dickie compulsively flexing his fingers inside his gloves.

They're ready, Jurens thought. *In the zone. Good men.*

Jim MacGregor leaned against the bulkhead, one hand resting on the sound-powered phone. "What's it gonna be when you get back, gentlemen? Coffee or hot chocolate?"

In unison, the team said, "Chicken soup."

MacGregor laughed, and Jurens said, "Habit."

The sound-powered phone trilled. MacGregor snatched it up, listened for half a minute, then hung up. "We're there. Conditions outside: Depth to the surface is thirty feet; you have a quarter moon, medium cloud cover, and light surface fog; water temperature is steady at fifty-one degrees—"

"Lost a degree," Smitty muttered.

"—current is running fore to aft at six knots for a total of ten knots; no surface, subsurface, or visual contacts; the beach appears clear; sea state is five."

Up from four, Sconi thought. *Gonna be rough out there.*

"Wind is gusting to twenty-five miles per hour, waves four to six feet, medium chop. That's it. Any questions?" MacGregor asked.

There were none.

"Master Chief, you're first."

Jurens climbed the ladder into the trunk and sidestepped to allow room for Smitty. A pair of hands poked through the hatch with a large rucksack. Jurens took it. The hatch closed with a thud.

"I hate this part," Smitty murmured.

"Yep," Jurens replied.

"Going from one coffin to an even *smaller* coffin."

"But then we're out in the big blue."

"Thank God."

They ducked under the bubble hood, a curved shell enveloping the upper third of the tank. During an emergency egress, this air pocket would be used by sailors to don their Steinke mask; in the SEALs's case, it allowed them to conserve the oxygen scrubbers on their rebreathers until they exited.

Inside the hood, Jurens could hear the muffled gurgle of the ocean outside *Columbia*'s hull. He looked across at Smitty, who gave him a thumbs-up. Jurens reached down and pushed the Diver Ready button. Two seconds passed. The lights blinked out. They were in total darkness. A red battle lantern glowed to life.

From the bulkhead speaker, MacGregor's voice: "Divers stand by. I am flooding the tank."

With a *whoosh,* the chamber began filling. Frothy water began climbing their legs.

"Divers, the tank is flooding."

Jurens keyed the squawk box. "Confirm tank flooding."

He felt the icy chill through his wet suit and could taste the metallic tang of compressed air around him. His ears began squealing. He worked his jaw until he got a *pop*. The pain receded. The water reached his thighs, then his crotch. He felt his testicles shrink into his belly.

With a sucking *plop,* the water enveloped the bubble hood.

The "Flood Complete" light flashed to green.

Jurens placed the regulator in his mouth and drew in a lungful of air; it was cold and coppery. He climbed the ladder to the outer hatch. Now came the hard part. With his feet braced against the ladder and his shoulders against the hatch, he turned the wheel and pushed it open.

Bubbles rushed past him and disappeared into the darkness. With a *clunk,* the hatch popped into the locked position. He poked his head through.

Half-expecting to get the slipstream in the face, he was surprised to feel nothing: The dunce cap was doing its job. He was surrounded by blackness; errant bits of phosphorescent plankton zipped past his mask, and for a dizzying moment he felt like he were hurtling through a star-filled void.

He clipped his D-ring to the cleat then climbed out and laid himself flat on the hull. The current tugged at the edges of his body. He could feel the throbbing of *Columbia*'s engines.

Smitty appeared, clipped his D-ring to the cleat, then down the length of Jurens's body until he, too, was lying flat on the deck. Jurens felt a double squeeze on his calf: *Secure.* He reached forward and closed the hatch.

The slipstream hit them full force. Sconi could feel it rippling around him, tugging at his limbs, trying to dislodge him. Ahead, in the blackness he could make out the shadow of *Columbia*'s fairwater.

They waited, clinging to the hull until finally the hatch opened again. A hand appeared out of the opening; Jurens took the proffered D-ring and locked it into place.

The process was repeated until Zee and Dickie were clinging to the hull behind Jurens and Smitty. Jurens felt another squeeze on his calf—*all secure*—then reached into the hatch, dragged out their two equipment bags, and locked them down before closing the hatch.

Jurens glanced at his watch. *Come on, Archie, turn this thing. . . .*

Suddenly he felt a shiver run through the hull. The fairwater began tilting to port, banking like the stabilizer of some great aircraft. Jurens started counting. *Four one-thousand, five one-thousand. . . .*

Behind him, as planned, each man was sequentially releasing his grip on the boat and grasping the next man's ankles. Jurens strained under the weight *Seven one-thousand . . . eight. . . . Now!*

He let go.

38

Washington, D.C.

THE COVER-UP—A TERM THAT LATHAM RELUCTANTLY DECIDED applied to what he and Holystone were doing—went relatively smoothly.

In the aftermath of the running gun battle with the Zis, he'd sat on his stairway, staring at the body of Grandpa Zi. In death, the man hadn't looked the least bit dangerous.

Cahil had arrived twenty minutes later, taken the Zis' keys and left. He called fifteen minutes later. "Found it, Charlie. About a quarter mile away. I've got the registration; the name looks bogus, but the address looks genuine. This thing has been sanitized. The plates looked altered and all the VIN tags are missing. I'm going through it once more, then head over to the address."

"Thanks, Bear."

"No problem. You okay?"

"A little shaky."

"You've got a right to be. Talk to you later."

Latham called Dutcher and filled him in. "Cahil's going to check the address."

"Okay," Dutcher said. "Two things: Which cell phone are you using?"

"One of yours."

"Good. Once you and Paul have your stories straight, use your home phone to call the police. What're you going to tell them?"

"I was out late, came home, and was attacked by unknown assailants. I killed one of them and my partner killed the other. I'll have to tell Harry a little more than that, but he'll back me."

WITHIN THE HOUR, THE HOUSE WAS BUZZING WITH ACTIVITY AS crime-scene specialists, a homicide detective from the Montgomery County sheriff's office, and the medical examiner went about their work. Owens sat with Latham as the inspector interviewed him. "So you and your partner were doing . . . what?" asked the inspector. "Having a beer, right?"

"Right."

"At Finnegan's in Chevy Chase?"

"Right."

"You get a call from your neighbor about a leak and hurry home. Your partner follows to see if he can help, you pull into the garage and. . . ."

For the third time, Latham took him through the confrontation.

"You have no idea who these people are?"

"No."

As the lie came off his lips, Latham felt a twinge of guilt, but he suppressed it: This was his case; these people had invaded his house, tried to kill him—and would have killed his family had they been here. This case belonged to him.

The inspector asked a few more questions, then left to supervise the CS team.

Once alone, Owens asked, "Is this them, Charlie?"

Latham nodded. "I'm pretty sure. We were calling them Grandpa and Grandpa Zi. Harry, they were hunting for me—maybe Bonnie and the kids, too."

"You must have struck a nerve. Is your story going to hold up?"

"Bonnie and Paul are clear and Finnegan's is always busy. My worry is the press. If the *Guoanbu* gets wind of this, they'll shut down whatever they've got cooking."

"I'll talk to the sheriff and the ME. I'll tell them we think it might have something to do with a former case of yours and we need time to dig into it. They'll probably identify them only as 'unidentified intruders.' "

"Good."

"Let's say you're right and these two killed the Bakers. . . . have you figured out why?"

"How much do you want to know?"

"Just tell me if you're getting close. I can keep running interference, but not for much longer."

"We're getting close, Harry. Real close."

IT WAS NEARLY DAWN WHEN EVERYONE FINISHED THEIR WORK and left. The ME was the last to go, wheeling the sheet-covered body of Grandpa Zi out the front door. Randall arrived a few minutes later.

As Latham got into the car, he asked Randall, "How is she?"

"Alive, but just barely. Her brain's mush, Charlie."

Latham could hear the anguish in Paul's voice. This was only the second time he'd fired his weapon outside the range; the last time had been the previous year during a raid of a terrorist safe house. The difference was, this had been a woman—an old woman, at that.

He squeezed Randall's shoulder. "She would have killed me, Paul. Bonnie and the kids, too, if they'd been here—just like the Bakers."

"Yeah, I guess. But, God, she's just—"

"Listen: Old lady or not, she was a killer, plain and simple."

Randall swallowed hard and nodded. "Yeah, you're right. Okay, where to?"

"Holystone."

DUTCHER AND THE OTHERS WERE WAITING IN THE CONFERENCE room. The first tinges of sunlight were filtering through the floor-to-ceiling windows. Oaken sat before a computer perched at the edge of the table. Everyone stood clustered behind him.

Dutcher looked up as Latham walked in. "How'd it go?"

"I think we're okay. They'll want to talk to me again, but Harry's going to cover me." He nodded at the computer. "From the Zis' house?"

Cahil nodded. "Walt's trying to break their security program."

A thought flashed into Latham's head. "Walt, stop."

"What?"

"Tell me about the program." Oaken did so. "Sounds like the same setup Baker's computer had," Charlie said.

"You broke it?"

"One of our tech people did. Lemme make some calls."

LATHAM CALLED WHULFORD AT HOME, WHO GOT DRESSED, DROVE to the Hoover Building, and looked up James Washington's phone number. It was five-fifteen when Latham made the call.

A groggy voice answered. "Yeah, hello."

"James, this is Charlie Latham. I don't know if you remember me—"

"Yes, sir, of course. What can I do for you?"

"Sorry about the time, but I need your expertise. The hitch is, you can't tell anybody about it."

"Is this about your daughter? Something to do with that?"

"Yes."

"Then we never talked. What's up?"

"I've run into another version of the security program you broke for me. Can you help?"

"No problem."

"Here, I'll give you to the guy you'll be talking through it."

THIRTY MINUTES LATER, IT WAS DONE. THE CONTENTS OF THE Zis' hard drive was transferred to Oaken's hard drive. Oaken pulled up the new directory on the screen. "Not much here. . . ." he said, scanning the file names. "Hold on . . . what's this?"

"What?" Dutcher asked.

"This folder's got about twenty gigabytes of ASF files in it."

"Which means?"

"ASF is a video format." Oaken clicked open the folder. "This could be something. Dates, times, locations. . . . Looks like they go back six or seven years. When were the Bakers killed?"

Latham told him.

"Jesus, that's the label on this file."

Dutcher leaned closer. "Let's see it."

THE ON-SCREEN COUNTER TOLD THEM THE VIDEO WAS FORTY minutes long, but after only five minutes, they'd seen enough. "Shut it off, Walt," Dutcher whispered. "My God."

"Why would they tape it?" Cahil murmured. "What possible use could it be?"

"We'll never know," Latham said. "He's dead, and if she survives, she'll likely be a vegetable."

Dutcher said, "What else, Walt?"

"There's a couple dozen files. None look more than a few minutes long. You guys go grab some breakfast; I'll sort through them."

TWENTY MINUTES LATER OAKEN CALLED THEM BACK INTO HIS office. "I started from most recent and worked my way backward. They taped a lot of meetings with Baker. They always used the same setup: Grandma Zi did the face-to-face stuff, Grandpa Zi taping. But take a look at this one. . . ." Oaken double-clicked on a file. The screen filled with snow, then turned into a shot of a parking ramp at night.

"That looks like a metrorail platform," Latham said.

"My guess, too," Oaken replied. "Shot from ground level, out a car window. Take a look at the person meeting Grandma Zi."

The camera zoomed in on the platform until they could make out two figures standing at the railing. The dull yellow light from the streetlamps illuminated their faces. After a few moments, the camera zoomed in.

"There's no sound?" Cahil asked.

"No. They probably deleted it. More deniability that way."

"Okay, that's Grandma Zi. I can't make out the other person."

"Wait . . . here it comes. . . ."

The other face, this one belonging to a man in his early sixties, swam into focus.

"Name that face, anyone?" Oaken asked.

"I can," said Dutcher. "Howard Bousikaris, chief of staff to President Phillip Martin."

Before anyone could react, Oaken's phone rang. He answered it, then handed it to Dutcher, who listened, then hung up and turned to Tanner. "Mason. He wants to see us. Walt, you'd better come, too. How long will it take to transfer all the Zis' files to a laptop?"

"Twenty minutes."

"Do it."

Tanner asked, "What's going on, Leland?"

"They just deciphered Soong's message."

39

Langley

CIA HEADQUARTERS WAS QUIET, WITH ONLY A FEW EARLY RISERS in the hallways. Sitting with Mason at the conference table were George Coates and Sylvia Albrecht. As Tanner took a seat, he realized all three were staring at him. *Whatever it is,* he thought, *it's bad.*

"Something tells me I'm off your Christmas card list," he said.

Mason smiled, but there was none of it in his eyes. "We need you to go through your conversation with Soong again, from start to finish."

Tanner did so, retelling it exactly as he had the previous times.

"No way you misunderstood?" Mason said. "Added anything, left anything out?"

"No."

"Soong's exact words were, 'Ming-Yau Ang and Night Wall.' You have to be sure."

"If I weren't sure, I would have said so. What's going on?"

Mason hesitated, then nodded at Sylvia Albrecht, who began.

"Nineteen years ago, Ming-Yau Ang was an operations analyst in China's Ministry of Defense," Albrecht began. "He was accused of spying for the Soviets, then summarily tried and executed. They never found out how long he'd been working for Russia, or what he'd passed. They swept it under the rug and it eventually faded.

"The truth is," Albrecht continued. "Ang was working for both the Russians and us."

"A double," Dutcher said.

"Yes. And with doubles you can never be sure of who's working who. We took his product, but we were always skeptical. We were feeding Ang material to pass to the Russians as Chinese product."

"And for safety's sake you had to assume the Russians were returning the favor," Tanner said.

"Or the Chinese," Oaken added.

"Right on both counts. Since all the product Ang dealt with was long-term strategic stuff, there was no way we couldn't be sure he was tampering with the product before it reached its destination."

Tanner understood the quandary. If Ang's job had dealt with tactical plans—an upcoming PLA divisional exercise, for example—the CIA could have fed him a "tweaked" plan and waited to see if the Russians reacted appropriately.

Albrecht said, “Ang was a good asset, but because we couldn’t entirely trust any of his product, he was never stellar. I doubt there were any tears shed when he went down.”

Mason took over the story. “Here’s where it gets interesting. ‘Night Wall’ is the name of a PLA operation Ang worked on, but it was tightly compartmentalized, so he could only give us bits and pieces. The overall plan was restricted to ministerial level. What he did give us seemed genuine enough, but as Sylvia said, there was no way we could take it on face value.”

“What did he claim Night Wall was?” Dutcher asked.

“Night Wall—the literal translation is ‘Wall of Night’—was a war game for the theoretical invasion of eastern Siberia.”

Uh-oh, Tanner thought. “What kind of invasion?”

“No idea. You have to understand: Back in the eighties, these kinds of plans were common. We did it, the Russians did it—everybody. It was just part of playing the game.”

“Letting the other guy know you could do it if you had to,” Oaken said.

“Exactly. You drew up a plan, war-gamed it, then shelved it. Ang’s handlers probably thought Night Wall as just another notional scenario—important, but not earth shattering.”

“But not anymore,” Dutcher said.

“Not anymore,” Mason agreed. “I’ll give you one guess who Ang claims authored Night Wall.”

Tanner didn’t have to guess. “General Han Soong.”

“The one and only. Two things: Soong designed it, and he probably knows Ang fed it to us. So, unless we’re wrong—and I pray to God we are—Soong’s message is pretty clear: Night Wall is real and the Chinese have taken it off the shelf.”

“The question is, Why? Why now?”

“I think we might be able to answer that,” Dutcher said. “Dick, you may want to excuse George and Sylvia for this.”

Coates said, “Now, hold on—”

Mason raised a hand, silencing him. “Why, Leland?”

“What I have to say . . . It might be better for them if they don’t hear it. If you choose to tell them afterward, that’s your business.”

"That bad?"

"That bad," Dutcher replied.

The DCI turned to his deputies. "George, Sylvia, give us a few minutes. Stay close."

Once they were gone, Dutcher said to Oaken, "Walt, give Dick the condensed version."

Oaken spent the next twenty minutes taking Mason through the convoluted path they'd been following: the Baker murders and Latham's suspicion of the *Guoanbu*'s involvement; Cahil's hunt for Skeldon and subsequent discovery of Sampson and Kycek; Oaken finding a link between Skeldon's Siberia survey and the process called TASSOL that Baker had been working on; and finally, Latham's identification of the Zis as the *Guoanbu* agents who'd murdered Baker. "Then, of course," Oaken concluded, "there's what we found in the Zis' home."

"What?"

Oaken opened his laptop, powered it up, then slid it across to Mason. "Hit Enter to start it; Spacebar to pause."

Mason tapped the keyboard and leaned back to watch. When the laptop beeped, indicating the video was finished, Mason glanced up at Dutcher.

"The woman's name is Siok Hui Zi, one of the agents linked to Baker. The man with her . . . well, you know who he is."

Mason nodded. "Yeah, I know him. That slimy son-of-a-bitch. . . ."

"The questions we have to answer are, what is Bousikaris doing for the Zis, and what is their leverage on him?" Dutcher said.

"Or on Martin," Mason added. "If somebody was squeezing Martin, Bousikaris wouldn't hesitate to jump into the fray. I may have a guess about what Bousikaris was doing for them."

"Jerking the rug out from under Latham's investigation," Oaken predicted.

"Besides that."

"What?" Dutcher said.

Mason waved his hand. "Later. How's Charlie?"

"He's fine; his family's fine," Dutcher replied. "We're still waiting for word on Grandma Zi, but it doesn't look good."

"Too bad Randall's such a good shot."

"Charlie would argue that."

"I guess he would. Walt, how solid is the connection between Baker and Skeldon?"

"The payoffs are fully documented and traceable. If this went into court—"

"It won't."

"Hypothetically, then. If it went to court, it would play out like this: Sampson and Kycek were hired by Skeldon, who was hired by Baker, who was in turn spying for the Chinese government. For whatever reason, the *Guoanbu* decides Baker needs to be eliminated, and the Zis are given the job. They kill Baker and his family, hoping it'll be written off to random violence."

"When was Bousikaris's first meeting with them?"

"Three weeks ago."

Dutcher said, "That mean something to you, Dick?"

"Maybe. Keep going. What do we know about this shale oil process."

"TASSOL. I'm still working on it, but we can logically assume it's revolutionary. If not, why would the Chinese go to all this trouble?"

"Makes sense. Okay, following your logic, whoever owns and controls this process can count on trillions of dollars in oil revenue and political clout that would rival that of the Mideast."

Tanner said, "Wars have started for less. A lot less."

"That they have," Mason replied. "So, the Chinese know Siberia's shale oil reserves are untapped—trillions of barrels of oil locked in the ground beneath the tundra with no way to get it out."

"Until now," Oaken said.

"Until now. What we don't know is when and how the Chinese are going to move."

"Judging by Soong's urgency," Tanner said, "I'd sooner rather than later. As for the how, only he knows the answer to that."

"Which means he probably knows how to stop it." Mason sighed, then looked at Tanner. "You still think you can get him out?"

"Yes."

"How soon can you pack your bags?"

40

Bay Ridge, Maryland

WALKING UP THE COBBLESTONE PATH UP TO HIS PARENTS' house, Tanner realized this had become something of a ritual for him. Invariably, whether returning from a mission or preparing to go on one, he found himself drawn home—to that part of his life that had nothing to do with "spies and bad guys." If the worst ever came to pass, he didn't want his last contact with them to be a phone call or a "sorry we missed each other" voice mail.

Before retiring from his post at the Naval Academy in Annapolis, his father, Henry Tanner, had taught history for Olive Branch Outreach, moving his family to a new country—a new adventure—as the whim struck them: Kenya in the spring; Switzerland in the fall; Australia the next summer; Beirut when it was still known as the "Paris of the Mideast," before being ravaged by decades of civil war.

Where such upheaval would have left some children confused and standoffish, under Henry and Irene's loving guidance Tanner had thrived. By the time they had returned to Maine for Briggs's entry into high school, he was a well-rounded and even-keeled teenager.

The front door swung open and Irene Tanner, wearing an apron and a single oven mitt, rushed out. After a long embrace, she studied him at arm's length. "You're not getting enough sleep."

"I know," Tanner said, then smiled. "I've taken up drinking; I think that'll help."

"Oh, stop it. Your hair looks lighter."

"I've been getting some sun."

"And the stubble? Are you growing a beard?"

"I'm thinking about it."

"I won't even recognize you," Irene said, clicking her tongue.

Let's hope it has the same effect with the Guoanbu *and the PSB,* Tanner thought. The beard was starting to itch and the blond highlights made him look like a California surf bum.

Irene said, "Did you eat the pie I left you?"

"Yeah, thanks; it was delicious. I had to use a blowtorch to get the wrapper off, though."

"Oh, shush. I get the same guff from your father."

Behind her, wearing his ever-present cardigan and half-moon reading glasses, Henry Tanner stepped onto the porch. He smiled. "Coming or going this time?"

"A little bit of both."

"How soon?" Irene asked.

While his parents knew his job entailed often dicey, and always secretive, work, neither of them pressed him for details. Nor did they smother him in worry, which had to be tough, especially for his mother. He did his best to downplay things, but he suspected they weren't fooled. Parent's intuition.

Briggs said, "Day after tomorrow."

"For how long?" Irene asked, picking at her apron.

He felt an ache in his chest. "Two weeks at most. When I get back, we'll have a clambake."

Irene smiled. "We'd like that. Well, come on in. We're having tater-tot casserole."

AFTER DINNER, TANNER AND HIS FATHER SAT IN THE SUNROOM drinking coffee while Irene dallied about, making an edible care package for Briggs. Every few minutes, she would come in to ostensibly look for something, touching Briggs's shoulder or head as she passed.

When he and his father were alone, Henry asked, "Where're you off to?"

"Asia."

"Big place," Henry said. "Take care of yourself."

"I always do," Tanner said. Then, in the back of his head: *You were careful last time and it almost wasn't enough.* Startled, he suddenly realized that a large part of him was dreading going back. He was afraid, plain and simple.

The Soong defection had been his first deep-cover job with ISAG, and it had nearly set the tone for the rest of his career. Not only had he left behind a man he'd come to call a friend, his wife, and a woman with whom he'd fallen in love, but he'd almost gotten himself killed in the process.

Stop it, Tanner commanded himself. *Get it out of your head. That was then; this is now.* The question was, What was he going to do with *this* chance?

With that realization, he felt his mind click over into that familiar mode he'd come to call "narrowing." Thoughts of routine daily life would soon start to fade: Mowing the lawn, fixing that loose shingle, paying bills—all of it would be irrelevant once he landed in China.

When it was over and he was back home, the lawn would still need mowing and the shingle would still be loose—and his parents would still be waiting with an open door and hot food.

HE STAYED FOR ANOTHER HOUR THEN SAID HIS GOOD-BYES, ACcepted a shrink-wrapped apple pie from Irene, and drove to Holystone. As he'd expected, everyone was there: Dutcher, Oaken, Cahil, and Charlie Latham; unexpectedly, however, Mason was seated at the conference table. As he walked in, all eyes turned to him. He stood awkwardly for a moment, then set the pie in the middle of the table.

"Don't tell me I'm the only one who remembered this was a potluck."

Chuckles broke out around the table.

"Have a seat," Dutcher said. "Dick's got something we need to know about."

"You all know about Howard Bousikaris and his involvement with the Zis," Mason said. "What we don't know is how it started or what's driving it. I believe—as does Leland—that Bousikaris is simply playing middleman for Martin. We're further convinced there's a strong possibility Martin is being manipulated by the Chinese government."

"Into doing what?" Oaken asked

"As we speak, a battle group is en route to Russia's eastern coast, and a SEAL team is on the ground southwest of Nakhodka-Vostochny to provide targeting support for an attack sub. The goal of the mission is to sink a ship named the *Nahrut* when it pulls into port." Mason briefly explained the events that led first to the SEALs's mission, and then the commitment of the *Stennis* group. "We're still in the dark about their precise role in China's scheme, but you can be sure it's a disaster in the making."

There was silence in the room.

Mason continued: "I'm giving each of you a chance to bow out. If, on the other hand, you choose to stay, there'll be no turning back. What has to be done, can't be done in half measures. If it goes wrong and we fail, there's a good chance we'll all end up in prison. Briggs, in a way, you're lucky: You'll be out of the country."

Tanner smiled. "Saved by a well-timed vacation."

Cahil spoke up. "All these long faces and grim talk is depressing me. Let's get on with it."

Oaken nodded. "I agree."

"Charlie, how about you? You didn't sign on for this."

"As far as I'm concerned, this is all part of the Baker case. Count me in."

Mason nodded. "Then we're all agreed?"

He got four nods in return.

"Now that everybody's on board," Tanner said, "what do you have in mind?"

"It's pretty simple, really," Mason replied. "We're going to stage a coup."

41

***And there it is,* Briggs thought. They'd all just crossed** the point of no return. In the eyes of the law, they were now coconspirators. Traitors. Tanner idly wondered if the death penalty was still used in cases of treason. *In for a penny, in for a life sentence,* he decided.

In the real world, few things are as black and white as the law aspires to be. Right and wrong are more often separated by degrees, rather than poles. If the ends were important enough and the means palatable enough, occasionally you had to take the shadier path. As far as Briggs was concerned, good guys still wore white hats, but sometimes when the fight was over, those hats needed a little dry cleaning.

If Mason's suspicions about Martin and Bousikaris were correct, there was no time for investigations, or probes, or a media-spun scandal. They had to move now, and move quickly.

"Define 'coup,' " Oaken said to Mason.

"Relax. I'm not talking about grassy knolls and book depositories."

"Glad to hear it. Then how're we going to do it?"

Dutcher answered. "We're going to convince Martin it's in his best interests to step down."

"Given his ego, that's gonna be a neat trick," Cahil said. "From day one he's been talking about the 'Martin Legacy'; he's obsessed with it. And if he's sold his soul—sold out the country, for God's sake—there's nothing he won't stoop to. He won't go quietly."

"Dick and I will worry about that."

"In the meantime, what are we doing?"

"That depends," Mason said. "How are your acting skills?"

Cahil groaned. "I had a feeling this was coming."

"As of now, you're Stan Kycek," Mason said. "Wherever Skeldon is and whatever he's doing, he's playing a role in China's game. You're going to have to find out what that is."

"According to Kycek, Skeldon will be calling in the next couple days," Cahil said. "I'll lay odds he's heading into Siberia, or he's already there."

"Agreed," Dutcher said. "Siberia is the prize."

"Which brings us back to the two big questions," Oaken said. "We're assuming Martin was coerced into committing the battle group and the SEAL team. If so, how are we going to find out how it all fits together?"

"If Leland and I do our parts, we may have that answer very soon."

"Assuming Bousikaris and Martin even know themselves."

"Right."

Oaken scratched his head. "We're talking about a full-fledged invasion. The Federation may be a shadow of its former self, but it's no pushover. It's still the big Russian Bear. The Chinese can't expect to simply march into Siberia, plant their flag, and start building refineries."

Tanner recognized the expression on Oaken's face. It was his "something don't fit and I want to know why" expression. He was digging in his intellectual heels.

"China knows all that, I'm sure," Dutcher said. "Whatever Night Wall is, they're confident it will give them the edge. The answer to how we defend against it lies with Soong."

And Soong is locked away inside a prison somewhere in the middle of five million square miles of Chinese territory, Tanner thought. *And he's old, and frail, and even if I manage to reach him, will he have the strength to make it out alive?*

Mason turned to Tanner. "Seems like we've been down this road before, doesn't it, Briggs?"

"It does indeed."

"Like it or not, this comes down to you. Unless we put a stop to this thing, I fear we're gonna find ourselves in the middle of a shooting war."

Beijing

Thousands of miles away, a man Tanner had never met was about to seal his fate.

In the weeks following their meeting at Yuyuan Lake, Chang-Moh Bian had heard nothing from Roger Brown. As instructed, Bian had done his best to forget the affair and go about his life. "You've done your part," Roger had said. "Unless something changes, we won't be needing you anymore."

The words had been music to Bian's ears. All the sneaking around, worrying about whether he was being watched, holding his breath whenever he saw a PSB officer. . . . It was finally over.

And then, the signal came.

As was his routine, Bian was riding the bus to work when he saw it. As he got off at Xizhimen Station to change lines, he froze, staring at the back of a nearby bench. Jammed into the wood were two thumbtacks, one red, one blue.

Heart in his throat, Bian called in sick, hurried home, and dug through the notes he'd jotted for himself. They wanted another meeting.

THREE DAYS LATER, HE GOT UP EARLY, FORCED HIMSELF TO EAT a light breakfast, then set out.

He boarded the bus at Chaoyangbei Street near his apartment and took it into Old Beijing. Over the next two hours he changed buses three times, getting off at one stop, walking to another several blocks away, then boarding again.

Certain he'd followed the procedures correctly, he disembarked at Dongsi Beidajie, hailed a pedi-taxi—the modern name for a rickshaw—and asked to be driven to a coffee shop near Longfu Hospital, where he got out and walked inside.

He chose a table near the window and ordered a cup of tea. The café was busy, full of Westerners and Chinese alike, which was precisely the point, he assumed. *What had Roger called it? "Cover for status."* If either of them were questioned, they had a legitimate reason for being at the café.

He sat for ten minutes, glancing at his watch, his heart pounding.

Outside, Brown appeared on the sidewalk. He stooped to tie his shoe.

I'll stop to tie my shoe. When I do, get up and start walking toward the door.

Bian stood up, dropped a few *yuan* on the counter, and headed for the door.

Not too fast, not too slow. . . .

Bian forced himself to slow down, sidestepping other diners in the aisle.

Brown was crossing the sidewalk now, coming toward the door.

When you reach the door, be on the left side; drape your coat in front of your body and let your right hand dangle by your side, palm open and toward me. I'll place the packet in your hand.

Brown reached the door. He pulled it open. The greeting bell tinkled. Bian bumped into a young pregnant woman, excused himself, kept going.

Don't avoid eye contact; just a cordial smile and move on.

He and Brown met at the door and exchanged smiles. Bian felt something rectangular pressed into his palm. He closed his hand around it, then turned sideways and stepped onto the sidewalk.

There, Bian thought. *Done. Now just switch your coat to the other arm—*

The toe of his shoe struck a crack in the concrete. He stumbled. The pavement rushed toward him. He reached out to brace himself. The packet—a micro cassette tape case, he now saw—slipped from his hand and clattered across the sidewalk.

Someone stopped beside him and leaned down to help.

"No, thank you, I'm fine, really. . . ."

Bian scurried after the case. He scooped it up and stuffed it into his pocket.

Behind him, he heard, "Sir?"

It's them, it's the police. . . .

Bian spun.

An elderly woman stood on the sidewalk, holding his coat. She smiled a toothless grin and handed it to him. He grabbed it, muttered a thank-you, then turned and hurried away.

SITTING ON A BENCH ACROSS THE STREET, MYUNG NIU OF THE People's Security Bureau, saw it all.

After reporting his accidental encounter with Bian at Yuyuan Lake, Niu had been given permission to oversee the surveillance of Bian. Niu had no idea where, if anywhere, it would lead, but in the competitive world of the PSB, you didn't pass up a chance to distinguish yourself. If Bian's activities were determined to be proper and innocent, Niu had lost nothing. If, however, Bian was engaged in something illegal—something the State considered a capital offense—Niu's name would be mentioned in high circles.

And now this.

Watching the cassette slide across the pavement, Niu instantly realized what he'd just seen. Moreover, he recognized the man Bian had just "bumped into" as the same one from Yuyuan.

It took all his self-control to not arrest Bian on the spot.

They knew who he was, where he lived, where he worked. He wasn't going anywhere. The other man, however, was another story. He was obviously a *waiguoren,* but beyond that, he was a mystery.

Not for long.

Niu stood up and walked down the block to a phone booth. He connected with the exchange operator and recited a number. Waiting for the call to go through, he scanned the café's interior until he spotted the American sitting in a booth near the back.

Good, Niu thought. *Sit there and enjoy your meal. In ten minutes I'll have a dozen men here. Then we'll find out who and what you are.*

• • •

Five hundred miles northeast of Beijing, inside a camp known only by its numeric designator of "Laogi 179," General Han Soong stared at the wall of his cell and felt a wave of despair wash over him.

Four thousand five hundred and six days. Twelve years staring at the same walls, eating the same food, listening to the light buzzing above his head. . . . A dozen summers and winters, gone. His wife, gone.

His first winter in prison, they'd awoken him in the middle of the night, dragged him outside into the wind and snow, and shoved him aboard a helicopter.

When they arrived at their destination he was led into a white-tiled room with fluorescent lights and a dozen stainless-steel tables. It was a morgue, he'd realized. All the tables were empty, save one, which was covered by a white sheet. They led him forward and pulled off the sheet.

It was his wife. She was pasty white, her once shining hair dull and brittle.

"She died four days ago. You may pay your respects. You have two minutes."

Soong stood stiffly by the table, blinking back the tears. He said a private prayer for her, then turned and walked out.

My Lord, Soong thought, *should I have gone with Briggs?* Freedom had been within his grasp. But what of Lian? She was all he had left. Without her at his side, freedom would have been hollow.

What if she too were dead? What if she'd died and they'd never told him?

Stop it. Lian is alive; she's alive and we are going to be together again.

Briggs will come back for both of us.

42

Beijing

It was six p.m. local time when Tanner's plane touched down at Beijing's Capital Airport.

Once off the jetway, he found himself on a narrow concourse bordered by iron barricades. Painted on the floor were two stripes, one red and one green, each leading to Customs gates.

Overhead, a speaker crackled to life. A singsong voice recited something first in Chinese, then French, German, and finally English: "Welcome to Beijing. Travelers with declarations, to the red area; travelers without declarations, to the green area. Have all documents ready for inspection."

Tanner chose the red line, waited his turn, then set his duffle bag on the counter.

"Bu dui!" the customs agent barked. *"Bu dui!" No, not good!*

"Shanme?" Tanner replied, deliberately mutating "what" into the word for "moldy noodles."

"Not time for bag," the agent said in English. "Put on floor until ask. Papers please."

Along with his passport, Tanner handed over the plethora of forms he'd filled out on the plane: entry registration, health card, luggage declaration, temporary visitor (business) entry visa, letter of invitation, photographic equipment permit request, and an emergency contact sheet.

The agent scanned the documents. "What is your name?"

"Ben Colson."

"Your letter of invitation is three months old."

"This is the earliest I could be here."

"Who is this? Who gave invitation?"

"He's a deputy minister in Sichuan Province," Tanner replied.

In truth, the man didn't exist, but the gamble was a safe one given the number of ministers, deputy ministers, and associate deputy ministers in China. More importantly, the letter was printed on the correct stationery and covered with half a dozen "chops," or bureaucratic routing stamps.

"He oversees a cultural exchange program," Tanner said. "When he heard about my book—"

The agent waved his hand, bored. "Book? What book?"

"It's called *Glorious Zhongguo*."

"You are declaring a camera. Where is it?"

Tanner produced the camera, a top-of-the-line digital Nikon.

"Photographing of restricted areas is forbidden: Police stations, government buildings, military bases—all forbidden. You must have camera when leave. If not, you will be fined."

"I understand."

"Now bag."

Tanner set his duffle on the counter. The agent unzipped it, rummaged inside for a moment, then withdrew a copy of *U.S. News and World Report*. "What is this? Why did you bring this?"

"I wanted something to read."

The agent flipped through it, frowning and shaking his head. "This is not allowed."

"Why?"

"Political. It is political."

Tanner had half-expected this, but it still surprised him. The fact that he could probably buy the very same magazine in one of the airport's shops told him the magazine itself wasn't the issue, but rather that he, an arrogant *waiguoren,* or "far country person," had dared bring it into the country.

The agent rifled through the rest of his bag, studying his razor, tapping his comb against the counter, unfolding his map and holding it up to the light, unrolling his socks. . . . The process continued until Tanner felt the first flutter of fear in his belly. *It doesn't mean anything. You're American and you've rubbed him the wrong way, nothing more.*

The agent finished with his bag, then stuffed the contents back inside and shoved it across the counter. He stamped each of Tanner's documents and handed them back. "Welcome to China."

He hadn't walked fifty feet when two charcoal-suited Chinese men stepped in front of him and flashed their IDs. They were plainclothes PSB inspectors.

"Good evening," the taller one said in English. "Your passport and entry documents, please."

Tanner handed them over. "Have I done something wrong, Officer?"

The inspector gave the paperwork a cursory glance, then handed them to his partner. "You will please come with us, Mr. Colson."

"Am I under arrest? Have I done something wrong? Perhaps I made a mistake on my—"

The inspector stepped forward and cupped Tanner's elbow. "Please come with us."

They led him through a locked door and down two flights of stairs to a small, windowless room with a table and three chairs. Sitting in the corner was the suitcase he'd checked aboard the plane.

Bad sign, Briggs thought. They'd seized his bag *before* they had approached him, which meant this wasn't a random stop. Though not yet ready to push the panic button, he felt himself tensing.

He scanned the room for cameras or peepholes; there were none. It was just him and these two inspectors. If the time came, he'd have to disable both of them quickly.

He rehearsed it in his mind: *Search them for anything pertaining to him, take the documents and luggage, hail a cab, get into the city, find the cache drop and pray Mason's embassy people have already stocked it, then go to ground. . . .* With any luck, an hour after leaving the airport he would be lost in Beijing's ten million-plus population.

He prayed it didn't come to that. His job was going to be hard enough by itself; doing so while being hunted as a fugitive would make it nearly impossible.

"Please sit," the lead inspector said.

Tanner did so. The inspectors remained standing, the tall one at the table, his partner beside the door. *Smart boy,* Briggs thought. *Have to reach him before he can get out the door. . . .*

"Where are you staying, Mr. Colson?"

"The Bamboo Garden Hotel on Jiugulou Street."

"You list your occupation as photographer. Is that correct?"

"Yes, that's correct."

"Tell us about your book."

"It's not my book, actually. I was hired by the house—"

"The what?"

"The publisher—Random House in New York."

"Please continue."

"It's a portrait on China called *Glorious Zhongguo.*"

"You used the traditional name for our country—why?"

"It's what you call your country; it seemed appropriate."

"Quite so. The word *China* is a Western invention. Did you know that?"

"No."

"You are an employee of this publisher?"

"No, I'm freelance—I work for myself."

"You are an entrepreneur?"

"I guess you could say that."

"We have entrepreneurs now, you know."

"I've heard that." *He's fishing,* Tanner thought. Was this *waiguoren* an advocate for the spread of the disease known as capitalism, or did he recognize the sanctity of Chinese culture and tradition?

"What's your opinion of China's entrepreneurial system?" the inspector pressed.

"I don't really have one. I just take pictures. I let the politicians worry about that other stuff."

The inspector stared at him for a moment. "Spoken like a true artist, Mr. Colson." He reached down, picked up Tanner's duffle, and placed it on the table. "May I?"

"Help yourself."

The inspector unzipped the duffle and pulled out the Nikon. "Very nice. How much memory?"

"Eight megs," Tanner replied.

"You can take many photographs with this?"

"A couple hundred on the normal setting."

"Technology is wonderful, isn't it?"

Another lure. "It can be; it also has its downside. There's a lot to be said for the simple, uncomplicated life."

The inspector returned the camera to Tanner's duffle and returned it to the floor. He then reached into his lapel pocket and withdrew a sheet of paper, which he placed on the table before Tanner. "This is a statement that you will not, under any circumstances, take photographs of police stations, government buildings, military facilities, or any other similarly restricted areas. If you do so, you may be subject to arrest and imprisonment. Do you understand?"

"Yes."

"Then please sign." Tanner did so. "Furthermore, you will be prepared at all times to present upon request, your camera, film, and permit to any local official. Do you understand this also?"

"Yes."

"Then please initial here."

Tanner did so.

"Thank you," the man said, then gestured to his partner, who stepped forward and handed Tanner his documents and passport. "You are free to go. Enjoy your stay in Beijing."

Tanner gathered his luggage, climbed the stairs to the main concourse, and stepped outside.

The sidewalk teemed with milling passengers. Taxis honked back and forth. Many in the crowd—Beijing natives, Tanner guessed—were wearing white surgical masks. Except for rare days when the wind was blowing right, Beijing lived under an near-constant smog warning. Tanner looked to the southwest, toward the city proper, and saw a grayish brown cloud hanging over the skyscrapers. Already he could feel his throat stinging.

He made his way to the curb and spotted a free taxi across of the lane.

"*Wanshang hao!*" the driver called through the side window. *Good day*. "Taxi, sir?"

"Yes."

Tanner climbed in the back. "Where go?" the driver asked.

"Tingsonglou Hotel."

"Mei wenti!" No problem. "Huang tou tai gao le."

It took Tanner a moment to piece together the words. *Huang tou tai gao le. . . .* The literal translation was "Blond hair too tall." Evidently, the driver considered him something of a freak.

With a blare of his horn and a shout out the window, the driver swerved into traffic. Within minutes they were away from the airport and heading toward the city.

In the back, Tanner stared out the window. He looked down at his hands. They were shaking.

Welcome to China, Briggs.

43

Ulaanbaatar, Mongolia

AS TANNER WAS HEADING TOWARD BEIJING PROPER, CAHIL WAS suffering through a white-knuckle landing aboard a Soviet-build Anatov-27 whose floor had more patches than an Appalachian quilt.

He gripped the armrests tighter and glanced at his seatmate, an elderly Mongolian man wearing purple pants, a yellow tunic and a splotchy fur hat. He reminded Bear of a Mongolian Willy Wonka.

"Boombity, boombity, boom," Willy yelled over the roar.

It was a fair impression of the sound the wheels were making on the rutted landing strip.

"Yeah," Cahil replied. "Boombity."

Abruptly the engines died away, leaving behind only the sound of the thumping tires. Cahil realized the pilot had shut off the engines to conserve fuel, a priceless commodity in Mongolia.

As the plane coasted to a stop, Cahil felt a tap on his shoulder.

"No more boombity," Willy said with a toothless grin. "Stop now."

"Never volunteer yourself, Bear," Cahil muttered.

THE ANSWER TO THE GAME CAHIL HAD COME TO CALL "WHERE in the World is Mike Skeldon?" had been answered two days earlier by a static-filled, ten-second phone call.

With Dick Mason and the CIA's resources at his disposal, Cahil had moved Kycek to a safe house in rural Virginia, where a team from Langley's Science and Technology Directorate set up a phone-router for Kycek's home number in Asheville. From Monday morning forward, all Kycek's incoming calls were automatically routed to a switchboard in the safe house's basement.

Promptly at noon on Tuesday, a call came in. As instructed, Kycek let it ring three times, then picked it up. As he did so, the CIA technician flipped on the recorders and the speakers.

"Hello?" Kycek said.

"Ready to travel?" the voice asked.

"I'm ready."

"Tomorrow morning, Ronald Reagan. Go to the TWA desk; there'll be a ticket waiting for you."

"Okay," Kycek said. "Uh, should I bring anything?"

"Yeah: warm clothes."

The line went dead.

Kycek hung up. Cahil turned to the technician, who said, "Not enough for a solid trace, but it was overseas, that's for sure."

"Warm clothes," Kycek said. "Wonder what that means? Russia, you think?"

Cahil shrugged and clapped him on the shoulder. "Not your worry anymore," he replied, then thought, *Yeah, definitely Russia. But where and why?*

• • •

RUSSIA VIA LOVELY MONGOLIA, CAHIL THOUGHT AS THEY SLOWED beside the gray terminal building. Painted on its front in bright red and black was a fur-hatted Mongol on a galloping horse. Cahil assumed it was the Mongolian state seal. Just to be sure, he tapped Willy and pointed.

"Suhe Baator," Willy explained. "Suhe the Hero."

"The liberator of Mongolia," Cahil replied.

"Yes, yes! Great liberator. *Kharasho!*"

Kharasho was the Russian word for "good." Though the Russians had been gone for over a decade, their legacy lived on. Many Mongolians still spoke a mixture of Mongol and Russian along with a smattering of Dorbet, Buryat, and a dozen other dialects.

The plane shuddered to a stop. As if on cue, the passengers leapt up. The door was flung open by the lone flight attendant.

When Bear reached the door, instead of stairs he found a telescoping aluminum ladder leaning against the Anatov's fuselage. He climbed down, then let himself drop the last few feet to the ground, stirring up a cloud of fine, gray dust.

Despite himself, he smiled. "One small step for man. . . ."

WITHIN MINUTES THE PASSENGERS, AIRCREW AND MAINTENANCE people had disappeared into the terminal building and Cahil found himself alone with the dust and the plane. A gust of wind blew across his face and he shivered. From horizon to horizon, the sky was a pristine, unblemished blue. The travel book he'd read on the flight called Mongolia "The Land of the Million Mile Sky." He now saw why.

These were the steppes of the Mongol hordes. Seven hundred years ago, Genghis Kahn and his tribe of bantam-size horsemen rode out of these grasslands and conquered half the known world. It must have been an awesome sight, Cahil thought: the bleak green hills, the blue sky, and in between, tens of thousands of Mongols, spearheads jutting skyward like the branches of a moving forest.

Maggie would love this, he decided. She was a born and raised Montanan, a child of Big Sky Country. Of course, Montana had nothing on Mongolia. This was nothing *but* sky—millions of square miles of it. Thinking of her and the girls, he felt suddenly lonely.

They're fine, he told himself. *They're fine, and you'll be back to them soon.*

The airport sat atop one of the foothills in the Hentiyn Nuruu mountain range; below lay Ulaanbaatar proper. Aside from a few multistory buildings and coal-belching smokestacks, most of the city's structures were squat affairs similar.

The air was filled with the tangy scent of what he guessed to be mutton, the cornerstone of Mongolian cuisine: Mutton, mutton fat, and mutton juice combined with gnarled potatoes, bland radishes, and soggy cabbage.

He followed the road down out of the foothills, across a bridge spanning a muddy river, and reached a road his map called Engels Avenue. Somewhere in the distance he heard strains of music, and it took him a moment to recognize it: "Hey Macarena. . . ." Ulaanbaatar, it seemed, was several years behind the newest tunes. Bear imagined a group of squat legged, dusky cheeked Mongol teenagers dancing the Macarena and found himself laughing.

He veered left down Engels and soon reached the Ulaanbaatar railway station.

He checked his watch: 11:30. Skeldon's written instructions, which had been attached to the ticket at Dulles, had been curt: *Go to the train station and wait. You'll be met sometime after noon.*

Bear mounted the deserted platform, explored a bit, checked the train schedule (the next arrival was due in in three days from Ulan-Ude, Russia), then found a bench and sat down.

AT THREE O'CLOCK, A GREEN, RUSSIAN YAZ TRUCK—THE SOVIET version of the U.S. Army's deuce-and-a-half—screeched to a stop beside the platform. The driver's door opened and a man climbed out.

The mysterious Mike Skeldon, Cahil thought.

He matched Latham's description to a tee: a few inches over six feet, rangy but muscular, blond buzz cut, and a hawk nose. As Skeldon walked toward the platform, Cahil could see his eyes scanning the ground around him. *The LRRP on patrol.* Retired or not, Skeldon was still a soldier-scout at heart.

Skeldon mounted the platform steps and walked to Cahil's bench. "You've lost weight."

And you've lost your Southern twang. The persona of Joe-Bob the Handyman was gone.

"Thanks. You trying to pick me up?"

"You've lost weight," Skeldon repeated impassively.

"How do you know?"

"I know."

"I went to Jenny Craig, so what?" Cahil growled. "Look, I've been flying on a death trap for the last six hours. Can we save the quiz for later?"

"No. Where'd you go to college?"

"Purdue. Dropped out in my senior year, joined the navy, and went into EOD—Explosive Ordinance Disposal."

"Separation date?"

"My DD-two-fourteen says May ninth of eighty-nine, but they got it wrong. It was the tenth."

Skeldon asked him a few more questions, then nodded. "Grab your bag and follow me."

SKELDON DROVE AWAY FROM THE RAILWAY STATION AND TURNED onto Peace Avenue. The road teemed with goats, horses, automobiles, and pedestrians, all of whom seemed to be obeying their own personal traffic laws. "No traffic police, I assume?" Cahil said.

"Nope," replied Skeldon.

"How many people in the city?"

"Half a million. About forty percent of them live on steppes just outside the city in *gherrs.*"

"What's a *gherr*?"

"It's what we call a 'yurt'—you know, those teepeelike things."

"All year around—summer or winter?"

"Summer's about a month long here; blink and you miss it. Mongols are tough."

"Genghis Khan."

"Yep. Tough."

An hour later they were twenty miles outside the city and traveling northeast on a rutted dirt tract. On either side of the road the steppes and rolling hills spread to the horizon.

"Can you tell me anything about where we're going, what we're doing?" Cahil asked.

Skeldon glanced at him, hesitated a moment, then replied, "We're headed to Naushki, on the Russian border. Once we're across, we'll link up with our team outside Kazachinskoye."

"Never heard of it."

"You and six billion other people."

"You said 'team.' I thought it was just you and me."

For the first time since they met, Skeldon laughed. "You kidding me? For where we're headed, we're gonna need all the help we can get."

44

Germantown Memorial Hospital

NEITHER DUTCHER NOR MASON WERE UNDER ANY ILLUSION: THE course they'd chosen could not only land them in prison, but could, if ever made public, shake the country to its foundations. Love him or hate him, Phillip Martin was the democratically elected president of the United States. Neither of them were comfortable in the knowledge that what they were planning was nothing less than a coup d'état.

"We can dress it up and dance it around all we like," Mason confided in Dutcher, "but the plain truth is, we're talking about overthrowing our own head of state."

"I can live with it," Dutcher replied. "Can you?"

"Ask me later."

EXACTLY AT NOON, GENERAL CATHERMEIER PUSHED THROUGH the door of the hospital room. Standing beside Grandma Zi's bed were Dutcher, Mason, and Latham.

"Thanks for coming, Chuck," said Mason.

"What the hell's going on?" He walked cautiously toward the bed, his eyes on the old woman lying there. At the head of her bed, an EKG monitor beeped every few seconds, accompanied by the rhythmic hiss of the ventilator. "Dick, why am I in a hospital, and who is this woman?"

"Bear with me, Chuck."

"You call me out of the blue, give me this mystery summons . . . Christ almighty, all this cloak-and-dagger crap. . . ." Cathermeier looked at Dutcher. "Leland?"

"You've got to trust us, Chuck."

Cathermeier frowned, the sighed. "What happened to her?"

Latham answered. "General, we haven't met. I'm Charlie Latham. I'm an agent with the FBI. This woman was shot by my partner a few nights ago. She was trying to kill me."

"This old woman? Why?"

"That's a question best answered by our guest of honor," Mason said, glancing at his watch. "Leland, call the doctor; let's get this ventilator unhooked."

BOUSIKARIS ARRIVED FIVE MINUTES LATER. AS DID CATHERMEIER, the chief of staff hesitated at the door, a mixture of anger and confusion on his face, then shut it behind him. "What is this? Dick, why—"

"Come in, Howard," Mason said. "We have something to discuss."

"Why am I here? This is a hospital. If we have something to discuss, call my secretary—"

"This is a topic best kept between us."

"Is that so? And what might that be?"

"Your betrayal of your country, Howard."

"I have no idea what you're talking about."

"And your association with agents of the government of the People's Republic of China."

"Nonsense! What agents?"

"This woman, for one."

"I've never seen her before in my life. Dick, I don't know what game you're playing, but you've lost your mind—all of you. I'm going to make sure the president hears about this."

Bousikaris turned and headed for the door. Latham got in front of him and held up a photo.

"Do you recognize this man?"

Bousikaris glanced at the picture, hesitated for a moment. Dutcher saw a flicker of surprise in his eyes. *Now he'll decide,* Dutcher thought. *Bluff it out, or work an angle and hope to save himself.*

"Never seen him before," Bousikaris said. "Now remove your hand—"

"I think you do," Latham pressed. "He's in the morgue downstairs. I killed him. And my partner shot this woman. They invaded my house, Mr. Bousikaris. They came to kill me and my family—just like they killed Larry Baker, his wife, and their two daughters."

"Who? Baker . . . you mean the Commerce—"

"That's right," Mason said. "Not only did you and Martin climb into bed with foreign agents, but murderers, as well."

"I have no idea what you're talking about."

"She and her husband taped everything—including your meetings and the murder of the Baker family. When she recovers, she's going to point the finger at you."

"Recovers? Look at her; she's a vegetable."

"Is she? She's not going to be much to look at, and she probably won't be able to feed, dress, or wash herself, but she'll be able to answer questions."

"I don't believe you."

"That's your choice. I'm more concerned with what the attorney general and the American public are going to believe. You've conspired with a pair of mass murderers to betray your country, Howard. The moment those accusations become public, your life is over."

"You wouldn't dare."

"Goddamned right I would," Mason replied. "In fact, if I had my druthers, we wouldn't even be having this conversation. Use your brain. Once the newspapers sink their teeth into this, you're going to be the most reviled man in America."

Bousikaris was shaking his head. "No."

"They'll play a few seconds from the Baker tape, then mention your name, and it'll all be over. Two hundred sixty million Americans will want your head on a stick."

"You don't understand—"

"What's to understand? Your loyalty to Martin? Martin works for the people of this country; so do you. You sold them out and now it's time to pay."

Bousikaris shuffled to the chair and slumped into it. His overcoat slipped from his arm and piled around his feet. "What do you want?"

"All of it. We want to know exactly what you and Martin have been up to."

TWO HOURS LATER, BACK AT THE HOLYSTONE OFFICE, THEY HAD it.

Bousikaris, his face blank, his voice monotone, answered their questions without hesitation.

He took them back to the beginning: Martin's assault of his secretary; President Haverland's vow to see Martin's campaign die before it got off the ground; the last-minute influx of capital from the PAC; and finally, the visit from the PRC's ambassador.

"It was all very subtle," Bousikaris explained. "We knew that each one of the ambassador's 'requests' was actually another demand, and we knew what would happen if we didn't go along."

"They would expose the true source of the donations?" Mason said. "They weren't afraid of the repercussions that would bring them?"

"They must have done their homework; they knew Phil would play along. He's so fixated on his damned legacy. . . . You know, the irony is, he could've been a great president. Not anymore."

Dutcher said, "They never gave any hint of what was behind their requests?"

"No. The sarin purchase . . . the ship in Nakhodka . . . It all had a ring of truth to it—which was probably the point, of course."

"To make it easier for you to say yes with a clear conscience."

"Yes."

"What's Redmond's role in this?" asked Mason.

"Nothing. Redmond would wear his pants backward if Phil told him to."

"And the battle group? The business about the reactor accident in Chita?"

"The Chinese want the group there as a calming influence—at least that was their explanation. The reactor accident is real. As for the Chinese casualties—if there are any. . . . It would be impossible to pin down, really. There's no census of the Chinese diaspora in Siberia."

"What about the Security Council meeting?"

"It probably went exactly as they wanted it to go; they didn't want to settle anything."

Mason looked at Dutcher and said, "That'll be their reason—the heartless Russian Bear."

ONCE SURE BOUSIKARIS HAD GIVEN THEM EVERYTHING, LATHAM led him to an empty office with a couch. The chief of staff looked like a shell of himself, shuffling along, his shoulders slumped.

"I almost feel sorry for the guy," Latham said when he came back. "He's been running around for years trying to save Martin from himself, and it just came crashing down on him."

"We might want to keep an eye on him," Dutcher said. "In his state of mind . . . Who knows."

Latham nodded. "I'll watch him."

Mason turned to General Cathermeier. "Chuck, you asked me why all the cloak-and-dagger crap. Now you know why."

"I almost wish I didn't. In essence, what you're saying is our president is a goddamned puppet for the Chinese government."

"That's only the half of it," said Mason. He spent the next ten minutes explaining the connection between Baker, Skeldon, and Han Soong. "Cahil should have already met Skeldon in Mongolia, and Tanner's already on the ground in Beijing."

"Your theory has a lot of gaps in it."

Before either of them could respond, Walter Oaken, who'd disappeared into his office when they arrived with Bousikaris, returned. "Maybe not anymore," he said. "I have a theory."

"Have a seat," Dutcher said. "What've you got?"

"Actually, it's not so much a theory as it is guesswork."

"Go ahead," said Mason.

"Okay." Oaken cleared his throat. "I put myself in China's shoes. The first thought I had was, why try to tackle Russia all by themselves? They may win, they may not. Given how much China has invested in this, those are crappy odds. The Russian Bear may be a little anemic, but a bear is still a bear. Knowing that, the Chinese had to ask the next logical question: How do we even the odds?

"Surprise is one way, but given the number of troops and equipment they'd need to pull off the invasion. . . . Well, you just don't move that many bodies and tanks without somebody noticing. Tactical nuclear weapons is another way, but what's the point of capturing territory that's been turned into a radioactive cesspool?

"If you remove those two equalizers, that leaves one: Overwhelming numerical superiority. To get that, China would have to have been dumping more money into war making."

"Which we know they haven't done," Mason said.

"Right. So their only other choice is to find an ally with enough military might to tip the scales in their favor. But who? Who, among the powerhouse nations, would have anything to do with an invasion of Russia?"

"No one," Dutcher answered.

"Not knowingly, at least. Don't you see? We're China's ally." Oaken started ticking items off on his fingers: "The shale oil process was leaked to China by an employee of the U.S. Commerce Department; we have a team of U.S. Navy SEALs on Russian soil, and a U.S. Navy submarine in Russian waters, both getting ready to launch an attack on the biggest commercial port on Russia's eastern coast; as we speak, a U.S. Navy battle group is steaming toward that same coast; and finally, a former U.S. Army Special Forces soldier is headed into Russia to do God knows what."

"We're being sandbagged," Dutcher said.

"Exactly. By the time China makes its move into Siberia, they'll have us looking like we're involved up to our necks. In Moscow's eyes, it'll be us and China against them. And you know what happens when you corner a bear."

Mason nodded. "It fights back."

Moscow

For Ivan Nochenko, election day in the Russian Federation had passed like a surrealistic dream.

To Bulganin's credit, despite being virtually assured of victory, he'd played the perfect challenger for the media, circumspect in his confidence and fervent in his esteem for the democratic process. Even so, Nochenko had seen the gleam in his pupil's eye, as though Bulganin were enjoying a joke to which no one but himself was privy.

By ten p.m. local time, both the print and electronic media had begun to officially call the election in Bulganin's favor.

By eleven, a crowd of five thousand Bulganin and RPP supporters were milling and dancing about Red Square chanting, "Russian Pride . . . Russian Pride!" Vodka bottles appeared and were passed from hand to hand, between stranger and friend alike. Under the watchful eyes of militia riot-control troops, barrel bonfires were lit and soon flickering shadows swirled over the façade of Lenin's Mausoleum and the arcading of St. Basil's Cathedral.

In his office two miles away, Bulganin stood, arms clasped behind his back as he watched the television coverage. He barked out a laugh. "There's nothing more heartening than a happy Russian! Look, Ivan, do you see?"

Nochenko nodded. "Yes, I see."

Bulganin's secretary rushed into the room. "Sir! Channel Four . . . it's the president."

Bulganin clicked the remote and the channel changed to show the incumbent Federation President standing at the podium on the floor of the Duma. ". . . you have spoken, my fellow Russians. It is with both respect and sadness that I hereby congratulate my opponent, Vladimir—"

"Ha!" Bulganin snapped. "About time!"

My God, Nochenko thought. *It's done.* He felt momentarily dizzy.

From the other room, a cheer arose from Bulganin's staff, followed by applause.

Bulganin clicked off the television. He stared at the blank screen for a few moments, then took a deep breath and turned to face Nochenko. "Ivan," he said solemnly.

Nochenko nodded. "Yes."

"We've done it."

"Yes. . . . Mr. President."

Bulganin's face split into a broad grin and he strode forward and clasped Nochenko by the shoulders. "We've done it, Ivan! Now we can get started. We have much work ahead of us—great work! Starting tomorrow, we put the Motherland back onto the road to greatness! God help those who stand in our way!"

45

Beijing

ONE OF THE FEW REMAINING GARDEN COURTYARD-STYLE HOTELS in Beijing, the Bamboo Garden Hotel, is surrounded on all sides by *hutongs*, or narrow alleys, thick rows of juniper hedges, and tall spruce trees. The red-lacquered front door is guarded by a pair of stone lions and the narrow street outside is covered in a layer of dust blown in from the Gobi Desert by what the Chinese call the "yellow wind."

After checking into his room, Tanner pulled out his cell phone—a Motorola satellite phone that had been specially modified by the CIA's Science & Technology wizards—and dialed. The number was local, an Internet line maintained by a Langley front company. After a single ring, the line clicked open. Briggs punched in a five-digit code, then disconnected.

Embedded in each of the five tones was a frequency spike designed to interrupt the carrier signal at a particular modulation. The first and last tones were called "shackles," the electronic equivalent of the "Start" and "Stop" inserts in old-style telegrams. Once decoded at Langley, the four remaining tones would match up to a list of phrases and words maintained by the Op Center's duty officer.

The message he'd sent was one of a dozen he'd memorized before leaving:

SAFE, ON THE GROUND, PROCEEDING.

He checked his watch. He had three hours before his meeting with the embassy's contact. He set his watch alarm, stretched out on the bed, and drifted off to sleep.

He rose at four, took a shower, and changed clothes, then left the Bamboo Garden and walked six blocks to the Drum Tower at the intersection of Gulou and Dianmenwai streets.

Built by Kublai Khan in the 1200s, the tower had once served as Beijing's version of Big Ben, sounding each passing hour with the beating of giant drums. Tourists, mostly Westerners, walked around the red-painted base, gaping up at the layered pagoda roof and the balcony encircling the top. As Tanner had hoped, few people were braving the long, sixty-nine-step climb to the parapets.

He took a few pictures for good measure, then stepped inside, mounted the narrow steps, and stared upward. Once at the top, he circled the lone drum on display, took a few minutes to read the placard, then walked to the balcony railing and looked out.

He could see all of Old Beijing, Beihei Park, and, a mile or so to the south, the Forbidden City, with its sprawl of courtyards, watchtowers, and bridges. He walked along the railing until he could see the Bell Tower a block to the north.

He watched the people milling about the tower's base, concentrating on Chinese faces until he spotted the one he was looking for. Chang-Moh Bian sat on a bench east of the tower on Baochao Hutong. Using Bian as his center point, Tanner scanned the surrounding streets for signs of surveillance.

It was a nearly impossible task. The *Guoanbu*'s Ninth Bureau, officially known as the Antidefection and Countersurveillance Bureau, was good at its job; they knew Beijing's layout, its customs, the ebb and flow of its citizens. If there was a Ninth Bureau team here, the only way Tanner might see it was if someone made a mistake and gave themselves away, which was unlikely.

Also, the very nature of Chinese customs gave any surveillance team an advantage. In China, staring at a foreigner or even following them about is not considered rude. Chinese are curious by nature and feel no need to either hide it or apologize for it. In fact, such overt interest is considered complimentary.

Briggs would have to rely on his instincts to tell him whether he was being stared at because of curiosity, or because he was a target; whether the person or persons following him were simple gawkers, or professional watchers.

When only five minutes remained before the official wave-off time, Tanner descended the tower steps and walked east on Gulou Dondajie, then turned north onto Baochao.

Bian was still sitting on his bench. He glanced nervously at his watch, then looked over his shoulder. Brown was right. Everything about Bian's demeanor cried, "Arrest me!"

Taking pictures as he went, Tanner strolled around the Bell Tower until he stood beside Bian's bench. He turned to Bian and asked in English, "Pardon, is this the Bell Tower or the *Zhonglou*?"

Bian hesitated, then said. "They are the same, though the Drum Tower has been here longer."

Tanner opened his map and stepped closer as though asking for directions. "Get up and walk north to Doufuchai Hutong," he said with a smile. "Once there, turn left and follow it to Xidajie. I will meet you in Guanghua Temple in thirty minutes. Do you understand?"

"Yes. What—"

"We'll talk when we meet. Walk slowly, be casual. Go on."

Bian stood up and started toward Doufuchai. Tanner waited sixty seconds, then followed.

HE TRAILED BIAN AT A DISTANCE, STOPPING FREQUENTLY TO LOOK in shop windows or take a picture, all the while keeping Bian in his peripheral vision. It took Bian less than ten minutes to reach Guanghua Temple. Tanner waited until he was inside and out of sight, then started "quartering his tail," retracing their route, weaving his way north and south along the streets parallel to Doufuchai Hutong as he watched for surveillance. Twenty-five minutes after his initial departure, he was back at the Bell Tower.

As far as he could see, no one was showing any interest in either Bian or himself.

He walked two blocks down Gulou Dondajie and turned onto Houhai Beiyan, which took him to the rear entrance of Guanghua Temple. He found Bian in one of the gardens, standing at the railing beside a pond. Bright orange carp swam lazily in the water.

"Hello," Tanner said.

Bian's hands trembled on the railing. "Hello."

Briggs reached over and placed his hand on Bian's forearm. "You've got to relax."

"Funny, that's what Roger said the last time we met."

"It's good advice. We're almost done. I just need a little bit of information."

"Roger also said that."

"I promise you, once you and are I finished, your part is over. You have my word."

With this, Bian seemed to relax. He took a deep breath and released his grip on the railing. "What kind of information do you need?"

"You told Roger you don't know where Soong is. Explain that."

"Someone has been passing messages between myself and General Soong."

"Who?"

"A guard at the camp where he is being held. He is a distant relative of the general's."

Good news, bad news, Tanner thought. Good news because he now had a contact on the inside, someone with access to Soong; bad news because that contact was linked to Soong. Either the *Guoanbu* had made a mistake in the screening process for the camp's guards, or they had not, and the guard was working for them—either wittingly or unwittingly.

"What's his name?"

"Kam Hsiao."

"Does he know someone is coming for Soong?"

"I assume so," said Bian.

More bad news. "And he's willing to help?"

"Yes."

"How can I reach him?"

"He's in the city. The guards are on two-week rotations; he goes back in a few days."

Tanner nodded. "Give me his address, but don't tell him I'm coming."

TANNER'S WORRIES ABOUT THE SKILL AND ADVANTAGE OF THE *Guoanbu*'s Ninth Bureau watchers were well founded. Three hours after he and Bian parted company at Guanghua Temple, the team's report was lying in front of MSS director Xiang. "It appears our young officer Niu has good instincts," he said, staring at a photo of Bian and Tanner at the Bell Tower.

"What do you want to do?" Eng asked. "By itself, Bian's contact with Brown is enough to arrest him. He's obviously conspiring to—"

"Obviously. What we don't know is what they're up to. That's what we must find out."

"I agree."

"What's their interest in Bian? He's a nobody, a functionary. His job gives him access to nothing of interest; he's got nothing to offer. What do we know about the man he met? It looks like he was carrying a camera. That means tourist, or journalist. Where is he staying, what's his name?"

"We don't know," Eng replied.

"Why not?"

"The team lost him after they parted at the temple."

"Lost him, or he got away from them?"

"He took no obvious actions to lose them, but—"

"But he's gone," Xiang finished, then was silent for a few moments. "We know he's a Westerner, we know he has a camera, and we can safely assume he arrived within the last week. Contact Customs and Immigration and have them pull all the entry visas that match that criteria. We'll check passport photos until we find one matching Bian's new friend."

46

Bay of Vrangel, Russia

JURENS COULDN'T SHAKE THE SENSE OF DÉJÀ VU THAT HAD BEEN tickling his subconscious since they had come ashore. He'd visited the Bay of Vrangel before—at least hypothetically, that is.

Of the hundreds of exercises Jurens had participated in over the years, one was strikingly similar to their current mission: The Soviet Union has crumbled and into the power vacuum has fallen a rogue's gallery of leaders and factions vying for control of the country. One of these factions seizes the port of Nakhodka-Vostochny and shuts it down. In response, and at the request of Russian moderates, the United States sends a navy battle group to force open the port. At its head is a SEAL team tasked with mapping and destroying the bay's obstacles in preparation for an amphibious assault.

The exercise itself, which lasted three long, cold weeks, had been conducted in the Aleutian Islands; the bay had been much smaller and the port imaginary, but the terrain and climate were similar enough to give Jurens a few flashback memories.

This was no exercise, he reminded himself. They were on Russian soil, watching a harbor and waiting for a ship called *Nahrut* so they could sink it. This was as real as it got.

The commercial port of Nakhodka-Vostochny was the largest in the Russian Far East. Nestled within the Bay of Vrangel, it boasted thirty-six berths, over 130 acres of terminals, bunkers, warehouses, a terminus connection to the Trans-Siberian Railway, and a mechanized army of loading equipment, including heavy-lift extension cranes, straddle carriers, and top loaders.

The spot Jurens had chosen was a thick cluster of scrub pine surrounded by boulders at the tip of Cape Kaminski on the bay's north side.

Icy wind whipped at Jurens's face, bringing tears to his eyes and worming its way beneath his camo hood. He suppressed a shiver, then parted the branches of the blind and raised his Night Owl binoculars. The bay's surface was choppy, the swells running three to four feet, and despite the sun, a patchy fog clung to the surface. In the distance, he could hear the wail of ship's whistles and the clanging of buoys.

He scanned toward the mouth of the bay. Somewhere out there, *Columbia* was waiting for the launch time. When that time came, the Harpoons would cut between the two capes, skimming low on the surface at over four hundred knots, their gray-and-white camouflage rendering them nearly invisible in the fog.

"Target, Skipper," Dickie called.

"Where?"

"Twelve degrees off the cape. I only got a glimpse of her bow, but it looks like ours."

He swiveled his binoculars around until he spotted a rust-streaked cargo carrier materializing out of the fog. She was two miles away and turning wide to clear the shoals along the headland.

"See a name?" Smitty whispered.

"No, not yet. . . ." Jurens scanned back along the bow. "There, I've got it: N-A-H-R-U-T. That's her. She's early—almost twelve hours."

FORTY MINUTES LATER, HAVING PICKED UP HER HARBOR PILOT AT the mouth of the bay, *Nahrut* dropped anchor just south of center channel a quarter mile from the port. Another hour passed as *Nahrut*'s crew went through the motions of securing the ship and then, as twilight began to settle over the bay, a cargo net was rolled down her side and her launch was swung out on its davits.

"Going on liberty," Smitty said. "I wonder what happens on a Saturday night in Nakhodka."

"Don't know," Dickie replied, "but you can bet it involves alcohol—lots of alcohol."

Jurens scanned the ship's railing, watching the crewmen climb over the side one by one. A face caught Sconi's eye. He backtracked. "This is interesting. . . ."

"What's up?" said Smitty.

"You see the guy standing at the cargo net, second from the right—the dark-skinned one."

"Yeah, I see him."

"You don't recognize him?" asked Jurens.

"Nope."

"Unless my memory is off, that's Sunil Dhar, our sarin buyer."

"His unlucky day," said Smitty.

"Maybe not," Jurens replied.

In truth, Jurens wasn't supposed to know Sunil Dhar's name or what he looked like. Whether conscious of it or not, Cathermeier's inclusion of Dhar in his brief was a consolation of sorts; when it came to putting men in harm's way, he was a firm believer in full disclosure.

Sconi had a decision to make. Though their orders said nothing about Dhar, he was a target of opportunity. The Kashmeran had been a player in the world's underground arms market for twenty years; his wealth of knowledge would be invaluable to U.S. intelligence.

"What're you thinking, Skipper?" asked Zee. "We paddle over there and snatch him?"

"It would be a shame to waste the chance," Smitty added.

Jurens was inclined to agree, but grabbing Dhar would complicate their job, not to mention their infiltration. As if reading his mind, Dickie said, "We've done it before, we can do it again."

Call it fate, Jurens decided. *Nahrut*'s early arrival and the lack of an open berth had just offered them a chance to destroy her without any collateral damage to the port. Sitting at anchor with her crew ashore, *Nahrut* would slip beneath the waves and their job would be done.

He unfolded his map and spread it on the ground. "Smitty, is your Russian still pretty good?"

"Sehr gut."

"That's German, Smitty."

"Just a joke. It's passable."

"Okay, we'll assume Dhar is going ashore. How long for you and Zee to slip down there?"

"Gotta figure forty minutes transit time, plus another ten to scout security."

Jurens checked his watch. "Two hours there and back?"

"No problem."

"Get your gear together. I'm calling *Columbia* and moving up the launch. I want you back here no later than midnight."

TWO MILES EAST OF THE BAY AND 160 FEET BELOW THE SURFACE, *Columbia* was hovering silently in the water, as she had been for the past six hours. In the Control Room, Kinsock was going over the daily reports when the intercom buzzed. "Conn, Sonar."

Kinsock reached up and levered the switch. "Conn, aye. Captain here."

"Skipper, Chief Boland. Got a minute?"

"On my way."

Kinsock walked out of the Control Room and pushed through the curtain into Sonar. *Columbia*'s Sonar Chief was standing at one of the consoles. "What've you got, Chief?"

"Something a little odd," Boland replied, pointing to the "waterfall" scope; slicing through the cascade of green snow was a thin vertical line: a frequency spike. "It's real faint. Frequency reads like a Kilo-class submarine. The bay's acting like a sound funnel, so its hard to guess the range."

"Plenty of Kilos out there on patrol, Chief; we bypassed two of 'em on the way up the coast."

"What's weird is that every ten seconds or so, the spike sort of . . . jiggles out of its frequency."

Kinsock thought for a moment. "The Russians have sold a lot of their Kilos to the Chinese and North Koreans. I wouldn't be surprised if they made some modifications to the power plant. Would that account for it?"

"Maybe. . . ."

"But maybe not," Kinsock finished. "You worried about this, Chief?"

"Not yet, but . . ." Boland shrugged.

Kinsock clapped him on the shoulder. "Keep an eye on it, see if you can pin it down."

"Aye, Skipper."

The intercom squelched again: "Captain, XO here. Radio's got traffic for you."

"Right. Meet me there."

MacGregor was waiting when Kinsock walked into the Radio Room. "It's Sickle," the XO explained. "Secure SAT-COM. They've authenticated; it's Jurens."

Kinsock keyed the handset. "Sickle, this is Blade, over."

"Blade, this is Sickle: Oscar-Golf-Sierra is delta, I say again, delta. Adjustment to follow: zero-one-zero-zero, break, two-one-zero-zero."

Kinsock mentally translated Jurens's message: *On-ground situation has changed. Request you adjust your schedule: new launch time one a.m. local, new pickup time, nine p.m. local the next night.*

He keyed the handset. "Roger, Sickle, standby."

MacGregor said, "Wonder what's changed?"

"The target's probably early. It's his call; he's on the ground. How far to our launch point?"

"Two thousand yards. No problem."

"Get the firing team together," Kinsock said, then keyed the handset: "Sickle, Blade, over."

"Go ahead."

"Affirmative on your request, will adjust accordingly."

"Roger. Sickle out."

AS SMITTY AND ZEE PICKED UP THE CAPE TOWARD THE PORT complex, Jurens and Dickie kept them apprised of Dhar's movements. To their advantage, the Kashmiri stayed aboard *Nahrut* until well after dark, taking the last launch ashore. "Alpha this is Bravo, over," Jurens said. "Say location."

"Ridge above the north side terminal. One of the warehouses looks like it's been converted into a rec center; that's where most of the crew seems to be headed."

"Freddy's coming ashore; he's about five minutes away from the pier."

"Roger. We're gonna look around. If security's light, we might do it now. Otherwise, we'll wait until he leaves."

"Roger, keep me posted."

"Alpha out."

SMITTY AND ZEE MADE THEIR WAY THROUGH THE TREES UNTIL they were behind and above the recreation center. Below them, an embankment sloped down to a concrete tarmac; fifty yards beyond that was the rear of the building. They could hear voices laughing and shouting in Russian.

"I don't see a fence," Smitty whispered.

"Me neither. The front looks pretty well lit-up, though," Zee replied, then pointed to the roof. Mounted at ten-foot intervals along the front edge were spotlights.

Smitty's earpiece came to life: "Alpha, Freddy has landed; headed your way."

"Roger," replied Smitty. He swung his Night Owls toward the pier road. After a few seconds, Dhar appeared in the yellow glow of a streetlight walking toward the rec center. "There he is."

"What's the plan?" asked Zee.

"Improvisation. Sit tight, Zee. If I need help I'll scratch my head."

Smitty crawled down the embankment to where the trees gave way to loose rock, then started crab-walking down. His feet started sliding. He dropped onto his butt and rode to the bottom.

"Hey, you," a voice called in Russian. What're you doing?"

Shit!

A man wearing a white chef's hat and holding a bag of garbage was standing in the rec center's open back door. "What were you doing up there?"

Smitty rose to his feet, stumbled, then pretended to zip up his pants. "What's it to you!" he slurred. "Can't a man take a crap anymore?"

"We've got toilets, idiot!"

"No kidding. You wanna come over here and wipe my ass, too?" Smitty started unbuttoning his pants and pulling them down. "Come on, then, come over here!"

The chef shook his head, then tossed the garbage bag toward the Dumpster. "Asshole!"

He shut the door.

Smitty let out a breath, and keyed his mouthpiece. "Zee, where's Freddie?"

"Two minutes away."

Continuing his wobbly gait, Smitty made his way to the back of building, then flattened himself against the wall and slid forward until he reached the corner. The shouts and laughter were louder now, interrupted every few seconds by rock music as the front doors opened to admit or expel a patron.

Smitty peeked around the corner. Sunil Dhar was walking across the parking lot. Smitty pulled his hood around his face, took a breath, then stepped into view, careful to stay at the edge of the light.

When Dhar was ten feet away, Smitty whistled softly. "Dhar . . . here."

Dhar stopped. "Who is that?"

"A friend. Get out of the light, for God's sake."

"What do you want?"

"I've got a message from Valerei."

"I don't know any Valerei."

"You're not here on business with a certain colonel?"

"Who are you?"

"A friend, I told you. Do you want the message, or not? Get out of the light, man! You want everyone to know our business?"

Curious now, Dhar walked forward but stopped just out of arm's reach. "What message?"

"The MVD knows about the transaction; they're going to be waiting at the warehouse."

"How did this happen?"

"I don't know. That's a question for the colonel. I can take you to him."

Dhar looked around, nervous again.

He's not going for it, Smitty thought. He was going to have to do it the hard way. Smitty looked around. Aside from a pair of stevedores nearing the front doors, the lot was empty. He kept one eye on them and another on Dhar, who was starting to shuffle his feet nervously.

"Look," Smitty said. "I've got his phone number."

The two stevedores reached the door, pulled it open.

"Here, talk to him yourself."

Smitty reached into his pocket, then extended his hand. Instinctively, Dhar looked at it. Smitty curled it into a fist and lashed out, striking Dhar on the point of the chin. The Kashmiri slumped forward. Smitty caught him, hefted him over his shoulder, then turned around and started trotting.

"Bravo, this is Alpha," he radioed.

"Go ahead," Jurens replied.

"Got Freddie, en route."

WITH ONLY TWENTY MINUTES LEFT BEFORE *COLUMBIA*'S LAUNCH, they slipped back into camp. Smitty dumped Dhar's still unconscious body onto the ground, then plopped down and accepted a canteen from Jurens. "Problems?" Sconi asked.

"Nah, he just took a little convincing. The crew still ashore?"

"Yep. Come on, help me with the LTD. Dickie, Zee, pick a spot and keep your eyes peeled."

Jurens and Smitty removed the Laser Target Designator from its waterproof case and started assembling it.

Powered by a nickel-cadmium battery and mounted on tripod legs, an LTD is nothing more than a night-vision scope joined with a frequency-adjustable laser, a concept similar to that of a laser sighted rifle: Wherever the laser dot goes, the bullet follows. In the case of an LTD, the laser can be seen only by a missile seeker programmed to search for it.

The team's job was simple: Keep the *Nahrut* "painted" with the electromagnetic bull's-eye so *Columbia*'s Harpoons would be able to distinguish her from the other ships at anchor.

Smitty flicked on the battery. "Power's up."

Jurens put his eye to the scope. Slowly the blackness resolved into a green glow. To his left, the lights of the port reflected off the dark surface of the bay. "Steer me."

"Twenty degrees left; make it bearing . . . two-one-zero true."

Jurens swung the scope around, watching the compass pointer rotate past one-eighty, then two hundred. . . . "Okay, I've got her." He adjusted the focus knob and *Nahrut*'s port bow came into view. He tracked backward along her forecastle to the midships hatch.

"Okay, Smitty, gimme the dot."

A red dot appeared in the reticle.

Jurens thumbed the knob, edging the dot downward until it covered the crease where the main deck and exterior bulkhead met. He pulled away from the eyepiece. "I'm set." He grabbed the SATCOM handset: "Blade, this is Sickle. The band is ready to play. I say again. . . ."

". . . THE BAND IS READY TO PLAY, OVER."

Aboard Columbia, Kinsock keyed the handset. "Sickle, Blade, roger. Guests en route. Out."

Kinsock turned to MacGregor, "Start the firing plan, Jim. Diving Officer, take us to periscope depth, all hands prepare for missile launch."

47

NMCC

CATHERMEIER AND MASON LEFT HOLYSTONE AND DROVE TO THE Pentagon.

Finally convinced of not only Mason's suspicions about Martin, but also that the premise of *Columbia*'s mission was bogus, Cathermeier wasn't about to let it continue. Whatever else China had up its sleeve was yet to be seen, but by calling off the attack on *Nahrut*, Cathermeier might at least be able to impede their plans.

What he couldn't know was that it was already too late.

THE PENTAGON'S NERVE CENTER, THE NATIONAL MILITARY COMmand Center, is divided into three main areas: the Emergency Conference Room, or ECR, "The Tank," or the Joint Chiefs secure conference room, and the Current Actions Center, or CAC, a large room filled with communications consoles and computer terminals. Mounted on one wall are three projection screens, one displaying the readiness conditions of various U.S. military theaters, the other two showing maps and satellite feeds.

Cathermeier and Mason walked in and walked directly to the CAC watch officer, an Army major. "What can I do for you, General?"

"Send an ELF to Blade," Cathermeier replied, referring to Extremely Low Frequency message, a slow but effective method of communicating with submerged submarines. "Have her surface for traffic."

Nakhodka-Vostochny

With Sunil Dhar bound, gagged, and still unconscious in the corner of the their lay-up, Jurens and his men lay on their bellies at the edge of the blind, Night Owls raised and focused on the mouth of the bay. In the greenish glow Jurens could just make out the light of Ryurik, the village at the tip of the cape and beyond the black line of the horizon.

"Sickle, this is Blade, over."

Jurens grabbed the handset. "Go ahead Blade."

"En route. Time to target, seventy seconds. Heads down, over."

Sconi smiled. *Thanks for your concern, Archie*. "Roger. Sickle out."

He powered up the LTD and peered through the eyepiece. The glowing red dot was holding steady on the *Nahrut*'s midships hatch. As a target point, it couldn't be better. After their terminal pop-up, the Harpoons would bore into *Nahrut* at an angle and explode at her waterline, breaking her in two.

Forty seconds passed.

Zee called out, "Target, Skipper!"

"Where away?"

"Bearing one-seven-five. Boy, they're really moving!"

Jurens swiveled his Night Owls around.

Flying at over four hundred knots and skimming a bare six feet over the water's surface, the lead Harpoon appeared out of the fog, barely visible against the night sky. As Jurens watched, the second Harpoon came into view, two seconds behind the first and staggered to the left a few feet.

Two miles from *Nahrut* and passing the tip of the cape, the Harpoons executed their first and only waypoint, turning ten degrees to the northwest and lining up on Nahrut's bearing, their seeker's homing in on the LTD's signal.

One mile and twelve seconds from impact, the lead Harpoon popped up to a height of fifty feet, followed a second later by its mate. Jurens watched, waiting for them to tip over toward *Nahrut,* but they continued flying high and level.

Malfunction? he thought. *Come on, nose over. . . .*

And then they were past *Nahrut* and streaking toward the port.

He snatched up the handset. "Blade this is Sickle, drop-kick! I say again, drop-kick!"

It was too late. Two hundred yards from the wharf, the missiles split, the lead Harpoon turning west toward the port's tank farm, the trailing Harpoon east toward a line of ships sitting at berth.

"Jesus Christ. . . ." Smitty muttered.

In a double bloom of fire, the Harpoons struck home and detonated.

EIGHT MILES AWAY, *COLUMBIA* HEARD JURENS'S CALL FOR MIS-sile destruct, but Archie Kinsock had his own problems. Fifty seconds after launching the Harpoons, he was descending and turning east toward deeper water when the squawk box crackled: "Conn, Sonar, contact! Probably submerged vessel, close aboard! Bearing zero-four-four. He's right on top of us, Skipper."

"All stop!" Jurens ordered.

"All stop, aye."

"Conn, Sonar, torpedo in the water, torpedo in the water! Same bearing!"

Kinsock turned to the diving officer. "All ahead flank, full down on the down planes, come right to course one-nine-zero!"

The DO repeated the order. The helmsman and planesman hunched over their controls.

"Launch noisemaker!" Kinsock ordered.

"Noisemaker away."

"Fire control, open doors on stern tube and fire snapshot."

"Snapshot, aye!"

"Sonar, Conn, talk to me." Kinsock called.

"Torpedo's gone active, sir! It's got us!"

"Conn, aye."

"Noisemaker away, Skipper."

"Launch another."

Coming to full speed, *Columbia* pitched over into a spiraling turn. The deck shuddered as compressed air jettisoned the torpedo from the stern tube. "Torpedo away."

"Cut the wires."

"Conn, Sonar, it didn't go for the noisemaker, Skipper. It's coming in!"

"Time?"

"Ten seconds."

"Launch another noisemaker!"

"Noisemaker away."

"Conn, Sonar: Five seconds . . . four. . . ."

Time seemed to slow for Kinsock. Heart pounding in his throat, he looked around the Control Room, taking in the faces of his crew. *If it's gonna happen*, he thought dully, *let it be quick.*

He snatched the IMC handset: "All hands brace for shock!"

48

Kazachinskoye, Russia

ASIDE FROM HAVING TO WAIT SIX HOURS—TWO ON THE MONgolian side, four on the Russian side—at the border, the crossing went smoothly. There'd been bribes to be paid, forms to be filled out, and officials to wheedle, but watching Skeldon work, Cahil realized the former Ranger had done his homework.

The trip from Ulaanbaatar had taken the rest of the day and part of the night as they traversed the dirt tracts that passed as highways on the Mongolian steppe. They pushed on at a steady forty mph, weaving their way ever northward through the cities of Mandal, Baruunharaa, Darhan, past marshes, peat bogs, and rolling hills. And grasslands—in every direction, as far as Cahil could see.

Now, two hours north of the border, Skeldon pulled off the road outside Kazachinskoye and stopped at an abandoned farmhouse. By Cahil's map, they were eighty miles north-west of Lake Baikal at the southern edge of the Great Siberian Basin, a plateau of taiga forest and crisscrossing rivers.

Skeldon stopped the Yaz beside a ramshackle barn and shut off the engine.

"What're we doing?" Cahil asked. He felt the tickle of fear on the back of his neck.

"We're waiting," Skeldon replied, a half smile on his lips.

Suddenly, out the truck's window, the brush along the barn began to move, slowly taking the shape of six men in camouflage gear. Cahil saw six pair of eyes staring back at him.

"Our team, I assume," he whispered.

"Yep. Spooky, ain't they?"

Skeldon restarted the engine and steered the Yaz into the barns, shut off the engine again, but left the headlights on, then got out. "Might as well get out and stretch," Skeldon said. "From here on, it's straight driving."

Cahil climbed down. Piles of moldy straw lay stacked along the walls. Dust motes drifted in the Yaz's headlight beams.

Skeldon was talking to one of the men, the leader of the group, Bear guessed. Only slightly surprised, he saw the man was Chinese. He heard Skeldon say the word, "colonel" but could hear nothing more of their conversation.

The other five men, also Chinese, were shrugging off their gear and stacking it in piles. Each of them carried an M-16 assault rifle, and as Cahil stepped closer, he realized the rest of their equipment was also American-issue: From web-belts, to boots, to grenades, every piece was standard U.S. issue.

Just like me and Skeldon, Cahil thought. *Is that why they were here? Were they nothing more than window dressing?*

Once done piling their gear, the commandos stripped off their camouflage clothing, beneath which they wore rough, twill shirts, sweaters, coats, and corduroy pants. Seeing the transformation, Cahil realized that at a distance each of the men could pass for any number of Russia's native peoples: Buryats, Evenks, cross-border Mongols.

The commandos moved efficiently and with a minimum of talk as they lifted open a hatch set in the barn's floor, revealing a root cellar. They set up a line and began hauling up wooden crates.

Helping Skeldon transfer fuel from the jerry cans to the Yaz's tank, Cahil watched from the corner of his eye as they began stacking the crates in the truck's bed. Each bore a U.S. Army stencil. The contents ranged from MREs, to 5.56 mm ammunition, to portable tactical radios.

The commandos closed the cellar door and piled the last three crates into the back of the Yaz. Cahil glanced up and read one of the stencils:

COMPOSITION 4, 12—1 POUND BLOCKS
STANDARD CHEMICAL DETONATORS, 16 EACH

C-4 plastic explosives, he thought. *Five crates . . . sixty pounds' worth; enough to turn the Sears Tower into a pile of bricks.* He nudged Skeldon and nodded at the crates.

"Mind your business," Skeldon muttered.

"This is my goddamned business," Cahil whispered back. "I wanna know—"

"Not now—later."

WITH THE COMMANDOS IN BACK AND CAHIL AND SKELDON UP front, they pulled out of the barn, back onto the main road, and started north again. The moon was full and bright, the sky sprinkled with stars.

They were well into the Russian steppes now, but unlike the flatlands of Mongolia, the terrain was all trees—millions of square miles of larch, spruce, and conifers stretching in every direction. Stark crescents of snow dotted the hillsides bordering the road, and the Yaz's headlights flashed over ice-filled ruts in the road.

He now understood why the Russians viewed Siberia with equal parts love and fear. It was beautiful, but its vastness was overwhelming. It was no wonder why many of the old Soviet gulags didn't bother with fences—the land itself was the prison.

After a few minutes, Skeldon turned to him. "You need to learn to keep your mouth shut, Kycek. These aren't the kind of people you want to piss off."

"No kidding. Look, this whole thing is making me nervous. Nobody said anything about a goddamned commando mission. When are you gonna tell me what's going on?"

"You'll know tonight. You can see it for yourself."

CAHIL DOZED FITFULLY UNTIL SKELDON WOKE HIM JUST AFTER dawn. "Coffee?"

"Thanks." Cahil sat up and looked around. Aside from the sunlight, the land looked the same as it had hours before: a sea of trees. "How far have we gone?"

"About a hundred twenty miles."

"Aren't there any checkpoints, military posts?"

Skeldon laughed. "Out here? Twenty years ago, maybe, but not today. How would they pay for it? You gotta remember, man, Siberia is almost fourteen million square miles. From Moscow to Vladivostok it's six thousand miles. That's twice the width of the U.S. Starting to get the picture?"

"Yeah: It's big."

"Bigger than big. It can swallow you whole. In some places, if you wander ten miles from civilization, you might as well be on the moon."

"Sounds like you've spent some time here," Cahil said.

"Some."

Time to push a little bit, Bear thought. If nothing else, he wanted to know Skeldon's story. What had brought him to the middle of Siberia, playing guide for a team of Chinese commandos?

"You're ex-military, huh?" Cahil said.

"What makes you say that?"

"The way you carry yourself. You can take the man outa the military, but you can't take the military out of the man."

Skeldon gave a half-smile. "I guess. Yeah, I was army."

"Grunt?"

"What is this, you writing a book?"

"Just trying to pass the time. We got a long drive ahead of us. What're you worried about? You think I'm gonna sell your story to the *National Enquirer*?"

Skeldon laughed. "That'd be something to see." He looked sideways at Cahil, then shrugged. "I was a Ranger—a Lurp before they got absorbed."

"Then the boonies don't scare you much. Hell, this place must feel downright comfortable."

"Better than being in the city, that's for sure."

"How long were you in?"

"Sixteen years."

"Why'd you get out? You were only four shy of retirement."

"They didn't gimme a choice," Skeldon said, bitterness creeping into his voice. "They booted me with a medical discharge."

"What happened?"

"We were on a live-fire exercise in Panama City. I caught a sliver of shrapnel in the head. They took it out, said I was fine, but about a month after I left the hospital I started getting these migraines. Hurt so bad I couldn't walk, couldn't see. The docs poked and prodded me for a couple months, tried all these different drugs on me, but nothing helped. About six months after the accident, my wife tells me she's taking the kids and leaving."

"Why?"

"She said I'd changed," Skeldon said. "I still remember how she put it: 'You ain't been right in the head since you got hurt.' I was mean to her, I yelled at the kids, I forget how to do things—simple stuff, like how to get to the grocery store."

"Was it true?" Cahil asked.

"I guess so. She loved me, so I figured, why would she lie? Friends were telling me the same thing, too, but I didn't see it. By then, the headaches were coming almost every day."

"The doctors couldn't give you anything?"

"Most of what they gave me left me so doped up I couldn't spell my name. I tried acupuncture, meditation, yoga—all that crap, but nothing worked. The only thing that makes it bearable are these."

Skeldon reached into his jacket pocket and handed a bottle to Cahil.

It was Percodan, a prescription painkiller. "This is heavy stuff," Bear said. "Addictive."

"No shit. It's better than feeling like there's an ice pick jammed into your brain."

"How many of these do you take a day?"

"Depends on the day. On average, about a dozen. The pain's still there, but those take off the edge. The downside is, they give me pruritus."

"What's that?"

In response, Skeldon rolled up the sleeve of his field jacket. His forearm was covered in scabbed-over scratches. "Makes me itchy. I scratch in my sleep. I go to bed at night, and when I wake up my sheets are bloody."

"Jesus. Looks painful."

"I hardly feel it," Skeldon said, then grinned. "I ain't much to look at on the beach, though."

Cahil couldn't help himself; he broke out in laughter, and after a few seconds Skeldon joined in. After a few moments, Cahil said, "I can't believe the army didn't help you."

"The army washed their hands of me. I get a disability check every month, but that only covers about a week's worth of pills. The way the army sees it, what happened to me is just part of the risk: Sorry son, you got unlucky. Here's a few hundred bucks."

Now it all made sense, Cahil thought. Everything Skeldon had ever cared about was gone: the army, his wife and children. . . . And all he had to show for it was pain. With nothing else in his life, he'd turned back to the only thing he knew: being a Lurp. Who paid him, and why, was irrelevant.

Cahil felt sorry for him; in other circumstances he might have reached out to help. But in his withdrawal from life, Skeldon had gotten himself involved in something very big and very dangerous.

Bear wondered how much Skeldon knew about his paymasters and their plan. And if he knew, did he care one way or another?

THEY DROVE FOR TWELVE HOURS, NORTHEAST THROUGH IRKUTSK and deeper into the Great Siberian Basin along the river Minya. With one eye on the map and one eye on the landmarks, Cahil ticked off villages as they went: Podgar, Yermaki, Korotkova, Sharabora, Andronovka. The land never changed and the trees never thinned, an unbroken blanket of green beneath the sky.

By late afternoon, they'd reached Yakutia's Chono River Basin.

Skeldon left the main road for a winding, dirt tract that took them deeper into the forest.

This area of the Chono Basin was dominated by a vast reservoir system that extended over a hundred miles from Lake Vilyuy in the north and down to Lake Ichoda in the south, where it split into hundreds of smaller rivers that fed the southern half of the basin.

As the sun was dipping toward the horizon, Skeldon pulled off into a small clearing and shut off the engine. He banged his fist on the cab's wall then got out. Cahil followed. One by one the commandos jumped down and began unloading crates from the Yaz.

"This is it," Skeldon said to Cahil. "Home sweet home."

"For how long? When are you going to let me in on the big secret?"

"Now's as good a time as any."

Skeldon walked to where the commandos were working, spoke with the colonel for a few seconds, then gestured for Cahil to follow. After a quick compass check, Skeldon found a trail leading into the forest, and set off.

The grade increased until they were pulling themselves along from tree to tree. After a mile, the slope eased and the trees thinned, revealing an escarpment. "Watch your step," Skeldon said. "It's a hell of a drop."

He led Cahil down a trail along the cliff face. Bear glanced over the edge, but could see nothing of what lay below, so thick were the trees. In the distance, he could hear the rush of water. After another hundred yards, the path came to a thumb of rock jutting from the cliff.

"Take a look," Skeldon said.

Cahil walked to the edge and peered over. A few hundred yards below, a river wound its way through a jagged-walled canyon. "What am I looking for?"

"Look upriver. You'll have to lean out a bit. Here, I gotchya." Skeldon grabbed the back of Cahil's belt. "Go ahead."

Cahil hesitated.

"Relax, Stan, I didn't drag your ass across Siberia just so I could drop you off a cliff."

Cahil planted his feet and slowly leaned outward.

Straddling the mouth of the canyon like a great stone castle was a hydroelectric dam. A mile wide at the top and sloping to a wedge at the bottom, the dam seemed to sprout from the canyon walls. Along its walkway were eight generator towers, each joined to the next by a network of power lines.

"The Chono Dam," Skeldon said. "Second largest in the world. Five hundred feet tall, just over a mile wide, and a hundred feet thick. Eight hydroelectric generators for a total of fifteen thousand megawatts. The reservoir is twelve miles wide, forty long, and averages about four hundred feet deep. It's like a man-made ocean."

"Pull me in." Back on solid ground, Cahil said, "You seem to know a lot about it."

"I sure as hell hope so."

Afraid he already knew the answer, Cahil dreaded asking the next question. "Mike, what are we doing here?"

"It's simple: We're gonna blow it up."

49

Beijing

KAM HSIAO'S APARTMENT WAS LOCATED IN BEIJING'S DABEIYAO District in a neighborhood of faceless gray brick apartment buildings and bustling *hutong* markets.

Tanner left the Bamboo Garden late in the afternoon and walked to the Forbidden City, where he strolled the courtyards and museums until the sun began to set, then boarded a bus at the entrance to Tiananmen Square, took it into Dabeiyao, and got off at the Majuan Terminal.

He spent the next0 hour circling the streets near Hsiao's building, looking for signs of surveillance but seeing nothing, which he took with a grain of salt.

This was the part of the job Briggs hated most: the constant, gnawing uncertainty. Living with it for any extended period meant you either developed a "if it happens, it happens" attitude, or you turned into a walking ball of neuroses. So far, he hadn't fallen into the latter trap, but he could feel the fear lurking at the edges of his mind, waiting for a chance to take over.

Once the street was clear, he crossed over and walked into the apartment's lobby. He trotted up two flights, then down the dimly lit hall to Hsiao's door. He hesitated, suddenly remembering a joke a CIA veteran used to tell at ISAG: *How do you know when you're under surveillance by the KGB?* Answer: *When a dozen of them rush through the door and dogpile you.*

Tanner knocked.

The door opened, revealing a slim, clean-cut man in his early twenties. He had large ears and, Tanner thought, sad but honest eyes.

"Yes, can I help you?" he said in English.

"Bian sent me. I believe you and I share a mutual friend."

Hsiao cocked his head, confused, then his eyes widened. "Oh! Please, sorry, come in."

Tanner stepped inside. Hsiao shut the door. The apartment had three rooms: a small kitchen, a living room, and a doorway leading to what Tanner assumed was a bedroom. The walls were a stark white, as were the floors, all of which were linoleum.

Hsiao gestured to one of two chairs. "Please sit. Would you like some tea?"

"That would be nice, thanks."

Hsiao came back a few minutes later with a tray holding two ceramic mugs. "It's young hyson," Hsiao said. "Organic, no pesticides. Very good."

"Hyson—green tea?"

"Yes."

Tanner smiled and raised his mug in thanks. "My favorite. Your English is very good."

"The army offers a course; it's very popular. I've been studying for three years."

"You're in the PLA?"

"Yes, a corporal. I have to tell you, I'm very afraid, Mr. . . ."

"You can call me Ben."

"Ben. I'm very afraid."

"That's okay. So am I."

"You don't look afraid," Hsiao said.

"I have a good poker face. Plus, I make it a point to have a good cry once a day; it seems to help."

Hsiao nodded sympathetically. "I see." Then he saw Tanner's smile. "You're joking."

"Yes."

With that, the tension eased. Hsiao let out a chuckle. "That's very funny. I suppose we should talk about . . . what we need to do."

Tanner nodded. "First, I want to make sure you're ready for this. It's a big risk."

"I know."

"Are you sure? Do you know what will happen if you're caught?"

"I know exactly what I can expect. I see it almost every day. I've made up my mind. General Soong is a good man and he doesn't deserve what's happened to him. Tell me how I can help."

Tanner decided he would trust Hsiao, not only because he had no other choice, but because his gut was telling him he could. He extended his hand to Hsiao, who took it firmly.

"Okay," Briggs said. "Welcome aboard."

"A board? What board?"

"It's just an expression. We're a team now, you and I."

"Ah! Good! How do we start?"

"I want you to tell me everything you know about the camp."

For the next ninety minutes, Tanner questioned him about every aspect of the camp: physical layout, terrain and climate, security measures, daily routines, emergency procedures. . . . Hsiao answered all the questions quickly and precisely. The only thing he didn't know was what Tanner needed most of all: the camp's location.

"There are two guard rotations that switch off every two weeks," Hsiao explained. "We're flown to the camp in a helicopter with blacked-out windows."

"How long is the trip?"

"We're not allowed to wear watches. If I had to guess, I would say the flight lasts between three and four hours."

"What kind of helicopter?"

"MI-Eight—I think you call it a Hip."

"Hip" was the old-style NATO nickname for the MI-8, a Russian built helicopter with accommodations for thirty passengers and a cruising speed of about 150 mph. If Hsiao's estimate was correct, that meant the camp was somewhere within a six hundred-mile radius of Beijing.

"What about your gear? What do you take with you?"

"Nothing. Everything is supplied once we reach the camp. In fact, we're searched before we board the helicopters. You were thinking of a homing beacon of some kind?"

"Yes."

"Impossible. The helicopters are thoroughly inspected."

"Where do you take off from?"

"A small air base to near the Miyun Reservoir."

"After you take off, do you hear a lot of jet noise—other airplanes?"

Hsiao thought for a moment, then nodded. "Yes, yes. How did you know?"

"Just a guess," Tanner replied. They were routing the Hip into Capital Airport's airspace to lose them in the commercial traffic. "Anyone trying to track you by radar would lose you."

"Ah, I see. Very smart."

Tanner's options were dwindling. He couldn't track Hsiao . . . he couldn't track the helo—at least not by traditional means. He'd have to give it some thought.

"How tight is security at the air base?" he asked.

"Average, I would say. You want to get in?"

"I might."

"I sometimes stand guard duty there when I'm off rotation. I can show you just where to go."

TANNER STAYED FOR ANOTHER HOUR, FIRST DISCUSSING COMmunications procedures in case they needed to talk again, then deciding on a way to establish communication when—if—Tanner reached the camp.

Once back at the Bamboo Garden, he opened his Motorola, dialed a number, and waited through two minutes of squelches as the call was bounced from satellite to satellite, then to NSA headquarters in Ford Meade, Maryland, and finally to Holystone.

"Holystone, Shiverick," Oaken said.

"Oaks, it's me."

"Hey, traveler. Are you on the Motorola?"

"Yes."

"Hold on." Tanner heard a beep as Oaken switched to a secure line. "Everything okay?"

"Yep. I need a favor," He explained his conundrum with Hsiao's transport helo. "We can't do it electronically, so why not chemically?"

"You're thinking some kind of paint job?"

"If we can get Dick to give us a bird's eye, it might work. I'd also need a recipe."

"I'll make some calls. Give me a few hours and I'll get back to you."

The Motorola's vibration ringer woke Tanner just before dawn. "Yes."

"Okay, we're set," Oaken said. "Dick's going to do some shuffling and get your coverage."

"And the recipe?"

"That, too. Got your shopping list ready?"

Tanner turned on the bedside light, grabbed a pad and pen to copy down all the items. "You're sure about the ratios? I don't want to end up a human torch."

"They're straight from the official cookbook. When do you plan on going in?"

"Tonight or early tomorrow morning. They're scheduled to take off at dawn."

"We'll be watching," Oaken replied.

THREE MILES AWAY AT THE *GUOANBU*'S HEADQUARTERS, XIANG was arriving for the day. As he'd expected, he found Eng in a conference room surrounded by stacks of manila file folders.

"Any luck?" Xiang asked.

"Two hundred fifty-seven Westerners arrived in the city during the period you indicated," Eng answered. "Of those, there's no way to know which of them are here on business or pleasure without checking each file."

"What about camera permits?"

"Same thing. There are no separate records."

"What about Bian? Any activity since his meeting with our mystery man?"

"Nothing. We've got a team watching him day and night, but so far he's behaving."

"What about his embassy contact—this Brown fellow?"
"He hasn't left the embassy since."
"Then it all comes down to Bian's mystery man."
"Which works in our favor," Eng answered. "He's an illegal and he's on our ground. If we catch him—when we catch him—we can dangle him like a hooked fish."
Who was he? Xiang wondered. Better question: Why was he here? True enough, Bian was a known supporter of Soong, but that didn't make him unusual. Even after twelve years, the general's supporters were still pressuring the government to commute his sentence. Were Bian's activities connected to Soong, or was it something else?
It didn't matter, he decided. He couldn't take the risk. "I think it's time we got proactive."
"How so?"
"Arrest Bian. Let's see how much he'll endure before giving us his new *waiguoren* friend."

50

Nakhodka-Vostochny

WITH THE SUNRISE, JURENS AND HIS TEAM GOT THEIR FIRST clear view of the port.

Whether by design or by accident, the Harpoons had impacted critical areas of the complex.

At the port's easternmost berth, the first Harpoon had struck a crude oil carrier, triggering a chain of explosions that had rippled from ship to ship down the wharf.

The second Harpoon had traveled inland several hundred yards, then plunged into the tank farm, igniting three tanks and puncturing six more, releasing a flood of flaming oil and diesel fuel that had spread through the port like a molten river, touching off flash fires wherever it touched.

Along the waterfront, dozens of ships still burned, adding their smoke to the pall that hung over the bay. Most of the heavy-lift cranes had toppled onto their sides like giant Tinkertoys, crushing beneath them warehouses, straddle carriers, and sheds

Through his Owls, Jurens could see figures shuffling along the waterfront. There seemed to be no organized fire fighting or rescue effort under way. *Probably not enough left alive for that,* he thought. Part of him wanted to take his team and go down to help, but he knew it was impossible.

"Is that snow?" Smitty muttered, looking up.

Jurens looked up. Bits of white fluff drifted before his face. He held out his hand, caught a flake, and tasted it. He spit. "Ash."

Smitty leaned closer to Jurens. "What the hell's going on, Skipper?"

"I don't know, but I'll tell ya what: Harpoons are smart birds; what they did last night . . . it's a one in a million chance. They just don't go haywire like that."

"Agreed."

"That leaves one option: Somebody else with an LTD took control and guided them in." As smart as Harpoons are, they don't discriminate between targeting signals. First come, first served.

"The best place for that would be closer to the mouth of the bay," Smitty said. "If I had to guess, I'd say . . . there." He pointed to the opposite cape.

They were in trouble, Sconi realized. They'd been set up. Someone not only knew they were here, but also why. They—whoever *they* were—had lain in wait for *Columbia* to launch her missiles, then taken control of them and guided them onto their own targets.

Answers would have to wait. Right now, they had to leave before the hills were crawling with Federation Army relief units.

"Zee, how're we doing? Any word from our ride?"

"Still nothing, Skipper. SATCOM's working fine; we're getting a clean bounce off the satellite, but she just ain't answering. Want me to keep trying?"

"No, leave it for now," Jurens said, then turned back to Smitty, "We gotta start thinking worst-case. If *Columbia* is gone—"

"Gone how?"

"I don't know, and it doesn't matter. If she's gone, we're gonna have to find our own way out."

"Long swim."

"Too long. First things first: I want to have a talk with Dhar."

"You think he knows something?"

"There's one way to find out."

Jurens picked up his MP-5, walked over to where Dhar was lying, and knelt beside him.

Dhar stared at him. "What?"

"I'm going to be straight with you: We're in trouble. Somebody's set us up—all of us, including you. In a couple hours, troops are going to be hunting for us."

"Why? I don't understand."

"We're being framed for this disaster."

"By who?"

"You tell me."

"I don't know."

"Who hired you?" Jurens said.

"The JRA."

"You're sure about that? Think hard."

"I'm sure."

"Okay," Jurens said with a shrug. He flicked off the MP-5's safety. "Sorry about this, but you're extra baggage." He pressed the muzzle to Dhar's forehead.

"Wait, wait! I can help you! Maybe . . . I may know something."

"Then share it."

"The man who approached me claimed to be JRA, but I've done business with JRA before, and something wasn't right about this one, so I did some digging. It took me a couple months, but I discovered the man was working for the Chinese—the *Guoanbu*."

"But you still went through with the deal."

"They paid me, why wouldn't I? Besides, you don't understand. If I'd backed out, they would have killed me just for good measure. As it is, I'm probably a dead man anyway."

You play, you pay, Jurens thought. Dhar's life had finally caught up with him. "Is that all?"

"That's it, I swear. What're you going to do with me?"

"Since you've been honest with me, I'll be honest with you. We're going to take you with us, and providing we get out of this alive, you'll be turned over to the CIA, who'll milk you for every bit of info you've got. After that. . . . I guess that depends how useful you are to them."

Dhar considered this for a moment, then nodded. "I could do worse."

Maybe you deserve worse, Jurens thought. "Zee, get Mace on the line. I think somebody's going to want to hear this."

Langley

At eight a.m. Beijing time the Chinese government drew its line in the sand.

Reading identical statements, both China's foreign minister and its ambassador to the United States decried the Russian Federation's lack of concern for the safety and welfare of Chinese citizens living within its borders, and set a deadline of forty-eight hours.

"If this deadline should pass without President Bulganin fully admitting the Federation's role in the deaths of nearly two thousand Chinese citizens, as well as agreeing to allow Chinese government inspectors full access to facilities employing Chinese citizens, the People's Republic of China is prepared to take whatever steps necessary to ensure the welfare of its people."

From the audience a CNN reporter shouted, "Mr. Ambassador, has your government ruled out any options? Is military force a possibility?"

"We have not ruled out any options. That President Bulganin has so far refused to acknowledge his country's role in these deaths is no surprise; Russia has a long history of covering up disasters."

"What type of military force would your government consider and when might it take place?"

"Those are not issues I will discuss."

"Is an evacuation of Chinese citizens living in Russia a possibility?"

"Again, we are not ruling out any options. We are committed to—"

Mason muted the TV, then turned to Dutcher. "Well, what do you think?"

"That's how it will start: a mass evacuation," Dutcher predicted. "They'll call it a humanitarian mission, but it'll be their way of getting their foot in the door."

Mason nodded. "From what little we know about Bulganin, I don't see him backing down. Less than a month into his presidency, it would be political suicide."

"Agreed. He's going to give the Chinese exactly what they want, and the poor bastard doesn't even know it. What worries me is, how is he going to react once they make their move?"

"That's anyone's guess." Mason sighed. "Dangerous goddamn game they're playing."

Mason's intercom buzzed: "Mr. Director, General Cathermeier on line two."

"Thanks, Ginny." Mason punched the speaker button. "Chuck, I've got Leland here with me."

"You two better get over here. We've got problems."

DUTCHER AND MASON FOUND CATHERMEIER IN THE SECURE CONference room standing before a map of Russia's eastern coast. He turned as they entered. "We've lost *Columbia*."

"What?" Mason said. "When?"

"About an hour after she launched her missiles. The message came over VLF. What little we got was garbled. They were under attack, they said."

"By whom?" Dutcher asked.

"No idea, but now they're off the air. We've sent a surface-for-traffic message over ELF, but we're not even getting a signal confirmation."

"Which suggests her transponder is damaged or—"

"*Columbia*'s gone. Destroyed."

Dutcher said, "Have we heard from Jurens and his team?"

"No, but I wouldn't expect to yet. If they know about *Columbia*, their doing E&E," Cathermeier replied, referring to evasion and escape: clear the area and find another lay up. "If they don't know about *Columbia*, they're probably in transit to the pickup point."

"Let's hope they know," Mason said. "Best not to have them exposed."

Dutcher asked Cathermeier, "Who knows about all this?"

"Us three and the CAC duty officer. I can't keep it from Martin and Bousikaris for long."

"How far is the battle group from *Columbia*'s last known position?"

"Three days. I could break away one of the subs to hunt for her, but that'll only leave one covering the whole group. If the Russians come out to meet us in any force, we could have a problem. You know, I can't help but wonder if this is part of China's plan."

"We had the same thought: *Columbia* mysteriously sinks after launching a missile attack against a Russian port. More proof we're in bed with China."

"Either that or another chance to pull us into the fight," Mason said.

The intercom came to life: "General, we've got secure traffic. Eyes only for you."

"On my way."

The duty officer, an army major, walked over. "Sickle on SATCOM, General."

Cathermeier picked up the handset and keyed the button. "Sickle this is Mace, say status, over."

"Mace, this is Sickle. We are intact and operational. Standby to copy sitrep in three parts."

Cathermeier glanced at the duty officer, who nodded. "Recorders on."

"Ready to copy, Sickle."

"Sitrep: reference my grid one-four-six-nine-two. Target is foul; birds astray; see grid for result. *Break,* Blade unavailable, cause unknown; request instructions. *Break,* Kashmiri intercepted; ID confirmed as papa romeo charlie. Copy all, Mace?"

"Roger, copy all. Standby." Cathermeier turned to the duty officer. "Major, match Sickle's coordinates and check to see if we have any satellites overhead."

"Yes, sir."

Mason said, "Okay, so they know about *Columbia*. What's the rest about?"

"Something went wrong with the launch. The Harpoons malfunctioned."

Dutcher said, "How could that happen?"

The watch officer interrupted, "General, the NRO has a real-time feed from a Keyhole over the Sea of Okhotsk. The angle's going to be a bit oblique, but it should work."

"Put it on the big screen."

The screen turned to snow, then resolved into an overhead picture of Russia's eastern coast. "Overlay Sickle's grid," Cathermeier ordered.

The screen refocused. The Bay of Vrangel appeared, bracketed by Cape Kamensky and Cape Petrovosk. The water of the bay was an indigo blue, the land mostly green with splotches of brown. In the crook of the bay was the white concrete expanse of the port.

"What the hell . . . ?" Cathermeier muttered. "Major, what do you make of that?"

"Looks like smoke, General. Lots of it. I can see ten—no, twelve smoke columns, and flames at the western end of the pier. Damn, there's nothing left standing."

"Transmit those coordinates to the NRO," Cathermeier ordered. "I want a damage analysis as soon as possible." He turned to Dutcher and Mason. "That's what Jurens meant. Somebody got ahold of those Harpoons and diverted them—probably right into the tank farm, judging from the damage."

Mason said, "That business about the Kashmiri. He's talking about Sunil Dhar."

"That's my guess," Cathermeier said, then recited: "Kashmeran is papa romeo charlie. . . ."

"People's Republic of China," Dutcher said. "It was a setup from the start."

"It's starting," Mason said. "We've got to move on Martin before it's too late."

EIGHT THOUSAND MILES AWAY, *COLUMBIA* WAS ALIVE, BUT barely so, lying on her port side at the edge of the continental shelf.

The torpedo should have killed them, Kinsock knew. What he would only later realize was that Jurens's decision to push forward the missile launch had given *Columbia* a fighting chance at survival.

Wary of her target's sensors and determined to launch a killing shot at point-blank range, the attacker had for hours been closing on *Columbia*'s position, creeping along at three knots, riding the currents and hiding in thermal layers. *Columbia*'s premature rise to periscope depth caught the attacker four thousand yards out of position, giving Kinsock those vital seconds he needed for evasive manuevers.

After launching its torpedo, their attacker had disappeared as quickly as it had appeared, slipping into the depths as Kinsock struggled to get his wounded boat pointed in-shore and away from the continental shelf and the crushing depths beyond.

As they spiralled downward, the sonar techs kept their headphones on, ignoring the chaos around them and trying to identify the rapidly fading signature of their attacker. In the final seconds before they struck bottom, *Columbia*'s sonar chief managed to record an ever so faint shaft whine to their southeast. However fleeting the contact, it was enough to identify the boat as the same mysterious Kilo they'd detected soon after arriving on station.

Kinsock stood in the wardroom and read the damage report as his department heads waited for him to finish. Throughout the control center, crewmen were running diagnostic tests and talking quietly amongst themselves. Occasionally the deck would tremble as *Columbia* settled into the silt.

"What's the plant status, Chief?" asked Kinsock.

Columbia's engineering officer flipped open his notebook. "Reactor's on line, all boards are green. Same with generators and all auxiliary equipment."

"Hull breeches?"

"Six minors but the pressure hull seems mostly intact. There's nothing we can't handle unless we go any deeper. Then things are gonna start to pop. I've got watches set on each of the sites and rovers looking for trouble spots. The worst is the screw: At least two of the blades are gone. The aft trim tank is holed, and we're getting pinhole leaks near the thrust block."

"So, bottom line, main propulsion is out."

"We got the power, but no screw to put it to."

"Outboards?" Kinsock asked, referring to *Columbia*'s two retractable thrusters used for pier-side maneuvering.

"Both are okay as far as we can tell. Skipper, you're not thinking about—"

"Just brainstorming, Chief."

" 'Cuz those thrusters are louder than hell. If we start 'em up, we're just asking for company. Besides, the best speed they can give us is four knots."

"I know that, Chief."

"Yeah, I guess you do. Sorry, Skipper."

"Forget it. Jim, how's command and control?"

"Not bad, all things considered. We're still running diagnostics, but so far the only major damage is to communications. Both our VLF and ELF are out. Weapons and sensors read okay, but neither of them are much use while we're on the bottom."

Kinsock nodded. "Okay, first we need to let somebody know we're here. Next, fix our leaks so once we get moving we can get a little depth under us." The engineer started to open his mouth, but Kinsock pushed on. "Chief, if we have to take on a little water to do it, fine. Right now, we're sitting ducks. If we can get some sea around us, we might be able to hide until the cavalry comes. Hell, even if all we can do is get off this shelf and float at zero-bubble, our chances are a lot better."

Kinsock looked from man to man. "Questions?" There were none. "Jim, get a SLOT buoy ready for launch. Time to let the folks at home know we ain't dead."

Nakhodka-Vostochny

Two hours after sunrise, an MI-6 "Hook" cargo helicopter from Vladivostok set down amid a minihurricane of embers and disgorged its two dozen passengers, a mix of emergency medical personnel, firefighters, and soldiers. They immediately spread out and went to work, some searching for survivors while the rest began setting up a base of operations from which the relief effort would be coordinated.

All but a few of the warehouses and storage bunkers were still burning, and every few seconds there came the groan of wrenching steel as another structure collapsed into rubble. Puddles of burning oil dotted the concrete, making the worker's every step treacherous as they picked their way through the wreckage, calling out for survivors and tagging corpses for later recovery.

At the port's easternmost end, Private Vasily Tarknoy of the Federation Army was walking along the waterfront, gaping at the skeletal remains of the ships that had not yet sunk. The oil tanker that had taken the brunt of the Harpoon impact rested on the bottom with only the tip of its mast jutting from the water. Every few seconds a geyser of bubbles would erupt from the hulk and spew a cloud of oily mist into the air. Through the ash on the water's surface, he could discern the outline of the ship. It reminded him of the pictures he'd seen of the *Arizona* Memorial at Pearl Harbor.

He was passing a jumble of wreckage that appeared to have been a storage shed when something caught his eye. There was a glint of glass amid the debris. He leapt across a small stream of burning oil and knelt. The metal was still hot. He pulled on his gloves and pushed aside the wreckage until he was able to reach the object.

The object looked vaguely like one of those large scopes used by bird-watchers. There seemed to be writing on the scope. He wiped away the soot until the letters were readable.

Tarknoy's grasp of English was poor, but good enough. He stood up and fumbled for his radio. "Major, this is Tarknoy. I think I've found something you should see."

51

Beijing

XIANG MARVELED AT BIAN'S FORTITUDE.

Given the man's panic when they'd arrested him, Xiang felt sure he would have confessed quickly.

They were in their fifth hour of interrogation—the last two of which had been physical—and still Bian had revealed nothing about either Brown or the man he'd met at Guanghua Temple.

Xiang leaned against the wall, smoking a cigarette and watching impassively as the interrogator reapplied the electrode to the sole of Bian's foot. In his writhing, Bian had proven surprisingly strong, having already dislodged the electrodes three times.

Then again, Xiang reminded himself, intense and extended pain tends to transform people, and he wondered idly if the pain might be steeling Bian's will. There was no mistaking the transformation Bian's feet had undergone: Both soles were blackened and split and dripping clear, lymphatic fluid.

They will probably have to be amputated, Xiang thought idly

He caught a whiff of burnt flesh and took another puff on his cigarette to block it out.

The interrogator tightened the straps around Bian's calves, then turned to Xiang. "We're ready. I don't think there's much feeling left in his feet, though."

"Up the voltage."

After another twenty minutes, Bian's screams died away and he began mumbling incoherently.

Better, Xiang thought. Speech was always the first hurdle. If you could get the subject talking—even nonsense—you were making progress. If this failed, Xiang knew that Bian had a daughter in Nanjing; if he were unconcerned about his own life, perhaps he would feel differently about hers.

". . . won't catch him . . ." Bian murmured suddenly.

Xiang stepped forward. "What, Bian? Did you say something? Catch who?"

Bian's eyes fluttered open. "You won't catch him."

"Who? Your friend from Guanghua Temple? The American?" It was a stab in the dark, but Bian rewarded him with a slight shift in his eyes. "We photographed you two together. We know what he looks like, we know when he came into the country, and we know he's an American. We're already closing in on him. Why put yourself through this?"

Bian shook his head.

"Hit him again," Xiang ordered.

As the electrodes began sizzling, there was a knock at the door. Xiang opened it. Eng was standing there with a manila file. "What is it?" Xiang asked.

"His medical file. Check page three; you'll find it useful."

Xiang closed the door and scanned the file, pausing on the third page. According to his doctor, Bian suffered from hypertension and arteriosclerosis, which in turn had caused him ongoing problems with thrombosis and angina, both potentially lethal heart problems. The fact that the interrogation hadn't prompted an attack said much about Bian's resilience.

But everyone has their limits, Xiang thought. He picked up the wall phone, explained what he needed, then hung up.

The male nurse arrived fifteen minutes later and wheeled a cart to Bian's side. Xiang pulled up a stool and sat down.

"Bian! Bian, wake up . . ." Xiang slapped his face. "Wake up!"

Bian's eyes popped open. "What? I told you . . . won't catch him . . ."

"Yes, I know. Are you listening to me, Bian, can you hear me?"

"Yes, I hear you."

"I understand you have a heart condition. You're taking several medications for it."

Bian's head lolled to one side. "So?"

"So, I have all your medications right here."

"Don't need them."

"You will."

Xiang nodded to the nurse, who inserted a syringe into a vial, extracted some of the liquid, then jabbed the tip into Bian's arm. "Ah! What is that?"

"Epinephrine," Xiang answered. "You probably know it as adrenaline."

"No! Don't do that . . ."

Xiang nodded at the nurse, who pushed down on the plunger.

Bian began bucking against his restraints. "No, no, no!"

Xiang grabbed Bian's head. "Can you feel it? Your blood pressure is rising, your heartbeat is climbing, your blood vessels are constricting. . . . Can you feel it yet?"

Beads of sweat appeared on Bian's forehead. His pupils contracted to pinpricks. A muscle in his cheek twitched. He opened his mouth to speak, but all that came out was a gasp. "Ahh . . . !"

Xiang leaned closer. "Now you can feel the pressure—like a block of stone on your chest."

"Oh, God. . . ."

"Tell me what I want to know."

"No!"

"Tell me what I want to know and I'll help you."

"No!"

"Tell me what I want to know and I won't have to pay a visit to your daughter in Nanjing."

Bian's head snapped around. "Leave . . . her . . . alone . . . ahhh!" He threw his head back, gasping for breath.

Xiang nodded to the nurse. "Give him some more."

"Don't!" Bian cried.

As the nurse gave the injection, there was another knock at the door. Xiang opened it.

It was Eng: "I think we have him." He handed Xiang a file. "He's traveling under the name Ben Colson; he listed his occupation as a photographer. I'm still trying to track it down, but he presented a letter of invitation at Customs."

"Probably a fake," Xiang replied. *China has more ministers than a dog has hairs*. He flipped open the file and looked at the passport photo. "That's him. Good work. Where is he staying?"

"The Tingsonglou."

"Gather a team. We leave in ten minutes."

Eng nodded and left, Xiang shut the door.

Bian was convulsing. His back was arched, his head rolling from side to side. Xiang walked over and grabbed Bian's head to still it. "We've got him, Bian," he whispered. "You went through this for nothing. All this pain—for nothing. Remember that."

Bian rasped, "My daughter. . . ."

"What's that?"

"Leave her alone."

Despite his frailty, the man had held up well. "Very well," he said. "She'll be unharmed."

Xiang started toward the door.

"Sir?" the interrogator called. "What should we do with him?"

Xiang saw the electrodes still attached to Bian's feet. "Give him the full treatment."

"But, with his heart . . . it will kill him."

Xiang shrugged. "The price of fatherhood."

Miyun Reservoir, North of Beijing

As Xiang and his team were racing toward the Bamboo Garden, Tanner was climbing a hillside north of the Miyun Reservoir. Behind him, the moonlight reflected off the water's surface.

He was on the last leg of a journey that had begun six hours before at Ritan Park, where he'd flagged down a taxi and asked to be driven to Taishiyun, a village northeast of the reservoir. Once there, he strolled the town's *hutongs* until dusk, when he hired another taxi to the reservoir.

"You want wait?" the driver asked as he dropped Tanner off.

"No, thanks. I have friends picking me up in about an hour."

"You wait in the dark?"

"I want to photograph the sunset. I'll be okay, thanks."

The driver shrugged and pedaled away.

As darkness fell, Tanner hunkered down in the underbrush and waited until the last few visitors left the beach and drove away. At nine p.m., a local PSB car rolled by, shined its lights along the trees, then kept going.

Once it disappeared around the corner, Tanner started moving.

He reached the top of the slope and paused to catch his breath.

Fifty feet ahead lay the barbed-wire fence of the air base's perimeter. As Hsiao had described it, the air base was only large enough to accommodate helicopters, with three landing pads and a cluster of hangars and maintenance buildings. Flashing blue-green lights outlined each pad.

Following Hsiao's directions, he followed the fence until he came to a rusted steel sign hanging from one of the posts. In Mandarin, it read WARNING: GOVERNMENT FACILITY. STAY OUT.

The bottom three rings securing the fence to the post were missing. He pushed the mesh inward and ducked through.

FORTY MINUTES LATER, HAVING DODGED THREE TRUCK-MOUNTED patrols, Tanner lay on his belly in the shadows along a storage shed. Across the road stood a hangar; the placard above the door read "Shiyi"—the number eleven in Mandarin.

Stacked against the outer wall were a line of wooden crates, several of them reaching to within a few feet of the roof's overhang. Astonished as he was at the lapse in security, Tanner was only too glad to take advantage of it.

So far Hsiao's information was proving out. Tanner was glad: It felt good to have an ally. Though he wasn't ready to put his life in the young soldier's hands, Hsiao's stock had just gone up.

He lay still for another fifteen minutes. Two patrol trucks came and went, but the road was devoid of foot traffic.

He got up and sprinted across the road. He mounted the first crate, chinned himself to the next one, then crawled onto the roof and shimmied forward until he reached the skylight. It was unlocked.

He lifted it open, peeked inside, then slipped through feet first.

THE CLIMB DOWN THROUGH THE GIRDERS TOOK LESS THAN A minute.

In the center of the hangar stood Hsiao's MI-8 Hip helicopter. At nearly twenty feet tall and sixty feet in length, it rose over him like an olive green monster. Its rotors drooped a few feet over his head.

He crouched down, opened his rucksack, and withdrew a liter-size bottle filled with a brown liquid straight from the CIA's "Cookbook o' Skullduggery," as Oaken called it.

The recipe had called for ingredients ranging from ground, match heads to acetone, to mineral spirits. Having no clue about the theory behind the process, Briggs could only rely on Oaken's directions as he spent most of the afternoon measuring and mixing the various parts until they became what he now had in the bottle.

According to Langley's Science and Tech gurus, the compound would remain stable until heat—such as from a helicopter's turboshaft exhaust stack—was applied to it, at which time it would begin deteriorating molecule by molecule. Just as sunlight through a prism is divided into its various wavelengths, so too would the compound systematically break down into a unique chemical signature.

As Tanner crouched on the hangar floor, two hundred miles above him a Keyhole "Prism Forte" satellite was aligning its ISA, or Infrared Spectrometer Array, to look for the chemical signature of his compound. When the Hip lifted off, the ISA would lock onto the trail, then pass it to the Keyhole's main camera, which would track it to the camp.

With the bottle and a paintbrush tucked under one arm, Tanner climbed onto the Hip's weapons rack. He popped the bottle's top, nearly gagged at the smell, then squirted some onto the exhaust stack and began spreading it on.

Fifteen minutes later he'd covered the stack with four coats of the compound, each of which went on the color of molasses but dried clear—and mercifully odorless—within minutes.

He climbed down, repacked his rucksack, and headed for the ladder.

At the Bamboo Garden, Xiang's team was tearing apart Tanner's hotel room. The mattress, bedcovers, and wall hangings lay strewn on the floor.

"Nothing, sir," one of the searchers reported.

"Bag up all his personal belongings and take them back to headquarters," Xiang ordered. "I want everything checked again."

"What now?" Eng asked. "He could be anywhere."

"Circulate his photo to all the PSB and PAP stations in the city. He'll turn up. In the meantime, tell the perimeter team to pull back. He may still come to us."

Xiang flipped open Colson's file and studied the passport photo. Something about the man's face looked familiar. *I know you, don't I?* Xiang thought.

52

Chono Dam, Russia

SEPARATED FROM DUTCHER AND THE OTHERS BY THOUSANDS OF miles, and with no way of telling them about Skeldon's plans for the dam, Cahil was wracking his brain for options.

The scope of China's plan was mind-boggling. Knowing Moscow's reaction to an invasion of Siberia would be to immediately dispatch reinforcements to Yakutia, Sakha, and Irkutsk, China had decided to create a geographical roadblock of stunning proportions.

Trapped behind the Chono Dam lay a system of waterways and lakes roughly a fifth the size of the Great Lakes. Once released, the flood would roar down the narrow Chono River gorge and into the Central Siberian Plateau, gaining momentum and speed as its force was multiplied by not only the flatness of the land itself, but by the major rivers that crisscrossed it: the Nyuya, the Lena, the Vitim, the Ineyke—all would merge into a juggernaut of water rushing south toward a four hundred-mile stretch of the Trans-Siberia Railway—Moscow's primary means of getting reinforcements into Siberia.

The flood would slowly dissipate as Siberia's web of minor rivers and tributaries absorbed the deluge, but that would take weeks, during which the Federation would be faced with not only one of the greatest disasters in Russian history, but also an entrenched enemy force.

Whether Skeldon knew that the dam was just a cog in a larger plan, Cahil didn't know, but certainly he didn't understand their presence here was integral to the drama to come.

Cahil wasn't sure how it would happen, but as the effects of the disaster were fully realized, word would reach Moscow: Bodies were found near the dam—two Caucasian and six Chinese—all wearing U.S. Army uniforms and carrying U.S.-issue equipment. The heavy-handedness of the revelation would be lost in the ensuing outrage. The United States would be accused of not only being in cahoots with China, but also of unleashing the disaster that had crippled Moscow's ability to repel the invaders.

THE MORNING AFTER SKELDON SHOWED HIM THE DAM, THEY awoke before dawn, had a quick breakfast of MRE chipped beef on toast and hiked into the forest, heading roughly northeast.

After an hour, Skeldon stopped before a wooded slope, glanced around, then started pacing off distances. Cahil realized he was following a mental map.

Skeldon stopped, walked to a section of the slope, then got down on his knees and parted a clump of bushes. He rummaged around for a moment, then wriggled backward, dragging a rock the size of a manhole cover. He pushed it aside and turned to Cahil. "Come on."

"Come on where?"

"You'll see. Just follow me and stay close."

Skeldon dropped to his belly and crawled into the bushes. Cahil followed.

A few feet into the undergrowth Cahil came to an opening in the rock. As Skeldon's feet disappeared inside, Cahil clicked on his flashlight and wriggled after him. The tunnel continued for ten feet, then widened into a cave tall enough for them to stand in.

"What is this place?" Cahil asked.

"A side tunnel. This used to be part of a silver mine. It's been abandoned for about sixty years."

"How'd you find it?"

Skeldon grinned, his face appearing skeletal in the flashlight beam. "Like you said, I've spent a fair amount of time over here. Come on, we've got about a mile to go."

Before Cahil could ask any questions, Skeldon started down the tunnel, his flashlight bouncing off the rock walls.

The floor was flat and well worn. Occasionally Cahil's beam would pick out the stub of a candle or a pick hammer nestled in a crag in the wall. After twenty minutes, the tunnel began a series of turns, snaking east and then west as the floor began to slope downward. The air grew cooler.

"You're not claustrophobic, are you?" Skeldon called over his shoulder.

"Nah," Cahil replied. *But the day is young.* He could feel the press of thousands of tons of rock above him. He suppressed a shiver and kept walking.

FINALLY THE TUNNEL OPENED INTO A CAVERN ABOUT THE SIZE of a basketball court. Stalactites glistening with water drooped from the ceiling, reaching in some places nearly to the floor. Skeldon led him to the far wall and shined his flashlight along its base. Bored into the rock at forty-five-degree angles were six evenly spaced holes, each about the diameter of a telephone pole.

"You made these?" Cahil asked.

Skeldon nodded. "Yep. It was a pain in the ass to get the depth right."

"What—"

"Shhh! Listen." Skeldon pressed his ear to the wall. He gestured for Cahil to do the same. At first Cahil heard nothing. Then, faintly, he could make out the distant rush of water.

"That's the river," Cahil said.

"Yep. Only about twelve feet of rock between us and the dam's footings."

"When did you drill the holes?"

"Last year."

Last year, Bear thought. *My God. . . .*

The Chinese had planned their operation down to the finest detail. Cahil now had the answer to one of his lingering questions: How they were planning to destroy the dam. These six bore holes, each packed with a portion of the C4 the commandos had loaded aboard the Yaz, would work as shaped charges. Detonated simultaneously, the charges would fracture the dam's base, sending a shock wave of cracks upward and outward. From there, the weight of the reservoir's water would do the rest.

Moscow

The strain was beginning to show on Bulganin, Nochenko thought.

It was understandable, of course: Less than ten days in office and the new president was facing a spate of crises: an angry and aggressive China; a major far-eastern port razed to the ground; and a U.S. battle group steaming ominously toward the Siberian coast.

Bulganin's eyes were red-rimmed and his hair jutted from his head at wild angles. Behind Bulganin, the ever-present Pyotr stared fixedly at the far wall.

Like the mausoleum guards, Nochenko thought. *Bloody thug.*

Bulganin pointed at the wall clock. "Where are they? I summoned them over an hour ago!"

It had only been twenty minutes, Nochenko knew, but he thought better than to argue the point. "Don't worry, Vlad, they're—"

The intercom on Bulganin's desk buzzed; he punched it. "Yes!"

"Marshal Beskrovny and—"

"Send them in."

The four men that made up Bulganin's National Security Council strode into the office and stopped in a semicircle before his desk: Premier Andrei Svetlyn, Foreign Minister Dmitry Kagorin, Defense Minister Marshal Victor Beskrovny, and Director of the SVR, Sergei Fedorin.

All but Beskrovny were recent appointees. Until ten days ago Kagorin and Svetlyn had both been serving as deputies for the men Bulganin summarily dismissed upon taking office. Whether they kept their new posts depended, Nochenko knew, on how well they served as conduits for Bulganin's decrees. In discussing their promotion with Nochenko, Bulganin had fallen short of admitting he was looking for "yes men," calling them instead "loyal servants."

A forty-year veteran of the Russian army, Marshal Beskrovny had served as either Defense Minister or Chief of the General Staff for both Mikhail Gorbachev and Boris Yeltsin, and was a popular figure among the people. Beskrovny was, in Bulganin's words, a "true hero of the Motherland."

Sergei Fedorin was the wild card. In the final days before the election the SVR director had helped Bulganin's cause by publicly recognizing his lead in the polls. As was expected, Bulganin had reciprocated by letting Fedorin stay on. For now.

"Beware the spies," Bulganin had told Nochenko, quoting yet another Stalinism. "Their eyes are sharp, their hearts black, their knives always ready."

Bulganin glowered at his cabinet, letting them squirm for a few moments. "Let's hear it. Kagorin, what do we know about this Chinese absurdity?"

"Beijing is declining all our attempts to communicate," the foreign minister answered. "As it stands, their deadline will expire in twenty hours."

"Any sign of what they plan to do then?" asked Nochenko.

Marshal Beskrovny answered. "Aside from a slight increase in their command structure's alert status, nothing has changed. Across the board, there's no movement of military units."

"Fedorin? You agree?"

"I do," the SVR director replied. "If they're planning a military response, it won't come quickly. They don't have the units in place to do anything significant."

"More Chinese inscrutability," Bulganin said. "All bark, no bite. Very well, let the deadline pass. I won't be dictated to by those little bastards! If they think they can bully me into taking the blame for those mishaps, they are mistaken. What of the U.S. carrier group, Marshal?"

"If it maintains its current course it will be off our coast in three days. According to their Pentagon, the group is on routine maneuvers—"

"That's a lie."

"If so, their purpose is plain: They're hoping the show of power will calm Beijing's fire a bit."

"Very kind of them, but we don't need help handling the Chinese. I want to be kept informed, Marshal, do you understand? Every hour, I want to know what the group is up to."

"Yes, sir."

"Now: Nakhodka-Vostochny—what happened? What's the extent of the damage?"

"Severe," Beskrovny replied. "First reports describe the port as 'flattened.' "

"Flattened? *Flattened!* What does that mean? What could do such a thing?"

"Mr. President," Nochenko answered, "relief crews have just arrived on scene, so it will be a while before we start getting firsthand accounts from survivors. But, as I understand it, the port does handle a lot of petroleum products."

Bulganin glanced at Marshal Beskrovny. "Is this true?"

"Yes, sir. A petroleum-related accident might explain the damage, but Ivan's right: We won't *know* anything until the crews have a chance to—"

Bulganin's intercom buzzed. "Yes?"

"Mr. President, I have an urgent call for Marshal Beskrovny."

"Transfer it in."

When the phone trilled, Beskrovny picked it up, listened for a full minute, then said, "How certain are you, General? Who confirmed it? I see . . . yes, of course. We need to be sure. If there's a mistake—" Beskrovny went silent again, then said, "Very well, I'll be back to you shortly."

"What?" Bulganin asked.

"That was the Far East District Commander in Vladivostok. One the relief workers found a . . . device that looked out of place, so he reported it."

"What kind of device?" Ivan Nochenko asked.

Beskrovny hesitated. "It's been identified as what's called an LTD—a laser target designator. They're used to guide missiles onto targets."

"What!" Bulganin roared. "How—"

Nochenko cut him off: "What else, Marshal?"

"The device is standard U.S. military issue."

"American?" Bulganin murmured, the muscles in his jaw bunching. "The Americans did this?"

"We don't know that, Mr. President," Beskrovny replied.

"Then explain the presence of the device."

"I can't. Not yet."

"Do we posses any of these . . . LTDs?"

"No, sir."

"Any reason why one should be in the port?" Bulganin pressed.

"No, sir."

"Would a missile attack explain the devastation?"

"It might. It would depend on—"

"This LTD—it's operated by ground troops?"

"Yes, sir, but—"

Bulganin held up a hand, silencing Beskrovny. "That's enough! I've heard enough!" He began pacing. "Those bastards . . . those rotten, backstabbing bastards—"

"Mr. President," Nochenko said.

"—attack us without provocation. . . . *Cowards!*"

"Mr. President!"

Bulganin stopped. "What?"

"I agree, it looks bad, but we need to proceed cautiously—"

"Ivan, didn't you hear? There are enemy soldiers on Russian soil! American soldiers!"

"Let the relief crews do their job. Let Marshal Beskrovny and Director Fedorin investigate the matter. If the Americans are responsible, they will pay, but we must be sure."

Bulganin stared at him. "Can't you see the obvious—any of you? They did this. They are responsible. They think I'm weak; they thought this was the perfect time to—" Bulganin stopped talking, closed his eyes for a few moments, then opened them, suddenly calm again. "Fine. Very well. Conduct your investigation. You have twenty-four hours to report back to me."

Both Fedorin and Beskrovny nodded. "Yes, Mr. President."

"In the meantime, I want two things from you Marshal Beskrovny: One, hunt down those soldiers. They must not be allowed to escape. Is that understood?"

"Yes, Mr. President."

"Second: I don't want that battle group approaching our coast. Mark my words: None of this is a coincidence. You don't see it, but I do. I don't want them anywhere near our soil. If they try it, make them pay for every inch!"

53

Beijing

IT WAS FOUR A.M. WHEN TANNER STEPPED OFF THE BUS TWO blocks from his hotel. He was exhausted and ready for a couple hours of sleep. When he awoke, hopefully Oaken would have the camp's location.

He walked southeast through a maze of dark *hutongs*, lined with boarded-up vendor's stalls and quiet courtyards. Aside from the occasional grunt of a pig or the squawk of a chicken, all was quiet.

Two hundred yards from the Bamboo Garden, he was turning onto Jiugulou when he caught a sudden whiff of cigarette smoke. A mental warning flag popped up. It was nothing concrete, but rather an intuitive punch in the stomach. Having learned the hard way, he'd come to trust the feeling.

He stopped, slowly stepped into a doorway alcove, and crouched in the shadows.

Two minutes passed. Abruptly, down the street in another alcove, the orange tip of a cigarette glowed to life. *Just a local having a smoke,* Briggs thought, but remained still nonetheless.

After another minute the cigarette glowed again. In those few seconds he caught the glint of olive-drab uniform pants with a red, vertical stripe: *People's Armed Police*. Tanner's heart filled his throat. What were the chances of a lone PAP officer stopping for a break in a darkened doorway just a hundred yards from his hotel?

They'd found him. A dozen questions swirled in his brain. Had Hsiao or Bian burned him? Had they been taken? Or was it something else, a mistake he'd made?

He continued to scan the street and slowly, one by one, he picked out another six men—two PAP officers and four PSB plainclothes—hidden along the street in front of the Bamboo Garden.

Six on this street, probably twice that many inside. . . .

The ambush had to be a *Guoanbu* operation; only they could coordinate both the PSB and PAP like this. It would only be a matter of time before they began circulating his photo to the city's local PSB stations—if they hadn't already started. From there his alias and picture would trickle down to street level until every bus and cabdriver had it.

Get out, Briggs.

Moving slowly, he slipped back around the corner. Heart pounding, eyes darting into the darkness around him, he started walking west, forcing himself to keep an easy pace. Suddenly, a voice came out of the darkness of a *hutong* entrance: "Stop, sir!"

He stopped in his tracks. *Don't run. Wait.*

"Sir, may I see your papers, please?"

He doesn't know it's me, Briggs thought. *Still a chance.*

Hands shaking, Tanner turned toward the voice. It was a uniformed PSB officer. Head tucked into his chest, Briggs patted his coat pockets. "Yes, Officer, I have them right here." He took a step toward the man. "Yes, here they are. . . ."

As the officer extended his hand for the papers, Tanner sent a straight punch into his solar plexus, then reversed his hand and slammed the butt of his palm into the man's chin.

The officer let out a gasp, then crumpled. Briggs caught him in a hug, then dragged him into the alley, and laid him down.

The thought of killing him flashed briefly through Tanner's mind, but he dismissed it. It was unnecessary; alive or dead, the officer would be found within a few hours. The incident would be linked to him. Besides, Tanner thought, before this was over there was going to be plenty of mayhem to go around; there was no sense adding to it before he had no other choice.

He dragged the officer deeper into the *hutong,* stuffed him behind a cluster of garbage cans, then smoothed his clothes, stepped back onto the street, and kept walking until he reached Xitau, where he found another doorway and ducked inside.

He pulled out the Motorola, dialed Hsiao's number. "Hello?" Hsiao answered groggily.

"It's me," Tanner said. "You recognize my voice?"

"Uh . . . yes. What—"

"How is everything?"

"What?"

"I said, 'how is everything?' "

"Oh . . . everything is awful."

He's okay, Briggs thought. A standard "fine" response would have meant "trouble; go away."

"And you?" Hsiao asked.

"The same. That makes two of us," Tanner replied. This too was code: *Don't know about Bian; check, but use caution.* "I'll be in touch. Take care of yourself."

"You, too," Hsiao replied.

AS THE FIRST HINTS OF THE DAWN WERE APPEARING ON THE horizon, Tanner stepped onto Deshengmen Avenue, flagged down a pedi-taxi—which was the last tier of transportation providers he felt would get his photo—and asked to be taken to the Ditan Gymnasium.

Once there, he walked west to Qingnianhu Park and followed the footpath around the lake to the visitor's pavilion, a large, open-air amphitheater containing rest rooms, city map displays, and rental lockers. He found the correct locker, inserted his key, and opened the door.

Inside was a expedition-size, waterproof backpack. *Thank God. . . .*

As promised, Brown and his people had deposited his cache.

Before leaving Washington, Tanner had given Mason a wish list of emergency items. Given not only the *Guoanbu*'s ultra-secret attitude toward the camp, but also the fact that Beijing had slowly but surely closing urban *laogis* in favor of more remote locations, he felt certain that sooner or later he'd find himself in the wilds of the Chinese countryside.

He took the backpack into a bathroom stall and took a quick inventory of the pack's contents. Everything was there.

He stripped off his clothes and pulled on a pair of gray, cotton canvas pants, a matching anorak-type tunic, and a baseball cap, which he pulled low over his eyes, as was the current fashion in Beijing. He hefted the backpack over his shoulder and walked out.

TWENTY MINUTES LATER HE WAS ABOARD A RUSTY, SINGLE-speed bicycle he'd found leaning against a tree on Huangsi Boulevard, heading north toward the edge of the city. Head down, baseball cap over his eyes, he pedaled for an hour as the sun rose and throngs of fellow cyclers and taxis began filling the streets around him.

At nine he pulled into Shahe, a suburb twelve miles north of Beijing, leaned the bike against the first bench he saw, and walked on. He found the train station two blocks away and slipped into the bathroom, where he changed back into his regular clothes. A Westerner walking around dressed as a native was bound to arouse suspicion.

At the ticket window he bought tickets for three trains, each leaving within the next twenty minutes: One to Chaoyang, another to Shanghai, and a third to Tianshui. Hopefully, if he didn't draw attention to himself, there would be no witnesses to confirm which train he'd boarded.

Half mental coin-toss and half hunch that Soong's camp lay somewhere to the north, Tanner chose the train bound for Chaoyang. As the speaker gave the last boarding call, he got up from his bench and boarded the last car.

Most of the seats were empty. A dozen or so people in peasant dress sat staring out the window or chatting quietly with their seatmates. No one gave him a second look. He found an empty row near the back and sat down.

He took a deep breath and leaned his head back. *Almost out. . . .*

The loudspeaker above his head blared to life, made a clipped announcement in Mandarin, and then the train started moving. With each clack of the wheels over the joints, he felt himself relax a bit more.

He pulled out his phone, paused a moment to mentally organize his message, then dialed the number and waited. When he got the tone squelch, he punched in the code and hung up.

He glanced out the window, watching the countryside slip past with increasing speed.

Come on, keep moving. . . .

Every mile he could put between himself and the city, the better chance he had of staying alive.

BACK IN BEIJING, THE PSB OFFICER HE'D DISABLED WAS FOUND by a street sweeper. Twenty minutes after the call arrived, Xiang was on the scene. The officer was sitting against the *hutong* wall being attended by an emergency medical technician.

"What happened?" Xiang asked Eng.

"We don't know yet; he's just coming around. This close to Colson's hotel, though—"

"Yes, it's him," Xiang said tiredly. There hadn't been a mugging of a PSB officer in thirty years; this was not random. "Another hundred meters and he would have walked right into us!"

Xiang walked over to the officer and dismissed the EMT. Xiang questioned the dazed man for ten minutes, frequently having to repeat questions. "You're certain you didn't get a look at his face?"

"No, sir, I'm sorry. I asked for his papers and then . . . I don't—"

"Did he seem nervous? In a hurry?"

"No, sir. He was just . . . walking."

Very cool, this one, Xiang thought.

"It happened so fast. . . . I was reaching for his papers and then . . . I woke up here."

"Very well. Go to the hospital, have yourself checked."

Xiang walked a few feet away, Eng trailing behind. "Where do we stand with the photo?"

"We're distributing them now. The airport and all the train and bus stations are covered."

"Widen it," Xiang ordered. "I want every taxi driver to know his face. Someone has seen him. He's only a few hours ahead of us; if we move quickly, we'll have him before the day is out."

CIA Operations Center

DDO George Coates happened to be in the center when Tanner's message arrived. The duty officer called from the communications desk: "Mr. Coates, traffic on Pelican." Pelican was the computer-generated code word for Tanner and the Beijing operation.

Coates walked over and scanned the message. "Goddammit, call Dick Mason. If Dutcher's up there, have him come along."

They walked in five minutes later. "Pelican," Coates said, handing over the message. It read,

> BURNED, CAUSE UNKNOWN. GONE TO GROUND. WILL CONTACT FOR STEERING.
> BRAVO YANKEE.

"He's safe at least," Dutcher said. The "Bravo Yankee" sign off was what's called a "no duress" signal. It was Tanner's way of letting them know he was in fact free, and not being coerced into transmitting. "That's the most important part."

Dutcher meant it, but beyond that he felt events were quickly slipping away from them: China's deadline was less than a day away and as they'd predicted, Bulganin wasn't backing down; Jurens and his team, though safe for now, were stranded on Russian soil with no way to get out; and finally, he, Mason, and Cathermeier were still days away from being ready to confront Martin. If their plan was to succeed, one more coconspirator had to enlist.

The only good news—if it could be called that—had come from *Columbia* the day before: Kinsock and his crew were alive, but their position was perilous. Though wary of leaving the battle group with only one sub for cover, Cathermeier had ordered *Cheyenne*, another LA-class attack boat, dispatched toward the coordinates given by *Columbia*'s SLOT buoy.

Cathermeier was not hopeful. Unless Kinsock could get *Columbia* moving under her own power and into deeper water where *Cheyenne* could protect her, little could to be done for the boat until a rescue mission could be coordinated—itself a dicey proposition given her proximity to the mainland.

And now Briggs, Dutcher thought. On the run, alone and hunted by the *Guoanbu,* the PAP, and the PSB, he'd be lucky to get out alive, let along reach Soong.

"Yeah, he's safe," Mason agreed, "but for how long? How long can he last?"

54

Beijing

XIANG'S FEELING THAT HE KNEW HIS QUARRY HAD EVOLVED INTO a certainty.

By noon, Colson's picture had been distributed to every taxi and bus driver, to every train station, and to every PSB officer, from foot patrols to branch commanders. He'd disappeared. The coolness of the man, his ability to simply fade into Beijing's background, reminded Xiang of another cat-and-mouse game he'd played with another agent twelve years ago.

Marshal Han Soong's mysterious benefactor.

He picked up the phone and called for Eng. His assistant arrived a minute later. "Yes, sir?"

"Pull the case file from Soong's defection."

The file was exhaustive except when it came to Soong's intermediary. They had one photo, a black-and-white half profile of a Westerner. Xiang laid it beside Colson's passport photo and stared at them until both images were etched in his mind.

He closed his eyes and let the photos merge, using his imagination to rotate them, change the angles and lighting. . . . He spent ten minutes like this, waiting for his subconscious to do the work.

Add a decade to the age, lighten the hair, give the face a beard. . . .

Xiang's reverie was broken by a knock on his door. "Come!"

It was Eng. "Sir, are you—"

Xiang silenced him with a raised finger.

It's you, isn't it? You came back for him, you stupid son-of-a-bitch. You came back. . . .

"That's him!"

"Who?"

"His name is Briggs Tanner—Soong's long-lost friend."

"How do you know his name?" Eng asked. "Soong never gave us—"

"My God, the arrogance! I'll say this: He's patient. Twelve years and he still came back."

"How do we know that's why he's here? It could be anything—"

"No. Soong's the reason." Xiang's phone rang and he snatched it up. "Yes?" He listened for a minute, then said, "I'm on my way." He hung up. "We have a lead."

"Where?"

"The Shahe train station. A ticket agent remembers seeing Tanner earlier this morning."

FORTY MINUTES LATER THEY ARRIVED AT THE STATION.

The PSB officer who reported the sighting was waiting in the office. Sitting on a stool in the corner was an old woman in a ticket-agent apron. She glanced at Xiang, then cast her eyes downward.

"Tell me," Xiang said to the PSB officer.

"She sold him three tickets: Chaoyang, Shanghai, and Tianshui. We're questioning passengers who might have been here at the time, but so far we haven't determined which train he boarded."

"Smart move, buying three tickets," Eng said.

"We'll cover them all," Xiang said. "Where are the trains now?"

"The Chaoyang and Tianshiu have already arrived. The Shanghai one is still en route."

"Eng, have it stopped and searched."

"Yes, sir."

"Then contact the PSB commandant in Chaoyang and Tianshiu and have them cover the stations. I want everyone questioned, from the ticket agents to the janitors. If Tanner was on one of those trains, someone had to have seen him. If need be, we'll put people on every connection."

Does he know where the camp is? Xiang wondered. *No, he couldn't. No chance.*

Then where was he going? If anything, time and experience would have made Tanner wilier, more resourceful. He was moving with purpose, but what was it? Had the ambush at the hotel scared him off? Xiang doubted it. So, if he wasn't running, what was he doing?

It didn't matter, he decided. Before the day was out they would have him. Of course, he'd said the same thing twelve years ago. Tanner hadn't been supposed to escape then, either. "Eng, assemble a search team. Call General Shiun at Fifteenth Army and tell him I want a company of his Dragons—"

"Paratroopers?"

"That's right. And a pair of helicopters—Hinds. If Tanner manages to slip us again, we'll hunt him down the old-fashioned way."

Chaoyang

The loudspeaker above Tanner's head blared to life again, made another curt announcement in Mandarin, then went silent. He was unable to decipher most of it, but caught the word "Chaoyang."

He opened his map and did a quick calculation. *Good.* His ruse at the Shahe Station had bought him almost 220 miles. He was refolding his map when the vibration ringer on the Motorola went off. He pulled it off his belt and read the LED screen: Pager message. He punched up the message:

TRACK SUCCESSFUL.
CAMP AT 47° 35'N—129° 27'E
GOOD HUNTING, STAY SAFE.
—W.O.

Briggs smiled. *Bless you, Walt.* He dialed the routing number, punched in the codes for "Message Received" and "In

Transit," then hung up, reopened his map and plotted the coordinates.

No, that can't be right. . . . He plotted them again, and came up with the same answer. *Good God. . . .* His journey had just started.

The camp was far to the north, deep in the forests and mountains of the Heilongjiang Province.

He had another three hundred miles to go.

WITH A GREAT SIGH OF STEAM, THE LOCOMOTIVE SLOWED BESIDE the red-and-green-bannered platform and jolted to a stop. The car's occupants got up and started filing toward the door. Tanner followed.

Chaoyang lay at the heart of Liaodong Province, a farming region mostly bordered by the forests of the Changbei Massif to the east and the rolling foothills of the Chingan range to the west.

Briggs kept his face in his map as he passed the conductor's assistant and stepped down onto the platform. He blinked against the bright sun and pulled up his collar. The temperature hovered around fifty degrees. A brisk spring day.

He found the ticket office and repeated his Shahe ruse, buying tickets for Shenyang to the east, Datong to the west, and Fuxin to the northeast, which would be his next destination.

If he could make it that far, his choices of routes and connections into Heilongjiang Province increased, thereby making it harder for Xiang to track him.

Thirty minutes passed before the loudspeaker announced boarding for Changchun. He waited for the third call, then boarded and walked to the rearmost of the train's eight cars. Only six other people occupied seats. Several of them clutched chickens or potbellied pigs in their laps.

As he passed, an old woman gave him a gap-toothed grin. *"Zao shang hao." Good morning.*

Briggs nodded and smiled back, surprised to feel a flood of gratitude wash over him. However small, the human contact felt good. To her, it didn't matter that he was *waiguoren.*

"Ai, ai!" the woman called to him. She reached into her pocket, pulled out an egg, and handed it to him. *"Hao chi, hao chi!"* Good eats.

Tanner took the egg and patted her hand. During hard times this one egg might have been an entire meal for her. He said, *"Xiexie buxie, ma pengyou."* Providing he'd gotten the inflection right, he'd said, "Thank you, old mother." If he'd botched it, he'd just called her a horse.

The woman smiled back. *"Bu kegi, huang tou!" You're welcome, blond hair.*

They shared a laugh, then Tanner wandered to the back of the car and found an empty seat and waited, coiled like a spring, until the train began moving.

AN HOUR LATER AND FIFTY MILES OUT OF CHAOYANG, THEY WERE entering a wooded valley north of Jiudaoling when the train suddenly lurched, followed by the shriek of metal on metal. The train began slowing. The other passengers started murmuring and looking around.

Briggs opened his window and stuck his head out.

Ahead lay a road junction; sitting across the tracks was a black Peugeot. One man sat behind the wheel, while two more, each wearing charcoal gray suits, stood at it's side.

PSB. Someone at either Shahe or Chaoyang had identified him.

The screeching continued until the train ground to a halt fifty yards from the Peugeot.

Two of the PSB officers walked to the locomotive, had a brief shouted conversation with the engineer, then boarded the first car. Moments later, Tanner heard some shouting from the cars ahead and caught a few snippets: "Stay seated . . . have papers ready. . . ."

The locomotive's whistle blew and the train started chugging forward again. Whether it was due to a mistake on the part of the officers, or to an engineer dedicated to his schedule, Tanner had just gotten a break. He knew he couldn't elude them on the train, but if he could get off without them noticing . . .

He looked up the aisle. The old woman was leaning out, looking back at him.

She frowned, worry lines around her eyes. *"Ni?" You?*

He nodded and said, *"Shi."* then added a phrase he hoped translated into "egg thief."

The old woman laughed uproariously, then glanced through the adjoining car's vestibule. She pushed her palm at him several times and said, *"Zou, zou." Go, go.* With the chicken clutched to her chest, she stood up and began waddling up the aisle.

She's going to run interference for me, Briggs thought. *"Bui shi!"* he called. *No, don't.*

She turned and shooed him. *"Zou!"*

She disappeared through the doors.

The only way he could help her now was to not be found. Hopefully, none of the other passengers would report her complicity. They were looking at him, eyes wide, but he saw no anger, merely worry.

He opened the rear door and stepped onto the platform.

On either side, the ground raced past, a blur of green underbrush. Cold wind whipped around him. About a hundred yards from the tracks was a line of thick fir trees.

With one hand on the railing, Tanner descended the steps then leaned out. The ground was mercifully flat, but that was no guarantee. Movie portrayals aside, jumping from a moving train—a moving anything, for that matter—was no easy stunt. At this speed, he would hit the ground at nearly quadruple his weight.

From the train came more shouts and the sound of a chicken squawking. He peeked through the door. The PSB officers were in the next car forward.

Time to go.

He leaned out, took a deep breath, and jumped.

The ground rushed toward him. He tucked himself into a ball, rounding his shoulders and covering his head with his hands. He began tumbling. He let himself go limp. On the second revolution, his tailbone slammed into the ground.

With a grunt, all the air rushed from his lungs.

After a few seconds he stopped rolling and lay perfectly still, willing himself to meld into the ground. *Don't move, don't move. . . .*

"Aiyahhh!" came a shout. Tanner lifted his head. Framed in one of the train's windows was one of the PSB men. *"Aiyahhh!"* he shouted again.

Dumbfounded, Tanner watched as the man pulled open the window and began crawling through, legs first. On his belly, he extended one leg, then the other until he was dangling from the pane. The man dropped. He hit the ground and began tumbling, limbs flailing like those of a rag doll.

Tanner didn't wait to see his landing. He snatched up his backpack and started running.

55

Behind him, a shout in English: "Stop! Stop there!"

Seconds later Tanner heard the double crack of gunfire and felt something tug at his sleeve.

Son-of-a-bitch. He put his head down and kept running.

In seconds he reached the tree line. Darkness enveloped him. The air cooled. He spotted a game trail and followed it. Behind him came the crunch of footfalls and more calls of "Stop!"

He glanced over his shoulder. He caught a glimpse of the PSB man twisting and ducking through the trees as he struggled to catch up. The trail led deeper into the forest. Soon the ground began to slope downward.

He started down the embankment, lost his footing on the pine needles, and started skidding. His hip slammed into a tree trunk. He gasped, rolled away, scrambled to his knees and kept going.

The path widened suddenly. The trail forked, north and south, both following the edge of a swamp. Half-dead sycamore trees lined the bank, their exposed roots jutting from the mud.

At a sprint, Tanner reached the edge of the bank, dropped hard onto his butt, and slid feet-first into the water. He resurfaced, snatched a breath, then ducked under and scrabbled back to the bank. As he'd hoped, the water had undercut the mud, leaving behind nooks among the tree roots. He wriggled himself into the darkened interior and went still.

He heard the pound of footsteps on the trail above. They paused at the fork for several seconds, then resumed, heading north.

Atta boy, keep running—

The footsteps stopped.

Following my prints, Tanner thought. He closed his eyes, straining to listen.

There was ten seconds of silence, then the footsteps came again, moving slowly toward the bank. Above his head, a twig snapped.

Ever so slowly, Tanner shrugged off his backpack and wedged it between the roots. He took a breath, ducked under, then peeked out.

And found himself staring at the toe of a shoe.

With one hand shading his eyes, the PSB man scanned the water. In his left hand was a revolver.

The PSB man looked down. They locked eyes.

"Aiyahhh!"

The man raised his gun hand, bringing it level with Tanner's head. Briggs launched himself from the water, locked his hands around the man's ankles and pulled. The man dropped to his butt. Tanner flipped him onto his belly, then dropped his weight, levering him into the water. The gun slipped from the man's hand and plunged into the murk.

Sputtering, the man thrashed to the surface. Tanner ducked under, hands groping. His fingers touched metal. He grabbed the gun, missed, tried again. His palm closed over the gun's checkered grip. He pushed off the bottom and broke the surface, gun leveled in what he hoped was the right direction.

The man was standing five feet away, shaking his head clear of water. He glared at Tanner. Briggs gestured toward the bank. The man didn't move. He reached into his coat pocket and withdrew a slender object. With a click, the switchblade popped open.

"Don't," Tanner warned. "*Bu shi.*" No.

Knife held before him, the man started toward him.

"*Bu shi!*" Tanner said again. "Stop."

The man muttered something in Chinese, then in English: "Surrender!" and kept coming.

"Goddammit, don't!" Briggs shouted.

The man lunged forward. Tanner pulled the trigger—and got a dull *click*.

Empty cylinder.

The man was falling toward him, knife arcing downward.

Tanner ducked left but lost his balance and slipped under the surface. The man plodded through the water, stabbing and slashing at Tanner's legs. Briggs felt a sting in his left calf, rolled away, then stuck his arm out of the water and pulled the trigger.

Click.

Again.

The gun boomed.

A quarter-size hole appeared in the man's chest. He stumbled backward, blinked his eyes a few times, then fell backward into the water, dead.

He searched the body, but found only a few *yuan* notes and a PSB ID card; he pocketed both. Then he steered the corpse under the shelf and wedged it into the root system.

Dragging his pack behind him, he crawled up onto the bank, stripped off his clothes, and sat down to examine the cut on his calf. It was deep, about three inches long, and in need of stitches. He unzipped the pack, pulled out the medkit and set to work closing the wound with tape sutures.

The ground around him was a muddy mess of overlapping footprints and scuff marks that no amount of camouflage would cover. When Xiang's team got here, they'd read the signs clearly.

Maybe there was a way to use that.

He needed to put as much distance between himself and this spot as quickly as possible. The question was, how far and how long could he run? When Xiang and his searchers got here, they would ask the same question; their answer would decide how far out they cast their initial net.

Briggs ripped the dressing off his wound, retrieved a small squeeze bottle of saline solution from the med-kit, and emptied it. Teeth gritted against the pain, he squeezed the cut until the blood began flowing again, then held the mouth of the bottle beneath it. When he had about three ounces, he screwed the top on, then redressed the cut.

He stood up and put his weight on the leg: a little pain, but not bad.

From the pack he pulled out a set of camouflage BDUs—pants, shirt, field jacket—and got dressed. He slipped on a dry pair of wool socks, followed by a one-piece Gore-Tex thermal underwear suit, then pulled on his boots, then covered his face and hands with black grease paint.

Next, using strips of black duct tape, he secured the bottle upside down to his right calf. He stomped his foot. Blood onto the ground. *Good enough.*

He checked his map, took a few compass readings, then cinched the pack onto his shoulders and starting jogging.

Darkness was falling when Xiang's helicopter landed in the field beside the tree line.

He and Eng were met by a soldier in camouflage dress with a lieutenant's insignia on one collar and a black dragon pin on the other. As Xiang approached, the lieutenant snapped to attention and saluted.

"Sir! Lieutenant Shen, Company B, Flying Dragons. General Shiun sends his regards."

"How many man do you have?"

"Sixty. Half are here, the other half are on their way."

"Show me what you have."

Shen led them into the trees and down the trail to the swamp. "We found the body stuffed under a shelf in the bank," Shen explained. "He was shot once. His gun and ID card are missing. According to the PSB commander in Chaoyang, the man's name was Peng. He'd been on the job only a year."

"How is that relevant?" Xiang asked.

"I just . . . I thought you'd like to know, sir. He was one of ours."

"Let his family mourn him." Xiang shined his flashlight around. "There was a struggle here."

"Yes, sir."

"Was he killed here or in the water?"

"In the water, I believe. There's blood on the ground, but not enough."

"Then it's Tanner's blood. He's hurt."

Shen nodded. "Yes, sir. Come this way."

They walked down the trail. Shen pointed to the ground. "He came this way. Take a look at the right print. . . . See it? Compare the heel depth to the left one."

Xiang squatted down. "It's deeper."

"He's favoring his right leg—limping badly. See the blood splotches beside the heel?"

"Yes."

"He's seeping blood from a wound on his right leg. Whatever it is, it's bad. I sent a tracker to scout his trail; the blood keeps going."

Good, Xiang thought. *At least the late Officer Peng marked him for us.* "How far could a man in that condition get?"

"What kind of man?"

"Your caliber, perhaps better."

Shen cocked his head. "He's been running for four hours, tired and in pain, losing blood. . . . Plus, he'd probably stay in trees, which would slow him down. . . . I'd say twelve miles at most. If you can get me some dogs and handlers, I'll have him for you by dawn."

"Get started," Xiang ordered. "You'll have dogs within the hour."

56

Chono Dam

A FEW HOURS AFTER HE AND SKELDON RETURNED FROM THE silver mine, Cahil was set to work.

With a few murmured orders from their colonel, the commandos began laying crates at his feet: C4, detonators, detcord, and six pieces of heavy, steel pipe, each closed at one end, about a foot long, and a few inches smaller in diameter than the bore holes in the mine.

They want me to build shaped charges, Cahil thought.

A shaped charge is designed to focus explosive force in a specific direction. On a small scale, antiterrorist units use them to knock down doors; on a larger scale, military demolition teams and miners use them to punch holes through obstacles and solid rock.

The idea here would be to slide the charges into the bore holes until they were resting against the bedrock. Upon detonation, the force of each charge would have nowhere to go but through the rock and into the dam's footings, setting off a shock wave that would ripple and crack the rest of the dam. With each charge packing ten pounds of C4, it would have enough force to create a car-size crater.

Cahil stared at the crates for several moments, his mind whirling. He was in an impossible position. He couldn't build these charges—or at least he couldn't build them to work—but if he chose either of those options, he had little doubt they'd kill him on the spot. They'd come here to not only destroy the Chono, but to die here as well. For all he knew, they were perfectly capable of building the charges themselves, and his participation was simply more window dressing.

So where did that leave him? Counting Skeldon as an enemy, the odds against him were seven to one. But should he count Skeldon as an enemy? He was assuming so, but was he certain?

The colonel walked over, gave him a grim stare, and gestured to the crates: *Get started.*

SKELDON WALKED OVER AND SAT DOWN. "HOW GOES IT?"

"Getting there," Cahil replied.

"What is that you're using—steel wool?"

Cahil nodded. "For the best effect, the inside of the pipe needs to be completely smooth."

"Why?"

"You never handled shaped charges in the Lurps?"

Skeldon smiled. "Hey, man, we were all booby traps and small IM stuff," he replied, referring to improvised munitions. "We left the bunker busting to the engineers."

"The theory's pretty simple: The bowl—in this case, this pipe—acts as a lens to focus the explosion. If the pipe isn't smooth, some of the force might get redirected."

"Gotcha. Want some help?"

"Sure. Start with the next pipe."

AFTER WORKING IN SILENCE FOR A FEW MINUTES, CAHIL DECIDED to dive in. It was time to find out where Skeldon stood. "Mike, what do you know about these guys?"

"Not much. They're special forces types, that's obvious."

"They're called Flying Dragons; they're paratroopers—the cream of Chinese special forces."

"How the hell do you know that?"

"Mike, you know they're going to kill us once we're done, don't you?"

Skeldon's head snapped. "Keep your goddamned voice down," he whispered. "That's crap—you're full of crap."

"You think so? How do you imagine it happening? We blow up the dam, have a little lunch with our new friends, then drive south and share a tearful good-bye at the border?"

Skeldon frowned, clearly uncomfortable. "Yeah, something like that."

"Nothing like that. Once we set these charges, we're dead men."

"Who the hell are you? Where's all this shit coming from?"

"I can tell who I'm not: I'm not Stan Kycek—"

"What the hell—"

"My name is Ian Cahil, and I work for our government."

Skeldon tensed, preparing to stand. Cahil clamped a hand onto his thigh. "Sit down."

"Go to hell."

"Mike, I have no intention of dying here. I've got a wife and two kids back home, and I want to see them again. Now *sit down*, or I'll kill you before you reach your feet."

Skeldon stayed seated, but stared Cahil in the eyes. *Measuring me,* he thought.

"I mean it," Bear pressed. "Better I kill you now; it evens my odds."

After a few moments, Skeldon picked up his pipe and began working. "Okay, start talking. Where's the real Kycek?"

"In a CIA safe house, thanking his lucky stars we got to him before he left."

"How'd you find him?"

"It's a long story."

"I wanna hear it."

"You know about Baker?"

"What about him?"

"He's dead—he and his family."

"What?"

Cahil spent the next twenty minutes taking Skeldon through the Baker case, from Latham's entry into it, through his trip to Asheville and his discovery of Lamar Sampson and Stan Kycek.

He ended by explaining the scope of the Chinese plan: the SEALs at Nakhodka-Vostochny; the battle group; China's ultimatum to Russia; and finally, the reason they were sitting in the middle of Siberia making improvised shaped charges.

The one item he left out—Martin's complicity in the affair—was something Skeldon could not know about.

"I don't believe it," Skeldon said.

"Why would I lie?"

Skeldon sighed and shook his head, frustrated. "I don't know. Are you lying?"

"No. It's time for you to decide, Mike: Whose side are you on? If we don't stop this here, there's gonna be a war. I need your help. I can't do it alone."

Skeldon stared at him. "We're in some deep shit, aren't we?"

"Yep."

Skeldon chuckled humorlessly. "I guess there's some loyalty left in me after all. Okay, Ian Cahil, what do you want to do?"

Washington, D.C.

The Towncar carrying Mason, Dutcher, and Cathermeier pulled up to the side entrance of the Naval Observatory at the corner of Massachusetts and 34th and stopped. Also known as the Admiral House, the white-brick Victorian was the official residence of the vice president of the United States.

Flanked by two Secret Service agents, the chief of the detail stepped forward and opened the door. "Evening, Gentlemen. If you'll follow me, please."

Always discreet, Dutcher thought. If the agents were at all curious why their boss was receiving a late night visit from the director of central intelligence, the chairman of the Joint Chiefs, and a long-retired CIA veteran, they gave no indication of it. If the matter didn't involve the safety of their charge, it didn't involve them.

They were led through the French doors into the foyer, then down a long hallway. The agent stopped before a door, knocked once, then opened it. He gestured for them to enter, then closed the door behind them.

With its green-baize wall coverings and heavy, brocade drapes, Vice President David Lahey's study reminded

Dutcher of a reading room in an old gentlemen's club. Oil paintings depicting various naval battles decorated the walls. A fire burned in a flagstone hearth.

At forty-two, Lahey was one of the youngest vice presidents in contemporary history, and since joining the Martin ticket, had struggled to shrug off the shadow of the "Quayle Syndrome." Lahey was bright, down-to-earth, and like Martin's former boss, President John Haverland, dedicated to the value of service—all of which had thus far been obscured by the debate over Lahey's age.

The rumor among Washington insiders was that Martin and Lahey's relationship was strained, and Dutcher suspected it was because Lahey was realizing what many people already knew: Consummate politician though he was, Phillip Martin was about as genuine as a nine-dollar bill.

Lahey came from around his desk and greeted them, shaking hands first with Cathermeier, then Mason, then finally Dutcher. "Leland, I don't think we've met. Welcome."

"Thank you, Mr. Vice President."

They arranged themselves in a semicircle of wingback chairs beside the fireplace. Lahey poured each of them a cup of coffee, then said, "Leland, did Chuck ever tell you how we met?"

"He told me you were friends, but nothing else."

"We were both serving at the National War College over at Fort McNair. Chuck was a colonel, I a lowly second lieutenant. One day we were war-gaming a problem involving the Balkans—"

"Macedonia," Cathermeier corrected him.

"That's right—Macedonia. Idiot that I am, I decided I understood the scenario better than Chuck, and before I knew it we were in a shouting match. Here's this roomful of army and navy officers watching some fresh-mouthed lieutenant flushing his career down the drain."

"What happened?" asked Dutcher.

"I'll tell you what happened," Cathermeier answered. "David turned out to be right. We played out both our solutions—his worked, mine didn't."

"Dumb luck," Lahey said. "Afterward, Chuck walks up to me—with the whole room still watching, mind you—apologizes, then hands me his fountain pen, and says, 'My sword, sir.' "

Dutcher and Mason burst out laughing.

"I still have that pen," Lahey said. "I carry it everywhere."

Cathermeier said, "I'm still hoping to win it back some day."

"Not likely," Lahey shot back

After a few moments of laughter, Lahey poured himself another cup of coffee. "I have to admit, gentlemen, you've piqued my interest. When Chuck asked for this meeting, I wasn't quite sure what to think. Who's going to put me out of my suspense?"

As planned, Cathermeier took the lead. Given his relationship with the vice president, he had the best chance of getting Lahey to listen. "David, we've got a problem with Martin."

"Then you've joined a sizable club. Many people do."

"It goes beyond personality, I'm afraid."

"Go on."

It took thirty minutes for Cathermeier to lay out their evidence. Occasionally, Dutcher or Mason would interrupt to clarify a point, but Lahey himself never spoke, simply listening, his face unreadable, until Cathermeier was done

Lahey stood up, walked to the fireplace, and stared into the flames.

Dutcher held his breath. This was the watershed. All Lahey had to do was pick up the phone and they were finished. Dutcher studied Lahey's face, looking for a sign.

"Leland, Dick, you were wise to let Chuck do the talking. If anyone else had brought this to me. . . . I'm not going to ask if you're sure about this. I can see by your faces that you are. When does China's deadline expire?"

Mason said, "Four hours."

"Do we have any idea what will come after that—or how soon?"

"No, sir."

"I want to talk to Bousikaris myself."

Cathermeier nodded. "We thought you might. He's in the car."

LAHEY REMAINED SEATED AS BOUSIKARIS ENTERED. "COME ON in, Howard." Dutcher, Mason, and Cathermeier stood behind Lahey's chair, hands clasped. "Have a seat."

Bousikaris's eyes were bloodshot and droopy. As he sat down, his shoulders slumped forward.

"Is it true, Howard?"

Bousikaris nodded. "Yes, sir, I'm afraid it is."

"Look at me, Howard." Bousikaris stared at his lap. "Howard: Look at me." Bousikaris did so. "If you're under duress, being pressured somehow into—"

"No."

"If you are, say so now. This is serious business we're talking about. Is everything they've told me the truth? Martin, the election, China—everything?"

"Yes."

Lahey sighed. "Jesus, Howard, how in God's name did you let this happen? You're smarter than that. Do you know what you've done? Do you have *any* idea?"

Bousikaris nodded; his cheek twitched. "I'm sorry."

"Unfortunately, sorry isn't enough. You and that . . . narcissistic *son-of-a-bitch* have brought us—and maybe the whole world—to the brink of war. Get out of here, Howard."

Once Bousikaris was gone, Lahey said, "Gentlemen, I wish there were time for me to absorb this, but I suspect time is the one thing we don't have. What are we going to do, and what's my part?"

Mason answered. "It's pretty straightforward, Mr. Vice President. You're going to have to take over the country and stop a war."

57

China

THOUGH TANNER HAD NO WAY OF KNOWING IT, HIS RUSE AT THE swamp had done its job.

As he was approaching the eastern outskirts of Fuxin, Xiang and his searchers were following his trail twenty-five miles to the south, certain their injured quarry could not be far ahead.

But the price for Briggs had been high.

Aside from hourly five-minute breaks to drink from his canteen, eat a handful of trail mix and a few bites of jerky, he'd been running for six hours through the forests and valleys that bordered the rail line between Jiudaoling and Fuxin.

Always keeping the tracks in sight, he stayed just outside the tree line, using the moonlight to pick his way along. After an hour, his face and hands were scratched bloody and his shins bruised from multiple falls. His BDUs became splotched and stained with tree sap, pine needles, and leaves.

Three hours into his run, the pack's straps began chafing his shoulders and before long he could feel blisters forming. With nothing to be done about it, he kept running. He focused his mind on his breathing, using its rhythm to blot out everything but the trail ahead and the forest's night sounds.

Halfway through every hour he would stop, backtrack a few hundred yards and sit still in the undergrowth, listening and watching for signs of pursuit. Twice he saw the twinkling of aircraft strobes to the south and caught the faint *thumping* of helicopter rotors. He heard the distant howling of dogs, but couldn't be sure whether they were tracking hounds, or local pets. To be safe, he assumed the former.

Dogs could be both a blessing and a curse, he knew. While dogs were nearly impossible to elude without a substantial head start, search parties that used them tended to rely too heavily on their cues. Without a good mix of both ground-scent and air-scent dogs, searchers could easily get mired in following dead ends and tangents.

Through the night and into the early morning hours, Tanner kept running, counting his strides to keep pace, listening to his breathing, watching for obstacles and avoiding open ground—all the while covering a mile every ten minutes—all the while pulling farther and farther ahead of his pursuers.

WITH DAWN STILL A COUPLE HOURS AWAY, HE EMERGED FROM the forest on a ridge overlooking the small town of Xinqiu north of Fuxin.

He got out his binoculars, found the train tracks leading in from the south, and followed them until he spotted an old clapboard terminal building on the northern edge of the town. A single light shone through one of the station's windows: the conductor's office, he assumed. Sitting on the tracks closest to the platform was a caboose; ahead of it, a string of ten cars—four passenger, five freight, and a tender—and a locomotive with smoke wafting from its stack. The number on its side read 17.

Gearing up for departure? Tanner wondered. The kernel of a plan formed in his mind, and he played with it for a few minutes before deciding it was worth a try.

On the secondary track behind the station was a line of fifty or sixty empty freight cars. Tanner studied each one, estimating its length, then made a quick calculation. *Fifty cars, each roughly thirty feet long. . . .* The string was over a quarter mile long. *Even better.*

Thirty minutes later he was lying on his belly in the bushes across from the station.

Nothing was moving and aside from tinny strains of *beiqu*, or Chinese opera, music filtering through the office window, all was quiet. In the distance, a train whistle wailed and then faded.

After a few more minutes of watching, he got up, ran across the tracks, and knelt beside the platform where he could see through the lighted window. Inside, an elderly man sat dozing in a chair, his feet propped on the desk.

Tanner spotted the schedule board: Train 17 was at the top of the list: Yingkou—0550.

Yingkou was a port city on the Bo Hai Gulf about one hundred miles to the south. He checked his watch: ninety minutes until departure. He would be cutting it close, but the risk was worth it.

He collected half a dozen small stones, then crept to the rear of the caboose, mounted the steps to the platform, and slipped inside. Hunched over, he walked down the aisle to the vestibule, opened the door, and stepped through. He clicked on his penlight and shined it over his head. He popped open the maintenance hatch, pushed his pack through, then chinned himself up and out onto the roof.

Crouching at the edge of the car, he tossed his pack across the gap onto the platform roof as gently as he could. He dropped onto his belly and went still. One minute passed . . . two. . . . The *beiqu* from the office continued uninterrupted.

Briggs took a deep breath, then leapt across, using his hands to distribute the impact.

He crept across the roof until he was centered over the office, then lay on his belly and shimmied to the edge. From his pocket he withdrew the PSB man's ID card, took aim, and flicked it onto the platform.

He crossed to the opposite side of the roof where the empty freight cars began, then repeated the earlier process, first tossing his backpack onto the car's roof, then leaping across to join it.

Almost there.

He pulled the stones from his pocket, chose the biggest one, took aim, and threw. It struck the platform with a thud, bounced twice, then smacked into the station wall. From the office there was a shout of surprise and the clatter of chair wheels on the wooden floor. The *beiqu* music stopped.

The office door opened, casting a yellow patch of light on the platform. The conductor stepped out and looked around.

He walked to the edge of the platform, stopped with his foot almost touching the ID card, and scanned the tracks.

Come on, Tanner urged. *Look down. . . .*

The man looked around for a few seconds, then turned back. Then stopped. He looked down and bent over, picked up the card, then walked back inside.

Good man, Tanner thought.

He stood up, donned his pack, and started jogging down the car's roofs. When he reached the last one, he climbed down the side ladder to the track bed, and started running north.

TWENTY-SIX MILES TO THE SOUTH, XIANG WAS FOLLOWING A service road along the rail line. Lieutenant Shen drove while Eng sat in the backseat. Behind were a pair of army trucks loaded with the rest of the paratroopers.

To the east, Xiang could hear the braying of the tracking dogs.

Enough of this, he thought. "Stop."

"Sir?" said Shen.

"Stop driving!" Shen slammed on the brakes. "What is it, sir?"

"How far have we come from the swamp?"

Shen unfolded his map. "Almost sixteen miles."

"A long way for an injured man, wouldn't you say?"

Shen shrugged.

"Who's your second-in-command? Who've you got with the dog handlers?"

"Sergeant Hjiu."

Xiang picked up the portable radio. "Xiang to Hjiu, do you read me?"

"Yes, sir, go ahead."

"Stop everyone where they are. We're coming to join you."

Shen pulled the vehicle as close to the tree line as possible, then they got out and walked the rest of the way. Hjiu was in a clearing of trees. "Where's the track?" Xiang asked.

"This way."

Hjiu led them down a trail to where the lead handler was giving his dog some water. "He's heading in roughly the same direction," Hjiu reported. "Roughly northeast. The scent is still strong."

Xiang turned to the handler. "Is there still blood?"

"Here and there, but not as much anymore."

"What about the tracks themselves?"

"Pardon, sir?"

"Any sign that he's favoring either leg?"

"No, sir. The strides are long and even. The dogs have a strong scent, though—"

"Dammit!" Xiang roared. "It was a ruse! He was never injured."

Lieutenant Shen said, "But the blood—"

"Who knows. . . . it doesn't matter. We're wasting our time! He's had almost eight hours. He could be anywhere. Shen, order your men back aboard the trucks!"

THEY WERE ON THE OUTSKIRTS OF FUXIN WHEN THE LEAD TRUCK flashed its headlights. Shen pulled over; the truck's driver jogged up. "A call on the base radio, Director Xiang. Peng's ID card was found."

"Where?"

"At the Xinqiu train station, just north of Fuxin—less than an hour ago. The conductor found it and called the PSB branch in Fuxin."

"That's impossible!" Shen said. "There's no way he could cover that distance on foot."

"Why not?" Xiang replied. "Could you? Could one of your men?"

"Yes, sir, but we're—"

"And so is he—if not better."

"It's almost fifty miles!"

"And he's had almost twelve hours."

"Yes, but—"

"But nothing. You're thinking with your pride, Shen. Tanner made us think what he wanted us to think—he tricked us into wasting our time."

"Perhaps, now he's spent. Running that far probably cost him every ounce of energy he had."

"On that, we agree," Xiang replied. *And tired men make mistakes*. "How far to Xinqiu?"

"Ten miles."

"Let's go."

TWENTY MINUTES LATER THEY WERE STANDING ON THE XINQIU platform with the conductor. The sun was fully up. A thin fog hovered over the ground. Down on the tracks, Shen and the handlers were working the area around the station. The dogs yipped excitedly and ran in circles.

"Where did you find it?" Xiang asked, studying the card.

"Over there," the conductor said. "Near the caboose."

"Caboose? What caboose?"

"For the Seventeen. It left about forty minutes ago."

"Hjiu! What've you found?"

"Strong scent, sir. It looks like he laid in those bushes over there, then walked to the platform and then back around to the tracks. But from there—"

"The trail disappears," Xiang finished.

"Yes, sir."

"Where's that train headed?" Xiang asked the conductor.

"Yingkou. It should arrive in about . . . an hour."

Eng said, "Stop the train?"

"No," Xiang answered. "Let him think he's safe. Call for the helicopter, then get Yingkou's PSB commander on the line. We'll grab him when he steps off the train."

FIVE MILES TO THE NORTH, TANNER WAS STILL RUNNING, BUT nearing the point of collapse. Ahead, the trees thinned out and gave way to a bowl-shaped meadow carpeted in orange poppies and bisected by a gurgling stream.

He picked out a particularly thick fir tree, then stuffed his pack beneath it and crawled under. Next, he took his knife, and, crawling around the trunk, partially sawed through a dozen boughs until they drooped to the ground.

One more thing to do before sleep, Briggs thought.

He pulled out the Motorola and dialed a number from memory. It was time to use the names Fong had given him. After three rings, the man named Yat Kwei answered. *"Ni hao!"*

"Ni hui yingwen ma?" Tanner replied. *Do you speak English?*

"Yes, I speak English. Who is this?"

"You don't know me. A man gave me your name, suggested I contact you."

"What man?"

"Zhimien; I met him in Taipei. He said you would be able to help me."

Kwei hesitated. "I know Zhimien. Are you in Beijing?"

"No," Tanner replied. "I had to leave the city unexpectedly. I had some . . . problems."

There was a pause on the other line; Tanner hoped Kwei was making connections. "You're American?" he asked.

"Does that matter? Zhimien, told me you don't care—"

"No, no, of course it doesn't matter. It's just that the police are looking for an American here. I was wondering perhaps—"

"Look, dammit!" Tanner snapped, forcing a little panic in his voice. "What does it matter? I have money. If you can help me, I'll pay you."

"Relax, friend. I'll help you. Tell me what you need."

"Passage aboard a ship—any ship, I don't care—as long as it's leaving Yingkou today. And documents, I need documents to get aboard. Can you do it?"

"Of course," Kwei said smoothly. "No problem. Are you in Yingkou now?"

"No."

"When will you be there?"

"The schedule said eight-fifty. I think . . . I think we left on time, so it should be about then."

"Good. I'll need time to contact the right people. Can you call me later, say in a couple hours?"

"Yes."

Tanner said good-bye and hung up.

Now let's just hope Kwei is as untrustworthy as Fong described.

58

China

TWO HOURS AFTER CURLING UP IN HIS BLIND AND DROPPING instantly asleep, Tanner was awoken by the Motorola's vibration alarm tickling his belly. He reached down, shut it off, then lay still for a few minutes, listening to the sounds of the forest and taking stock of his body.

He was in pain. From his head to his feet, he felt every scrape, bruise, and ounce of impact his feet and knees had taken during his long run. Starting at his toes, he slowly worked his way up his body, contracting and relaxing the muscles and tendons and ligaments, testing them for injury. Aside from the pain—which he hoped would work itself out as he began moving—he seemed intact.

He rolled onto his belly, parted the branches, and peeked out. *All clear.* Pushing his pack ahead of him, he crawled out and rearranged the branches to a natural position.

He spent fifteen minutes stretching and warming his muscles until finally the pain began to subside and he could move without wincing. He had a quick breakfast of trail mix, jerky, a pair of Excedrin, and washed them down with a liter of water.

He checked his watch: *Time for another performance.*

He pulled out the Motorola and dialed Yat Kwei, who answered immediately. *"Ni hao!"*

"It's me," Tanner said. "You recognize my voice?"

"Yes, of course. Where are you?"

"In a minute. Did you get the papers?"

"I'm working on it. They should be ready by this afternoon. The ship I have in mind departs at six tonight."

"Good. I'm going to need the time. I had to leave the train near Gaokan."

"Never heard of it."

"It's about fifteen miles north of Yingkou," Tanner replied.

"What happened?"

"Nothing. Train stations make me nervous. I'll go the rest of the way on foot. I'll call you at three about the documents. Will you be coming yourself?"

"No," Kwei said. "One of my associates. Don't worry, he knows nothing about you."

"That's fine," Tanner said tiredly, letting his voice crack. "I just want to get out of here."

Tanner said good-bye and hung up. He strapped on his pack then started trotting north.

Yingkou

The Number Seventeen train sat beside the platform, hissing and steaming as the engine cooled. Mixed in with the still-disembarking passengers were a dozen plainclothes PSB officers.

He's not there, Xiang thought. There wasn't a Caucasian face anywhere to be seen. Xiang felt himself flush. *Another damned trick! But what?* There were two options: He'd jumped off the train somewhere between here and Xinqiu, or he'd never been aboard the train at all.

There was a larger concern also, Xiang realized. Though still hundreds of miles from the camp, Tanner seemed to be moving in that general direction. Did he know its location, and if so, how? *Irrelevant,* Xiang thought. *Assume he knows and act accordingly.*

Eng had already argued that they should simply move Soong, but Xiang refused to consider it. He'd be damned if he was going to let Tanner make him jump through hoops.

Let him reach the camp, if he can. If he does, I'll fill the forest with hunters and tracking dogs. He won't last an hour.

TEN MINUTES LATER THE TRAIN WAS EMPTY. THE PSB OFFICERS boarded it, searched it from end to end, and found nothing. Behind Xiang, Eng walked up carrying a cell phone. "Sir?"

"What?"

"Headquarters got a call about an hour ago from a man named Yat Kwei."

"So?"

"Kwei is a small-time racketeer; he deals in forged documents . . . immigration papers and the like."

"How nice for him. Get to the point."

"Kwei's been a stringer agent for us for the last twenty years. He got a call a few hours ago from a man claiming to be American. The man was looking for documents and passage aboard a ship."

This caught Xiang's attention; he faced Eng, saw the smile on his assistant's face. "And?"

"The man claimed he was in trouble and that he needed to get out of the country. He told Kwei he was aboard a train bound for Yingkou—"

"You're joking."

"No, sir." Eng handed him the cell phone. "I've got Kwei's number."

THE CONVERSATION LASTED FIVE MINUTES. GRINNING, XIANG hung up and tossed the phone to Eng. "He jumped off near Gaokan. He's smart, but not smart enough. Never trust anyone, and if you have to trust someone, make sure it's not a goddamned criminal! We've got him!"

"Gaokan is only fifteen miles away," Eng replied. "With the helicopter—"

"No. He'll be calling Kwei this afternoon to arrange a meeting. We'll be there."

• • •

Having not heard the howling of dogs since leaving Xinqiu, Tanner was starting to relax.

They'd bought his ruse, but for how long? Xiang was no dummy. Upon realizing he'd been duped, he and his team would return to Xinqiu, unravel his disappearing act, and start after him again.

How many tricks did he dare play? *Fool me once, shame on you; fool me twice, shame on me*. Tanner didn't care much about shame, of course, but for his plan to work, he had to keep Xiang guessing. Every misdirection and delay he could cause brought him a step closer to the camp.

From the start, Briggs had known his biggest handicap was his very goal. That Xiang had found him at all suggested he had inside information, which implicated either Bian or Hsiao—or both. While certain neither man had knowingly betrayed him, he was sure one of them had led Xiang to him. Bian was the most likely candidate. The old man's heart was in the right place, but Roger Brown had been right: Bian was an accident waiting to happen. If in fact Bian had been arrested, Briggs had to assume he'd given them everything—including why he was here.

He hoped Bian hadn't tried to hold out; he prayed they hadn't killed him. *But what was worse for Bian?* he wondered, *Death or the* laogi*?* It was a question he might want to consider himself—though he doubted he'd be given a choice. If he were caught, Xiang would probably execute him on the spot and bury him in a shallow grave.

He kept his pace slow and easy—averaging four miles per hour—but before long this too became a challenge as the terrain grew hillier and the meadows and plains gave way to jagged ridges, deep valleys, and ever-thickening forests of spruce, walnut, and pine. The air was growing colder as well, and in some spots he could see crescents of snow clinging to the hillsides.

At noon he stopped to eat and catch his breath. A quarter mile away was a lake, and beside it, climbing away from the shore, train tracks. Any train attempting it would slow considerably during the climb.

He pulled out his map and traced the tracks north away from Xinqiu, mentally ticking off towns as he went: Wuhuanchi . . . Ping'an . . . Zhangwu—that sounded familiar. *Zhangwu. . . .* Though not completely sure, he seemed to recall seeing Zhangwu on the Xinqiu station's schedule board.

It was another big risk, but worth it, he decided. Even if time were not a factor, he couldn't run all the way to the camp; his body would shut down long before he got there.

Why walk when you can ride, Briggs?

NINETY MINUTES LATER HE HEARD A TRAIN WHISTLE IN THE DIStance. Beyond the curve of the lake, puffs of black smoke rose above the treetops.

Heart in his throat, Tanner watched the curve. If the train was all passenger cars, he was in trouble. One freight car was all he needed. If it happened to be hauling feather pillows, all the better. . . . Despite himself, excited by the prospect of giving his feet a break, Tanner let out a laugh.

Led by its angled cow catcher, the gleaming black and red locomotive rounded the bend and started up the grade. Its whistle blew again, echoing off the valley walls. Tanner counted cars as they came into view: One . . . two . . . three, all passenger cars. Five more appeared . . . seven.

There! At the tail end were two top-loader freight cars and a caboose.

The train continued to slow, steel wheels grinding against the tracks as the engine struggled to negotiate the slope. As it drew even with him, Tanner pressed himself deeper into the grass.

Have to be fast . . . get along side quickly, into the blind spot, and go for the caboose.

The chugging of the engine was thunderous, wheels clanking.

At the right moment, he leapt up and sprinted up the slope. His feet slipped on the gravel. He fell to one knee, got up, kept running. He thrust out his arm and clamped it onto the step rail, then heaved himself onto the steps. He reached between the cars, grabbed the access ladder, then climbed up and into the top loader.

59

Washington, D.C.

"LET'S HAVE IT," PRESIDENT MARTIN SNAPPED. "GENERAL, what the hell happened up there?"

"What happened, Mr. President, is what happens anytime you aim a battle group at another nation's shores," General Cathermeier replied. "They send out their ships and planes and it turns into a game of chicken. They were trying to warn us off—make sure we know they're not pushovers."

"By crashing into one of our planes? That's absurd."

The night before, a flight of four Russian Mig-31 Fulcrum fighters had come out and tried to buzz the battle group. That close to the Russian mainland, the group's commander had been expecting the visit and ordered the group's BARCAP—or Barrier Combat Air Patrol, in this case a pair of F-14 Tomcats—to intercept the intruders.

"At this point, it looks like an accidental bump," Cathermeier said. "One of their pilots took it a little too far and misjudged his approach."

"Not according to the Federation's foreign minister," Martin growled. "They're claiming it was our fault! What the hell are they doing out there?"

He's crumbling, Mason thought, seeing Martin with new eyes. Either the job was more than he'd bargained for, or he was starting to realize the deal he'd struck with the Chinese had been a terrible mistake. Mason suspected it was a combination of both. Martin had neither the temperament nor the character for the job.

Though Martin didn't know it, Mason, Cathermeier, and Dutcher had decided this meeting was his last chance to fix the situation before they moved on him. Not that it would matter in the end, Mason knew. Whether it was now or weeks from now, Martin had to go.

As planned, Bousikaris was absent from the meeting, having ostensibly gone to the dentist with a cracked molar. Martin alone would seal his fate.

Mason said, "Mr. President, we have the option to pull the group back, slow it down."

"No."

"It would give the Russians room to breathe."

"I said, *no,* dammit! Dick, I'm getting tired of repeating myself around you. I'm the commander in chief. I'll decide when and if it's time to move the battle group. Now, General, tell me about this business with the Chinese airliners. When did this happen?"

"During the night. As best we can tell, there were four aircraft in the group, all Russian-built Antonov An-12s—we call them Cubs. They're troop and cargo transports designed—"

Martin rolled his hand. "Go on, go on."

"About thirty minutes after the deadline expired, they lifted off from Hailar in northern China."

"They didn't waste any time, did they?"

"No, sir. According to the Chinese Foreign Ministry, the lead aircraft contacted Chita air control prior to crossing the border and identified the group as unarmed transports on an evacuation mission."

"Evacuation? Of what?"

"Of the Chinese living in the Chita area, Mr. President. The Russians are claiming the opposite—that the planes never made contact and ignored repeated attempts to contact them."

"Who's lying? Dick?"

"No way to tell," Mason replied, but thought, *the Chinese, of course*. "Any transcripts or recordings from either won't be accepted by the other."

"Go on, General."

"Getting no response to their hails, Chita scrambled a pair of Mig-23 Floggers to intercept the flight. About sixteen miles north of the border—"

"In Russian airspace," Martin clarified.

"Correct. The Floggers joined on the Chinese Cubs. They tried to establish radio contact; failing that, one of them pulled alongside the lead Cub and tried to establish visual contact. Here's where it gets fuzzy," Cathermeier continued. "The Chinese claim the Floggers fired on them from behind, without any attempt to establish contact; the Russians claim the opposite, of course.

"Either way, there was an explosion on or near the one of the Cubs. It tipped over, went into a flat spin, and crashed."

"From what altitude?"

"Twenty-five thousand feet. The Russians are looking for the site."

"They won't find much," Mason said.

"No shit," Martin replied. "Well, I've been on the phone all morning with State. The Chinese are screaming bloody murder, and their ambassador is on his way over here as we speak. What I want to know from you two is, where's this going?"

It was a genuine question, Mason realized. Looking into Martin's eyes, he saw uncertainty and fear. Whether the man understood his own role in the unfolding disaster, Mason wasn't sure, but so far Martin was showing no signs of changing course.

Neither Mason nor Cathermeier answered Martin's question.

"I want an answer, gentlemen. Where is all this going?"

Last chance, Mason thought. "Mr. President, it's my opinion that the Chinese are not going to back down. Whether we're seeing their true motives or not, I don't know, but the fact that they moved so quickly after the deadline is telling.

"Their position will be clear: Russian negligence has killed thousands of Chinese citizens; every step of the way, the Federation has refused to work with them to remedy the situation; and now, they have attacked an unarmed, clearly identified group of transports sent on a goodwill mission to rescue Chinese citizens."

"Which might all be true," Martin said.

"Perhaps," Mason countered, "but I don't see it that way. As I said, it's my opinion this is just part of a larger plan for the Chinese. They're not going to back down until they get what they want, and they'll do whatever it takes to get there."

"To what end? What larger plan?"

Mason shrugged. "Bottom line, Mr. President: I have two recommendations. Remain neutral in this—both militarily and diplomatically. And two, do whatever it takes to get both sides to step back and take a breath before it's too late."

Martin looked to Cathermeier. "General?"

"I agree. If we don't take steps to cool the situation, it's going to escalate."

Martin sighed heavily, then nodded. "That's all gentlemen. Stay close to your phones."

Moscow

The tirade had so far lasted twenty minutes and showed no signs of slowing.

From his chair, Ivan Nochenko watched Bulganin pace the room, one hand clasped behind his back, the other gesticulating wildly as he shouted.

Nochenko had seen him in such moods before, but this one had a different feel to it. Bulganin's speech, his demeanor, the very inflection of his words had a disconnected quality to them, as though he were summoning them by rote from some corner of his brain.

Earlier this morning Bulganin had ordered Pyotr to double his personal guards and to search the staff's belongings upon entry and exit of the building. Only at Nochenko's intercession had Bulganin excluded he and the rest of the members of the National Security Council.

Pyotr now stood behind Bulganin's desk, watching the room with a hawk's eyes.

"Let us review," Bulganin said. "Not only are the Americans threatening our coast with their ships, but they've put soldiers on our soil, destroyed a port, and now, just hours ago, they downed one of our aircraft in international airspace."

Defense Minister Beskrovny spoke up. "We're looking into that, Mr. President, but initially it appears to have been an accident."

"Believe that if you like, Marshal," Bulganin shot back. "What about the Chinese? It's not enough they accuse us of murdering their citizens, but now they invade our airspace on a so-called rescue mission. What kind of aircraft were they, Marshal?"

"Antonov transports. Unarmed and empty, it appears."

"So it appears," Bulganin repeated. "I wouldn't be surprised if they destroyed their own aircraft just to give themselves a reason."

"A reason for what?" asked SVR director Sergei Fedorin.

"That's what I want you to tell me! Do you have any answers?"

"Not yet, Mr. President."

And understandably so, Nochenko thought. These incidents had occurred one on top of the next. There had scarcely been time to digest the information, let alone draw conclusions.

Even so, Nochenko was worried. Farfetched though it seemed, Bulganin's statement about the Chinese planes couldn't be discounted. All these events were related somehow; there was a pattern to them, but Nochenko had yet to piece it together. *Coincidence is the mother of deception.*

Moreover, the events seemed to be keeping pace with one another—disastrous stepping-stones leading toward some unknown goal. Whatever that was, a theme was emerging: provocation and escalation. But who is the provocateur? China or the U.S.? Or both?

Nochenko broke in: "Mr. President, I have a suggestion."

"Go on."

"There's a trend of escalation going on. Whether intentional or unintentional, we can't be certain, but we must choose our next steps carefully. The best course is to not feed the fire. Let Minister Kagorin contact the Chinese ambassador and—"

"And what?" Bulganin snapped. "Grovel? Show them we're frightened? I don't think so. Frankly, I'm surprised at you. We've been *attacked*! Am I the only one who sees that?"

Bulganin looked from man to man. "Am I alone in this, gentlemen? Do any of you care about the security of your country? If not, say so now, and I'll find someone to replace you. Anyone?"

No one spoke.

"Good," Bulganin said, then clasped his hands behind his back and stood tall. "Here are my orders: Minister Kagorin, you will contact the Chinese ambassador; we will give them one more chance to moderate their position. Director Fedorin, these events are connected. I want to know how and why. Marshal Beskrovny, until further notice, I want interceptors patrolling our border with China day and night. I want the American battle group stopped before it comes within one hundred miles of our shore. Finally, I want every Military District from here to Vladivostok brought to full alert—including the Rocket Forces."

Beskrovny stepped forward, his face drawn. "Mr. President—"

"That's an order," Bulganin said.

"If we bring our nuclear forces to alert, the Chinese will reciprocate."

"Let them. Perhaps it will scare some sense into them."

Nochenko interrupted: "Vlad—"

Bulganin glared at him.

"—Mr. President. . . . Please reconsider."

"I've made my decision. Marshal Beskrovny, are your orders clear?"

"Yes, Mr. President."

"You will carry them out?"

"Yes, Mr. President."

Bulganin rapped his desk with a fist. "Good. You're all dismissed."

60

Chono Dam

WITH SKELDON NOW ON HIS SIDE, CAHIL'S CHANCES OF STOP-ping the dam's destruction had improved, but he still faced tough odds. They were not only outnumbered, but without weapons.

With no way to fight, Cahil had turned his mind to sabotage, but as the first day passed and moved into the second, the Chinese colonel began inspecting his work on the charges. The man knew his business, Cahil immediately realized. There was no way to make the charges both defective enough to fail, and convincing enough to pass muster.

"We're going to have to take them on," Cahil whispered as he and Skeldon worked.

"With what, sticks?"

"Either that or your charming personality."

Skeldon grinned at him. "Smart-ass."

"Do we know what they're waiting for? A signal, or are they on a timetable?"

"I'm betting a signal," Skeldon said. "I've been watching their radioman; he's been making contact every four hours since yesterday."

"Then we might be coming down to the wire," Cahil said. "How's your head?"

"Hurts, but no more than usual." Skeldon paused, frowning. "Here's a thought: What if we take some of my pills and slip them into their—"

"I considered that," Cahil said, "They're too sharp. I haven't seen them let down their guards once. Besides, they eat in shifts. We'd only get a couple of them before they caught on."

"Then what're we going to do?"

Cahil thought for a few moments. "Is there any way we can get back into the mine? Can you tell them I need to see the boreholes again?"

"What did you have in mind?"

Cahil explained briefly, and Skeldon said, "There's one way to find out."

THE COLONEL GAVE THEM PERMISSION, BUT ORDERED ONE OF THE commandos to escort them.

Once through the entry hole and into the main tunnel, they began walking, Cahil in the lead, followed by Skeldon, then the commando, who carried his M-16 at ready-low with the safety off. Cahil studied the walls and ceiling, hoping he'd recognize what he was looking for when he saw it. About halfway to the cavern, he spotted it: A bowl-shaped shelf jutting downward from the ceiling.

"Hold up," Bear called as he drew even with the shelf. Skeldon stopped, as did the commando, who backed up a few feet, M-16 pointed in their general direction. "I've got a rock in my boot."

He went through the motions of fixing his boot, then stood up. As he did so, he reached up and grabbed the shelf. "Boy, that's handy, ain't it?"

Skeldon nodded. "Sure is."

THEY SPENT TEN MINUTES IN THE CAVERN AS CAHIL PRETENDED to study the boreholes, then retraced their steps to the outside. Once back in camp, he and Skeldon returned to work on the charges.

"Think you'll be able to spot it?" Cahil asked him.

"Yep. Why that spot?"

"You saw how it was angled down?" Skeldon nodded. "It will work just like a shaped charge. If we time it right, whoever's behind us will take the brunt of the explosion."

"I like it. So what do we need?"

"A few ounces of C4."

"What about a detonator?"

Cahil smiled. "I thought you might be able to use your winning personality to steal one."

Nakhodka-Vostochny

Though Cathermeier's words had been oblique, the message for Jurens and his team had been clear: Columbia *is gone, either missing or dead; don't count on extraction anytime soon.* It wasn't exactly what Sconi had wanted to hear, but he was unsurprised. However bad their own situation, it was obviously worse elsewhere.

Time to get wet and go home, he thought. The idea of continuing this game of hide-and-seek with the Russian troops didn't appeal to him. Confident as he was in his team, he also knew a good commander didn't pit himself against a force many times his size unless he had no choice.

Shortly after midnight, Smitty and Zee slipped back into their camouflaged bolt-hole above the road junction. Parked fifty yards below their perch was a Federation Army truck and a squad of eight soldiers. Laying on his belly, Jurens surveyed the road block through his Night Owls.

"They're new," Smitty whispered. "How long've they been here?"

"About an hour. So far they don't look inclined to send out patrols, but the night is young."

"And if they do?"

"We let them slip past us."

"And if they don't?"

Jurens gave him a glance. They both knew the answer to the question: Kill the squad as quietly as possible and move on. Jurens hoped it wouldn't come to that. "What'd you find?" he asked.

"Not our ride home, but maybe the next best thing."

"Where and what?"

"About three miles south of here there's a small cove with a pier. We counted eight boats moored alongside."

"What kind?"

"Mostly small trawlers and a few skiffs. Good enough to get us into international waters."

"See any Indians?"

"They're thick, Skipper. All the road junctions are covered. We had to bypass three foot patrols on the way back. When we make our move, we better not be in a hurry."

Jurens nodded. "Nice work. Get some sleep. You've got the four to six watch."

Smitty crawled away.

How many out there looking for us? Jurens wondered. At least a company, and more coming into the port every hour, it seemed. No matter how good his team was, it was only a matter of time before some patrol stumbled onto them.

USS *Columbia*

Columbia had been resting on the bottom for two days, and like Jurens, Archie Kinsock was itching to move. *Two days of sitting, listening to the hull settle deeper into the silt, feeling the deck tremble with every strong current. . . .* And waiting—waiting for the eerie whistle of an active sonar scouring the seabed for them.

So far the crew had handled the stress well, but sooner or later the boredom and uncertainty would take its toll. Aside from the SLOT buoys—which provided only one-way communication—their link to the outside world was gone. If they hadn't already, some of the crew would start to worry they'd been abandoned. They knew better, of course, but unlike knowledge, which is born of logic, despair and fear work on those dark places in your brain where logic doesn't live.

In their case, there was only one cure against despair: action.

Get off the bottom, get moving, and take our chances, Kinsock thought.

MacGregor walked over to the status board where Kinsock stood. "He's back," the XO said.

"Is he all right?"

"Cold but fine."

"Thank God."

Two hours earlier Kinsock had sent the boat's diver, Gunners Mate John Howley, out the escape trunk to determine whether the hatches to the maneuvering thrusters were clear. Sitting as they were in the silt, one or both of them might be buried.

"Remind me to put him up for an accommodation," Kinsock said. "How'd it look?"

"The port-side hatch is clear; starboard is partially blocked, but by only a couple inches of silt. Howley said it's fine, almost powdery."

"That's the best news I've heard in a while. Get down to engineering and tell the chief we're in business. Next high tide, we fire up the thrusters and drive outa here."

61

Yingkou

TEN MINUTES AFTER THREE, XIANG'S CELL PHONE TRILLED. IT WAS Kwei: "He just called."

"Where is he?" Xiang asked.

"In the city somewhere, but he refused to say. He'll be at the Liaobin ferry terminal at five."

"We'll find it," Xiang said. "Is he expecting you?"

"No, I told him one of my people would be coming, a man named Lin. That way, you can—"

"Good thinking. If you hear from him again, call me immediately."

"Of course."

Xiang hung up and turned to Eng. "Liaobin, two hours."

THE FERRY WAS HALFWAY ACROSS YINGKOU HARBOR WHEN XIang's phone rang again. "Yes?"

It was Shen. "We have a problem. One of the trackers was walking his dog north of the station and he got a hit on Tanner's scent."

"What! How sure are they?"

"Very. The dogs went crazy. I think I know how he did it," Shen said, then explained Tanner's ruse. "We followed the trail for about a mile. He's still headed northeast."

Xiang paused, thinking. *He's been toying with us since he jumped off the damned train! He's wasted our time, split our forces. . . .* "Lieutenant, split your men into two trucks. I want one team to follow the rail line north, the other to stay on Tanner's scent. Somewhere, the two are going to meet."

"How do you know that?"

"He's got over two hundred miles to go. He's not going to run all of it. Get moving!"

Shijiapu, China

Two hundred miles northeast of Xiang, Tanner was nervous. Whether from cynicism or a sixth sense, he couldn't quash the feeling that things were going too smoothly. His luck had held out too long.

Upon jumping into the freight car, he'd found it loaded not with feather pillows, but stacks of rotted railroad ties. Though the ride had been far from comfortable, he'd fallen quickly asleep inside the makeshift cave he'd created in the car's bottom corner, and dozed intermittently, watching the sky and listening to the train's wheels thump over the joints.

Once past the incline by the lake, the train had steadily picked up speed as it began a winding course north and east through the towns of Zhangwu, Baojiatun, Jinjiazhen. Shortly after his call to Kwei, he passed out of Liaoning Province and into Jilin.

According to his map, the camp was 250 miles away.

XIANG'S HIND LANDED IN A SMALL CLEARING SOUTH OF THE LAKE. A truck drove him the half mile to the rail line where Shen was waiting. Despite the late afternoon sunshine, Xiang could feel a chill in the air. He pulled his coat tighter around him.

"The trail ends here," Shen reported. "He must have laid in the grass here—probably guessing the train would have to slow on the incline—and jumped aboard as it passed."

"Could he have walked the rails? Can the dogs track scent on steel?"

The dog handler nodded. "Yes, sir. Not as well, but they can. There's been no rain, no wind to speak of. . . . If he'd done that, the dogs would have caught it."

"Then he's aboard another train," Xiang said. He turned to Eng. "Call the Fuxin station. I want a complete map and schedule of every route north of Xinqiu." Then to Shen: "Lieutenant, you, twelve of your best men, and the dog teams come with me. Eng will arrange transport for the rest."

"Where're we going?"

"We're flying straight up this line and stopping every train we come across."

SIXTEEN MILES NORTH OF CHANGCHUN, TANNER'S LUCK RAN OUT.

Sunset was less than thirty minutes away when he heard the distant beating of helicopter rotors. He closed his eyes and strained to listen, hoping against hope the sound would fade into the distance. It didn't. *Coming closer,* he thought. *From the south.* He climbed to the top of the car and peeked out.

Three hundred yards behind, sunlight glinting off its cockpit, a Hind helicopter raced toward the caboose. Briggs ducked as it swept overhead. The Hind drew alongside the locomotive, then banked hard, circling and descending over the tracks. The whistle blared. The train lurched forward, slowing.

Tanner didn't have time to think. He ran forward, leaping from tie to tie until he reached the front of the car, then slipped over the side and down the access ladder into the caboose buffer.

He leaned out, looked ahead. Wind whipped his face. A half mile ahead of the locomotive, the Hind had come to rest across the tracks, its rotors still spinning. The train was slowing rapidly and great billows of steam drifted back along the cars.

Tanner jumped. He landed hard on his shoulder and hip, then found his feet and tried to stand. White-hot pain shot through his feet, into his legs, and up his back. He collapsed. Instinctively, he knew what was wrong. *Stupid!* Lying still for hours inside the top-loader, his muscles had stiffened.

He dropped to his belly and looked around. Bordering the tracks was a field of waist-high millet. This early in the season, it was still green and tender, and would betray his passage as clearly as a neon arrow. But there was nowhere else to go.

Down the tracks, the Hind's side door opened and soldier's began leaping out, followed by a pair of dog handlers. The dogs tugged on their leashes and barked. The cockpit door opened and out stepped Xiang; he talked with one of the soldiers, who turned and began barking orders.

Time to go, Briggs.

Jaw clenched against the pain, he crawled up the embankment and onto the tracks so the caboose would temporarily shield him from the soldiers. He forced himself upright and started running.

"HALF YOUR MEN TAKE THE RIGHT SIDE, THE OTHER THE LEFT," Xiang ordered Shen. "One dog handler per team. I want a sentry posted on each car. If he jumped off, the dogs will find his scent; if he's still aboard, we'll search it car by car."

IN THE END, IT WAS THE DOGS THEMSELVES THAT BOUGHT HIM the time he needed.

Shaken and disoriented from the helicopter ride, the dogs spent ten minutes running around in circles before the handlers were able to bring them under control. By the time they started moving down the tracks, Tanner was a mile away, his body limbering with every stride.

Every few seconds he would glance over his shoulder, and when he saw the first soldier appear alongside the train, he dropped onto his belly and crawled for the edge of the millet field, where he turned himself around and backed feet-first into the grass, closing the stalks behind. After ten yards of this, he raised himself into a crouch and started picking his way east.

Behind him, the sun was dropping toward the horizon.

Half a mile into the millet field, he heard the dogs start to howl, followed by excited shouts. He felt a ball of fear explode in his chest. He stood up and started sprinting with everything he had.

"HE'S STICKING TO THE RAIL LINE," SHEN TOLD XIANG OVER THE radio. "His scent is strong; the dogs have him. He can't be far ahead."

"Run him down!" Xiang said.

Fifteen minutes later: "He's veered into the millet field. He's heading east."

"Keep going," Xiang ordered. "We're going airborne."

TO HIS WEST, TANNER HEARD THE ROAR OF THE HIND'S ENGINES spooling up, followed moments later by the *thump* of rotors heading in his direction. *Outa time, outa time. . . .*

He crashed through the edge of the field and found himself standing at a junction of two dirt roads. He stood rooted, panting hard, heart in his throat. Twilight had fully fallen now, with only a few tinges of orange sunlight showing to the west. Behind him, the barking had changed into a series of long, overlapping wails. Then voices, shouting in Mandarin: *This way . . . hurry!*

Tanner looked left, right. *Decide, Briggs! Do something!*

Beyond the road stood a line of fir and through them he caught a glimpse of water. He felt a flood of relief. The ex-SEAL in him took over: *Water is safety; head for the water.* He sprinted across the road and through the trees and found himself at the edge of a muddy, fast flowing river. Head down, he dove in.

SIXTY SECONDS BEHIND HIM, SHEN AND THE DOG TEAM EMERGED from the millet field. The dogs led them straight to the riverbank. Shen grabbed his radio.

"He's in there," Shen reported when Xiang arrived. "He couldn't have been more than a few minutes ahead of us. I've got my men spreading out along this bank, but we need to cover the other side. The current's running fast, so we need to hurry.

"Split your men; the helicopter will ferry them across."

Shen nodded, then passed the order to Sergeant Hjiu, who ran off.

"Where does this river lead?" Xiang asked.

Shen pulled out his map. "Southeast for ten miles. This could be a problem. . . . It splits into three tributaries just north of this lake. If he makes it that far, we'll have triple the shore to cover."

Xiang studied the map. On the lake's shoreline were four towns, each with a population of twenty thousand or more. Shen was right: they had to find Tanner before he reached the tributaries, and certainly before he reached the lake. If he made it that far he could disappear into one of the cities.

"Eng, how long before the rest of Shen's company arrives from Xinqiu?"

"Within the hour."

"Good. Until then, we'll use the Hind and patrol the river."

"Yes, sir." Eng ran off.

Xiang walked to the bank. He knelt and dipped his fingers into the water. It was cold. That was good. The more miserable Tanner became, the sooner he would try to get out.

62

THIRTY FEET UPRIVER, HUDDLING BENEATH A TANGLE OF TREE limbs beside the bank, Tanner could hear only snippets of Xiang's words over the rush of the current, so strong it pushed his body nearly horizontal. Already, the icy water was numbing his fingertips and ears. He closed his eyes and tried to steady his breathing. The cold felt like a vice around his chest.

Until the moment he'd plunged into the river and realized the strength of the current and the temperature of the water, Tanner had intended to float downstream for a distance, then climb out on the opposite bank and keep going. Instead, he'd turned and started paddling hard upstream, gaining mere feet for every dozen strokes until finally he spotted the branches and latched onto them.

Now he wondered if he'd made a terrible mistake. If Xiang chose this spot as the hub for their search, he'd have to either try to crawl out and slip away or let go and take his chances downstream.

Either way, he couldn't remain in the icy water for long.

FIVE MINUTES AFTER THE HIND FERRIED SHEN'S MEN TO THE opposite bank, it returned and landed at the road junction. Over the beat of the rotors, Tanner heard a barked order, but caught only bits of it: "Two . . . here . . . watch."

He slowly turned his head until he could see Xiang and another man jogging toward the helo. Two soldiers remained behind at the river's edge.

The Hind lifted off and flew upriver a few hundred yards, then turned and started downriver at a near hover. The belly spotlight clicked on and began tracking across the water's surface.

Eyes squinted against the downwash, Tanner waited until the beam was nearly upon him then took a gulp of air and ducked under. The light swept over the tangle of branches, started to move on, then stopped. The water went translucent. Leaves and silt swirled around his face.

Come on . . . there's nothing here. . . .

The water went dark. Tanner resurfaced. The beam was moving downriver.

From his left, a flashlight beam played over the branches as one of the soldiers walked along the bank. He called to his partner, "Check upstream."

A laugh in reply. *"Xi wang ni war de hao!" Have a good time!*

The soldier slipped from Tanner's peripheral vision. He waited until the crunch of footfalls faded then dug his fingers into the mud and gently pulled himself onto the bank. Ten feet to his right, the remaining soldier stood smoking, his AK held at ready-low.

Shivering now, Tanner clenched his jaw against it and began inching his way along the bank. From the corner of his eye, he could see the patrolling soldier's flashlight playing along the water's edge. Suddenly the beam lifted, turned.

Coming back this way.

It took all his self-discipline to not get up and run. He kept crawling, gaining six inches at a time until he'd reached the soldier's blind spot. Slowly, eyes fixed on the man, Tanner rose into a crouch. He coiled himself, sure the soldier was going to turn.

He didn't.

Tanner sidestepped left, paused, took another step, paused. The patrolling soldier was fifty yards away, his flashlight beam skimming ever closer. *Gotta go, gotta go. . . .* Tanner turned, scuttled into the trees along the road, and dropped onto his belly. Heart pounding, he waited for a shout.

None came.

At the bank, the two soldiers joined up.

On trembling legs, Tanner crept across the road, then started running north.

Against every rule he knew but beyond caring, he ran straight down the center of the road for an hour, listening as the braying of the dogs and the thumping of the Hind's rotors slowly faded into the distance.

All the terror and frustration and exhaustion of the past two days rose into his throat. He wanted to scream. He swallowed it and kept running, and slowly the emotion subsided. With it went all his energy. As if someone had pulled a plug, he suddenly felt numb.

His boot struck a rock. He tripped and sprawled into the dirt.

Stay here, a voice in the back of his head told him. *Sleep. You've gone far enough.*

He rolled himself onto his back and stared up at the stars.

You've done all you can. It's time to let go.

Then, a different voice: *If you quit, they'll find you and kill you.*

"No," Tanner murmured. "Get up, Briggs. Get off the road."

He rolled his head to the left and saw a steep embankment of stunted pines bordering the road.

Get up, Tanner commanded. *Climb the ridge into the next valley. More places to hide there. Find a place, then sleep.* He rolled onto his belly, forced himself to his knees, then planted a boot in the dirt, then pushed himself upright. He staggered a few steps, then caught himself. His vision sparkled.

Now run. Don't think, just run.

He pointed himself at the embankment and started up.

TEN MILES TO THE SOUTHEAST, XIANG AND SHEN STOOD ON THE lake's shoreline, watching the Hind hovering over the water, its spotlight slicing through the darkness.

"There's no way he could have slipped through," Shen said. "The dogs have been up and down both sides of river; there's no scent."

"Then where is he?" Xiang demanded.

"There's one possibility: he swam with the current and beat us here."

"Ten miles, in this water?" Xiang said. "I don't think so."

"Then what?" Shen snapped. "Perhaps he's a ghost; perhaps he sprouted wings and flew away."

"Watch your tone, Lieutenant."

Shen sighed. "I'm sorry, sir. It's frustrating. We have no trail, no scent. . . . We were three minutes behind him and now he's gone!"

"He won't get out of the country; in fact, I doubt he'll even try—not yet at least," Xiang replied. "We have a critical advantage; I think it's time we use it."

"What advantage?"

"We know where he's going."

63

THOUGH LATER HE WOULD BE ABLE TO RECALL ONLY FUZZY IMages of the hours following his escape from the river, upon reaching the crest of the ridge, Tanner hadn't stopped as he'd promised himself, but kept going, putting one foot before the other until finally his body gave out.

Running on force of will alone, he stumbled down into the next valley, up the next ridge, then down again before collapsing. He crawled off the trail, covered himself with loose branches, then slipped into unconsciousness.

When he awoke he felt a flash of panic. It was daylight. The sun filtered through the trees, casting stripes on the ground. He blinked against the glare and looked around. *Oh God. . . .*

Less than three feet from his face were a pair of boots. Silhouetted by the sun was a man-shaped figure. As Briggs watched, the boots shuffled forward, and slowly the tip of a walking staff slipped through the branches and jabbed him on the forehead.

Tanner grabbed the staff, jerked hard, felt it come free, then swung, striking the leg in front of him. As the man fell, Tanner rolled out and scrambled to his feet.

Sitting on the ground before him was a gaunt Chinese man in his early fifties. He rubbed his leg and stared up at Tanner in terror. "Aiyah . . . aiyah!" He began crawling backward.

"Deng. . . . Hen baoqian. . . ." Briggs called. *Wait, I'm sorry.*

He bent over and laid the stick on the ground. As he straightened, he felt a wave of pain burst behind his eyes. His vision blurred and he felt bile rising into his throat. Before he could catch himself, he lost his balance and toppled backward onto his butt.

"Ni you shemma bing?" the man said.

Tanner tried to focus on the words. *What's wrong . . . you . . .*

Tanner felt his forehead; his skin was hot and clammy. His calf felt like it was on fire. He pulled up his pant leg and ripped off the bandage. The knife wound was swollen red and seeping pus.

"Ahh!" the man gasped, then pointed at Tanner's leg. Looking at Tanner for permission, he gestured to himself, then at the wound. Briggs nodded. The man crawled over.

The man touched the wound with his fingertips, then sniffed them and wrinkled his nose. He felt Tanner's forehead. *"Fa shao." Fever. "Shen-chu she tou lai."*

Tanner shook his head, not understanding. The man stuck out his own tongue, then pointed at him. Briggs reciprocated and the man studied it. "Ahh . . ."

"I'm sick," Tanner said in English.

The man nodded. "You sick." He grabbed his walking staff and Tanner's backpack, then helped Tanner to his feet. *"Lai, lai." Come, come.*

Tanner knew better than to argue; it was all he could do to stay upright. He started walking.

• • •

THE MAN LED HIM DOWN THE VALLEY FLOOR, THEN TURNED ONTO a path. Judging from the angle of sunlight, Tanner assumed it was shortly after dawn. He'd slept for almost ten hours. Where was Xiang?

The path opened into a sloping meadow bordered by a narrow dirt tract to the west. Nestled in the center of the meadow were a cabin and barn made of thatch-and-mud bricks and flagstone shingles. A pen with two chickens and a goat sat beside the barn.

The man called out. The door opened and out stepped a young boy and girl, both between eight and ten years old, and a woman, also in her mid-fifties. They stopped and stared at Tanner.

"Bang zhu!" the man called. *"Bang zhu!"*

As one, the children and the woman ran forward, relieved the man of the staff and Tanner's backpack then led the way into the cabin, which was divided into a small kitchen, a front room, and a communal bedroom. The only light came from two large windows in the kitchen.

The man led Tanner to a cot against the front-room wall and gestured for him to lie down. His vision swam and sparkled, and he felt another wave of nausea grip his belly.

The man began barking orders and Briggs found himself at the center of activity. A pair of hands stripped off his field jacket while another removed his boots and socks and while a third rolled up his pant leg. In seconds he was covered in a heavy woolen blanket.

As had the man, the woman examined the knife wound, felt his forehead, and looked at his tongue, making "ahh" and "eeeh" noises as she went. After a brief murmured conference with the man, she nodded and rushed off into the kitchen.

The man shooed away the children, who'd been kneeling beside the cot, staring at Tanner and giggling. As they scampered away, the old man shrugged an apology at him.

"It's okay," Tanner said. *"Huang tou tai gao le." Blond hair too tall.*

The man cocked his head, then smiled. *"Huang tou tai gao le,"* he agreed.

• • •

TANNER SLEPT FITFULLY FOR SOME TIME, AND WAS AWAKENED by a stinging sensation on his calf. He opened his eyes and looked down. Kneeling at his feet, the man was applying a compress to the wound.

"Pool-tyce," the man said.

Pool-tyce . . . ? Poultice, Tanner realized. "You speak English?"

"Little English."

"Where did you learn?"

"Eh? Oh. . . ." The old man called out and the young girl scampered into the room carrying a trade paperback. She held it up: *Harry Potter and the Sorcerer's Stone.*

"Good old Harry," Tanner said.

The girl nodded vigorously. "Good old Harry!" she repeated, then ran off.

Tanner laughed; the effort took his breath away. "Your daughter?" he asked.

"Daughter, yes."

"What's your name?"

The man thought for a moment. "Tun-San. You?"

"My name is. . . . My name is Briggs."

"Briggs. Where from?"

"America."

Tun-San's eyes widened. "America . . . no joking?"

"No." Tanner suddenly felt guilty; he was putting these people at risk. If Xiang discovered they'd helped him. . . . "Tun-San, it would be best if no one knew I'd been here."

It was too much for the man's vocabulary. He shook his head. "Not understand."

Using a combination of English and Chinese words and hand gestures, Tanner got his point across. Tun-San looked him in the eye. "You . . . ah . . . criminal?"

"No," Tanner replied. "I'm trying to help a friend. He's in trouble."

Tun-San considered this, then nodded solemnly. "I tell no one."

Tun-San lifted the poultice away, looked at it, then set it aside. He pulled another from the bucket between his knees, wrung it out, and reapplied it to the wound.

"Bad come out," he told Tanner.

AFTER TWO HOURS OF TREATMENT WITH THE POULTICE, TUN-SAN woke Tanner from his light sleep.

"Look leg," he said.

The swelling and redness were almost completely gone. Tun-San gently pressed the cut, but instead of pus, all that came out was a dribble of bright, red blood. Briggs reached down and touched the flesh; it was cool. "How did you do that?" he asked. "What was—"

"Herbs," Tun-San said, then rattled off a list of ingredients. Tanner recognized a few of them—Chu-hua, ginseng, forsythia, willow—but most were unfamiliar to him.

"Ah, here, drink."

Tun-San's wife, Wu, appeared beside the cot carrying a quart-size bowl of steaming, greenish brown broth. Tun-San propped Tanner up with a pair of straw pillows and she placed the bowl in his hands. They both watched him expectantly.

He sniffed the broth, then drew his head back. It smelled like unwashed socks, dirt, and hot gin.

Seeing Tanner's expression, Tun-San chuckled and said something to his wife, who gave him a withering stare. *Making fun of her cooking,* Tanner guessed, then smiled.

Clicking her tongue, she urged him to drink.

He lifted the bowl to his lips and sipped. The broth tasted exactly as he imagined unwashed socks, dirt, and hot gin would taste. It burned all the way down to his belly, then seemed to surge into his head. He blinked his eyes and groaned.

Tun-San hurried into the kitchen and returned with a cool, wet towel, which he draped across Tanner's forehead. After a few seconds his vision cleared. He felt Wu's eyes on him.

"All," she ordered. "Drink all."

• • •

TUN-SAN SAT BESIDE THE COT AS HIS WIFE FED TANNER BOWL after bowl of what he'd mentally dubbed "sweat sock soup." Halfway through the second bowl, his taste buds went mercifully numb.

After the first hour, he signaled that he needed to relieve himself. With Tun-San's help he hobbled onto the porch and urinated into a steel pail until it was full

Tun-San nodded approvingly and patted him on the back. "Bad out," he said.

The process went on for another six hours until Briggs had consumed nearly two gallons of the broth and made a dozen trips to the pail. To his amazement, with each urination he felt progressively better. His headache and fever began to fade and he felt the strength returning to his limbs.

Occasionally, after he'd finished outside, Wu would retrieve the pail, pour some of the urine into a clear jar and examine it in the light, clicking her tongue and squinting.

By mid afternoon, she ordered him out of bed and to the kitchen table. Tanner stood up, testing his legs. Aside from a slight ache in his calf and some residual body weakness, he felt remarkably good.

Wu placed a plate of boiled vegetables and fried rice before him. He suddenly realized how hungry he was and began eating, not stopping until he'd consumed two platefuls and downed three glasses of goat's milk. Through it all, Wu stood, arms akimbo, and nodded. When he was done, she cleared away the dishes and set a clay mug before him.

"Cha lu," Tun-San explained.

"Green tea?" Tanner said.

"Yes, green tea with . . . ah. . . ." He made a buzzing sound.

"Honey?"

"Yes! Honey!"

It was delicious. He finished three mugs before he could drink no more.

Wu pointed to the door and said, "Use pail, then bring."

When he returned, she repeated her inspection process, squinting at the specimen for several seconds before turning to him. "Better," she proclaimed, then asked. "Feel better?"

"Much better," Tanner said. "Thank you, Wu."

Mere thanks wasn't enough, he knew. Not only had these people probably saved his life, but they'd given him a mental boost he hadn't even realized he needed. It felt good to be surrounded by friendly faces for a change. White skin, blond hair and all, they'd seen someone in need and had helped. "Thank you both," he repeated.

For the first time since Tanner had arrived, Wu smiled. "Happy to do."

LATER, HE AND TUN-SAN SAT ON THE PORCH TOGETHER. "WHERE your friend?" he asked.

"I'll show you," Tanner said. "Where's my pack?" Tun-San went inside and returned with it. Tanner pulled out the map, took a moment to orient himself, then pointed. "He's right here."

Tun-San peered at the map. "How far?"

"About a hundred seventy kilometers."

"Eh?"

"A hundred seventy *gong li.*"

Tun-San traced his finger along the map, muttering to himself and measuring distances with his thumb. "Five hours," he said.

"Pardon me?"

"Be there *zhong tou*—five—hours."

"I don't understand."

Tun-San stood up and grinned. "Come."

Tanner followed him to the barn. Tun-San unlatched the doors and swung them open.

Sitting inside was a rust-streaked, powder blue 1952 Chevrolet pickup truck. Aside from the cab, which was pitted with rust holes, the rest of the truck seemed to be constructed solely of bamboo and what looked like several miles of bailing wire. In the place of rear tires were a pair of wagon wheels. The doors had been removed; in their places, a pair of horizontal bamboo rods.

To Tanner, the truck looked like something out of a *Gilligan's Island* episode.

Beaming with pride, Tun-San opened the hood.

Instead of a traditional engine, a motorcycle engine was suspended from the mounting brackets by yet more bailing wire. A rubber belt like those found on industrial timber saws connected the engine to the drive axle. Jutting from the top of the contraption was a rope cord connected to a T-handle—the starter, Tanner realized.

Tun-San pointed at the engine. "Triumph, nineteen sixty-five."

"Triumph motorcycle engine?"

"Yes."

"It's amazing, Tun-San. You built this?"

He nodded. "Four years."

"It runs? It goes?"

"Oh, yes. I show. I can take you to your friend."

Tanner shook his head. "No. Thank you, but no. If you're seen with me, you'll get into trouble."

Tun-San waved his hand like an old Jewish mother. "No trouble. I drive, you hide."

Tanner was torn. If by accepting the offer he brought harm to Tun-San and his family, Briggs would never be able to live with himself; on the other hand, he doubted he had the strength to reach the camp on foot—not quickly, at least. Tanner extended his hand. "Thank you, my friend."

Tun-San took it. "You welcome, my friend."

After saying good-bye to the children, Tanner accepted a small jug of sweat sock soup and a set of stern dosage instructions from Wu. On impulse, he gave her a hug, evoking a giggle from her.

"I'm happy to have met you," Tanner said. "Thank you for everything."

"Yi-lu ping-an," she replied. *Have a good trip.*

• • •

WITH THREE CRATES OF EGGS AND TWO FIVE-GALLON GAS CANS resting on a bed of straw in the back and Tun-San at the wheel, Tanner pushed the surprisingly buoyant truck out of the barn. He got into the passenger seat and, at Tun-San's urging, pressed his foot on the brake pedal.

Tun-San got out, lifted the hood, then reached inside and heaved on the pull cord. With a throaty roar and a puff of smoke, the engine fired to life. Tanner felt the rear wheels churning on the ground. Apparently, Tun-San's chariot had only two gears: forward and stop.

Tun-San slammed the hood and leapt into the driver's seat. He gripped the wheel with both hands then nodded to Tanner, who took his foot off the brake. The truck lurched forward.

"See?" Tun-San said. "Runs good."

64

NMCC

"HOW MANY SHIPS IN THE SAG?" MASON ASKED.

An hour before, the commander of the *Stennis* group, Commodore Scott, reported a Surface Action Group of Russian warships steaming north toward the group's picket ships, while *Cheyenne*, patrolling ahead of the group, was engaged in a game of cat and mouse with a Russian Akula.

"We're still trying to identify the individual elements," Cathermeier replied, "but according to the most recent flyover, it looks like a good chunk of the Russian Pacific Fleet—might be as many as eighteen warships, from Krivak-class frigates to Kirov cruisers."

"How much distance between them and us?"

"Less than ninety miles."

"Too close. If somebody pushes the panic button, they could be mixing it up in minutes."

"The Sea of Japan just ain't big enough for all that firepower," Cathermeier agreed.

"What about the rest of the Federation?" Dutcher asked. "How widespread is this alert?"

"Across the board. We've got reports of increased radio traffic in every district from Moscow to Vladivostok—all branches, from ground forces to rocket forces."

"Tactical or nuclear?"

"Both. Leaves and furloughs are being cancelled; interceptors are sitting hot on runways at Chita, Ulan-Ude, Irkutsk, and Vladivostok; they're also putting up BARCAPs along the border," Cathermeier said, referring to Barrier Combat Air Patrol; once a navy-specific term, it had become a generic description of any airborne line of defense.

"What about the Chinese?" Mason asked

"Mirror image," said Cathermeier. "We haven't seen much ground movement, but every air base in the Beijing and Shenyang military regions is on full alert—same with the First, Fifth, and Twenty-Third Army Groups nearest the Mongolian salient."

"Where exactly?"

Cathermeier turned to the watch officer. "Put up a topographical map of Heilongjiang." The major tapped his keyboard and a map appeared on the screen. Using a laser pointer, Cathermeier traced the Chinese-Mongolian border as it swept upward, forming a bulge into Siberia. "The First, Fifth, and Twenty-third all have their bases in this area south of the Hinggan Mountains."

"That makes sense," Mason muttered.

"What do you mean?"

"The shale oil deposits Skeldon mapped start north of Hinggans, just inside the border."

"Well, if that's going to be their penetration point, then they've got a tough job ahead of them," Cathermeier replied. "Just getting there by ground would take four days, which would give the Russians time to shift. If that's their plan, it's flawed."

Mason considered this. "How would you do it?"
Cathermeier chuckled. "I wouldn't."
"If you had to."
"I'd have to give it some thought, but I'll tell you this: I'd make damned sure I had surprise on my side. The Russian's know how to defend their soil."
"The Chinese have to know that," Dutcher said.
"You'd think so."
They talked for a few minutes more, then Mason led them into the Tank and shut the door.
"Any word from Tanner or Cahil?"
"Nothing from Ian and nothing from Briggs since his last message," Dutcher replied. "If he hasn't been captured, he's probably still en route to the camp."
"I hate to say it, but I don't think we should count on either of them. We have to move now. Martin's not going to back down; he's watching a war unfold before his eyes and he's still more worried about covering his ass."
"When do you want to do it?"
"Tonight. I'll call Lahey."

Moscow

It was past midnight when the knock came at Ivan Nochenko's door. He got up, threw on his robe, and peered through the peephole. Standing in the hall were Sergei Fedorin and Marshal Beskrovny. Both wore street clothes. Nochenko unlocked the door and opened it.
"May we come in?" Beskrovny said.
"Yes, of course."
They stepped inside and Nochenko gestured toward the kitchen table. Fedorin and Beskrovny sat down. *Something's wrong,* Nochenko thought. "What is it? Has something happened?"
"That's why we're here," Fedorin said. "We're hoping to stop something before it starts."
"I don't understand," Nochenko said. That wasn't entirely true; part of his brain knew why they'd come. "What are you talking about?"

Beskrovny said, "Ivan, you know President Bulganin better than anyone, yes?"

"I suppose so."

"How does he seem to you?"

"He's under a lot of stress, if that's what you mean."

"We're all under stress," Fedorin replied. "We're more concerned with him."

"He's going through an adjustment period. This early in office, it's to be expected—especially given the circumstances—the Chinese, the American battle group . . ."

"You're not concerned?"

"Of course I'm concerned. Stop mincing words! Say what you came to say."

Fedorin and Beskrovny exchanged glances. Beskrovny cleared his throat. "We feel the president is leading the country down a very dangerous path. We feel he's . . . unbalanced."

There it is, Nochenko thought. He felt a flash of anger, but before he could open his mouth to speak, the emotion was gone, replaced by a strange clarity. All the doubts and fears about Bulganin he'd been suppressing came back in a flood.

Unbalanced? Nochenko thought. Vladimir Bulganin was far beyond unbalanced. He'd known that for a long time. *Not only known it,* he thought, *but ignored it. Maybe even helped it along.*

And for what? Nochenko thought. For the challenge of it. Like some half-baked god, he'd been trying to create a king from a lump of clay, but instead he'd created a golem, a monster born of desire and vanity and delusion.

"Are you all right?" Beskrovny asked. "You don't look well."

Nochenko took off his glasses and rubbed the bridge of his nose. He had to step carefully here. If Fedorin and Beskrovny were heading in the direction he suspected, his role as Bulganin's chief advisor would be not only pivotal, but perilous.

"I'm fine," Nochenko replied. "Let's suppose you're right. What do you propose?"

"That depends on what happens in the coming days," said Fedorin. "If he continues on the same course, our options become limited. Neither Victor nor myself can refuse his orders—not without being dismissed."

"Which he would do without hesitation."

Beskrovny nodded. "And then appoint more . . . pliable men in our places. That's the rub, you see. Whatever is behind this business with China and all the rest of it, we haven't seen the worst of it. Events are not going to slow down and wait for Bulganin to get his house in order."

"In other words, while he's sacking you, the missiles are flying."

"That's a very real possibility."

And if the missiles do start flying, Nochenko thought, *the country is going to need men like Fedorin and Beskrovny.* He wondered if that was part of their message to him: *Your golem is out of control. We know what we're willing to do to save Russia. What about you?*

"Tomorrow I'll speak with him," Nochenko said. "Perhaps he'll rethink his stance."

"Perhaps," Marshal Beskrovny replied.

"And if he doesn't?" Fedorin asked.

Your golem, Ivan.

"Then we'll meet again and . . . discuss alternatives."

65

Anjia, Heilongjiang Province, China

NOT LONG AFTER THEY HAD LEFT, TANNER DISCOVERED THAT Tun-San was familiar with their route.

As it turned out, three times a year he would travel to Harbin armed with a shopping list from other nearby farmers. At over three million people, Harbin was a strange and wondrous place, and Tun-San had become something of a hero for his tri-yearly quests to what many of them still called Pinkiang, the city's name when Heilongjiang Province was still known as Manchuria.

Tun-San followed the meandering dirt roads with confidence, never once consulting Tanner's map. Before long, Briggs learned his secret.

"Rock shape like bird," Tun-San would call out, pointing. Or, "Two trees leaning."

As the pickup chugged along, eating up the distance at a slow but steady twenty-five mph, Tun-San called out landmark after landmark, explaining to Tanner why it was special and how he used it to navigate. Some of them he used only during summer months, others only during the rainy season when his normal route was flooded.

Aside from a handful of peasants, Tanner saw very few people on the roads, oftentimes going for an hour without seeing a soul. At those times, Tun-San would invariably spot the pedestrian first and call out, "Duck," and Tanner would crouch on the floor until he got the all clear.

Outside Yushu, twenty-five miles from the southern border of Heilongjiang Province, they started an impromptu game of "Name That object" as Tun-San pointed at a low-flying hawk. *"Niaor!"* he called.

"Niaor," Tanner repeated, then said, "bird."

The game continued until they reversed roles and Tun-San pointed and called out, "Cow!"

"No," Tanner replied. "Cucumber."

Eyes narrowed, Tun-San glanced sideways at him. "Cucumber?"

Tanner smiled. "No, cow."

"Yes. Cow," Tun-San replied, then started laughing.

TRUE TO TUN-SAN'S ESTIMATE, FIVE HOURS AFTER THEY LEFT, they arrived on the southern outskirts of Anjia, a tiny village of less than two hundred people. Tun-San pulled over and shut off the engine. Outside, dusk was falling and Tanner could see black-bellied clouds piling up on the horizon. A gust of wind cut through the cab, sending a tingle up his neck. "Rain's coming."

"Very much rain," Tun-San agreed. "Map, please?"

Tanner unfolded it and set it on the seat between them. He clicked on his flashlight.

Tun-San traced his finger along the map. "Anjia . . . here. We . . . here. Your friend?"

Tanner pointed to a spot in a valley to the northeast. "Here. I can walk the rest—"

"No."

"It might be better if—"

"Quiet, cucumber man," Tun-San ordered, then barked out a laugh.

FOUR MILES NORTH OF ANJIA, TUN-SAN TURNED EAST OFF THE main road onto a narrow track barely wider than the truck. Night had fallen, and with it the wind had risen. Briggs could smell ozone in the air, a sure sign rain wasn't far off.

Suddenly a pair of headlights glowed to life in front of them. "Duck!" Tun-San called.

Tanner hit the floorboards. Hands held before him against the glare, Tun-San jammed on the brakes. The truck shuddered to a stop with the back wheels still churning.

"Can you tell who it is?" Tanner whispered.

"Army truck."

Army truck. This close to the camp, it had to be a roadblock. If they had dogs, it was all over.

An amplified voice called, *"Ting!" Stop!* followed by another order Tanner didn't catch.

"They say come ahead," Tun-San muttered.

"Do it," Briggs said. "After a few feet, steer toward the edge of the road until your front wheel is in the grass, then shut off the engine and tell them you've stalled. Do you understand?"

"Yes." Tun-San glanced down at him and covertly extended his hand; Briggs took it. "Luck to you, *huang tou tai gao le*," Tun-San said.

"And you, my friend. Thanks for everything."

As Tun-San started moving forward, foot pressed on the brake to keep his speed down, Tanner turned around so he was facing the door opening. Tun-San began easing to the right. Tanner watched the strip of dirt disappear and change to grass. Tun-San cut the wheel and shut of the engine.

Tanner slithered out the door, doing his best to stay behind the tire. He felt the glare of the truck's headlights on his face. He let himself slide down the embankment and into the taller grass at the bottom.

"My truck has stalled," Tun-San called in Mandarin. "Sorry."

"Stay there. Make no sudden movements," the amplified voice ordered.

In the glare of the headlights Tanner saw a pair of shadows moving toward Tun-San's truck. Working by feel, he opened his pack and pulled out the revolver. He opened the cylinder: four rounds. It wouldn't be enough against soldiers armed with AK-47s, he knew, but he'd already made up his mind: At the first sign they were going to take Tun-San, he would intervene.

Shoot the first two, grab one of their AKs, then pray you get the drop on the others. . . .

The soldiers walked up, one on each side of the truck, and began questioning Tun-San. He played the lost farmer well, showing the perfect mix of fear and respect. After searching the truck, they accepted a crate of eggs, then helped him get the truck turned around and started again.

With a wave out the door, Tun-San chugged back down the road and disappeared.

Tanner lay perfectly still for ninety minutes, listening to the soldiers talking and laughing.

There were four of them. Though he was only able to catch snippets of their conversation, the primary topic of discussion seemed to involve him—"the American agent"—and what they would do to him if they caught him. Though Briggs knew it was nothing more than soldierly bravado, it set his heart pounding nonetheless. He was well and truly alone.

Every half hour he heard the squelch of a radio and a brief exchange: "Post four, all clear. . . ."

Tanner listened closely, committing the words to memory.

A light rain began to fall, pattering the grass around him. In the distance he heard the rumble of thunder. Up the road, the soldiers hurried for the truck's bed; three got in the back while one remained outside. He sat on the front bumper and smoked, rain poncho hiked over his head.

Tanner began creeping forward.

The cover of rain sped his progress, but it still took him forty minutes to cover the one hundred yards to the truck. As he drew even with it, he heard the squelch of the radio: "Post four. . . ."

The soldier on the bumper raised his radio. "Post four, all clear."

"Very well."

Moving inches at a time, Tanner began dragging himself up the slope until his outstretched fingers felt dirt. The soldier was five feet away now, with his arms resting on his knees and the AK leaning against the bumper.

Nice and easy, Briggs. Don't rush it. . . .

If the soldier sounded the alarm, he'd have a firefight on his hands.

Tanner stood up, stepped forward, and knelt beside the soldier. "*Ni hao,*" he whispered.

The soldier snapped his head around. Tanner stuck the barrel of the revolver in his face. The man's eyes bulged. "No sound. One noise and you're dead. *Dong?" Understand?*

The soldier nodded. "*Dong.*"

Tanner gestured for him to lower himself to the ground, which he did. Tanner pointed at his hood: *off*. With trembling hands, the soldier complied. "Hand me your rifle," Tanner whispered.

As the soldier turned to reach for it, Briggs reversed the revolver in his hand and smacked the butt behind the soldier's ear. Tanner caught him as he fell, then laid him flat and took his radio.

From the truck: "Okay out there?"

"Hao, hao," Tanner replied. *Yeah, yeah.* Disgruntled solder in the rain.

Briggs picked up the AK and crouched down to wait. Nothing moved. After five minutes he heard snoring coming from the truck.

The radio squelched: "Post four, report."

He paused to rehearse his lines, then keyed the radio: "Post four, all clear."

"Very well."

Tanner quickly disarmed the remaining three soldiers—Flying Dragon paratroopers, he saw—then had them climb out and march to the front of the truck. Seeing their comrade laying in the dirt, the team leader, a sergeant, knelt beside him. He glared up at Tanner.

Briggs shook his head. "He's alive. *Ni xing shem ma?"*

"My name is Hjiu," he replied in English. "I know who you are."

"Good for you," Tanner said. "Open my pack, Sergeant. Inside you'll find some duct tape."

CARRYING THEIR STILL-UNCONSCIOUS COMRADE BETWEEN THEM, Tanner marched them into a field beside the road, where he had them lie down on their sides next to one another. He ordered Hjiu to bind the other's hands, feet, and mouths and then, satisfied with the job, did the same to Hjiu. Finally he taped them together, back to back, wrists to feet, until they were all immobilized.

Once done, he knelt down beside Sergeant Hjiu. "Sorry about the rain."

Hjiu mouthed something behind the tape; Tanner peeled it away. "Yes?"

"You will kill us now?"

"What for?"

"They told us you would."

Briggs shrugged. "They lied."

Back at the truck, Tanner gathered the AKs together, removed the magazines, then tossed the rifles into the back. He climbed into the cab, started the engine, then did a Y-turn on the road and headed north.

Ten miles to go.

66

***Laogi* 179**

TANNER DECIDED THAT IF THERE WERE ANY SILVER LINING TO THE nightmare he'd gone through over the past three days, it was that his perspective had undergone a metamorphosis. He now realized that conscious effort aside, he hadn't been able to completely silence the cold voice of pessimism in his head, and that part of him had expected to get caught long before now.

In retrospect, all of it seemed surreal: his hurried flight from Beijing; his battle with the PSB man at the swamp; his torturous overnight run to Xinqiu; his leap from the train north of Changchun and subsequent race to the river; and finally his collapse near Tun-San's farm.

And yet, the voice was still nagging him: Yes, he'd beaten not only the odds but also his pursuers; and yes, he was just miles from his destination. But what had he actually accomplished? He'd managed to reach the most heavily guarded prison camp in all of China. *Now what?*

AFTER LEAVING THE SOLDIERS UNDER THE TREE, HE DROVE NORTH-west through the rain to the outskirts of Beiyinhe, where he turned east and followed the road as it wound along a series of ravines—marking several on his map as he went—until he was west of the camp.

Without fail, every half hour the radio crackled to life and each time he gave his "all clear" report and got a "very well" in reply. Though he knew sooner or later the next guard rotation would arrive to discover their comrades, and his ploy would be over, he was determined to squeeze from it every hour and every mile he could.

At last the road led him down into a wooded valley. Bordered by a cliff on one side and a fast-flowing river on the other, the shoulders narrowed until the trees were scraping the doors.

He drove until he found a still part of the river wide enough and deep enough for his needs, then turned the wheel and eased the truck forward until the tires teetered at the edge of the road. He shut off the engine, shifted into neutral, and set the parking brake. Once he'd cleared the cab of his belongings, he reached in and released the brake.

Slowly at first, then with increasing speed, the truck rolled down the embankment and into the water. He watched as it sunk hood-first beneath the surface and disappeared from sight.

Another mystery for Xiang to solve. If Tanner were lucky, once they failed to find the truck in the immediate area, they would expand the search, wasting more time and resources. Better yet, Xiang might begin to question whether he had remained in the area at all.

For what felt like the hundredth time, he hefted the pack over his shoulder and started jogging.

FOUR MILES FROM THE CAMP HE CAME TO A SWITCHBACK IN THE road. From habit he stopped short, dropped onto his belly, and peeked around the bend. A hundred yards away an army truck straddled the road. Like the first one, this roadblock was also manned by four soldiers. Here, however, all four stood outside, ponchos drawn over their heads and rifles held at the ready.

He backed around the bend, wriggled across the road, and down the embankment to the river's edge, where he carefully cut free half a dozen branches. With them spread across his body, he slipped into the water, gasping as the coldness enveloped him, and pushed himself off the bank.

Within seconds the current caught him and began drawing him downstream.

Three miles beyond the roadblock the river forked. On impulse, he crawled out and onto the island between them. He was only a mile from the camp, and his subconscious was talking to him.

This was too easy. Knowing the camp was his ultimate destination, surely Xiang would have taken better measures than roadblocks. Did the *Guoanbu* director imagine he would bump into one of them and surrender? There had to be more: Roving patrols, hidden observation posts—something.

He checked his watch: one a.m. Dawn was five hours away. If Hsiao had managed to make the necessary changes, his duty shift began at six a.m. Tanner needed to be in position before that.

The rain continued to fall, churning the river's surface and dripping off the leaves. The air had grown noticeably cooler, and he could see faint tendrils of vapor escaping his mouth with each breath.

He looked downriver, scanning the banks and trees. They were out there. But where?

AFTER SCOUTING NEARBY TO MAKE SURE HE WASN'T SITTING ON top of an OP—observation post—he opened his pack and pulled out the woolen blanket he'd taken from the truck's cab. It was old, threadbare in some spots, and standard-issue olive drab—it was perfect. He spent ten minutes dirtying it with mud, dirt, and ground leaves, then took his knife and went to work.

He cut away a rough oval big enough to cover his mouth and nose; it would not only break up his features, but the wool would also filter the moisture from his breath, reducing any telltale exhalation. He then slit the edges of the blanket at random intervals to also break up its form.

What he'd just made was a homemade gillie cape like the kind used by snipers. Worn as a coat or a cape, a well-designed gillie is all but indistinguishable from its surroundings. Particularly at night, the human is drawn to shine, movement, and shape. Though not perfect, if he used the gillie correctly it would render him just another piece of the landscape.

Once satisfied with his work, he draped the blanket over his shoulders, tucked its edges under his pack straps, and slipped back into the water.

In the end, patience saved him.

He spent the next four hours picking his way along the forest floor and the river's banks, at times covering only a few feet at a time before stopping to watch and listen.

Less than a half mile from his starting point, he came across the first OP. Manned by two paratroopers laying perfectly still inside a clump of ferns, it was so well concealed that Briggs had crawled to within thirty feet of it before spotting a faint glint of moonlight on blued metal. *Gun barrel.*

Inch by inch, he eased himself back down the slope until he was out of sight, then turned and started crawling again, circling wide around the OP before returning to his course along the river.

Three more times he encountered similar posts and three more times he repeated the painstaking process of bypassing each until finally, at five-thirty, he saw a glimmer of yellow light through the trees to his right. After another fifty yards of crawling, he came to the edge of a tree line.

And suddenly, twenty feet in front of him, it was there.

As Hsiao had described it, *Laogi* 179 was nestled at the narrowest end of a wooded valley about a quarter mile across. The camp itself was a rectangle with twelve-foot high razor fencing and guard towers at each corner. The main gate lay on the south side and provided access to the only road leading to and from the camp.

The inner compound was made up of four long, wooden barracks, three for guards and support staff, and a fourth, which he guessed contained the prisoner's cells. Set apart from the barracks at the opposite end of the camp were four barnlike storage buildings and a wooden water tower. Beside these was a concrete landing pad big enough for two helicopters and a small hangar.

A Hind-D sat on the pad with its rotors tethered to the securing rings.

Xiang was here. What did that say? Either he knew how valuable Soong was, or he was taking this hunt personally—or both. Did he simply want to be there when Tanner was caught, or was he here to make sure nothing went wrong?

Another curiosity Tanner had been wrestling with was why Xiang hadn't simply moved Soong. Perhaps Xiang's pride and vanity were calling the shots. The *Guoanbu* director wasn't going to let anyone dictate his decisions, let alone the man who'd beaten him before. Moving Soong would have been tantamount to admitting defeat.

Good for him, Briggs thought. While Xiang was fighting his personal battle, Briggs was going to slip in, steal Soong, then slip out again.

Now all he had to do was come up with a plan to make it happen.

IN THE HALF HOUR BEFORE HSIAO'S SHIFT STARTED, TANNER LAY in the undergrowth watching the camp come alive as the first trickle of dawn light seeped through the forest.

He studied the guards, how and where they moved, their routes and checkpoints. They were very good, he immediately realized—thorough and observant. If he stayed around long enough he would eventually find a weakness in their security, but that would take time he didn't have.

The trick would be not only getting in, but reaching Soong and then escaping without raising the alarm. If even one shot were fired, he'd be finished. Well-trained as they were, the guards would undoubtedly respond smoothly and quickly to any emergency.

At five minutes to six, a group of twelve or so guards emerged from one of the barracks and walked into the compound. One by one Tanner scanned faces through the binoculars until he spotted Hsiao. Several of the guards broke off and headed for a line of outhouses beside the storage buildings.

Latrines, Briggs thought with a smile. *Latrines and a water tower. No plumbing.*

The seed of an idea planted itself in his brain.

AT THE BEGINNING OF EACH GUARD SHIFT, HSIAO HAD EXPLAINED back in Beijing, a "fence check" was performed by each shift's two junior members, which in this case meant Hsiao.

As advertised, Hsiao and another guard walked out the main gate, then separated and began slowly walking along the fence, inspecting it for gaps, weak points, and signs of tampering. As he drew even with Tanner's position, Briggs whispered, *"Ni hao." Good morning.*

Hsiao stopped in his tracks, but kept his cool and didn't turn around. He knelt beside the fence as though checking it. *"Ni hao,"* he whispered back.

"How are you?"

"Awful."

"Glad to hear it."

"And you?"

"The same. What did you find out about Bian?"

"He was arrested; aside from that, I was unable to find out anything."

No, no, no. . . . "I'm sorry."

"So am I. Now, more than ever, we must free the general. We owe that to Bian, at least."

"No second thoughts?"

"No, but I've decided I want to come with you."

Tanner smiled to himself. "I thought you might. I'm glad to have you. Is Xiang here?"

"Yes, last night, with about two dozen paratroopers."

"I assume that's his Hind on the pad; what about in the hangar?"

"The camp's Hoplite is kept in there."

Tanner knew the Hoplite; it was boxy and slow, but durable. "Did Xiang bring dogs?"

"No, no dogs. Two things you should know: there's a rumor that Soong's daughter is here."

She's here . . . my God. Lian is here. "He brought her here? Why?"

"I don't know."

The only advantage her presence might give Xiang was blackmail. Soong wouldn't leave without her and Xiang knew it. By dangling her in front of Soong, perhaps Xiang was sending a message: I've got my hands on her throat, leave and she dies.

The son-of-a-bitch. . . . Tanner shook it off. *Don't let it throw you off. Get out of your head and focus on the job.* "What else?" he asked.

"They found a group of soldiers from one of the roadblocks. I assume that was you?"

"Yes. Are they looking for the truck?"

Hsiao nodded. "I was in the control center when word arrived about the roadblock. Xiang and the paratrooper lieutenant—Shen, I think—were arguing over what it meant. Xiang thinks you're still in the area; Shen thinks you're running. They haven't decided what to do yet."

Confusion and uncertainty—good. Maybe he could get some more use out of that.

"You better keep walking," Briggs said. "Stop on the way back."

TWENTY MINUTES LATER HSIAO AGAIN STOPPED BESIDE TANNER, this time pretending to fix something with his boot. "How are you going to do this, Briggs? I might be able to cut the fence—"

"No. I might have an idea. Tell me everything you know about your sewage system."

"Huh? Our sewage system?"

"That's right."

Hsiao gave him the information. Tanner asked a few questions, then mentally dissected the plan for weaknesses, of which there were plenty, but he dismissed them and decided that, given a bit of luck and good timing, the plan could work.

It was all about odds, he knew. As with anything, there were no absolutes. What were the odds a guard would follow the exact same route every time? Even with the odds heavily in your favor, the guard, being human, might change his mind at the last minute, or get different orders, or find his way blocked. . . . The variables were endless.

All Tanner could do was hope the odds fell in his favor and trust that when they didn't, his skill and experience would be enough to make up the difference.

"Why all these questions?" Hsiao asked. "What are you planning?"

Tanner told him.

Hsiao's face went pale. "You . . . you are not serious, are you?"

Serious, but not looking forward to it, Briggs thought. "I am. Can you get the things I need?"

"Yes."

"Good. Be ready. If all goes well, we'll be on our way tonight."

"How? I don't understand what you're planning."

Tanner smiled. "I'm still working on it. Ask me again in a few hours."

67

White House

AS DIRECTED, HOWARD BOUSIKARIS ARRANGED THEIRS TO BE Martin's last meeting of the day.

It was nine p.m. when Dutcher, Mason, and Cathermeier were ushered into the Oval Office. The room was dim except for a pair of brass floor lamps casting soft light into the corners, and a green visored banker's light on Martin's desk. As always, Bousikaris stood beside Martin's elbow.

As they were shown in, the president looked up. "Good, gentlemen, come in. I'm hoping we can make this short; I've got a late supper scheduled with Senators Petit and Diaz."

Dutcher glanced at Bousikaris, who shook his head: *meeting cancelled.*

"Let's sit by the fire, shall we?"

Once they were all seated, President Martin gave Dutcher an appraising stare. "The mysterious Leland Dutcher. I understand you helped my predecessor on a few occasions."

"Yes, sir. I was honored to serve," Dutcher replied, and meant it.

John Haverland had been, and still was, albeit now out of the public eye, a man of integrity. Though Haverland had been too discreet to say as much, Dutcher always suspected he'd regretted not only bringing Martin aboard as his VP, but also positioning him for a run at the White House.

A terrible mistake, Dutcher thought, *but hopefully a correctable one.*

"Speaking of serving," Martin replied, "I don't recall seeing your name on the schedule. Did you stow away in Dick's pocket?"

"No, sir, I was invited."

Martin narrowed his eyes at Dutcher. "Not by me."

Too much ego, not enough substance, Dutcher thought. *A hollow man squabbling over petty control issues.* For a brief moment Leland felt sorry for him. For Martin, every moment of every day, was consumed with worries over his image. It had to be a maddening existence. The problem was, unlike many people who fight similar demons, Martin had sold his own country in pursuit of a legacy his very character would never support.

"I asked him to come," Bousikaris said. "Leland has some experience with both China and Russia; his perspective might be useful."

"Fine. So, gentlemen, where do we stand? Any change in either country's posture?"

"Before we get to that," Mason said. "I have something you might want to take a look at." Mason opened his briefcase, withdrew a file folder, and handed it to Martin.

Frowning, Martin took the folder, flipped it open, and began reading. After thirty seconds, he snatched off his glasses and glared at Mason. "What is this?"

"That's an affidavit signed by your chief of staff."

Martin turned in his chair and looked at Bousikaris. "Howard, what the hell—"

Mason broke in: "Currently four copies of that affidavit exist: The one you're reading and three others, each of them sealed and notarized. One is—"

"What in God's name are you doing?" Martin growled. "This is a dangerous game, Dick. One phone call from me and—"

"Phil," Bousikaris said. "Listen to what they have to say. If you make the wrong decision now, you'll regret it."

"Are you threatening me, Howard? You little mealy-mouthed asshole! How dare you!"

"I'm telling you it's over, Phil Your only chance—*our* only chance—of not ending up in jail is to listen to what they have to say."

Jaw muscles pulsing, Martin said, "Go on, Dick. Keep digging your grave."

"One of the affidavits is in the CIA's chief counsel's office safe; the second in the safe of an assistant director at the FBI, the third in a safe-deposit box," Mason said. "If in two hour's time each of us fails to make a phone call, the affidavits will be distributed."

"To whom?"

"One will go to the attorney general, the other to the director of the FBI, the third to the editor in chief of *The Washington Post*. In short, the affidavit outlines your collusion with the People's Republic of China, starting with its donations to your campaign—"

"I never knew it was them. That was—"

"To your agreement with China's ambassador to commit U.S. military assets to further China's strategic aims. The affidavit also contains a report from a decorated Special Agent with the FBI detailing his investigation into the murder of a Commerce Department official and his family—"

"What? That's nonsense. I don't know anything about—"

"—who were murdered by agents of China's Ministry of State Security—the same agents that served as intermediaries between Mr. Bousikaris, yourself, and China's ambassador."

Martin stared at Mason, then chuckled and tossed the folder onto the coffee table. "Wonderful story. Problem is, gentlemen, you've forgotten something: If you follow through on your threat, your names will come out as well. You'll be lucky to survive it. You sink me, you sink yourselves."

Dutcher said, "Small price to pay to stop a war. I for one would rather take my chances than to see you stay in this office another day."

Martin glanced at Cathermeier. "And you, General? I can't believe you, of all people, would betray me. I'm your commander in chief, for God's sake. You're sworn to follow my orders."

"And you're sworn to uphold the Constitution and to put this country's welfare above everything else—including yourself," Cathermeier responded. "I've had a good career—a good life—and if in the process of tossing you out on your ass I lose all of it, I'll still call it a fair trade."

"You're a disgrace! All of you! You're all traitors, and I swear on my soul I'll see you pay—"

"An empty oath," Mason said. "You've got no soul to swear on. The only question that remains is, are you going to go willingly or kicking and screaming?"

"Go to hell!"

Mason shrugged. "Once you're out of here, perhaps, but not before."

Martin looked at Bousikaris. "Howard, how could you do this to me? I trusted you. Of all the people who would want to see me fail, I never thought you'd be one of them."

Bousikaris looked down at the carpet and Dutcher saw a tear at the corner of his eye. "I'm sorry, Phil," he whispered.

"I am. We made a terrible choice, and there's no running away from it. We could have done the right thing; we could have told them to go to hell and let the chips fall where they may. But we didn't."

"You little weasel! That's fine, I don't need you." Martin turned back to the others; he leaned forward, elbows on his knees, and grinned. "You think you're ready to take me on? I am the president of the *goddamned United States*! I'll have you hauled out of here in handcuffs, and then we'll see what you're made of!"

Martin stood up and started walking toward his desk.

"Just so we're clear on this," Dutcher said. "Whether you have us arrested or not, nothing will change. The affidavits *will* go out. By tomorrow morning you'll have the attorney general, the Justice Department, the FBI, and every newspaper and television reporter in the country sitting in your lap. And that's just day one; day two will be worse still, and so and so forth until you're drummed out of office and hung in effigy from every tree in every town in this country. You'll go down in history as the most corrupt president in our nation's history—and that's if you're lucky. More likely, you'll end up in jail. So go ahead and make your call. Maybe it's fitting that you seal your coffin."

With one hand hovering over the phone, Martin shook his head and smiled ruefully. "I'll give you this: You boys know how to tie a good knot." Martin walked back to his chair and sat down. "So you've got me over a barrel. What's it going to be? You all want influence . . . special consideration? You've got it. What's your pleasure, gentlemen?"

Amazing, Dutcher thought. Martin was still trying to play his own game. Despite it all, he truly thought they were just like him.

Dutcher glanced at Mason and Cathermeier, who both shook their heads sadly.

"How about it, gentlemen?" Martin said. "You've won your little victory. Now it's time to collect. It's not often I admit to being bested, so don't squander it."

Bousikaris stepped forward. "Phil—"

"No, Howard, I know when to bend a little. Let them enjoy their time in the sun."

Mason sighed, then looked at Bousikaris and nodded.

Bousikaris picked up the phone, spoke into it for a few seconds, then hung up. Thirty seconds later the door opened and David Lahey walked in. "Good evening, Phil."

"What're you doing here?" Martin said. "Dick, this is between us. David's got nothing to do with this."

"He's got everything to do with it. He's your replacement."

"What? Oh Jesus, give it up, gentlemen! You can't really expect me to simply step down."

"That's exactly what we expect. Next week you'll hold a press conference. Citing a cancerous brain tumor—a cerebella astrocytomas, to be exact—you have transferred power to Vice President Lahey. While the tumor is not fatal, the doctors have told you it will eventually begin to affect your judgment and therefore your ability to carry out your duties. For the good of the country, you are tendering your resignation."

"No one will buy that."

"Of course they will," Dutcher replied. "Most of them gladly."

For the first time, Martin lost a bit of his swagger. He spread his hands. "You can't do this. Please. . . . Don't do this to me."

"You did it to yourself," Cathermeier replied.

Mason said, "Make your decision. If you take the option we're offering, you get to retire to your farm in New Hampshire and write your damned memoirs; if you go against us, your life is over. It's time to decide, Phil."

As though suddenly deflated, Martin leaned back in his chair. He stared at the carpet for nearly a full minute. "Okay," he whispered. "You win. What do you want me to do?"

THIRTY MINUTES LATER THEY WERE JOINED BY THE WHITE House's chief counsel and the director of the Secret Service. As they entered, both men were visibly wary. For Martin's part, he played his role well, sitting tall in his desk chair, the commanding and brave president.

"Now that we're all here, I have an announcement to make. What I'm about to tell you is very difficult. Aside from Howard, my wife, and my personal physician, no one else knows about this."

Martin went on to explain his condition, the type of tumor involved, and then his prognosis, never once missing a beat. It was a masterful performance, Dutcher thought. It was no wonder how Martin had risen so high in politics; he was a chameleon of the highest order.

"And so," Martin concluded, "next week I will be resigning the presidency. Effective immediately, however, I wish to formally turn over my duties and responsibilities to Vice President Lahey."

The room was silent. The director of the Secret Service was the first to break the silence. He stepped forward. "Mr. President?"

Dutcher held his breath. This was the point of no return. If Martin chose to damn the consequences and turn on them, it would happen now. Dutcher had no idea what the duress code word would be, but within seconds of Martin's using it, they would find themselves surrounded by a dozen Secret Service agents.

Martin paused a few seconds, then shook his head. "Relax, Roger. I appreciate your concern, but this is my decision, and as painful as it is, it's the right thing."

"Very well, Mr. President."

Martin turned to the White House counsel. "Lorne, how do we make this official?"

CONSIDERING THE GRAVITY OF THE EVENT, THE TRANSFER OF power from Martin to Lahey was surprisingly simple, Dutcher thought. There would be further bureaucratic hoops through which to jump, of course, but an hour after giving the order, Martin was signing the last of the documents transferring the powers of office to David Lahey. The documents were then witnessed and signed by both the chief counsel and the director of the Secret Service.

"Is that it?" Martin asked.

"Yes, sir," said the chief counsel. "That's it."

"Thank you both. Roger, please inform my detail that President Lahey's personal detail will arrive shortly for a transfer of duties."

"Yes, sir."

"That's all, then. You can go."

Once they were gone, Martin let out a heavy sigh, pushed himself away from the desk, and stood up. He turned to Lahey and gestured to the chair with a flourish. "David, the mantle is yours."

Lahey merely nodded.

Martin looked at Dutcher, Mason, and Cathermeier each in turn. "I assume, gentlemen, that you have no problem with me retiring to my bedroom?"

Mason shook his head.

As Martin headed for the door, Mason called, "Phil."

"Yes?"

"Make no mistake: Tomorrow or ten years from now, the affidavits will still be there. Between the three of us, we'll see to that."

Martin nodded wearily. "I know, Dick. I'll be a good boy, I promise."

As the door shut behind him, there was a long, awkward silence in the room. Finally, Lahey walked to one of the wingback chairs and sat down heavily. "Jesus Christ."

"Yeah," Mason said.

"I actually feel a little sorry for the bastard. I can hardly believe it, but I do."

The intercom on the desk buzzed. Everyone glanced at it, but no one moved.

"I believe that's for you, Mr. President," Leland Dutcher said.

"Yeah, I guess it is." Lahey walked to his desk, picked up the phone, listened, then nodded to Cathermeier. "For you. I sure hope this isn't a bad omen."

Cathermeier took the phone, listened for a few moments, then hung up.

Mason said, "What is it, Chuck?"

"The Chinese have planes in the air. They're headed toward the Russian border."

68

***Laogi* 179**

TANNER SPENT THE FIRST HALF OF THE DAY ASLEEP, CURLED UP inside the rotted bole of a black walnut with underbrush and branches piled around him for camouflage.

A little after noon he woke up, coded a message for the Motorola, and sent it home. He then ate his last remaining rations of trail mix and beef jerky and washed it down with some of Wu's sweat sock soup spiked with honey; it tasted almost pleasant.

At two, he left his cave and headed out, crawling deeper into the forest. His destination lay two miles to the south and he had three hours to get there, but without knowing what kind of daylight patrols Xiang had set, he wanted to allow plenty of time.

It turned out to be the right decision.

THE FOREST SURROUNDING THE CAMP WAS THICK WITH XIANG'S paratroopers as roving patrols had been dispatched to augment the OPs. A few hundred yards from his starting point Tanner again found himself playing a nerve-wracking game of hide-and-go-seek.

The paratroopers were good, but, as before, Tanner used patience to his advantage. Patrols came and went, oftentimes passing within feet of him as he lay under his homemade gillie cape, holding his breath until their footsteps faded and he could continue on his way.

At four-thirty he reached the edge of the woods. Ahead lay a clearing at the center of which was a wide, sand-filled pit; to his right, back toward the camp, was the road Hsiao had described. Briggs was about to grab his map to confirm his location when the stench of feces filled his nostrils. A spurt of bile filled his mouth; he swallowed it.

This has to be the right place, he thought.

Now he waited.

THIRTY-FIVE MINUTES LATER HE HEARD THE ROAR OF A TRUCK engine echoing through the trees. Tanner peered down the road. The tanker truck, driven by a guard from the camp, chugged around the bend and pulled into the clearing. Black hoses dangled like tentacles from their mounts on the holding tank, bouncing and swaying with each bump in the road. With a grinding of gears, the truck stopped, did a Y-turn and backed toward the pit, stopping a few feet short of the edge.

The guard shut off the engine and got out. He wore rubber chest waders and elbow-high gloves. He walked to the rear of the truck, unhooked one of the hoses, and dropped it into the pit.

Tanner got to his feet and sprinted to the truck's front bumper, where he dropped to his belly. Beneath the length of the truck he could see the guard's feet shuffling as he readied the vehicle.

With a whine, the tank's pump kicked on. The man's feet backed away from the hose and stopped beside the rear tire. The hose convulsed a few times, then came the sound of gushing water. And then, the odor—the sickly sweet stench of feces, urine, and garbage.

Tanner felt his belly heave. He set his teeth against it.

Forget it, he ordered himself. *This is your way in*.

He crab-walked around to the passenger side, mounted the access ladder, and climbed to the top of the tank. He laid himself flat and shimmied forward until he could see the guard's head. The man was smoking as he watched the hose, seemingly transfixed by the effluent gushing into the pit.

Tanner reached out and lifted open the tank's hatch. A cloud of fat, blue-backed flies burst from the opening; it took all his self-control to not drop the lid. *Don't think, just do it. . . .* Fingers clenched around the strap, he lowered the pack through the hatch until he felt it bump the ladder, then clipped the D-ring to a rung and released it.

Eyes fixed on the guard below, Briggs turned the AK so it hung across his chest, then dropped his feet through the hatch. He took one final breath of fresh air, then started downward.

THE TANK'S INTERIOR WAS A PERFECT ECHO CHAMBER, AMPLIfying the rhythmic grinding of the pump. He closed the hatch and the tank fell into complete blackness. Tanner felt a flash of claustrophobia. He closed his eyes, pressed his gillie mask tighter over his nose, and concentrated on his breathing until the panic waned. He clicked on his flashlight and felt instantly better.

The tank was half full of fecal bilge, a brown-green quagmire that lapped at the sides of the tank with a sickening, gurgling sound. A miniwave of it washed over the bottom rung and left behind an oily deposit on his boot. At the rear of the tank the fluid whirl pooled around the vent valve.

Slowly but steadily the effluent level began to drop. A sporadic sucking sound echoed through the tank. The pump chugged and groaned. Tanner felt like he was trapped inside the belly of some prehistoric beast.

After another ten minutes, the tank was finally empty except for a half-inch of waste. Briggs stepped down, careful of his footing on the stainless-steel surface.

With a great sucking *whoosh,* the last of the tank's contents disappeared through the valve. The pump went silent. The cab's door opened, then shut. The truck's engine growled to life, and as Tanner reached out to steady himself on the ladder, it began moving.

He spent most of the twenty-minute trip perched on the ladder, holding the hatch open a few inches and breathing fresh air. He couldn't remember a more beautiful smell and vowed to never take it for granted again.

With more grinding of gears, the truck began slowing, then came to a stop. Outside, a voice—the driver's, he assumed—called out in Mandarin. Another voice answered, followed by the squeaking of steel hinges. *The main gate,* Briggs thought. The truck lurched forward again.

Inside—

The truck lurched to a stop. Silence. Then footsteps clanking on the access ladder outside. *What the hell is this . . . ?* Hsiao had mentioned nothing about anyone inspecting the inside of the tank. Briggs unclipped his pack from the ladder, unzipped the side pocket, pulled out the revolver.

The hatch opened. A shaft of sunlight knifed through the darkness.

Tanner raised the revolver and pointed at the opening.

A hand appeared and gave the thumbs-up sign. A moment later, Kam Hsiao's face appeared in the opening. He spotted Tanner, gave him a brief nod and a smile, then withdrew.

The hatch clanged shut. Then Hsiao's voice: "All clear! Drive on!"

AFTER A FEW MORE STOPS AND TURNS THE TRUCK WAS BACKED into the garage and the barn doors shut behind it. Briggs remained inside the tank for another ten minutes until certain he was alone, then climbed the ladder, popped the hatch, and peeked out.

Aside from some daylight showing around the edges of the doors and through a small, tarnished window in the rear, the garage was dark.

He grabbed his pack, climbed down the ladder, and dropped to the floor.

Hsiao's directions took him into the garage's small office, where he found a battleship gray desk, a chair, a filing cabinet, and a mangy, threadbare rug covering the floor. Tanner lifted its corner and there, set into the floor just as Hsiao had promised, was a hatch. He grabbed the handle and lifted, exposing the dirt foundation. A gust of cold, musty air blew past his face.

Built in the early fifties, all of the camp's buildings had been equipped with crawl spaces for easy access to the electrical conduits and plumbing. Chosen twice a month by lottery, three guards were forced to inspect each building's crawl spaces for rodent infestation and weather damage.

"It's the least favorite duty in the camp," Hsiao had explained, "Believe me: no one will go there unless they have to. You'll be safe."

Tanner dropped his pack and AK through the hatch, then stepped down. The opening came up to his waist. He reached back, grabbed the corner of the rug, then pulled it over the hatch as he closed it behind him.

A few feet into the crawl space Briggs found a black plastic garbage bag—the items he'd asked Hsiao to gather. He took a quick inventory and found everything there—including a surprise: a small tinfoil package. Inside was a hunk of roast pork tenderloin, some grilled broccoli, and fried rice.

Good ol' Hsiao.

Despite the grumbling in his belly, Briggs resealed the food and set it aside. *First work, then eat.*

He had a lot to do if he was going to be ready for tonight.

69

NMCC

LED BY GENERAL CATHERMEIER, NOW-PRESIDENT DAVID LAHEY, Dick Mason, and Leland Dutcher walked into the center. "What's happening, Commander?"

The CAC duty officer, a female navy lieutenant commander, walked over. "I have a briefing ready, General. If you'll follow me."

She led them into the tank and waited for everyone to find a seat, then walked to the wall screen, which showed a map of the Chinese-Russian border stretching from the western corner of the Mongolian salient to Birobijan, Russia's Jewish Autonomous Oblast, in the east.

"As of now," the duty officer began, "we're showing two squadrons of aircraft moving toward the border. Initial composition of the group appears to be a mix of A-501, Russian built A-50 birds, and defense fighters."

Lahey interrupted. "Pardon me, Commander, but I'm a little rusty. Could you translate all that into English for me?"

"Yes, sir. A-501s are Israeli-made AWACS radar planes used to coordinate air-to-air fighters. They can spot and track targets from hundreds of miles away and then vector fighters to intercept them. The use of such planes is critical if an attacker hopes to gain air superiority.

"A-50s are similar to AWACS, but they serve in more of an ELINT role—electronic intelligence gathering. Similar to that of the AWACS, their job is to detect enemy radio and radar transmissions, and in some cases jam them. A-50s are old, but still useful; they can be used to direct ground-attack aircraft toward ground-to-air missile sites, as well as fighters toward enemy AWACS."

"Unless I'm wrong, doesn't that tell us something?" Lahey said.

"Yes, sir," Cathermeier replied. "Whatever the Chinese are planning, they're making it their first job to gain air superiority over Siberia. If they can wipe the skies of Russian fighters, that makes everything else easier."

"But we still don't know what that is."

"No, sir. Commander, anything new on ground forces in the salient?"

"Very little movement. All of it's consistent with the increased alert status, but not a coordinated push toward the border. Even if they moved now, the first mechanized division wouldn't reach the border for three days."

Dick Mason said, "That's damned odd."

"Go on, Commander," said Cathermeier.

"Fighter bases throughout the Beijing and Shenyang military regions are on full alert. We expect once the AWACS and ELINT planes get on station with their midair refuelers, we'll see a surge of fighters and interceptors moving toward the border."

"They're trying to get the Russians to commit their own fighters and AWACS early," Dutcher said. "Get them up, make them wait, expend resources, then swoop in."

Cathermeier nodded. "I agree. And they'll have no choice but to do it. These days they haven't got enough ground, radar stations to cover the whole salient. Commander, any statements from either Moscow or Beijing?"

"Not a peep, sir."

"Bad sign," Mason said.

"There's more," the duty officer said. "As of an hour ago, satellite surveillance showed a Chinese surface-action group from the PLAAN's North Sea Fleet moving out of the East China Sea and into the Korean Straits."

"Moving toward Vladivostok," Cathermeier muttered.

"Explain," Lahey said.

"Our joint battle group is currently steaming. . . ." Cathermeier looked to the duty officer.

"One hundred fifty miles, steaming east at twelve knots."

"A hundred fifty miles off the Russian coast; in response, the Russians sent out their own SAG—surface action group—to meet us, which is. . . ."

"One hundred seventy miles south of us, steaming north at fifteen," the duty officer replied.

"They're closing the box," Cathermeier said.

"Explain," Lahey said.

"Geography is against us. Vladivostok is in the Sea of Japan, which is a tight fit for a battle group. To the north, the waters continue to narrow between Sakhalin Island and the Russian coast. Now, squeeze into that space our battle group, the Russian and Chinese SAGs. . . . We'll be scraping paint with each other. Worse still, we've got no way of withdrawing except by going south—through the Russian group. Commander, what's the size and makeup of the Chinese SAG?"

"Sixteen ships, consisting mainly of Haizhou-, Shenzhen- and Luda-class destroyers plus an odd mix of medium and light frigates."

"By itself, not much of a match for us," Cathermeier told Lahey, "but throw the Russians into the mix. . . . It's a disaster waiting to happen."

"Which is probably their intention," Dutcher replied. "To the Russians, it will be more evidence that we're in bed with China: A U.S. battle group and a Chinese SAG off their coast, and Chinese fighters threatening their southern border."

"Not to mention the attack on NV," Mason added.

"A joint invasion," Lahey murmured. "If I were sitting in Moscow myself, I'd probably see the same thing. Christ almighty."

There was a knock on the conference room door; a marine lieutenant poked his head in. "Director Mason, message for you."

"Thanks." Mason took the message, read it, then looked at Cathermeier. "General, can you excuse the commander for a moment?"

"Sure. Thank you, Commander. Anything else?"

"No, sir."

Once she was gone, Mason held up the message. "From Tanner."

"Thank God," Dutcher said, leaning forward. "What's he say?"

"He's alive and at the camp. He's making his move tonight, his time."

"How?"

"He didn't say."

Lahey said, "Excuse me, gentlemen, what are we talking about?"

Mason responded. "Tanner is the man we sent in after General Soong. A few days ago in Beijing he was burned; he went on the run. He's managed to reach the prison camp where they're holding Soong."

"And this Soong—he's the one you think might hold the key to what China's up to?"

"Yes, sir. We hope."

"Well, then let's say a little prayer for both of them," Lahey replied. "In the meantime, we have to slow this thing down. What are our options?"

"Diplomacy is out," Dutcher said. "At this stage, China's got too much. They're not going to stop."

"I agree," Mason said.

"Then Moscow," Lahey said. "We've got to make the Russians see the bigger picture."

"That's a toss-up. Vladimir Bulganin is something of an enigma, and so far he isn't showing the greatest restraint. He's already got his forces at full alert, ready to pull the trigger."

David Lahey sighed. "Well, then my introduction to the game of international diplomacy is going to be an interesting one. Let's get President Bulganin on the phone."

Moscow

"What does this mean? How far from the border are they?" cried Vladimir Bulganin. "Is this an attack or not!"

Marshal Beskrovny hesitated. "Not an attack, Mr. President, but it certainly appears like the precursor to one. These radar and signal-gathering aircraft that—"

"Gathering what?"

"Electronic intelligence from radio transmissions, SAM sites—"

"Our defenses, you mean."

"Yes, sir. The radar aircraft they've got up are most often used to coordinate fighter aircraft."

Bulganin began pacing, his hands clasped behind his back. ". . . going to attack," he muttered to himself. "The yellow bastards are going to attack us!"

For the first time in days, Ivan Nochenko agreed with Bulganin. They were seeing the opening moves of an air campaign. *But why?* he wondered. *To what end?* So far, Beijing had rebuffed their every attempt to communicate. This wasn't about the Chinese diaspora in Siberia; the reaction was too disproportionate. Then what?

"That may be, Mr. President," said SVR director Sergei Fedorin, "but I remind you, we're seeing virtually no movement of ground forces on their side of the border. If they are planning to invade, it can't be coming anytime soon—a week, at least."

"You're splitting hairs, Fedorin! Air . . . ground. . . . They're both an invasion of the Motherland! Good lord, are you both blind? All of you? Are you suggesting we should simply open the doors for their aircraft? Perhaps *thank* them because they're not sending tanks?"

"That's not what we're saying," Beskrovny countered. "Our point is, we have time to examine the situation—to plan the appropriate response."

"I'll tell you what the appropriate response is," Bulganin shouted. "It's the same that Koba gave Hitler sixty years ago: We crush them!" Bulganin began pacing again, gesticulating wildly. "This time, though, it will be different. This time, we're not going to give up an inch of ground! Not an *inch*! The moment their fighters cross into our airspace, we'll swat them from the sky!"

Both Fedorin and Beskrovny glanced at Nochenko, who stepped closer to Bulganin's desk. "Mr. President."

". . . let them try, if they have the stomach for it. We will—"

"Mr. President!"

"What!"

"Please, I ask you again: Listen to Marshal Beskrovny. Our country—the Motherland—is in a dire position, but we have alternatives. We must choose carefully. If not, this conflict could turn fatal for everyone involved."

"You mean nuclear, don't you?"

"Yes, sir."

Bulganin squared off with him, chest to chest. "Does that frighten you, Ivan?"

"Yes, sir, it does."

"You're weak."

"Sir—"

"You haven't the stomach for the hard choices. None of you do! Those little devils to the south understand only force, don't you see? If we show the slightest weakness, they will exploit it. And the Americans! They're as two-faced as always. For all we know, they're working with China. It makes sense, after all: Wait until that weak nobody from Omsk comes into power, then attack. The shoemaker from nowhere will surely crumble. He'll be so scared he'll probably hand us the keys to the Kremlin!" Bulganin tapped his chest with a thumb. "They're wrong! They're in for a surprise!"

Bulganin's desk intercom buzzed. "Sir, the president of the United States is on line one. He urgently wishes to speak with you."

Bulganin's eyes narrowed. "Well, gentlemen, speak of the devil. . . . Send it through."

The phone buzzed and Bulganin snatched it up. "President Bulganin here."

There was a few seconds pause as the interpreters exchanged the words.

"Mr. President, this is David Lahey."

"Who?"

Nochenko whispered, "The vice president."

"Lahey?" Bulganin replied. "Why in the hell am I talking to you? Where is President Martin?"

"President Martin is unavailable, sir. He's asked me to stand-in for him."

"What is this nonsense? Unavailable—what does that mean?"

"He has a medical condition that required care. Please believe me when I tell you I have full authority to speak for, and act on, the behalf of the government of the United States."

"Very well. What would you like to say?"

"As I'm sure you are, we're aware of the Chinese aircraft moving toward your border, and we share your concern over it. I'd like to discuss how we might work together to defuse the situation."

"You can defuse the situation by withdrawing your battle

group from our waters," Bulganin replied. "Once you have done that, you can further defuse the situation by explaining why you attacked and destroyed the port of Nakhodka-Vostochny."

There was a five-second pause. "President Bulganin, I—"

"You didn't think we knew about that, did you? Well, we do. Your words are meaningless, Lahey. They contradict every action your country has taken in the past two weeks."

"If you'll give me a chance," Lahey said, "I might be able to provide an explanation."

There was a knock on Bulganin's office door. A messenger walked in and handed Marshal Beskrovny a message. Bulganin put his hand over the phone. "What is it? What have you got there?"

"A reconnaissance flight out of Vladivostok has sighted a PLAAN surface group moving north through the Korean Straits."

"Moving north?"

"Yes, Mr. President."

"Toward us," Bulganin muttered. "How far away? How many days?"

"At present speed, thirty hours."

"Bastards!" Bulganin returned to the phone: "Lahey, I've just been informed a group of Chinese warships is steaming toward our coast. Is this another coincidence, or is this just yet another piece of the plan?"

"There is no plan, Mr. President. You have to believe me."

"I don't have to do anything, Lahey. I can see what's happening! We're done talking, you and I. Good day!"

Bulganin slammed down the phone and turned to Beskrovny. "How many hours did you say?"

"Thirty. Mr. President, perhaps we should reestablish communication with—"

"No. They're trying to buy time, to keep us from reacting until it's too late. If those Chinese ships are allowed to link up with the American group, we'll be outgunned. That's when they'll make their move over the border!"

Bulganin paced behind his desk and leaned on it, thinking for a moment. He then rapped the top with his fist. "We must move now, before the Chinese get into position. Marshal, order our ships to close with the American battle group and prepare to attack."

70

***Laogi* 179**

LYING ON HIS BELLY IN THE CRAWL SPACE, TANNER WORKED steadily into the night, assembling half a dozen crude flash-fire bombs from Hsiao's supplies.

Similar to the device he'd used to cripple Solon Trulau's yacht in Jakarta, each bomb consisted of two sets of ingredients: a base and a catalyst. Alone, each was stable, but combined they were volatile. In this case, he was using a mixture of petroleum products he'd found in the garage along with some chlorine-based cleanser used to clean the inside of the tanker truck.

Once certain the chemicals were correctly blended, it was time for a test.

A few feet down the crawl space he dug a small hole in the earth and then, arm outstretched, spooned into it a couple drops of the base, followed by a drop of catalyst. With a small *poof*, a blue white flame filled the hole. Tanner quickly covered it with dirt and the flame died.

Now for the vessels.

He lit the sterno can, then placed on top of it the small sauce pot Hsiao had stolen from the kitchen. Into this he dumped the half a dozen candles and the contents of four tins of shoe polish.

Once the mixture was completely melted, but not yet boiling, he removed the pot and began the molding process. It took an hour, most of the mix, and a lot of kneading, but in the end he'd created twelve golf ball–size shells.

Careful to keep them separated, he filled half of them with the base, the other half with the catalyst, then, using the last of the wax, he sealed each shell. He let them fully harden and then duct taped them together in pairs, one base and one catalyst.

In theory, upon impact each shell would shatter, mixing the chemicals together. The resulting flash fire would be brief, but strong enough to ignite almost anything it touched.

Tanner scrutinized his handiwork. As long as he placed them well and timed his movements right, they would do the job, he decided. Even so, the biggest variable was out of his control. He could only hope the guards responded like the well-trained professionals they were.

AN HOUR LATER HE HEARD THE GARAGE DOOR OPEN ABOVE HIM, then close. Footsteps clicked on the floorboards above. "Everything is awful," a voice called.

Hsiao. "That makes two of us," Tanner called back.

The hatch opened and light poured into the crawl space. Tanner shimmied over to the opening to find Hsiao squatting beside it. "Are you ready?" he asked.

Tanner nodded. "What did you find out about Soong and his daughter?"

"The general is in his regular cell. Two of Xiang's paratroopers have been posted outside his door, though."

"I'll handle them."

"Soong's daughter is being kept in a bunk room in the same building as the control center."

Tanner nodded. "When do you go on duty again?"

"I managed to change places with another guard. I have the roving patrol starting at midnight."

"That didn't raise any suspicion?"

Hsiao shook his head. "A group of us play mah-jongg every evening; I told him I didn't want to miss the game."

"Good. Can you stop by here?"

"Yes, but only for a moment. If I miss a checkpoint by even a few minutes, the alarm sounds."

"I'll only need you for a minute," Tanner said, then explained what he had in mind. "I assume the control center has an incoming phone line? You know the number?"

"Yes."

"Good. You might want to practice your acting skills. What're the chances they'll buy it?"

Hsiao smiled, shrugged. "I know the guard manning the control center tonight. His name is Wujan. He's . . . how do you say it? *Er bai wu*."

Tanner smiled back; he knew the phrase. *Er bai wu* literally meant 250—on an intelligence scale of 1000, Wujan was three-quarters stupid. "If you can fluster him a bit, it would help."

"I'll try." Hsiao took a deep breath and let it out. "I'm a little scared, Briggs."

"Just a little? Then you're doing better than me," Tanner replied, only half joking.

After all the hardship he'd endured to get here, his success or failure would soon come down to a period of a few minutes. If he succeeded, they would be a step closer to freedom; if he failed, Soong and Lian would spend the rest of their lives here and he and Hsiao would be executed.

He gripped Hsiao's forearm and gave it a squeeze. "It's almost over. Hang in there."

"Okay. See you a little after midnight."

TANNER DOZED INTERMITTENTLY UNTIL HE AGAIN HEARD THE GArage door open and footsteps entering. He checked his watch: 12:40. He felt his heart rate shoot up. Almost time.

The hatch opened and Tanner crawled over.

Hsiao said, "Ready?"

"Yeah, you?"

"I think so. Tell me again what you want me to say."

Tanner went over the wording once more. "Keep it short. Act excited as if you're on the run."

"Okay, okay. I'm ready."

Tanner pulled out the Motorola and dialed the number. Once it began ringing, he handed it to Hsiao. They pressed their heads together so Tanner could hear.

"Administration, Corporal Wujan speaking."

"Wujan, this is Sergeant Jong."

"Uh . . . pardon? Who's this?"

"I'm one of Director Xiang's men, dammit! We've found the missing truck in a ravine about three miles east of Beiyinhe. We think we've found the American's trail, but we need help."

"Uh . . . okay. . . ." Wujan replied. "Where are you?"

"On the outskirts of Beiyinhe. We have a witness who thinks they saw the American."

"What was your name—"

"Hurry! We need help. Three miles east of Beiyinhe! The American can't have gotten far!"

"Okay, but what—"

Hsiao handed the phone back to Tanner, who disconnected. "Perfect."

"Do you think it will work?"

"It'll get a reaction, that's certain," Tanner replied. "Whether it's the kind we want, we'll know shortly. Go back to your rounds. When the fireworks start, sound the alarm, wait for the commotion to start, then meet me in the hangar."

"Right." Hsiao closed the hatch and left.

One more miscue, Tanner thought. Success now hinged on one thing: Whether upon receiving the news Xiang would ask, or fail to ask, that one critical question.

INSIDE THE CONTROL CENTER, CORPORAL WUJAN WAS TORN BEtween confusion and terror. Though he missed part of the message, the gist of it had been clear: *Someone had found the American! Where had the man said? Beiyinhe?* This was important . . . had to remember that part. With someone as important as Director Xiang involved. . . . Perhaps there was a commendation in it for him.

Wujan picked up the phone.

• • •

Two minutes later Xiang and Eng barged into the control center. The base commander was already there. Xiang asked, "When did it come in?"

"Minutes ago," replied the base commander. "One of Shen's men called in and reported finding the truck near Beiyinhe."

"Three miles to the east of Beiyinhe," Wujan added nervously. "He was very clear about that. He said they may have found the American—or, no, his trail. They found his trail."

"How far away is that?" Xiang asked the base commander.

"Ten miles to the southwest."

"Contact the patrols outside the camp and tell them to move in closer."

"Why?"

"If this is a ruse, Tanner will use it to try to slip into the camp. Eng, go get Shen. Have him gather ten men and meet me at the helicopter pad."

71

Tanner crouched beneath the crawl space hatch in his yellow coveralls and matching flash hood, waiting and listening. The backpack and AK were slung over his shoulder. In his right hand he carried his gillie blanket, rolled into a tube with the revolver stuffed inside; in his left hand, a gas mask.

As Hsiao had explained, the coveralls, flash hood, and gas mask were standard attire for the camp's fire-fighting squad, which consisted of a handful of guards specially trained to respond to fires and general minor disasters that came with living year-round in the wild's of northeastern China. Aside from the camp commander himself, members of the fire squad outranked everyone during emergencies.

Tanner was about to find out if that was true.

FIVE MINUTES AFTER HSIAO PLACED HIS CALL, TANNER HEARD the electrical whine of the Hind's turbo-shaft engine being powered up, followed moments later by voices shouting to one another:

"No packs, just weapons!"

"Move, move, move!"

Briggs popped open the hatch, boosted himself up onto the floor, and stood up. He raced to the garage doors and peeked through a crack. Shrugging on their coats and packs, paratroopers were racing out of the barracks toward the landing pad. Xiang and another man—the leader of the paratroopers, Tanner assumed—stood beside the Hind's door until the last man was aboard, then climbed in and slid shut the door.

The Hind's rotors spun to full speed. The pilot lifted off, rotated in place to clear the hangar roof, then banked right and disappeared over the treetops.

Briggs started his mental clock. *Five minutes for them to reach the false dump spot, another five to realize it's a ruse, another five back to the camp. . . .* He could count on fifteen minutes, no more.

He pulled the first flash bomb out of his pack and hurled it across the garage, where it hit the wall and ignited in a flash of blue flame. Within seconds, smoke began to drift across the garage.

Tanner jogged to the rear of the garage, pried open the window, leaned, and heaved a second flash bomb against the wall of the adjoining storage shed. It ignited, sending a splash of flames up into the eaves. He turned right and threw another bomb against the shed closest to the hangar.

Around him the garage was thick with smoke, the far wall half engulfed in flame.

He pushed his backpack through the window, followed it, then dashed along the rear of the sheds until he was kitty-corner to the hangar. He removed the last three bombs, gingerly tucked them inside his coveralls, then strapped the AK to his pack and tossed the bundle overhand toward the hangar wall, where it bounced into the shadows.

Suddenly the *whoop, whoop, whoop* of an alarm began blaring. Voices started shouting. Smoke was wafting across the compound. He could see the first tendrils of flames beneath the garage's eaves.

He donned his mask, tucked his gillie blanket under his arm, and ran into the compound.

He headed straight for Soong's barracks. A dozen guards, many still in their long underwear, were stumbling out of bunkroom barracks, staring at the smoke and flames.

"Huo zai!" someone shouted. Fire! *"Huo zai!"*

"The hangar's in danger!" another voice called. "Someone get the pilot, hurry!"

Tanner strode up to the group and gestured wildly. "Move it! Move, move!"

The men hesitated for a moment, then scrambled in different directions.

Tanner kept jogging, mounted the barracks steps, and pushed through the door. A pair of men rushed past him into the compound. Mentally following Hsiao's map, Tanner turned left down the hallway, then right, then left again. Before him lay a door labeled with Mandarin characters. He could only decipher one word, but it was enough: "sublevel."

He backed up a few feet, threw a flash bomb down the hallway, then pushed through the door and trotted down the steps to the sublevel.

It was quiet here, the earthen walls absorbing all but a few shouts from above. He took a moment to get his bearings, then started jogging. *Right . . . left . . . another left. . . .*

He turned the corner and skidded to a halt. He was standing in a short hallway at the end of which was a lone wooden door. On each side of the jamb stood a paratrooper, an AK-47 across each body. They eyed Tanner with a mixture of fear and uncertainty.

"Ni shi shei?" one of them asked. *Who are you? State your business.*

"The camp's on fire!" Tanner shouted through his mask. "Get the general!"

He started toward the door, but one of the paratroopers moved to block him. "No one enters, but the camp commander, you know that!"

Out of choices, Briggs thought. He threw up his hands. *"Er bei wu!" I'll find him!*

He turned, jogged down the hall and around the corner. He stopped, jammed his hand inside the blanket, and gripped the revolver. *Gotta be quick . . . can't miss . . . four shots, two apiece. . . .*

He took a breath, spun around the corner. He took two bounding steps, dropped to one knee.

Muffled by the blanket, the revolver's report was barely audible. He fired twice into the nearest paratrooper's chest, then adjusted his aim and put two more into the second man. They both crumpled.

Tanner tossed away the revolver and snatched up one of their AKs. He fired a three-round burst into the door's top hinge, then the bottom. With a crash, the door dropped off its hinges and swung inward, ripping the knob and lock out of the jamb as it fell.

Tanner stepped through the door.

Curled into a ball in the corner was General Han Soong. He stared wide-eyed at Tanner. "What?" he cried. "What is it?"

Seeing his friend, this once proud man, huddled like a frightened child, filled Briggs's chest with emotion. *My God, what had they done to him?* He ripped off his gas mask. "Hello, Han."

Soong blinked once, then again. "Briggs? My God, Briggs. . . ."

Tanner walked over and knelt beside him. "Good to see you again."

"And you!"

"Feel up to a little traveling?"

"Yes, of course. My God, yes!"

"Then we better move; we haven't got much time."

"What about Lian? I have no idea where they're keeping her! Briggs, I can't leave without—"

"You won't have to. She's here."

"Here? What do you mean? I don't—"

"Later, Han. We have to go—*now*."

"Of course. What do you want me to do?"

"Nothing. Play dead."

With Soong dangling over his shoulder and covered by the gillie blanket, Tanner climbed the stairwell to the main floor, retraced his steps to the entrance, and charged into the compound.

The garage and the storage sheds were fully engulfed. Despite the coveralls, he could feel the heat of the flames on his skin. Black smoke roiled across the compound, so thick he could see little past the few feet before him. The guard towers had turned their spotlights onto the garage and burning embers and ash swirled in the beams. Bodies rushed by on all sides, fading in and out of the smoke. Someone jostled him from behind, then was gone. Disembodied voices called out to one another.

From across the compound he heard another turbo-shaft engine grinding to a start. *The Hoplite*. Following procedure, the camp's pilot and ground team were moving the helicopter from the imperiled hangar and warming up the engines should it need to be evacuated.

Using the sound as his guide, Tanner pushed on through the smoke. As he passed the garage, a man in red coveralls and a gas mask—the leader of the fire team, Tanner assumed—grabbed his arm. "You! Where are you going?"

Tanner shouted a garbled response, then jerked his thumb at Soong's limp body and kept going.

"Wait! Come back here!"

After ten more paces he felt his feet hit concrete. *The landing pad*. He adjusted course and a few seconds later the hangar doors materialized out of the smoke.

The nose and most of the cockpit of the Hoplite were halfway out the doors. Two soldiers—one of them Hsiao—were bent over the nose wheel's tow bar, struggling to pull the Hoplite onto the pad. Tanner ran around to the already open cabin door.

The pilot jerked around in his seat. "Hey!"

"Injured!" Tanner shouted, and waved him back to the controls. He lay Soong on the cabin floor and tucked the AK beneath him. Briggs lifted the corner of his mask and pressed his mouth to Soong's ear, "Stay on your belly. Keep your face hidden. I'll be back."

He followed the fence away from the garage until he saw a wooden wall off to his right. He turned toward it. *The control center.* He mounted the steps, pushed through the door, and started down the hall. *Radio room, first door on the left. . . .*

"You!" came a voice from behind. "I asked you, what are you doing?"

Tanner turned. The fire-team leader stood in the open door. Briggs again shouted nonsense and turned to go. The man chased after him. "Stop right there! Who are you? Show me your face!"

Tanner turned, took a quick step toward the man, and kicked. The top of his foot slammed into the man's knee, shattering the joint. As he screamed and fell forward, Tanner met him, slamming his knee into the center of his forehead. He toppled over sideways and went limp.

"Hey! *Hey!*"

Briggs turned. Standing outside the radio-room door was a guard. In his left hand he held a Makarov 9 mm pistol. "Stop right there! Don't move!"

TEN MILES TO THE SOUTHWEST, XIANG'S HIND WAS LANDING ON the road beside the ravine. As soon as the skids touched the dirt, Shen and his men jumped to the ground and scrambled down the bank and into the ravine.

Barely aware of his surroundings, Xiang remained sitting in the cabin. *Something's not right about this . . . what is it? Think!* What had Corporal Wujan said? *"One of Shen's men had called. . . ."* Not radioed—*called!* Was it a slip of the tongue?

Xiang got up and walked into the cockpit. "Contact the camp, get a status report!"

"Yes, sir," the pilot replied. Ten seconds later. "Sir, there's no answer."

No, no, no. . . .

Panting, Shen appeared in the Hind's doorway. "There's nothing down there!"

"I know," Xiang growled. "That bastard! Damn him! Get your men—"

"What the hell is that?" the pilot cried, pointing out the window.

To the northeast, an orange glow hung over the treetops.

"Get your men aboard!" Xiang shouted. "He's set the damned camp on fire!"

TANNER GAUGED THE DISTANCE BETWEEN HIMSELF AND THE man. *Too far*. He'd be dead before he made it halfway. Briggs noticed the corporal's patch on the man's sleeve. *Wujan. . . .*

"Wujan, help me!" Tanner cried. Pointing a finger at the fire chief's body, he pressed his back against the wall and began sliding toward Wujan. "That's . . . that's the American!"

"What? He's—"

From the corner of his eye, Briggs saw Wujan's gun hand droop ever so slightly. He snapped his hand forward, grabbed Wujan's wrist in an overhand grip, and wrenched. As Wujan stumbled forward, Tanner hit him, driving his fist into the point where his jaw met his ear. Wujan slumped forward, unconscious.

Tanner took the gun, stuffed it into his pocket, and stepped into the radio room. He pulled out his next-to-last flash bomb and threw it against the wall above the radio set. Liquid fire splashed over the set and ignited the wooden table. Briggs ran back into the hall.

There were two remaining doors, both on the right side.

Briggs pushed open the first one: mops, buckets brooms. . . . He moved to the next door and turned the knob. It was locked. He backed against the wall and slammed his heel against the knob plate. The wood splintered, but held. He kicked again, then a third time. The jamb tore loose. The door swung open.

Heart in his throat, Tanner rushed inside.

Lian Soong sat in a wooden, hardback chair in the center of the room with her hands clasped in her lap. Though it had been twelve years since Tanner had last seen her, she seemed to have changed very little: petite, smooth, white skin, silken black hair . . . *My God, Lian. . . .*

She stared up at him with an expression Tanner could only describe as apathetic. *She no longer cared,* he thought. Broken and obedient, she was resigned to the course her life had taken. *What had they done to her? To both of them?*

Briggs took off his mask. "Lian, it's me. It's Briggs."

Her eyes went wide for a moment, then she cocked her head. "Briggs."

Not a question, but a statement.

"Yes, Lian. I have your father outside. We're getting out of here. All of us."

"Briggs," Lian repeated, as though reconnecting memories in her mind. "It's you."

Tanner stepped forward and knelt before her. He took her hands in his own. "It's me."

Lian looked into his eyes, then smiled tentatively. "He told me you were coming back for us."

AS WITH HER FATHER, TANNER DRAPED LIAN OVER HIS SHOULDER, then ran into the hall. Gray smoke poured from the radio-room door. One wall and part of the ceiling was aflame. He ran out the door, down the steps, and into the compound. He sprinted through the smoke, dodging bodies, until he reached the landing pad. The Hoplite was there, rotors turning at idle. Busy checking gauges, the pilot never saw him climb into the cabin. He laid Lian on the cabin floor next to her father.

"Both of you lay perfectly still," he shouted to them.

Briggs leaned out the cabin door, looking around. "Hsiao!"

Hsiao materialized out of the smoke with Tanner's pack in his hand. Briggs took it, pulled him aboard, and slid the door shut.

"What're you doing?" the pilot called. "We don't have orders to—"

Tanner drew the Makarov and pointed it at him. Careful to stay below the windshield, Briggs crouch-walked into the cockpit. He jammed the gun into the pilot's side. "Do you speak English?"

"Yes."

"Good. Listen carefully: I can fly this helicopter—not as well as you, but I could—so I don't need you. Do you understand?"

"I understand."

"Make one wrong move, and I'll shoot you dead."

"I understand."

"Good. Liftoff."

"Now?"

"Now."

SIX MINUTES AFTER THE HOPLITE DISAPPEARED OVER THE TREE-tops, Xiang's Hind landed in the middle of the compound amid a tornado of black smoke and embers. Shen slid open the side door and he and Xiang jumped to the ground. Xiang coughed and squinted his eyes against the smoke.

Xiang stared in silence at the chaos around him. All but two of the camp's buildings were in flames. Now just a charred skeleton, the garage had collapsed in on itself. Portions of the septic truck were visible through the timbers; the silver tank glowed red through the patches of soot. Members of the fire team and partially dressed guards hurried to and fro.

Xiang felt a flash of rage, but it passed almost immediately. In its place came a detached calm. It was remarkable, really. He had underestimated Tanner every step of the way. The man had wasted their time, divided their forces, disappeared and reappeared like a ghost. . . .

None of that matters now, Xiang thought. True enough, he had lost this battle, but not yet the war. It wasn't over. Tanner wasn't as smart as imagined.

Eng appeared out of the smoke. "The Hoplite's gone, sir. We tried to stop it, but. . . ."

"I know," Xiang murmured. "Lieutenant Shen!"

"Sir!"

"Send some men to Soong's cell."

"Yes, sir." Two minutes later Xiang got the answer he expected: "He's gone," Shen reported.

Xiang nodded.

Shen stared at him. "Sir?"

"What?"

"Your orders?"

Xiang pulled himself erect. "Yes. I assume the Hind has the RFDF unit?" he asked, referring to Radio Frequency Direction Finder.

"Uh . . . yes, sir—for locating search-and-rescue beacons."

"That'll do," Xiang said. "Gather your platoon. We're going on a hunting trip."

72

Chinese-Russian Border

AS TANNER AND HIS PARTY WERE LIFTING OFF FROM THE CAMP, nine hundred miles to their northwest the first wave of Chinese fighters—three regiments of nine squadrons apiece for a total of 120 aircraft—approached the border in stacked formation, layered from twenty-five thousand to thirty-five thousand feet in the darkened night sky to confuse Russian ground-radar stations.

Once over the border, the wave split, the uppermost layer of the more advanced J-10 and J-12 interceptors breaking off into individual flights of four planes and climbing to their maximum ceiling, where they again split, half the flights to the east, the other to the west, all still pushing northward, all under the guidance of the Chinese AWACs loitering in the relative safety of Chinese airspace.

Below them, the lowermost layer of aging J-5 and J-6 fighters—essentially Chinese versions of Russian MiG-17s and 19s—went to full throttle and closed with the Russian's ready-alert defending force, an enhanced regiment of SU-27 Flankers and MiG-21 Fishbeds.

Mindful of the Chinese interceptors orbiting high above, the Russian ground and air radar stations immediately realized the dilemma. While more than a match for the Chinese J-5s and 6s, the defenders were still outnumbered two to one and had no choice but to devote their attention to the leading edge of attackers, all the while knowing a full regiment of AWACS-guided J-10s and 12s hovered twenty thousand feet above, waiting to swoop into the fray.

Within minutes of the first missile exchange, the Russian defenders had cut the Chinese's first wave by more than half. But the cost was high, as the Russian regiment had lost ten of its thirty-six planes, six Fishbeds and four Flankers.

At a prearranged signal, the few remaining aged Chinese fighters turned south and headed for home, drawing a portion of the defenders into a game of pursuit. Seeing this, the Chinese AWACS ordered the J-10s and J-12s into the fray.

Sweeping in from above in a pincer movement, the interceptors slashed into the now-spent defenders. Plane to plane, the Russian Flankers and Fishbeds are well matched against their attackers, but the odds had not only reversed, but worsened. For every Russian fighter there were three Chinese.

One by one the defenders were blotted from the sky. Streams of tracer shells crisscrossed the darkness accompanied by blooms of orange. Crippled and flaming planes tumbled toward earth.

Out of fuel, and ammunition, and luck, the remaining Russian fighters broke off and turned north. Of the thirty-six that had lifted off forty minutes before, only eight survived.

NMCC

"Is this a real-time image?" David Lahey asked, nodding to the large view screen.

"Yes, sir," replied Cathermeier. "Keyhole satellite."

Along with the rest of the CAC's personnel, Lahey, Dutcher, and Mason stared, dumbfounded, at the screen. Though the image was rendered in mostly black, here and there they could see the twinkling of city lights far below—Chita, Kungara, Hailor. Above them blooms of orange and yellow dotted the sky.

"My God," Dutcher murmured.

Lahey said, "General, each one of those is an explosion—a plane?"

"Yes, sir. We'll have a better idea within the hour, but at least initially it looks like a full division of Chinese fighters crossed the border north of the Hingann Mountains right about . . . here—a fifty-mile stretch between Igrashino and Dsahlinda.

"Again, once we're able to firm up the BDA—battle damage assessment—we'll have better figures, but we've got to give this round to the Chinese. The Federation could only concentrate a regiment in that area, so the odds were against them from the start. Round two is still a toss-up."

"Round two?" Lahey asked. "Are you telling me this isn't over?"

"Not even close. The Chinese will keep coming, and if they use the same strategy—"

"Which is?"

"They swarmed the Russians with older fighters; they're no real match for their interceptors, but the Russians can't ignore them either."

"So while they're busy with the PLA's second-string planes, the starting team waits and watches for its chance to swoop in."

"Exactly. It's gonna cost the Chinese a lot of planes and pilots, but at last count the Beijing and Shenyang military regions had about fifteen hundred older MiGs and Sukhoi fighters at their disposal."

Dick Mason said, "Cannon fodder."

"Yep. A lot of them are nearly obsolete, but in quantity—in a close-in dogfight—they're still dangerous. You get enough ants together, they can take down an elephant."

"How long can the Chinese keep it up?" Lahey asked.

"It depends on how much they're willing to sacrifice. By the numbers, the Chinese can pour more planes more quickly into the area than can the Russians. The problem is, if the Russians decide to wait until they've gathered the planes they need to make it a real battle, the Chinese will have tactical air superiority—in other words, to gain time the Russians might have to surrender some sky for a while."

"Which will make it twice as hard to retake once they're ready," Dutcher added.

"Right. On the other hand, if the Russians choose to meet every wave the Chinese send across the border, their numbers will slowly but surely get whittled down."

David Lahey stared at the screen. Finally he said, "What can we do to help?"

"Right now, nothing. The only possible asset we have in the area is the battle group."

"How many planes?"

"*Stennis* could put eighty or ninety in the air. But, sir, there are several problems with that idea. One, unless the Russian surface group breaks off, we're going to find ourselves in a major sea battle in a matter of hours; if we strip the group of its planes. . . ."

"I understand. What are the other problems?"

"Distance. Even if the Russians agreed, it's still a thousand miles from the coast to the battle area. Our planes would need refueling points, alternate airfields, ground control passovers—"

"And if we had all that?" Lahey pressed.

"That's a mighty big 'if,' sir."

"Humor me. Could we make a difference?"

Cathermeier thought for a moment then nodded. "Yes, it would make a difference. The Tomcats and Hornets aboard *Stennis* are more than a match for anything the Chinese can put in the air."

Lahey considered this for a few moments. He looked to Dutcher and Mason. "Thoughts?"

"Tough sell," Dutcher replied. "Especially given Bulganin's reaction to your first call. Still, it's worth a try. The alternative is much worse."

"Dick?"

Mason nodded. "I agree. Bulganin's about as unpredictable as a shark, but he's got some good people around him. If he listens to them. . . . maybe."

Lahey nodded and turned to Cathermeier. "General, let's try this again. Get President Bulganin on the phone."

They settled around the head of the Tank's conference table and waited in nervous silence for two minutes before the intercom buzzed: "General, we're linked with Moscow—line three."

Lahey punched the button for speakerphone. "President Bulganin, this is Vice President Lahey, can you hear me?"

"Yes, yes, I hear you," Bulganin growled. "What do you want? As I'm sure you're aware, my country is under attack. Speak quickly, Lahey."

"Mr. President, I have reason to believe both our countries are being drawn into a conflict neither of us wants. I will be glad to outline my reasons for believing that, but right now it's important we get control of this situation before it's beyond control."

"What situation do you mean, Lahey? Your battle group looming off our coast, the attack on Nakhodka, or your ally's incursion into our airspace? Which is it?"

"Mr. President, despite appearances, I promise you we are not working in conjunction with the People's Republic of China. Circumstances have been manipulated to implicate my country—"

"Oh, I see," Bulganin replied. "You are claiming your country is the victim here? You have stones, I'll say that much, Lahey. While our brave pilots are fighting and dying at the border, you're crying about the wrong done to you! How dare you!"

"No, sir, you've misunderstood. Your country has been attacked without provocation; I fully recognize that. All I'm asking is that we explore a joint solution to—"

"Withdraw your battle group immediately and I may consider your words."

"As I said, the proximity of your surface group makes withdrawal difficult. If you will—"

"Order our ships to retreat?" Bulganin finished. "And give you a chance to attack? I think not! You have my conditions, Lahey. Order your aircraft carrier to withdraw immediately, or it will be attacked! If you fail to give the order it will only prove what I already know: You and those yellow devils are together in this!"

"Mr. President—"

"Will you give the order or not?"

"Yes, I will give the order, but you must first divert your surface group so my carrier will have room to maneuver—"

"To launch an attack!" Bulganin countered.

"No!" Lahey cried. "Mr. President, you have to listen to me—"

"No, we are done talking, Lahey. I won't let you distract me again!"

The phone went dead.

Lahey stared at the buzzing phone, then leaned back and sighed. "Why won't he listen?"

"He doesn't sound stable," Dutcher said. "His thought process was convoluted . . . disjointed."

Mason nodded. "I agree. I fear he's bought into the ruse."

"General, how long before our ships and the Russian surface group is engaged?"

"Two hours at most," said Cathermeier. "I can order them north, but the less water they have to maneuver in, the less able they'll be to defend themselves. It's either that, or we hold our ground and mix it up with them, or try to fight our way through their line."

"Not much of a choice," Lahey said. "Either way, we get bloody."

Moscow

"It's a another trick!" Bulganin shouted. "Why can't you see that?"

Marshal Beskrovny shook his head. "Sir, I disagree. I think we should listen to his proposal. It costs us nothing. If he's telling the truth, it certainly sheds a different light on the situation."

"You're blind! Fedorin, certainly you see my point! Tell him!"

The SVR director spread his hands. "With respect, Mr. President, I have to agree with the marshal. There may be some credence to what Lahey said. Consider their carrier group: They're more than a match for our surface group, yet they haven't attacked. They continue to withdraw north—"

"They're buying time so the Chinese can continue with their air attacks—"

"I don't think so. As the carriers withdraw north, their effectiveness dwindles. The closer they let our ships get, the better our chances. They know this, yet they haven't attacked. That, I think, is significant."

Nochenko spoke up. "I agree, Mr. President—Vladimir. Please think! Are the Americans truly our enemy in this? If there's even a chance—"

Bulganin smashed his fist into the desktop. "There is no chance! *No chance!* My God, I'm surrounded by blind men! The Motherland is under attack from all sides and no one sees it but me!" Bulganin spun toward Beskrovny. "General, how many planes did we lose in the air engagement?"

"Twenty-eight."

"Twenty-eight planes and twenty-eight pilots—gone! And what are the Chinese up to now?"

"There are indications another sortie will be launching in a few hours."

"Exactly!" Bulganin said. "There you have it: Another attack, more brave pilots dead. I won't have it! We're going to put a stop to this, right now." Bulganin walked to the conference table and leaned over the map. "Show me where their planes are coming from, General."

Beskrovny pointed to several spots on the map. "Here—the foothills of the Hingann mountain range. They have air bases at Gulian, Changying, Pangu, and Ershizhan."

"Four air bases."

"Yes, sir."

"How far from our border?"

"The closest is forty kilometers; the farthest, seventy."

"Excellent!" Bulganin replied. "Well within range."

Fedorin said, "Of what, Mr. President?"

"An air strike of our own, of course. Four strike groups, four weapons. General, I'll leave the details to you, but I imagine air-launched cruise missiles are the best approach. Only one has to get through, after all. Our fighters can slip into their airspace, launch the missiles, then slip out again."

"What are you talking about?" Ivan Nochenko asked.

"Ivan, haven't you been paying attention? These four air bases are the crux of the problem. As long as they're allowed to operate, the attacks will keep coming. Once they're gone, the Chinese attack will be toothless. We'll have the upper hand."

"And how do you plan to do this?"

"Very simple. Four bases, four tactical nuclear warheads. We'll blot them off the map."

73

Chono Dam

THE SIGNAL THE CHINESE COMMANDOS HAD BEEN AWAITING came shortly after dawn.

Cahil and Skeldon were sitting on their log, putting the finishing touches on the sixth and final charge when the team's radioman leapt up and began chattering excitedly. The rest of the paratroopers crowded around as the colonel received the report. After a brief celebration of backslapping and smiling, the colonel ordered them back to their tasks. He walked over to Cahil and Skeldon.

"Done?" he said.

"Yes," Bear replied.

The colonel called two paratroopers over, who picked up the charge and carried it to where the others lay. "We leave in twenty minutes," he told them. "Be ready."

With that, the colonel turned on his heel and began barking orders. Two paratroopers stood up. One of them hoisted a charge over one shoulder, a roll of detonation cord over the other, while the second man shouldered the remaining two charges. They filed out of the camp and down the trail in the direction of the mine.

"What the hell is this?" Cahil whispered to Skeldon.

"Don't know."

Much of their plan depended on them moving as a group to the mine and then setting the charges. The night before, Skeldon had managed to steal a chemical detonator from one of the crates, providing them the final piece for their own charge—the six-ounce chunk of C4 they'd culled in bits and pieces from the main charges. Cahil could feel the disk of plastique pressing against the skin of his belly. He resisted the impulse to finger the detonator in his pocket.

As the three commandos disappeared down the trail, he felt his heart sink. *Stupid, Bear. Never assume.* With three of the charges already set and the commando team split, would they be able to reach the wall in time?

"That's a problem."

"Big problem," Skeldon agreed. "You think they'll come back?"

"I doubt it. That radio call means they're on a deadline now."

Which meant that whatever else the Chinese had planned for Siberia was probably under way. *What about Briggs?* Cahil wondered. As had been the case the year before during the Beirut operation, he had no way of knowing what was happening to his friend. The feeling of helplessness tore at his heart. Was Briggs alive, dead, or a prisoner of the *Guoanbu*?

He'll make it, Bear told himself. *And so will you.* There was just one more hurdle to cross: take on six heavily armed commandos, stop the dam's destruction, then get out of the mine alive and find a Russian who wouldn't shoot him on sight. *Simple.*

"By the time we get there," Cahil told Skeldon, "the first three charges will be primed."

"What do you want to do?"

"Stick to our plan and pray."

Nakhodka-Vostochny

As Cahil and Skeldon were readying themselves for their do-or-die gambit, 1500 miles to their southeast, Sconi Bob Jurens and his SEAL team were preparing to make their own move.

Two hours before dawn, still hidden in their blind above the Federation Army roadblock, Jurens decided it was time to move. Throughout the night, reinforcement troops had been pouring into the area. In the space of an hour, he'd watched five trucks pass through the roadblock, each one loaded with a squad of soldiers. In the distance, he could hear voices calling to one another in Russian. Twice, foot patrols passed so close they'd heard the hiss of radio static and the crunch of footfalls.

Sooner or later a patrol would stumble upon their position and the mission would in an instant turn into a full-fledged firefight with several hundred Federation soldiers. Given such an inevitability, Jurens decided he'd rather join the battle on his terms. If they had any chance of escaping this, it would be by fire-and-maneuver tactics. Hit hard and disappear like ghosts.

He scanned the terrain through his Night Owls. Cape Kamensky was rugged and hilly, dotted with boulders, scrub pines, and slopes of loose slate and gravel. The roads wound around and up the peninsula like stripes on a barber pole, finally ending at the junction below them. To their southeast he could make out the small fishing pier Smitty had found on his reconnoiter the previous day. Jurens counted eight boats: six fishing trawlers and two skiffs.

Watching them roll with the swells, Sconi felt that old familiar draw: Water was safety; water was cover. Most of all, water was their way home.

He lowered his binoculars and wriggled back into the blind. Smitty, Zee, and Dickie gathered around him. Sunil Dhar sat a few feet away, arms wrapped around his knees.

Jurens pulled out his map and clicked on his hooded penlight. "Smitty, that fishing pier—what d'you think? Three miles?"

"Give or take."

Jurens nodded. "That's where we're headed. We'll move fast and straight. Unless we have no choice, we'll bypass any patrols."

"And if we can't?" Dickie asked.

"Then we take them out. Shoot-and-scoot; we can't give them time to get coordinated." With only four of them, any patrol they might encounter would likely have them outnumbered. "Either way, we need to reach the pier, snag a boat, and be on the water while it's still dark. If we don't make it into international waters before daylight, we've got problems. Any questions?"

There were none.

Jurens turned to Dhar. "Nobody's gonna stop you if you run. I assume you'd rather go with us than take your chances with the Russians?"

Dhar nodded vigorously.

"Then keep up. We'll try to protect you, but if you fall behind, you're on your own."

"I understand."

Jurens folded up his map. "Zee, get on the Satcom and call home; give them our plan, tell them we're on the move."

USS *Columbia*

"Conn, Engineering."

Archie Kinsock keyed the squawk box. "Go ahead, Chief."

"We're all set down here, Skipper. Just finished the last diagnostic check on the maneuvering thrusters. Everything reads green. You give the word, and we'll have them powered up in thirty seconds."

"Good. How about our leaks?"

"Under control."

"And if I need to put a little depth under us?"

"I've got men stationed at each location; we'll do our best to stay on top of them."

"Conn, aye. Stand by for my order."

Kinsock and MacGregor leaned over the chart table. Their position beside the continental shelf was circled in red; south of them, also marked in red pen, was the International Waters boundary.

"Fifteen miles," Kinsock muttered.

"Long way at four knots," MacGregor replied. "Even if we catch a current, we're looking at four hours. A lot of time to attract attention."

"Well, jeez, aren't you a ray of sunshine," Kinsock said with a grin.

"I try my darndest."

"We'll take our time. As long as we can get moving and stay at zero bubble, we can drift our way out. Four hours or four days, it's better than sitting here waiting for the other shoe to drop."

Saying the words, Kinsock felt another pang of guilt. The idea of leaving behind Jurens and his team grated on him, but his first responsibility was to *Columbia* and her crew. He had no doubt that given a choice his men would vote to try and rescue the SEALs, but the bird on Kinsock's collar didn't allow him the luxury of risking a hundred men to rescue four.

Pete Cantor, one of Kinsock's first COs, had been fond of telling his junior officers that "the obligations of command and the comfort of personal conscience are often at odds." It was, Archie thought now, a fancy way of saying, "You don't have to like it; you just have to do it."

As if reading his mind, MacGregor said, "I hope to God they're okay."

"Amen," Kinsock murmured. "Okay, let's get to it." Kinsock reached up and keyed the squawk box. "Sonar, Conn."

"Sonar, aye."

"How're we looking, Chief?"

"Five surface contacts on passive: The two hospital ships that came into port last night haven't moved from their anchorages. As for the other three, I make them a Krivak and two Osa patrol boats, but they're a good twelve miles to our northeast. As long as they stay there, we should be okay."

"Any subs in the area?"

"Not for the last four hours, but I wouldn't swear on anything."

Kinsock understood. Simply by the nature of its propulsion and engineering systems, a surface ship twelve miles away was easier to detect than a sub lurking a mile away. "What're the maneuvering thrusters going to do to your ears?"

"We'll be deaf while they're running. If you can shut them down occasionally—"

"That's my plan."

"Then we'll keep listening."

"Conn, aye."

Kinsock grabbed the handset and switched to the shipwide 1MC. "All hands to general quarters. We're going to make our move, gentlemen. It's time to head for home."

74

China

Hoping to pull off one last bit of illusion, Tanner ordered the pilot to climb to two thousand feet and head southeast toward Mudanjiang, the last major city before the Russian border and Vladivostok. The Russian port was, he thought, the most logical destination for someone trying to flee China in a hurry.

"We can't outrun the Hind," the pilot said. "They've got forty knots of airspeed on us."

"I know," Tanner said. Despite that, he felt light, almost buoyant, and it took him a moment before he realized why: He was alive—*they* were alive, and with each passing minute their chances of staying that way improved. Whether they would make good their escape was another matter, but this certainly was better than being hunted like an animal through the wilds of Heilongjiang Province.

"Why don't you just give up?" the pilot asked. "If you know you can't make it—"

"I'm a cockeyed optimist," Tanner said. "Keep flying."

Once sure they were headed in the right direction, he called Hsiao to the cockpit to watch over the pilot, then went back into the cabin. Tears streaming down his face, Han Soong sat on the floor with his daughter wrapped in his arms.

He reached out a hand to Tanner. "Thank you, Briggs. Words can't describe my gratitude."

Briggs gripped his shoulder. "No need, old friend. I'm just sorry it took me this long to get here. Lian, are you okay?"

She raised her head from her father's chest and nodded. "I can't believe this is real. Are we really free?"

"Almost, but not quite."

"How long?"

"With a little luck, two hours."

With a lot of luck, Briggs thought.

ONCE THEY WERE FIFTY MILES FROM THE CAMP, TANNER REturned to the cockpit. "How're your night-flying skills?" he asked the pilot.

"I'm fully qualified."

"Night vision?"

"I have a headset, but. . . ."

"But it's scary as hell."

"Yes."

"Sorry, but you're gonna have to get used to it. Put them on, then shut off your navigation lights and descend to thirty feet."

"Thirty feet!"

Tanner nodded. "Don't trim any trees."

Once the pilot had donned his headset and began his descent, Tanner reached over to the IFF—Identification Friend or Foe—unit on the console and flipped the power off.

"What're you doing?" the pilot cried. "They'll shoot us down."

"That's a very real possibility," Tanner said.

Regardless of nationality, all military aircraft carry some type of IFF unit designed to transmit a coded ID signal when interrogated by friendly units. By shutting down the unit, Tanner had not only turned them into an unidentified aircraft eligible for attack, but he'd made them virtually invisible to commercial airport radars that track by IFF tag rather than radar return. By ordering the pilot to hug the earth, he was hoping to also slip beneath the radar coverage of nearby military bases and get lost in the ground clutter.

If Tanner had any luck left at all, Xiang would use the Hoplite's last known IFF position and course as the starting point for his search.

"Thirty feet," the pilot called. "It's too low . . . I can't keep this up."

"What's your speed?"

"One-fifty."

Tanner took a moment to study the map and make a few rough calculations. "Cut back to one-twenty and turn northeast . . . make it course zero-three-five. Once you find the Songhua River, turn north. Stick to it and stay low."

DELAYED BY A REFUELING STOP AT AN AIRSTRIP OUTSIDE FANGzheng, Xiang's Hind was thirty miles to Tanner's southwest, but the Hind's greater airspeed was steadily cutting the gap. In the cabin under the glow of red lights, Shen and his platoon of twenty-four paratroopers were checking their weapons.

"Director Xiang?" the pilot called.

Xiang knelt in the cockpit door. "You have the beacon?"

"No, sir, nothing yet. We just got word from Fangzheng Control. They have an IFF tag matching the Hoplite. It's on our zero-seven-one, about thirty miles away."

"Course and speed?"

"One-six-zero, speed one hundred fifty knots—almost redline for a Hoplite."

"He's running. What's in that direction?"

"Changting, Mudanjiang, then the border."

"Vladivostok?"

"Yes, sir."

Nearest major civilization, Xiang thought. It made sense. "How long before we intercept?"

"Twenty minutes."

TEN MINUTES LATER: "DIRECTOR XIANG, WE'VE GOT A PROBLEM."

"What?"

"Fangzheng reports the Hoplite stopped squawking and dropped off the radar."

"Which means?"

"It means he's gambling," the pilot replied, then explained Tanner's gambit. "If the pilot's any good, he might be able to pull it off."

"And if he doesn't?"

"They'll either crash or pop up on radar."

"Keep heading toward their last known position. What are the biggest commercial radars in the region?"

"Tieli, Jiamusi, and Hegang."

"Can they track by return?"

"Yes."

"Contact them and have them look for a target without IFF."

"Yes, sir."

Xiang walked back into the cabin and sat down. *Turn on the beacon, damn you. . . .*

• • •

To his credit, the pilot had nerve, Tanner decided.
Hands white around the collective and cyclic controls, sweat rolling down his neck, the pilot kept the Hoplite at near wave-top height over the Songhua River, winding northeast up the valley, dodging trees and slipping past cliff faces.

The lights of early morning fishing boats slipped beneath the windscreen, appearing and disappearing in the same second. On either bank of the Songhua, Tanner could see the twinkling of distant lights and he tried to match them against the towns on the map: Qinghe, Hongkeli, Yong'an. . . .

Occasionally the Hoplite's ESM panel would chirp, indicating they'd been painted by a random radar wave, and Tanner would wait, breath held, hoping against hope the tone didn't change to a steady "lock on" pulse.

A few miles north of Jaimusi, Tanner had his head in the map when the pilot suddenly cried out.

"Oh, God!"

Tanner looked up. Before the windscreen, a massive rock spire jutted from an island in the middle of the river. The pilot banked hard. Tanner lurched against his restraints. The Hoplite's engines roared in protest, the rotors beating the sky to gain altitude. The ESM panel began chirping. At the last moment, the pilot rolled the helo nearly onto its side and the spire flashed past the windscreen.

Tanner glanced at the altimeter: 200 feet. "Dive, dive!" he ordered. "Back on the deck!"

Once they were back at treetop height, the pilot said, "Sorry, sorry. I just. . . ."

"Forget it. How's our fuel?"

"Not good. Two hundred kilometers, give or take."

Tanner eyed the ESM panel. *Had they raised any flags?* "Go to full throttle," he ordered.

Orbiting in a fuel-saving hover eighty miles south of Tan-ner, Xiang's pilot called out, "Contact! We've got contact! Jiaumsu Control reports unidentified aircraft just popped up on their radar!"

"How far away?"

"A hundred and thirty kilometers—about ninety kilometers south of the Birobijan border. They're smart; they're sticking to the river valley."

"Go after them!" Xiang ordered. "How long until they're into Birobijan airspace?"

"Twenty-five minutes."

"Can we catch them?"

The pilot paused to study his knee-board map. "Just barely. We should overtake them about twelve kilometers south of the border. Sir, if I may: Why risk it? Shuangyashan can scramble a pair of interceptors and overtake them in six minutes."

"There are no interceptors, dammit!" Xiang growled. Virtually every plane the PLAAF had was committed to the Hingaan salient. "Just keep flying; we'll get them ourselves."

A button on the cockpit console began blinking red, accompanied by a steady beeping. The pilot pressed a few buttons and read the screen. "RFDF just popped on," he said. "What's the frequency of your beacon?"

"Forty-two point five gigahertz."

"That's it." The pilot pressed more buttons. "Same course and speed as Jiamsu's bogey."

"That's them!" Xiang shouted. "We've got them!"

75

China, seventeen miles south of Birobijan, Russia

"WE'VE GOT WEATHER AHEAD!" THE PILOT CALLED OVER HIS shoulder.

Tanner walked into the cockpit. The pilot pointed to the windshield. Swirling out of the blackness, ice pellets peppered the windscreen, their rapid-fire ticks sounding like a

Geiger counter gone haywire. Even over the thump of the rotors Tanner could hear the wind howling.

"Barometer's dropping, too," the pilot said. "It's a front, all right." Suddenly the Hoplite lurched sideways. The pilot compensated and they leveled off. "Wind shear!"

"What's air temperature?"

"Two degrees centigrade."

Just above freezing, Briggs thought. "Climb to a hundred feet," he ordered.

The pilot sighed. "Finally."

"Don't thank me. When we're ten miles from the border, I want you to take it back down."

"In this weather? We're gonna die!"

"Maybe so," Tanner replied, "but at least it won't be in China."

TWELVE MILES FROM THE BORDER, RED LIGHTS BEGAN FLASHING on the ESM console. A rapid chirping filled the cockpit. From the tone, Tanner knew immediately it wasn't a standard radar warning.

"Fire control," the pilot announced. "From our six o'clock . . . he's close!"

"What kind?"

The pilot punched a few buttons. "Raduga-F. It's the Hind! He's locked onto us!"

Tanner knew the Hind was primarily an antitank gunship, but its 20 mm nose gun was equally effective against air targets. A three-second blast from the 20 mm would slash the Hoplite in half.

"He won't shoot," Briggs replied. "Not yet. He'll try to force us down first. Descend."

As the Hoplite nosed over and dove downward, Tanner turned and yelled back into the cabin. "Hsiao, get everyone strapped in. It's gonna get rough!"

The chirp of the ESM grew louder. *Getting closer,* Tanner thought. *Was he guessing right? Would Xiang shoot first, or try to force them down?*

"Fifty feet!" the pilot yelled.

"Keep going!"

Through the windscreen, Briggs could see the ice pellets had changed to snow. The flakes swept past the nose like miniature stars and for a moment he felt dizzy, as though looking into a kaleidoscope. He glanced at the pilot; he, too, was staring, transfixed, at the effect.

"Watch your gauges," Tanner said.

"Sorry . . . sorry! Twenty feet . . ."

"A few feet. . . ."

Tanner could see the earth now, a carpet of blackness below them dotted with clumps of trees and rolling hills. The ground loomed before the windshield until the Hoplite's belly seemed to be skimming the dirt. "Pull it up!"

The pilot eased back. "Ten feet! I can't do this!"

"Yes you can."

The ESM grew louder, the chirps overlapping one another.

"They're going to fire!"

"Keep going. How far to the border?"

The pilot glanced at this console. "Two miles! What about Russian SAM sites?"

"This is Birobijan. There are no SAMs," Tanner called back. *I hope.*

In the eyes of the post-Soviet government, Birobijan was not only one of the Federation's poorest oblasts, but also a disposable buffer between it and China. The chances of anything but token units being assigned to this section of the border were slim.

"You sure about that?" the pilot asked.

"Just fly. If we get across the border, we're home free."

IN THE HIND'S COCKPIT, THE PILOT SAID, "WE'VE GOT A GUN lock, sir."

"How far from the border?" Xiang asked.

"Thirty seconds. I'm firing!"

"No, I want them alive!" *You're not getting away—not this time!*

"They're almost across!"

"Then follow them," Xiang ordered. "We'll overtake them and force them to land."

"That's Russian airspace! You don't have the authority to—"

Xiang drew his pistol and let it dangle beside his leg; the pilot glanced at it. His face went pale. "Is this enough authority for you?" Xiang asked.

"You're crazy."

"And I'm also in charge. Now, follow them!"

"WE'RE CROSSING THE BORDER!" THE HOPLITE'S PILOT YELLED. "They're not breaking off!"

"What?"

Suddenly the ESM panel went silent. In its absence, the cockpit was eerily quiet. Random ice pellets ticked off the windscreen and the wind whistled through the cabin door. Beyond the windscreen the snow was thickening.

"Where are they?" the pilot said.

"Close," Tanner said. He stood up and peered through the windshield. "Turn on your landing light for a second."

The Hoplite's nose beam glowed to life, illuminating the ground below. The terrain had become more rugged: jagged mountains cut by steep river valleys, all covered by a thick layer of snow.

"Okay, turn it off—"

Out of his peripheral vision he saw a dark shape materialize out of the darkness.

"There he is," Briggs said.

The Hind pulled ahead until it was at their 2 o'clock. Its landing lights blinked twice, then twice more. The cockpit's interior light clicked on. Inside, the pilot jerked his thumb downward.

"He's signaling us to land," the pilot said.

"Keep flying."

"They're giving us a chance! Listen, maybe your government can negotiate for your—"

"My government will be lucky to find out where my body's buried." *And Soong and Lian go back to the* laogi *where they'll rot away and die.* "Keep flying."

The Hind matched their course for another thirty seconds, then abruptly banked away and disappeared into the darkness.

Ten seconds passed. Both Tanner and the pilot scanned the sky outside the windshield. In the cabin, Hsiao stood at the door window, face pressed to the glass.

Briggs called, "Anything, Hsiao?"

"No, nothing—there! Right side, right side!"

Rotors thumping, the Hind dropped out of the darkness and swooped across their nose. The pilot pulled back and banked right. "Whoa!"

"He's coming around again," Hsiao called. "Behind us! He's making another pass!"

This time the Hind came from the left and above, dropping across the windshield, so close Tanner could see the tail number.

"He's going to bump us!" the pilot shouted.

"Hsiao, do you see him?"

"Wait . . . wait. Yes! He's below us!"

"Climb!" Tanner ordered the pilot. "Fast as you can!"

The Hoplite's nose canted upward. Tanner gripped the armrests tighter. In the cabin, Lian cried out. Tanner glanced back. "Hsiao?"

"We're okay! Everybody's okay!"

"Where is he?"

"I don't know!"

Tanner stood up and stooped closer to the windshield outside. As he did, the bulbous nose of the Hind appeared out of the blackness below, matching their angle of ascent. With a sudden surge of power, the Hind shot ahead and upward, banking as it went.

"He's too close," the pilot yelled. "He's going to hit us . . . !"

The Hoplite lurched sideways as though struck by a giant hammer. A shudder tore through the fuselage and they tipped sideways, then back upright. A light began flickering on the console; then two more, followed by a buzzing.

"What is it?" Tanner said.

"Oil pressure's dropping! The temperature on the number two engine is redline!"

Another light; more buzzing. "Fire warning!" the pilot shouted. "We're losing altitude!"

Tanner turned around: "Hsiao?"

"I'm looking! Yes, I see it . . . there are flames coming out of the stack."

"We're finished," the pilot said. "We're going down."

A jagged valley appeared before them. Steep-walled, forested cliffs swallowed the Hoplite. Through the darkness and swirling snow, Tanner glimpsed a clearing.

"There," he said, pointing. "An open spot!"

"I see it! I see it!"

Ten feet from the ground, a wind gust hit them broadside and pushed them toward the cliff face. The pilot compensated and banked the Hoplite onto its side. The ground rushed toward the windscreen. "I'm losing it!"

"Pull up!"

In the final seconds, Tanner turned in his seat and shouted, "Hold on!"

One of Hoplite's rotor blades struck the ground and they began tumbling.

76

NMCC

"GENERAL, WE'VE GOT NEW SATELLITE IMAGES COMING UP," THE CAC duty officer called.

"Put them on the big screen," Cathermeier ordered. Eight black-and-white images, each two feet square, appeared on the monitor. "What are we looking at, Commander?"

"Two pictures each of four air bases just north of the Hinggan Mountains," she answered. "Gulian, Changying,

Pangu, and Ershizhan. We're reasonably sure these are the primary launch points for the Chinese sorties."

"Good God, look at that," Mason murmured.

In each photo the tarmacs were covered with lines of black dots.

Each dot a plane, Dutcher thought. "Looks bigger than the last sortie."

"Initial estimate puts the combined total at five regiments—two hundred aircraft."

"Composition?" asked Lahey.

"Almost identical. MiG Seventeens, Nineteens and some a mix of older Sukhois."

"More cannon fodder," Mason said.

Lahey asked, "Commander, any estimate of how long before they liftoff?"

She cocked her head, thinking. "Using their first sortie as a guide . . . four hours, give or take."

"Makes sense," Cathermeier said. "Dawn attack."

"Can the Russians handle it?" Mason asked.

"They'll try, and the Chinese will lose a lot of planes, but the PLAAF has the numbers on its side. The Russians have no other choice but to play their game. If they split their force and go after the high-orbiting J-tens and -twelves, they'll get overwhelmed by the front wave."

"Lose-lose," Lahey said.

"Exactly. Now, once they can throw some MiGs into the fight that have stand-off missile capability, their chances improve. Problem is, will they come soon enough, and in enough numbers?"

"Stand-off missile capability," Lahey repeated. "Like our Tomcats and Hornets?"

"Yes, sir."

Lahey thought for a moment, then sighed. "Though I don't hold out much hope, I've got to try to reason with Bulganin again. Together, if we can somehow blunt this next Chinese sortie. . . ."

"Its unlikely he'll even entertain the idea," Dutcher said. "He's made up his mind: We're the enemy."

"I have to try."

"It's worth a shot," Mason agreed. "But even if he agrees, it doesn't solve our larger problem: The Chinese aren't going to stop. For argument's sake, let's say we repel this next wave. . . . What about the one after that, and the next? The Chinese have everything riding on this; they've gotta have more up their sleeve than an air campaign."

Cathermeier nodded. "It's the old maxim: Until you take the soil you haven't won the war."

"Tanks and infantry," Lahey murmured.

"Yep. And once that starts, it's going to make these air skirmishes look like a snowball fight."

Moscow

Ivan Nochenko stared out his office window at the night-lights of Moscow and beyond. Light now swirled against the glass like moths fluttering to a light.

It's very simple. . . . We'll blot them off the map. . . .

"I did this," Nochenko muttered. He felt drugged; everything around him seemed hazy, as though time was moving erratically around him. "This is my doing."

After Bulganin's cruise-missile proclamation, they'd stood frozen in place, staring at him.

To Nochenko's initial surprise, neither Fedorin or Beskrovny put up any argument, and in that moment he knew they'd turned a corner. Lost in his world of paranoid delusions, Vladimir Bulganin was about to start a nuclear war. The time for talking was over.

After giving the order and seeing there was no dissent, Bulganin had been buoyant, joking and slapping them on the back, chillingly oblivious of what he'd just done.

Once dismissed, Nochenko, Fedorin, and Beskrovny returned to Nochenko's office. He dropped wearily into his chair and stared, slump shouldered, at his desk blotter.

"The man's insane," Sergei Fedorin murmured. "He's going to kill us all."

Beskrovny said, "The only question left is how it will happen. The Chinese will respond in kind—that much is certain—but will it be against tactical targets or population centers?"

"What does it matter? Millions are going to die. Whether it's today or spread out over a few weeks, what does it matter?"

Beskrovny nodded. "You're right, of course. If I refuse to carry out his plan, he'll simply have me arrested and take direct command. Some idiot colonel in Kungara or Urasha will get the order, snap off a goddamned salute, and launch the strike."

"Then what do we do?" Fedorin said. "We're running out of time."

Nochenko lifted his gaze from his desk and said, "I'll take care of it."

"What?" Beskrovny said. "How? He doesn't listen to a word we say. What makes you think you'll have any more luck if you try again?"

"I'll take care of it," Nochenko repeated. "I understand Vladimir. We simply haven't been taking the right tack with him." Seeing the doubt written on their faces, Nochenko forced a confident smile. "Gentlemen, trust me. I'll take care of it. In the meantime, Victor, go through the motions of ordering the strike."

"What?" Beskrovny cried.

"If he sees you're dragging your feet, he'll do just as you said and replace you. Make the preparations, but don't order the release of the warheads. Victor, please, do as I ask. I'll take care of everything."

"How, exactly?" Fedorin said.

"That's not your worry. I'm asking for your trust. Russia is going to need men like you in the coming days. This crisis will pass and when it does, your expertise will be instrumental in repairing the damage that's already been done. So, I'm asking you, can I count on you?"

Beskrovny and Fedorin exchanged confused glances, then nodded.

• • •

WHO IS WORSE? **NOCHENKO WONDERED, STARING IN THE BLACK**ness. *A paranoid schizophrenic with delusions of Stalinhood, or a blind, ego-driven old fool? His is a sickness of the mind; mine a sickness of conceit. Without me, he wouldn't be here. Without me, the world wouldn't be teetering at the brink of a nuclear war.*

Every step of the way he'd ignored Bulganin's rantings, his vicious mood swings, his Cold-War mentality. . . . Worse still, after the Irkutsk Massacre, when his conscience had finally risen up and refused to be silent, he'd tricked and cajoled and deceived himself back into ignorance.

I've done this, Nochenko thought again. *This is my responsibility.*

AT FOUR A.M., BULGANIN RECALLED THE THREE OF THEM TO HIS office.

Nochenko found his president pacing near the window, occasionally peeking out the curtains and muttering to himself. As usual, Pytor stood against the wall behind Bulganin's desk, eyes scanning the room. Another two guardians stood on either side of the door, hands clasped behind their backs.

"Ivan!" Bulganin shouted. "Where are. . . . There they are. Good, gentlemen, come in."

Beskrovny and Fedorin walked in and stopped in front of Bulganin's desk.

"Marshal, how go the preparations for our strike?"

"Everything is proceeding, sir. The strike will lift off from Urasha in eighty minutes."

"Excellent!" Bulganin boomed, clasping his hands in excitement. "Little devils are going to find it difficult to carry on their little scheme once those air bases are gone, eh Marshal?"

"Yes, sir," Beskrovny replied with a stiff nod, then a glance at Nochenko.

Bulganin's intercom buzzed. "Mr. President, Vice President Lahey is on line three."

Bulganin threw up his hands. "Ah! What does this rube want now? All right, send it through!" When the phone rang, Bulganin pushed the speaker button. "What now, Lahey?"

"Mr. President, I have a proposal for you. I have General Cathermeier, my chairman of the Joint Chiefs here with me. Do you have someone similar there with you?"

"My defense minister, Marshal Victor Beskrovny is standing beside me. Why, Lahey, what game are you playing now?"

"No games, Mr. President. I'm going to let General Cathermeier explain my proposal. Marshal Beskrovny will be able to advise you as to its soundness."

"Get on with it."

"President Bulganin, this is General Cathermeier. Our satellite intelligence shows activity at four Chinese air bases north of the Hinggan Mountains. We believe they're preparing to launch another air attack against you."

"Yes, yes, we're aware of that," Bulganin barked. "Make your point."

"Our proposal is this: With your permission and with the support of your refueling facilities, we are prepared to dispatch from our carrier group a support force to aid you in defending against the next attack."

"That's nonsense," Bulganin shot back. "We will not—"

Marshal Beskrovny interrupted: "General, this is Beskrovny here. Tell me, what kind and how many aircraft are you talking about?"

"F-14s and F/A-18s. Approximately thirty aircraft."

"What percentage of the group's total aircraft does this represent?"

"Over fifty percent, sir."

"That would leave your carriers largely undefended, would it not?" Beskrovny asked.

"The group would still have the support of its surface vessels, but yes, those aircraft are critical to the group's defense."

"These Tomcats and Hornets would be equipped with stand-off missiles?"

"Yes, Marshal. Phoenix air-to-air missiles with a range of one hundred plus miles. We feel these aircraft could make a real difference in the coming fight."

Beskrovny nodded thoughtfully, then said, "General, will you excuse us for a moment?"

"Of course."

At Beskrovny's urging, Bulganin muted the phone, then said, "Surely you're not taken in by this, Marshal?"

"Sir, I think we should consider the proposal."

"Absolutely not."

"You heard the man—they would be stripping their group of almost every aircraft it has."

"And sending them, fully armed, into our airspace. As the Chinese attack us from the south, the Americans attack us from the east. They're asking us to agree to our own envelopment. Surely you can see that." Bulganin glanced at Fedorin and Nochenko. "You must see that."

Fedorin said, "Mr. President, we're not going to win this next air encounter. We haven't yet got the forces in place to do anything but stall the Chinese. These American fighters would tip the scale in our favor. We have to consider—"

"They have attacked us once already. I will not open the doors for a second strike."

"Mr. President, I may have a solution that will ease your mind. May I?"

Bulganin grumbled, but nodded.

Beskrovny unmuted the phone. "General Cathermeier, would you be willing to provide us the individual IFF codes for your aircraft so we may track them more effectively?"

"Yes, sir."

"And agree to allow them to be tracked by SAM site radars while they are crossing our airspace to the battle area?"

There was a short pause. "Yes, sir, we can do that as well."

"Thank you. One more moment, please." Beskrovny muted the phone again.

"That means nothing," Bulganin said. "They agreed too quickly to your demands. They're still playing their games—I'm sure of it."

"And I'm sure they're not," Beskrovny replied. "Mr. President, for God's sake. . . ."

Watching the exchange, Ivan Nochenko again felt the druglike haze settle over him. His vision tunneled and sounds around him seem to fade, as though he were underwater. He watched Bulganin's lips moving, his bulging wild eyes and flushed face, and realized for the first time what Beskrovny and Fedorin had themselves been witnessing: a ranting madman.

In that same moment Nochenko felt what he could only describe as a sad affection for Vladimir Bulganin. *My golem,* he thought. Had he not interfered, would Bulganin have simply lived and died a shoe-factory foreman in Omsk, bothering no one but those forced to listen to his silly diatribes? *I did this. My responsibility . . . mine and no one else's.*

Caught up in the argument, no one saw Nochenko leave. The two guardians at the door stared at him as he stepped out, but they said nothing. Mind blank, moving like an automaton, Nochenko walked down the hall to his office, opened the door and walked inside. He strode to his desk. He bent over and opened the bottom drawer.

The gun, a 9mm Makarov semiautomatic, was exactly where he'd left it the night before. He inserted the magazine, cycled the slide, and flicked off the safety. He slid the gun into his belt beside his hip, then smoothed his suit jacket and headed for the door.

". . . NO!" BULGANIN WAS SAYING WHEN NOCHENKO STEPPED back into the office. "We don't need their help, and we certainly don't need their trickery. You may be fooled by them, Marshal, but I am not so gullible. Ivan, there you are. Where did you go off to? As I was saying, General, we're—"

I created him. . . . Beskrovny and Fedorin will do their duty. Now it's time to do yours. . . .

Nochenko strode forward, eyes fixed on Bulganin. *Must get close . . . must be sure . . .*

"—done arguing about this! I've made my decision. The attack will continue—"

Bulganin picked up the phone: "General Cathermeier, your offer is declined. If your aircraft approach our coast, they will be shot down. As for your ships—"

Bulganin glanced up, saw Nochenko striding toward him.

Do your duty. . . .

"Ivan, what in the world is wrong with you?"

Nochenko reached into his belt, drew the Makarov, raised it. Out of the corner of his eye, he saw Pyotr moving, reaching into his own coat, his gun coming clear and turning toward him. . . .

"Gun! Mr. President, get down . . . !"

Still clutching the phone, Bulganin cocked his head. "What is this, Ivan? Why—"

"Mr. President, *move*!"

Too late, Nochenko thought in the final seconds.

He raised his gun and began pulling the trigger.

INSIDE THE NMCC'S CONFERENCE ROOM, THE SOUND OF GUNFIRE burst from the speakerphone. Lahey jumped to his feet. "What the hell is that? President Bulganin! What's going on?"

There was a moment of silence, then three more shots. Silence again. In the background, a moan, followed by confused shouting and the sound of footsteps.

"Hello? Is anyone there?" Lahey called. "Can anyone hear me?"

FROM A RANGE OF FIVE FEET, NOCHENKO HAD FIRED FOUR ROUNDS into the center of Vladimir Bulganin's chest before Pyotr got off his first shot. The bullet tore into Nochenko's side below his nipple, the second into his neck just above his collarbone. As he fell, he turned the gun on Pyotr and fired three more shots. Two missed completely, but the third found its mark, striking Pyotr in the center of the forehead.

Having dropped to the ground at the first shot, Beskrovny and Fedorin now raised their heads and looked around. Guns drawn, a dozen guardians had flooded the room. Bulganin lay on his back on the carpet, a pool of blood spreading beneath him like a pair of black wings.

From the phone, a voice: "Anyone hear me? President Bulganin . . . Marshal Beskrovny. . . ."

Fedorin was the first to regain his composure. "Victor, talk to them. Take charge. Do what needs to be done. I'll take care of this," Fedorin said. "Hurry, Victor, time is short!"

Stepping over Nochenko's body, Beskrovny grabbed the phone receiver. "I am here, Mr. Lahey," Beskrovny said, panting. "There's been an . . . incident here."

"What's happened?"

"President Bulganin and his chief bodyguard are dead. They've been shot."

"By whom?"

"One of his advisors—Ivan Nochenko. He's dead as well."

"Are you injured, Marshal?"

"No."

"Who's there with you?"

"Sergei Fedorin. Is your General Cathermeier still with you, Mr. Vice President?"

"I'm here," Cathermeier answered.

"Until things get sorted out here, it seems I'm in charge. General, does your offer still stand?"

"It does."

"Then on behalf of my country, I accept. When we're done here, I'll alert my district commanders. General Chonyesky in Vladivostok will make the necessary arrangements; he'll contact you with the necessary radio frequencies."

"Good, Marshal. Your ships are still steaming toward our group, however. If you can divert them so our carrier can maneuver—"

"I'll do better than that, General. I'm ordering my ships south. If the Chinese want to reach our coast, they're going to have to fight their way through."

"Let's hope it doesn't come to that."

Another voice came on the line: "Marshal Beskrovny, this is Dick Mason of the CIA."

"Yes, Mr. Mason."

"We feel that these air sorties are just the spearhead of the Chinese attack, but we've seen no movement from PLA ground units. Mechanized infantry, tanks . . . all of it is sitting still."

"That has puzzled us as well. They must have a . . . what's the phrase? A trump card?"

"Exactly right. I suggest we put our heads together and figure out exactly what that is before the Chinese play it."

77

Birobijan, Russia

TANNER AWOKE TO THE FEELING OF ICY WETNESS CREEPING OVER his scalp.

He forced open his eyes, blinking until his vision focused. For several dizzying seconds he couldn't remember where he was. *The Hoplite . . . we crashed.* The cabin seemed to be sitting upright and, aside from a floor-to-ceiling crack in the fuselage, seemed mostly intact. Faint moonlight and puffs of snow filtered through the crack.

Tanner reached up and touched his scalp. Half expecting to see blood, he was surprised to find nothing on his fingertips. He pushed himself upright. The cabin floor was covered in two inches of icy water. Lying about the cabin were Hsiao, Soong, and Lian. Hsiao groaned and rolled onto his side.

"Hsiao," Tanner called. "Hsaio, can you hear me?"

Hsiao's eyelids fluttered open. "Briggs. . . ."

"Are you hurt?"

"No, I don't think so. . . ." Hsiao sat up. "I'm wet . . . why—"

"I don't know." Briggs looked around until he spotted his backpack. As he crawled toward it, the cabin floor rocked under his weight, as though it were resting on a fulcrum. He opened the pack, pulled out a flashlight, and clicked it on. "Help me check Han and Lian."

They crawled over to them and after a few minutes of coaxing, both of them started coming around. Lian had a large bruise on her cheek and two of her fingers appeared to be broken. Tanner cradled her in his lap. "Anything else hurt?"

"No, I don't think so. Your cheek, Briggs."

Tanner reached up and felt his face; the cheekbone was swollen and crusted with what he assumed was blood. "It's just a cut. Han, how're you doing?"

"I don't know," Soong answered. "My legs . . . something doesn't feel right."

Tanner crawled over and shined the light over Soong's legs, both of which were submerged in the water. As he lifted them up, he felt them bend in mid-shin. Soong screamed.

"They're broken, Han," Tanner said.

From outside there came a loud *pop*, followed by a grinding sound like stone on stone. The cabin trembled around them. Tanner's eye was drawn toward the door; a small geyser of water was spurting past the weather stripping. "Nobody move," Briggs ordered.

"Why?" Lian asked. "What's going on?"

"We landed on a frozen river. We're sinking."

As if on cue, there came another *pop*, then a second. The cabin rolled sideways, throwing Tanner against the bulkhead. He slipped and plunged into the water. Lian screamed.

"Everybody stay still, grab on to something," Tanner said. He reached out, lifted the door handle, and shoved. It opened a few inches, then stopped. Water gushed through the opening and began rising. "Hsiao, grab my pack and pass me the AK."

Hsiao did so. Tanner slammed the rifle's butt into the window. The cabin lurched and settled lower. The water reached his knees.

"Hurry, Briggs. . . ."

Tanner hit the window again, cracking it. On the fourth strike, the glass shattered outward. He knocked loose the rest of the shards and peered out. He turned back.

"The ice is about three feet below the window. When you're out, lay flat so your weight is distributed. Hsiao, you first, then Lian, then Han. Once you're out, start belly crawling away from the helo. Come on, Hsiao."

Hsiao crawled through the water. Tanner boosted him through the window, then stretched out his hand to Lian. "You're next."

"I'm scared, Briggs."

"You're fine, come on."

Once Lian was through, Tanner grabbed his pack and shoved it into Hsiao's waiting hands. He crawled over to Soong; he was shivering, his face twisted in pain. Briggs said, "Some rescue, huh?"

"You've done wonderfully. I knew you would get us out."

"Out, but not quite in one piece."

Soong forced a grin. "Alive—that's what counts."

"Are you ready?"

"I think so."

Tanner put one arm under Soong's shoulder blades, the other under his buttocks, then lifted him up and began scooting on his knees toward the door. He slipped Soong's head and shoulders through the opening. "Got him," Hsiao called. With he and Lian pulling, Tanner eased Soong's legs outside.

"Come on, Briggs."

Tanner was halfway through the window when he remembered: *The pilot* . . . He started wriggling backward, lost his footing, and plunged back into the water. The flashlight slipped from his hand and dropped into the water. The cabin went black. With another grinding crackle the cabin rolled onto its side and began sinking.

"Briggs, hurry—"

Hsiao's voice was cut off as the window slipped beneath the surface. Tanner plucked the flashlight from the water and shook it off. Water gushed through the window opening. He scrambled forward into the cabin.

The pilot was still strapped into his seat, limp and hanging against his restraints. The right side of his head was bloody. Tanner felt his neck for a pulse; he was alive. Using the armrest as a step, he climbed over the pilot, grabbed the door latch, then turned it and shoved. The door swung open.

"Briggs?" Hsiao called. "Is that you?"

"It's me. Keep going. I'll be right behind you."

Briggs chinned himself level with the door, then rolled out onto the fuselage. The Hoplite wallowed from side to side, its roof and belly scraping the edges of the ice hole. Trapped air hissed from the crack in the fuselage. Two of the rotor blades were underwater; the third, which had been sheared off at the halfway point, jutted skyward. Down on the ice, Lian and Hsiao were crawling away, dragging Soong between them.

Tanner sat in the doorway with one foot braced against the frame. He reached down with one hand, gripped the pilot's collar, and then unlatched the restraint with the other. The pilot's weight dropped. Tanner heaved against the weight, using his leg as a lever until he could grab the pilot in a bear hug and roll back onto the fuselage.

Dragging the pilot behind him, Briggs shimmied down the fuselage, letting its natural slope ease them onto the ice. He started crawling.

He got twenty feet before he heard a final hiss of trapped air. He turned in time to see the Hoplite slowly sink from view until only the tip of a rotor was visible.

FIFTY YARDS FROM THE HOLE, TANNER CALLED A HALT AND GATHered everyone in a circle. Still spread flat, they joined hands.

"Now what?" Hsiao asked.

Tanner opened his pack and pulled out the Motorola. Immediately he could feel the case was cracked. He turned it over and found the rear plate shattered; the nicad battery was missing. He rifled through the pack, removing its contents one by one. The battery was gone.

"It's not working?" Hsiao said.

"Not without the battery. Looks like we're going to have to make our own way."

Testing the ice before him with the butt of the AK, he slowly stood up and took a few tentative steps. The ice seemed solid.

"Hsiao, see what you can do about the pilot's head. Han, Lian, are you okay?"

"Cold but okay," Soong answered.

"I'm going to scout ahead, then we'll see what we can do about finding some shelter. Stay here and stay still. I'll be back."

Tanner had only a vague idea where in Birobijan they were, but judging from the width, they'd probably crashed into a tributary of the Bira River. From shore to shore it was nearly three hundred yards, and both shores were lined with cliffs that sloped upward to jagged, tree-lined ridges.

Though dawn was still an hour away, the sky was partially clear, revealing a star-stippled sky and a full moon bright enough to read by. The earlier storm had left almost a foot of snow that swirled across the ice with the gusting wind.

The good news was, they were out of China and in relatively friendly territory. The bad news was, given the remoteness of Birobijan they could be fifty miles from the nearest civilization. Cold and wet and tired, with two of them injured, they wouldn't make it five miles. If he could at least get them off the river, into some rudimentary shelter and build a fire, they might have a chance.

He skate-walked forward, probing ahead with the AK's butt and listening to the ice grate and moan around him, ready to drop flat at the first sign of cracking. A hundred yards from the group, he came to a bend in the river. As he came around it, he found himself staring at an island rising from the channel.

About one hundred feet long and forty feet wide, it was roughly oval in shape, and thick with trees and undergrowth that climbed away from the beach in terracelike strata. Though the trees themselves were heavy with snow, Tanner was guessing the undergrowth would have some nooks and crannies dry enough to provide shelter.

He was about to turn around and call to the others when something caught his eye.

He cocked his head, looking more closely at the island. *Something there. . . .* He couldn't put his finger on it, but there was a pattern to the underbrush. Slowly at first, and then more steadily, he began to see it: Straight lines, angles, corners. . . . As if there were a structure hidden by all the foliage.

He scanned the island for a few more moments, then suddenly saw it: What looked like the skeleton of a massive barrel lying on its side. But instead of staves it was joined together by . . . what?

Fins—horizontal fins.

The image was familiar somehow, but each time he reached for it, it slipped from his grasp

Come on, what is it . . . ? Then, from his subconscious, thoughts began to bubble forth: *Tom Sawyer . . . Huck Finn . . . the Mississippi River. . . .*

"That's it," Tanner said aloud. *How in the world. . . .*

He was looking at the waterwheel of a paddle boat.

FIVE MILES TO TANNER'S SOUTH AND EAST, KYUNG XIANG'S HIND sat in the small clearing the pilot had managed to find after their collision with the Hoplite. Armored as it was, the Hind had survived with only a rough landing and a damaged rear tailfin. The pilot reported he would be able to make the repair, but it would take several hours.

"What about communications?" Xiang asked.

"We lost our VLF antenna, along with most of our tactical frequencies," the pilot told him. "I'll start rotating through the emergency frequencies, but—"

"Fine, fine," Xiang said. "What about the beacon?"

"That shouldn't be affected." The pilot powered up the RFDF console and adjusted it to the correct frequency. The beacon showed as a spike radiating from the center of the screen. "There it is—northwest of us . . . make it bearing three-four-zero."

"How far?"

"Signal's pretty strong," the pilot replied. "Not more than ten miles."

Xiang walked out of the cockpit into the cabin. Two of Shen's men—one with a broken collarbone, the other with a concussion—lay on the floor. Xiang stepped over them and hopped to the ground. The remaining paratroopers were squatting in the snow in groups of twos and threes.

"Report, Lieutenant."

Shen said, "Twenty-six men, two injured."

"Good," Xiang said. "Get them up and moving. We have a trail to follow."

78

Russia

TWENTY-FIVE THOUSAND FEET ABOVE THE RIVER IN WHICH TANner and his party had just crashed, the flight of thirty F-14 Tomcats and F/A-18 Hornets, two EA-6B Prowler electronic-warfare planes, and two E-2 Hawkeye AWACS from *John Stennis* were arriving on-station three hundred miles north of the Chinese-Russian border.

Having made contact with their Russian ground controllers, the fighters left their Hawkeyes behind and climbed to their sustained combat ceiling of 52,000 feet—almost ten miles above the earth's surface—then throttled back into an energy-saving loiter and began their waiting game, mere ghosts at the edge's of the Chinese ground and AWACS radar.

THIRTY THOUSAND FEET BELOW THEM AND TWO HUNDRED MILES to the south, the leading edge of the Chinese fighters was approaching the border. As predicted, it was four regiments strong, almost two hundred fighters spread across a fifty-mile front, led by a spearhead of aging MiG and Sukhois designed to entangle the defenders and absorb their punishment. Above and behind them, the two remaining regiments of J-

10 and -12 interceptors circled with their AWACS, waiting to be directed into the fight.

Sixteen minutes after sunrise, they crossed the border.

Five miles into Russian airspace they encountered their first defenders, a squadron of Floggers and Flankers climbing from their bases to intercept. Three miles from one another, forces exchanged their first missile volley, but within seconds they had closed to dogfighting range. The Chinese's three-to-one advantage quickly began to take its toll. As ordered, the Russian pilots put up a brave fight before reluctantly turning tail and heading north, drawing the Chinese force with it.

Orbiting at the rear of the attacking wave, the Chinese AWACS detected a second flight of Russian MiG-25 Foxbat interceptors one hundred miles to the northwest. Seeing the classic pincer movement unfolding, the AWACS planes vectored half of the J-10s and -12s toward the approaching Foxbats.

Fifty miles into Russian airspace, the Chinese force left the periphery coverage of their ground radar stations. Safe in their assumption of coverage from their orbiting AWACS, the spearhead of the wave pushed on, the leading edge pursuing the retreating Floggers and Flankers while the split force of J-10s and -12s closed on the still-unsuspecting Foxbats.

At a prearranged signal from the Russian ground controllers, the two Navy Prowlers that had been loitering fifty miles southeast of the Chinese AWACS loosed a volley of four HARMs—or High-Speed Anti-Radiation Missiles—each of which was designed to home in on the radar signatures of the Chinese AWACS. Even as the HARMs left their rails and began streaking toward their targets, the Prowlers turned on their powerful jammers.

Focused on the battle below them, the four Chinese AWACS failed to react quickly enough to the cloud of white noise suddenly filling their radar screens. It took a precious ten seconds for them to burn through the interference and see the missiles coming. Hoping to throw the missiles off their scent, the AWACS shut down their radar.

It was too late. The HARMs had already switched to terminal homing mode. No longer a mere radar signature inside each missile's electronic brain, but rather physical targets, the HARMs ignored the ploy and kept going.

Each HARM found its target, and ten seconds after the first explosion the Chinese attack force found itself without radar coverage, naked, and virtually blind.

At a signal from the Prowlers, the E-2 Hawkeyes turned on their radars. Having already been fed the location of each of the Chinese J-10 and -12 fighters, it took only seconds for the Hawkeyes to sort out the radar picture and give the Tomcats and Hornets their attack vectors.

Twenty thousand feet above the Chinese wave, the navy fighters moved into firing position, made one last check of their targets' locations, then fired their first volley of missiles.

Having lost not only their protective radar umbrella but also their source of stand-off targeting information, the Chinese fighters were forced to depend on their own short-range targeting radars. Even so, whether from bravery or confusion or overconfidence, the Chinese wave pressed on toward the last known location of the MiG defenders.

Well beyond the radar range of the Chinese fighters and traveling at three thousand miles per hour, the fifty-four Phoenix missiles launched from the Tomcats and Hornets tore into the split force of Chinese J-10s and -12s, instantly blotting forty-six of them from the sky and leaving the remaining forty-two in disarray.

With a go signal from the Hawkeyes, the earlier decoy force of Russian Foxbats turned hard east and went to afterburner, closing the distance to the Chinese interceptors in less than ninety seconds. Though at a slight numerical disadvantage, the Foxbats used the attacker's confusion to quickly make up the difference. One by one, Chinese fighters began plummeting to earth.

Meanwhile, the Tomcats and Hornets launched their remaining missiles at the leading edge of older Chinese fighters still in pursuit of the first Russian defenders. In groups of twos and threes, the older MiGs and Sukhois were blown from the sky.

Twelve minutes after the battle began, it ended. Of the two hundred fighters that crossed into Russia, only thirty-two returned to Chinese airspace.

NMCC

"It worked!" David Lahey boomed and clapped Cathermeier on the back. "General, it worked!"

"Yes, sir, it did. This time."

"What do you mean?"

Cathermeier pointed to the Keyhole image on the big screen. "Unless I'm mistaken, those black shapes south of the Hinggan Mountains are more fighters. Commander?"

"I agree," said the duty officer. "I make it at least two divisions coming north from Beijing."

"How many planes?" Lahey asked.

"Another two hundred fifty."

Mason said, "Replacements for their losses. They aren't wasting much time."

"If we had any doubt about their commitment to seeing this through to the end, we don't now," Dutcher said. "We just decimated four regiments and it didn't phase them."

The duty officer called, "General, I have Defense Minister Beskrovny on the line."

Cathermeier picked up the phone and said, "Congratulations, Marshal."

"And to you, General. It seems we've bought ourselves some breathing room."

"I fear that's all we've done."

"We've seen them. How long do you estimate before they're ready to launch the next wave?"

"Five hours, no more," said Cathermeier.

"I agree. Not enough time for your fighters to return to *Stennis*, reload, and return."

"I'm afraid not."

"Well, we'll have to make due with what we have."

"Will it be enough?"

"I wish I could say yes, but I'd be lying. We'll do our best, however. I'll be in touch, General."

"Good luck."

Cathermeier disconnected and turned to the group. "I don't envy his position."

"There's nothing we can do to help?" Lahey asked.

"Not in the near term. We have to face facts: the Chinese are going to see this through to the bloody end, and right now there's not much we can do about it."

79

Birobijan

TANNER STARED AT THE PADDLE WHEEL, HIS BRAIN SLOWLY CONnecting lines and angles until he could make out the entire underlying form. A dozen questions jockeyed for position in his head. *How long had it been here? Where had it come from? How had this half-jungle island, half-ship hybrid come to be?*

As for the first question, the earliest steam paddle wheel had been built in the early 1800s, so if by some quirk of history one of them had found its way here, this vessel could be almost two hundred years old. Tanner doubted that, but it piqued his curiosity all the more.

As for the last question, if he were right and this were a tributary of the Bira, the answer might lie with the history of the river itself. Given that much of the Bira wound through the mountains and was fed by often torrential spring runoff, the river often changed course and depth every spring. From year to year lakes become mere bulges in the river; bulges in the river, deepwater lakes.

Assuming the paddle wheel had been here long enough, it may have simply become a self-evolving part of the ecosystem: Pushed from sandbar to sandbar, with each spring flood depositing onto its decks yet another layer of silt that eventually became soil strong enough to catch and nurture seeds blown by the wind, the paddle wheel became a living island. Grass would have grown, followed by vegetation, then finally small trees.

Tanner could see it in his mind. Just as a sunken ship becomes an ecosystem to the plants and fish beneath the surface, this boat had over time mutated into just another among the hundreds dotting the Bira River.

Whatever its history and origin, Tanner knew this boat meant one thing for them: shelter.

IT TOOK ONLY A MINUTE TO GATHER THE OTHERS AND MAKE THEIR way back to the paddleboat. With Soong on Tanner's back and the pilot on Hsiao's, they climbed off the ice near the waterwheel and picked their way through the outer ring of vegetation into the interior. The paddle wheel's once-white hull was now mottled in shades of brown, green, and black. It had sunk so deeply into the sandbar that only the upper edge of its gunwales were visible. The handrail was still intact, albeit thick with vines and creepers.

With some help from Hsiao, Briggs boosted himself onto the gunwale, pried apart the vines, and poked his head through. It was the main deck. He stuck his leg through the opening until his foot found the handrail, then climbed over and dropped to the deck below. His feet sunk two inches into the dirt.

The first thing he noticed was the drastic temperature difference; it was ten degrees warmer here than on the river. The wind had died to a whisper. To his left and right—fore and aft—the main deck stretched into the darkness, a leafy tunnel broken only by overgrown doorways leading into the superstructure. The deck was a carpet of thick ferns and grass.

Tanner poked his head out. "Hsiao, can you and Lian hand me Han and the pilot?"

"Sure."

They jostled both men through the opening. Tanner laid them onto the deck, then helped Hsiao and Lian over the railing. "Briggs, what is this place?" Lian said.

"It's an old steam-driven paddle wheel boat."

"What's it doing here?" said Soong.

"I have no idea, and right now that doesn't matter. Let's find a way inside and get warm."

AT MIDSHIPS THEY FOUND A PASSAGE THAT LED THEM TO A WIDE alleyway running the length of the boat, with entrances at the forecastle and afterdeck. Like everything else, the alleyway's bulkheads were splotchy with mildew and moss. Both sides of the passage were lined with closed doors.

Tanner clicked on his flashlight and shined it into the darkness. "Come on," he whispered.

They started forward, stopping every few feet to rattle doorknobs. Briggs found the sixth door unlocked, but jammed shut by a mound of topsoil. He and Hsiao dropped to their knees and dug until they'd cleared a path, then wrenched open the door.

Inside, they found a well-appointed cabin, with two triple-tier bunk beds, a pair of hardback captain's chairs, and a small, potbellied stove. The ceiling planks, warped and cracked from untold years of rain, had been infested by root systems from the decks above. The air was thick with the musk of decaying vegetation. Thousands of snakelike tendrils covered every inch of the ceiling as well as the upper reaches of the bulkheads. Briggs felt a shiver on the back of his neck.

He waved Hsiao and Lian into the room. Lian gasped as she saw the ceiling.

"Just roots," Tanner explained. "Hsiao, let's get Han and the pilot onto those bunks."

Once everyone was situated, Tanner made a quick search of the cabin, but found little of use except for an ancient oil lantern. He shook it gently; it was full. After some tinkering and several lighting attempts, the lantern sputtered to life and filled the cabin with a warm, yellow glow.

"Han, how're you doing?" Tanner asked.

"My legs are beginning to hurt badly."

"They're starting to warm up, which is a good sign. Can you manage?"

Soong forced a smile "Of course. Compared to my previous living conditions, this is luxurious."

"Hsiao, what about him?" Tanner asked, nodding to the pilot.

"He's got a laceration in his scalp, but the bleeding has stopped. He probably has a concussion. Rest is the best thing, I think."

"Good." Tanner turned to Lian and wrapped an arm around her shoulder. "And you?"

She smiled shyly at him. "I'm fine. Thank you for asking."

"Hsiao, see what you can do about getting that stove going. I'm going to have a look around."

WHERE THE ALLEYWAY EXITED ONTO THE FORECASTLE HE FOUND a spiral ladder leading upward. Like the main deck's handrails, the steps and balustrade were snarled with creepers. Rising beside the ladder, sapling rose upward and disappeared into a canopy of green.

He climbed to the next deck, where he found himself in another fore-to-aft alleyway lined with cabin doors. He walked aft, shining his light over the doors and trying to quash the tingle of fear in his belly. The ship was a ghost town, each closed door a potential tomb.

He spotted a vine-encrusted life ring on the bulkhead. He pried away the growth until he could read the stencil: SS PRISCILLA.

Thanks for your hospitality, Priscilla, Briggs thought. *Whoever and wherever you are.*

He found another ladder and climbed upward until he came to a partially closed hatch. He braced his back against it, then coiled his legs on the steps and heaved. With a grinding of steel, the hatch popped open. A small avalanche of dirt poured onto Tanner's head. He shook it off and climbed through the opening.

He found himself starting at the ship's wheel. He was on the bridge. Through the soiled windows he caught a glimpse of the trees and vegetation on the forecastle. Aside from what little sunlight made its way through the canopy, the bridge was otherwise as dark.

Near the port bridge wing door was a raised pedestal chair. With a start, he realized the seat was occupied. Hand resting on the butt of the Makarov, he clicked on his flashlight and shined it over the figure. His beam picked out the glimmer of bone and the black hole of an eye socket.

Could this be the captain? Tanner wondered. Heart pounding, he stepped closer.

The skeleton sat perfectly upright in the chair, fully clothed in thick wool pants, a parka, and a fur cap, all so rotted Briggs could see patches of bone through the material. Clutched in the skeleton's lap was a square package of what looked to be sealskin.

One eye watching the skeleton's face, Tanner tentatively reached out and pried the package free. He backed up to the windows for more light. It was in fact sealskin, hemmed at both ends by rawhide stitches. He opened his knife, plucked loose the seam, and unraveled the rest.

Inside was a leather-bound book, roughly the size of a paperback and two inches thick. It was remarkably dry, with only the faintest water damage on the cover. He opened it to the first page. There was an inscription:

JOURNAL OF ANDREW GALBRETH HADIN
VOYAGE OF THE *PRISCILLA*, August 1909

Tanner felt his breath catch in his throat. "Dashing Andy. I'll be damned."

Like most people, Tanner loved a good mystery, and the disappearance of Andrew Galbreth Hadin was one of the greatest of the twentieth century, along with Amelia Earhart's and Jimmy Hoffa's.

Hadin and his crew of forty men had sailed from Lake Baikal in late summer of 1909, ostensibly on a mission for the Smithsonian to collect specimens from the wilds of Siberia. Knowing Hadin's penchant for the dangerous and outlandish, U.S. newspapers didn't buy the explanation and soon after his departure rumors began circulating about the true nature of the expedition.

While most modern-day scientists have generally come to agree that the 1908 Tunguska Event had been caused by an asteroid impact, in 1909, less than year after the explosion, whatever had happened in the remote forests of Siberia was still a mystery. Something had flattened half a million acres of trees and created shock waves that had been felt all the way to Belgium, and no one knew why.

Many newspaper editors and fans of Hadin's surmised that Tunguska was the real driving force behind his voyage, and that he'd taken on the Smithsonian's mission merely as a way of bypassing Russian bureaucracy and secrecy surrounding the event.

Four months after Hadin's departure, the *Priscilla* was officially declared missing. The Russian government sent out search parties along Hadin's supposed route, but found no sign of the boat or her crew. A handful of Hadin admirers and emulators also attempted mounted searches for the billionaire, but they too failed.

"You're a long way from home, Andy," Tanner whispered. As the crow flies, they were 1100 miles from Lake Baikal and probably twice that by water course. "How did you get so lost?"

Briggs opened the diary and thumbed through the pages; every one was filled with Hadin's precise handwriting. He scanned the entries, reading as he went:

Yablonovyy Mountain Range, 9 September 1909

Left the damned gorges behind this morning. The Pris *got rather banged up in all the rapids, but we're already making repairs and should have everything mended soon.*

Our maps, I fear, are woefully inaccurate. Of course, it doesn't help matters that Tunguska isn't clearly marked on any of them. All we can do is trust the word of natives we pass along the way. Even Nogoruk seems a bit lost at times, but I'm not worried. . . .

Vitim River, 28 September 1909

Woke up to frost on the bridge windows this morning. It certainly gets colder here earlier than I'd imagined, but the crew is a hardy bunch and seem to be in their element.

Had to backtrack twice today after taking the wrong branch. Lost hours. Damned frustrating. Making good progress, however, and I feel we'll reach our goal before another month passes.

East of Ogoron, 19 October, 1909

Ran into first ice on the river today. Sat immobile until sun began to break up chunks and we were able to push forward. . . .

Engrossed, Tanner kept reading, his heart sinking with each entry. Hadin and the *Priscilla* had kept pushing eastward as autumn descended upon them and his entries reflected his frustration and confusion as they slowly became lost in the expanse of Siberia. Toward the end of October, his location entries became more and more vague until they finally started reading "Location Unknown."

Despite this, Hadin forged on, still confident they would find their way. In twos and threes the crew began abandoning *Priscilla* in hopes of reaching civilization before winter swept down on them. Finally only Hadin, his guide Nogoruk, and four loyal men remained behind.

Briggs flipped to the last entry:

Location Unknown, spring of 1910

Nogoruk and others gone forty days now. Haven't seen a soul since. Priscilla *is a ghost ship. Food running low, and despite my best efforts, radio still inoperative. Generator contraption should work, but it doesn't; I'm obviously missing something. Tried my hand at hunting yesterday; no luck.*

Miss Nogoruk. Good man. Loyal to the end, he'd refused to leave until I made it an order. As he and the others disappeared into the trees along shore, he turned and waved. "I'll come back for you!"

I believe him. I'm not worried.

He'll be back with a fresh crew and supplies and we'll start the journey anew.

Tanner closed the journal. *What a god-awful way to die,* he thought. The loneliness must have been overwhelming. And yet, to the very end, Hadin had been optimistic. What of his family? It must have been torturous for them, waiting and praying for news—good or bad—about his fate.

Briggs slipped the diary into his breast pocket. He would make sure it reached Hadin's family. Though almost a century had passed, they would finally know his fate.

Curious about Hadin's comment regarding the radio, Tanner wandered around until he found the radio room one deck below the bridge. Inside he found the transceiver missing from its mounts, the cables ripped from the bulkhead.

"Generator contraption . . ." he murmured. "Engine room."

He found the engine room a jungle unto itself. Water from the sandbar had seeped through the *Priscilla*'s rotted hull, creating a swamp. The creepers lining the bulkheads and catwalks joined with the roots poking through the ceiling to form a cave.

Following his flashlight beam, Tanner searched the catwalks until he was at the very stern of the boat. Below him he could see the giant cogs of the reduction gear; aft of these lay the telephone pole–size shaft leading to the waterwheel.

Sitting on the uppermost catwalk, he found the generator Hadin had mentioned. A makeshift hand crank jutted from the side of the rusted machine. Amid the tangle of electrical cables was an ancient Marconi radio the size of a small steamer trunk.

Hadin's contraption, Tanner realized. *A hand-powered generator.*

A pair of cables led upward from the radio, spiraled around the catwalk support, and disappeared through a ragged hole in the ceiling.

He traced the cables to the roof of the bridge. The sun had risen. Aside from a line of scrub bushes and small trees lining the railing, the roof was mostly open. Despite the chill wind, the sun felt good on his face.

The cables ended at a pile of rusted, steel rods, wire mesh, and wire. It took Tanner several minutes of sorting before he realized the mess had been Hadin's attempt at making an antenna. Where Dashing Andy had gone wrong, Tanner didn't know, but he realized the idea might be worth a second shot.

HE WAS CLIMBING DOWN THE AFT LADDER WELL WHEN SUDDENLY a snippet from Hadin's diary popped into his head: *"I'll come back for you!"* It had been Nogoruk's promise to Hadin. It had also been his promise to Han and Lian twelve years ago. His mind flashed back to his first sight of her at the camp, sitting in the chair, her hands clasped in her lap as she looked up at him. . . .

"He told me you were coming back for us."

". . . were coming back for us," Tanner murmured.

Were—a certainty. Not "would," as if repeating an as yet unfulfilled promise, but "were," as if describing something already happening. Briggs suddenly felt dizzy. He sat down on the steps. Even as half of his brain was putting together the pieces, the other half was arguing against the conclusion.

You're wrong, Briggs. You're exhausted and not thinking straight. You're wrong.

"He told me you were coming back for us. . . ."

HE RETURNED TO THE CABIN TO FIND HSIAO SITTING BESIDE THE stove nursing a small fire. Tanner shivered as the warmth hit him. Soong and Lian were both asleep, Lian curled up on the bunk above the still-unconscious pilot. Tanner stood staring at her face. *God, let me be wrong.*

"Briggs. . . ." Hsiao whispered. "Briggs . . . ?"
"Yes?"
"What did you find?" Hsiao whispered.
"A way to phone home, I hope. I'll need your help in a few minutes."
Tanner knelt beside Soong's bunk. Hsiao had splinted his legs with slats from the bunk then secured them with duct tape. Briggs gently shook Soong awake. "Sorry to wake you."
"What is it? Is everything okay?"
"We need to talk. Keep your voice down. Tell me what happened the day you were arrested."
Soong frowned. "I was taken to *Guoanbu* headquarters and—"
"What about Miou? She wasn't arrested at the apartment, was she?" Tanner asked.
"No. One of her friends was sick; she decided to take some soup to her."
"She hadn't planned on it?"
"No, it was last minute."
"What about Lian?"
"I don't know," Soong answered. "The last time I saw her was at our apartment that morning."
"You never saw her again—never spoke to her?"
"No."
"You're sure?"
"Yes, Briggs. Please, what is—"
"Not even by letter or through an intermediary? Last night was the first time you'd seen her or spoken to her since you were arrested? You have to be sure, Han."
"I am, Briggs. She's my daughter. I would remember."
Tanner nodded and forced a smile onto his face. "Okay, thanks."
"What's this all about?"
"Nothing—just trying to refresh my own memory. Go back to sleep."
In a daze, Tanner shuffled out of the cabin and stood in the alleyway, listening to the wind whistle down its length.

He pressed his back against the bulkhead and slid down to the deck.

It hadn't been Fong, after all, Tanner thought. Fong had been just a bit player; a conduit.

It had been Lian from the start. Lian had betrayed her own mother and father to the *Guoanbu.*

My God. . . .

Briggs hung his head between his knees and wept.

80

***AM I WRONG ABOUT THIS?* TANNER WONDERED.**

Had Lian's words at the camp been merely a slip of the tongue? As much as he wanted to believe so, the hollow feeling at the pit of his stomach told him otherwise.

Many things made sense now. From what little the CIA had been able to gather following Ledger's failure, Tanner knew that Soong's wife, Miou, had not been arrested at their apartment, but rather at a friend's. He'd always assumed the *Guoanbu* had followed her there, but now he wondered. If they'd had her under surveillance, why not take her as she stepped onto the street? The answer: Just as Fong's feeding of the *Guoanbu* had relieved them of having to keep Briggs under constant surveillance, Lian's had made it unnecessary to follow Miou. They knew about her unexpected trip that morning. Lian had told them.

He now also understood why Xiang had brought Lian to the camp; she was his insurance policy in the event Tanner managed to rescue Soong. What Briggs had mistaken for a leverage gambit was in fact Xiang's ultimate leash on his prisoner.

They were in real trouble, he realized. How long did they have?

Hsiao appeared beside him. "Briggs, are you okay?"

"Yes."

"You don't look it."

Tanner pushed himself to his feet. "Hsiao, I have to do something—something I don't want to do. I'll need your help."

"Of course. Tell me what you need."

"Just do what I tell you."

They walked back into the cabin. As Hsiao woke Soong, Tanner gently shook Lian until her eyes opened. "Get down," Tanner told her.

"Why?"

"Please get down, Lian." She climbed down from the bunk and stood before him, frail, delicate, her doe eyes staring up at him. "What's the matter, Briggs? What are you—"

"When I found you at the camp, you said, 'He told me you were coming back for us.' "

"Did I?"

"Yes. What did you mean?"

From his bunk, Soong said, "Briggs, why are you—"

Tanner held up a silencing hand.

"I don't remember saying that," Lian replied.

Tanner took a step toward her. "I'll ask you again: What did you mean?"

"If I said it, I must have meant my father. He promised me you would come back for us."

"When did he tell you that?"

Lian shook her head. "I don't know." She looked at Soong. "Father. . . ."

Soong said, "Briggs, she must have imagined the words. From a dream, perhaps."

"No, I don't think so." He turned back to her. "You meant Xiang, didn't you? Xiang told you I was in China, and that I was coming for you and your father."

"No."

"That's why he brought you to the camp."

"I don't know what you're talking about."

"He wanted you at the camp, and I know why."

Lian shook her head; tears welled in her eyes. "That's not true. I've been a prisoner—"

"You're lying," Tanner said, his chest aching. "Hsiao, search her."

"What?"

"Search her."

Soong said, "Briggs, why are you doing this? Lian would never—"

"I'm sorry, Han. Go ahead, Hsiao."

Hsiao stepped forward and began patting down Lian's clothes. As he moved down her body, Tanner studied her face. In the blink of an eye, her expression hardened into a mask of hatred, her eyes narrowing as they bore into his. It was as though he were looking at a different person. In that instant he knew with sickening certainty that he was right about it all.

As Hsiao reached the top of her trousers, he stopped and frowned. He reached into the waistband and withdrew a black box the size of a cigarette pack. He backed away from her and handed the box to Tanner. It was a radio beacon.

Briggs dropped it to the floor and crushed it under his heel.

Lian Soong glared at him. "It's too late," she said. "He's on his way."

"Lian, what is that?" Soong said. "What is he talking about?"

Tanner said, "It's a beacon. She's drawing them to us."

"No, that can't be." Soong looked at her. "Lian, it's not true. Tell me it's not true."

She glowered at him. "Of course it's true! You're a traitor!"

"What?"

"You betrayed Zhongguo! You sold yourself to the West like a common whore!"

Eyes brimming with tears, Soong looked to Tanner. "Briggs, they've done this to her. They're making her say these things."

"I wish that were true," Tanner whispered. "This started a long time ago—before the defection, didn't it, Lian?"

"Lian . . . My God, what happened to you?"

"*You* happened to me!" she snarled. "Since I was old enough to listen, you were always talking about the glory of the Middle Kingdom, about patriotism and loyalty—about how we had to defend our way of life. And then those . . . rabble-rousers at Tiananmen came along and suddenly all your talk was for nothing!"

"Lian, those were students—young people like yourself. Our government murdered six thousand people who were guilty of nothing more than speaking their minds!"

"They were trying to destroy our way of life! For eighteen years I listened to you talk about patriotism only to watch you betray it all over some morally corrupt thugs!"

"They were slaughtered, Lian!"

"And rightly so! They were traitors—just like you! As far as I'm concerned, you should have gotten the same punishment!"

"No, Lian—"

"I would have gladly pulled the trigger my—"

Tanner snapped, "That's enough. Not another word!"

"And you!" Lian snapped. "You're no better! You're scum!" She spat at him.

Soong gaped at her, then looked to Tanner, his face etched in agony. Briggs could think of nothing to say; there was no way to ease his friend's pain. Han had wasted away in a dank cell for the last decade, su[cf4]rviving on the hope of being reunited with his daughter, only to find it was her betrayal that had imprisoned him and killed his wife.

Tanner couldn't decide if Lian's hatred was inherent or had been cultivated by the *Guoanbu*, or was a mixture of the two. *What about her feelings for him? Had it all been an act—the affair, their love—everything?* His heart was pounding so hard he could hear it in his ears. *Put it away, Briggs. No time for this now.* Xiang was coming.

"Hsiao, get the duct tape out of my pack. Bind and gag her."

Soong said, "No, Briggs, don't—"

"She'll betray us again if we give her the chance, Han."

"Please, don't hurt her."

"I'm not going to hurt her."

Once Hsiao was finished binding her, Tanner asked him, "How good are you with electronics?"

Hsiao shrugged. "I used to tinker with shortwaves when I was a child."

"Good enough. Grab one of the AKs and the lantern, then take Lian down to the engine room. On the upper catwalk there's a hand-powered generator and a radio—one of the old-style vacuum sets. Look it over and see what you can do. Take this, too." Tanner handed him the Motorola.

"And do what?"

"We can't be sure until we try, but aside from a missing battery, the phone might be salvageable. If we can jury-rig the transformer to regulate the power, we might be able to put out a signal."

"I'll see what I can do."

Once they were gone, Tanner knelt beside Soong's bunk. He put his hands on Soong's shoulders. "I'm so sorry, Han. I wish to God it weren't true."

"As am I," Soong whispered. "I can't believe it, Briggs. They did something to her. She wouldn't say those things otherwise." He hesitated. "But that only explains part of it, doesn't it?"

"Yes."

"After I told her about my plans, she went to the *Guoanbu* on her own. Oh, God. . . ."

Soong broke down in tears. Tanner embraced him. "We can't take her with us, can we?"

Tanner shook his head. "No. Han, this invasion your government is planning—do you know how to stop it? Can you tell my people?"

"Yes, I think so."

"How? You've been in prison since—"

"Night Wall was originally mine; they changed very little of it. I know because for the last decade Xiang has been picking my brain . . . bragging as 'his' plan progressed. It makes him feel superior, I think. Have they already started, do you know?"

"Probably, but how far along they are, I don't know."

"Then we have to move quickly. How many men will Xiang have?"

"A Hind can carry a platoon. Thirty men, perhaps—paratroopers, probably."

"Too many for you to fight alone."

"I don't plan on fighting them. Come on, let's get out of here."

ONCE IN THE ENGINE ROOM, TANNER FOLLOWED THE GLOW OF Hsiao's lantern to the upper catwalk. Hsiao was hunched over the generator. Briggs laid Soong down on the grating. Lian sat against the railing and glared at Tanner. Part of him wanted to return her gaze, to study her eyes for even a hint of the woman he thought he knew, but he quashed the impulse. That Lian was gone, perhaps never having existed at all.

He turned to Hsiao. "Any luck, Hsiao?"

"Whoever's boat this was spared no expense: The generator is mostly made of aluminum. There's some rust, but I found an oilcan down below, so I think I can get the crank moving. As for the radio, I think I can rig a crude transformer and get power to it, but it could be tricky. If I guess wrong, the power might destroy the phone's circuits."

"Do your best. How about the cables?"

"They're in surprisingly good condition—high-gauge copper. A little splicing here and there, and it should be no problem. We're going to need an antenna, though—"

"I'll take care of that."

Hsiao gestured for Tanner to follow him down the catwalk, then stopped and whispered, "Are we sure Xiang is coming? How do we know the Hind even survived the collision?"

"Because they're built like flying tanks," Tanner replied. "If we survived, they did."

"How long have we got?"

"I don't know. It's safer to assume not long. If you get the radio going, I want you to stay here and keep transmitting as long as you can."

"What are you going to be doing?"

"Hopefully making things difficult for Xiang and his men. If I'm lucky I might be able to run them around for as long as I can."

"And when you can't anymore?"

"I'll come back here. We'll use this as our retreat," Tanner said, then cast his flashlight around. "We're going to need an emergency exit. . . . Come on."

They followed the catwalks down the bilges where the grating had become a quagmire of mud and decaying plants. Moss and lichen coated the bulkheads.

At the very stern of the boat, where the shaft exited the hull, Tanner found a maintenance hatch. Tanner crouched down and kicked the hatch until it splintered and broke outward. He pried free the remaining slats, then with the flashlight in his teeth, wriggled through.

He emerged inside the waterwheel. Above his head lay one of the massive, horizontal fins. Through the tangle of foliage he could see patches of sky. He pushed his way through the undergrowth until he emerged outside.

Blowing snow swirled in front of his face. He squinted his eyes against the sunlight, looked around, then wriggled backward, pulling the brush closed behind him. Hsiao asked, "How's it look?"

"It leads down to the ice. When we make our break, that'll be our exit. If I'm not here, you'll have to handle Han yourself. Can you do it?"

Hsiao nodded. "I can do it. And once we're outside?"

"Run for the river bend, then get ashore and keep going. I'll buy you as much time as I can."

CARRYING A BUNDLE OF LOOSE CABLE AND THREE BALLAST stones he'd collected from the bilges, Tanner left Hsaio working in the engine room and climbed to the bridge roof, where he first untangled the mass of rods and mesh, then began untangling the cable, counting arm lengths until he knew how many feet with which he had to work.

Knowing the frequency the CIA had assigned his phone, he turned his attention to determining what size of antenna he would need. The calculation was fairly straightforward, but exhausted as he was he couldn't wrap his mind around the numbers, so he knelt down and traced the formula in the dirt until he had the answer.

He measured off the correct lengths on the cable, cut three sections of it, then shimmied up the smokestack and crimped each cable end to the stack's fluted chimney, tight enough that they wouldn't come undone, but loose enough that he could adjust them. He climbed down and jiggled each cable until all three were spaced evenly around the chimney.

Next he sorted through the pile of rods until he found the three sturdiest ones, then paced twelve feet out from the stack's base and pounded each rod into the dirt with a ballast stone. Once satisfied they were all of equal height, he crimped the remaining cable ends to the tips of the rods.

Finally, he gently placed a ballast stone at the base of each rod until the cables were taut.

What he'd just built, he hoped, was an inverted dipole—or a "big top"—antenna. While he knew the satellite was somewhere up there in a stationary orbit, he wasn't sure where exactly. Though not the most efficient of antennas, the big top was their best bet, as it radiated into the atmosphere in all directions. Now all they had to do was get the frequency right and cross their fingers.

He was turning back to the pilothouse door when something caught his eye.

A half-mile astern, a lone man in camouflage gear appeared from around the river's bend. As Tanner watched, five more joined him, then ten. One of them pointed in his direction, then turned around and shouted something.

Out of time, Tanner thought.

81

Chono Dam

SURROUNDED IN FRONT AND BACK BY A PAIR OF COMMANDOS, Skeldon and Cahil carried the remaining three charges down the trail to the mine's entrance. The colonel brought up the rear. Cahil could feel the man's eyes on his back. *Marching us to our deaths,* he thought. *Not if I can help it. . . .*

As planned, Skeldon, with a charge balanced on each shoulder, walked ahead of Cahil. Bear could feel the C4 disk rubbing against his belly. He mentally rehearsed his movements.

Have to be very quick, Bear. Once he made his move he would have but seconds before the commandos' confusion turned to action. There was, he realized, a very real possibility he'd be shot before he got two steps. If so, he could only pray Skeldon would somehow see it through to the end.

Forty minutes after leaving the camp, they stopped in front of the mine's hidden entrance. The point man knelt down, rolled the stone aside, then wriggled into the tunnel, followed by the next man.

"Push your charges through," the colonel ordered Skeldon.

Skeldon dropped to his knees and slid his charges into the hole. A pair of hands appeared and dragged each inside. Cahil followed the same procedure and then the colonel ordered them into the tunnel. Once everyone was through and standing inside the cave, Skeldon and Cahil hefted their charges and the group started out again.

The point man's flashlight danced over the rocky walls. The scrape of their boots echoed down the tunnel, each man's step raising a tiny cloud of dust. A breeze blew past

Cahil's face, cooling the sweat on his forehead and chilling his neck. He shivered.

How far? he wondered. He eyed the passing walls, searching for his landmark.

After another two minutes, he saw it: a dumbbell-shaped bulge in the wall. A few steps ahead, Skeldon passed it. His right index finger tapped twice on the charge. He'd seen it.

Cahil started counting steps. Sixty-two paces to the ambush point.

He glanced over his shoulder. The tail man and the colonel walked with their M-16s at the ready, fingers resting on the triggers. *Gotta be quick. . . .* In the confines of the tunnel, an M-16 blast would send bullets ricocheting off the walls, each a tumbling piece of deadly shrapnel looking for flesh.

The tunnel began sloping downward. The air grew cooler. Cahil could smell musty water.

Getting closer. Forty-three . . . forty-four. . . .

When they reached the ambush point, Skeldon wouldn't wait to see if he was moving; he would simply attack the two lead commandos and trust Cahil was doing his part.

Fifty-four . . . fifty-five . . . fifty-six . . . Just yards now.

Cahil reached up and undid the button on his shirt, rubbed a finger over the C4 disk.

The tunnel turned sharply right, then straightened out.

Sixty. . . . Where is it, where is it?

He reached into his belt, palmed the detonator cap, then pressed it into the C4. He gently folded the disk in half and closed his fist around it.

Sixty-one. . . . There!

Ahead, hanging low from the ceiling, was the rock shelf. The point man's beam flashed over it, then moved on, rounding the corner. Skeldon passed beneath the shelf.

Now!

Cahil let the charge slip off his shoulder. It hit the dirt floor with a thud. He danced backward a few steps as though trying to save his toes. The commando behind him backed up.

"Sorry," Cahil said.

"Pick it up!" the colonel barked.

With the C4 balled in his right first, Cahil knelt down beside the charge. *Ready, ready. . . .* He glanced back, taking aim, then closed his eyes briefly and said a quick prayer.

From ahead, a surprised shout: "Aiyahhh!"

Cahil lashed out with a mule kick that slammed into the commando's belly. The man stumbled backward into the colonel, who struggled to raise his M-16. Cahil cocked his right arm and threw the C4. Even as it slammed into the shelf, he dove forward.

A flare of light filled the tunnel, followed by a muffled explosion. Smoke billowed around him. As it cleared, he looked ahead and saw a pair of flashlights lying in the dirt; in their shadowed beams Skeldon and one of the commandos were locked together in struggle. The other commando lay on the ground, his head partially crushed beneath Skeldon's pipe charge.

Out of the corner of his eye Cahil saw movement behind him. He spun. The commando he'd kicked shuffled through the smoke, his M-16 dangling from one hand. His right arm was missing at the elbow; blood gushed from the stump. His jacket front, neck and face were a mass of bloody pockmarks. He took two more steps, then groaned and collapsed.

Cahil scrambled over to him, snatched up the M-16, and charged around the corner.

Skeldon was lying on the ground. A commando stood over him, M-16 raised.

Cahil took aim, fired. The man fell backward.

"You okay?" Bear asked, snatching up a flashlight.

"Yeah."

"Grab his weapon and flashlight. We've gotta move; the others had to have heard the shots."

With Cahil in the lead, they raced down the tunnel, their flashlight beams bouncing off the walls.

"How much farther?" Skeldon called.

"Should be coming up. When we get into the cavern, we'll split. You go right, I'll go left!"

"Right!"

They were approaching the last bend in the tunnel when Cahil saw pale, crimson light ahead. He stopped, dropping to one knee. Skeldon did the same. Cahil crawled forward to the bend.

Spaced at even intervals, four sputtering red flares dotted the cavern floor, casting the stalactites and stalagmites in eerie relief. Near the far wall, behind a row of small boulders, a pair of lanterns glowed yellow against the rock. A shadow of a figure hunched beside one of the bore holes. A few feet away a head popped up from behind a boulder, then ducked down again.

Cahil crawled back. "One's on lookout, the other's rigging the last charge."

"What's the plan?"

"No plan. Hail Mary. We rush them and hope one of us reaches the charge."

"Not exactly what I'd call a brilliant plan."

"Sorry, I'm all out of brilliant. Concentrate your fire on the lookout."

"Right. Ready when you are."

Together, they rose into a crouch. Cahil mouthed a silent three-count, then they stood and charged into the cavern. Skeldon veered right, toward the nearest boulder, Cahil straight ahead.

The lookout popped up from behind his boulder. Fire winked from his muzzle.

Cahil dove behind a stalagmite. Bullets pounded into the rock.

To the right, Skeldon opened fire. Cahil rolled left, fired off a dozen rounds, then rolled back.

"I'm going!" Skeldon called. "Gimme cover!"

"No, wait!"

It was too late. Skeldon was already on his feet and sprinting forward in a weaving run.

Seeing Skeldon, the lookout opened fire. From the corner of his eye Cahil saw Skeldon stumble and go down. *No, no, no. . . .* Bear took aim, fired. The lookout toppled over.

"Mike!"

With a groan, Skeldon pulled himself to his knees, then to his feet, and began shuffling forward. He dragged his right leg behind him. He glanced back at Cahil; his face was twisted in pain.

Ahead there came a flare of white light. *Detonator cord,* Bear realized. The charges were lit.

The last commando rose beside the wall. He saw Skeldon and turned that way, M-16 coming up. Cahil jerked his own weapon to his shoulder, took aim, fired. The man crumpled. Cahil started running. Skeldon covered the last few feet to the wall, tried to hurdle the line of boulders, but fell forward.

Cahil was there in seconds. Both commandos were dead. Skeldon lay on his side, groaning, but still trying to crawl forward. The bullet had shattered his tibia; a jagged piece of white bone jutted from his pant leg. "The charges!" he rasped.

Cahil spun. The hissing end of each length of det cord had already disappeared into its respective bore hole; white light sparkled from the mouths; dangling from each lay the straps the commandos had used to lower the charges into place.

"You get those," Skeldon said. "I've got this one."

Cahil dropped his M-16 and rushed to the first hole. He knelt down, grabbed the strap, and began reeling it up. The glowing end of the det cord came into view; it was two feet from the charge. He grabbed it, jerked hard. *Snap!* It came free.

A few feet away, Skeldon straddled the bore bole, his good leg braced against the wall, the other flailing in the dirt as he heaved at his strap. Tears streamed down his face. Each time he leaned forward to pull, his shattered leg bowed in mid-calf and Cahil could see a jagged tip of tibia jutting from the rent in his pant leg.

Bear forced himself to look away. He dove for the second strap. *Faster . . . faster . . .* From out of the dark hole came the flaming end. Cahil grabbed it, wincing as the heat seared his palm. He jerked hard. *Snap!*

"Help me," Skeldon called. "Ahhh!"

The end of the last det cord was jutting from the hole; it was six inches from the charge. With one hand wrapped around the strap, Skeldon leaned forward, his fingers stretched toward the charge.

"Hang on!" Cahil yelled.

From across the cavern came the *crack crack crack* of gunfire. Bullets thunked into the wall above Cahil's head. He felt a sting in his bicep. He dropped to the ground and turned.

The colonel, his face and neck slick with blood, staggered across the floor toward them.

"I've got this!" Skeldon yelled. "Get him!"

Cahil dove for his M-16. As his hand touched the stock, the colonel hurdled the boulders and landed in a crouch. He swung his barrel toward Skeldon.

Cahil fired. His three-round burst stitched up the colonel's back, the last bullet slamming into the back of his head. He dropped forward.

"Cahil . . . !" Skeldon had managed to pull the charge into his lap. The det cord sizzled. He stared at it for a split second, then looked up at Cahil. "Too late."

The end of the det cord disappeared into the charge.

In that last second, Skeldon stared at him with an expression that Bear could only describe as sad resignation. "Sorry," he said, then tucked the charge against his chest and rolled away, pointing the charge toward the cavern's far wall.

"Mike . . . !"

Bear pushed himself upright and dove over the boulder. He would never remember hearing the explosion, only the shock wave as it picked him up and hurtled him into the darkness.

82

Nakhodka-Vostochny

Jurens and his team bypassed the first roadblock with-out incident and made good time for the next hour until Smitty, who was walking point, called a halt with a raised fist. As one, they dropped to their bellies. Dhar, fourth in the line, froze. Jurens grabbed his pant leg and pulled him down.

Sunrise was less than an hour away now, and Jurens could see faint gray light filtering through the canopy above. Dew and frost clung in patches to the ground; he could feel the cold seeping through his BDUs.

Smitty turned and signaled: *Road; enemy foot patrol approaching; squad-size, heavily armed.*

Dammit, Jurens thought. They were in a bad spot. If not for their hurried pace, they would have seen the patrol long before now and had time to set up in a defensive ambush position; as it was, they were bunched up with lousy fields of fire and only one route of retreat.

Sconi signaled back: *Proceed when clear.*

Smitty nodded and turned back. Jurens wormed his way left a few inches until he could see the edge of the road. Now he could hear what had caught Smitty's attention: the murmur of Russian voices and the crunch of boots on gravel.

Thirty seconds later, a pair of booted feet passed before the trail not two feet from Smitty's face. The soldiers were moving slowly and in a modified squad wedge. This wasn't another bored patrol, Jurens realized, but a hunting party. Aside from an occasional whispered exchange, they made no sound. Sconi counted feet as they passed: eight men.

After what seemed like ten minutes, the last soldier passed the trail head. Smitty waited another two minutes, then crawled onto the road to reconnoiter. Without turning, he signaled back: *All clear.*

Smitty rose to his feet, hunch-walked across the road, MP-5 tracking side to side, then disappeared into the underbrush on the other side. Dickie crawled forward, then crept across to join him, followed by Zee, then Dhar.

Jurens would never know how Dhar managed it, but half-way across the road he stumbled and sprawled in the dirt. He gave a sharp cry of pain. Dickie and Zee slipped out of the bushes, grabbed his collar and pulled him down the slope.

Jurens lay still, listening.

Then, from up the road, he heard the scuff of boots and a harsh whisper:

"Shtoh . . . gdeh?" What . . . where?

Jurens knew immediately what was happening. The squad had left behind a trailing OP, or observation post, designed to watch for enemy movement in the wake of the main force's passage.

Ten seconds passed. From Jurens's left came the sound of boots crunching on the gravel. A pair of man-shaped shadows slipped across the trail. The two soldiers stopped in front of him and knelt.

Very slowly, Jurens eased his MP-5 up and took aim.

"Shtoh?" one of the soldiers asked. *Where?*

The other one pointed toward where Smitty and the others had crossed into the underbrush. Rifles held before them, they began creeping toward the spot. They stopped, peered into the foliage.

Nothing to see, Jurens thought. *Keep walking—*

"Stope!"

In unison both soldiers jerked their rifles to their shoulders.

Jurens and Smitty fired simultaneously. Sconi's three-round burst impacted the back of the first soldier's head. The second one, his chest similarly riddled, crumpled. As he did so, his rifle discharged. The single *crack* echoed through the night air.

Smitty and Zee were out of the trees in an instant, providing cover for Jurens's crossing. Sconi sprinted across the road, paused to snatch up the soldier's rifles, then slipped into the brush. Smitty and Zee each grabbed a soldier by the collar and pulled them out of site as Dickie tossed dirt over the blood stains and drag marks. Once done, they all gathered in a circle.

"So much for stealth," Dickie said.

"What'd they see?" Jurens asked.

In response, Smitty jerked his head toward Dhar, who said, "Sorry."

From up the road they heard the sound of a truck engine revving. Excited voices shouted to one another.

"Time's up," Smitty said.

"What's the plan, boss?" asked Zee.

"Run for all we're worth. It won't take them long to find these two; by then, we best be on a boat and heading to sea."

USS *Columbia*

"On my mark," Archie Kinsock called. "Three . . . two . . . one—Blow ballast!"

"Blow ballast, aye," the chief of the watch replied from the control panel.

A shudder rippled through *Columbia*'s hull as compressed air rushed from the flasks and expelled the boat's water weight. The deck rolled beneath their feet; Kinsock and MacGregor grabbed at the chart table to keep their balance.

Kinsock kept his eyes fixed on the depth readout. The diving officer leaned over the helm console, his hands resting on the shoulders of the helmsman and planesman. Five seconds passed. Ten.

Lift, lift, lift . . . Kinsock chanted to himself. *Up baby*. . . .

As if following his orders, the readout clicked from 160 to 158.

"We're moving," the diving officer called. "One fifty-seven . . . fifty-six."

"Trim us out, Chief. Even keel."

"Aye, sir."

Eyes fixed on his gauges, the chief punched a series of buttons. With a groan, *Columbia* rolled slightly to starboard, her deck coming level. "Coming level."

The diving officer called, "One hundred fifty and rising."

Kinsock keyed the squawk box. "Engineering, Conn."

"Engineering, aye. Chief here, Skipper."

"We're off the bottom, Chief. Deploy the thrusters."

"Stand by."

A few seconds passed and then Kinsock heard a faint hum as the thruster doors opened and the outboards deployed. "Conn, Engineering. Thrusters locked and ready. On your order, Skipper."

"Conn, aye. Diving officer, bring us to PD."

WITHOUT PROPULSION TO GIVE HER HEADWAY, *COLUMBIA*'S climb to periscope depth became a careful dance of cooperation between the chief at the ballast controls and the diving officer, who passed a continuous stream of murmured orders to the planesman and helmsman.

Columbia wallowed and tipped as she rose through the currents and thermal layers.

"Coming to PD," called the diving officer.

"Gimme zero bubble."

"Zero bubble, aye," replied the chief. "Zero bubble. Steady at depth."

"We've got a drift. Southeast at two knots," the diving officer added.

"Aye. Up scope."

With a hum, the periscope ascended from the well. Kinsock caught the grips and put his face to the viewer.

His first sight of the surface in three days took his breath away. The water was a cobalt blue, rolling and choppy with the wind tearing the crests into spindrift. He duck-walked the scope from the northeast to southeast; the horizon was clear of ships. He turned landward, skimming the viewer first over Cape Kamensky and then past the mouth of Vrangel

Bay. Aside from a flurry of tugboat and ferry activity nearer the port, the surface was clear.

Kinsock closed the grips. "Down scope. Raise the antenna." He turned to MacGregor. "Jim, go to Radio; time to tell home we're alive."

"Aye."

Two minutes later, MacGregor called: "Conn, Radio. Skipper, you better take a look at this."

"On my way."

When Kinsock pushed into Radio, MacGregor handed him a flimsy message:

WELCOME BACK COLUMBIA. CLEAR AREA ASAP. TACTICAL SITUATION DIFFICULT; WILL ATTEMPT
DISPATCH ESCORT YOUR POSITION. PROCEED WITH CAUTION. SICKLE SITREP: OPERATIONAL;
ATTEMPTING EXFILTRATION; DESTINATION: 42° 44' N/
132° 51' E, GRID REF 12 ECHO
DISCRETION YOURS. LUCK.

"I'll be damned," Kinsock muttered. "They're alive."

"And making a run for it," MacGregor replied. "What'd that mean: 'Discretion yours.' "

"It means we can either clear out and save our asses or go get Jurens and his men."

"I vote for both."

They returned to the Control Center and walked over to the chart table. Kinsock quickly plotted the message's latitude, longitude, and grid coordinates. "It's a fishing village," he said.

"Makes sense. Steal a boat, get into international waters. How far away are we?"

Kinsock measured the distance. "Two miles southeast."

"What do you think?"

Kinsock looked around the Center, his eyes resting briefly on each of the watch standers. *One hundred twenty men,* he thought. *All trusting me to get them home. And if this* was *a democracy? What would be their vote? Run away or go back?*

Even before he asked the question of himself, Kinsock knew the answer.

"The hell with it," he said. He keyed the squawk box. "Engineering, Conn. Power up the thrusters, Chief. Diving officer, make your course two-one-zero. We've got passengers waiting."

WITH SMITTY STILL ON POINT, JURENS AND HIS TEAM WERE halfway across the last road above the village when an army truck skidded around the corner and stopped fifty yards away. Soldiers began jumping from the back and running toward them. Behind them, up the embankment, gunfire raked the trees and punched the dirt at their feet.

"Go, Smitty, go!" Jurens called.

Smitty took off with Zee and a wide-eyed Sunil Dhar on his heels. Firing from the hip, Jurens and Dickie sprinted across the road and down the opposite slope. Bullets crashed into the trees around them, each impact sounding like a whip crack. Branches and leaves rained down on them.

"Keep going!" Jurens ordered Dickie.

Jurens dropped to one knee, plucked a grenade off his web belt, and tossed it through the canopy toward the road, then kept running. With a *crump,* the grenade exploded. Cries of pain and anger filtered through the trees.

Jurens crashed from the tree line and onto the beach. Dickie was waiting. Smitty, Zee, and Dhar were thirty feet ahead, running toward the pier some one hundred yards distant. To the left, Jurens heard an engine revving.

A truck screeched to a stop on the beach road. Sconi turned, fired half his magazine into the cab. In twos and threes soldiers leapt from the tailgate and began climbing down the rock wall. As each landed, he dropped to one knee and began firing. Jurens counted ten soldiers, then fifteen . . . twenty. Up the embankment, soldiers were crashing through the trees, calling out to one another.

Jurens and Dickie took off, heads down as they sprinted for the pier. Still in the lead, Smitty mounted the planking and kept running. Dhar tripped, fell. Zee stopped, grabbed him by the shoulder, and began dragging him.

"I can't!" Dhar cried. "I can't run anymore."

"Then crawl!" Zee shouted. "*Move!*"

Dickie caught up to them, hitched one arm beneath Dhar's arm and together they began dragging him. Running beside them, Jurens turned and fired from the hip. Two soldiers went down. He ejected the spent magazine, slammed another into the butt, kept shooting.

From the pier he heard the throaty roar of an engine. At the end of the pier Smitty stood at the controls of a trawler. "Come on, come on . . . !" He mounted the transom, brought his MP-5 to his shoulder, and began firing three-round bursts over their heads.

"The hell with this!" Zee yelled.

He handed his MP-5 to Dickie, then heaved Dhar over his shoulder. Dickie lagged back with Jurens, both of them firing together. There were nearly forty soldiers on the beach now. Sergeants and officers were shouting orders, trying to organize their fire.

"How many grenades you got?" Jurens called.

"Two!" Dickie replied.

"Use 'em!"

As Jurens provided cover, Dickie tossed both grenades. *Crump, crump!* Double geysers of sand erupted amid the soldiers. With Dickie in the lead, he and Jurens turned and charged down the planking. Dickie cried out, grabbed his leg, stumbled. Jurens caught him. They kept running.

Ahead, Zee was five feet from the boat's transom when suddenly his arms went wide and he pitched headfirst onto the planking. Dhar landed in a heap on top of him.

"Zee's down!" Smitty called and leapt onto the dock. He grabbed Dhar and gave him a shove; he tripped over the gunwale and crashed to the deck. Smitty turned back for Zee. A bullet struck him in the upper chest; he spun and plunged into the water.

"Get him!" Jurens ordered Dickie.

As Dickie tossed both his MP-5s onto the afterdeck and dove into the water, Jurens dropped to one knee, turned, and poured fire onto the beach. He plucked his own remaining grenades from his belt, tossed one toward the soldiers, then rolled the last down the planking. It exploded, disintegrating a ten-foot section of the dock.

He turned, grabbed Zee by the collar, and staggered the last few feet to the boat. Zee was unmoving; there was a ragged bullet hole between his shoulder blades. *No, no, no. . . .*

At the transom, Dickie struggled to climb aboard with Smitty, who clutched the gunwale with both hands. His face was ghostly white. Watery blood coated his neck. Dickie reached over, grabbed his belt and heaved. Together they rolled onto the deck.

"Catch!" Jurens called. He tossed his MP-5 to Dickie, then dragged Zee to the edge of the dock and jumped onto the afterdeck. He and Dickie grabbed Zee's shoulders and pulled him aboard.

"Get us outta here!" Jurens ordered.

Dickie ran for the cabin. Jurens snatched up his MP-5, fired three rounds into the stern cleat, shredding the mooring line, then turned and did the same for the forward cleat.

"Go, Dickie!"

Dickie shoved the throttle to its stops. The trawler surged forward. Bullets thunked into the transom and gunwale, sending up a shower of wood chips. The cabin windows shattered. Dickie dropped to his knees, one hand on the wheel as he steered blindly.

Jurens felt a hand on his shoulder. He turned. Smitty gave him a wan smile. "Good to be on the water, boss," he murmured. He coughed and a pink, frothy bubble burst from the hole in his field jacket. *Sucking chest wound.*

"Amen, Smitty. Hang on, bud."

"How's Zee?"

A few feet away, Zee lay on his back. His eyes stared sightlessly at the sky. *No, God, Zee. . . .* "Don't worry about him; he's fine." He tore his eyes away, then opened Smitty's pack and withdrew a field dressing. "Dhar! Take this, put pressure on his wound."

"What? Where."

"There, goddammit, stop the bleeding! Turn him on his side."

Abruptly the gunfire stopped. Jurens peeked over the transom. On the beach, a single soldier was standing ahead of the others. He held a long cylindrical object to his shoulder. Jurens recognized it.

"RPG!" he shouted. "Dickie, help me!"

Together they dragged Smitty and Zee toward the cabin door.

From behind there came a *whoosh*. Jurens spun. A smoke trail arced across the water.

"Down!"

The rocket-propelled grenade slammed into the starboard corner of the transom. The boat rocked hard to port, then righted itself. Shrapnel and wood splinters peppered the cabin. The smoke cleared.

A four-foot section of the transom had been blown off. The deck was listing sharply. Water poured through the splintered gunwale. The engine whined and sputtered.

Back on the dock, a half mile away, the soldier's were racing toward the remaining boats.

With a final cough and a burst of black smoke from the exhaust, the engine quit. As Jurens watched, the top of the transom slipped beneath the surface. The deck began sloping to starboard.

Jurens turned to Dickie. "What's your vote? Here, or in the water?"

Dickie gave him a game smile. "The water. It's the only way to go."

"You take Zee; I'll grab Smitty. Smitty, how 'bout it? You up for a swim?"

"Always, boss."

"Dhar, can you swim?"

"Barely."

"Do your best. Don't put up a fight when they try to take you. Tell them we kidnapped you."

"What will they do to you?"

"As far as they're concerned, we destroyed their port, killed their men. You do the math."

"Certainly they won't—"

"Of course they will."

Dickie called, "Here they come."

A half mile astern, the soldier's boats were pulling away from the docks.

Beneath Jurens's feet, he could feel the deck settling lower. Seawater lapped toward the cabin door. "Time to go," he said.

"Wait!" Dhar called out. "What the hell is that?"

"What?"

"There!"

Jurens followed his extended finger. Fifty yards to their right, a periscope jutted from the ocean, a curve of white water trailing behind it. As Jurens watched, transfixed, the periscope rotated toward them, then stopped. A light blinked twice, then twice more.

God bless, Archie.

"That," Jurens replied, "is the man I'm going to name my firstborn after."

83

Birobijan

TAKING THE STEPS TWO AT A TIME, TANNER RUSHED BACK DOWN to the engine room and climbed the catwalks to where Hsiao was kneeling. He'd managed to connect the generator cable to the radio's transformer, which in turn was linked to the Motorola by a pair of fine, copper wires.

"They're here," Tanner said.

"I told you he would come," Lian said. "You're not going to get away. You won't live to see another hour—none of you!"

Briggs ignored her and focused on Hsiao. "Any luck?"

"Perhaps. Listen."

Hsiao began slowly turning the generator's hand crank. Tanner knelt down and pressed the phone to his ear. At first he heard only static, then in the background came a faint pulsing squelch.

"That's a carrier wave," Briggs said.

"Is it the right one, though?"

"It's all we've got. How's your Morse code?"

"It's been a while—since boot camp—but I think I can manage as long as it's short."

"Just two words: Pelican and Dire. Keep sending it over and over."

"That's all?"

"If someone's listening, it should be enough—I hope." Tanner unzipped his pack and pulled out his supply of AK magazines—six of them, each containing thirty rounds—then checked over both weapons. He handed one to Hsiao. "You've got twenty rounds. Use them wisely."

"I'd prefer to not have to use them at all."

"Keep thinking good thoughts. I'll hold them off as long as I can, then come back here. If I can't make it, I'll fire six shots in sets of two. If you hear that, get out."

Hsiao nodded. He looked Tanner in the eye and extended his hand. "Good luck."

Briggs took his hand. "You, too; thanks for everything. We wouldn't have made it this far without you." He turned to Soong. "Han—"

"Don't say it. Just go and come back safely."

"Okay."

Tanner faced Lian. He could think of nothing to say to her. She glared at him, and he felt her hatred down to his very core. *Put it away, Briggs. She's gone. Put it away; you'll have time later.*

He stood up, tucked the magazines into his belt, and headed for the door.

ONCE BACK ON THE BRIDGE, HE DROPPED INTO A CROUCH AND waddled out the door to the aft railing.

The soldiers had paused at the river bend. In the middle, two men stood together conferring, one in camouflage gear, the other in civilian clothes. The soldier, Tanner assumed, was the platoon leader, which meant the other man was probably Xiang. Standing behind them was the team's radioman.

They spoke for a few more moments, then the platoon leader turned and barked an order to his men. His voice echoed across the ice. The men began spreading out in a staggered line abreast. It was a smart move, Tanner knew. The less they bunched up, the harder a time a sniper would have.

Briggs dropped onto his belly and wriggled back from the rail so they would have a more difficult time pinpointing his muzzle flashes, then settled into a firing position. He tucked the stock into his shoulder.

The morning sun was at his back. Light sparkled on the river ice and the air was dead calm. Both conditions would work to his advantage, he hoped, as the soldier's vision would be degraded by the glare and the lack of wind would better echo his shots.

Regardless of nationality, soldiers share a universal fear of snipers. These paratroopers would probably react better than most, but watching helplessly as comrades are struck dead by phantom bullets tends to shake even the best troops. Even so, Briggs doubted he'd get more than three or four men before the platoon scattered and began laying down suppressing fire.

They were seventy-five yards away now, spread in a staggered line about one hundred yards long. Xiang, the platoon leader, and the team's radioman had moved to the rear. *Which one first?* Tanner thought. He desperately wanted it to be Xiang, but he knew better. Once under fire, the troops would look to their leader. He had to be the first target. The radioman would be second; the psychological effect of losing their communications would further unnerve the platoon.

Briggs laid his cheek against the stock and took aim. *Breathe and squeeze, breathe and squeeze. . . .*

• • •

LIEUTENANT SHEN PULLED OUT HIS COMPASS AND TOOK A BEARing on the opposite ridgeline. Walking beside him, Xiang said, "Well?"

"We're on their track." Two hours after leaving the Hind, they'd spotted the Hoplite's rotor blade jutting from the hole in the ice and gone to investigate. "At least one of them had to have been injured in the crash," Shen said. "That had to slow them considerably."

"Considering they shouldn't have gotten even this far," Xiang said, "that's a rather stupid statement, don't you think?"

"I suppose."

"Lieutenant!" Ahead, Sergeant Hjiu was waving. "Come take a look at this!"

They jogged forward to where Hjiu was standing with a group. "What is it?" Shen asked.

Hjiu was pointing upriver to a tree-covered island rising from the ice. "What do you make of that?"

Xiang said, "It's an island, so what?"

"No, sir, look more closely," Hjiu said. "You see the straight lines, the tiers. . . ."

"Yes," Shen murmured. "I see it now. It's man-made. . . ."

"A boat," Hjiu said.

"Check the bearing," Xiang said.

Shen did so. "It matches. If they survived the crash, they'd have been wet and cold, and—"

"Looking for shelter," Xiang finished. "Let's check it out."

Shen nodded. "Sergeant Hjiu, spread the men out and start them forward."

"Yes, sir."

They were seventy-five yards away from the island when Xiang heard a double *crack*. As did a dozen others, he looked down, sure the ice was giving way, then dropped to his belly to distribute his weight. Beside him, he saw Shen and his radioman do the same.

"Shen, do you see anything?"

Silence.

"Shen, answer me—"

Xiang saw blood spreading from beneath Shen's body. Xiang glanced at the radioman; he lay on his back, dead eyes staring at the sky

Crack! Crack!

To the right, another man dropped, then a third.

"Sniper!" Sergeant Hjiu shouted. "Sniper!" Hunched over, he scrambled back to Xiang, grabbed Shen's collar, and started running toward the shoreline. "Come on! Move!"

Xiang turned and chased after him.

THEY WERE WELL-TRAINED, TANNER SAW. AT THE SHOUT OF "sniper," there'd been the barest of hesitation before the platoon broke into two sections, each heading for an opposite shoreline. Despite the ice, they covered the distance in less than twenty seconds and slipped into the trees.

Tanner waited and watched for movement.

From the left shore, a lone soldier leaned out from behind a tree. Tanner took aim and fired. The soldier toppled over and rolled onto the ice. To their credit, the paratroopers kept their cool; there was no shouting, no panicked movement.

After thirty seconds, a voice from the right shoreline barked an order; a second voice called back. Tanner missed most of words, but the one he caught was enough: "encircle."

From both shorelines, he saw movement in the trees as each group began making its way up the slope. Tanner spotted a leg sticking out from behind a tree trunk. He adjusted his aim and fired once. The bullet struck the leg's thigh; it jerked behind the trunk.

Five down, Briggs thought. *Time to move*. Once fully under the cover of the trees, the paratroopers would converge on the paddle wheeler from both sides for a simultaneous charge.

Tanner backed away from the railing and started crawling toward the pilothouse door.

CIA Headquarters

Case Officer Karen Hensridge had just come on duty as the OpCenter Duty Officer, or OCDO. Already bored, she stood at the communications console looking over the previous watch's log entries. Aside from the routine daily traffic, there wasn't much going on in the intelligence world today—a couple of embassy contact reports and info requests from field personnel, but little else.

The joys of OpCenter duty, Hensridge thought. All case officers had to go through OCDO qualifications, and only the greenest case officers—the ones who hadn't yet sat through a dozen mind-numbing shifts—looked forward to the experience. However, if you wanted to get promoted up through the CIA's Operations Directorate, OCDO was part of the price.

"Say, Karen, you got a minute?" one of the communication techs asked her.

"Got more than a minute, Kent. What's up?"

"Listen to this."

He handed her his headset, which she put to her ear. "Sounds like static to me."

"No, listen deeper. Behind the static."

Hensridge closed her eyes, trying to mentally blot out the hissing. She was about to give up when she heard it—a series of clicks embedded in the carrier wave. "It's repeating," she said.

The tech nodded. "Five second intervals."

"Can you amplify it, maybe bring it to the front?"

"Hold on."

The tech tapped his keyboard and the static faded slightly. The clicking was more prominent now. Unconsciously, Hensridge began drumming her fingertip along with it. She opened her eyes. "Gimme your pad, quick!"

As the series repeated itself, she began doodling, trying to ferret out the pattern. In a flash, it struck her. "Dots and dashes. . . . It's Morse code."

"You're kidding?"

"No."

She copied down the series, then snatched a binder from the shelf above the console and began rifling through pages until she came to the reference section. The Morse code page was yellowed from neglect, but still readable.

"P-E-L-I-C-A-N . . . D-I-R-E," she recited. "Pelican. . . ." She grabbed another binder, this one the OCDO daybook, and flipped to the "Comms" section. "Pelican" was at the top of the list. "Jesus!"

"What?"

Hensridge reached for the phone.

MASON WAS IN THE TANK WHEN COATES'S CALL CAME through. Mason put him on speakerphone.

"Dick, we think Tanner's made contact."

Dutcher was on his feet instantly. "Where, how?" he demanded.

"Morse code, of all things. We're working on triangulating the signal, but it looks like it's coming from Siberia just north of the Chinese border. Khabarovsk region, probably."

"How long till you can pinpoint it?" Mason said.

"Five minutes, maybe less."

"Did he give anything else? Whether Soong was with him . . . their condition?"

"No, just the word *dire*."

"Call me the second you know."

Mason disconnected.

"He's in trouble," Dutcher said.

"But alive." Mason turned to Cathermeier. Mason said, "Can we get Beskrovny on the phone?"

"Goddamn right we can!"

The CAC duty officer made the connection and routed it into The Tank. Mason called, "General Beskrovny, can you hear me?"

"I can hear you. Who is this?"

"Dick Mason, CIA. We've got a situation we need help with."

"Go ahead."

"It's rather complicated. . . . Ten days ago we sent a man into China to rescue an imprisoned PLA general."

"Who?"

"Han Soong."

"He's alive?"

"Not only is he alive, but we think he may have the answer to what China is up to."

"And you're just telling me this now?" Beskrovny snapped.

"Until now, there was no point. We'd lost contact with our man, but we just heard from him. We believe he's managed to cross the border into your country—somewhere in Khabarovsk."

"With Soong."

"We hope so. His situation may be grave, however. If we give you the coordinates, can you—"

"Of course," Beskrovny said. "I'll call the Khabarovsk garrison commander."

"We'll get back to you."

Five minutes later Coates called with the coordinates. As Mason recited the numbers, Cathermeier plotted them on the map. Once done, he got Beskrovny back on the line and repeated the coordinates "They're in Birobijan, Marshal, about seventy-five miles northwest of Novotroitskoye."

"I know the area. I'll get the helicopters moving."

As the phone line went dead, Dick Mason sighed and turned to Dutcher. "I know I shouldn't be surprised, but I can't believe it. He made it out. Jesus."

Dutcher nodded. *Hang on, Briggs.*

Birobijan

Tanner was only halfway to the pilothouse hatch when he heard a double *thunk* behind him. He glanced over his shoulder in time to see a pair of grenades arc over the handrail and roll to a stop beside the smokestack. Briggs dove for the hatch.

The grenades exploded in quick succession, each a muffled *crump*. Shrapnel struck the open hatch like a flurry of hail. A few still-sizzling chunks landed on the deck beside Tanner. He crawled to the hatch and peeked out.

The underbrush and trees lining the railing were shredded and blackened. The smokestack, along with his makeshift antenna, lay in a smoking heap. *So much for the phone call,*

Briggs thought. There was no reason to loiter now. Xiang and his men would be coming. The only questions were, would they charge in force, or send a recon team, and could Briggs lure aboard the bulk of the platoon before making a run for it?

Tanner dropped through the hatch to the deck below, ran to the spiral stairwell, and down to the main deck. Once there, he sprinted down the main alleyway to the midships intersection, stopping short of the corner. He dropped to his belly, crawled ahead, then peeked out.

Noise. Port side.

Beyond the vine-entangled handrail he could hear the soft crunch of footfalls. A few seconds passed, then a pair of hands emerged from the foliage. One of them gripped the railing, the other parting the leaves to make an opening. A head emerged, then a torso. The paratrooper moved slowly, quietly, his eyes scanning for movement. Once he was crouched on deck, he gave a soft bird whistle. A second paratrooper crawled over the railing and dropped beside the first.

Wait, Tanner commanded himself. He could feel sweat rolling down the back of his neck. His heartbeat rushed in his ears. *Were there more coming?* he wondered.

After another ten seconds, no one else had joined the first two. That answered his question: Xiang was taking his time before rushing in. They sat crouched together, unmoving, AKs tracking up and down the deck.

Moving with exaggerated slowness, Briggs edged the barrel of his AK around the corner and pressed his cheek to the stock. He took aim, took a breath, then squeezed off a round. Even as the first paratrooper fell back, Tanner adjusted his aim and fired again. The second man slumped over.

Beyond the railing, a voice called in Mandarin: *"Shinkao!" Report!*

Hunched over, Tanner rushed to the bodies. On each he found a pair of grenades and a spare AK magazine. He pocketed everything, then grabbed their weapons and tossed them down the deck, out of site. He grabbed the first body by the arms and dragged it around the corner, then came back and did the same with the second.

More voices now. Boots pounded through the underbrush. Four to six men, Tanner estimated.

Gunfire erupted, slashing through the vines and foliage. Leaves fluttered and branches dropped to the deck, revealing patches of daylight. Bullets pounded into the exterior bulkhead. The fusillade lasted ten seconds, then went silent.

Thunk . . . thunk . . . thunk. . . .

Tanner knew the sound: More grenades.

A shouted order: "Go, go, go. . . ."

Here they come. . . . Their recon party having failed, the paratroopers would come in force now, trading bodies in an attempt to overrun him.

He ducked down, covering his ears. Three overlapping explosions shook the deck beneath his feet. A cloud of smoke and debris rushed the alleyway. Shrapnel ripped into the wood beside his head.

He ejected the AKs magazine, slammed home a fresh one, then peeked around the corner. The alleyway's walls looked as though a giant rake had been dragged over them. Through patches in the smoke he could see the handrail trembling under the weight of multiple bodies. A pair of hands appeared, then another, and another. . . .

From the starboard side he heard more grenades crash through the vines and bounce against the bulkhead. *"Kuai pao, pa xia!"* a voice shouted in Mandarin. *Run, take cover!*

Crump, crump, crump. . . . More smoke billowed. *Wait, Briggs. . . .* The urge to run was strong. He quashed it. *Wait. . . . Now!*

He spun around the corner, dropped to one knee, and opened fire. Using three-round bursts, he raked the railing until his magazine was dry. He ejected it, inserted another, kept firing. Bullets sparked off the steel railing. Chunks of foliage disintegrated, revealing more daylight.

He pulled back around the corner and glanced over his shoulder. Four paratroopers were climbing over the railing. One of them saw him and jerked his rifle up. Tanner ducked away. Bullets shredded the wood over his head. Briggs felt a sting on the back of his neck; he reached up and his hand came back bloody. *Splinter.*

"Zai Nar! Zhua Zhù!" There! After them!

From the corner of his eye, Tanner saw a grenade bounce off the bulkhead and roll to a stop a few feet away. He kicked it with his heel, sending it back around the corner. *Crump!* Screams of pain echoed down the intersection. He turned and sprinted down the alley and the engine-room hatch.

Halfway there, he stopped and knelt. He pulled out a grenade, jerked the pin, then pressed it spoon-down into his last boot print and covered it with a small mound of dirt.

Behind him, voices.

He spun, fired a dozen rounds at the paratroopers standing in the intersection. They scattered.

He sprinted the last ten feet to the engine-room hatch, heaved it open, and stepped through. He closed the dogging lever and leaned on it. "Hsiao!"

"Here!" Hsiao's flashlight shone down from the upper catwalk. "Briggs, the phone—"

"I know, forget it. Come help me."

Before Hsiao reached him, Tanner heard a muffled boom from the alleyway as his booby trap detonated. Hsiao jogged up. "What—"

Tanner held up a silencing finger. He pressed his ear to the hatch. Five seconds passed, then, from the other side, came whispered voices. He felt the dogging lever rise; he leaned on it. He grabbed Hsiao by the shirtfront and jerked him toward the hatch. At that instant, multiple AKs opened fire, tearing holes in the bulkhead on either side of them.

Hsiao stared wide-eyed at him and mouthed, "Thanks."

"My pleasure," Tanner replied, then explained what he wanted to do.

"Got it. Ready when you are."

Briggs gestured for him to lean on the lever, then backed up, took aim on the weakened bulkhead, and fired off half a magazine, further widening the gash in the wood. He pulled out a grenade, popped the pin, and shoved it through the hole.

"Pa Yia!" Take cover!

Boots pounded. The grenade exploded. Shrapnel peppered the hatch.

"Now!" Tanner rasped.

With their feet on its lowermost rung, he and Hsiao mounted the railing beside the hatch, gripped the top rung, and heaved back. Under their combined weight, the corroded steel groaned and began to bend down

"Harder!" Tanner urged.

The hatch buckled against Tanner as multiple bodies crashed against it. The dogging lever jiggled; Briggs took a hand off the railing and leaned on it.

"Pull, Hsiao!"

Using their legs as levers, they began bouncing up and down in unison. With a shriek, the railing folded over until it lay across the hatch's jamb.

"Go, go!" Tanner ordered.

With Hsiao in the lead, they raced to the upper catwalk. Soong, struggling to raise himself to a sitting position, said to Tanner, "Good to see you."

"Good to be alive. You ready to travel?"

In response, Soong turned to Lian. Eyes welling with tears, he studied her face.

Looking for his little girl, Briggs thought.

"Lian. . . ." Soong pleaded.

She turned her back on him and stared at the far bulkhead. Below, there came a sharp *gong* as the hatch crashed open against the railing. Through the quarter-inch gap Tanner could see bodies pressed against the steel.

Soong tore his gaze from his daughter and looked up at Tanner. "I'm ready."

Hsiao knelt down and hefted Soong onto his back.

Tanner said, "Go to the tunnel and wait for me."

Hsiao nodded. "Okay."

As they passed him, Soong grabbed his hand. "We go together, right?"

Tanner squeezed his hand and smiled. "I'll be right behind you."

Moving at a hurried waddle, Hsiao started down the ladder. Once they were out of sight, Tanner knelt down beside

Lian. She glared back at him. "You won't make it out of here."

Briggs shrugged. "Maybe not."

He drew his knife. Eyes wide, she jerked back. In one smooth motion, he cut her hands free, then stood her up and walked her behind the generator. He retaped her hands to the railing.

"Stay behind this and stay down," Tanner said.

She blinked at him; cocked her head. "What?"

"When they break through there might be some shooting."

"Why do you care?"

"Because I think—I hope—that somewhere inside you is the woman I fell in love with."

"You're wrong."

Below, bodies crashed against the hatch. With each collision, the railing buckled and trembled.

"Maybe so, but that's a chance I'm not willing to take."

As had Soong, Briggs studied her eyes one final time. She met his gaze evenly. For the barest moment he thought he saw a flicker of emotion there, but then it was gone. "Goodbye, Lian."

He got up and trotted down the catwalk.

As he reached the tunnel's mouth, the engine-room hatch banged open.

With a jarring crash, the catwalk tore from its mounts and plunged to the deck below. Screaming, two paratroopers tumbled over the edge. Two more faces peeked around the jamb. Flashlights clicked on and pierced the darkness.

"Go," Tanner whispered. "Head straight for the river bend, then into the trees."

Hsiao nodded, then backed feet-first into the tunnel, reached out, grabbed Soong under the arms, and pulled him through and out of sight. Tanner turned and took aim on the hatch above. The paratroopers parted and a lone man stepped to the threshold. Though only partially lit from behind, the face was unmistakable: *Xiang*.

Tanner laid the AKs front site over Xiang's sternum and curled his finger around the trigger.

"Lian!" Xiang called. "If you're there, call out."

Silence.

Tanner hesitated. *Why wasn't she answering?* His heart thudded. *My God, was she—*

"Lian, you're safe now," Xiang shouted. "If you can speak, tell me where they are!"

Still no answer.

Suddenly, from outside, came three rifle cracks. Xiang jerked his head around, then turned and disappeared aft, the paratroopers quick on his heels.

Tanner dove for the tunnel and started crawling.

He emerged from the relative dark of the underbrush into dazzling sunlight. An icy wind blew across his face. He shivered and blinked his eyes until his vision cleared.

Fifty yards onto the ice and halfway to the river bend, Hsiao was running backward and firing from the hip at the paddle wheel. Soong clutched doggedly to his back, his legs swaying from side to side. Bullets punched the ice around Hsiao's feet.

Briggs rolled onto his back and pushed himself out until he could see the upper decks. Four rifle barrels jutted from the shattered pilothouse windows, fire winking from their muzzles. Tanner pulled out his second-to-last grenade, pulled the pin, let the spoon pop free. He counted two seconds, then lofted the grenade in a high arc. It exploded in midair before the windows.

"Go, Hsiao, run!" he called.

With a wave, Hsiao turned and started waddle-running toward the river bend.

Briggs got up and started after them. He'd covered forty yards when the firing resumed. In his peripheral vision, he saw bullets striking the ice, each a miniexplosion of snow. Something plucked at his sleeve. He glanced back. Muzzles flashed from the bridge wings. Near the waterwheel, soldiers emerged from the underbrush and began to give chase.

Thirty yards downriver, Hsiao and Soong reached a berm of fallen trees trapped in the ice. The glistening trunks jutted from the snow, a natural fortification in the otherwise flat landscape. It was as good a place as any to make a stand, Tanner decided. Whether it would change the ultimate outcome, he didn't know, but he was determined to give Hsiao and Soong a fighting chance.

Ahead, Hsiao glanced over his shoulder, caught Tanner's eye, raised his hand in salute, then disappeared around the bend. Briggs put everything he had into a final sprint. Twenty yards to go.

Something slammed into him from behind. Off balance and spinning, he stumbled forward. Ten feet short of the berm, he sprawled into the snow. He pushed himself to his knees, trying to stand. His left leg buckled. He looked down. There was a bullet hole in his upper thigh.

Pushing off with his good leg, he dragged himself forward. The berm was five feet away. Bullets raked the tree trunks, snapping off branches and sending up plumes of snow. Behind him, voices shouted in Mandarin. The firing was steady now, the single cracks now a fusillade.

Go, Briggs. Get up!

He tossed the AK over the berm, jammed the toe of his boot into the ice, got traction, then shoved. His hands touched the trunk. He got to his knees and threw his good leg over the trunk.

He felt a sudden stab of heat in his back. He pitched himself headfirst over the berm.

The entire left side of his torso burned. Working on instinct, gasping through the pain, he grabbed his last grenade, pulled the pin, and tossed it over his head.

Crump!

The gunfire ceased. Tanner rolled onto his side and peeked over the trunk. Twenty feet away, three paratroopers lay sprawled around the grenade crater. A few seconds passed, then he heard a grating sound, like stone on stone. Fissures appeared in the ice around the crater and began spreading outward like roots. The shattered ice began to wallow with the current. One by one, each of the bodies slid beneath the surface.

At the paddle wheeler the remaining soldiers—a dozen, Briggs guessed—stood on the bridge wing. At their head, binoculars raised, was Xiang. He pointed toward the berm, then barked an order.

Tanner rolled back out of sight. His vision sparkled. He tried to fill his lungs, but it felt like he was trying to suck air through a sponge. *Punctured diaphragm*, he thought. *Maybe lung*. He tore open his field jacket. There was a quarter-size hole beneath his bottom rib. He touched the skin; it was hot. *You're bleeding inside,* he thought dully. *Not good, Briggs. . . . Have to slow it down. . . .*

Jaw set against the pain, he began scooping up snow and packing it against the wound. Almost immediately the snow turned crimson. *Snow cone,* he thought, then chuckled. *Cherry snow cone. . . .* Then, from the still-lucid part of his mind, *You're going into shock.*

In the distance he heard a hollow *thunk.*

He peeked over the berm. A dark object was sailing through the air from the paddle wheel. It took a moment for Tanner to realize what he was seeing: *rifle-grenade*. He watched, transfixed, as it dropped toward him and slammed into the ice. He rolled into a ball.

The explosion rippled beneath him. Snow billowed over the berm. His vision contracted and started to dim at the edges.

Thunk.

The second grenade impacted to his right. With a sound like a steamroller crushing a bed of glass, the ice began shifting beneath him. Icy water bubbled between his legs.

Thunk.

Snow erupted to his left.

With a grating *pop,* the ice gave way. He felt himself sliding. He grabbed for the trunk, but it rolled away. He slipped into the water up to his waist; the cold sucked the air from him. He glanced around for something to grab. There was nothing. He clawed at the ice. The water reached his chest, then his neck.

He looked back at the paddle wheeler's bridge wing. Smiling triumphantly, Xiang lowered his binoculars. He turned to the soldiers, mouthed an order, and pointed in Tanner's direction. A single soldier stepped forward and raised his rifle.

Here it comes, Briggs thought. *Would he hear the shot?* he wondered, *or would there be nothing?* Alive one minute, blackness the next.

Suddenly, from beyond the river bend, came the thumping of rotors. The sound grew until it was a roar. A blizzard of snow and spray washed over him. A shadow blotted out the sun. He looked up to see the olive-green belly of a helicopter stop in a hover above him. Jutting from the cabin door was a 12.7 mm machine gun. It began coughing. Fire flashed from the muzzle. Spent shells rained down on him, sizzling as they hit the water.

Bullets pounded into the paddle wheeler's bridge. Xiang and the paratroopers scattered. One of them, too slow, was struck in the chest and his upper torso disintegrated in a plume of blood.

Tanner saw a face appear out of the cabin door and look down at him. *Hsiao. . . .* A horse-collar attached to a rope dropped into the water beside him. The machine gun kept coughing. Hsiao was mouthing something: *Grab it. . . . put it around you, Briggs!*

His eyesight contracting to pinpricks, Tanner reached out, grabbed for the horse collar, missed it. His hand felt encased in lead. He felt the water engulf his throat and slosh over his chin. *Try again . . . come on. . . .* He threw his hand out, snagged the rope with a finger, and dragged the horse collar to him. He stuck one arm through it, then the other, then clasped his hands.

As the blackness closed in around him, Tanner felt himself rising into the air.

84

NMCC

Lahey, Dutcher, Mason, and Cathermeier sat around the table staring at the phone. Mason shoved out his chair, stood up, and began pacing. "Where the devil are—"

"General Cathermeier, I have Marshal Beskrovny on secure line two."

Everyone stood up. Cathermeier punched the button. "Victor, can you hear me?"

"I can hear you, Charles. We have them. They just landed at our base in Novotroitskoye."

Dutcher let himself drop back into his chair. He closed his eyes. *Thank God. . . .*

Cathermeier said, "How many?"

"Three. General Soong, a man claiming to have helped him escape, and your man—Tanner."

"Everyone's all right?" Mason asked.

"General Soong's legs are broken; the guard is fine. But Tanner. . . ." Beskrovny hesitated.

Dutcher thought, *No, God, no. . . .*

"He is badly wounded. He's in the infirmary as we speak. I'm very sorry, but it sounds grave."

Standing beside Dutcher, Mason clapped a hand on his shoulder.

"I see," said Cathermeier. "Please tell your people to do their best for him, Victor."

"Already done, my friend. We should have three-way communication set up with Novotroitskoye within minutes. They're bringing Soong to the base commander's office now."

Ten minutes later the link was established. Over the speaker, Soong called, "Who am I speaking to, please?" Cathermeier listed the people in the room. "The Russian commander here tells me my country has already begun the attack," Soong said.

"Yes, sir," Cathermeier replied, then recounted the air skirmishes that had taken place over the last few hours. "We're assuming they're just the opening moves to a larger plan, but we don't know what that is. We're seeing no movement of tanks or infantry."

"And you won't—at least not until the next phase is complete."

"Please explain that. Are we seeing your plan here—Night Wall?"

"They're calling it something different now—Rubicon, I believe—but yes, essentially it is the plan I authored two decades ago."

"How do you know that?" Mason asked. "If you've been in prison for—"

"The man in overall charge of the operation—Kyung Xiang—has spent the last decade planning Rubicon. He took Night Wall—a plan I prayed would never be used—and put it into action. Whether from vanity or cruelty, he's been diligent about keeping me informed. Given the nearness of my escape twelve years ago, I suspect he holds a special hatred for me."

"Do you know how to stop it?"

Soong hesitated. "Stop it? No, I'm sorry, I don't. I know its Achilles' heel, however."

"That'll do," Cathermeier said. "Let's hear it."

SOONG KNEW ANY INVASION OF SIBERIA THAT INVOLVED A HEAD-on tank and infantry assault was bound to fail. Not only were the Russians tactically adept standing toe-to-toe with invaders and slogging it out, but the very spirit of the army depended on such clarity of purpose: Us versus Them, invaders of the Motherland and her valiant defenders.

In 1812, when Napoleon invaded Russia, he was turned back at Moscow; in 1941, Hitler's *wehrmacht* marched on the Motherland only to be defeated by an army that not only absorbed some of the bloodiest punishment in history, but also eventually laid waste to Hitler's eastern front. Vowing to avoid a similar fate, Soong had turned his attention to what he called "strategic irregular warfare."

"Russia knows how to fight on multiple fronts hundreds, sometimes thousands, of miles long," Soong continued. "Armies clashing into one another in a battle that requires stamina, resources, and the willingness to sacrifice life for territory. Of course, I knew we would have to eventually take and hold the ground, but I envisioned that coming well after the main phase of battle had been joined."

"Joined by whom? With what?" Cathermeier asked.

"Airborne troops—paratroopers trained to fight at battalion strength complete with light artillery, antitank and air-defense companies."

Over the speaker, Beskrovny asked, "How many?"

"Ten divisions. Nearly one hundred thousand men."

"That's impossible," said Cathermeier. "That would take an air armada of. . . ."

"Eight hundred planes," Soong answered. "Not impossible, General. Difficult, but not impossible. In China, we have a saying: 'Water is patient; its anvil, the rock, soft.' Patience can solve any problem. Xiang and my former colleagues in the PLA have long been preparing for this battle."

Mason said, "Eight hundred planes and a hundred thousand men are tough to hide. Certainly we would have seen indications—"

"Only if you'd been diligently assembling the pieces for the last ten years," Soong said. "For example, I think if you go back and dig deeply enough, you'll find that *Guoanbu* front companies have been buying up old transport planes for many years—obsolete AN-twelves from Estonia's air force; C-eight Buffalos from Canadian freight companies; Seven-oh-sevens from bankrupt airlines— Anything big enough and durable enough to a single round trip."

"That's what this opening air gambit is all about? To make way for a massive airborne drop?"

"That, and to ensure our strike aircraft can support them once they're on the ground. As the Russians wait at the border for our tanks, they suddenly find themselves fighting an enemy from within. Every critical point in Siberia would be under almost simultaneous attack—rail junctions, supply depots, airports and air bases, command and control centers. . . . I think you get the point."

"It's bold," Beskrovny admitted. "General, what would be the battalion's composition?"

"Each is made up of three rifle companies, each equipped with light mortars, and two defense companies—one antitank and one air defense. They are trained to fight not only at battalion strength—roughly five hundred men—but also as a part of a divisional force should it become necessary to link pockets into a larger front."

There were several seconds of silence as everyone absorbed this. Finally, Cathermeier said, "Your impression, Victor? Is it feasible?"

"As General Soong said, it would be difficult, but not impossible. Providing the PLAAF did in fact gain air superiority, *and* if they managed to put the troops on their targets. . . . I have to say, we would be in trouble. Ten divisions is nothing to take lightly; and once their tanks and mechanized infantry started rolling. . . . It pains me to admit it, but I don't know that we could stop them."

For the first time since the discussion had begun, Dutcher spoke up. "General Soong, there's one thing that confuses me. If this airborne assault is the lynchpin to their plan, it already must be under way. It must be assembling somewhere."

Cathermeier said, "Good point. We've seen no movement of that size. Where are they hiding?"

"That's the Achilles' heel I spoke of," Soong said. "You see, I know exactly where they are and how to find them. Now, whether it will do us any good is another matter altogether."

• • •

NOVOTROITSKOYE'S BASE COMMANDER QUICKLY FETCHED SOONG a map of the Russian-Chinese border and the Mongolian salient. "There will be twelve bases," Soong said. "All in the foothills of the Hingaan Mountains, all within a hundred miles of the Russian border."

"How do you know their locations?" Marshal Beskrovny asked.

"In his arrogance, Xiang never bothered changing the locations I originally laid out for Night Wall. I can give you the latitude and longitude of each."

"I'm still confused," Cathermeier said. "You said twelve bases. If my math is correct, each one would have to be large enough to accommodate some seventy transport planes and over eight thousand troops—not to mention support staff. Again: You can't hide something of that size."

"You can if you put it underground," Soong countered. "Each of these bases has been under construction for a decade, disguised as strip mines or quarries. They're carved into the bedrock of the Hingaan range—each one a small, self-sufficient city complete with hangars, elevators, crew quarters, ventilation systems, mess and recreation halls. . . . In fact, General Cathermeier, when I was imagining these bases, I used your own Cheyenne Mountain as my model."

"Glad to hear we could help."

Mason asked, "How deep underground are they?"

"Roughly thirty feet below the bedrock."

"Like hardened silos," Beskrovny said.

"Exactly so," Soong replied. "They were designed to withstand near–full nuclear strikes. And therein lies our problem, you see. Simply knowing their location may not be enough."

David Lahey spoke up. "What about that, General?"

"I'd have to see surveillance photos, of course, but if what General Soong says is true, conventional munitions won't be enough. General, you said nuclear—I assume you're not talking about tactical weapons, but strategic?"

"Correct. Anything short of the megaton range would be useless."

"Not much of a choice," Beskrovny said. "Either we stand by and watch helplessly as Chinese paratroopers drop into my country, or we start a nuclear war."

Mason said, "There may be a third option."

"What's that, Dick?" asked Cathermeier.

"Toothpick."

Cathermeier sighed, shook his head. "Jesus."

"What's Toothpick?" asked Lahey.

THE PROJECT CODENAMED TOOTHPICK BEGAN IN 1983 AS AN offshoot to Reagan's Strategic Defense Initiative, Mason explained. Having been proven impractical for ABM, or antiballistic missile defense, space born kinetic-energy weapons were scrapped in favor of particle and focused radiation weapons until the wholesale scaling down of the U.S.'s nuclear arsenal began in the '90s. Recognizing the need for semismart, autonomous conventional weapons that could be employed in low-intensity conflicts, Toothpick was taken off the shelf in 1993.

Based on a KH-12 spy satellite platform, Toothpick consisted of a "nested drum" of five hundred fifty pound "spikes," each made from an alloy of super-dense, heat-resistant tungsten, tantalum, niobium, cobalt, and nickel.

Receiving input from a constellation of surveillance and weather satellites, Toothpick's targeting computer at NORAD was designed to calculate a target's location, air temperature and wind layering, earth rotation, and atmospheric turbulence to arrive at the optimal aiming point for Toothpick's designator, a blue green argon laser able to penetrate fog, rain, snow, and clouds.

Costing a mere $3,000 apiece, each six-foot spike consisted of little more than a teardrop head, fins, and a rudimentary seeker designed to guide the spike down the beam like a pea through a straw.

"Six feet and fifty pounds?" said Lahey. "Forgive me if that doesn't sound very impressive."

"It's all about speed and focus," Cathermeier said. "Toothpick orbits at about twenty-five miles—roughly one hundred twenty thousand feet above the earth. By the time one of the spikes hits the ground, it's traveling at nearly eighteen thousand miles an hour—or five miles a second. You get the kinetic energy equivalent of a ten thousand pound blockbuster bomb."

"In other words," Mason added, "All that destructive power—millions of pounds of pressure, heat, and energy—is focused into an area the size of a dinner skillet."

Lahey stared at them. "I think I'm starting to get the picture. How many of these things do we have?"

"Three in orbit," Cathermeier said. "The first live-fire test is scheduled for next month."

"So we have no way of knowing whether it will even work."

"No, sir, we don't. Given our alternatives, though, I suggest it might be time to find out."

Lahey turned and stared at the wall map for several seconds. He turned back to Cathermeier. "How long do you need?"

The ambassador of the People's Republic of China stepped off the elevator in the White House's subbasement and was met by a pair of Secret Service agents who escorted him down the hall to an oak-paneled door bearing a small placard reading SITUATION ROOM. One of the agents punched a code into the pad beside the knob, then pushed open the door and nodded to the ambassador.

The ambassador stepped through. The room was darkly paneled with subdued track lighting along the walls and a long, diamond-shaped conference table in the middle. High-backed leather chairs ringed its perimeter. Sitting at the far end of the table was David Lahey; standing behind him, Leland Dutcher and Dick Mason.

"Please come in, Mr. Ambassador," Lahey said, gesturing to a chair.

Visibly wary, the ambassador pulled out a chair and sat down. "Where is President Martin?"

"President Martin is indisposed," Lahey replied. "As of last night, he transferred to me all the powers of the presidency."

"I . . . I don't understand."

"You had an arrangement with Phillip Martin. I'm here to tell you it's over. I'm going to give you the benefit of the doubt and assume you're not privy to the whole of your government's plans for Siberia, but trust me when I tell you: Your role in this fiasco is enough to land you in prison for the rest of your life."

"First, Mr. Lahey, I don't know what you're talking about," replied the ambassador. "Second, I have diplomatic immunity; the worst you can do is expel me."

"Don't push your luck. You played intermediary for a pair of *Guoanbu* spies who not only conspired to blackmail a president of the United States, but who also slaughtered an entire family—including two little girls. We're well beyond expulsion at this point, Mr. Ambassador, so choose carefully your words. They may decide your fate."

The ambassador lifted his chin indignantly. "Why have you summoned me here?"

"Your country is preparing to conduct a full-scale invasion of Russia."

"I know of no—"

"I'm offering you a chance to put a stop to it before it's too late."

"Me? I have no authority to—"

"I realize that. But you can forward my offer to your premier." Lahey gestured to the phone beside the ambassador's elbow. "Simply pick up the phone and the call will be put through."

The ambassador chuckled. "And what do I tell him—that you want him to call off an imaginary invasion? I can't do that."

Lahey stared hard at him for several seconds, then looked over his shoulder at Dutcher. "Leland, if you would." Dutcher walked down the table, laid a sheet of paper before the ambassador, then returned. "If you'll look, Mr. Ambassador, you'll see that sheet lists twelve latitude and longitude coordinates. Each represents a secret underground air base your government has built in the Hingaan Mountains."

Lahey pressed a button in the tabletop and one of the wall's panels retracted, revealing a sixty-inch television monitor. Centered on the screen was a black-and-white image of the Mongolian salient and Hingaan Mountains.

"The bases in question are highlighted by the red circles you see, labeled one through twelve. Each facility holds some eighty to one hundred transport planes and over eight thousand airborne troops—all awaiting the order to drop into Siberia."

"I don't see anything," the ambassador replied. "This is nonsense."

Lahey folded his hands on the table and leaned forward. "Again, Mr. Ambassador, I'm going to give you the benefit of the doubt. Pick up the phone and relay our terms to your premier. If your government fails to do as we ask, we'll destroy each of these bases in turn, then move on to the PLA's command and control facilities."

The ambassador spread his hands. "Mr. President, I—"

"I won't ask again."

"I cannot help you."

Lahey punched a button on his phone. "General Cathermeier, are you there?"

"Yes, Mr. President."

"Proceed with the first target."

"Stand by." Twenty seconds passed. "First salvo en route. Impact in forty-two seconds."

"Very well." Lahey turned to the ambassador. "Keep your eye on the easternmost base, Mr. Ambassador."

Cathermeier called, "Twenty seconds to impact."

The ambassador said, "What am I—"

"Just watch."

The image shimmered, then refocused, tightening on the red circle labeled "1."

"What am I looking for?" said the ambassador. "All I see is what looks like a . . . quarry."

Cathermeier's voice: "Ten seconds . . . five . . . four . . . three . . . two . . . one."

On the screen, a black speck suddenly appeared in the center of the red circle. Then two more, then five. Within ten seconds, the white area within the circle was filled with dark specks. In slow motion, a grayish cloud began spreading outward from the circle's perimeter. The smoke cleared, revealing a rubble-filled crater.

The ambassador's mouth worked, but no words came out.

Lahey said, "Mr. Ambassador, the rubble inside that crater is all that remains of a division of airborne troops, their planes, and the base's six hundred support personnel. There are eleven more facilities like this one, and we'll destroy each of them in turn until the invasion is halted."

"This is a trick."

"No."

"You're bluffing, then."

His eyes never leaving the ambassador's, Lahey said, "General Cathermeier?"

"Sir."

"Prepare the second package."

"Yes, sir."

"Wait!" the ambassador cried. He stared openmouthed at the screen. "My God. . . . That's truly an air base? That crater was . . ."

"Yes."

"Lord, what have you done?"

"Nothing compared to what we're prepared to do, Mr. Ambassador. Your country's little adventure in Siberia is over. The only question that remains is, How many Chinese soldiers and airmen have to die before your government realizes it?"

The ambassador tore his eyes from the screen and looked at Lahey. He closed his eyes for a moment, then reached for the phone.

EPILOGUE

CHINA'S INVASION OF RUSSIA ENDED WITH A WHIMPER.

Alerted to the alleged demise of their base, PLAAF surveillance planes were quickly dispatched to the area. The pictures they returned with were quickly sent up the chain of command and landed on the desk of the premier two hours after Toothpick's first salvo.

The cornerstone to their Rubicon gambit, the PLA's decade-long marvel of engineering had in the space of ten seconds been turned into a crater. Every blade of grass, every tree, every slab of concrete was dust. Not a single aircraft or soldier survived.

Further satellite and aerial reconnaissance showed no evidence that nuclear weapons were involved; rescue workers found no signs of radiation. Nothing could explain the utter destruction that had befallen their installations—nothing but the ambassador's testimony that the United States caused it.

With no other course left open, the premier acceded to David Lahey's terms.

Two days later, under the watchful eyes of Russian and American strike aircraft orbiting above, the troops and support personnel of the remaining eleven bases were shuttled south to Beijing, two airplanes at a time.

With the images being transmitted to PLA headquarters in Beijing, the remaining underground bases, now ghost towns, were one by one destroyed by Toothpick's deadly rain.

• • •

SPARED THE BRUNT OF THE EXPLOSION BY MIKE SKELDON'S SACrifice, Ian Cahil survived with only a broken collarbone, several dozen scrapes, and some bruises. Twelve hours after clawing his way out of the partially collapsed vent tunnel, he drove Skeldon's truck to a village called Tas-Yuryakh sixty miles east of Chono Dam and pulled to a stop before a ramshackle hut that served as the village's general store, barbershop, and administration building, and walked inside.

The proprietor, a toothless old man smoking a pipe, gaped at him.

Putting on what he hoped was his most amiable smile, Bear cleared his throat and said, "Can you please tell me where the nearest phone is? I seem to be a little lost."

INTIMIDATED BY *COLUMBIA*'S TIMELY AND DRAMATIC APPEARance in front of them, the soldiers in pursuit of Jurens and his team stopped and began circling at a distance as the commander in charge pondered his next step. To nudge him in the right direction, Archie Kinsock called out his twelve-man Security Alert Team, which emerged from the fore and aft escape trunks, trotted to the foredeck, and snapped into parade rest formation, M-16's held across their bodies.

Eyeing each other across the water—Kinsock standing on *Columbia*'s monolithic fairwater, the Russian commander at the stem of wooden skiff—the two men came to an unspoken agreement. *Columbia*'s raft was sent across to Jurens and his team, who were pulled aboard and ferried back.

Columbia's escape from Russian territorial waters was a close-run race. Alerted to her presence by the Federation ground commander at Nakhodka-Vostochny, the Krivak frigate and two Osa patrol boats to the northeast came about and headed down the coast at flank speed and were soon joined by the lone Akula *Columbia* had encountered days before.

With the pursuers closing the noose around his boat and no chance of evading them, Kinsock sent a flash message to the NMCC reporting their situation. What he wouldn't know until days later was that General Cathermeier had already informed Marshal Beskrovny about *Columbia*'s peril. Aware that *Columbia* had played a role—albeit an involuntary one—in the destruction of Nakhodka but determined to avoid the war China was so desperately trying to manufacture, Beskrovny sent his own flash message to his Far East District Commander. With both the Krivak and Akula closing to within firing range of *Columbia*, each captain got the same baffling yet unequivocal order: Let the American submarine pass unmolested.

Four hours after rising off the bottom, *Columbia*, tooling along on the surface at four knots, exited Russian territorial waters, where she was met by *Cheyenne*, dispatched from the *Stennis* group to serve as her escort. An hour later an SH-60 Seahawk from *Stennis* picked up an unconscious but stable Smitty and flew him to the carrier for treatment.

Jurens and Dickie, both uninjured but sick at heart, remained aboard *Columbia* to see Zee's body back to Pearl, where they were met by his wife, his four-year-old son and two-year-old daughter.

As for Sunil Dhar, he was met pierside by two men in dark suits who ushered him into the back of a nondescript government sedan and whisked away.

Rappahannock River

In the end, it had been a bizarre confluence of irony and luck that had saved Tanner's life.

The first bullet had torn through his right buttock, missing his pelvic bone by a quarter inch, then blasted out of the front of his thigh. The second shot was more serious, having entered his lower back and cutting a ragged groove through both his diaphragm and spleen before exiting his abdomen.

Already slipping into shock, Tanner's plunge into the icy water pushed him toward the edge of hypothermia, slowing both his respiration and circulation as his body began to instinctively shut down nonessential systems. The snow he'd packed around his wound further slowed the bleeding of his ruptured spleen. By the time Hsiao pulled him aboard the helicopter, Tanner's heartbeat and respiration were nearly undetectable.

His stroke of luck came in the form of Novotroitskoye's base doctor, a former army field surgeon who'd served during the Soviet Union's invasion of Afghanistan. He'd seen and treated the worst of wounds in the worst of conditions. Upon seeing Tanner, he wasted no time, bypassing traditional treatment methods for those he'd successfully used so many times on the battlefield.

Keeping Tanner in a limbo of near-hypothermia, the doctor packed the major arteries in his arms and legs in ice, then took him straight to surgery, repairing the gash in his diaphragm and removing his spleen in a record thirty-four minutes. As the last stitch was closed, he ordered Tanner transferred to a warming table, covered with blankets, and pumped full of intravenous fluids.

For two days Briggs lay unconscious, his lungs and heart pumping at bare sustenance levels.

As the doctor predicted, on the third day Tanner's natural healing system took over and he regained consciousness. "Welcome back," the doctor said with a smile.

Tanner blinked his eyes open. "Where am I?" he rasped.

"Under the care of the greatest doctor in all of Siberia, that's where."

"Glad to hear it. How long have I—"

"Three days. This afternoon we'll have you up and walking—with a cane, mind you—and by the end of the week you'll be well enough to leave for your cell at the *gulag*."

"What?"

"Just a joke."

"Very funny."

The doctor shrugged. "As I understand it, there's an American transport plane waiting for you."

"Where are my—"

"Friends? They're outside, waiting to see you."

"They're okay?"

"Compared to you, they're Olympians."

Tanner nodded, then laid his head back and closed his eyes. "Good."

• • •

TWENTY DAYS AFTER ENTERING CHINA, TANNER WAS BACK home.

Kam Hsiao and Han Soong were secreted in a luxurious CIA safe house in rural Maryland, where they would spend the next few months, after which both would receive new identities, homes, and vocations if they so chose. Either way, Dick Mason said, both men would never want for anything again. Along with Tanner, Cahil, Mike Skeldon, and Charlie Latham, Soong and Hsiao had helped prevent what could have easily become the third world war.

Kyung Xiang had vanished. As Tanner and the others were en route back to Novotroitskoye, the base commander had ordered a pair of Havoc helicopter gunships loaded with soldiers back to the Bira River. Xiang, his remaining paratroopers, and Lian Soong were gone, as was Xiang's Hind. The Hoplite pilot was found alive in the cabin where they'd left him and was returned to the border.

In subsequent meetings between the U.S.-Russian delegation and its Chinese counterpart, questions about Xiang were deflected with the vague comment, "Former-director Xiang is unavailable at this time." Recognizing diplomatic subtlety when they saw it, State Department analysts took it to mean Xiang had either already been executed, or he was already locked away in a dank *laogi* cell.

For Tanner's part, he spent his first days home savoring hot showers, home-cooked meals, dry clothes, and a bed with soft sheets and thick blankets. After his time in China, each experience seemed new. He vowed to never take such amenities for granted again.

All in all, he decided, it felt good to be alive.

IT WAS JUST AFTER DUSK WHEN TANNER ARRIVED HOME FROM his second-to-last physical therapy session. Though the damage to his leg was neither permanent nor disabling, the bullet had badly torn muscles and tendons in its passage. Tanner had rid himself of the cane the previous week and now walked with only a slight limp. Ignoring warnings to the contrary, he'd started swimming in the mornings and running in the evenings—or as Cahil had called it, "hobble-jogging." Tanner found every stroke and step painful, but each day he awoke feeling a bit more like himself.

He pulled into the driveway behind the lighthouse, got out, then grabbed the mail from the box and walked around the deck to the back door. A wind was coming up and he could smell rain in the air. The hanging baskets swung in the breeze.

Leaving the screen door open for some fresh air, he dropped the mail on the kitchen counter then checked his voice mail. There was one message: Oaken had found Andrew Galbreth Hadin's descendents. His three great-grandchildren, the oldest of whom was the director of the Hadin Museum, all lived in Long Island, New York.

"I didn't contact them," Oaken said. "Thought you'd like to do that yourself. Anyway, gimme a call when you get a chance, and I'll give you the info. Bye."

Tanner almost hated parting with Hadin's diary; it had been his constant companion over the past several weeks as he'd sat in the hospital's whirlpool or laid for hours as the flexor machine stretched and contorted his leg. He read and reread the diary from cover to cover, each time feeling a bit closer to Hadin. Their stumbling upon the *Priscilla* had not only saved their lives, but possibly hundreds of thousands of others as well. In a way, Hadin was again the dashing hero, albeit eighty years after his death.

Tanner grabbed an apple from the fridge, then shuffled through the mail. Bills, junk mail, a mailer insisting that he "may already be a winner" . . . and a padded, manila envelope. He checked the front; there was no return address. He tore open the top.

Inside was a black, unlabeled, VHS tape.

Curious now, he took the tape into the living room, slipped it into the VCR, then grabbed the remote and hit Play. There was ten seconds of blackness, then the picture swam into focus. A dark object swung before the lens. The camera retreated until he recognized it: a shoe.

The angle widened and began to pan upward.

"Good God," Tanner murmured.

The shoes had feet in them. The camera skimmed up past a pair of calves, then thighs and torso, then finally to the neck and face.

Briggs felt his stomach heave into his throat. *Oh, God. No, no. . . .*

Suspended from a noose, her face bruised and bloody, was Lian Soong.

Tanner snatched up the envelope, turned it over. The postage stamp bore no cancellation mark. Someone had delivered the envelope in person.

"She hardly struggled at all," a voice called behind him.

Briggs felt a shiver trail down his spine. He turned around and looked up.

Standing at the loft's railing was Xiang. He held a small-caliber automatic in his right hand. It was leveled at Tanner's chest.

Briggs stared at Xiang, unable to speak. The room swirled around him. He glanced back at the television; Lian's face filled the screen. After a moment, the screen went black.

Tanner turned back to Xiang. "You did that?" he whispered.

"Yes."

"Why? For God's sake, why?"

"She'd served her purpose. I was done with her."

You're lying, Briggs thought. Xiang had killed Lian as punishment for her silence at the paddle wheel. Her refusal to pinpoint their location had bought Hsiao and her father the time they'd needed to get away. Whatever her reasons, in that last act of defiance, Lian had again become the daughter Soong had thought he'd lost, and the woman Tanner had feared never existed.

And Xiang had killed her for it.

Briggs felt a ball of hot rage explode in his chest. *Focus, Briggs. He's come here to kill you. Think!* Tanner took a step forward, blocking the television screen. He fingered the remote's volume button to it's highest setting. Set on the VCR channel, the screen flickered silently.

"You came all this way for revenge," Tanner said. *Play him along, Briggs.*

"That's right!" Xiang growled. "Why not?"

"I'll say this much: You plan a pretty lousy invasion, but you sure can hold a grudge."

"Shut your mouth! You destroyed my life! I can never return to China. I'll be hunted until the day I die. Everything I struggled for is gone, and it's your doing!"

"Glad I could help."

"Tell me: Where did they put Soong and the other one—the guard from the camp?"

Holding the apple in his right hand, Tanner held it up for Xiang to see, then took two slow steps to the left and set it on the dining table. The door was seven feet away now.

"That's your plan?" Tanner said. "Once you're done here, you're going to hunt them down?"

"Yes."

"You'll never find them."

"I will if you tell me."

"That's not going to happen."

"It could mean the difference between living and dying," Xiang said.

"Even if I believed that, I wouldn't tell you."

"Are you certain you don't want to reconsider?"

Tanner shook his head.

"Very well."

His gun never leaving Tanner's chest, Xiang started toward the stairs.

Behind his back, Tanner aimed the remote at the TV. *Wait . . . wait. . . .*

Xiang reached the head of the stairs, placed his foot on the top step.

Tanner punched the channel selector. Static blasted from the TV. Xiang flinched, spun that way.

Tanner sprinted for the door. Four shots boomed. The French doors shattered. The paneling beside Tanner's head splintered. Half hobbling, he put his head down and bulldozed into the screen. With a ripping sound, the mesh parted. Entangled in his arms and legs, the frame ripped off its track.

He lurched onto the deck, shrugged off the frame, then turned and staggered to the beach stairs.

"Stop!"

Crack!

The balustrade beside him shattered.

He was five feet from the top step when he felt a stab in his calf. Pain seared up his thigh. Only partially healed, it was more than his leg could bear. It buckled beneath him and he collapsed.

"Don't move!" Xiang ordered. "Stay right there!"

Footsteps clicked on the wood behind him.

Don't give him the satisfaction, Tanner thought. *Get off your knees.*

Briggs reached up, grabbed the deck railing, and struggled to his feet. His calf burned as if coated in acid. He shifted his weight to his good leg and rotated himself around.

Xiang was standing a few feet away, gun leveled. "Almost," he said.

At close range Tanner now recognized Xiang's gun. It was a compact .25-caliber Sig Sauer. *Seven- or eight-round magazine?* he wondered. Seven. Xiang had already fired six. The man had just broken a cardinal rule: count your shots; know your reserves.

It was cold comfort. No matter what Tanner did, he was going to get shot. At this distance, Xiang couldn't miss. The only question was, Could he cross the gap fast enough, throw off his aim enough to avoid a fatal wound? There was only one way to find out. Tanner steeled himself for it.

"Do me a favor," he murmured, letting his shoulder slump.

"Why should I?"

"Because you've won. You can afford to be gracious."

"What is it?"

Tanner pointed to his forehead. "Make it quick."

Xiang considered this for a moment, then shrugged. "Have it your way."

Xiang jerked up his pistol. As the barrel came level with his chin, Briggs ducked and pushed off the railing with everything he had, aiming his shoulder for Xiang's belly. The gun roared. Tanner felt a hammer blow to his chest. His shoulder slammed into Xiang's solar plexus. They stumbled backward. Before his leg could buckle, Tanner wrapped him in a bear hug and pushed off, driving Xiang back.

Xiang began flailing with his gun hand, pounding the butt into Tanner's neck and face and shoulders. Briggs felt the skin on his cheek split open. He held on. Xiang cocked back his leg and slammed his knee into Tanner's groin. Pain erupted in his belly. He reached up, groping for Xiang's eyes, his throat, anything. *Hold on, Briggs.*

"Bastard!" Xiang roared.

He kneed Tanner again, then again, then a third time, driving him backward across the deck.

Tanner felt his foot slip off the edge of the deck and onto the top step. He glanced down between his legs and saw his foot teetering on the edge of the step. Below him, the stairs dropped sharply to the beach. *You're going, Briggs,* he thought. *Take him with you. . . .*

He took a breath, corralled his last bit of strength, and pushed off into his good leg. He lifted Xiang off the ground, turned, and pitched himself down the stairs.

Locked together, they tumbled end over end. His vision became a blur of dark sky, steps, wooden railing, and flashing foliage. The impacts came one on top of the next, the wood gouging into his head, shoulders, and back. Tanner bit his tongue, tasted blood. His heartbeat thundered in his ears.

Then, suddenly, it was over.

He lay motionless for a few moments, then forced open his eyes. He was lying ten feet from the bottom of the stairs. Somewhere in the distance, a thousand miles away, he heard the *swoosh-hiss* of waves. Then, another sound: a gurgling.

A few feet away, Xiang lay on his side and stared up at him with bulging eyes. His upper arm hung across his chest while his lower one, pinned against the steps by his body, twitched spasmodically.

For a moment Tanner's brain couldn't make sense of what he was seeing. Something was wrong . . . something about the way Xiang was lying. Then he saw it. *Good God. . . .*

The violence of the fall had wrenched Xiang's head nearly 180 degrees. His chin was resting on his shoulder blade. He coughed, a wet gurgle. Froth bubbled from his lips. His eyes, filled with a mixture of terror and confusion, darted around him, then returned to Tanner's face.

Shot, Briggs thought. *You're shot*, again. . . .

He touched his chest, expecting to feel warm, wet blood. There was nothing. He probed his jacket until he found the bullet hole and, beneath it, a hard object. He reached into his pocket.

Hadin's diary. The bullet had cut an oblique groove through the leather cover and half the pages before exiting the spine and punching out the side of his coat. *Good ol' Dashing Andy.*

Beneath him, Xiang gurgled again. Wincing against the pain, Tanner scooted forward, dropped to the next step, then another until he was sitting beside him. Xiang's lips curled into a snarl. He stared into Tanner's eyes and tried to mouth something.

"What?" Briggs said.

Xiang tried again. This time Tanner caught it: *Damn you. . . .*

Xiang hung on for several minutes, as each breath became more labored than the last. Tanner watched, unable to tear himself away as the life steadily slipped from Xiang. In the final seconds Xiang locked eyes with him, gave a final cough, twitched, and went still. His dead eyes gazed at the sky.

"Almost," Tanner murmured. "But not quite."

Tanner reached up, grabbed the railing, pulled himself upright, and began climbing.